THE
PUSHCART PRIZE, XXVII

2003
PUSHCART
PRIZE XXVII
BEST OF THE
SMALL PRESSES

EDITED BY BILL HENDERSON
WITH THE PUSHCART PRIZE EDITORS

Note: nominations for this series are invited from any small, independent, literary book press or magazine in the world. Up to six nominations—tear sheets or copies, selected from work published, or about to be published, in the calendar year—are accepted by our December 1 deadline each year. Write to Pushcart Press, P.O. Box 380, Wainscott, N.Y. 11975 for more information, or contact us at w.w.w.pushcartprize.com

© 2003 Pushcart Press
All rights reserved, which includes the right to reproduce this book or portions thereof in any form whatsoever except as provided by the U.S. Copyright Law.

Acknowledgments

Selections for *The Pushcart Prize* are reprinted with the permission of authors and presses cited. Copyright reverts to authors and presses immediately after publication.

Distributed by W. W. Norton & Co.
500 Fifth Ave., New York, N.Y. 10110

Library of Congress Card Number: 76–58675
ISBN: 1–888889–33–0
        1–888889–35–7 (paperback)
ISSN: 0149–7863

For
Hannah Turner,
who makes it all possible
and in memory of
William Phillips (1907–2002),
a Founding Editor
of this series

INTRODUCTION

by BILL HENDERSON

Every year it gets harder to contain my enthusiasm for the writers in the current Pushcart Prize. It seems that never before in the 27 year history of this annual collection has the talent been more stunning, more surprising.

Maybe after all these years, and Pushcart's featuring thousands of writers and hundreds of presses, I am getting soft in the head, losing my judgment, beginning to dotter about. And perhaps too I am losing my financial sense: a short book is much cheaper to produce than a hefty one. But here we have it, one of the biggest books in the series, well over 600 pages and as far as I can judge it, worth every page, every sentence, every comma.

As a reality check, and to back our soon to be announced Pushcart Prize Fellowships (about which more later), I recently asked writers who have been featured in the first quarter-century of Pushcart Prizes to comment on the project. "The best series . . . incredibly good," said the poet Gerald Stern. "A heroic work," said T.C. Boyle. "Urgent and absolutely necessary," remarked Mary Karr. "The most creative, the most generous, and the most democratic of any of the annual volumes," wrote Rick Moody. More than twenty-five writers joined the acclaim. So we must be doing something right here, Pushcart and its band of 200 plus contributing and staff editors.

For me one of the truly right things we do is to recognize new talent. And this edition is a winner in every way: more new writers than I can remember in any past edition. Most of these people I have never heard of. And I am stunned by their power, intelligence, compassion. Not since the early Pushcart Prize volumes that featured unknowns named Ray Carver, John Irving, Tim O'Brien, Lynne Sharon

Schwartz, Andre Dubus, Jayne Anne Phillips, Charles Baxter, Susan Minot, Mona Simpson, Richard Ford, D.R. MacDonald and others have I been so impressed with new talent.

And that's saying a lot for today's writers. These are tough times. The commercial tide is running hard the other way. Writers are seen as mere fillers for spaces between the ads and the graphics in pop mags. If you don't have a bankable name or gimmick, it's almost impossible to find ready access to a commercial book publisher.

But the times are tough in other ways too. The late R. V. Cassill, author of many acclaimed story collections and novels, a retired professor of English at Brown, described the situation like this in *The Norton Anthology of Contemporary Fiction,* which he co-edited with Joyce Carol Oates: . . . "writers have found their voices amid a blab and clatter of media noise unlike anything known before; of the dud eloquence of public discourse in advertising, sports and manipulative politics; of instant folklore, junk mail and junk values trickling down through literary and academic decadence; and through cosmetic heroism and the tyrannical buzzwords of received ideas . . . Our best writers had to find their way through clouds of murk. And they must be sought there by the unflaggingly hopeful readers of this student generation."

❖   ❖   ❖

.What is always helpful to writers, particularly new and young writers, is food and shelter. Food to fuel the soul, shelter to keep the writing implements and paper out of the rain. For this reason, Pushcart has started The Pushcart Prize Fellowships. Our goal in the years ahead is to raise an endowment of many millions of dollars to provide grants (money to live on) for new authors that are recognized by this series and elsewhere.

This is a project that everybody can help out with. If you have some loose change or a spare million send it to the endowment. Or if you know of likely contributors (individuals or foundations), mail us their names and addresses and we will forward information about the Fellowships. All gifts are tax deductible, and all gift-givers will be recognized in future editions of the Pushcart Prize. Our address: Pushcart Prize Fellowships, PO Box 380, Wainscott, NY 11975

❖   ❖   ❖

Every year new poetry co-editors select the Pushcart Prize poems. I doubt if any other series ever has had the assistance of such distinguished poets (the names of past poetry co-editors are listed in "The People Who Helped" section). This year they were joined by Pattiann Rogers and Carl Phillips, who performed a mammoth and impossible job with grace, and justice.

The latest collection by Pattiann Rogers is *Song of the World Becoming: New and Collected Poems 1981–2001* published by Milkweed in 2001. In a starred *Booklist* review, Donna Seaman commented: "Rogers possesses the philosophical elegance of Stevens, the body awareness of Sharon Olds, and the keenness of Mary Oliver, but her penetrating vision, avid imagination, and open-winged exaltation are all her own."

She is the author of seven books of poetry, the first of which, *The Expectations of Light*, was published in 1981.

In 1994, Rogers published a book of new and selected poems, *Firekeeper* (Milkweed Editions), that went on to be a finalist for the Lenore Marshall Poetry Prize and one of *Publishers Weekly's* best books of the year.

Rogers has won several awards for her work, including the Hokin Prize, the Tietjens Prize, and the Bock Prize from *Poetry*, three awards from The Texas Institute of Letters, two Strousse Awards from *Prairie Schooner*, The Theodore Roethke Prize from *Poetry Northwest* and five Pushcart Prizes.

Rogers has been the recipient of two NEA Grants, a Guggenheim Fellowship, and a Lannan Poetry Fellowship. In May, 2000, she was a resident at the Rockefeller Foundation's Bellagio Study and Conference Center in Bellagio, Italy.

In addition to her books, Rogers' poems have appeared in the *Paris Review, New Yorker, New Republic, Hudson Review, Yale Review, Orion, Tricycle,* and other magazines and journals.

Rogers has been a visiting writer at numerous universities and colleges and was Associate Professor at the University of Arkansas from 1993–97. She lives with her husband, a retired geophysicist, in Colorado. She is the mother of two grown sons.

Carl Phillips is a professor in the Department of English, and the African and Afro-American Studies Program at Washington University in St. Louis. He is also director of the Writing Program there.

He holds a B.A. degree magna cum laude in Greek and Latin from Harvard, and graduate degrees from Boston University and the University of Massachusetts.

His books include the just-published *Rock Harbor* (Farrar, Straus

11

and Giroux), *The Tether* (FSG 2001, winner of the Kingsley Tufts Prize), *Pastoral* (Graywolf, 2000, winner of the Lambda Literary Award in Poetry); *From The Devotions* (Graywolf, 1998, Finalist for the National Book Award) and *Cortège* (Graywolf, 1995, a finalist for the National Book Critics Circle Award).

His poetry has appeared in *The Pushcart Prize, Best American Poetry, The Vintage Book of African-American Poetry* and *Making Callaloo: 25 Years of Black Literature* (St. Martins) and many other anthologies, as well as in *Agni, Atlantic Monthly, Boulevard, Daedalus, Doubletake, Field, The Journal, The Nation, Parnassus: Poetry In Review, TriQuarterly* and elsewhere.

The Tether was named one of the best books of poetry for 2001 by the *Los Angeles Times. Pastoral* was a finalist for the *Los Angeles Times* Book Award in 2001 and was selected as one of the year's best books of poetry by the *Washington Post Book World* and *Publishers Weekly.*

✧   ✧   ✧

I am profoundly honored that Carl Phillips and Pattiann Rogers have joined us this year and also that so many outstanding editors have continued to help us with their nominations and advice through so many years.

Here then are the results of our efforts: 67 authors from 52 presses,* 12 of them new to the series—Barrow Street, New Orleans Review, Northeastern University Press, Parkett, Post Road, Quaderai Di Yip, Shearsman, Bridge, Fence, Fugue, Jubilat and Lyric.

These authors and editors are true heroes in dark times that desperately need their light.

✧   ✧   ✧

* *note: over 8,000 nominations yearly arrive from both print and on-line journals*

THE PEOPLE WHO HELPED

FOUNDING EDITORS—*Anaïs Nin (1903–1977) Buckminster Fuller (1895–1983), Charles Newman, Daniel Halpern, Gordon Lish, Harry Smith, Hugh Fox, Ishmael Reed, Joyce Carol Oates, Len Fulton, Leonard Randolph, Leslie Fiedler, Nona Balakian (1918–1991), Paul Bowles (1910–1999), Paul Engle (1908–1991), Ralph Ellison (1914–1994), Reynolds Price, Rhoda Schwartz, Richard Morris, Ted Wilentz (1915–2001), Tom Montag, William Phillips (1907–2002), Poetry editor: H. L. Van Brunt.*

CONTRIBUTING EDITORS FOR THIS EDITION—*Kent Nelson, Michael Dennis Browne, Roger Weingarten, Philip Appleman, Joan Swift, Jim Barnes, Jane McCafferty, James Reiss, Kevin Bowen, Rachel Hadas, Daniel Hoffman, Jess Row, Jean Thompson, Marianne Boruch, David Rivard, Robert Cording, Debra Spark, Jeff Dolven, Chard deNiord, Thomas Lux, Elizabeth Spires, Margaret Gibson, Kathleen Hill, Judith Kitchen, Jane Brox, Madison Smartt Bell, Billy Collins, William Heyen, Alice Mattison, Lee Upton, Gary Fincke, Grace Schulman, Tom Filer, Kirk Nesset, Sharon Solwitz, Christopher Buckley, Timothy Geiger, Gibbons Ruark, Vern Rutsala, Len Roberts, Andrew Hudgins, Joe Ashby Porter, James Harms, Charles Harper Webb, Alan Michael Parker, Marilyn Hacker, Sylvia Watanabe, Mark Cox, Robert Gibb, Glenna Holloway, Michael Waters, Michael Heffernan, Lance Olsen, David Romtvedt, Marvin Bell, David Kirby, Colette Inez, Janice Eidus, Gary Gildner, Paul Zimmer, Erin McGraw, Kevin Prufer, Michael Martone, Judith Taylor, Laura Kasischke, Jeffrey Harrison, Kathy Fagan, Daniel Orozco, William Wenthe, Wesley McNair, Gerry Locklin, Natasha Trethewey, Peter*

13

Liotta, Kim Barnes, Susan Hahn, Linda Bierds, Mariko Nagai, Robert Wrigley, Melissa Pritchard, Josip Novakovich, Bernard Cooper, Maureen Seaton, Kay Ryan, Martha Collins, Fred Leebron, Molly Bendall, Claire Bateman, Reginald Gibbons, Anthony Hecht, David Plante, Ed Ochester, Christina Zawadiwsky, Molly Giles, Gerald Shapiro, Kathy Callaway, Michael Collier, Rachel Loden, Tony Ardizzone, Edward Hirsch, Robert Boswell, Katrina Roberts, Henry Carlile, Tony Quagliano, Lynne McFall, Lou Mathews, John Drury, Talvikki Ansel, Bret Lott, Christopher Howell, William Olsen, S.L. Wisenberg, Jack Marshall, Stuart Dischell, Rita Dove, E.S. Bumas, Richard Jackson, Antler, Debora Greger, Peter Orner, Stephen Corey, Jacqueline Osherow, C.E. Poverman, Pamela Painter, Thomas E. Kennedy, Ted Deppe, Pinckney Benedict, M.D. Elevitch, Barbara Selfridge, Philip Dacey, Joe Hurka, Eleanor Wilner, Lucia Perillo, Arthur Smith, Jim Daniels, Pamela Stewart, David Baker, Maura Stanton, Sherod Santos, Renée Ashley, Mike Newirth, Karl Elder, Katherine Min, Michael Bowden, Joy Williams, Marilyn Krysl, Daniel Henry, Dewitt Henry, Mark Wisniewski, Marianna Cherry, David St. John, Rosemary C. Hildebrandt, Maxine Kumin, Jeannette Barnes, Richard Garcia, Cathy Song, Bruce Holland Rogers, John Kistner, Stacey Richter, Elizabeth McKenzie, Kristin King, Dan Masterson, Jessica Roeder, Philip Levine, Jeffrey Hammond, George Keithley, Edith Pearlman, Rick Bass, Elizabeth Graver, Beth Ann Fennelly, Mark Irwin, Tom Paine, Robert McBrearty, David Wojahn, Bob Hicok, Ron Tanner, Diann Blakely, Eamon Grennan, Forrest Gander, Herb Francis, Salvatore Scibona, Claire Davis, Jane Hirshfield, Cleopatra Mathis, Bonnie Jo Campbell, Bruce Beasley, Reginald Shepherd, Cyrus Cassells, David Madden, Laurie Sheck, Ed Falco, Kim Addonizio, Richard Burgin, Joyce Carol Oates, Barbara Hamby, Susan Wheeler, Dorianne Laux, Wally Lamb, Nancy Richard, Paul Maliszewski, Rosellen Brown, Richard Kostelanetz, Renée Ashley, Laurie Lamon, Richard Tayson, Marie S. Williams, Caroline Langston, Kenneth Gangemi, H.E. Francis, Robert Phillips, Stephen Dunn, Nancy McCabe, Donald Revell, John Allman, Jana Harris, David Jauss, Jim Moore, Dan Chaon, Jewel Mogan, Mary Kuryla, David James Duncan, Bert States, Jim Simmerman, Carol Potter, Joan Murray, Pat Strachan, Virginia Holman, Clarence Major, Sharon Dilworth

PAST POETRY EDITORS—H.L. Van Brunt, Naomi Lazard, Lynne Spaulding, Herb Leibowitz, Jon Galassi, Grace Schulman, Carolyn

Forché, Gerald Stern, Stanley Plumly, William Stafford, Philip Levine, David Wojahn, Jorie Graham, Robert Hass, Philip Booth, Jay Meek, Sandra McPherson, Laura Jensen, William Heyen, Elizabeth Spires, Marvin Bell, Carolyn Kizer, Christopher Buckley, Chase Twichell, Richard Jackson, Susan Mitchell, Lynn Emanuel, David St. John, Carol Muske, Dennis Schmitz, William Matthews, Patricia Strachan, Heather McHugh, Molly Bendall, Marilyn Chin, Kimiko Hahn, Michael Dennis Browne, Billy Collins, Joan Murray, Sherod Santos, Judith Kitchen.

ROVING EDITORS—*Lily Frances Henderson, Genie Chipps*

EUROPEAN EDITORS—*Liz and Kirby Williams*

MANAGING EDITOR—*Hannah Turner*

FICTION EDITORS—*Jack Driscoll, David Means, Monica Hellman, Bill Henderson*

POETRY EDITORS—*Pattiann Rogers, Carl Phillips*

ESSAYS EDITOR—*Anthony Brandt*

EDITOR AND PUBLISHER—*Bill Henderson*

CONTENTS

THE
PUSHCART PRIZE, XXVII

EVERYTHING RAVAGED, EVERYTHING BURNED

fiction by WELLS TOWER

from FENCE

Just as we were all getting back into the mainland domestic groove, somebody started in with dragons and crop blights from across the North Sea. We all knew who it was. A turncoat Norwegian monk named Naddod had been big medicine on the dragon-and-blight circuit for the last decade or so, and was known to bring heavy ordnance for whoever could lay out some silver. Scuttlebutt had it that Naddod was operating out of a monastery on Lindisfarne, whose people we'd troubled on a pillage-and-consternation junket in Northumbria after Corn Harvesting Month last fall. Now bitter winds were screaming in from the west, searing the land and ripping the grass from the soil. Salmon were turning up spattered with sores, and grasshoppers clung to the wheat in rapacious buzzing bunches.

I tried to put these things out of my mind. We'd been away three long months harrying the Hibernian shores, and now I was back with Pila, my common-law, and thinking that home was very close to paradise in these endless golden summer days. We'd built our house together, Pila and I. It was a fine little wattle and daub cabin on a pretty bit of plain where a wide blue fjord stabbed into the land. On summer evenings my young wife and I would sit out front, high on potato wine, and watch the sun stitch a brilliant orange skirt across the horizon. At times such as these, you get a big feeling, like the gods made this place, this moment, first, and concocted you as an afterthought just to be there to enjoy it.

I was doing a lot of enjoying and relishing and a lot of lying around the rack with Pila, though I knew what it meant when I heard those flint-edged winds howling past the house. Sons of bitches three weeks' boat ride off were fucking up our summer and were probably going to need their asses whipped.

Of course, Djarf Fairhair had his stinger out even before his wife spotted those dragons winging it inland from the coast. He was boss on our ship and a fool for warfare. His appetite for action was so terrifying and infectious, he'd once riled up a gang of Frankish slaves and led them south to afflict and maim their own countrymen. He'd gotten in four days of decent sacking when the slaves began to see the situation for what it was and underwent a sudden change of attitude. Djarf had been fighting his way up the Rhine Valley, making steady progress through a half-assed citizens' militia of children and farmers, when the slaves closed in behind him. People who were there say he turned absolutely feral and began berserking with a pair of broadaxes, chewing through the lines like corn kernels on a cob, and that when the axes broke, he cut loose with a dismembered human head, so horrifying those gentle provincials that they fell back and gave him wide berth to the ship.

Djarf was from Hedeby-Slesvig up the Slie fjord, a fairly foul and rocky locality whose people take a worrisome pleasure in the gruesome sides of life. They have a habit down there if they don't like a child's looks when he slides from the womb. They pitch him into the deep waters and wait for the next one. Djarf himself was supposedly a colicky, peaked baby, and it was only the beneficence of the tides and his own vicious tenacity that got him to the far shore when his father grew tired of his caterwauling and tried to wash him from the world.

He'd been campaigning for payback ever since. I was with him on a search-and-destroy tour against Louis the Pious, and with my own eyes watched him climb up over the soldiers' backs and stride like a saint across men's heads, golf-stroking skulls as he went. On that same trip, we ran low on food, and it was Djarf who decided to throw our own dead on the fire and have at last night's mutton when their stomachs burst. He'd been the only one of us to dig in, apart from a crazy Arab along as a spellbuster. He reached right in there, scooping out chewed-up victuals with a shank of pine bark. "Faggot greenhorns," he called us, the firelight twitching on his face. "Food's food. If these guys hadn't gotten their threads snipped, they'd tell you the same thing."

24

So Djarf, whose wife was a rotten, carp-mouthed thing and little argument for staying home, was agitating to hop back in the ship and go straighten things out in Northumbria. My buddy Gnut, who lived just over the stony moraine our wheat field backed up on, came down the hill one day and admitted that he too was giving it some thought. Like me, he wasn't big on warrioring. He was just crazy for boat. We used to joke and say Gnut would ride a boat from his shack to his shithouse if somebody would invent one whose prow could cut sod. Gnut's wife had passed years ago, dead from bad milk, and now that she was gone, the part of him that felt peaceful in a place that didn't move beneath him had sickened and died as well.

Pila saw him coming down the hill and frowned at me. "Don't need to guess what he'll be wanting," she said. She scowled and headed back indoors. Gnut ambled down over the hummocky earth and stopped at the pair of stump chairs Pila and I had put up on the hill where the view was so fine. From there, the fjord shone like poured silver, and sometimes you could spot a seal poking his head up through the waves.

Gnut's wool coat was stiff with filth and his long hair so heavy and unclean that even the wind keening up from the shore was having a hard time getting it to move. He had a good crust of snot going in his mustache, not a pleasant thing to look at, but then he had no one around to find it disagreeable. He tore a sprig of heather from the ground and chewed at its sweet roots.

"Djarf get at you yet?" he asked.

"No, not yet, but I'm not worried he'll forget."

He took the sprig from his teeth and briefly jammed it into his ear before tossing it away. "You gonna go?"

"Not until I hear the particulars, I won't."

"You can bet I'm going. A hydra flew in last night and ran off Rolf Hierdal's sheep. We can't be putting up with this shit. It comes down to pride, is what it comes down to."

"Shit, Gnut, when'd you get to be such a gung-ho motherfucker? I don't recall you being so proud and thin-skinned before Astrud went off to her good place. Anyway, Lindisfarne is probably sacked out already. If you don't remember, we just about pillaged the living shit out of those people on the last swing through, and I doubt they've come up with much in the meantime to justify a trip."

I wished Gnut would go ahead and own up to the fact that his life out here was making him lonely and miserable instead of laying on with this warrior-man routine. I could tell just to look at him that most days he was thinking of walking into the water and not bothering to turn back. He wanted back on the boat among company.

Not that I was all that averse myself, speaking in the abstract, but I was needing more sweet time with Pila. I loved that girl even more than she probably knew, and I wanted to get in some thorough lovemaking before the Haymaking Month was under way and see if I couldn't make us a little monkey.

But the days wore on and the weather worsened. Pila watched it sharply, and a sort of hysterical sadness welled up in her, as it often did when I'd be leaving. She cussed me on some days, and others she'd hold me to her and weep. And late one evening, far toward dawn, the hail started. It came suddenly, with the hard, terrifying scraping sound a ship makes when its hull hits stone. We hunkered down in the sheepskins, and I whispered soothing things to Pila, trying to drown out the clatter.

The sun was not yet full up in the sky when Djarf came and knocked. I rose and stepped across the floor, damp with cool morning dew. Djarf stood in the doorway wearing a mail jacket and shield and breathing like he'd jogged the whole way over. He chucked a handful of hail at my feet. He had a wild grin on his face. "Today's the day," he said. "We got to get it on."

Sure, I could have told him thanks anyway, but once you back down from one job, you're lucky if they'll even let you put in for a flat-fee trade escort. I had to think long term, me and Pila, and any little jits we might produce. Still, she didn't like to hear it. When I got back in bed, she tucked the covers over her face, hoping I'd think she was angry instead of crying.

The clouds were spilling out low across the sky when we shoved off. Thirty of us on board, Gnut rowing with me at the bow and behind us a lot of other men I'd been in some shit with before. Some, like Ørl Stender, were men with families and cried when the boat left the shore. Ørl fucked up the cadence waving to his son, who stood on the beach waving back. He was a tiny one, not four or five, standing there with no pants on, holding a baby pig on a hide leash, sweetly ignorant of the business his father was heading off into.

Most of the others onboard were young men, brash and violent children, so innocent about the world, they would just as soon stick a knife in you as shake your hand.

Gnut was overjoyed. He laughed and sang and put a lot of muscle into the oar, me just holding my hands on it to keep up appearances. I was limp with grief and missing Pila already. The hills humping up behind the beach were a shrill green hue, vivid and outrageous, an angry answer to all of that gray water that lay before them. I watched the beach for Pila and her bright white hair. She hadn't come down to see me off, too mad and sad about me leaving to get up out of bed. But I looked for her anyway, the land scooting away from me with every jerk of the oars.

If Gnut knew I was hurting, he didn't say so. He nudged me and joked, and maintained a steady patter of inanities, as though this whole thing was a private vacation the two of us had cooked up together. "If you had to live on the ship, but you got to have a magic basket full of your favorite food, but only one favorite food, what would it be? I'd have black pudding. Black pudding and plums. So all right, you get two foods." Or: "If someone put a curse on you, and you had to have horns like a goat, and shit little shits like a goat, would you rather have that, or a seven-foot dick that you had to have hanging out of your pants at all times?" And so on.

Djarf stood at his spot in the bow, all full of vinegar and righteous enthusiasm at being back on the sea. Slesvigers, as you know, will bust into song with no provocation whatsoever, their affinity for music roughly on a par with the wretchedness of their singing. Djarf screamed out the cadence in a sickening, wobbly melody that buzzed into the ears and stung you on the brain. His gang of young hock-choppers acted like it was the best thing they'd ever heard, and they piped up too, howling like spaniels whose nuts hadn't dropped yet.

Three days out, the sun punched through the dirty clouds and put a steely shimmer on the sea. It cooked the brine out of our clothes and got everybody dry and happy. I couldn't help but think that if Naddod were really as serious as we were all sure he was, this crossing would have been a fine opportunity to call up a typhoon and hold a massacre. But the weather held, and the seas stayed drowsy and low.

We had less light in the evenings out here than at home, and it was a little easier sleeping in the open boat without a midnight sun. Gnut and I slept where we rowed, working around each other to get comfy on the bench. I woke up once in the middle of the night and found Gnut dead asleep, muttering and slobbering and holding me in a rough embrace. I tried to peel him off, but he was a big man, and his hard arms stayed on me sure as if they'd grown there. I poked him and jabbered at him, but the dude would not be roused, so I just tried to work up a little slack to where he wasn't hurting my ribs, and I drifted back to sleep.

Later, I told him what had happened. "That's a lot of horseshit," he said, his broad, loose cheeks going red.

"I wish it were," I said. "But I've got bruises I could show you. Hey, if I ever come around asking to be your sweetheart, do me a favor and remind me about this."

He was all upset. "Fuck you, Harald. You're not funny. Nobody thinks you're funny."

"I'm sorry," I said. "Guess you haven't had a whole lot of practice lately having a body beside you at night."

He got quiet and rested on the oar a second. "That's right," he said, turning his face away. "I haven't."

Thanks to an easy wind blowing from the east, we crossed fast and sighted the island six days early. One of the hockchoppers spotted it first, and when he did, he let everyone know it by cutting loose with a battle howl he'd probably been practicing in his father's pigyard. He drew his sword and swung it in figure eights above his head, causing the men around him to scatter under the gunwales. This boy was a nasty item, a face like a shoat hog and a vibrant beard of acne ravaging his cheeks. I'd seen him around at home. He had three blackened, chopped-off fingers reefed to his belt.

Haakon Gokstad looked up from his seat in the stern and shot the boy a baleful look. Haakon had been on more raids and runs than the bunch of us put together. He was old and creaky and worked the rudder, partly because he could read the tides by how the blood moved through his hands, and also (though you'd never say it when he could hear) because those old arms were poor for pulling oars. "Put your ass on that bench, young man," Haakon said to the boy. "We got twelve hours' work between here and there."

The boy colored. He let his sword arm hang. He looked at his friends to see if he'd been humiliated in front of them, and if he had, what he needed to do about it. The whole boat was looking over at him. Even Djarf paused in his song. The other kid on his bench whispered something and scooted over. The boy quickly sat and grabbed the oar, head bowed. The rowing and the chatter started up again.

You could say that those people on Lindisfarne were fools, living out there on a tiny island without high cliffs or decent natural defenses, and so close to us and also the Swedes and the Norwegians—how we saw it, we couldn't afford *not* to come by and sack every now and again. But when we came into the bright little bay, a quiet fell over all of us. Even the hockchoppers quit grabassing and looked. The place was wild with fields of purple thistle, and when the wind blew, it twitched and rolled, like the hide of some fantastic critter shrugging in its sleep. Red wildflowers spurted on the hills in gorgeous, indecent gouts. Apple trees lined the shore, and there was something sorrowful in how they hung so low with fruit. We could see a man making his way toward a clump of white-walled cottages, his donkey loping along behind him with a load. On the far hill, I could make out the silhouette of the monastery. They hadn't got the roof back on from when we'd burned it last, and with orphaned roof joists jutting up, it looked like a giant bird's nest whose occupant had left for distant shores. It was such a lovely place, and I hoped there would still be something left to enjoy after we got off the ship and wrecked everything up.

We gathered on the beach, and already Djarf was in a lather. He did a few deep knee bends. He got down on the beach in front of all of us and ran through some poses, cracking his bones and drawing out the knots in his muscles. Then he closed his eyes and said a silent prayer. His eyes were still closed when a man in a long robe appeared, picking his way down through the thistle.

Haakon Gokstad had a finger stuck in his mouth where one of his teeth had fallen out. He removed the finger and spit through the hole. He nodded up the hill at the figure heading our way, "My, that sumbitch has got some brass," he said. Then he put the finger back.

The man walked straight to Djarf. He stood before him and removed his hood. His hair lay thin on his scalp and had probably been blond before it went white. He was old, with lines on his face that could have been drawn with a dagger point.

"Naddod," Djarf said, dipping his head slightly. " 'S'pose you've been expecting us."

"I certainly have not," Naddod said. He brought his hand up to the rude wooden cross that hung from his neck. "And I won't sport with you and pretend the surprise is entirely a pleasant one. Frankly, there isn't much left here worth pirating, so, yes, it's a bit of a puzzle."

"Uh-huh," said Djarf. "Can't tell us anything about a hailstorm, or locusts and shit, or a bunch of damn dragons coming around and scaring the piss out of everybody's wife. You don't know nothing about any of that."

Naddod held his palms up and smiled piteously. "No, I'm very sorry, I don't. We did send a monkeypox down to the Spanish garrison at Much Wenlock, but honestly, nothing your way."

Djarf's tone changed, and his voice got loud and amiable. "Huh. Well, that's something." He turned to us and held up his hands. "Hey, boys, hate to break it to you, but it sounds like somebody fucked something up here. Old Naddod says it wasn't him, and as soon as he tells me just who in the motherfuck it was behind the inconveniences we been having, we'll get back under way."

"Right." Naddod was uneasy, and I could see a chill run through him. "If you're passing through Mercia, I know they've just gotten hold of this man Ethelred. Supposed to be a very tough customer. You know, that was his leprosy outbreak last year in—"

Djarf was grinning and nodding, but Naddod looked stricken.

Djarf kept a small knife in his belt, and in the way other men smoked a pipe or chewed seeds, Djarf stropped that little knife. It was sharpened down to a little fingernail of blade. You could shave a fairy's ass with that thing.

And while Naddod was talking, Djarf had pulled out his little knife and unzipped the man. At the sight of blood washing over the white seashells, everybody pressed forward, hollering and whipping their swords around. Djarf was overcome with a sort of crazed elation, and he hopped up and down, yelling for everybody to be quiet and watch him.

Naddod was not dead. His insides had pretty much spilled out, but he was still breathing. Not crying out or anything, though, which you had to give him credit for. Djarf hunkered and flipped Naddod onto his stomach and rested a foot in the small of his back.

Gnut was right beside me. He sighed and put his hand over his eyes. "Ah, shit, is he doing a blood eagle?"

"Yeah," I said. "Looks that way."

Haakon spit again. "He don't need to mess with that. Damn tedious waste of time."

Djarf held up his hand to quiet the crowd. "Now I know most of the old-timers have seen one of these before, but it might be a new one on some of you young men." The hockchoppers elbowed each other, giddy with anticipation. "This thing is what we call a 'blood eagle,' and if you'll just sit tight a second you can see—well, it's a pretty wild effect."

The men stepped back to give Djarf room to work. Djarf placed the point of his sword to one side of Naddod's spine. He leaned into it, and worked the sword in gingerly, as though he were doing elaborate embroidery on a piece of rare silk. He went at it slowly, delicately crunching through one rib at a time until he'd made an incision about a foot long. He paused to wipe sweat from his brow, and made a parallel cut on the other side of the backbone. Then he knelt and put his hands into the cuts. He fumbled around in there a second, and then drew Naddod's lungs through the slits. As Naddod huffed and gasped, the lungs flapped, looking sort of like a pair of wings. I had to turn away myself. It was very grisly stuff.

The young men roared, and Djarf stood there, flushed with pride, conducting the applause. Then, at his command, they all broke out their sieging tackle and swarmed up the hill.

Only Gnut and Haakon and Ørl Stender and I didn't go. Ørl watched the others flock up toward the monastery, and when he was sure no one was looking back, he went to where Naddod lay dying, and struck him hard on the skull with the back of a hatchet. We were all relieved to see those lungs stop quivering. Ørl sighed and crossed himself. He said a funerary prayer, the gist of which was that he didn't know what this man's god was all about, but he was sorry that this humble servant had gotten sent up early, and on a bullshit pretext too. He said he didn't know the man but that he seemed nice enough, and he probably deserved something better the next time around.

"Hell of a rigged-up-ass excuse for a raid," Haakon grumbled.

Gnut smiled and squinted up at the sky. "Have you ever seen a day like this? This is a heck of a fine day. Let's go up the hill and see if we can't scratch up something for a picnic."

It was all the same to him, a month away from home for neither moral purpose nor riches. He did not have a wife waiting on him who was pissed already and would require extravagant palliating with Northumbrian booty.

We hiked up to the little settlement on the top of the hill. Some ways over, where the monastery was, the young men were on a spree, shouting and setting the trees on fire, dragging out the monks and pulling blood eagles.

Our hands were sore from the row over, and we paused at a well in the center of the village to wet our palms and have a drink. We were surprised to see the young hockchopper from the boat bust forth from a stand of ash trees, yanking some poor half-dead citizen along behind him. He walked over to where we were standing and let his victim collapse on the dusty boulevard.

"This is a hell of a sight," he said to us. "You'd make good chief-tains, standing around like this, watching other people work."

"Why, you little turd," Haakon said. He took his hand off his hip and backhanded the boy across the mouth. The fellow lying there in the dust looked up and chuckled. The boy squealed with rage, plucked a dagger from his hip scabbard, and stabbed Haakon in the stomach. There was a still moment. Haakon gazed down at the ruby stain spreading across his tunic. He looked greatly irritated.

A sweet, angelic expression of overmastering anxiety crept across the young man's face as he realized what he'd done. He was still looking that way when Haakon cleaved his head across the eyebrows with a single, graceful stroke.

Haakon cleaned his sword and looked again at his stomach. "Sumbitch," he said, probing the wound with his pinky. "It's deep. I believe I'm in a fix."

"Nonsense," said Gnut. "Just need to lay you down and stitch you up."

Ørl, who was softhearted, went over to the man the youngster had left. He propped him up against the well and gave him the bucket to sip at.

Across the road, an old dried-up farmer had come out of his house. He stared off at the smoke from the monastery rolling down across the bay. He nodded at us. We walked his way.

"Hullo," he said. He looked hard at my face. "Hm. I might recognize you."

"Could be," I said. "I was through here last fall."

"Uh-huh," he said. "Now that was a hot one. Don't know why

you'd want to come back. You got everything that was worth a shit on the last going-over."

"Yeah, well, we're having a hard time figuring it ourselves. Just supposed to be an *ad hominem* deal on your man Naddod. Wrong guy, as it turns out, but he got gotten anyway, sorry to say."

The man sighed. "Doesn't harelip me any. We all had to tithe in to cover his retainer. Do just as well without him, I expect. So what are you doing, any looting?"

"Why?" I said. "You got anything to loot?"

"Me? Oh, no. Got a decent cookstove, but I can't see you toting that back on the ship."

"Don't suppose you've got a coin hoard or anything buried out back?"

"Ah, a coin hoard. Jeezum crow, I wish I did have a coin hoard. Coin hoard, I'd really turn things around for myself."

"Yeah, well, I don't suppose you'd own up if you did have."

He laughed. "You got that right, my friend. But I guess you got to kill me or believe me, and either way, no hoard." He pointed at Haakon, who was leaning on Gnut and looking pretty spent. "Looks like your friend's got a problem. Unless you'd like to watch him die, why don't you bring him inside? Got a daughter who's hell's own seamstress."

The man, who was called Bruce, had a cozy little place. We all filed in. His daughter was standing by the stove, and she gave a nervous "pip" when we came through the door. She was a small thing and looked neither young nor old. She had a head full of thick black hair, and a thin face, pale as sugar. She was a pretty girl. So pretty, in fact, that it took a second to notice she was missing an arm. We all balked and had a look at her. Haakon took his hand off his stomach and gave a boyish wave. Ørl farted anxiously. But Gnut, you could tell, was truly smitten. The way he looked, blanched and wide-eyed, he could have been facing a wild dog instead of a good-looking woman. He rucked his hands through his ropy hair and tried to lick the crust off his lips. Then he nodded to her and uttered a solemn "hullo."

"Mary," Bruce said. "This man has developed a hole in his stomach. I said we'd help fix him up."

Mary looked at Haakon. "Aha," she said. She lifted his tunic and surveyed the wound. "Water," she said to Ørl, who was looking on.

Gnut eyed him jealously as he left for the well. Then Gnut cleared his throat. "I'd like to pitch in," he said. Mary directed him to a little sack of onions in the corner, and told him to chop. Bruce got a fire going in the stove. Mary set the water on and shook in some dry porridge. Haakon, who had grown rather waxen, crawled up on the table and lay still. "I don't feel like no porridge," he said.

"Don't worry about that," Bruce said. "The porridge is just for the onions to ride in on."

Gnut kept an eye on Mary as he bent over a small table and overdid it on the onions. He chopped and chopped, and when he'd chopped all they had, he started chopping the chopped-up ones over again. Finally, Mary looked over and told him, "That's fine, thank you," and Gnut laid the knife down.

When the porridge was cooked, Mary threw in a few handfuls of onion and took the concoction over to Haakon. He regarded her warily, but when she held the wooden spoon out toward him, he opened his mouth like a baby bird. He chewed and swallowed. "That doesn't taste very good," he said, but he kept eating anyway.

A minute passed, and then a peculiar thing occurred. Mary lifted Haakon's tunic again, put her face to the wound, and sniffed at it. She paused a second and then did it again.

"What in the world is this?" I asked.

"Gotta do this with a wound like that," Bruce said. "See if he's got the porridge illness."

"He doesn't have any porridge illness," I said. "At least he didn't before now. What he's got is a stab hole in his stomach. Now stitch the man up."

"Won't do any good if you smell onions coming out of that hole. Means he's got the porridge illness and he's done for."

Haakon looked up. "Oh, you're talking about a pierced bowel."

"Yes," said Bruce. "Pierced bowels, the porridge illness."

Mary had another sniff. The wound, evidently, did not smell like onions. It only smelled like a wound. She cleaned him with hot water and was able to stitch the hole to a tight pucker, after telling Gnut about fifty times, thanks very much, she could manage without his help.

Haakon fingered the stitches, and, satisfied, passed out. The five of us stood around, and no one could think of anything to say.

"So," Gnut said in an offhand way. "Were you born like that?"

"Like what?" Mary said.

"Without both arms, I mean. Is that how you came out?"

34

"Sir, that is a hell of a thing to ask my daughter," Bruce said. "It was your people that did it to her."

Gnut said, "Oh." And then he said it again: "Oh." And then really no one could think of anything to say. Finally, Gnut stepped around the table and quietly let himself out. Then we heard him out in the yard, cussing and kicking things. He did that for a minute or two, but he was calm when came back in, and silent again.

Then Mary spoke. "It wasn't you who did it," she said. "But the man who did, I think I'd like to kill him."

Gnut told her that if she would please let him know who it was, he'd consider it a favor if she'd let him intervene on her behalf.

She thanked him and Gnut nodded and grunted.

I said, "I would like a drink. Ørl, what have you got in that wineskin?"

"Hmph," Ørl said. The skin hung from his shoulder, and he put his hands on it protectively.

"I asked what have you got to drink."

"I've got some carrot brandy, for your damned information. But it's got to last me the way back. I can't be damp and not have something to take the chill off."

Gnut was glad to have something to raise his voice about. "Ørl, you're a son of a bitch. This man's daughter got her arm chopped off on our account, Haakon is maybe gonna die, and you can't even see your way to splash a little booze around. Now, that is the worst, the lowest, thing I've ever heard."

So Ørl opened up his wineskin, and we all had a dose. It was sweet and potent and we drank and laughed and carried on. Haakon came to, and in the mawkish way of someone who has almost died and sees the world through new eyes, he made a sentimental toast to what a splendid day it was. Bruce and Mary got loosened up and we all talked like old friends. Mary told a funny story about a filthy-minded apothecary who lived down the road. She was having a good time, and did not seem to mind how Gnut was getting all up in her personal space. No one looking in on us would have known we were the reason this girl was missing an arm, and also the reason, probably, that nobody asked where Bruce's wife had gone.

It was not long before we heard Djarf causing a commotion at the well. Me and Gnut and Ørl stepped outside. He had stripped to his waist, and his face and arms and pants looked about how you'd figure. He was hauling up buckets of cold water, dumping it over his head, and shrieking with delight. The blood ran off him pink and watery. He saw us and came over.

"Hoo," he said, shaking water from his hair. He jogged in place for a minute, shivered and then straightened up. "Mercy, that was a spree. Not much loot to speak of, but, damn, a hell of a goddamn spree." He did another deep knee bend, massaged his thighs and spat a few times. Then he said, "So, you do much killing?"

"Nah," I said. "Haakon killed that little what's-his-name lying over there, but no, we've just been sort of taking it easy."

"Hm. What about in there?" he asked, indicating Bruce's cottage. "Who lives there? You kill them?"

"No, we didn't," Ørl said. "They helped put Haakon back together and everything. They seem like very nice people."

"Nobody's killing them," Gnut said darkly.

"So everybody's back at the monastery, then?" I asked.

"Well, most of them. Those young men had a disagreement over some damn thing or other and fell to killing one another. Gonna make for a tough row out of here. Pray for wind, I guess."

Brown smoke was heavy in the sky, and I could hear dim sounds of people screaming.

"So here's the deal," Djarf said. "We bivouac here tonight, and if the weather holds, we shoot down to Mercia tomorrow and see if we can't sort things out with this fucker Ethelred."

"I don't know," Ørl said.

"Fuck that," I said. "This shit was a damn goose chase as it is. I got a wife at home and wheatstraw to bale. I'll be fucked if I'll row your ass to Mercia."

Djarf clenched his jaw. He looked at Gnut. "You too?"

Gnut nodded.

Djarf yelled. "Aaaaah! You motherfuckers are mutinizing me? You sons of bitches are mutinizing my fucking operation?"

"Look, Djarf," I said. "Nobody's doing anything to anybody. We just need to head on back."

"Motherfuck!" Djarf yelled. He drew his sword and leaped around the yard, striking at the earth and chunking up his gobs of sod. Then he snorted and ran at us with the sword raised high, and Gnut had to slip behind him quickly and put a bear hug on him. I went over and clamped one hand over Djarf's mouth and pinched his nose shut with the other, and after a while he started to cool out.

We let him go. He stood there huffing and eyeing us, and we kept our knives and things out, and finally he put the sword back and composed himself.

"Okay, sure, I read you," he said. "Fair enough. Okay, we go back. Oh, I should have told you, Olaffsen found a stash of beef shells somewhere. He's gonna cook those up for everybody who's left. Ought to be tasty." He turned and humped it back toward the bay.

Gnut didn't come down to the feast. He said he needed to stay at Bruce and Mary's to look after Haakon. Bullshit, of course, seeing as Haakon made it down the hill by himself and crammed his tender stomach with about nine tough steaks. When the dusk started turning black and still no Gnut, I legged it back up to Bruce's to see about him. Gnut was sitting on a hollow log outside the cottage, flicking gravel into the weeds.

"She's coming back with me," he said.

"Mary?"

He nodded gravely. "I'm taking her home with me to be my wife. She's in there talking it over with Bruce."

"This a voluntary thing, or an abduction-type deal?"

Gnut looked off toward the bay as though he hadn't heard the question. "She's coming with me."

I mulled it over. "You sure this is such a hot idea, bringing her back to live among our people, you know, all things considering?"

Gnut's voice grew quiet. "Any man that touches her, or says anything unkind, it will really be something different, the sort of shit I'll do to him."

We sat a minute and watched the sparks rising from the bonfire on the beach. The warm evening wind carried smells of blossoms and wood smoke, and I was overcome with a feeling of deep satisfaction. It had been such a pleasant day.

We walked into Bruce's where only a single candle was going. Mary stood by the window with her one arm across her chest. Bruce, we could see, was having a fit of anxiety, and when we came in he moved to block the door. "Get back out of my house," he said. "You just can't take her, with what little I've got."

Gnut did not look happy, but he shouldered past and knocked Bruce on his ass. I went and put a hand on the old farmer. His whole body had gone tight with grief and fury.

Mary did not hold her hand out to Gnut, but she did not cry when Gnut put his arm around her and moved her toward the door. The

37

look she gave her father was a wretched thing to see, but still she went easy, because with just one arm like that, what could she do? What other man would have her?

Their backs were to us when Bruce grabbed up an awl from the table and made for Gnut. I stepped in front of him and broke a chair on his face, but still he kept coming, scrabbling at my sword, trying to snatch up something he could use to keep his daughter from going away. I had to hold him steady and run my knife into his cheek. I held it there like a horse's bit, and then he didn't want to move. When I got up off him he was crying quietly. As I was leaving, he threw something at me and knocked the candle out.

And you might think it was a good thing, that Gnut had found a woman who would let him love her, and if she didn't exactly love him back, at least she would, in time, get to feeling something for him that wasn't so far from it. But what would you say about that ride back when the winds went slack and it was five long weeks before we finally fetched up home? Gnut didn't hardly say a word to anybody, just held Mary close to him, trying to keep her soothed and safe from all of us, his friends. He wouldn't look me in the face, stricken as he was with the awful fear that comes with getting hold of something you can't afford to lose.

Things got different then and they stayed like that. Not long after we got home, Djarf had a worm crawl up a hole in his foot and had to give up raiding. Gnut and Mary turned to homesteading full time, and it got to where we just stopped talking because those times we did get together he would laugh and chat a little bit, but you could see he had his mind on other things.

Where had the good times gone? I didn't know, but when Pila and me had our little twins and we put a family together, I got an understanding of how terrible love can be. You wish you hated those people, your wife and children, because you know what awful things the world will do to them, because you have done some of those things yourself. It's crazy-making, but you cling to them with everything and close your eyes against the rest of it. But still you wake up late at night and lie there listening for the creak and splash of oars, the clank of steel, the sounds of men rowing toward your home.

Nominated by David Plante, Marianna Cherry, Fence

THE LIMIT

memoir by CHRISTIAN WIMAN

from THREEPENNY REVIEW

I don't understand anything . . . and I no longer want to understand anything. I want to stick to the fact . . . If I wanted to understand something, I would immediately have to betray the fact, but I've made up my mind to stick to the fact.
— Dostoevsky, *The Brothers Karamazov*

I

I WAS FIFTEEN when my best friend John shot his father in the face. It was an accident, I'm certain, and but for the fact that I'd dropped a couple of shotgun shells as I was fumbling to reload, the shot could have been mine. I sometimes wonder what difference that might have made.

We were dove-hunting, catching them as they cleared the edge of the small tank on John's family's property outside of town. Surrounding the tank was a slight rise of brush before the fields, and John's father, a country doctor who shared a small practice with my father, had wandered off through the brush behind us to check the fenceline. I was close to my limit that afternoon, which I'd never gotten, wearing one of those hunting vests with pockets big enough to hold a dozen or so birds. I remember the full feel of it, reaching in every so often to touch the little feathery lumps as they cooled. It was nearly dusk, my favorite time in west Texas, the light like steeping tea, shadows sliding out of things.

I'd been hunting for a couple of years. It seems odd to me now that I was allowed to have a gun, as my family's history was not a placid one, and I myself was prone to sudden destructive angers and what my grandmother would call "the sulls." I have more than one vivid memory of being in my bedroom as one of these angers subsides, books and clothes scattered on the floor, a chair and dresser overturned. I take the shotgun from under my bed and pump a shell into the chamber—roughly, so everyone in the house is sure to hear. No one comes. No one ever comes. I set the stock on the floor, lean my chin on the top of the barrel, stretch my arm down toward the trigger I can't quite touch, and wonder if this is something I'll grow into.

Theatrics, that gun aimed at my parents more than myself, with a kind of calculated malice that, twenty years later, makes me wince. My mother was terrified of guns. That my brother and I weren't allowed to have toy guns as we were growing up, yet both got shotguns as gifts in our early teens, is ironic, I suppose, though in that flat world of work and blunt fundamentalism in which I was raised, where in grade school county history lessons I learned the virtues of a man who'd slaughtered three of the seven white buffaloes known to exist, where one branch of my family had spent their happiest years in a town called Dunn, it has only a sad sort of retroactive irony.

My mother's hatred of guns was something more than the expression of a delicate feminine sensibility. Her own mother had been murdered in front of her and her two brothers when she was fourteen. The killer was her father, about whom I know only that he was compulsively itinerant, almost certainly manic-depressive, and for the month or so prior to the act had been living apart from his family. He walked in the back door one evening and killed his wife as she was cooking dinner, waited while his children ran out into the fields, then laid down beside her in some simulacrum of spent desire and shot himself in the head.

This was just a story to me; less than that, really, since it wasn't so much told as breathed, a sort of steady pressure in the air. I don't remember it ever being mentioned, and yet I also don't remember a time when I didn't know about it. It had more reality for me than the night in my infancy when my father, who was also given to the sulls, went into his room and didn't come out for several months, for I have no memory of this and didn't learn of it until after I'd left home; but less reality than the aunt, Opal, who'd committed suicide before I was born. Supposedly, the whole extended family had conspired for a time to create their own private climate of calm, eradicating all

40

hints of darkness from their lives like a country rigidly purging its past, steering conversations toward church and children, hiding the knives. It was hunting, as one might imagine, that proved most difficult in this regard, though Opal's husband was very careful to make sure their two sons kept their guns "hidden" under the beds, the shells all locked up in a little chest to which he had the only key. It seems not to have occurred to anyone that they might simply stop hunting and get rid of their guns. It was Texas. They were boys.

My family was so quiet about these matters that I thought they were something we were supposed to be embarrassed about. I learned early and no doubt too well that only certain kinds of violence were acceptable, both as topics of conversation and as actions. I loved the story of the uncle who, frustrated by a particularly recalcitrant cow, slammed his fist into its skull so hard that the cow dropped immediately to its knees like some ruined supplicant. I loved my immense, onomatopoetic uncles, Harley and Burley, who'd storm into town after months on offshore oil rigs, the nimbus of gentleness around each of them made more vivid and strange by their scars and hard talk, the wads of cash they pulled from their pockets like plunder.

And though I was mildly, reflexively disciplined by my father after the one truly serious fight I had growing up, when I was consumed with an anger that still unnerves me and continued to beat a cowboy I'll call Tom even after I'd broken bones in my hand and every blow was doing me a lot more damage than it was doing him, I was alert to the tacit masculine pride. Even the principal who meted out our corporal punishment for fighting on school grounds whipped our backsides with a kind of jocular aggressiveness that amounted to approval.

But anything that suggested madness rather than control, illness rather than health, feminine interiority rather than masculine action, was off-limits. Or perhaps not so much off-limits as simply outside of the realm of experience for which we had words, for I don't remember *resisting* discussing these things, really, or having them deflected by adults. Later, when I would begin to meet other young writers who, like myself, generally had more imagination than available experience, the events of my family's history would acquire a kind of show-and-tell exoticism, little trinkets of authenticity brought back from the real world. That it wasn't a real world, not yet, that it had no more reality for me than what I read in books, didn't seem to matter too much at the time.

41

Now it does. At some point I stopped talking about my family's past and began reinventing it, occasionally in what I wrote, but mostly just for myself, accumulating facts like little stones which I would smooth and polish with the waters of imagination. I chose them very carefully, I realize now, nothing so big that it might dam up the flow, nothing too ugly and jagged to be worn down into the form I had in mind. Psychoanalysis is "creating a story that you can live with," I have been told, and perhaps that's what I was doing, though in truth I think I wanted less a story I could live with than one I could live without, less a past to inhabit than some recreated place I could walk finally, definitively away from.

The bullet hole between my grandmother's shoulder blades, then, and the way she crumples faster than a heartshot deer. I can see my grandfather stepping away from the door, can see the look in his eyes, which, I know, is meant to assure his children as they back slowly out of the room that he is as baffled and saddened by this as they are, that they needn't be afraid, that he would never, never hurt *them*. He walks heavily across the room, steps over his wife, and, in some last gasp of that hopeless hardscrabble sanity his children will inherit and pass on, turns off the stove so the dinner won't burn, then lies down beside her on the floor.

I can see my Aunt Opal, too, gathering the laundry, humming something, deciding at the last minute to wash the coats. She is not beautiful but there is something of the landscape's stark simplicity about her face, a sense of pure horizon, as if what you saw were merely the limit of your own vision, not the end of what is there. As she shakes out her husband's coat, a single forgotten shotgun shell falls out of the pocket onto the floor. I can see the dull copper where the light dies, the little puckered end of the red casing. *Oh, Honey,* she says as she picks it up, bemusement changing to concern on her face, concern to pain, *it's not your fault. It's no one's fault.*

Lately, though, more and more, it's John I see, standing stolid and almost actual in his boots and hunting vest, lifting his shotgun to his shoulder and laughing as I fumble to load mine. He is physically very similar to me but at ease in his body in a way I'll never be. He does not yet inhabit that continuous present that precludes remorse, but already he is all impulse and action, whereas I am increasingly deliberate, increasingly interior. There is some inner, inarticulate anger we share, though, and recognize in each other. When John's begins to slip out of control, the results for the people around him will be immediate, palpable, and utterly disastrous. My own implosion will be no more noticeable to the people around me than something I've imagined.

The gun that goes off in my ear now is a fact. It is muted by all the intervening years, by all that has happened, both internally and externally. Still, the authority of its report surprises me, as does the strangely muffled shout that seems to occur at almost exactly the same time, as if the dove, which once again John has not missed, which as I look up is plunging downward, had a human cry.

II

I don't want to kill myself. I never have, though for a time not too long ago the act emerged in me like an instinct, abstractly at first, and with a sort of voluptuous, essentially literary pleasure. (Nietzche: "The thought of suicide is a powerful solace; it enables a man to get through many a bad night.") Gradually the thought became more painful as it became more concrete, more dangerous as it became more familiar, more alienating as it became more my own. I thought of it as a kind of cancer in my mind, because eventually no matter what I was doing—teaching a class, sitting at a dinner party, trying to write, waking every hour of every night to check the clock—that was what I was doing, attending to that slowly clarifying imperative that beat itself out inside me as steadily and ineluctably as my own pulse.

I told no one. I couldn't. On the couple of occasions when I'd made up my mind that I would tell friends what was happening, my heart began to race, I had difficulty breathing, and I simply had no language for what I needed to say. Also, even during the worst of it, I always doubted the validity of the feeling, suspected that, like the impersonal stories I used to tell about my distant familial history, it might just be a bit of disingenuous self-dramatization. Despite the fact that I've had relatives on both sides of my family commit suicide, despite my knowledge that my father has resisted the impulse all his life, and my sister has twice attempted the act, I suspected I might be faking, using the thought of suicide as a way of avoiding the more mundane failures of my life. I wasn't going to tell anyone until I was *sure*. But how does one prove such terror is real except by committing the act itself?

My father knew, not definitively, perhaps, but with something like that visceral sense by which an artist comes to recognize the flaws in anything he's made. Our relationship is as fitful as ever—we go months without talking to each other—but there is more ease between us now, more forthright affection and trust. I think this has more to do with him than me. During the fifteen years or so when our relationship consisted of little more than holiday exchanges of information, he endured a divorce, bankruptcy, the loss of his medical practice, the death of his second wife, divorce again, back surgery, an almost fatal rattlesnake bite, a heart attack (from the volume of serum given to counter the snakebite), cancer, a plane crash, alcoholism, the estrangement and self-destruction of his children, and no doubt several other calamities which he's managed to keep secret. It was a run of luck that would have mellowed Caligula.

During the approximately six months that I was—what to call it?—thinking, sinking, we talked on the phone twice. On both occasions he asked me, out of the blue, and with a sort of mumbling quietude that I've begun to recognize in my own voice at emotional encroachments, "Do you ever think of doing away with yourself?" That's just the way he said it, "doing away with yourself," which led me to make a snide, annihilating comment about the linguistic imprecision and general uselessness of psychiatry, because in his late forties that's what my father had become, a psychiatrist living on the grounds of a state hospital, where suicide was as ubiquitous and predictable an impulse as hunger, where even the doctor whose place my father had taken, whose office he used and whose bedroom he slept in, had "done away with himself."

Some families accumulate self-consciousness in the way that others accumulate wealth (and perhaps one precludes the other). A man who eats and works and copulates all with same bland animal efficiency somehow sires a son who, maddeningly to the father, pauses occasionally in the midst of plowing to marvel at the shapes in the clouds, or who sometimes thinks fleetingly that perhaps there is an altogether different order of feeling than the mild kindliness he feels toward his wife. He in turn has a son who has the impulse to be elsewhere—geographically, sexually, spiritually—but not the wherewithal to wholly do so, who lives the impulsive, appetitive lives of his own children in the fixed world of his parents, and destroys both. A person emerging from the wreckage of this—and many simply don't—is likely to be quite solitary, given to winnowings and adept at departures, so absurdly self-aware that he can hardly make love with-

44

out having an "experience." He might even be, maddeningly to all concerned, a poet.

That I should have turned out to be a poet seems strange to me for all sorts of reasons—I don't relish poverty or obscurity, to name just two—but my background has never seemed one of them. Bookless though it was, my childhood, with its nameless angers and solitudes, its intimate, inexplicable violence, seems to me "the very forge and working-house" of poetry. Tellingly, my father, though he certainly never read poetry, is the one member of my family for whom my becoming a poet never seemed at all odd or surprising. I begin to understand this now. He knew—taught me—love's necessary severities, how it will work itself into, even be most intense within, forms of such austere and circumscribed dimensions that, to the uninitiated, it might not seem like love at all.

I am eight years old. My mother has been scratched by the kitten we've had for a month or so, and there has been a flurry of panic and activity as she has had the beginnings of a severe allergic reaction and been rushed to the hospital. I don't know where my brother and sister are, or why I've come home with my father, or if my mother is all right. I'm sitting on the couch, staring at the television, though it's not on. My father is looking for something in a kitchen drawer, now he's back in the bedroom looking for something else. My face is boneless, ghostly on the black screen. I'm hardly there. He walks past me with the kitten in one hand and a hammer in the other, opens the sliding glass door to the porch, closes it behind him. I shut my eyes, will myself away.

It's eight years later. My father is having an affair. He and my mother are at the edge of what will be a nasty, protracted, ruinous divorce in which their children will be used as weapons. It's the middle of the afternoon on a school day and I'm stoned, maybe on speed as well, I forget. Some little argument cracks the surface of civil estrangement we've tacitly agreed upon, and out of that rift all the old anger rises. I begin to curse at my mother in a way I've never done before or since, now I break something, now something else, and she's scared enough to call my father at the hospital and leave the house until he rushes home.

They come in together. I am sitting in the living room, seething, waiting. My father stands over me and quietly—guiltily, I realize, the first flaw in his hitherto adamantine authority—asks me what is going on. I tell him I'm ashamed of him. I call him a liar. I curse him in the harshest and most profane terms I can muster. He hits me open-handed across the face—hard, but with a last-minute hesitation in it, a pause of consciousness that seems to spread like a shadow across his face and, as he sinks into a chair, is to this day the purest sadness I have ever seen.

I stand up slowly. I am vaguely aware of my mother yelling at my father, of my sister in the doorway weeping. I am vaguely aware that our roles have suddenly and irrevocably reversed, that he is looking up at me, waiting for what I'll do. I hit him squarely between the eyes, much harder than he hit me. He does nothing but cover his head with his hands, doesn't say a word as I hit him again, and again, and again, expending my anger upon a silence that absorbs it, and gradually neutralizes it, until the last blow is closer to a caress.

That was the end of my childhood. My father moved out within a month or so, and in the same time I gave up drugs (well, close enough), began the exercise regimen that I've maintained for twenty years, and started assiduously saving for the tuition for my first year of college, to which I was suddenly determined to go, and which I would choose entirely on the basis of its distance from Texas. Once there I sometimes went months without talking to any member of my family, whose lives seemed to me as dangerously aimless and out of control as mine was safely ordered and purposeful. I began to read poetry, which I loved most of all for the contained force of its forms, the release of its music, and for the fact that, as far as I could tell, it had absolutely nothing to do with the world I was from.

And then one night John killed a man outside of a bar. I'd kept up with him somewhat, had been forced to, in fact, since in a final asser-tion of physical superiority he'd ended my lingering relationship with my high school girlfriend by impregnating her. I knew that he'd gone to work in the oil fields, and that he was deep into drugs. Our friend-ship had fallen apart before this, though, a slow, sad disintegration that culminated in a halfhearted, inconclusive fistfight on a dirt road outside of town. I forget the reason for the fight itself, and anyway it wouldn't be relevant. What we were trying to do, I think, was to for-malize the end of something that had meant a great deal to both of us, to attach an act we understood to a demise we didn't.

My mother called to tell me about it. John had gotten in an argument with a stranger that escalated into blows. They had been thrown out of the bar by bouncers and continued the fight in the street. In front of some thirty or forty people John had slowly and with great difficulty won the fight, beating the man until he lay on his back gasping for air. And whether the pause I've imagined over and over at this point is something that came out in the trial, or whether it's merely some residual effect of my friendship with John, my memory of a decent and sensitive person to whom some glimmer of consciousness must surely have come, what happened in the end is a fact. At nineteen years old, with his bare hands, in front of a crowd of people who did nothing, and with a final fury that must have amazed that man who was only its incidental object, John destroyed him.

Hanging up the phone, sitting there in my dorm room of that preposterously preppy college fifteen hundred miles away from my home, it all came back, the guns and the fights, the wreckage of my family, my friendship with John, the wonderment in his voice in the hours after that hunting accident when he kept saying, *I shot my father, I shot my own father*, as if he were trying out the thought, trying to accommodate it in his consciousness.

I did what I always do: I went for a run, thirteen miles through the hills of Virginia, much farther than I usually ran, but without difficulty, my heart a steady thump-thump-thump in my chest. It was not release. It was the same thing as my precipitous decision to get out of Texas, no different from what poetry would be for me for years, until I would finally find myself back home one day, living on the grounds of that state hospital, collecting facts. It was what suicide would have been the final expression of: flight.

III

Dr. Miller's face was obliterated. He walked out of the brush across from us and around the edge of the tank with the hesitant precision of someone making his way across a familiar room in the dark. Amid the blood and loose bits of skin there were clumps of pellets cauliflowering his cheeks and the sockets of his eyes, distorting his forehead and throat like a sudden, hideous disease, his dark shirt darker down his chest. His lips, too, were so misshapen that it was hard at first to understand the directives he was giving us, though he spoke calmly, deliberately, with the same west Texas mix of practical necessity and existential futility that no crisis could ever shock my own father out of.

He drove. I don't remember there being even a moment of discussion, though both John and I had our licenses by then, and though Dr. Miller had to lean over the steering wheel to see, wincing as the pickup jolted over the ruts and stones. I was sitting in the middle of the seat, John at the door. I kept trying not to look at Dr. Miller, kept thinking that his breaths were shorter than they should have been, that I could hear blood in his lungs.

There were two gates before we got to the road. At the first one, John simply leapt back in the truck as it was still moving, leaving the gate unlatched. Dr. Miller stopped, turned his head like some sentient piece of meat toward us, and said, "Close the gate, John."

At the second gate, after John had gotten out of the truck, Dr. Miller said without looking toward me, "You didn't fire that shot, did you?"

Could it be, in life as well as in writing, that our deepest regrets will not be for our lies, but for the truths we should not have told?

"He didn't mean to," I said, the words spilling out of me, "it was an accident, we thought you were in the south pasture, we didn't hear you, we. . ."

"It's my fault," Dr. Miller said peremptorily, putting his hand on my knee. "I know that."

About halfway through the ride John began to weep. He was leaning over against the door, and as his shoulders trembled up and down, it seemed years were falling away from him, that if he were to reach out it would be with a hand from which all the strength was gone, if he were to speak it would be in the voice of a child. I looked out at the fields that had almost vanished, darkness knitting together the limbs of mesquite trees, accumulating to itself the crows and telephone poles, the black relentless pumpjacks which, when John and I spent the night out here, beat into our sleep like the earth's heart.

Dr. Miller drove himself straight to my father, who was still at the office. My father registered no more alarm for Dr. Miller's injuries than Dr. Miller himself had done, though my father did, I noticed, immediately and carefully touch my face, my shoulders and arms, as if to ensure himself that I wasn't the one hurt.

John and I waited in my father's office. I sat in my father's chair behind the desk, John in the chair across from me, looking out the window. This is when I remember him saying, "I shot my father, I shot my own father," not to me, and almost as if it were a question, one that neither I nor anyone else could answer. Not another word

48

was said. I sat there watching the clock on the wall across from me, willing it to go faster, faster.

To be a writer is to betray the facts. It's one of the more ruthless things about being a writer, finally, in that to cast an experience into words is in some way to lose the reality of the experience itself, to sacrifice the fact of it to whatever imaginative pattern one's wound requires. A great deal is gained, I suppose, a kind of control, the sort of factitious understanding that Ivan Karamazov renounces in my epigraph. When I began to spiral into myself and into my family's history, it was just this sort of willful understanding that I needed. I knew the facts well enough.

But I don't understand, not really. Not my family's history and not my childhood, neither my father's actions nor his absence. I don't understand how John could kill someone, or by what logic or luck the courses of our lives, which had such similar origins, could be so different. I don't understand, when there is so much I love about my life, how I could have such a strong impulse to end it, nor by what dispensation or accident of chemistry that impulse could go away, recede so far into my consciousness that I could almost believe it never happened.

It did happen, though. It marked me. I don't believe in "laying to rest" the past. There are wounds we won't get over. There are things that happen to us that, no matter how hard we try to forget, no matter with what fortitude we face them, what mix of religion and therapy we swallow, what finished and durable forms of art we turn them into, are going to go on happening inside of us for as long as our brains are alive.

And yet I've come to believe, and in rare moments can almost feel, that like an illness some vestige of which the body keeps to protect itself, pain may be its own reprieve; that the violence that is latent within us may be, if never altogether dispelled or tamed, at least acknowledged, defined, and perhaps by dint of the love we feel for our lives, for the people in them and for our work, rendered into an energy that need not be inflicted on others or ourselves, an energy we may even be able to use; and that for those of us who have gone to war with our own minds there is yet hope for what Freud called "normal unhappiness," wherein we might remember the dead without being haunted by them, give to our lives a coherence that is not "closure," and learn to live with our memories, our families, and ourselves amid a truce that is not peace.

49

I hear my father calling me from what seems a great distance. I walk down the hall of the office that has long ago been cleared out and turned into something else. But here are my family's pictures on the walls, here is the receptionist's window where my sister and I would play a game in which one of us had some dire illness which the other, with a cup of water, or with some inscrutable rune written on a prescription pad, always had the remedy for. And here is John, small and terrified, walking beside me.

Dr. Miller is sitting up on an examining table, his face swathed in gauze, his shirt off, revealing a sallow, soft, middle-aged body. Its whiteness shocks me like a camera's flash and will be the first thing I'll think of when, within months, John tells me that his father has left for another woman. We stop just inside the door, side by side. My heart seems almost audible.

"Well now," my father says, smiling slightly as he looks to the table then back to us, "did you boys get your limits?"

Dr. Miller laughs, and John moves toward him.

He is all right. Everything is going to be all right. I stick my hand in my pocket full of cold birds to feel how close I've come.

Nominated by Threepenny Review, Talvikki Ansel

THE LACE MAKER

by CARL DENNIS

from SALMAGUNDI

Holding the bobbins taut as she moves the pins,
She leans in close, inches away from the fabric
Fretted and framed on the wooden work board.

A young woman in a yellow dress
Whose lighter hair, bound tight to her head
But flowing about one shoulder,

Suggests the self-forgetful beauty of service,
Service to a discipline. Just so the painting
Forgets the background to focus on her.

Here she is, so close to the surface
The painter could touch her if he stretched his hand.
Close work in sympathy with close work.

The sewing cushion holding the colored threads
Suggests a painter's palette. So Vermeer
Offers a silent tribute to another artist

Who's increasing the number of beautiful
Useless things available in a world
That would be darker and smaller without them.

This is no time to ask if the woman
Wishes she were rich enough to buy the likeness,
If Vermeer can afford the lace she's making;

No time to consider them bandying compliments.
They work in silence, and you may look on
Only if you quiet your thoughts enough

To hear the click of her needles as you lean in close
(But not so close that you cast a shadow)
And the light touch of his brush on canvas.

Nominated by Maura Stanton, Wesley McNair

SCORDATURA

fiction by MARK RAY LEWIS

from ONTARIO REVIEW

W<small>HEN YOU'RE SEVENTEEN</small> and you're the gay son of a Baptist preacher from Dallas Texas and you have a lisp and a drawl and a musical gift and you were named Oral because an angel told your daddy to do so in a dream, then New York City can seem like it's saving your life. But when you're twenty-four and an epidemic has claimed all your friends and all your friends' friends including your one-true-love who you abandoned after a final ultimatum seven months before he died because he was drinking two bottles of red wine a day and *not communicating* and only finding out later that he had been HIV positive, and being shunned at the funeral by his hip political activist mom as well as the very last of the mutual friends in favor of his new lover who was only there at the end, and your tests keep coming up negative and your ruddy good health looks back at you from the mirror like a screaming miracle, then, when that happens, New York City can seem small and exhausted.

So after finding the keys and the title left stealthily/anonymously in your mail slot and sitting in his Volvo P-1800 and leaning over and slobbering on the soft vinyl case of the cello in the passenger seat and driving all over New Jersey feeling the vibrations of his beloved Webber fuel injectors, looking for a good cliff to sail off but feeling sure that God would find a way to fuck with you, like He'd catch you halfway down and make you say that you love Him, and returning to your neighborhood and searching for parking and finally you double-park, slosh through the blackened snow, stuff a suitcase full of sheet music and a pair of organ shoes and head for home. It's what anybody might do, including you.

You arrive in the morning feeling long-dead and ready for scraps.

Your house has been converted into a Discipleship House. You knew this but it surprises you again. There are four Christian young men living on bunk beds in your old room and six Christian young women living in the remodeled basement and everyone is assigned a night to make dinner and another night to do the dishes and they smile at you and say sweet simple things and no one in your family asks about Micah, especially not your sister. There's a soundtrack running in your head as usual but this one is especially repetitive, a Philip Glass tape you found in the glove compartment and let loop all the way down the belly of North America. When people talk you smile and nod and treat them like they're speaking in the middle of a concert, or if they start to push it you exit to the piano or go for a walk among the lava rock lawns and naked oaks and blooming Judas trees; it is the most beautiful time of year in Texas. Afternoons you join your mother in the backyard where she is landscaping more ground than ever, as if in response to losing control of the house. She has always preferred to garden in silence. You refuse gloves or tools and go to a corner and dig in the dirt with your soft white fingers, accomplishing little.

You sleep on the long couch in your dad's study where Micah slept when he used to come down with you, before you realized that he enjoyed it all too much—the traditional family and the role of playing your buddy—he treated it all like a big joke, and in response they fell in love with him. Your head is three feet from the computer where your dad files his sermons and behind that a picture of him carrying a football in the same preseason exhibition game that brought him off the bench and clipped his career in the knees, and a black and white picture of him standing like Samson between two pillars of the portico of First Baptist and your mom a step below, three months pregnant with your sister Rose, and at the bottom of the picture is JFK and the others in the spotless convertible about to enter a dark canyon formed by Cahill Manufacturing and the Lone Star Bank.

You brought no clothes and it would take two of you to wear your dad's, so you pilfer the closet of dead-guy clothes donated by widows and you imagine you're them, both before and after embalming. You remember that weird Sunday morning scene of walking in on your dad holding a suit coat for Micah to put his arms through and slapping his shoulders, "Perfect fit!" You go to your dad's barber and ask for the same, "the medium cut." You shower two or three times a day and use up to ten Q-tips and trim your nostril hairs and keep the nails at the quick. You sleep for ten-hour stretches. Your cock doesn't wake up at dawn and you don't think you miss it.

Your sister and her husband come over from Southwestern Seminary for dinner on Fridays. She still has her vintage Mustang and long legs and timeless style—the tight jeans and boots and Western shirts and black leather jacket—but the glint of rebellion that was growing in her eyes is completely gone now, as you knew it would be. You remember when she came to visit in New York during spring break of her senior year at Wheaton. You put her up with your friend Exene and she stayed coked to the gills the whole week and one afternoon she walked in on you and Micah—or somebody opened and shut that door—and on the way to the airport Sunday morning you made the mistake of stopping by the Cathedral of St. John the Divine where she started crying and within six months she had rededicated her life.

Before the second Sunday your dad asks you to play a solo and you say yes and get the key to the church and the organ and practice in the crimson and white auditorium full of empty wooden pews and curtained on three sides by stained glass. You close your eyes and imagine you're the young J.S. Bach, ten years old, parents both dead, trudging through the dark forest, across meadows and wet marshes, trying not to destroy your leather shoes, miles and miles of silence except for the chattering people, then finally making it to the cathedral at Ohrdruf, and walking through the tall doors and into the huge bright ornate house of God, the music blasting from the tall pipes, the ultimate holiness overpowering you, dropping you to your knees.

Your mother tells you that your grandfather called but you don't call him back, then he leaves a message that he wants you to record what you play in the services. He's been trying to be grandfatherly since you and Micah flew down to play at his wedding when he married Edna Pearl. She was your grandma's best friend and they married less than a year after your grandmother died. Your dad didn't attend the ceremony.

Sunday your dad puts your name in the bulletin and below his own on the marquee out front in bold red letters, big enough that even JFK couldn't have missed them. After the service the old ladies with penciled eyebrows come through the reception line and fall all over you. One says, what about that nice cello player? Another duet sometime?

The next three weeks you stay at the organ through the whole service and your dad asks you to organize the music for the upcoming Easter Sunday. "You love Easter," he says.

"What about Bob Sullivan?" you say.

"He's still the hymn leader," he says. "Unless you can warble and sing out of the side of your mouth like that." He's a joker.

You relish the opportunity to pick only your favorite hymns and organize a total Bach-fest, nothing but Bach for the musically challenged. They'll think they stumbled into Notre Dame.

You ponder the poetry of it: the Crucifixion, the Resurrection, and the Ascension, plus a nod to the Second Coming and the Rapture of the Elect before the Great Tribulation.

Easter Sunday you wake to your dad playing boogie-woogie piano in the living room: *woke up this morning feeling fine, woke up with heaven on my mind.* You vacate the study and you find a bright blue Tuxedo coat among the dead men's clothes. It's gotta be forty years old. You match it with some black pants and walking out the door your dad stops you, carrying a bowl of cereal in one hand. Two Christian young women watch him from the table. "You know who that belonged to don't you? Deacon Whiteside. He wore it every Easter too."

"The Bubble Gum Man?" you say, just like a kid.

"Yup. You're asking for it, wearing that."

You stop by a station and spend money for the first time since you've been home. Gas and bubble gum. Standing at the pump you cringe at the clash between the coat and the car's forest green. You stuff the coat pockets with individually wrapped pieces and feel happy, or interested at least, driving the freeways downtown to church. It's sunny and beautiful just like it has been every goddam Easter Sunday your whole life. Your pockets and your cheeks are full of gum and staying on the right side of the road is no problem, it requires no special concentration. You pull past the marquee bearing the family name twice, as well as a quote from your dad: Jesus is King, Not Elvis.

You park in a staff-only spot up front and let yourself into the auditorium and practice for a while then you go to the old choir rehearsal room and lock the door until it's time to start playing the intro. On your way back into the auditorium Deacon Meinhart pulls you aside. "Schroeder" he calls you. He says the boss told him to give you the list of announcements and you pick up a bulletin and see that your name is there next to the announcements and you sit down at the organ and read over them. It's a small list of birthdays and hospitalizations, but you should've been asked first. You know exactly what he's doing and he's been doing it your whole life, since even before you were born. The weird thing is that now you don't seem to mind. *So what happened to Oral?* you hear one queer say to another queer at Cafe Pergolesi. *He went back to Dallas to become a preacher.*

You hate public speaking. Besides the speech impediment—which you forget about and some people actually like—you have a fear of losing control of yourself when addressing groups of people larger than, say, five. You like to attribute it to the time you were seven and you performed "We Three Kings" with your best friend Sean and his older brother for a Christmas concert. You and Sean had been covertly wearing panty hose every day for over a month since one Sunday playing at his house between services, he asked if you had ever worn them. No, you said, but you did not laugh at the idea. He pulled up his pant leg to show that he was indeed wearing a pair and he celebrated their warmth and comfortableness. Back at home you stole a pair from your mom's closet and it was December and they were warm, and comfortable, and it was all fine, until the middle of that song when you looked at him and his eyes said, *We're standing here in front of everyone in baggy purple robes and gold painted crowns and underneath it all we're wearing panty hose.* Then you had to stop singing and put your tongue into your lower lip to arrest the laugh and he looked up toward the ceiling lights and let out a painful sort of yelp and you pulled your crown down over your eyes and disintegrated, while his big brother plowed ahead—"field and fountain, moor and mountain, following yonder star."

You push the record button on the cassette player and begin with *Jesu meine Freude* a piece that you memorized a long time ago and you close your eyes and lean into the keys and skip tap on the foot pedals with your soft-soled shoes. Toward the end you hear a voice behind you and you glance back and there's a kid saying "Hey, do you have any gum?" You shift your hips so that your coat pocket slides off the edge of the bench and you nod your head to the side. "Can I have a piece?" the kid asks. "In the pocket," you say. The song is supposed to end but you improvise a coda so the kid will be able to make it back to his seat in time. "Hurry up," you say and you feel the pull of his hand rifling around. The kid is greedy. His hand gets stuck and you have to stop playing and slide off the bench to keep the coat

57

from ripping in half. Pieces of gum fly all over the stairs which causes a riot of children to the front of the auditorium. You empty your other pocket onto the stairs and turn the pockets out to show that you have no more. An adult emerges, gives you a look, and pinches the first kid who approached between the shoulder and neck, leading him out a side door. "Be sure to check for panty hose," you want to call after them, as Micah could've and would've, but not you.

Now it's time for the opening announcements that you never agreed to give and you're not up for it, so you go to your dad, Pastor Paul, sitting in a wooden throne chair to the left of the pulpit and say, "I can't do the announcements. I'll start laughing."

He raises an eyebrow. "Laughter is a good place to start," he says. He holds his hand over his lapel mike. His voice is rich with reverb, like there's a reed in his throat. He's incapable of whispering and as a kid you enjoyed making him try. "Believe it or not, these people enjoy laughter," he says.

Over his shoulder you can see your sister Rose in a choir gown, in the front row, shoulders back, posture perfect. Behind her is the beautiful white alcove where your dad baptized you when you were six. Above the baptismal font hangs a set of the thickest bass pipes, copper tinged with streaks of red-brown and green.

"No, I mean I'll really lose it," you say. "It'll be just like 'We Three Kings.' "

You used the Three Kings excuse once before when you were sixteen and already headed back east and you went to your dad's study less than an hour before the annual all-Youth-led service was to begin in order to tell him you would not be able to preach the sermon. That time it was a lie, but a merciful one.

"I'll take over if that happens," he says.

"No, sir," you say. "You should've asked me first. Maybe next week."

He doesn't say anything but takes the list from you.

You go back to the organ. He approaches the pulpit and sniffs the microphone then sniffs his lapel mike and bends over and sniffs the carpet around the base of the pulpit. A few people in the audience laugh. "What's that smell?" he says. "Oral, do you smell that?"

You ignore him and frown down at the keyboard. You recall a time he took the pulpit after you and Micah played and he said, "Wouldn't that cello-player make a fine son-in-law?" The congregation giggled, embarrassed for your sister, who turned red but not as red as you.

He takes a deep whiff and says, "Oh, oh. I'm sorry. I know what that is. Never mind. Deacon Fuller, could you close that door. I can't concentrate with the smell of my daddy's smoker wafting in here." Ha ha ha! Everyone laughs. "Yes that's Graydon tending his brisket, sending his regards down to the house of God. He says he has his calling and I have mine and last week when he invited me over for Easter I just couldn't refuse. The Bible says honor your parents that your days may be long on the earth and this afternoon I plan to do just that. Yes, a second and perhaps a third time, too.

"Wasn't that a fine piece of music Oral played? Purrr-dee. Uh! I was especially surprised by that ending, that last note in particular. Who would've thought? Those old composers are something else. I mean Mozart and Chopin and what-not . . . full of surprises." He holds his hand up to his brow and looks out at the congregation. "Are all the little munchkins back in their seats? Yes? We'll give them that one for free. Chalk it up to the Easter Bunny and sensory overload from all the colorful hats you lovely ladies are wearing. Plus Billy should probably get a prize. I don't know if you all made the connection but the legacy of the Bubble Gum Man lives on at First Baptist Dallas. Isn't that right Oral? I believe he's in it for good now. I don't think the munchkins are going to let him back down from his responsibilities hereafter." He holds up the list. "And do we have some birthdays to announce?"

Hymn #481, "Just a Closer Walk with Thee"

Instrumental, "Der Tag der ist so freudenreich"
(The Day Which Is So Rich with Cheer) J.S. Bach

Hymn #334, "Blessed Assurance, Jesus Is Mine"

Instrumental, "Wachet Auf, ruft uns die Stimme"
(Wake, The Voice Calleth) J.S. Bach

Pastor's Message, "Fourth and One on Your Own Thirty-five"
Scripture, John 16:2

It's not until near the end, actually into the altar call—you're already meandering around the keys to the melody of "Softly and Tenderly"—that he mentions AIDS. It sounds almost like an accident.

He's in the middle of an inventory of the obvious signs that the world is coming to an end—war, earthquakes, famine, disease . . . He doesn't say explicitly that it was sent to earth by God as a punishment to homosexuals, though perhaps he's emphasized that enough already. They know what it means—the wages of sin, judgment. You know what he means. But there's a hesitation, an almost-embarrassment in his voice, like he has lost his train of thought for a moment or is uncertain of his pronunciation.

After lunch Edna Pearl and your mom start clearing plates and your grandpa says, "I gotta go take my medicine and check on the bees. Oral? You up for a ride?"

"Sure."

"Bring the tape," he says.

"Well don't take too much of your medicine," Edna Pearl says from the kitchen. "He gets weird when he takes too much of his medicine." No one responds to her, ever.

In the mud room your grandpa stops and says, "Have you had sex recently."

"No sir," you say.

"That's what I thought," he says. "Me neither. Bees don't like the smell. Too much like bear."

You approach an old blue Dodge. "Four hundred dollars," he says, squaring his body to a side panel and banging it with a hard upper-cut. "Army surplus. I think they shot missiles at it, but by God they missed."

There's a wire hat rack with a thick hinge attached to the middle of the ceiling with two dirty cowboy hats in it. "I need one of these for my Volvo," you say.

"That's illegal in Texas," he says. "You have to go to Sweden if you want to do shit like that."

As he drives down a gravel road, he pulls out a pipe and a baggie of what looks like pot though it couldn't possibly be.

"Smoke a bowl?" he says.

"Good God," you say. "I didn't know you smoked pot."

"I suspect there's a lot you don't know about me," he says. "It's good for the eyes. I try not to enjoy the side effects. My acupuncturist gets it for me."

"Acupuncture?" you say. "What about Shacklee? The vitamins?"

He pulls a bottle of multivitamins out of a pocket in the seat cover.

"To keep the wheels from falling off I like a multi-leveled approach. Smoke?" he says.

"No," you say. By the time you felt ready to allow mind-altering substances into your life, marijuana had become the drug of the dying, a smell linked to the Perry Street Hospice. "I've probably had a contact high."

"Contact high?" he says. "That sounds like an urban myth. Like cows asleep standing up. Maybe narcoleptic cows. Maybe in Oklahoma."

He takes a hit and hands the pipe to you. It's the first time you've ever inhaled smoke, any smoke, directly into your lungs. You remember as a kid taunting the cigarette smokers who'd bolt outside after the church service—you'd brush by them and then cough and gag and fall down dead on the lawn.

"So what's up with your boyfriend?" he says.

You feel a searing in your lungs as you inhale too quickly and begin a coughing fit that lasts a good two minutes.

He pats you on the back with his free hand. "I've awoken a sleeping monster," he says.

You get momentary control and say, "I guess there's a lot you know about me that I didn't know."

"Sure," he says. "I'm your Grandpappy. I knew before you were ten years old. And I knew you were in for a hard ride."

"That's impossible," you say. "I didn't know until I was fourteen."

"You think so?" he says. "Different theories, I guess. So it's over with him . . ." He lifts a cassette out of the seat cover and reads it. "Micah."

"Over," you say.

"I'm sorry," he says.

You drive along in silence for a while.

"So," he says. "What is it you are doing now, may I ask? Is this a temporary thing, this living with your parents and devoting yourself to the First Baptist Dallas?"

You shrug.

"Seems kinda strange to me. I mean, from one P.K. to another. You never had the fortune of meeting your great-grandfather. Wonderful man. Used to like to grab me by the hair at the supper table. Sweet. A revivalist. Churches would call him when they wanted to be kicked in the ass. It was all about fire and brimstone, fear. When he visited a church it smoldered for weeks afterward. He could jump-start a dead horse. Shit. Your dad is different. A good guy, all in all. I suspect that makes it more difficult for you in some ways." He turns onto a dirt road. "It's been interesting watching you grow up, Oral. That is until you were fourteen and you stopped talking to me. Typical enough, though I could've done without the "Meat is Murder" T-shirts and calling me a butcher and all."

"Morrissey," you say, as excuse.

"But I don't remember you seeming too happy last time you were living at home and going to church three times a week, that is, right before you went to school up north. You were one wound up little fucker as I recall. But hell, I guess things change . . . people change . . . I don't know . . . Tell me, has the Southern Baptist Convention recently passed a resolution to embrace tolerance? Last time I heard they were packing gay Christians off to sexual reorientation camp. *Reorientation*," he says again. "Sounds pretty backward ass doesn't it? Pretty sick, actually. But what the hell do I know?"

"I'm like Bach," you say and you let that sink in.

"I don't follow," he says.

"I'm bringing spiritual sustenance to the dark forest." Your voice sounds trite but you go on. "I mean who really knows how Bach felt? What Bach wanted to fuck? No one."

"In other words you enjoy being a song and dance man for bigots, since after all there might be some historical precedent . . ."

"It's a great organ," you say.

"Yeah?" he says.

"In New York I played a 1901 Murray Harris, but only in a tiny soundproof room. I was limited to two hours. Organs are meant to be played at high volume in large spaces. Preferably a sanctuary."

"Are you sure there's not some sort of charge you're getting out of it? Some sort of, I dunno, like it's a big charade? It seems to me it could only end in disaster for everyone concerned. Especially you."

"I don't have anything better to do right now," you say.

"No?" he says. "Can't think of anything? Bet I could make you a list."

"I'm resting," you say. "Taking a sabbath."

"Good for you," he says. "But don't fall asleep. I remember how you'd cry as a kid and tell me you didn't want me to burn in hell. You'd get out your little Children's Bible. You could barely read but you'd open it up and point. Jesus Christ, it was unbearable! I mean, just don't forget where you come from." He slows to cross an abandoned railroad track. "Back by the pond near the house there's a certain fence post, a thick irregular one, covered in orange and green lichen, it's nice—I'll show you when we get back. Anyway, I walk out to that post every morning, first thing, before coffee. What do I do there? I don't know but I like to call it 'prayer.' I like the word. Although I'd never use it with your dad or any other Christian—they think they've got the patent. And I pray for you every day," he says.

"Really grandpa?" you say, and you feel like you're about eight and inside a black and white television set. *A boy is drowning Lassie? Ruff! How far away? Ruff, Ruff, Ruff. Three miles? Ruff!* "Good God, I'm stoned," you say. "Good God." It's way too bright in Texas. You open the glove compartment and grab a pair of sunglasses and pull the smaller, inside hat (Edna Pearl's?) out of the hat rack. It's too big for you, but it rests on the top of the sunglasses. A black cow watches the approach of the truck with big mellow eyes and it occurs to you that the son of man never had a grandpa.

You pull past a row of salt licks, white and scooped out like decaying teeth. He backs up to a wooden water tower and cuts the engine but leaves the battery running. "Do you have the tape?" he says.

"Yes."

"Put it in," he says. "I'm going to tell you about the birds and the bees. I need a soundtrack."

"Listen for a funny part at the end of the first chorale prelude," you say.

"Okay," he says. "So. In the hive there are three different castes or groups or what have you. There's the queen—always only one unless there's a big problem going on. There's the worker bees of which there are lots of subsets: home builders, field workers, nurse bees. They do everything including defending the hive and curing my arthritis with their venomous little kamikaze attacks. Then there's the drones. The drones do almost nothing, the bare minimum, the very least that they can get away with. They consider themselves the proud stewards of the royal jelly and if the hive needs to create a new queen, they have the power to do so. Their whole lives they dream of one day, that is, the day of the mating flight with the queen. Around here it happens in late fall but further north it happens in late summer. I try to wait until after to do my biggest extraction because the bees are most submissive then. It's when there's plenty of honey stored up for winter and things seem pretty calm and stable and the cracks are all caulked with propolis to keep out the weather and basi-

63

cally the workers are tired of taking care of the drones and they don't see the need to do it for another day. So the queen stops laying eggs and puts on something sexy and saunters out to the entrance of the hive and takes flight. Watching this the drones get horny as hell and go scurrying after. The queen flies up and around and around and she lets the drones mount her in midair, one at a time. One would hope that it's the best sex ever because when the drones go to pull out, the queen rips their dicks off with the super strong muscles of her vagina and calmly says, Next. And the next drone in line hops right up. The drone who just lost his dick tries to fly back to the hive—you can imagine it must be a terrible flight—but if he makes it he finds the worker bees are guarding the entrance, Sorry, no admittance. If he is insistent then they will bounce him off the landing board. The queen meanwhile keeps each of these dicks inside her and flies home and somehow catalogs them inside her so that later when she's fertilizing eggs she can actually pick the dick she wants to use."

You've doubled over on the bench seat, "Oh, that's the worst story I've ever heard," you say. "You got me high to tell me that?"

"Think about it. It's a good story. But don't go making a parable out of it. It's just weird, that's all," he says. "Now let's go get some honey."

He leaves the tape playing and the doors open. He opens the tailgate and hands you a safari-looking hat with a net and a pair of long suede gloves. You button the cuffs on your white shirt and tuck your pants into your socks. He takes out a tin cylinder with a spout at the top and bellows attached to the back side. He lights a piece of burlap and stuffs it in. He has you stand aside with your arms in the air and he runs it over your body like a metal detection wand. It makes you feel young and cooperative and a little giddy. He does the same to himself. You hear the end of the prelude and your dad sniffing the mike and joking about the brisket and you look at each other and laugh. You edited out the general announcements and a hymn so the tape goes immediately into the next chorale prelude. He takes a small pry bar out of the truck and holds it up. "The wonder bar," he says. He walks ahead of you past the wooden water tower and past a slimy green pipe dripping water into an old antique clawfoot bathtub.

"You could sell that tub for a lot of money in New York," you say.

"I'm kinda hoping it doesn't come to that," he says.

You go up a muddy cow-churned path and through a small grove of oaks. You can see the hives across a field about a hundred yards away, like stacks of unwrapped presents.

As you cross the field he says, "It's been the warmest winter on record. That means nectar."

He approaches the hives from behind. He takes the tin bellows and smokes the entrance and smokes all around the hives. You don't know why he's doing this but it seems perfect and holy and that association will dominate even later when you have your own hives in San Diego and neighbors call you to get swarms out of trees and you know that the smoke is meant to simulate forest fire. He pulls you to the front of the hive and points out a big odd-looking bee. A drone, he mouths through his veil. He takes the wonder bar and pries off the lid of the top super and the air becomes thick and frenetic with loud bees. He leans over and looks in to make sure all the bees have exited through the one-way excluder. He lifts a rack of comb out and it drips with honey. Bees fly all around your head, some land on his bare hands and crawl up his arm. He puts the rack back into the super and points down at a detached abdomen and stinger pumping venom into the underside of his arm. It looks sad and painful but he smiles. Arthritis medicine. He lifts the whole super and hands it to you and it is very heavy with honey. You can feel it in the muscles that line your spine to create the small of your thin back. He puts the lid back onto the top of the hive and points to the truck and asks you with his arms and face if you can carry it okay. No problem, you nod and turn in that direction. He goes along beside you and smokes you with the bellows again, then he turns back to the other hive. After the smoke clears a throng of angry and confused bees begins circling your head and crawling on the net in front of your eyes and your back is aching and your arms are quivering and before you're halfway across the field you know it was a mistake, that you've overestimated your strength, but then you begin to hear the tape playing the faint organ music and you concentrate on the different voices of the melody. *O Mensch bewein deine Sünde gross.* What does that mean? You try to forget about the pain in your arms and back. It's the end of the service. The altar call. The mike is mostly overpowered by the organ but you can hear your dad's voice in the background, tinny and small, not unlike your own voice. You step forward careful on the dry, uneven ground and the sermon that you spent so much time preparing for that youth service begins to play back to you.

Always always start with a joke. What joke? The hardest part. Buy a joke book. Find something with a sort of built-in irony to the end, like a boycott of Disney. Make them laugh and slowly hypnotize them and finally make them cringe, that's the idea. Use the Cruden's Concordance with the King James. Build a foundation on scripture. Revelations 3:15–16. Red letters: *I would thou wert cold or hot. So then because thou art lukewarm, and neither cold nor hot, I will spew thee out of my mouth.* That's the message to the church at Laodicea. The Lukewarm Church. And that's the message to you. You are the Lukewarm Church, make that clear. *We* are the Laodiceans, The Lukewarm Church. Then a sort of state of the sinful nation, bring in all sorts of random statistics, anything and everything, the decline of our great country through drugs and gangs, the Occult, new age and prostitution, abortion, infanticide, evolution, uppity women, prayer in schools, whatever. All the favorites. Throw some barbs that indicate the complicity of the church, the middle class, the status quo, backed up with more red ink—Mark 10:25: Easier for a camel to pass through the eye of a needle than a rich fucker . . . etc. But don't dwell on economics too much. Just get the general feeling of culpability. Then back to the decline of the nation. The liberal media, sex on TV, the movies, bad language, the Lord's name in vain, etc. A culture of heathens, turning away from God. Sodom and Gomorrah. Then the big move. Pull the screen down and tell Jeremy (acting as associate pastor) to hit the projector and show the slides of them homosexuals in San Francisco, the Folsom Street Fair, dragging each other around on leashes and chains, the hollow of a butt cheek stark against black leather chaps. And infiltrating the Boy Scouts of America! Sanctioned pedophilia, the Green Party in Germany, etc. Whip them into a frenzy and return again to the Church of Laodicea and the killer Sword Quote which you totally shout: Peace? Peace? No! Not Peace! But a Sword! I came to bring a Sword!

Then when they're really frothing at the mouth the big shocker: And guess what? There's an avowed ho-mo-sexual right here in our midst! Yes. Right here among us, people. Who? Who? Me. I am. That's right. I'm a faggot. Yes, you heard me. Now quick, come forward and kill me. I hate you mediocre fuckers. Your sex is so boring! It's as basic as plumbing! You idiots could never master queer sex, don't try it, you can't even clap through a hymn. So c'mon, stone me! Yes! Kill me!

And those that hadn't fainted already would rise up against you? Slay you?

No.

At first they would probably cheer, thinking you were acting out some live drama. They would chuckle at your squeaky, impeded voice. Then everyone would become embarrassed and ashamed. Silence. A few might laugh uncomfortably. A lone, sincere voice, "God help him." Then another, "Help him, Jesus." A pained, constipated look on the faces of those who thought they knew you, who thought they loved you. Most would stand and turn to go. Yes, the Lukewarm Church. Your dad would be the first to walk out the back door without turning to salt. Deacons would come forward, shaking their heads, disappointed and shy. They'd gently escort you off stage as Bob Sullivan led the remaining members of the congregation in some quiet hymn of mercy, something whiny like "There Is a Fountain."

Later everyone would smile with a wince and treat you like a misfortunate stranger, like a cripple. Someone would hand you the testimony of an ex-gay. Then they'd wait it out until you buckled and the orderlies came to take you away. Only a matter of time.

You are almost to the grove of oaks and the pickup is just below the embankment but you feel exactly like you did the time in eighth grade when you tried out for wrestling and they stuck everyone in a small padded room and cranked the heat up to suck out salt water and you pushed and pulled and pinned and stayed strong until the end and you were standing there listening to the closing remarks of the thick squat coach and next thing you were lying on your back on the mat with everyone in a semicircle above you and the coach was holding your feet off the ground and asking if you remembered your name. Your name? Would that be Oral?

But maybe you could've tapped into that vicious hateful side of them, that current of fear that saturates all of their politics and most of their beliefs . . . pricked the vein of their animalistic nature . . . because they are animals, Jesus came to earth as a man among animals, this you know. You close your eyes and plunge forward and concentrate on your dad's distant voice prophesying the end of time and the chorale prelude from *Das Orgelbuchlein* which means the little organ book and suddenly you see the congregation steaming and boiling and seething hot, rising up in a fury and grabbing anything they can—Bibles, hymnals, keys, lipstick, money clips, shoes, pencils, any-

67

thing, and they let it all fly as you grip your white pulpit full of honey. Yes! Yes! Finally! Stone me already! Yes! And you fall forward to the ground and roll over onto your back and throw off the veil and laugh and let the Texas sky shine on your hot face as everything flies through the air. You feel the venom pumping into your neck and your cheeks, then a figure stands between you and the sun. Your sister? Finally unable to bear it, rushing forward from the choir loft, awkward in her gown, gesturing with her hands, screaming Enough, No More.

Then you're being lifted out of murky water by big hairy-knuckled hands and strong Texas arms, water in your nose and your ears, and a windy wheezing voice and you know what your name is and your grandfather is saying it, *goddamn crazy fucking preacher's kid.*

Two years later you get a call with the bad news about your grand-dad, the heart attack, the hospitalization.

Your friends from the ad department of the free weekly put you on a plane to D/FW. At the hospital your dad spots you coming out of the elevator and he breaks from the family and crosses to you with a red, wet face. He pins you in a bear hug and speaks hoarsely into your ear. "It's wonderful. It's so wonderful. God is *so good,* son. My father, your grandfather, he confessed and repented and asked the Lord into his heart only moments before he passed away."

You exit down some stairs and out among the vents on the roof between two wings of the building. You hold your fist up to the blue sky and fast-moving white clouds and the stupid little birds and you say, "I'm so sick of You and Your Fucking Tricks." You see your sister watching you from a room window—serene, expressionless. You crouch at the edge and study the small brown pebbles. "That's it," you say. "I give up."

But it's not true, not for Oral. He gets sixty years of learning how to love this world before the moment he has to leave it.

Nominated by H.E. Francis, Joyce Carol Oates, Ontario Review

HOW TO MEDITATE

memoir by BRENDA MILLER

from FOURTH GENRE

DAY ONE

On ARRIVAL, huddle in the Volkswagen with your friends and eat all the chocolate in the car. Chocolate chips, old KitKats, the tag-end of a Hershey Bar—do not discriminate. Feel deprived, then light up your last Sherman, pass it around. Watch your fellow retreatants flow into the meditation hall. Note how elegant they look, even in sweatpants and black Wellingtons. Wonder where they get such nice sweatpants. Look down at your baggy jeans, your dim T-shirt and say, *I'm not dressed for this, let's go home.* Look beyond the meditation hall to the Navarro River, the cattails, the red-winged blackbirds. It will be raining, just a little.

Remember that you've forgotten dental floss. Take a deep drag off the cigarette and wonder what you're doing here. Take a close look at your companions in the car: your boyfriend Seth, who is so much older than you, and your friends John and Marybeth. Remember how the four of you, just days earlier, wound up tangled in a bed together, a soft bed with a down comforter, lazily stroking each other's limbs. Feel ashamed. Feel superior. Say, *Ready?*

A woman with bristled red hair leads you and Marybeth to the women's dorm. There will be a deck overlooking a marsh where the blackbirds clack and whistle in the reeds. Glance at the other women who are folding their extra pairs of sweatpants, their Guatemalan sweaters. Sit on the cot and pat it with one hand. It will be hard, unyielding, to help you obey the precept against lying in "high, luxurious beds."

Scope out the meditation hall. Set up your pillow, your blankets next to the wood-stove near the back door. Figure this will be a prime spot—easy in, easy out and smugly wonder why no one else has nabbed it. Realize your mistake when, during the first sitting period, heat blazes from the stove, frying the hair on your shins. Slide away a little, quietly as you can, and bump the knees of the woman next to you. Irritation rises from her like a wave. Start to apologize but choke yourself off mid-whisper.

Sit cross-legged on your pillow, your hands palm down on your knees. Breathe. Your teacher, who is from Burma, perches on a raised platform, his belly round, his knees hidden under his white robe. He speaks in a voice so deep it vibrates beneath your skin. He repeats the word: *equanimous, equanimous.* Invent a strange animal, an *Equanimous*, half-horse, half-dolphin, gliding through the murky sea of your unconscious. Feel where the breath enters and leaves your body just below the nostrils, like a fingertip tapping on your upper lip. Concentrate on this sensation. Within seconds find yourself thinking about Marybeth's hand on your breast. Go back to your breath. Find yourself thinking about pancakes, eggs, bacon. Go back to your breath. Spend your first hour of meditation this way. They call it "monkey mind." Picture your brain swinging through the banana trees, its little hands clutching the vines.

Feel the pain begin in your knees, between your shoulder blades. Shift a little and feel the pain travel up your neck, down into your hips. Open your eyes halfway and surreptitiously glance at the meditators around you. They look perfectly still, their backs straight, their *zafus* round and plump. Look at your own flat pillow spilling from beneath your thighs.

You don't have the right equipment for this. You'd better leave now, before you're paralyzed.

Day Two

Read the rules again: No talking, no reading, no sex, no drugs, no eye contact. Vipassana, they say, is the art of looking deeply. Be unsure about how deeply you want to look. Read the schedule six times—4 A.M.: waking bell, 4:30–5:00: chanting in the hall, 5–6: sitting, 6–7: breakfast, 7–9: sitting, 11:00: lunch, more sitting, nap time, more sitting, tea at 4:00, no dinner, Dharma talk at 7, more sitting. Add up the hours of meditation and come up with the number 16.

Figure this must be a mistake and perform the calculations obsessively in your head, your own private mantra. You're already so hungry it's difficult to concentrate. Think longingly about the chocolate in the car, and hate yourself for not saving just a little.

Go to breakfast. Hold a simple white bowl in your two hands. Stand in line with your fellow retreatants and note the radiant colors of their shawls, their scarves, the blankets they have draped over their shoulders. Shuffle your way to the breakfast table. There will be large urns full of porridge. Take some. Take too much. Take a banana. Realize that your boyfriend Seth is opposite you at the table. Watch his hand as it chooses a pear, puts it back, takes an apple, puts it back. Feel a surge of love and annoyance. Out of the corner of your eye see a glint of Marybeth's blond hair. See a flash of John's denim shirt. Feel grateful and angry at the same time.

Sit down at the long picnic table and begin to eat your food. Realize you need some honey and scan the table, spying it at the far end. How do you ask for it without speaking? You decide to get up and fetch it yourself, to avoid making an embarrassing faux pas. When you stand up your knees hit the table, knocking over your neighbor's teacup. Irritation rises from her like a wave.

Go back to your room and lie down. Fall asleep. Hear bells ringing in the distance. Know that you are supposed to be somewhere, then sit bolt upright and run to the meditation hall. Slow to a casual walk when you approach the doors. Stand and listen to the silence a minute. Listen to the breathing. Open the door, which creaks on its hinges. Tiptoe to your seat, aware of everyone aware of you, of your every move. Settle in. Breathe. Fingertip. Nostril. Etc. Feel an overwhelming desire to run screaming from the meditation hall. Think about pizza. A cigarette. A beer. Feel your breath for one, maybe two seconds. Feel your neck slowly seizing up. Fantasize about yourself paralyzed. Imagine Seth and John and Marybeth caring for you, running cool cloths across your forehead. Imagine the three of them kissing you all over your numb body, trying to restore feeling. Gasp when the bell rings. Hobble out of the meditation hall.

Go to lunch. Hold a simple white bowl in your two hands. Shuffle forward and ladle yourself miso soup, rice, some wilted bok choy. Take too much. Reach for the tamari. Notice Seth watching you from the opposite side of the table and dab it on sparingly. Sit down and eat slowly, slowly. Wonder if there's dessert.

When you wake up, you might hear two women whispering in the bathroom. If so, take the opportunity to feel superior. Calculate how long it's been since you've last eaten. 16 hours. This seems impossible. Wonder why everything adds up to 16.

Drape a blanket over your head and walk outside, toward the meditation hall. Notice the red-winged blackbirds, the budding lilac, the silver cast to the sky. You'll think it's beautiful. You'll think you'll have to get up earlier at home from now on. Pause for a moment and notice your breath, like a fingertip tapping on your upper lip.

When you enter the hall the chanting has already started. Your teacher seems to chant the word *Betamite* over and over, with variations in pitch and speed. Wonder what Betamite is. Think of it as a breakfast spread, sweet and salty at the same time. Think about breakfast. Calculate the amount of porridge you will ladle into your bowl. Top it with honey and a pear. Breathe. Notice yourself breathing. Notice yourself noticing yourself breathing. Your neighbor tips over, asleep, and wakes up with a stifled cry. Feel sympathetic. Smile a sympathetic smile to yourself.

In the afternoon take a walk down by the river. You do not have Wellingtons, so your feet get wet and cold. Your hands are freezing. You miss your friends. You feel alone in a way that is foreign to you. Try to remember if you've ever been so completely alone in your life, and realize how surrounded you've always been, how supported. Remember how you laughed in bed with Seth and John and Marybeth. Remember the release of it, how it felt not so much like sex, but like love multiplied ten-fold.

Wonder if you'll ever be able to speak again. Try it. Open your mouth. Feel a tiny bit of panic tremble beneath your upper arm. Feel hunger in your belly like a wild animal.

DAY FOUR

Just when you think you have it down, just when you've noticed yourself noticing your breathing for unbroken seconds at a time, your teacher tells you everything will change from now on. Now you must become aware of the sensations on the surface of your skin. Now you must scan your body, *sweep* your attention from head to toe, noticing the sensations arise and pass away. Arise and pass away. *Equanimous*.

Start with the top of your head. Feel your skull like a dumb shield, hard and unyielding. Feel nothing, then feel a slight tingling, a teardrop of sensation. Notice it. Move your attention like a scrim down the crown of your head, to the tips of your ears. Feel an overwhelming desire to run screaming from the meditation hall. Return to what you know. That fingertip. Settle in with the fingertip tapping on your upper lip. Feel competent. Feel sly.

Thirty minutes later open your eyes halfway and, without moving your head, try to see toward the men's side of the room. Move your gaze past young men with straight spines, men whose faces seem chiseled, calm, focused, unconcerned. Find among these men your boyfriend, Seth. See his furrowed brow, his downturned mouth, his clenched fists. See him trying so hard. Look past him for John. Try to find John anywhere in the room.

When you walk back to the dorm, see Marybeth flossing her teeth on the deck. Stop behind a tree and watch her floss and floss, the movements of her hand so practiced, her teeth so white. Feel at a loss when she turns around and heads back inside, the deck now so empty.

At lunch, take the right amount of salad, half a baked yam, stir-fried snow peas with tofu. Hold your bowl in both hands as you find your seat at the picnic table. Sit in the same seat every day, though you could sit anywhere you like. Try to eat with chopsticks, the way the people in radiant scarves do. Drop bits of food all over the table. Try to brush them away, casually, with the back of your hand.

You've memorized fragments of the people around you: a hand, a wrist, a thigh. You know their shoes: Birkenstocks, rubber boots, thongs. You recognize their smells: rose water, underarms, unwashed wool. Feel at home in this. Then feel surrounded by bits of people disintegrating.

At night, you'll have trouble sleeping, though you're so tired you think you might go insane. Breathe in and out. *Equanimous. Equanimous.* Your teacher's voice is the only one you hear all day, and so you listen carefully to every word he says. At night, when you cannot sleep, briefly worry about brainwashing. Think of your brains heaped in a sink, rinsed repeatedly in cool water.

At 5 A.M. you'll feel as though you're in a film. Drape your blanket over your head, clutch it closed at your throat, so you're cowled like a monk. Think of an appropriate soundtrack, something with gongs and birdsong. On your way to the meditation hall, you might see someone furtively smoking a cigarette. If so, feel superior. *Sweep* your attention from the top of your head to the bottoms of your toes. Make it to somewhere mid-torso before you begin craving kisses, wine, a cigarette.

After breakfast it's your turn for karma yoga, which means you have to wash the dishes. Stand at the sink with a man who, out of the corner of your eye, looks incredibly handsome, radiant. He moves efficiently through the kitchen, drying the dishes you hand him with a rough towel. Imagine the two of you communicating without words as you plunge simple white bowl after simple white bowl into the hot water. Imagine you are married to him, that you have a house in the country with two dogs and a meditation room. Imagine the children you will have together, their terrible beauty. Feel him close by your side. He hands back a bowl you haven't washed properly; a gob of gray porridge clings to the rim. Feel as though you want to die.

Walk to the meditation hall in the rain. Think, *equanimous, equanimous.* Feel the water evaporate from your skin as you *sweep* your attention from the top of your head to the bottoms of your toes. Think about Marybeth's hand on your breast, Seth's mouth on your lips, John's lips on your thigh. Try not to feel like a harlot. Try to remember how *natural* it all seemed at the time. Calculate how many different relationships must be nurtured in this foursome. Come up with the number 16.

At the Dharma talk that evening, discover that you will now have periods of "strong sitting." Now you must not move a muscle, no matter how painful the sitting becomes. Practice "strong sitting" for a half-hour before going to bed. As soon as you begin, feel an overwhelming urge to run screaming from the meditation hall. Feel a sharp pain radiate from your hip, your ankle. Resist the urge to move. Feel the tension in the room rise.

Then, inexplicably, feel your body relax. Feel the pain arise and pass away, arise and pass away, a continuous and fluid thing, impermanent. Begin to feel a glimmer of understanding. Begin to see your body in these terms, arising and passing away. Even the muscles.

Even the hard bones. Even the core of you. Begin to wonder if the body that melted under the touch of Marybeth's hand is the same body that now arises and passes away. Feel a bewildered sorrow. Return to your breath. Wait for the bell to ring.

DAY SIX

In the night, when you're not sleeping, have a terrible dream. Feel your body dissolve, turn into nothing but air. Not even air. Jerk yourself back. Lie there gasping for breath. Resist the urge to wake up Marybeth, to lie down next to her, to feel her impermanent skin against your own.

DAY SEVEN

Decide to ask your teacher about this experience. You will go up to him during the question/answer session after the Dharma talk. Spend all day worrying about this, about what exactly you will say, what words to use. Worry that your voice might sound harsh and ugly, like someone diseased.

Wait your turn. Kneel next to the stage, and know that Seth can see you, and Marybeth. Try to look serene. John, you think, has stopped coming to the meditation hall, has decided to find enlightenment on his own. Bad boy. Envy him his initiative.

Move forward on your knees. Kneel before your teacher. His face is large, larger than your head. His eyes are kind but almost all pupil, and you feel yourself drawn into them, spiraling the way you did in your bed last night. So lean back a little, take a deep breath. His wife, next to him, smiles at you and you suddenly want to cry. Say, *I felt myself.* . . . Start again. Say, *I have so much fear.* . . .

He laughs. Fear is fear, he says, impermanent, passing away. He waves his hand in the air and for a moment it seems to vanish in a flash of white. Thank him. Return to your place near the wood-stove. Breathe. Feel the fingertip tapping on your upper lip.

In the last meditation period of the day, have another dream. Think of yourself pregnant, squatting behind a chair, giving birth to a baby girl. Feel yourself split open. Feel the beating of your heart, your blood.

Day Eight

Breathe.

Arise.

Pass Away.

Day Nine

Begin to dread the breaking of Noble Silence. Begin to appreciate how much of your life is taken up with small talk and inconsequential matters. Swear you will get up earlier when you get home, you will speak only when necessary, you will be an equanimous person, even if you never touch Marybeth or John or Seth again. Work hard at your meditation, so hard you break out in a sweat during "strong sitting." In the afternoon, realize that Marybeth has been sitting behind you all along. Wonder how you missed her there, all this time. Before going to your seat, watch the back of her head, the set of her small shoulders. See her as a body already dead. See the flesh passing away until only a skeleton remains. Wonder how you will live your life from now on.

Begin to lift your head and look at your fellow retreatants. Notice that everyone seems a little worn down, pale, sallow. Look forward to washing your sweatpants, sleeping in your own bed. Wonder if you will be alone in that bed. Memorize a speech you will give to Seth, John, and Marybeth. Swear you will love them no matter what happens.

Eat a pear for breakfast. Some rice and tofu for lunch. Steal some floss from Marybeth while she's in the shower. Stop in your tracks at the whistle of a blackbird. Whistle back, a small sound made of nothing but air.

Day Ten

Break the Noble Silence. Feel the buzz in the room. Everyone's giddy. You've all just returned from a trip to a foreign land; you all have pictures to show, stories to tell. Even the strangers look familiar to you. Say *Don't I know you?* to everyone you meet. Notice the subtle glow around everyone's cheekbones. Sit with Seth and John and Marybeth at a round table on the deck. Hear the blackbirds yukking it up in the glade.

Well, Marybeth says, holding John's hand to her heart. *We've decided to have a baby!* A baby. The words seem so loud, so rough-hewn, you have trouble getting them from your ear to your brain. Marybeth's gaze slides across your face. John looks straight at you and grins. Seth puts a hand on your shoulder, and takes it away again.

Forget the speech you were going to give. Start to tell them about the night you dissolved in your bed, about your fear of becoming no one, but halfway through sputter to a stop. Try to feel your breath like a fingertip tapping on your upper lip. Feel an overwhelming urge to run screaming from the dining hall.

Walk a path through wet grass down to the Navarro River. Say good-bye to the blackbirds and their red shoulders. Think you will always remember this, and know that you won't. Feel yourself rising and passing away, there by the river. Look upstream and then down. Feel yourself like a boulder in the middle, worn by the rushing water. Hug yourself. Feel your hands strong against your upper arms, holding yourself in place.

Nominated by Daniel Henry, Bruce Beasley, Fourth Genre

THE SENSUAL WORLD

by LOUISE GLÜCK

from AMERICAN POETRY REVIEW

I call to you across a monstrous river or chasm
to caution you, to prepare you.

Earth will seduce you, slowly, imperceptibly,
subtly, not to say with connivance.

I was not prepared; I stood in my grandmother's kitchen,
holding out my glass. Stewed plums, stewed apricots—

the juice poured off into the glass of ice.
And the water added, patiently, in small increments,

the various cousins discriminating, tasting
with each addition—

aroma of summer fruit, intensity of concentration:
the colored liquid turning gradually lighter, more radiant,

more light passing through it.
Delight, then solace. My grandmother waiting,

to see if more was wanted. Solace, then deep immersion.
I loved nothing more: deep privacy of the sensual life,

the self disappearing into it or inseparable from it,
somehow suspended, floating, its needs

fully exposed, awakened, fully alive—
Deep immersion, and with it

mysterious safety. Far away, the fruit glowing in its glass bowls.
Outside the kitchen, the sun setting.

I was not prepared: sunset, end of summer. Demonstrations
of time as a continuum, as something coming to an end,

not a suspension; the senses wouldn't protect me.
I caution you as I was never cautioned:

you will never let go, you will never be satiated.
You will be damaged and scarred, you will continue to hunger.

Your body will age, you will continue to need.
You will want the earth, then more of the earth—

Sublime, indifferent, it is present, it will not respond.
It is encompassing, it will not minister.

Meaning, it will feed you, it will ravish you,
it will not keep you alive.

Nominated by Susan Wheeler, Lucia Perillo

LUNCH AT THE BLACKSMITH

fiction by CORNELIA NIXON

from PLOUGHSHARES

I THINK AT LAST I will give up the Blacksmith House. I've liked the place since college, when my best friend, Celia, and I would meet for coffee in those frugal, scrubbed pine rooms, full of the feel of long-dead Puritans, which we were not. You could smoke in public in those days, and we sucked unfiltered Pall Malls, the most kick for the buck, making sure that there was paint on us somewhere. Celia was beautiful, part Indian, part imp, with Coke-bottle green eyes and skin that somehow let you know it wasn't white, though it was nougat-pale, creamy. Her father and older brothers fished in Maine, and she liked to wear ripped jeans, flannel shirts, and stroll along beside the tweedy Harvard crowd with languid grace.

Underneath, hidden to everyone but me, she had a conscience worthy of Aquinas, and a deep God streak. She wanted to discuss the moral implications of our every act. Was it right to buy paint when you could give all your money to the poor? Was a portrait of a dying homeless person just sensation for itself? For years we wondered what she could do with a certain married professor that would be morally correct, yet satisfy her raging need to get into his pants.

"He tucked the label in my shirt," she said one day, upstairs in the Blacksmith House. "I felt his fingers on my neck. He went on staring at my canvas like it was nothing. I think he has some casuistical system worked out, wherein he can do anything so long as his motives are pure. He pretended to be calm and said something about Gauguin. 'What was his crime against perspective?' as if I might do it, too. As if his mission were to prevent me."

"What did you do?"

"I didn't know *what* to do. Do I have to say something, to keep from being wrong? Like *Keep your mitts off, buster?* Not as if I *mind*. Do I have to lie, to keep from tempting him?"

"Yes, you do," I said and gave her a hard look. It was one of our big subjects—lying from kindness, to protect someone, lies of omission. When did they become the same as any other lie?

She took the cigarette out of my hand and sucked on it. "But you never lie, do you? And you know it. Would you tell him you wanted him, and *therefore* he should keep his mitts off you?"

I reached across the table, pushed a silky lock out of her eyes. We touched each other all the time in public, made a point of it. We held hands, or stood with one arm draped around the other's neck. I was what some people would call a tall cool blonde, and we must have been a sight, Celia soft and dark, me all bones, entwined. Not even lesbians did that in public yet, and we weren't lesbians. I'd had a parade of men and boys, a new one every two months. Celia was not a virgin, but she wanted to get married, have a baby sometime soon. I wanted that life, too. It's just that our approaches were a little different.

"You can't tell him unless you want to seduce him. Because you know it would. He'd go insane." I had seduced a married professor myself, the year before, as Celia well knew.

Her laugh was soundless, like a bellows puffing in and out.

"Knowing I felt the same? But I keep thinking—what if he'd be happier with me? His marriage is hollow. He never sleeps. He reads all night. He drives me home three nights a week."

I nodded. Celia lived about three blocks from him, in a house with other students.

"And that's fine. So long as you never do a thing you couldn't look back and approve of fifty years from now." It was our principle, the one that stood to every test.

She closed her eyes. "Oh, God. Of course I can't. The guilt is even too much now."

She leaned forward, searched my eyes.

"You know what I wish? I wish we could be Catholics. They know exactly what a sin is and how to get absolved. Protestants have to obey the *spirit* of the law, and that's endless, because it's vague. And no one hears your confession. You carry the same sin year after year, and never get absolved. 'We are forgiven,' says some minister who hasn't heard your sin, and what is that supposed to do? It hasn't been removed. Not like when a priest has heard the whole earful, and he frees you from it. Go in peace and sin no more. Then it is truly gone."

I held my hand over her head. "Go in peace, my child, and sin no more."

She caught my hand and gazed into my eyes. "You laugh, but you know it helps, even if it's you. Do you really think I am absolved?"

"No one was ever more innocent than you."

"That's *now.*" She laughed her soundless laugh. "How will I ever keep from telling him?"

I grinned. "Just stare at that little bald spot on his head and think about Gauguin."

Celia stopped riding home with him. We graduated, wondered what to do. We both wanted to paint, but how were you supposed to eat?

There was art history, and we got fellowships to read a million books while grading freshman essays on the Post-Impressionists. We spent more years on Levi-Strauss and Baudrillard and Lyotard than anyone who'd ever held a brush. We took the same classes, and dominated them. Celia hated abstract art, except Rothko and Franz Marc, in whom she thought the spirit moved. She could say words like "numina" and "grace" with a straight face, while I tried out the tougher faiths of Marxism and cultural historicism.

"Art is hoax," I said, "and surplus capital, effluvia of luxury. Art is imperial aggression, very thinly veiled. The sun never sets on Jackson Pollock's empire anywhere."

Then I retired with Celia to the Blacksmith House, to discuss the hierarchical behavior everywhere in academe, and how there was no way to escape judging constantly. We wondered if we could foster our students without hurting them, and read each other's seminar papers before we turned them in. We talked an hour on the phone at night, even if we'd met that day. We wore each other's clothes.

"We need another year," she said one afternoon. "For this friendship to jell."

82

"To jell?" I said, a little hurt she could think so. How much more jelled could it get? She was already the best friend I'd ever had.

"I mean, for it to become strong and flexible, the reed that bends in gale-force wind. So even if one of us had to commit murder, we'd defend each other automatically. Three musketeers."

I picked a tobacco flake off my tongue. "You planning to murder someone soon?"

Her green eyes shone. She laughed her puffy gasps. "You never know."

Our second year in grad school, Celia met a future minister named Daniel, moved in with him, and took two incompletes. Her back hurt, she said, from so much reading, and she couldn't paint. She carried a pillow into class, and went to chiropractors instead of to the library.

"Paint gives me hives," she said. She went to herbalists, who made her give up cigarettes and coffee. She quit going to class. One day I saw her disappear into the big brick church on Harvard Square.

"We're off art, and into God," she told me when I asked.

"Okay. But what will you do now?" As far as I could tell, she wasn't doing anything.

I was too busy to pay attention for a while. I finished course-work, studied for my doctoral exams. I had to memorize the history of Western art and every theory about it. For a year, I hardly slept. I read. I smoked three packs a day, and knew what time it was by counting butts.

People fainted in the course of their exams and threw up in trash cans. The written part was sixteen hours long, plus three oral, two more when the art department challenged every word. By the time I finished, I knew nothing about anything, and staggered out to Celia in the hall. She waited with me while the art department debated my fate inside. Finally, the tall, gray-haired chairman came out from behind the beveled glass.

"It was a pass, but not as good as we expected it to be," he said mournfully.

Celia gripped my arm and led me out of there. She took me home to the apartment she now shared with Daniel, a decent place in an old house in Somerville. Daniel was extremely thin, with deep lines in his face, though he was only twenty-five, like us, with a blond shock of surfy hair. He gave a wry smirk as he held a champagne glass toward me. I reached for it, began to sob.

"It was too hard."

Celia crouched beside me, pressed her cheek to mine. "I know," she said.

And it was true. She did.

That summer, Celia married Daniel at her parents' seaside church, and stopped taking my calls. Daniel answered every time.

"She isn't here," he'd say. Or, "She's resting now."

"*Resting?*" I said. "*Resting?*"

Had Celia become an invalid? Did Daniel keep her locked inside their room? Even prisoners got one phone call. I phoned every day for weeks, but she did not call me.

"Hey, Daniel. Tell Celia I'm not calling back again. She'll have to get in touch with me."

"Okay," he said. But when my phone rang, it was never Celia.

A year later, I caught a glimpse of her in the chilly reaches of the Harvard swimming pool. She was hugely pregnant in a green tank suit stretched tight, and I watched her underwater do a dreamy breaststroke back and forth. In the locker room, we both stood at the mirror, several women in between, while she drew a faint brown line beneath her eyes and smudged it with a fingertip. I'm sure she saw me in the frame of her vision. But she did not turn her head.

I supposed it was the saga of my life, the way the boyfriends came and went, that looked especially boring from her new position on the inside of a wedding ring. I could almost understand.

But when I knew that Celia was gone for good, I was more crushed than I had ever been by any man. You *expected* that from lovers, but not from your best friend. I caught the flu, kept smoking, and it turned into pneumonia. I spent a month in bed, unable to catch my breath. I wasn't sure I wanted to. I wanted to find a deep woods, crawl inside a big black garbage sack, and put a gun inside my mouth. I wanted to dispose of my remains and never be identified. I had no messages to send to anyone.

Instead, I found a psychiatrist who took me on for charity at half the going rate, and spent a year weeping for Celia in his red wingchair. Dr. Douhomet was hairless as a frog, and hardly said a word, except "Time's up" and "Thirty-five dollars, please." Once, when I described the way that Celia and I had touched in public, he gave a small, superior smile.

"It was erotic, but not genital," he said and nodded with a click.

I shook my head. "It wasn't erotic. It was playful, and about defying categories. It wasn't easy to freak out the art department, but we tried. We wanted to show them even straight girls could do that. That there were more things in heaven and on earth than were dreamt of in their philosophy, Horatio. Or in *your* philosophy," I said with sudden energy.

He went on beaming his Olympian grin, and didn't say a word.

One afternoon I saw him drive his BMW convertible through Harvard Square, and I lit up like the preteen fan of some rock star. I ran a block to try to catch him at the light on Church, and when his car was gone, I laughed and laughed. So that was transference—and if I felt that way about a frog, of whom I knew nothing, it was a very strange experience. I supposed he wanted me to transfer onto him and somehow feel what I had felt for Celia, and cure myself by understanding it.

But the feeling I had on the street was nothing I had ever felt for Celia. I loved Celia, but I would not have chased her up the block. Sex was what gave you that crazy energy, and I had done stranger things for men I hardly knew. And after I had slept with them, I felt related to them, forever and ever, amen. It must be because my genes got mixed up in it, trying to fulfill their evolutionary destiny.

But I didn't feel that way for Celia. Evolution wasn't interested in friendship, and that gave it a democratic feel. Friends loved each other voluntarily, no matter how close they got. And that meant Dr. Douhomet had nothing he could do for me.

"I'm not coming back," I said the next week, in his chair.

His cheeks went purple.

"But you're finally getting somewhere!" he shouted. It was the first time he'd expressed emotion, while I'd been weeping for a year.

"That's okay. I feel much better anyway."

And it was true, when I walked out of his office, it cheered me up. I didn't need a shrink. I needed a friend to talk things over with, share the details of my life.

But I was wary, and I had a dissertation now to write, on the New York School. It took me five more years, and I was over thirty, so lonely I thought I might implode, before I had the heart to find another friend.

It was the week I broke up with my sweetest lover ever, a handsome pipe welder who sculpted on the side. Ricky had made me an eight-pound valentine of inch-thick sheet metal, with a small arrow he had somehow made to pierce right through. He'd done it tenderly, precisely, using his blowtorch. He made love like that, too. But he had gotten a vasectomy at twenty-three, and he was never going to marry me.

"You're never going to marry me, are you?" I said, one night on the phone.

"No," said Ricky in a voice of mild surprise. "Did I ever say I would?"

He hadn't, that was it. Now what was I supposed to do?

I needed someone I could tell it to. I thought of Katie, who was art director of a Boston magazine. Katie was thirty-eight, and lovely, confident, good at what she did. We had met socially, and she took pity on my student poverty, gave me castoff clothes. They were the best things I had ever owned, a wool Ralph Lauren skirt, a hand-knit harlequin sweater, fawn-brown Gucci loafers light as glove leather. For the shoes alone, I ought to call Katie.

We made a date for lunch at the Blacksmith House. I hadn't smoked since the pneumonia, and half of Cambridge had quit, too. Most restaurants around the square ignored the trend, went on as smoky dives where you could swill martinis, chew on fat and gristle in the dark. Only the Blacksmith had clean air, mesculin salads, homemade soup—which meant it would be packed with parents, kids in strollers, diaper bags. So I put on the Guccis early, dodged the icebergs crossing Harvard Yard, as snow began to swirl.

The tall, lean windows of the Blacksmith steamed, as frostbit people packed inside. Puffed coats stood eight-deep to the counter, babies squalled. I tried to wiggle into line. But someone dropped a bowl of lentil soup down the staircase, and the crowd recoiled, slipping on the oak floor.

I waited half an hour, and was almost to the register when Katie wedged inside. She looked about nineteen in a hooded car coat, tall suede boots, hair sprung out around her face in bright banana curls. She worked out hours every day with weights, got massages, facials, manicures. She had her pores vacuumed, hair lightened with special weaves. Unwinding her long scarf, she cried out in a cheerful voice, inches from a woman trying to pull a toddler out of its snowsuit.

"Sorry! The gynecologist ran late. I asked him to check out the bacteria in there, you know, take a smear and look under the microscope. And he said, '*Whew!* Have you got bacteria in there!'"

Katie was from Manhattan, and I'd noticed that New Yorkers could say anything in crowded restaurants, sure they'd never see the same people again. But Cambridge was about the size of an Upper West Side block, and I cringed as she shouted on.

"And I have this *thing* on my shoulder, this little nothing red spot. I showed it to him, hoping he would say it's definitely not herpes, and I should forget it right away. Know what he said? 'Yep! Sure looks like herpes to me!'"

Mortified, I stared into the deli case. What did I care what these people thought? I did, though. I cared. Holding up one foot, I pointed to the Gucci loafer, trying to distract her.

Katie smiled and nodded, shouted on. "He said it can be years in incubation, so there's just no way to tell who gave it to me. It could be some guy ten years back, who didn't know he had it. He may just be getting symptoms now, and *wham*, it's got me, too. The doctor says I shouldn't bother notifying guys I've slept with in the last few years, since they'll find out soon enough. Oh, lentil soup, how perfect, don't you think?"

The girl behind the counter had six rings through her upper lip, and she lifted it as if she hadn't realized women our age still had sex. I had once given that look to my mother and her friends, when they fixed their hair or shopped for clothes. Why do they bother? I had wondered then. Who's going to look at them?

"Two lentil soups," I said. I turned to Katie loyally. "I bet you're going to be fine."

She seemed to strain to hit a high note that went through walls. "No way. He said there's herpes now in half the single population. But even married people aren't quite safe, are they? Think of Bob's poor wife. You know, that guy I slept with last year? She's probably got herpes, too!"

The girl behind the counter slopped our soups in haste. Hoisting the tray, I turned to fight my way into the crowd. But it parted like the Red Sea, averted eyes on every side.

Upstairs, no one knew how dangerous we were. All the babies had been crowded into two small rooms, like steerage class in a potato famine year. The only empty table lay buried in coats, children squirming all around. We worked our way in, settled down beside a young blond woman with her sweater pulled up, one pink breast exposed. She looked like a Swedish grad student, and her tiny red-faced infant suckled audibly, so close I could smell milk.

I smiled at Katie, rolled my eyes. Of course we'd have to talk on neutral subjects here. Katie knew a lot about the art scene, and she had explained to me the process of full-color printing and the problem with the greens. Shaking out my paper napkin, I held my spoon above the soup.

"So, did you see that thing on Caravaggio, in *Art in America*?"

She brightened with delight. "By that dick Howard James? Oh, sure, you know who he is. He did those burning scarecrows under glass. 'American Gothic.' You know, you saw that. I knew him in SoHo, when he was sealing dead seagulls in Plasticine. And he not only *was* a dick. He had this huge one that he thought you were supposed to die for. He thought it was about pumping, you know? Pumping! Half an hour, in-out, in-out, in-out, on and on and on!"

Crowd noise ceased, and Katie could be heard in the next room at least.

"Does that do anything for you? You know, pumping?"

I took a slurp of soup and gestured to my full mouth. She leaned forward, yelled.

"What's that you're mumbling? I bet it's no. It doesn't do a thing for me, either. *Oral sex* is what I like. Licking, I mean. But most guys only seem to like it for themselves. It's been an age since I found anyone who'd give me cunnilingus, more than two minutes anyway. Have you? Do you have trouble finding men willing to lick you properly?"

She waited for an answer, as did everyone at every table on the second floor. A pierced and tattooed, gender-non-specific bus-person paused with a tray nearby, pretended to scan the room.

"Let's not talk about it here," I whispered.

"What?" She gaped at me. "Not talk about it here? Why ever not?"

I was miserable for days. I was not cut out for friendship, that was clear. Why couldn't I have talked to Katie and forgotten all those people listening? I was raised to be inhibited, by unhappy Protestants. Why couldn't I have shouted pump! lick! herpes!, told a few tales of my own? Maybe then I'd have a friend.

But I didn't have one, and now I was even more alone. I missed Ricky terribly. I'd been invited to an opening in the Back Bay, and he might be there. I knew I shouldn't go, but I put on his favorite dress, a knitted cream silk sheath, and the three-inch heels he said made my ankles unforgettable. Wrapped in my somewhat shabby overcoat, I took the T to Arlington and wobbled through the slushy streets.

I had almost reached the gallery when a cab pulled up in front and Ricky bounded out. He looked devastating, wide shoulders in a tweed jacket, curls on his strong brown neck. He turned back toward the cab, and Katie stepped out in a tight black dress and heels. Her ankles looked extremely good. Laughing, he put an arm around her, and they disappeared into the gallery.

My toes froze as I stood, and certain memories came back to me.

"You and Katie, what a team," he'd said, the night I introduced them, warm brown eyes gleaming. Once I went up to Vermont to see my family, and when I got back, neither of them told me they had met. Then Katie had a party, and I took Ricky. It was a November night, cold in her living room, and Katie shivered in a shimmering tube top. She fiddled with the radiator valve.

"Ricky!" she cried. "This thing doesn't work. You're the only one who ever made it put out any heat. What did you do?"

Ricky blanched, and so did I. He rushed in, and the two of them fussed with the valve, animated as if onstage. They shouted about a painting on the wall, which someone had given Katie. Ricky thought that it was bad.

"Really bad!" he cried. "Wretched!"

"Oh, not that bad!" she yelled.

"No, really bad!"

They laughed frantically. Now all I could think of was how Ricky's favorite brand of sex did not involve *pumping*.

I had a friend once, loyal and true. I was five, in a mill town, and Sue Ellen's family lived next door to mine. Two years older than I was, she still stuck with me all through elementary school. We talked for hours on her brick front stoop, about the strange things people did, and where pets went when they were dead, until she graduated into junior high and started to wear nylons and French heels, and smelled like Campbell's soup when it was warm. Then my father lost his job, and we had to move to my grandparents' farm. I never saw her after that, though we wrote for a few years, on the perfumed stationery our brothers gave us every Christmas and birthday.

In the country, I had cousins but no voluntary friends. Then Radcliffe took me on for charity, let me wait tables in the dorm. I made

89

friends with Amy, a small, dark, quiet girl I waited on, who was smart and funny when you got to know her, privately, and had the finest taste I'd ever even seen. She was from the Upper East Side of New York, and she got married after our sophomore year and moved back home.

I heard from Amy sometimes and had been to visit her and her husband, Alex, and their little boy. Amy had a gift for friendship, and I often cried when we talked, as if I were in therapy. She had in fact become a therapist, but had to limit her practice, while Alex was chief surgeon of a major hospital, and wrote books in his spare time, about medicine and ethics, life and death. "Poetry," *The New York Times* had called his last, which spent a few months on the bestseller list.

Why didn't I call Amy more? I picked the phone up, punched her number in.

"But how did you know?" she cried. "I'm coming up to Boston for a conference. Let's have lunch at the Blacksmith House."

I had no qualms. Amy was the most discreet person I knew, and she never even gossiped or said mean things about anyone. Merely being seen with her should raise me in the eyes of all those supercilious pierced persons in the Blacksmith House.

The day she met me there, she looked the way that I remembered, lovely and well-dressed. She could look natural inside a tailored skirt, a cashmere sweater, pearls, at eleven in the morning, in 1998, and I felt tasteless in my tight black pants and chunky shoes, like some fake teen. My hair had never once been so well-cut as hers, in a simple shape from some hairdresser whom you needed a hereditary link to see.

"You look wonderful," I said. "Mind if I just go shoot myself?"

"Don't do that, please. I like the way you look. It's so . . . *caj*," she said, meaning casual, and I felt a rush of pleasure. The last time I had seen her, we decided that should be the term for suave, cool style. I was touched that she remembered what we'd talked about.

We carried tea and mesculin salads up the stairs, and at first we had a good few feet between us and the nearest mothers with children. But soon a troop of Japanese tourists came shyly in. The Swedish grad student wedged next to me and flashed her young pink breast, as if we had agreed that she should always nurse by me.

"Are you all right?" Amy murmured. "Everything okay?"

I felt the urge to cry, because I missed Ricky and had no money for haircuts. But I held it off a moment, almost happy, knowing I could tell it all to her.

Suddenly she gave me a big blazing look. Her eyes looked huge and black, intense.

"Well, I'm not all right. Alex told me last weekend he doesn't want me anymore. We've only made love about twice in the past year, and I asked him why. I took my clothes off, waved my breasts around, and nothing happened. I asked if he has any sexual feelings, and he just looked uncomfortable." Her voice rose to a seagull's cry. "I think he's fucking someone else!"

At tables nearby, conversation ceased. I tried to notice only what she'd said. Alex was urbane and charming, asked intelligent questions about my work. The last time I saw him, he'd started to go bald and grown his hair long on one side to comb across. I caught a glimpse of him emerging from the shower, a wing of hair about a foot long jutted from his ear. Was that some kind of danger sign I should have recognized?

I kept my voice down. "Maybe he's just getting middle-aged. You've been married a long time."

Her voice stayed loud. "But I'm still horny, and why shouldn't he be, too? Bald guys have lots of testosterone. I bet he's having tooth-and-claw sex with some nurse right now. It makes me so angry! And horny! You know that awful kind of horny you get when you think that everyone is having sex but you?"

She gasped, and dropped her head back on her neck. Around the room, no one moved. The tattooed bus-nerd lingered near our table, stared. If Amy noticed, she didn't care.

"You know what I want to do? I want to masturbate some guy while telling him how much I hate him. Doesn't that sound great? Go fuck yourself, you say and yank on it. Go fuck yourself!"

Sometimes life presents you with a test, and you have ten seconds to pass or fail. I had failed most of them so far. Did it matter that I'd never wanted to do what she'd said?

"Wow, sure does!" I cried. "Jerk off the jerk! Only you shouldn't do it all the way. Just almost, and then say, 'My hand is tired.' Tell him you're going to find some guy who doesn't have to comb his hair across his big bald spot!"

She whooped. "Some guy about nineteen who wants it all the time!"

"He'll beg for it!"

"He'll be your slave!"

"And you can tie him up and torture him!"

Amy giggled, stared at me, along with everyone else in the Black-smith House.

"Well, I suppose, if that's what you like," she said demurely, sipped her tea.

A week later, another therapist told Amy that Alex did indeed have someone else. Not a nurse, but a psychiatrist whose name was practically a household word. She wrote articles for *The New Yorker* and commentaries for *All Things Considered*, and Alex had been seeing her for years. All the therapists in New York knew, except Amy. When she confronted him, he seemed relieved. He moved to an apartment near his hospital.

"Everyone knew but me!" Amy shouted on the phone. We had been talking for so long, the phone burned against my ear.

"Why didn't Alex tell you? What exactly was his plan?"

"He says they thought I was too vulnerable. *They* thought! Him and his concubine, like I'm this patient in their care! I think everyone's been doing that to me. Did you know he was seeing her? Would you have told me if you did?"

"No way." I felt a qualm. Could I have lied and kept it to myself, and would that have been better? I wished with sudden violence that I could talk to Celia.

"Are you glad you know? Do you still like the person who told you?"

"I do. I like her more. Where would I be without her? In the dark! When I think of everyone who knew and kept the truth from me!"

I took the train down to New York and sat up half the night on Amy's couch, talking it all through. Punchy in the dawn, we told each other jokes, about how many therapists it takes to change a light bulb, and how many art critics. I told the one about the penguin who tried to drive across a desert, but its car broke down. The penguin took the car to a garage and went into an ice cream parlor to cool off, and covered itself in vanilla ice cream.

"Looks like you blew a seal," said the mechanic, coming in.

"Naw," said the penguin. "This is just ice cream."

We laughed and squeaked. Amy tried to speak.

"What do you call that ugly piece of flesh on the end of a man's penis?"

I didn't know.

"That's . . . the man!"

A few weeks later, back in Cambridge, my phone rang at one a.m.

"I have to find a man," said Amy, in a panicked voice. "I want to have sex right this minute! How do you find men? Tell me quick!"

All the men I knew were either married, or untrustworthy, or recently divorced and needed time in the emotional deep-freeze. Half of them were my old lovers anyway, and I'd already told her what was wrong with them.

"I don't care! He can be a jerk, and live in Timbuktu. So long as he'll fuck me!"

Two weeks later, Amy had found Steve, a nice genetic researcher at NYU, younger than she was. She didn't call me for a week. I left messages, and she called back a few times. But she was busy now with Steve, and her divorce, and juggling her practice and her son. Soon we only talked to each other's answering machines.

I understood, though I was shocked to realize how few resources I had left. I had nothing but my dissertation, and even that was getting done. I applied for jobs, and went down to a conference in New York for interviews with two Midwestern schools. I called Amy, and she said she'd be with Steve all afternoon. But could I meet her around six at her favorite sushi place?

The sushi bar was tiny and crowded, and Amy was half an hour late. They wouldn't seat me until she arrived, so I had to stand. At last she breezed in through the bamboo-decorated door, flushed and grinning in a rumpled tweed suit, and they put us at a table about two feet wide, in the center of the tiny space. She looked great, but she'd been drinking martinis all afternoon and seemed unable to talk quietly. Her voice was high and powered by a laugh.

"God, isn't sex great?" she yelped. "Is it always so great for you? Is that what you've been doing all these years, fucking every afternoon?"

I murmured that, as she knew, I had not seen anyone for several months.

She shouted sympathetically: "But you have to find someone! If only I had known, I never would have waited for Alex to fuck me twice a year. I would have fucked the FedEx man. Surely you know someone you can fuck!"

I wondered if such things were shouted all over the country now, wherever women met. I couldn't take it anymore. I snapped.

"Let's not talk about this in a sushi bar, okay?"

"Okay, sure. Sorry."

Sake, she gestured to the waitress from across the room, holding up her hands to imitate the china bottle and the cup.

"If it makes you uncomfortable. But just tell me one thing." A giggle squirted out of her. *"Don't you think sex is great?"*

After that, I did without close friends. Sometimes I did talk to another grad student, Lisbeth, who was English and even more bitter than me about the years we'd spent in school. When we started, Lisbeth had been glamorous and willowy, but now she drank, and she was shapeless as a tube of pudding, with a red face and broken vessels in her cheeks. She liked to say things like, "Mmmmm, Dom Perignon, and such a *full* bottle!" She liked to slander women we both knew. She insisted so-and-so "would screw a bush if she thought there was a snake in it," or that no inch of someone else was untouched by the surgeon's knife. A man we both knew had a lovely wife, who happened to be rich, and of course Lisbeth said he'd only married her for money. I knew Lisbeth's intentions were not especially good, and I mostly steered clear of her.

My final year at Harvard came down to a pinched, reluctant spring. In June the sun burned through, and lilacs opened, sweet enough to make your temples pound. I got a job at one of the Midwestern colleges, where I would know no one. But my fellowship was over, and I had to go. I filed my dissertation, packed up my few things.

A few days before I had to leave, I walked through Harvard Yard. It was hot summer now, and I could smell cut grass, Chinese restaurant, hints of sewage from the Charles. Circling the square, I visited the stations of my youth. On the brick sidewalk, I could see Celia ahead of me look back laughing, in a ripped tank top and ragged cut-off jeans. The bricks were there, the yellow light on them. But where was Celia?

I'd been invited to a party, in a loft in Watertown. Everyone I knew in Cambridge would be there, and I was tempted not to go, avoid saying goodbye. But I had nothing left to do. At nine o'clock, I dressed and took a cab.

The loft was in a warehouse with big clanking metal doors, the room high-ceilinged as a barn, a hundred people packed inside. The first person I saw was Lisbeth, face already splotched. She held a drink in one fist and a burning cigarette.

"Fancy running into you like this!" she cried and kissed me on the lips, which no woman had ever done before. Startled, I stepped back. Her voice rose as if eager for an audience.

"And to think that I just had a call this very afternoon from Celia!"

Arrested, I stared like a cow unaware it has been shot in the head. Celia called *Lisbeth*?

"Oh, but how tactless of me. What a shock it must be for you to hear that. Can you ever forgive me? Here, let me get you a drink."

She took hold of my arm and dragged me off to find a double scotch. Then she backed me in a corner, stood too close, and offered me a cigarette.

"Pardon me, it slipped my mind. Your marvelous pure lungs, like Celia's. You two were always quite the pair! But you seem rather sensible, next to her. Poor Celia's *quite* batty, you know, up there in New Hampshire with those eight or nine small boys. I thought the worst was when she needed to be Born Again, as if once weren't bad enough. Tent meetings, all that, passing out for God, that sort of thing. And of course she's always been a positively *devoted* hypochondriac, exists on rice and greens."

She took a drink, and her shoulders shot up with eagerness to swallow it and tell me more.

"And now! The horror! She's become a Catholic. *A lay nun,* no less, part-time bride of Christ, and scribbled a book to enlighten the rest of us. *God Is My Co-Dependent,* I believe it's called, or perhaps it's *Going All the Way with God.* Still married to the country parson, though, alas."

I tried not to show that every word of this was more than I had ever heard. Lisbeth shrugged my murmurs off and stared into my eyes, as if she knew this news would hurt but still be good for me.

"Now, you do realize, I trust, my dear, that she is nothing to disturb yourself about. She has become a very ordinary housewife."

"Disturb myself about?"

She shook her head, as if to dislodge a fly. "Oh, you know, your lesbian period. We all knew about it at the time. Such a good idea, I always thought. So sensible of you! It's just that Celia couldn't bear it, though, you see. She *recoiled,* in fact. Oh, dear, I fear I *have* stepped in it, haven't I? Can you ever forgive me? Let me take you out to lunch, say, Thursday at the Blacksmith House?"

I escaped, and made no dates. I went home and tried to blot out Lisbeth's voice. Had everyone believed I was in love with Celia? Had Celia thought I was? I knew it wasn't true, and yet I couldn't sleep. I dreamed of sneering faces, murderers outside my door, and woke up every twenty minutes all night long.

In the morning, big white cruise-ship clouds stood motionless against a hot blue sky. I packed up my last things, and the phone began to ring. I had forgotten to unplug the answering machine. A woman's voice began to speak.

"I had to call. I had a message. It was very clear."

It was a dry Maine voice, full of salt cod. It took me several moments to be sure.

"It was the strangest thing. I was just praying, and I knew. I had to call."

I picked up the phone. My tongue wouldn't move.

"So, Celia. How've you been for six or seven years?"

Sharp intake of breath. "It hasn't been that long."

Who was I to argue with someone who heard from God?

"Okay. What did the message say?"

"They're not in words. It was just a feeling, that I had to talk to you. But when it happens, I don't question it."

I felt impatient with the call. Had she had my number all this time, like when I was plotting to dispose of my remains?

"So, hey, Celia. Why did you stop speaking to me?"

She seemed to expect this. "That's too big a question to answer on the phone. Meet me in an hour at the Blacksmith House."

"Okay," I said before I thought, and Celia hung up.

So she was in town. She had swooped in, and now I was to report as ordered. Had she come to prove me wrong about the democratic nature of friendship? Was I supposed to just eat mesculin salad with her as if nothing had happened?

Sweating, I drifted to the Blacksmith House. The moment I saw Celia, I felt calm. She did not look the way that I recalled. She *did* look like a nun, or an old-maid clerk in 1956—stick-thin, in a Peter Pan collar and lace-up shoes. Her hair was bowl-cut, but her eyes were still Coke-bottle green, and when she saw me, something impish flashed through them. She walked toward me with languid grace.

"But you look wonderful," she said, as if she had heard differently. She kissed my cheek, and laughed her airy laugh.

"Hey, thanks. Want some lunch? They make good salads here," I said, as if she'd never been there before. "I mean, they've gotten better lately."

"Sure." She laughed again, breathless, as if this were hilarious. She seemed astonished to be there with me.

We carried salads up the stairs. The place was packed, but without piles of snowsuits, there was more room. The baby of the Swedish grad student could now sit up. Most of the other mothers looked familiar, too. Even the Japanese tourists could be the same.

Celia showed me pictures of her two small sons, and Daniel, and the white church where he led the flock. Daniel was even thinner than before, his face ashen, as if he'd been incinerated from within. He looked ill in his white collar, and even in the Santa suit he had put on for a children's party at the church. But their boys were round and rosy, cheerful, with pink cheeks.

"And have you joined the Catholic Church?"

"Oh, yes!" She flushed with happiness, and told me all the steps she had gone through, and what a lay nun was, and that she hadn't taken vows and might not. But she said Daniel understood and even envied her.

I got us coffee, cream for her, the way she'd always taken it. She was pleased that I remembered, and gave me a searching glance. She played with the flimsy cream package.

"I should answer your question. I've thought about it now for years, of course. I'm not sure what to say."

"You don't have to, if you don't feel like it," I said in a rush, not meaning to. Of course she had to say. I had almost killed myself, but I was over it. What could she say now that would make a difference?

"Just tell me why you wouldn't take my calls. You could have explained. It's not like we weren't talking every day."

She waved one hand, laughed quick clean puffs. "I know, I know."

She seemed unable to go on. But something in her face told me I had to wait. I waited, wishing that I didn't need to know.

She did say something then. I know I heard it, saw her lips move and her eyes beseeching me. But seconds later I could not remember what it was. It may have been so vague my mind refused to take it in. Or maybe it was what I'd always thought, that, being married, she could no longer approve of me. Whatever she said, it might have held the secret of friendship.

But it was gone the moment she said it, and part of me began to keen, and shred its handkerchief, its plastic garbage sack. What did she say? It was as if no one was listening at all.

Celia seemed relieved, and talked with animation, asked questions about my life. I told her, leaving out the year with the psychiatrist, since it seemed rude to mention it. She talked about her children's choir, her husband's early midlife crisis, and how impatient she felt with it.

"He actually said lately that he doesn't know if he believes in God. As if he's twenty-two! The weekend he said it, we'd had this major breakthrough, too. I didn't think there were any more barriers we could overcome."

"What kind of breakthrough?" I said, not really following.

She flushed happily, began to shout.

"It was the most amazing thing. You know how, when you're fucking, and you feel the Holy Ghost descend? And your orgasm sends you up to a higher dimension?"

Around us, people froze. The same wait-nerd who'd been there every time appeared a few yards off, perforated ears opened wide.

I didn't pause. I shouted back.

"Your orgasm? The Holy Ghost shows up when you come? Do tell! How does it feel?"

I leaned back. I relaxed. At last I knew what was going on. I knew where we were headed to. Lifting my cup, I nodded encouragement, as Celia went on.

Nominated by Maura Stanton, David Wojahn, Don Lee, Ploughshares

TO BE HONEST

memoir by JEFFREY A. LOCKWOOD

from ORION

M Y JOB IS TO KILL.

But I usually describe my profession euphemistically as "applied
ecology" or "pest management." As an entomologist on the faculty of
the University of Wyoming's College of Agriculture, I work to develop new and better methods of managing grasshopper outbreaks
that would otherwise devastate the western rangelands that ranchers
depend on to feed their livestock. While agriculture brings forth life,
entomology is largely premised on taking life.

I flatter myself that I make substantial contributions to science by
refining the use of insecticides. But the bottom line is that I am an
assassin: my job is to extinguish life. I am expected to do it well—efficiently and professionally. This year, I will direct the killing of no
fewer than 200 million grasshoppers and more than a billion other
creatures, mostly insects. Their accumulated bodies will weigh over
250 tons and fill twenty dump trucks. That's a lot of killing, and each
year it gets harder.

I began to study grasshoppers in 1986, learning how they spent
their days. Few scientists have taken the time simply to observe
these insects, although this seemed to me a reasonable initial step in
getting to know them. During that first summer in Wyoming, I sa-
vored long, lonely hours watching grasshoppers in a field south of
Laramie. As the insects lounged in the soothing morning sun, or took
their siesta in the sizzling afternoon heat, I struggled to stay alert and
focused on my work, systematically recording their behavior for later
analysis. In the words of Konrad Lorenz, "It takes a very long period
of watching to become really familiar with an animal . . . and without

the love for the animal itself, no observer, however patient, could ever look at it long enough to make valuable observations on its behavior."

Our empathy for animals that are not soft and warm grows slowly; years of familiarity breed compassion. It might seem difficult to connect intimately with grasshoppers, but they are rather endearing when you give them a chance. We readily bond with infantile forms; the oversized head and eyes of a baby melt our hearts. It is no coincidence that Walt Disney chose a cricket for his first insect character—Jiminy's features trigger a subconscious parental instinct. Grasshoppers are innocent and affable creatures, although they can be a bit scrappy when crowding around a particularly tasty morsel (such as a recently deceased comrade).

Grasshoppers are also beautiful animals. On an afternoon's walk, I can find twenty or more species. *Dactylotum bicolor* is a garish pink, blue, and black pencil-stub of a grasshopper. Like Jack Sprat and his wife, the sleek, velvety black males of *Boopedon nubilum* are the antithesis of the obese, mottled-brown females. The size of a mouse, the wingless pink-and-green *Brachystola magna* lumbers across weedy fields munching sunflowers. Only a sharp eye can detect *Hypochlora alba*, a ghostly green grasshopper that vanishes as it tumbles into a patch of the cudweed that constitutes its only food. An adrenaline rush gives way to a sigh of relief upon finding *Aeropedellus clavatus*, an acoustical mimic of the prairie rattler. I can't help but wonder if all this splendor was a necessary consequence of evolution or whether it's simply a miraculous expression of joy.

When I started my research, I was largely an observer of the insecticidal spectacle conducted by various agencies and orchestrated by the U.S. Department of Agriculture. These programs were intended to protect the grass needed by livestock, and the USDA paid the entire cost of spraying pests on federal land, half the cost on state land, and one-third of the cost on private land. As a consequence, the killing fields were immense. The smallest operation permitted by policy was ten thousand acres, but this does not approximate the scope of effort brought to bear against a major outbreak. In 1985 and 1986, more than twenty million acres were blanketed with insecticide.

As a developing scientist new to such staggering proportions, I was anxious to innovate and explore novel approaches to improving grasshopper management. To my disappointment, any interest the

USDA had at the time in new ideas was subsumed by the enormous investments that fueled their control programs.

However, in response to economic and environmental concerns, the USDA was forced to abandon its subsidy program in 1996, a decision that effectively tripled the cost of grasshopper control for ranchers. This is where I came in. With my colleagues, I developed a method of application whereby insecticides are applied in strips at a fraction of traditional rates, with untreated strips in between. This wasn't rocket science, but it worked (largely because grasshoppers move readily into treated swaths, perhaps in search of a cannibalistic snack).

When we generated our first large-scale success on three square miles of rangeland, I knew something of what J. Robert Oppenheimer felt as the first atomic fireball blistered the New Mexican desert and he muttered, "I am become Death, the destroyer of worlds." Like myself, he never chose a target, ordered a strike, or pulled a release lever, but he provided those who make such decisions with the option. Recently, the method that we pioneered has been employed on a quarter of a million acres throughout the West, killing perhaps twenty billion grasshoppers.

Perhaps because I began relating to grasshoppers one at a time, my encounters with control programs have a haunting quality. Unable to fully grasp the number of individuals killed in a control program, the effect is similar to scanning a stadium packed with tens of thousands of individuals. As it's impossible to make out faces in such a crowd, they meld into an anonymous mass of humanity, a numerical attendance figure.

To conceive of the single largest spray program in the West, imagine a desolate tract of rangeland encompassing six million football fields. This area is so large that you would need a month to walk its border, and a company of gardeners equal to the population of New York City to mow its surface in a day. Over this area, we spread 375,000 gallons of insecticide, the amount of liquid that would be contained in a line of beer bottles 157 miles long—enough to give every person in the U.S. a heaping teaspoon. A few days later, we have killed five hundred billion grasshoppers. With this number of corpses, we could fill six hundred gymnasiums, and it would take a working surface of twenty square miles to stitch a quilt of their wings. Imagine giving each person on earth eighty of these small corpses.

Walking across the prairie after the first large-scale program that I had witnessed, I hardly noticed the corpses. But the stillness was profound. In a grassland swarming with life one day earlier, there were now no bees playing connect-the-dots with wildflowers, no ants staggering under their masochistic loads of seeds, no ground beetles lumbering in their search of a meal, no flies circling with their whining plea for a sip of sweat, and, of course, no grasshoppers erupting in pandemonium from beneath my feet. Like Lilliputian scenes from the suburbs of Hiroshima, the architecture remained but there was no movement and no sound, save the ghostly swaying of the grass and the eerie whisper of the wind. To hear the silence of Rachel Carson is to know the power of poison.

These days, the weapon of choice for most ranchers and local pest management agencies is diflubenzuron, a chemical that, even at very low levels, inhibits the formation or hardening of the insect's cuticle or exoskeleton. I am proud that we now use less than one percent of the amount of insecticide that was applied just ten years ago, but the quantitative success belies the qualitative effects. Within a week of treatment, the insects molt into deformed monsters, with grotesquely twisted wings and misshapen legs. Often, their hind legs fall off, as the cuticle is too weak to withstand the pressure of jumping. They become lethargic, appearing dazed or exhausted. Like forgotten war refugees, the amputees stagger about aimlessly. Each summer, I walk the prairie after spraying to see the gruesome results of a control program, so that I never forget what I have made possible.

The first time I fully sensed death at such a tremendous scale was during a sabbatical leave in Australia, a land known for its ability to touch the human spirit. My purpose in going there was to learn from the world's most efficient and effective locust control program. The Australian Plague Locust Commission's headquarters bears an uncanny resemblance to a war room, with color-coded targets on wall-sized maps, the static-laden chatter of radios, and a camaraderie reminiscent of a grizzled platoon. The formal lessons they offered me concerning logistics, communications, and survey were informative, but what I ultimately learned was not part of the structured tutorial.

The sparse grasslands that fringe the outback near Broken Hill are notorious for their capacity to foster locusts—the migratory, swarming form into which some grasshoppers develop under outbreak conditions. My introduction to these creatures occurred on an unusually wet, gray morning. My guide pointed at the birds swooping from a distant treeline to join a raucous flock, just visible as it churned in the clumped canopy of grasses. It was an enormous all-you-can-eat buffet of locust nymphs.

Nymphs are the immature, wingless stage of grasshoppers or, in this case, locusts. Although each one is only the size of a push pin, they form bands ten feet wide and a mile in length. With two thousand nymphs per square yard, a single band may include twelve million insects—roughly equivalent to the entire human population on the Australian continent. Warmed by the morning sun, the nymphal anarchy coalesces in a surging, leaderless mass—and the march begins.

On a quiet afternoon, the faint rustling of millions of mandibles grinding and bodies tumbling accompanies the sinuous band as it rolls across the grasslands. These waves of life are so thick that they can be seen from airplanes; at five hundred feet they appear as arching shadows with rings of bare soil in their wake, marking the places where they stopped and fed on previous days. Deep in the outback the adults are relatively harmless, but their flights take them inexorably toward the farmlands that border the arid interior of the continent. The swarms look like shimmering dust storms rolling over the baked grasslands. Grains of sand, stars in space, locusts in flight—the sheer numerical splendor is terrifying and joyous.

Early one morning we traveled to the site of a spray program. I had planned to lend a hand in the body count or "efficacy assessment," but I never got beyond trying to comprehend the essence of the massacre. I had observed such programs in the United States, but never one in which death was so apparent. Perhaps it was the recency of the insecticide application, my empathy after having been engulfed by a swarm the previous day, or my detachment from the farmers who benefited from the program, but I was stricken by the scene around me.

Everywhere locusts were lying in the burnt-red dust. Some were dead but many were still twitching in the spasms brought on by the neurotoxin. I am told that some bombardiers in World War II were unable to continue their duties once they witnessed the carnage on the ground. It was as if I had seen, *really seen,* for the first time, what it meant to dole out wholesale death.

When I was in fourth grade, my older brother, who occasionally thrashed me when we were younger, came to my defense against a seventh grade bully. The miscreant never again accosted me, but my brother did. As the love of a brother transcends the scraps and tussles of growing up, so my relationship with grasshoppers is conflicted, swinging between affection and aggression. In the midst of my own violence, I have defended them from government bullies who understand little of their nature and care even less.

In 1989, the USDA planned to import exotic parasites and pathogens to attack the native grasshoppers of the western states. These organisms, tiny wasps that lay their eggs in those of grasshoppers and fungi that invade the tissues of insects, were to be gathered from around the world and released on the prairie. Because it risked permanently damaging our vast grassland ecosystem, I engaged in a long, bitter, and eventually successful battle to stop this effort.

The program was missing important elements, such as a provision for protecting nontarget organisms. I found results of laboratory studies hidden away by the USDA that revealed that the wasp proposed for release would have parasitized a grasshopper species that suppresses snakeweed, a poisonous plant that induces abortions in cattle. Yet there would have been no way to put the genie back in the bottle if things were to go dreadfully wrong.

At least with insecticides, every use is an intentional act that invokes regulatory constraints. We can avoid national parks, wildlife refuges, and habitats where beneficial species reside—unlike parasites, which spread and invade without regard to such considerations. And we know that chemicals will eventually break down, whereas parasites and pathogens will increase in numbers. For all of the damage that we can do and have done with toxins, the potential for ill-conceived introductions of exotic species to disrupt natural systems is even greater.

Grasshoppers, unnoticed, sculpt the prairie, prune poisonous weeds, compost dead plants, and feed the birds. And with each passing year, the quiet chorus of their lives becomes more deeply instilled in my being, while the rousing refrains of their sporadic outbreaks continue to draw the attention of government agencies.

Taking life—like giving life—can be a sacred act. A friend of mine

104

who is an herbalist believes that one must harvest medicinal plants with thankfulness, understanding, and humility to access the full potential of the resulting extract. Indigenous peoples asked permission or forgiveness of the animals they hunted, and perhaps modern agriculture should act with such humility and grace when killing is necessary. Following the lead of native people, agriculturalists would do well to understand that the land is shared with other creatures, and their needs are worthy of our understanding.

At the beginning and end of each summer, I sneak away from my field assistants and collaborators to be alone, to pray. This is a time when I experience the fullness of the prairie, when I seek what lies at the core of my intentions as a scientist, and when I release the guilt and shame. The thought-words are different each time, but the question I ask myself persists—Why do I continue to develop the means of killing these creatures?

I justify killing grasshoppers because my intentions are purified by love for them. I am soothed by the notion that I mean well, that I foster a world in which there is less killing and fewer misunderstandings between species. I tell myself that intentions are all that we really control; outcomes are evasive and uncertain. But spraying thousands of acres with insecticides, regardless of intentions, is going to do a lot of harm. A Buddhist priest once told me that the Samurai were Zen masters—they killed with a depth of awareness we can barely imagine. The mindfulness of Buddhism allows one to be profoundly effective, but, he noted, you are still stuck with deciding what to do effectively. Slicing an enemy in half with perfect awareness still makes a mess.

Vignettes from a documentary on killing have haunted my memory for years. The film followed a condemned killer over the course of his last days. Ironically, I found the most compelling character to be not the convict, nor his family, nor the victim's family, but the warden. Here was a good and kind man burdened with the obligation of premeditated murder. The warden acted with dignity and compassion; he was gentle but not fawning, supportive but not patronizing, regretful but not apologetic. He struggled to make the most difficult of all social responsibilities as decent as humanly possible.

And so I ask who is taking the more meaningful role: the compassionate warden at the side of the condemned, making the execution more dignified and decent, or the protestors in the streets outside, shouting slogans against the death penalty? Perhaps I would be a better environmentalist if I refused to use insecticides, but would I be creating a more decent world for my fellow creatures if I left my job in protest? Or should I keep working to find ways of killing fewer creatures with more humane, less toxic methods?

I claim to be a compassionate executioner. After all, if somebody has to kill, it might as well be someone with an inkling of empathy. But to be precise, I am not the executioner—that would be the aerial applicator. In fact, I generally avoid the treatment programs. To sustain the analogy, I'm really in the business of designing less cruel electric chairs, and this sometimes seems even more perverse than pulling the switch. Perhaps it doesn't do the convulsing grasshopper (or inmate) a whole lot of good to know that I care, but maybe society can retain some of its humanity if I can make the act of killing less brutal and less frequent.

Inescapably, we live by death. I study how to kill better and less, but a little more of me dies with each field season. If my current projects succeed in reducing the amount of toxin needed to restore grasshopper infestations to naturally manageable levels, during the next outbreak we will reduce our insecticide use by ten thousand tons and limit our killing fields to less than half of their historical scale. Still, the carnage will not be avoided; that is the ugly middle ground called compromise. I am convinced that it is easier to be a member of Earth First! or the Chemical Manufacturer's Association than a member of neither. The atheists and the theists have it easy.

I sometimes wish I could throw myself at one of the extremes—environmentalism or anthropocentrism, mysticism or rationalism, religion or science. But to do so is to become truncated, half human. Some people can choose one or the other, but living and working with grasshoppers, knowing their beauty and innocence while being deeply responsible for their deaths, has shown me that both of these ways of knowing must be honored for our agriculture and our civilization to flourish.

Scientists have a unique opportunity in this venture: we can understand, connect with, and tell the story of the natural world. For those who are willing, it is possible to both comprehend the facts and transcend them for the sake of the spirit. And when we are open to this possibility, I have found that with time, technical data give way to a deeper kind of knowledge that relies on intuition, tradition, experience, and faith—and beyond knowledge lies the possibility of wisdom. For me, the data of "percent mortality" has given rise to the knowledge of how to control grasshoppers with minimal harm. My wisdom, however nascent, comes from seeing the death of grasshoppers and the integrity of their biotic communities (including the human elements), and realizing that we are all one, that we are diminished by their deaths and uplifted by their lives.

Scientists often attack spirituality, and I believe that the reason is fear—a sense of anxiety, even dread, that there remain elements and processes of the world that are fundamentally and ultimately beyond our capacity to control, quantify, or rationalize. I suspect that many scientists are hostile to mystical notions in order to prevent the impure thoughts of transcendent experience, the troubling touch of subjective feeling, and the unsettling whisper of spiritual insight from confusing the rational process of analysis. To focus on one-half of what it means to be human, they chant a mantra of materialism to deny anything that lies outside of science. Rather than sustaining the illusion of objectivity, they could open themselves to a respectful, caring, even loving relationship with the creatures they study. But then they would end up like me—attached to the creatures I kill, with all of the unrest that this entails.

Although ideals make for fine philosophical tracts and political treatises, real life is full of complexity, uncertainty, diplomacy, and nuance. I often encounter those who preach about how the world ought to be, but rarely do these futurists wish to engage in the actual work of getting us from here to there. Of course, the middle way risks the pitfall of rationalization, as we talk ourselves into perpetuating the status quo. I try to forgive myself and secure nature's pardon by contending that with each killing season we are one step closer to a just and compassionate future. And so I will continue to decimate grasshoppers for the benefit of agriculture and continue to mourn them for the sake of human culture.

But the putative virtues of "killing them softly" beg the question of why kill them in the first place. There are no comprehensive solutions to the universal dilemma that we must kill to live. No philosopher, theologian, artist, or scientist has offered a general solution to the mystery of suffering and death. Paradoxes are not solved—they are lived in, and perhaps lived through. The wicked irony embedded in this paradox is that I take psychic sanctuary in making my victims anonymous by numerical imaginings. On a recent trip to Australia, I watched an aerial spray program with detached interest, taking mental notes of logistical and methodological details. But I cringed when a colleague looked down at the parched soil and lifted his foot to grind a single nymph under his heel. It is harder to crush a grasshopper slated to be sprayed than it is to watch the airplane lay down a blanket of death.

My memory is drawn to the summer of 1992, when I stood on a desolate tract of sunburnt rangeland infested with Mormon crickets (which are actually a bizarre species of katydid, named for their legendary invasion of Mormon farms) near Edgerton, Wyoming. A dense band of insects numbering in the tens of thousands had been sprayed a few hours earlier, and I arrived to find them staggering about on the slopes. Humpbacked, wingless, with antennae streaming behind, it was as if a sadistic fisherman had dumped a net-full of melanic prawns on the prairie, where they flailed desperately.

The poisoned crickets were unable to hop uphill, so each movement brought them down into the ravines. In the dry creek beds they accumulated in what looked like stagnant black streams. On the hillside I lifted one cricket from within the sagebrush where it had become entangled. I grimaced at its convulsions, which were aggravated by my handling, then set it down on the dusty soil to resume its dying journey to the anonymous mass of writhing bodies at the bottom of the draw.

So in the end, how do I live as an assassin? I know that the grasshoppers' suffering and my pain are real. I know that they die so I might live. Grasshoppers are my ecological communion—their bodies are my life. Through them, I have found meaning in my work, experienced connectedness to other beings, and gained a sense of purpose in this world. Perhaps my destiny is that of the warden, to assure that these creatures do not die unknown, by the hand of a dispassionate executioner. To be mourned is to have one's life—and death—touched by another sentient being. Perhaps that is all that any of us can hope for.

But does one man's perspective offset the billions of deaths? I am suffocating under the expanding mass of corpses that pile onto my conscience each year. And so, I tell their story and mine—and ask something of you. At your next meal, say grace, give thanks, remember them.

Nominated by Orion

THE PAST

by CHRIS FORHAN

from BELLINGHAM REVIEW

How worthy of attention, the past. How much less
predictable than the present, all bluster and disarray—

rugs tumbling from open truck beds, roof and joist rot,
loose dogs and wind. The future is barren: white, odorless.

But what of the scent when Grandpa worked the cider press
years ago? That meant something. How much sweeter

the scent has grown. It seems to have lingered for weeks,
rising from the cellar, gathering in every room.

What of the year of the barley market downturn? The year
Joe Wilkey took to drink? Not so awful, really.

Every dawn, in memory, offers its drawn-out vowel
of possibility, each sunset steeps us

in deep burgundy and pink. The bedroom fire, the loss
of half the house, seems a small thing now,

though occasions of elation—the day
the aircraft carrier nuzzled the waves as it entered

the bay, or that youthful escapade
involving the slowly sinking rubber raft—

seem intricate and grim. They loom
like a grey, rain-drenched monument.

The spring of the trolley operators' strike—
when Father bought the Rambler—puzzles. Why recall it

with such clarity? Whatever we were going to be
is back there still, a bird flittering through a scraggly wood.

How small the desire we quell, indiscriminately licking
the swizzle stick of the present, when there's the past

to think of: how it casts its baffling shadow upon us,
how it goes on forever, and holds such promise.

Nominated by Laura Kasischke, Bellingham Review

THE MANDELBROT SET

fiction by JANET BURROWAY

from FIVE POINTS

MANDELBROT HAD AN ASS like a bifurcated cantaloupe, the two halves set side by side in the squishy paisley of his great room loveseat. Mandelbrot sat alone. His party furled around him, tinkling and chortling in the usual way; his choice of friends, his choice of rivals, half a gross of go-getters academic and political, divorcés, heirs and CEO's, the *crème de la* Birmingham, Alabama, each with a murderous desire for the esteem of colleagues they found contemptible. A merry band!

Nearest him, the batch from neuroscience had got into celebrity sightings and couldn't seem to find a way out. Franklin Yorke claimed to have bummed a light from Steve Martin in the lobby of the Lyric Hammersmith. Cantor Swinney had shared an elevator at the *Hotel des Artistes* with Francois Truffaut. Curvy Helga Koch had run into Dustin Hoffman in a hooded parka on Fifth Avenue, and in their moment of eye contact he had made a silent plea that she not blow his cover. She was proud to say that she had not. How they admired her! How they were invigorated to remember their moments with Debbie Reynolds, Dick Cavett, Doris Lessing, Henry Kissinger—not ten feet away in the street, the corridor, the bar, the dining room, the pool!

Mandelbrot alone sat despondent. A man of order and control. A man well-known for his unflappable, imperturbable, slightly cynical take on the world (some said his raised eyebrow, the single wafting lock on top of his bald head put them in mind of Jack Nicholson); a worldly man, slightly jaded, something of a roué, a bit louche at

111

worst, but through it all a mensch of regular habits, regular meals, regular bowels. Overwhelmed.

It was no one thing in particular. It was too much of everything. A cascade of last straws. Money, society, love, career, all just over the top of whelm, rendering his heart arrhythmic, his bladder in flood. Mandelbrot was overwhelmed with the futility of things. He thought of death. He! who had never given root-room to gout, hemorrhoids, hangover, peptic ulcer. Now he was aware of himself flaking off into the carpet, body ash and dandruff, psoriasis. He would flake away to nothing, so much organic gray confetti.

Mandelbrot was a flunky with a fancy handle, a monogrammable honorific; he was a Consultant, a Coordinator, an Associate, a Liaison. His job description said he had "primary responsibility for generating alumni enhancement and targeting growth potential in the community sector for developmental outcomes." This meant it was up to him to squeeze ten million a year out of somebody other than the Boosters, who had their own deep pockets. For this he was paid like six professors and worth every shekel.

For Mandelbrot believed in the primacy of fundraising. Fundraising explained nothing in the world. Fundraising was a self-referential science and could not be valued in terms of its application. Mandelbrot was a number cruncher, one of the best. Of course he was. He could slip a digit or finesse a stat faster than the eye could see. He had begun in pure math and proceeded to impure math, his detractors argued. Nevertheless. Number crunching was a good thing, a move toward abstraction, which is the direction of human intellect. Mandelbrot was a master of the abstruse abstraction. He could go on and on. *Of course I crunch numbers,* Mandelbrot said; *I keep them in the freezer and defrost them one at a time.* He ground his teeth for illustration, for emphasis.

Therefore he had brought oodles and oodles of endowment into a system nearly strangled by the tight-assed Legislature. He had got trucking magnates to ante up. He had got pharmaceuticals to grant and frozen chickens to bequeath. He had milked the mega-dairies. He had tickled misers till their coins fell out.

But this year he had come up short. He had not taken it to the hoop. In truth, he was two million shy of the projected goal, and the fiscal year-end just three weeks away. Never had this to him before happened. He was in Dutch with the Board of Regents, the Chancellor, the Provost, the President. He was their point guard off point.

If he didn't make up the deuce, his career would be on the downside, even the downsize! He would have the game to answer for.

This gig was a long shot. A last ditch. Based on no more than a titillating hint, offhandedly dropped by his beloved (!) Edie, that there might be a couple of mil untapped under the most unlikely mattress in mattressland. He had, it happens, rolled on that particular Dunlopillo—twice? three times?—how many! years ago? Which made it the trickier to dip into the kapok, so to speak. And yet, if Edie was right, it might yet prove the coup of coups, the *coup de grace*, the graceful coup. In any case it was already in progress, whatever it was, and must certainly run to its conclusion. Could he get up for it?

And then his marriage. *Mariage*! Mirage! In the area of interpersonal relations a little bravado had always been necessary—but sufficient. More than one woman had been polite about the size of his cock. More than one colleague had referred lip-smackingly to his *trophy wife*. Trophy! He might as well jerk off into the Ryder cup.

There she was, down the center of the room, the gorgeous Edie Mandelbrot née Lorenz, percolated into a satin strapless with, on each breast, a mad tendril of stitching no thicker than dental floss, swirling inward to nestle each nipple in an array of pastel colors. Booby colors. Edie scooped up a tray of canapés and insinuated them into a circle of investment bankers, lost her balance, juggled precariously a moment—almost lost it!—but contained, maintained. Laughed at self, deprecating, delicious. Even as he applauded her save, he imagined the stink of lox and capers in the carpet nap. Oh, Edie! If they only knew.

She was his third (the first had a Ph.D., the second money). A world class looker, flat-bellied, bumptious ass, tits out to here with aureoles like taffy targets. Butterfly tattoo on her adorable trapezius. At night she wore underwire contraptions and bikini panties in startling colors like stained glass, and she was easy in them, sitting cross-legged on her pouf to dig at her toenails or standing at the foot of the bed hanging her weight on one foot, taunting, amused. Was that it? Was that the point: amused? Still, she took trouble. She took her time. The trouble was that he would have to close his eyes and imagine her doing what she was actually doing, maybe in the burgundy red outfit instead of the lime green. He had to fantasize her sucking while she sucked. In the fantasies she meant it. In reality she was dog-paddling, polishing silver, pulling on a joint. As soon as he got active she just lay there, a lump. Amused?

113

All sixteen belltones of Westminster Abbey sounded. Now Edie had rid herself of the tray and was crossing to the front door for the fortieth or fiftieth time, a waste of effort since everybody came in anyway. But his Edie, she would play the hostess. She passed in front of the aquarium wall, flicked a finger as usual at the seahorses, who tumesced for her, and opened wide the door. Tantara! Here she was (at Edie's invitation), Helena Nagy, sleek in a floor length number, matte black panels falling plumb from a rhinestone cluster on each shoulder. And her young lover, according to Edie, who (Edie) had promised to spirit him (the young lover) away so he (Mandelbrot) could talk to her (Helena). Good God, a young giant, six foot twelve at least, a tumble of curly forelock and a wing chair's worth of shoulder. Cheshire smile. (Helena must be fifty if she's a day. He knew exactly. Fifty-two.) Bit of a dork, though. Made a show of bending over Edie's hand, who giggled and managed with a modest twist of her body to make her tits still more strangely the center of attraction.

Helena Nagy was nervous. Even at this distance she signaled sex. She ground her shoulders prettily, palpated her own black silk lungs. Did not so much listen to the others' prattle as auscultate it, ear pressed to the air in front of her. So: not wholly sanguine about appearing in public with her studly dalliance. In a state of turmoil, wanting but not wanting to be seen to want.

They three disappeared in the direction of the drink. Mandelbrot sat pat.

A complex system can give rise to turbulence and coherence at the same time. Dissipation is an agent of order. Over the vastness of his great room Mandelbrot surveyed the situation of his own making. They were cultured guys and gals! Multi-cultured, too. A Pakistani horticulturist, a black Dean. A Representative of Latin extraction. A lady novelist! Mandelbrot himself boasted a Jew *and* an Arab in his ancestry, not that those two progenitors had ever met. This was his crowd as he had envisioned it, the clique he fantasized as a child in that dank Queens basement, looking up at the world through shit-colored glass. His *place*, cleanly constructed as geometry! Why did his vision fail him now? No sense to it. Yet mood is random. Here around him his chosen few seemed rough, not rounded, scabrous, not smooth; a social circle pitted, pocked, twisted, tangled, intertwined.

The neuroscientists, for example, couldn't quit; any minute now they would self-destruct. Harvey Smale had seen Martin Amis jump-

114

ing into a Jag in Atlanta! Frank Houthakker shared a first-class flight with Larry Bird! Lori Crutchfield's grandmother was second cousin to Louisa May Alcott! Their cigarette smoke curled toward the cathedral beams. The pendulum of the grandfather clock boomed back and forth.

An impossible thing had happened. At that last opening of the door a butterfly had got into the room. Wrong time of day, wrong setting, a mortal miscalculation for a Monarch. Mandelbrot snatched at it for an ugly omen. The butterfly passed before the aquarium, the grandfather clock, rose in a drift of smoke from Chris Sierpinski's *con mille amores* and disappeared. The immediate effect was to get Mandelbrot off his ass. He lumbered up, a big man, no longer agile, and wended his way toward where he thought the wings had gone.

"Great Party, Benni!" Imelda Peano called. Mandelbrot flashed on her in some other elegant soirée, saying, "Oh, I knew Benni Mandelbrot *quite* well when he was alive."

No sign of the butterfly. Maybe he imagined it. Mandelbrot was no lepidopterist ("I had lunch with Nabokov at Cornell!" claimed Guy Scholz hysterically), but he thought he knew a Monarch when he saw one. No sign, however.

Once up, Mandelbrot continued to amble through the topology of partydom. He wandered in oscillating isolation. He encountered dynamical systems, robust and strange. There was instability at every point. The senators' aides were vying with each other on how many votes they could muster for the HMO's. The religion people were falling over themselves for a handle on humility. The phenomenologist was pitting his claims for perception against the Marxist's materialism. In the TV room a couple of tag-along teenagers were slopped in front of *Blow-Up*, immobile except that one foot of each was in competition for the hassock. On the screen the stills clicked forth one after the other in ascending scale. (Detail. Detail of detail. Detail of detail of detail.) On the floor three pre-schoolers whacked each other with Barbie dolls. (*What am I, a Day Care Center?*) There was a dog, unfamiliar, scratching fleas that no doubt had other fleas to scratch. Free enterprise also displayed itself in a pair of red ants squaring off over a crumb of hot dog bun. Unbeknownst to Mandelbrot, under the parquet, two rival armies of termite were at work on the central joist.

"Great party, Mandelbrot!"

"Benni, it's lovely here!"

Beset by random pressures, his trajectory took him past a voice just beyond the edge of recognition, clear in spite of the ice cubes clacking, the canapés gnashing, the decibelia of good times:

". . . won't be sitting so pretty this time next year."

Who won't? The remark had not been intended for his hearing. It cut. His heart in tachycardia, *rat-a-tat, boomararaboom,* Mandelbrot careered off toward the dining room.

And therefore encountered there the gorgeous three. Edie with her head atilt, radiant as a silver lining. The hunk towering and gesturing above his head with a slice of asparagus quiche as if he was about to slam dunk it. Helena Nagy against the pillar in a curve of question mark, a glass in one hand and a mini bottle of Perrier in the other.

She was very gone on the toy boy, that was apparent. She had the smell of sex on her, which is near enough the smell of terror. Internal, nay, subterranean agitation; a twitchy, musky lovely reek, exuding labyrinths. She hiccuped softly and stumbled on the vowel sounds of suffixes, *certainlay, delightfoil.* Ashamed of discovery—his, perhaps.

Or was it something else? She knew somehow that Mandelbrot planned to rob her pretty nest? Prey on her nest egg? Pry her fingers free? Would Edie have let something slip?

Not Edie, no. Here was Edie exuding nothing but hostessly luminosity. *Helena you know, of course* (of course!); *and this is Mitchell Figginbaum.* The hunk high-fived. The sleeve of his silky shirt was rolled up on a forearm like a hirsute two-by-four. Helena gave Mandelbrot a peck on the mandible.

"Helena," he said. "Surely we can find you something more exciting than that to drink."

"Oh, I'm easily excited," she skittered. Then registered an unintended *double-entendre*? Colored, maybe. Recovered quickly. "These are my two best students, you know." Blushed still more?

The situation was as follows: Edie had decided to improve herself via an Article and Essay Workshop. But would not insinuate herself into the U. at Birmingham lest others should think her nepotistical, Mandelbrot having some influence in that arena. Week after week she would rap out Personal Essays in the Persuasive or Descriptive mode, out of her repertoire of froufrou, trivia, trifles, furbelows and frivolalia. Week after week, Tuesday and Thursday afternoons, she would hop in her sassy little teal green T-roof SRX and toodle off

116

down the road to Hoover State. Young Figginhunk, her classmate, was also improving himself, being back from a comfortably warless stint in the U.S. Navy—spent, as far as Mandelbrot could ascertain, mostly on the Banzai Pipeline of Oahu. This world-experience rendered him, in Edie's gleeful opinion, sufficiently sophisticated to be sex partner for Helena Nagy. Who, however, was looking a little scrawny about the neck if she didn't mind his saying so (he did not say so).

"Edie is a natural ironist," Helena said, and for a brief, mad second he imagined Edie ironing his shirts. Whereas—his mother had done all that, back in the basement in Queens—he would cut off his left pinkie before he'd subject his wife to such lumpen humiliation. We all suffer a sensitive dependence on initial conditions.

He knew, however, where the picture came from. Mind trash, out of Edie's closet-cleaning this afternoon. Christ! The bed stacked with six department stores' worth of folded finery, every smidgeon paid for by yours truly the number-*crunchateur*. How did she find the time to sign the charge slips? "I didn't know what to wear tonight, and I got into this," she said. Helpless. Radiant. Awkward. The uncertainty principle has it that when you are observing a woman she is perforce not behaving normally.

Mandelbrot had no problem imagining Helena and Hunkenbaum in bed together. She was, as he recalled, quite frisky. (Or was that Fran Bourbaki?) What was harder to get his head around was the notion of Edie as Helena's confidante. But it must be so. For not only did his wife know of this unseemly May–October liaison, she also knew that her teacher had two million stashed in Apple stock. An *affaire* may be gossip fodder, but financial affairs of that magnitude are classified. That Edie was the vault in which such knowledge had been deposited endeared her to him the more, if more were possible. Into the ears of babes!

The question was (that is, before the real question: could she be parted from it?): how had an ass. prof come by that amount? On her salary? *Reparations?*—Mandelbrot had suggested: she *was* a refugee. But no, Edie didn't think so, just natural thrift. Helena never went anywhere. She didn't spend anything to speak of. A raincoat was a major purchase, Edie said. Helena had her little cottage that she'd had built to her own quaint Euro design. But that was in the early seventies, and it was a squidge of a place on a pine scrub acre of outskirts. Can't have cost very much. Lean living, then, leading to a fat portfolio, the same as he was always preaching to the BOR.

"Mitchell," Edie-ever-the-hostess was saying, "Would you like to see the house?" Which left him free to interpose, "Helena, come take a look at my hibiscus." And easy as taffy they pulled apart, the kiddies up the circular and the adults through the lanai.

Outside it was ravishing, Mandelbrot's estate. Beemers and Royces, natty Infinity sunroofs lined the drive. The academics' clunkers were exiled beyond the wall. This side, one Porsche, one Mercedes, one classic '57 Plymouth Fury, every boy's dream, the get-a-girl car. Ah! In those days! *You see that Fury over there? Get in.*

"Shall we walk this way?" he now unctuously proposed.

The drive was low-lit with state-of-the-art twilight-sensitive coolie hats. Cedars had been topiaried into phalluses, uncircumcised. Behind the house, the garden was laid out as a giant paisley—"Did you know that the paisley shape derives from the mango?"—though of course it also suggested a pear, a teardrop, a human liver, a human heart. Viburnum hedges at hip-height outlined the shape over a lush acre, one end fat and the other coiled on itself. Inside that, a ruching of rose bushes in pink and red, then the walkway studded with mosaic in miniature paisley pattern, the beds of impatiens and hydrangeas, day lilies, calla lilies, hyacinth, hibiscus. Inside it all, the paisley of pool like a glittering jewel on a dinner ring. Tiles, half-submerged, sported the seahorse motif again, picked out in chartreuse and cerulean glaze.

All this of course was surface. But Mandelbrot was deeply interested in surface.

Nor was this portion of the estate unpeopled, but callow bodies cracked the water, flapping, splashing. These were the fractious, fucktious, upwardly mobile silicon young. They had barely dipped a toe in divorce, betrayal, self-loathing, putrefaction. They trailed no real estate, they nursed no gall. They knew no erectile dysfunction. They had not been downsized! They wore bikinis, cutoffs, flattops, flipflops, toe rings, ankle bracelets. They were into marijuana instead of Marlboroughs. They were into Programming, gigabyte and megahertz variations. They were into Information Theory, Artificial Intelligence, media *blitzen*, Fuzzy Logic. They had so little history they couldn't tell the difference between a room of one's own and *lebensraum.*

118

"I wanted to mention . . . that I haven't said anything to Edie about . . ." Mandelbrot resorted to aposiopesis.

"Of course not. What would be the point?" Helena fell into step.

"Well, I know you're close."

"I like her a lot. She makes me laugh."

Laugh! Ironist! Amused? Mandelbrot would not pursue it. He had other fish to fry. "Well, in any case, it's a long time since. . . ."

"We were practically children then."

An ironist? "Still, I remember. . . ." He remembered nothing. Panic.

"I remember you called me *girl*."

"Did I? Good God. Were you offended?"

"I don't remember."

A young woman in vermillion hair said hotly to a balding boy, "I don't get why you're so big on the standard toolbar!"

They did not pause to hear the mystery solved.

"I gather," said Helena, "that you haven't read her pieces? She does domestic comedy in the Benchley-Bombeck range. The fleas of life, that sort of thing. She may be shy about showing them to you."

Edie shy! "Why? This comedy is at my expense?"

"Not at all, not at all." The suggestion made her hyperventilate. "I was thinking she should record a few and try them at NPR."

They mounted the gazebo with the onion top. Billows of cloud burbled up in the night sky, complex edifices without a hint of random. Giant water oaks forked and branched and twigged and leaved and veined.

All dross. All dross.

Under normal circumstances he would have psyched himself for some special spiel. Aimed just at her. He tried to remember something about their couple of—three?—nights together—how long? ago! She was frisky, right? Feisty. No? Tender. Athletic, perhaps. He couldn't quite bring it back. This being the case, he heaved his breath up in his deflated lungs and launched into a generic.

"Helena. If you could do one thing for young people today, what would it be?"

"I haven't thought about it."

"Perhaps you should. You know there's an information revolution going on. Our world is going to change in ways you and I cannot imagine."

"Oh, yes, we're going to die. It's famously difficult to imagine."

119

"Helena!" This was zigging into the undergrowth. He zagged. "It's well known you're one of the most dedicated teachers in the system. Edie says. . . ." Panic. Invention flagged. Mandelbrot had an extensive command of phatic phrases. He could filibuster a vapor out of a void. But he needed some nouns, however abstract! Some verbs, preferably passive! Whereas he hadn't the remotest recollection what Edie said about Helena, except that somehow she still snagged the studs and that she had stashed away in stock the precise amount of his shortfall. ". . . the young adore you. That must be what has kept you so young yourself."

"On the contrary, Benni, I'll tell you why teachers get burned out. If you're raising a child, everything that happens is a phase. You don't know what you're doing because you're always doing something new. But when you teach Freshman comp, it's like taking care of an eight year old, and then an eight year old, and then an eight year old. . ."

"I see."

". . . and an eight year old, and an eight year old, and an eight year old, and an eight year old, and an eight year old. . . ."

"I see!" he said with some vehemence. A gross misstep, that, vehemence toward a mark. Not that he thought of her as a mark. "Edie tells me . . ." he paused, more confident. This was what he did remember. "I've always been an IBM man myself, but Edie tells me you're into Apple." She looked at him. Behind her head a giant water oak branched and twigged. "An Apple for the teacher," he grinned.

"The life has its rewards, I grant you that."

Mandelbrot grinned anew and moved his elbow just discreetly in the direction of a rib-dig. "I think you're pretty well rewarded one way and another, eh?"

"How so?"

"Well, that's a helluva good looking young man you've got in tow."

She gave him a funny look. Compassionate, something of that nature. Pitying, in that ballpark. Possibly exasperated.

"You can say what you like" (said Mandelbrot, who was not saying exactly what he liked, but was wiggling on the hook while trying with unaccustomed incompetence to set the hook), "you can say what you like, but there's something special about the young."

She looked uncomfortable. Splotchy. A possibility of tic. A sidelong skittering glance. "Oh, I don't know, Benni," she sighed. Sick at ease, it seemed! Caught out robbing the cradle—was that so blooming bad? Better than grave robbing, ha ha! Hadn't she been a lot looser in days of yore, a bit of a flybynight, a bit of a social butterfly, a happy hippie? So changed? that she couldn't tweak to a hunk without this display of discombobulation? "There was a day I realized I'd been pulling backward, trying to be one of them. And it came to me that I was done with all that. I like the look of the young, but I no longer want to *be* one."

This was off-kilter, somehow. There was an undertext. She eyed him strangely. She looked out over the rough air of the bodies plashing. "You and I haven't always picked the most suitable companions."

This was a strange confession. "Lieutenant Figginbaum, I presume."

"I'm sorry, Benni."

Good God, what was she sorry for? She couldn't imagine that he'd descend to jealousy after all these years, a man of his experience. "I can handle it."

"I'm glad. To be honest, none of us were sure."

This tickled him. Or, no, his stomach tickled; there was a hint of butterflies. He decided to be blunt. He was blunt. "You *are* having an affair with young Mitchell."

"Oh! No, Benni. I'm not. I'm sorry." She didn't look sorry. She looked suddenly composed. She looked briefly toward the road. What did she look? Relieved. *Absolved.* "Dear Benni. I'm so sorry."

Understanding comes as a form of chaos. It may begin with no more disturbance than the sand-flick of a seahorse at the bottom of the sea. But it increases with the tide. Even as he saw again in his mind's eye the folded stacks of all she owned, there was disturbance in front of the house. A friction of fractal surfaces where the rubber met the road. Mandelbrot observed, at the crest of the drive, the little teal SRX tilt and hover. He couldn't see the driver's side, but out of the passenger window stuck a hairy arm, hooked over the roof in a j-shot. The T-roof hung there, revved. And ran.

Still—he would not let the knowledge break over him, not yet. He held the swell at the moment just before the whitecap crowns. He had always been interested in this moment, in the abstract. Philosophically. Scientifically. The calm before the storm. That second of hesitation before the donor bends to sign. The moment the diver bounces from the board and hangs outstretched. Michael Jordan treading air. Baryshnikov in flight. Not yet!

"You have Apple stock!" he asserted.

Helena furrowed, squinted. "I do?"

"Edie told me you'd invested in MacIntosh."

"She told you that?"

"Yes. Was that indiscreet?"

"It seems a bit—arbitrary."

"It's true, though?"

"For what it's worth."

"Quite a lot, I'd have thought, depending when you acquired it."

"Well, for me it's an extravagance. But Edie convinced me it was an investment. A real Burberry, shipped from Regent Street, with a zip-out lining."

"Say what?" he said.

"My new MacIntosh."

They wagged their heads this way and that.

Edie was still standing in his mind's eye among the folded clothes. Holding an angora sweater studded with a sequin paisley. No, seahorse. Butterfly? He remembered thinking that it was an odd time to sort out her closet, when the guests would be arriving in a few hours. He remembered rationalizing, then, that, anyway, the do was catered, the housecleaning was accounted for, the pool man had been and gone, the florist that very moment at work among the baby's breath. Edie was free of any need but to make herself sartorially scrumptious.

Now the wave crested. Now the surf churned. The MacIntosh was a cheap shot! A superficial culture clash! A minor mistranslation! But Edie stood among the silken stacks. Flustered. Footing something away beneath the bed, perhaps. The suitcase surely.

She wasn't sorting; she was *packing*.

She wasn't on a joy-ride, she was *gone*.

The surface of the human lungs is so fabulously folded, richly textured and enribbed, that its area approximates that of a tennis court. Mandelbrot was deeply interested in this surface at the moment. Mandelbrot wheeled and navigated the gazebo steps. He lunged for breath.

At the whiff of oxygen, synapses fired. The dendrites branched and put forth feelers, electrical impulses leapt from place to place such as universally happens when someone is in the process of learning something. The limbic system took up the alarm. The nerves sent signals through the gateways, making spasm in the muscles, clenching at the valves.

"Benni?"

He staggered up the path and past the tumbling tots of darkness. He gained the great room and flung back the door. There they all were, his set, his sidekicks, his society. Revealed to him for what they were. Quicksand. Offal. Carrion. Every one of them divorced, lapsed, terminated, corrupted, stuck. Not one among the mahogany and naugahyde who had not adulterously boffed some other, diddled this one on stock options, been screwed by that on a land deal, had fingers in till, nose up ass, tongue on boot, foot in mouth, hand on heart, heart in throat, heart on sleeve, heart in the wrong (!) place.

He may have seen the Monarch feebly flapping at the glass. Or that flutter may have battened on his chest wall from inside. You can't always be stopping to figure out the source of turbulence! He stumbled on and up.

"Benni, Benni?" Helena was his black wake. He fumbled at the bedroom door and achieved the walk-in, the stagger-in. The shelves were nearly empty, but you couldn't tell what had been taken because on the Axminster was dumped a mini-mountain of her stuff, the fulgent rubbish of a promising career in Consumerism. Even as he breathed in silken, woolen, flaxen reek, the hillock seemed to shift and body forth a flock of moths. Flock—nay—a company! A host!

"Are you . . . ?" Helena was frowning at him prodigiously. What he would never learn (and how much time was there left to learn?) because he would never ask (or because Helena wouldn't say, or both. Whatever!) was to what degree she was part of the plan and to what degree an innocent bystander. How much of the joke she was in on and how much a victim of it.

Edie! Edie!

According to Gleick, three tiny parachutes make up the gauzy heart valve. Luminous, they fold aside. In the His-Pukinje network, that ordered wilderness of paths, that methodical tanglement, the pumping chambers left and right coordinate their rhythm. The whoop and suck, the surf and tide, the stretch and squeeze of blood percusses from one side to another, and back, and through; the fluid pounds and whirls. Like earthquakes, like the stock market, the frequency spectrum of heartbeat timing is subject to fractal law. Many are the pathologies of arrhythmia: electrical alternans, ectopic beats, *torsades de pointes*, high grade block and escape patterns, atrial parasystole pure or modulated; Wenckebach rhythms simple or complex.

The most common of these is tachycardia leading to ventricular fibrillation. But there is absolutely no predicting when or whether this sequence will occur. The wave does not always crest. The storm does not always break. The Nasdaq skids in the snowbank, which may or may not avalanche.

Helena was leaning toward him. A halo of moth dust hung around her.

He saw himself reiterated, diminished, in the pupil of her eye. "Benni? Shall I get somebody?"

Somebody? Such as. . . ?

Going, going, going. Oh, my heart!

Nominated by Elizabeth Gaffney, Five Points

CAMP CEDAR CREST

essay by ALEXANDER THEROUX

from CONJUNCTIONS

Camp cedar crest was the first and last camp I ever attended. It was run by a couple named Beebe, had Catholic affiliations, and the counselors were seminarians, candidates for the priesthood who, for the duration of the summer, tyrannically ruled the hundred or so boys sent there, mostly from the inner city, to get them off the streets. It was an inexpensive place, predominantly for boys from poor families, and there were even charity cases. My parents sent me there for another reason: to be cured of wetting the bed. I had turned twelve years old that summer and had never been away from home before, and I remember when my parents dropped me off and drove away I had the sudden feeling of being deserted.

The word *priesthood* for some reason always, chillingly, gave me an image of cobras.

Was it because of the counselors? They wore black trousers and white T-shirts, and seemed always hidden, until, sliding out of some corner, they appeared, pimply-faced and tall with big black shoes and round miraculous medals around their necks. They were Irish and sex-starved and jut-jawed and repressed and angry and always spoke to us, overpronouncing words, as if talking to idiots. The worst one was Monsky, in charge of C cabin—mine. He had short hair, a fat humorless head, rather like a professional bowler's, and a feral-looking case of underbite, with fanged teeth. He was also humpbacked and mannerless and dyed his hair and had a missing kneecap and held his fork like a screwdriver.

He shouted at everyone and with disgust called us "quats" and could cagily pick out features in each of us to ridicule. I met Monsky right away because the first day I got there and was waiting for my cabin assignment he called me in and asked, "Why are you sitting on your footlocker like a fairy and not outside with the others?"

The camp was a circle of old barrack-type cabins in a clearance of a forest in Marshfield, Massachusetts. Dusty fields lay all around. At the end of the main field, in front of which stood a flagpole—we fell in at 6:30 A.M. for reveille—stood the administrative hall, where Bill and Phoebe Beebe, the administrators, ran the programs. Races, activities, things like that. Canoes were launched along the small river, a narrows beset with woody islets where the summer air was redolent of hot pine, spruce, and cedar. Blueberry bushes sprouted up everywhere. Spongy pine needles were lovely to walk on in those dark dingles and dales under the kind of tall, massive, sky-pointing evergreens that I knew could once be seen all over North America when it was a young and beautiful country. Nearby lay a malodorous marsh that stank at low tide and which we called Fart Harbor. I stared at the moon by night and communed with it. Mist gathered in valleys in the early morning. Most of the ballfield grass got yellow by the middle of July. It was, all in all, a green, deeply forested, and isolated place which became even more so in the rain-dripping darkness. I remember many warm lazy afternoons, a droning plane somewhere in the distance, writing postcards home. Many far miles away rose the kind of hills, I knew, that Indians once lived on, always facing south, near water. I knew about stuff like that. I don't know, maybe most everybody did. I had a book with photos, in his tent in the frozen wastes, of Richard Evelyn Byrd, whose name *wasn't* a woman's.

My favorite book, thick and green, was *Trader Horn*, about an adventurer who once made a comment on one page I remember regarding the lack of softness in nature. I wrote down words from it that I later kept. My favorite song was "The Heather on the Hill." My favorite painting was *Lady with an Ermine.* I had six rolls of Wheatsheaf pennies. A beautiful Korean girl named Sarah with an angel's features once gave me a valentine that I still have in a drawer. I wanted to know and I needed to feel and I felt I had to know the meaning of everything.

I can honestly say that most of the time I lived a dream life. So many times I saw people, strangers, passersby, and out of nowhere thought: *I will never ever see that person again.* Everyone always walked in different directions in the world, lost to logic or loyalty or luck. What was fleeting was temporary, and anything temporary broke my heart. Nothing one experienced ever remained permanent or recoverable, I realized with melancholy—not the moment, not the place, nothing. Whatever we encountered or passed by was immediately and forever in the past. I pondered in consequence and with mad concentration the way things used to be. I was always wasting my time as a young boy trying to squint back through space and time or some dimension, making an effort to look into and then past crowded neighborhoods and urban blight and city blocks in an attempt to see, as if by way of photographs, the ghosts of the past.

And I knew about druids. Who knew, I thought, maybe I was one once. I could read signs in nature. I wanted to sleep in the open air without a blanket, live in the woods, eat berries, and find mushrooms—I believed trees had rights—trek over trailless mountains and meet Pontiac's holy ghost, attaining the tippity-top of their highest mysterious peaks, silent in their primeval sleep. Be an explorer. That word. I loved it. And the word *scout*. I made friends, grew quiet in the presence of girls, whose beauty and mystery I loved and feared, but still, because I was going to be an author, I walked alone by the lake, tossing in stones, listening in silence in clearings, and taking long looks into the world. I got goose bumps.

Phoebe Beebe, who gave out mail in the high hall, where the chapel was—daily attendance was required—looked like a bag of russet potatoes with earrings. Augie Doggie had a joke about her and told it every day. "Why is it good Phoebe Beebe has the face of a vulture and the voice of a crow?" And we'd all sing in unison, "Because if you threw a rock at her, you could kill two birds with one stone."

There were campfires at night, when we all sat like Mohawks *sur leur derrières*, crouched, our knees as high as our ears, and fed the fire fat pine knots as we listened to scary stories about creepy madmen like Grippo and Three-Fingered Willy and Mr. Mendacino, a sentient vegetable, and Fat Ping, the Chinese warlord who bit people to death, and Dripple the Cripple, who strangled women and said, "Thuffer!" Sometimes we threw on pieces of old driftwood: Whoever has seen driftwood burn with all its magical lights, hissing and spitting sparks, odd bursts of powder, will never forget it. The moon would be out. Foxes barked some nights, and I think I heard coyotes. I felt the wind. It was wild and wonderful to be alive.

At times Mulligan and Obie, two of the nicer counselors, asked questions. I often knew the answers. It was because of my reading—

and knowledge of James Fenimore Cooper and spirits that came from the loveliness of the deep woods and being able to survive if I got lost on Mount Katahdin and all the time I put in dreaming, especially about Glooskap, an Indian spirit who never grew old and lived at the south end of the world with the lion and the wolf.

Curfew was for ten. And they were strict. "Don't you trust us?" asked Vinnie Mushpart, as in the dark we filed into the cabins by flashlight. "Yuh," said Atkins, "like a pink-faced prostikook doing pushups over twenty-dollar bills."

But I didn't mind the curfews. Or the work detail. Or even Monsky. (My nightly affliction was something else.) I had not only friends, but admirers for the first time. I knew things others didn't and it won me some esteem. A button is a good fish lure. Snow is a leavener for cooking. All seaweed is good to eat. Never plant a seed deeper than its width. Spring moves north about thirteen miles a day. The bark of a dead tree holds moisture on its northern side, and the center of the damp or rotten area is usually slightly east of north. I even knew that people wiped their bums with stones in Samoa, but that I didn't feel was right to mention.

We sneaked out and smoked pipes, not cornsilk as once I did at home, but Edgeworth in the blue pouch and Model tobacco, from a can with the cartoon of the bald old man with a mustache that the Jackdaws bought, two brothers named Shoffner who looked like birds of prey but were great at soap carving, where you glued together two or three bars, one on top of the other, for whittling totem poles or heads. I thought I'd never get as old as that old geezer on the Model can. My postcards home were speckled with nonsense, puns, and Latinisms. Sometimes Monsky stared at me in games. He was cruel and, I felt, dangerous.

I got to know my bunk mates. Billy Gilday could mouth and spit-shoot three hundred BBs into the hole of a Daisy rifle. There was Harshbarger, the Nazi, who went for "mailbox baseball," smashing them with a bat. Rappleye, a genuine mutant who had webbed toes, a twist of nature he often pointed to with pride. Snover. Brian Godalming, my friend. Fitler, who was always flipping a Zippo in his pocket. Richard Center went home with rheumatic fever and later died. Patroni. Slupski. Julie Zuk, from Danvers, who collected leaves (oak, maple, catalpa, etc.)—"telling leaves," he called it—and Mushpart, who, although he was thin as a reed, weak, and pale as the underbelly of a fish, would stand up during dinner and squeeze sandwiches through his fingers. There was Edd ("Bona") Harding. And even Blackerby who was from Athol and turned blue in the ocean and whom we called the "Unidentified Flying Oddball."

And Warren Ruck, who wanted to talk after taps. I remember him as a quiet, fragile, stuttering boy with exquisite but somehow feminine manners who always wondered why I got up from the breakfast table—the wood was always gluey—to get back to the cabin before the others. But inspection followed, and I had to open the window and talcum the sheets whenever I had an accident, which was all the time.

Cruel counselors mocked Ruck—and always, of course, us—about girls. They called him "SSSpeedo" and snatched his hat and played *salucci* with it and abused him and never picked him for patrol leader. Several times the counselors asked us if we wanted to become priests. But from the sound of the sheets shuffling at night, and from what I heard about it, there may have been sins being committed, which is why one Sunday after Mass, Phoebe Beebe had pamphlets called *The Difficult Commandment* passed around to all.

We often went to the old tractor shed, with its old tin signs advertising Moxie and Nehi that resonated when we bounced small green apples off them, me and Warren and Brian Godalming. We made gimp lanyards and twill-woven pot holders and rawhide wallets and leatherhead drums and birch birdhouses and talked about things like when is the best time to plant and where to build lean-tos or how the Pilgrims survived the first winter in Plymouth. "Eating groundnuts, birch syrup, pigweed, even antlers when in velvet," I said, which was true. I never said much about myself, having developed formidable defenses against reality at a very tender age. Bedwetters must. But I remember being very happy.

I was *prepared*. It's a concept young boys alone can understand: being prepared, not for anything in particular. But for everything. Like the Minutemen. Was it an escape mechanism? I ratholed all sorts of things in my khaki footlocker: pamphlets on ventriloquism and throwing your voice; baby powder; a rubber sheet; a jackknife; two bottles of Vitalis; an army compass; a flashlight; several packages of Clark's Teaberry gum; a copy of *Saint Among the Hurons*; bags of chestnuts; a hatchet; copies of my favorite comic books: *Strange Tales, Sad Sack, The Purple Claw, Wild Bill Elliott*. I had copies of Jimmy Hatlo's *They'll Do It Every Time*.

I wanted to be an author, mostly because, at least to me, writing books with quills by candlelight seemed to be about the best thing a person could do, no matter what, and also, I think, at least partially, because I had the same name as Alexandre Dumas. I once made a list:

Things in Nature That Hurt

> sunglare
> jellyfish
> horseradish
> hot peppers
> locust bark
> poison ivy
> dry ice
> yucca plants
> snakes
> onions
> rhubarb leaves
> mosquito bites
> thorns
> hail
> hornpouts

Camp food dorked. We marched to the dining hall every morning to "Fairest of the Fair," an old scratched 78 rpm record playing on a Victrola up in the wooden fire tower and blasted over a loudspeaker. I remember watery scrambled eggs and pancakes and clogged syrup-pourers and the scent of pine blowing through morning windows thrown wide open. Gilday once winkled some silverware and we made long spears, to fight saber-toothed tigers. We left messages in the woods by shaping tree limbs. Tapioca pudding we called "fish-eyes," doughnuts "shotputs," apples "Mrs. Beebe's Bubbies," and certain white round desert-dry cross crackers they gave us were impossible to eat with peanut butter without strangling. The soup was so thin, we used to say it was made from boiling the shadow of a pigeon that had starved to death. Sometimes we stole Oreo cookies, which we wolfed down with gulps of milk, trying to see who'd pass out and making a paste completely unspitoutable—"Look!" we gagged—and thick enough to brick up Fortunato.

Afterward came inspection, as I say, which terrified me. I came to align all my hopes to the fact of that, not so much never being known, as much as, if found out, then forgiven. I desperately shook powder over the stained sheets or doubled up the blanket or did both, praying to God under my breath that no one would notice my incontinence. It worked for a few days. But then my luck abruptly came to an end. I can still remember the morning. Monsky strode in and, jut-jawed, hump up, paused, flinging back the covers of my cot, singling me out in front of all the others, and screamed, "What is this? Come here, fart harbor, and explain this! Are you a fairy? Hand wash them blankets! Spray the slats, springs, and frames of this bed! Get them thoroughly wet, then borax them, hear me?" He called me a quat and a doughhead and a fairy and, in his mocking way, even managed to make my friends laugh at me. My face heated balloon red from humiliation, and, for a minute, in a hot flush of vertigo, I actually thought I had disappeared. Or was upside-down. I remember hearing only echoes in my head of his infernal shouts. "And spray that dog of a mattress! Do not soak it! Pay particular attention to seams and tufts! And brush the box springs, for godsakes, because they reek!"

As a punishment, I was forced for an afternoon, in front of the entire cabin, to sit on a stool and wear a rubber sheet around my neck.

Many things have happened to me in the intervening years, good and bad, but from that day on I was never the same person again. I was only worried. I never wrote home again, or if I did, I rarely told the truth. It was like I never was. And when I was given jobs, like putting para-crystals in the old storage rooms and cleaning the garbage pails with chlorine bleach and brushing the radiators and boraxing the toilet molding, I always wondered whose hands were doing the job and who was acting under my name.

I was going to say I never went out after that—but I wasn't even alive anymore—and yet I did go out once, to the top of the old wooden fire tower, where I sat alone for hours trying not so much to not be seen, though that, as to be able somehow to turn back time. The whole last week of camp it rained, and we stayed in those musty cabins with their cedar walls and silverfish in the wood and naked light bulbs, and it never seemed so lonely. I was so homesick that if anybody blew on me, I knew I'd start to cry.

The day my father came for me, I was so happy to see him I went mute. I could not talk. My throat was filled with tears. But I was cynical, too. Since I figured nothing ever came true, especially what you wanted, when I wanted something I prayed for it not to happen, so it would, like my father coming to get me. I never went to camp again. Nor did I dream again of woods or compasses or Glooskap or wolves or the best way off Mount Katahdin. I was a bedwetter, and so knew I was worthy of being neither an Indian nor an author.

One thing I never wondered anymore was what hurt most in nature, only because I knew. It wasn't jellyfish or locust bark or dry ice or thorns or eating rhubarb leaves. It was people. Camp, they said, always taught you something. And now I knew that they were right.

Nominated by Conjunctions

FROM THE PSALTER

by JENNIFER ATKINSON

from NOTRE DAME REVIEW

According to the lily, praise is an arrow, a song
Loosed from the recurved bow of its petals.

According to the dove in the far-off pine, sorrows
Are credits in the ledgerbook, tears pearls in an amethyst bottle.

According to the deer whom night has forsaken, best
Are the fields of half-ripe oats beset with quail easily startled.

According to the voice through the mask of feigned madness: I is
No more *I* than the star left is *star* when you lift the stencil.

According to the red field-lily, praise is a serenade
That beguiles the lover and beloved alike: open your mouth and be
    grateful.

Nominated by Jean Thompson, John Drury

CASUALIDADES

fiction by CAROLYN ALESSIO

from TRIQUARTERLY

ON THE STREET NEAR THE BUS STOP a group of teenaged boys stood in a circle, sharpening their rusted machetes. Berta pulled her market bag closer as she walked toward the bus. The *ladrones*, the thieves, weren't likely to rob anyone until payday—two days off—but Berta moved with caution. Three rotting onions knocked together inside her bag, next to a vial of medicine. She always carried old onions with her medicine because the people in her village were nosey and if they tried to look into her bag they would smell the odor and stay away.

This morning she had taken off work to go to the hospital on the hill for a checkup. She had not had a seizure for two weeks, but the medicine gave her gas, a constant rumbling that pained and embarrassed her. A week ago she had stopped taking the full dosage.

The faded green bus started uphill, groaning and halting. Berta looked in vain for an empty seat. The bus driver shifted gears jerkily, and Berta nearly stumbled. As she reached for the bar above to steady herself, a woman in an embroidered smock pulled her basket of chicks onto her lap and gestured at the empty seat next to her. Berta smiled and sat down.

At the sewing cooperative where she worked, none of the women wanted to sit by Berta anymore. Her seizures had increased in the past year, and the women had begun to treat Berta like someone they thought the priest should exorcise. She took to working alone, hunched over in a dim corner of the cinderblock building, but even that didn't work. Two weeks ago she had been cutting out striped *jaspe* fabric for a vest when the strange singing rose up inside her, the low song without words that always heralded her attacks. She tried to muffle the sounds, to quiet her trembling hands, but the rumbling notes escaped from her mouth and her fingers shook, releasing the scissors. They landed a foot away from her nearest coworker, Esperanza, but Esperanza screamed anyway. Later, when Berta opened her eyes, the women stood around her in a circle and the gringo boss told her that she needed medical attention.

A man sitting near the front of the bus stood up, pulled out a package of colored pencils, and began to call out their virtues. Berta shifted in her seat near the back, next to the woman with the basket of squirming, squeaking chicks. She wondered if they could smell her onions. The vendor walked down the aisle. In a clear plastic case he held a rainbow spread of pencils: red, light blue, green, yellow, and an orange that nearly matched the pair of vinyl shoes Berta wore, a purchase that had cost her a month's wages. "Good prices, a bargain," the vendor said, strolling up and down the aisle. Neither Berta nor the woman next to her looked as he passed, but inside Berta's head she had begun to draw, starting with a red pencil for the clay along the road, then moving upward, shading in the sky as it looked at daybreak, a blue-gray haze that covered the mountains and the inactive volcanoes. This was her view from the roof of her mother's house as Berta fed the roosters in the early morning. The bus lurched and Berta felt a nip from a chick at her elbow.

The seizures always began with singing, a low thrumming that started below her breastbone and traveled upward, swirling in gritty circles around her throat and emerging from Berta's mouth in syllables that many villagers thought were too low for a woman. Sometimes they started at work, but mostly the attacks happened at home, the strange song catching her as she leaned over the *pila* to wash a glass sticky with rice drink, or tend the fire for tortillas that her mother had started but forgotten to watch.

Berta's house was made of cinderblock and sheets of thin wood that darkened in the rain and shuddered during the windy season. She was twenty-nine and lived with her mother. Every other woman of her age in the village had a man and children; some even had grandchildren. Sometimes Berta babysat for her neighbors' children, not minding even when they rubbed their grimy hands in her long hair, but lately their mothers had been worried about the evil eye she might carry, and they asked Berta not to stare too long at their babies.

Berta had never been on a date and she rarely looked in the mirror. Mornings when she pulled her glossy long hair into a barrette, she remembered what her mother said once when Berta asked if she were pretty: *"M'hija,* you have beautiful hair."

Gray letters arched over the steel gate, announcing "El Hospital Mental Público de Guatemala." Berta had disembarked from the bus a mile before and walked uphill, muddying her lovely shoes as she trudged past a long shallow garbage pit whose odors mixed with the day's heavy humidity and clung to her skin. She approached the guard, who slouched against the bumper of a military truck. He stood up, crushed out a cigarette, and asked for her identification.

Berta reached into her bag for her medical card, the one that her gringo boss had gotten for her when he drove her there for her initial consultation. The guard glanced at the green cardboard pass, grunted, and motioned with his gun to the path beyond the gate.

The grounds were a maze of low, squat buildings connected by dilapidated paths. The grass looked tired, yellow-brown in patches. Berta stepped over snarls of dirt and roots.

A man with a ragged beard approached her, and began to ask for money in a high staccato voice. Berta shook her head no, but he persisted, calling her pretty, complimenting her hair. Berta's head hurt.

"Por favor," the man said to Berta, "just a few *quetzales.*" Berta sucked in her breath: she had never understood why her country's currency was named after the nearly extinct national bird.

The man reached for her arm, with a grip that was surprisingly tight.

Berta remembered her father before he left the family, on nights when his boss hadn't paid the workers their due at the coffee plantation. Drunk, he raced around the house, ripping laundry off the line, sometimes throwing pots into the street.

"Listen," she hissed now, turning around. *"No hablo español,"* she said, trying to sound nasal like the gringo boss at the sewing cooperative. "Speek Ing-lish."

The man loosened his grip, stood back and studied her. *"Gringa?"* he said, his heavy-lidded eyes widening.

"Sí." The laughter rose in her like odorless gas as she turned to look for the big building with the high padlocked gates.

The doctor didn't call her name during the first hour she waited, nor the second. When he finally got to her, Berta's back was stiff from leaning so long against the damp wall, and the doctor didn't even say her full name—Berta Francisca Torneo de Monterosso, but simply, Señorita Torneo. Her face burned as she got up to follow; everyone seemed to know just by looking at her that she was still Miss, Señorita.

The examining room was divided by a torn, faded curtain. Berta hesitated at the edge, noting the fabric's uneven cut, when the doctor waved her in.

The doctor spoke slowly and his lower lip was punctuated with dark indentations, like bruises on mangoes past their time. Berta wondered if he were nervous. He looked up from her file and said, "This is too early for your follow-up appointment."

Hands in her lap, Berta told him about the medicine's side effects. She tried to explain how she could not stand rumbling with gas out in public; making a rude sound at Mass just before the offertory, at work when she and the other women presented their wares to a traveling missionary group. Nearly whispering, she mentioned she had lowered her dosage, and had suffered a flare-up at work.

The doctor said, "Do you want the seizures to return?"

She shook her head. Outside an ice cream truck played a jangly, carnivalesque tune.

"Señorita," he said, "I could switch you to another medicine but you'd have different problems. Sleep too much, thirsty all the time. With all epilepsy medications," he said, sweeping his long thin arm across the desk, "there are *casualidades*."

Chances of side effects. She looked down at her market bag and the odor of old onions rose to her eyes.

A woman with matted hair pushed into the examining room, yelling that she had lost her son, and pulling at the dirty rags wrapped around her wrists.

The doctor glanced at her. "Suleni," he said quietly, standing up, "They need you down at lunch."

The woman stared, pulled at her wrists. "My son is missing," she said. "He doesn't know I've moved."

The doctor went to her, placed his hands gently on her shoulders. "Let's find a nurse," he said, leading her toward the doorway. "We'll be right back," he said without turning to look at Berta.

A moment later he returned. He did not sit down, but reached for Berta's file from the desk. "Well," he said, turning back to Berta, "you will try the medicine a bit longer?"

She stared at the barred window for a moment, at the dingy walls. She imagined her shiny long hair matted, and putrid rags wound around her wrists. The doctor looked at her and she nodded.

Berta reached for her market bag and stood, moving toward the door. The doctor's voice stopped her: "Before you leave, let's see you take your noon-time dosage."

The pills left a bitter white paste on her tongue. Berta stopped on the street near the bus stop to splurge and buy a Coke, but even as she sucked the sweet soda through the straw in the plastic bag, she could not rinse the sourness from her mouth.

On the ride home she dozed a little, leaning up against the window that rattled and shook as the bus plodded forward. The metal clasp of her crooked barrette pushed into her scalp so finally she sat up. At one of the stops a group of schoolchildren in uniforms got on, waking Berta with their laughing and talking. Judging from their pressed uniforms she guessed they lived in the village two bus stops beyond hers, a cleaner place where there were no sewage ditches and the dogs did not howl all night for food.

The children unwrapped bright red suckers and tiny taffy squares. Dry wind blew in from the windows and Berta remembered playing in the wind as a child, pretending as her skirt billowed out that she was a flower.

The bus pulled into the last leg of Berta's journey. One-room cinderblock houses and wooden shacks pressed up against the sides of the road, their doors only feet from the sewage ditch.

Berta straightened her blouse, and wondered if, when she returned to work, the other women would ask her where she had been. Maybe she could slip into the corner, and they would be too busy to notice as they stitched tiny brown-faced dolls onto barrettes to ship up North to the States.

A sharp pounding shook the bus as it pulled near the sewing cooperative. The bus slowed and everyone turned around to look. Two young men had climbed on the back, yelling and beating at the windows.

The stooped, gray-haired driver stopped the bus and stood up. He pulled a tiny knife from his pocket, stepped off the bus, and went around to the back. Berta heard shouts and curse words. Inside the bus she saw other passengers pulling their bags closer. She did not have to be told they had been stopped by *ladrones*.

Finally the driver returned to the front, but he was followed by a young man waving a machete. Berta recognized the tall *ladrón* with the unusual green eyes.

"Don't worry yourselves," the bus driver called out to the passengers, but the *ladrón* stamped on the floor with a ragged boot and pushed him back to his seat.

Another young man with a machete entered from the side, also carrying the bus driver's tiny knife. A schoolchild began to cry.

"Pass up your money," the green-eyed *ladrón* called, slightly slurring his words. Everybody began to dig in their pockets and purses. Berta heard muttering. Payday at the factories and fincas was not for two more days—most villagers were down to bus fare and enough for a few eggs. She thought the *ladrones* must be desperate, drunk or high on sniffing glue bought at the shoemaker's shop. Berta looked in her bag: two onions and a vial of medicine. She swept her hand beneath them, found a single *quetzal* note. She handed it to one of the *ladrones* as he passed down the aisle, scraping his machete along the floor. The bus driver slouched in his seat, holding his face in his hands.

Nobody had much more to offer than Berta: single *quetzal* notes were pressed into the ladrones' hands, some loose change. Even the schoolchildren with the nice uniforms only had enough for another bus fare or two: they had spent most of it on candy.

The *ladrones* counted the money at the front of the bus, cursing every time a handful of loose change appeared. Berta estimated that at most they would have enough for an evening or two of beer, the regular kind with the rooster's head on the label. They counted the money again, then the green-eyed one muttered something. They talked back and forth a little, conferring, and spitting in the aisle.

Outside the bus, people from the neighborhood were beginning to gather. Berta thought she saw Esperanza from the cooperative, the woman she had scared with her scissors. Nobody ever called the police in their village, because the police were scared of the *ladrones*, too. It was hard to enforce law in their village, and revenge only came rarely, usually in the form of a midnight beating in the garbage dump.

The *ladrones* stared at them and paced, walking up and down the aisles and panning the passengers with their too-wide pupils. Finally the green-eyed *ladrón* turned to the passengers and said, "Pass up your shoes."

Nobody spoke. Many of them had been robbed before, of bus fare, jewelry and even food, but Berta had never heard of this. She looked down at her own, orange vinyl shoes. Until she was twelve she had gone barefoot, like most of the other young women in the village. After that she had worn plastic beach thongs, the cheapest kind at the market. But a month ago, she had treated herself to these beautiful durable shoes, after finishing a shipment of 34 purses, 12 vests, and 25 barrettes. She still knew the numbers. The *ladrones* began with the schoolchildren, urging them to hurry as they passed up their dark-soled loafers. One child even passed up his socks.

Berta looked around. The adults with no shoes looked the most frightened. One woman had pulled several mangoes out of her bag as if to offer them in compensation. The others with shoes were taking them off, slipping their feet from plastic beach thongs, and unlacing boots in clumsy hurried movements. The muscular *ladrón* paced the aisles. His machete looked like it had once been used on a plantation.

Berta removed her shoes, stroking the smooth orange vinyl. The muscular *ladrón* hissed at everyone to hurry up. In the front of the bus the green-eyed *ladrón* was piling shoes into the T-shirts he and the other one had stripped off, makeshift knapsacks. Berta held her shoes for a moment longer in her lap, cradling them, then she slipped one into her bag. The other she slid beneath her shirt, hoping that in the commotion she wouldn't be noticed. The vinyl felt nice against her chest and she crossed her arms to camouflage.

The bare-chested *ladrones* now had full knapsacks. Outside the bus more villagers lined up, talking and wringing their hands. Berta thought she saw the priest, a friend of her mother's. She hated her town, herself, for always backing away from danger.

Everybody on the bus had bare feet now. The shirtless *ladrones* walked along, grabbing some shoes and purses that had not been handed up. The green-eyed *ladrón* stopped at Berta's seat. "Pass it," he said, staring at the bag on her lap. "Señorita," he said, grabbing her wrist, "Pass it here."

"Only vegetables," she began, but he emptied it. Three mottled, onions fell out and a medicine vial, then the thud of one orange shoe. The *ladrón* let the onions roll down the aisle in off-white rotations, but he stooped to pick up the shoe. Normally the drugs might have interested him, Berta thought, but now everybody was watching. He held the single shoe in his hand, gripping it by its muddy sole.

The other passengers turned around to stare at her, but Berta was used to this. She knew how to be a spectacle.

The shoe dangled in front of her head. "Your other shoe," the green-eyed *ladrón* said. His assistant walked toward them. "Hey crazy lady," the muscular *ladrón* said, a glimmer of recognition crossing his broad face, "give us the shoe."

Berta shook her head. Inside her blouse, the vinyl felt cool against her clammy skin. "Now," the green-eyed *ladrón* said.

"It's mine," Berta said, clutching the shoe to her chest, "*Mío.*"

The muscular *ladrón* moved forward, but the green-eyed *ladrón* waved him off. She could tell he thought he had a way with women. "Señorita," he said, in a voice that reminded her of her visit to the doctor, "your shoe, please."

Berta shook her head. He was so close she could smell the perspiration on his chest. He reached for a lock of her hair, not pulling as hard as she expected.

The bus was quiet. The green-eyed *ladrón* worked a strand of her shiny hair in his fingers, then muttered something to the muscular *ladrón* behind him. The muscular *ladrón* laughed, and Berta spit in the green-eyed *ladrón's* face.

Now he yanked her by the hair, pulling her down the aisle to an empty seat at the front of the bus. He tugged so hard her barrette snapped open and the orange shoe fell out from under her shirt. The muscular *ladrón* lunged for it, but the green-eyed *ladrón* shoved Berta to the floor, a handful of her hair still caught in his fist. Her head smarted and her hands felt numb. Outside the bus people had begun to shout. Breathing hard, the green-eyed *ladrón* laid her hair out straight on the seat. As he positioned his machete to cut her hair, Berta opened her mouth and began to sing.

Nominated by David Wojahn, Jean Thomspon, TriQuarterly

SOLATIUM

essay by PHILIP D. BEIDLER

from MICHIGAN QUARTERLY REVIEW

MORE THAN THIRTY YEARS LATER, and not a week goes by when I don't think of the dead Vietnamese boy at Gia Ray. Actually, I go through periods when I see him every day. I zip open the body bag, and out he comes, face first, the rest of him in a fetal crouch, arms and legs drawn up in front like some dreadful insect mutation. Later I find out that is what dead bodies often do. Everything—head, limbs, torso—is covered in a kind of viscous, translucent slime, the stuff they use in monster movies. A combination of mucus, chest fluid, urine, and dissolved fecal matter, it smells oddly sweet. Later I find out that is how dead bodies often smell.

It's dusk. Early in the day, I've sent this boy out on a helicopter with a depressed skull fracture. The mechanized unit in which I'm a platoon leader—tanks, armored personnel carriers, and assorted other vehicles—has been moving through his village, and a big tank retriever has knocked down the corner of an old, ceremonial stone gate. A heavy piece—about the size and weight of a cinder block—has fallen on the boy's head, basically caving in one side of his skull. When I pick him up and carry him to my track, I notice that the indentation is in the exact shape of the rock.

My next recollection has me inside a nearby firebase—Mary Ann I think it's called—kneeling on the helipad, with the boy in my lap and a PRC-25 radio beside me. I'm yelling into the handset, begging for an army medevac helicopter, a dustoff. Voices on the other end keep telling me that no dustoff is available, and that even if one is, I can't call a dustoff for a Vietnamese civilian. In between sessions of screaming at the bastards on the radio, I keep looking down at the kid, patting him and stroking him, telling him it's going to be all right, we'll get him out of there and somebody will take care of him. He seems to be just barely breathing. Under his short, black, shiny hair, I can see the big rectangular dent in the side of his skull.

As I remember, it's finally the brigade executive officer, a colonel, who with much impatience finally agrees to land his command ship and take the boy to the Vietnamese Army compound at Xuan Loc, about ten miles away, where they have their own medical evacuation unit. When the helicopter lands, I give him to one of the door gunners. I go back to my platoon.

In the years since, I have tried every way I can to put together the rest of that day, but it just doesn't exist. We may have patrolled the jungle with tanks and armored personnel carriers like we did most days or set up blocking positions for the infantry sweeping the other way. We may have done convoy escort or roadblock duty. It was bad country up there. On the roads, we kept passing burned-out hulks from the last American unit to operate in the place a year or so back a hot-shit armored cavalry regiment, commanded at the time by George Patton, Jr., that obviously had not won all that many hearts and minds. Once, in the middle of a jungle clearing, we found some kind of aircraft fuselage with French markings. Boy, I remember thinking, is this going to be a long war.

Whatever happened that day in late July or early August 1969, my platoon was back inside the firebase by late afternoon, setting up for night perimeter security. The boy was there waiting for us when we pulled in. Also waiting were orders to get him cleaned up and ready for a ceremony in the morning when he would be returned to his family for burial. Since I had the only field medic, he got the job. I went with him to see if I could help. I had a rule in the platoon that there would be times when I would never ask anyone to do something I wouldn't do. I decided this was one of those times. That was when I opened up the body bag. It was also when my medic went temporarily insane. He was a decent man and a brave soldier, the kind of medic everybody called "Doc," and he had been through a lot. He took what he saw as an insult to the dead. He screamed, he raged, he wept. He cursed every curse he could think of, mainly at the fucking ARVNs. It seemed to be a professional matter. Who would let something like that happen to a kid and then not clean him up? After a while, the thing seemed to pass. He settled down and went to work, wiping the boy's body and straightening his limbs. I of-

143

fered to stay and help or at least keep him company. He told me in a kindly voice that he wanted to do it by himself and that I should go on back to the platoon.

The ceremony didn't take place until midmorning. It probably took that long to gather up all the brigade bigwigs from the rear. The Vietnamese boy's parents were going to be brought in to the firebase to get him. They were also going to get something called a solatium payment. That was the official name for it. It was a cash payment made by the U.S. government to Vietnamese civilians who lost property or family members as a result of accidents of war. The figure, as I recall, was alleged to be around thirty-five dollars. The procedure was administered by a special staff officer in the brigade called the S-5. This was something the Army had added during the Vietnamese war. Traditionally, S-1 was personnel; S-2, intelligence; S-3, operations; and S-4, supply. In Vietnam, S-5 was the officer for civil affairs, providing civilian medical and dental care, rebuilding damaged property, involving villagers in agricultural and sanitation projects and the like. This was another one of the things the S-5 did—find Vietnamese civilians who had lost loved ones due to military operations and arrange solatium payments. He was also in charge of arranging the ceremonies, like the one they had at Mary Ann.

I watched from a distance. It was held in the back of a big armored command vehicle, full of radios and situation maps, with a ramp that dropped to the ground and a tent attached like an awning, making a kind of pavilion. Lots of high-ranking functionaries had flown in for the ceremony, including a couple of field grade officers from the brigade staff and the local ARVN commander. The S-5 did the honors. The parents looked numb and bewildered. They made strange smiles and bows. Every time they did it, the Americans started smiling and bowing, and then the parents smiled and bowed some more too. Besides the cash payment, the parents also got a couple of big ration supplement boxes like the kind they gave to units in the field once a week or so, sundries packs they were called, full of candy and snacks and toilet items, and each with about ten cartons of American cigarettes in all different brands.

That was it. An infantry company moved in to secure the firebase, and the next day I was back in the jungle with my platoon. Eventually I left the platoon and became the executive officer of my troop, a company-sized unit. When my year was up, I went home. I went back to graduate school and used my G.I. Bill to get a Ph.D. in English. I've spent my career teaching American literature in a university. As part of my work, I've written a good deal about the literature of the Vietnamese war. I suppose it's been my way of coming to terms with the experience. On the other hand, not much of it has dealt directly with what I did or what happened to me personally; and I can only infer that until lately, at least, I have wanted it that way.

I'm fifty-six now and a parent for the first time. My wife and I have a daughter who is seven. I have an obsessive fear that something bad is going to happen to her. There are times when I put her in the car to go somewhere with her mother or someone else I really trust and I worry that I'm never going to see her again. One weekend about two years ago, when my wife and I were at the beach and my daughter was staying with her aunt, I convinced myself that they were both going to be freakishly murdered. For a day and a half I sat in a chair, staring and mute, bludgeoned with medication. My wife took me home. A VA psychologist who has become a friend tells me this is all typical of what he calls "recurrent unpleasant thoughts," a form of PTSD, delayed stress disorder. It's all through the literature, he tells me. Deep down somewhere, he says, it's the dead Vietnamese boy at Gia Ray I'm thinking about. He's right, I've decided. I've also checked the DSM IV, and he's right there, too. It's all in black and white: intrusive memories; persistent anxiety; excessive vigilance.

Oddly, as many Vietnamese as we killed in what were called accidents of war, you don't see much written about solatium in the literature. A scene such as the one I witnessed appears in an early chapter of Josiah Bunting's novel *The Lionheads*, in which the major general commanding the fictional 12th Infantry Division and his chief of staff meet with a Vietnamese couple whose son has been killed and their house destroyed. The ceremony takes place in the general's imposing office at the division headquarters. "Mr. Tranh," says the general, addressing the father, "this is a great tragedy you've sustained, and we know what a blow it is for you. It's something we feel terrible about here. We want you to know that we have made arrangements with Captain Kramer to see that you get every assistance rebuilding your house. And it's a terrible, terrible shame about your son. I know how much you must have loved him." The general mentions that he also has sons. No, he replies to the Vietnamese father, they are not in the army. The chief of staff, a colonel, surprises everyone, including himself, by quoting some Lincoln he has learned at the Academy. "Nothing could beguile you from a loss," he intones, "as overwhelming as this one is." The bereaved parents receive the payment in an envelope embossed with the Lionhead crest. Type-written and carefully centered in capital letters, the envelope reads FROM THE MEN OF THE TWELFTH INFANTRY DIVISION IN DEEP CONDOLENCE. When the Vietnamese couple are escorted to the jeep that has brought them to headquarters, "a trailer has been attached to it, filled with tools, burlap sacks of rice, and some cartons of C-rations."

Misspelled as "solacium," the policy is also mentioned anecdotally in James William Gibson's *The Perfect War: Technowar in Vietnam*, where a former army enlisted man assigned to the U.S. civilian aid mission angrily remembers it as emblematic of the American bureaucratic attitude toward the Vietnamese: "an adult civilian over 15 years who was killed was worth $35 to their family; a child under 15 was worth $14.40. The United States government paid people off for their dead children, or their dead husbands and wives, or whatever, at the rate of $35 or $15, depending on their age."

Another brief reference appears in a Vietnam glossary as "Grievance Payment," under which are listed not only "Solatium," but also "Compensation Payment" and "Go-Minh Money." Solatium procedures, it says, involved "cash payments ranging from a few dollars to several hundred dollars made to Vietnamese as compensation for property damages to buildings, crops, farm animals, and personal possessions, and also for grief suffered as the result of the loss of a loved one." However, as with virtually everything involving money among Americans and Vietnamese, it goes on, a built-in potential for shamming and scamming quickly became a two-way street. Initially claims were to be made either directly to the U.S. Military or to the U.S. Mission through the Vietnamese district and/or province chief. In the latter case, there quickly arose a problem with fraudulent inflation of claims and awards, including the skimming of high percentages of payments into official pockets. As a result, eventually the Vietnamese government was required to have citizens submit claims directly to Americans. Thence, in the idea of applying for and receiving compensation directly from the Americans, arose the local nickname: "Go-Minh Money." In Vietnamese, it can be roughly translated as "extracting oneself from a predicament."

Ironically, the most detailed historical description of solatium policy now available probably comes from an official source, a Depart-

146

ment of the Army pamphlet entitled *Law at War.* Written by a Major General, George S. Pew, it is a history of activities during the period of Vietnam operations of the Army's legal branch, the Judge Advocate General Corps. Described under the heading of Claims Administration within a general framework addressing civilian problems caused by military operations, it is worth quoting in full:

> In South Vietnam it was the custom for a representative of the United States to pay a visit of condolence to a Vietnamese injured by military activities or to the survivors of a deceased victim, and for a small amount of money or goods such as rice, cooking oils, or food stuffs to be given. The visit and payment took place when U.S. personnel were involved in the incident that caused injury, regardless of who was at fault, and even if the incident was technically caused by combat. The donation was not an admission of fault, but was intended to show compassion. By caring for the victims, the United States could assist the civic action program in Vietnam. The recipient of the solatium payment would also be advised of the procedures required to present a claim against the U.S. government, if appropriate, and the location of the nearest U.S. foreign claims commission office.
>
> The condolence visit was successful in that the personal expression of compassion by a representative of the United States made a favorable impression on Vietnamese victims who had previously regarded the American claims system as efficient, honest, fair, and generous—but cold.

That, apparently, was the explanation of the scene I had witnessed at Firebase Mary Ann. Whether the desired results had been achieved I couldn't tell. As Michael Herr would say later, trying to read the war was like trying to read the faces of the Vietnamese, and trying to read the faces of the Vietnamese was like trying to read the wind. Still, the word stuck with me. Solatium. Obviously it was some kind of Civil Affairs policy term—another bright idea, no doubt, from the people who gave you Winning Hearts and Minds. And if it was a policy term, like anybody who had been in Vietnam for five minutes, I could rate the chances at around 100% that it was also some kind of bullshit language game. At the very least, it was obviously some kind of payoff. On the other hand, like anybody who had struggled through ninth-grade Latin, even I could see that it had something to do with solace.

Whatever uses the Army was trying to make of it, I wondered, how had a word of such strange beauty sneaked into the war? Everything else seemed such an acronym stew. MACV was Military Assistance Command Vietnam—the American advisory units helping the Vietnamese military forces who were allegedly fighting the war. USARV was United States Army Vietnam, the American military units actually fighting the war the Vietnamese military forces were allegedly fighting. ARVN was a South Vietnamese soldier. RFPF, pronounced Ruff Puff, was a militiaman. CIDG was Civilian Irregular Defense Group, in most cases mercenaries. LLDB were Vietnamese Special Forces, unless you served with them, in which case they became Lousy Little Dirty Bugouts.

In my own, much smaller acronymic universe, ACAV—Armored Cavalry Assault Vehicle—was an APC—Armored Personnel Carrier—mounted up with three machine guns instead of one. A worthless light tank called the Sheridan—a high-tech death trap if there ever was one—was officially an ARAAV—Airborne Reconnaissance Armored Assault Vehicle. RPG was rocket-propelled grenade, a deadly communist anti-tank weapon that a sixth-grader could operate. LAW was its American equivalent, Light Anti-Tank Weapon, small and disposable, but much more complicated to use, albeit with detailed instructions thoughtfully written on the side. The enemy was VC—Victor Charlie—although with increasing intimacy he could also become Charlie, Charles, Chuck, or Old Clyde. A lot of the time in the places where we operated he wasn't VC at all but NVA—North Vietnamese Army. Meanwhile, on his side, VC was NLF—National Liberation Front, and NVA was PAVN—People's Army of Vietnam.

In fact, if you got to thinking about it, almost nothing existed except in some strange combination of sounds and initials. H&I was harassment and interdiction, basically random artillery fire delivered on preplanned targets. R&R was rest and recreation. BMB was Brigade Main Base. REMF—pronounced the way it looked—was somebody who worked there—a rear-echelon motherfucker. The magic word for everybody was DEROS, the one in every soldier's dream: Date of Estimated Return from Overseas—assuming of course that you didn't go out first in a hospital plane or an aluminum casket.

Most of the time, even if something looked like a real word, chances were good that it was trying to say anything but what it meant. Pacification was forced resettlement. Revolutionary Development was political indoctrination. Search and Destroy became Search and Clear; Search and Clear became Reconnaissance in Force; Reconnaissance in Force became Ground Reconnaissance. The mission remained, of course, Search and Destroy.

For years I tucked "solatium" away, as if trying not to disturb it. On one hand, it just seemed a kind of beacon in the general muddle; on the other, I was almost afraid to find out what kind of linguistic freak show *it* would turn out to be. Eventually, I looked it up and found that my intuitions on both counts had been dreadfully correct. The good news was that it did have a direct connection with "solace"; indeed, by some accounts, the word "solace" itself actually derived directly from "solatium" as a past participial form of "solari," to comfort or console. The bad news was that it was a word found only in obscure legal lexicons, conceptually a bizarre inheritance of English law out of Scottish law, which in turn, because early Scottish lawyers did most of their study on the continent, derived from Roman law by way of the medieval church. **Solatium**, read the entry in West's Legal Dictionary: (se-lay-shee-em), *n.* [Latin "solace"] *Scots law.* Compensation; esp., damages allowed for hurt feelings or grief, as distinguished from damages for physical injury.

I shouldn't have been surprised. What I had seen, then, that morning at Firebase Mary Ann was the attempt during U.S. military operations in Vietnam to put a price on mental anguish. To say this another way, you weren't doing anything as crass as trying to pay somebody off for their actual loss of a loved one or some other kind of injury to family or property; you were trying to compensate them for their emotional loss, as if those could somehow be separated.

In all these respects, it was a very western concept, a function of what Frances Fitzgerald called "states of mind": a way of dividing up the world into reason and emotion, mind and spirit, body and soul, on the assumption that everyone everywhere was naturally inclined to think that way. Since the gospel of American progress—of moral assurance and rational certainty—assumed politically that anyone enlightened enough to want to be its ally—even the remnant of a three-thousand-year-old Asian culture—really wanted deep down inside to be a two-hundred-year-old western democracy, it only followed that they wished a similar vision of legal equity to be effected in their understanding of death. In sum, it must have once been exactly the kind of thing a McNamara, a Bundy, or a Rostow could have cooked up in a memorandum and then slept better knowing about. Now, like everything else in the war, mainly it just all seemed pointless and irredeemable.

Like most company grade officers, I got to see my share of dead people in Vietnam. So increasingly I wonder why over the years it's the dead boy at Gia Ray who keeps coming back to me and not the ambush patrol leader we picked out of a minefield a few days later with the back of his head blown off; or the ghostly-looking kid from Texas in a ditch later on, bled white from a single bullet; the heap of dead civilians who came back to earth one day after their Lambretta ran over a booby-trapped artillery round, or the God knows how many Vietnamese I saw on convoy runs with their brains all over the pavement. Surely it has to do with coming late in life to being a parent, to understanding that peculiar lesson in mortality no childless person, I honestly believe, can really comprehend. In my particular case, I also think it has to do with an analogous version of that lesson as embodied in words. Even longer than I've been a parent, I've been a teacher and a writer who has spent my life working with words, trying to comprehend their queer conjoinings of presence and evanescence, their power quite literally both to make and unmake the world in the space of a breath or a line: how they sound; how they look; what they can do; what they can't do; where they come from; where they go; the exaltations they inspire and the dishonesties they conceal; the corruptions they put on and the debasements they resist.

This one, as it turns out, still has a place in the government inventory—now on the Internet, not surprisingly, in an official Department of Defense dictionary of military and associated terms. "Monetary compensation given to alleviate grief, suffering, and anxiety resulting from injuries," the entry reads, "and property or personal loss." On the other hand, you still won't find it in the histories, or even in the personal accounts, like this one, except as some queer, haunted memory. Nor, of course, will you find it in the DSM IV. This is as it should be. I think that when the Army came up with the word solatium, it set some very strange magic loose in the world. For me it will always be a reminder, even amidst the latest revelations of the sheer amplitude and indiscriminacy of our killing and destructiveness there, of something every bit as horrifying—and that is of how totally, appallingly, even insanely resolute we remained in believing in our good intentions. Solatium. What's in a word, I ask, when now, as then, there's still so little solace for anyone, American or Vietnamese, who had anything to do with that war? As an American, still trying to come to terms with what we did there, I hang onto it for two very specific reasons. It won't bring that boy back; and it won't make him go away, either.

Nominated by Michigan Quarterly Review

THE CHURCH OF OMNIVOROUS LIGHT

by ROBERT WRIGLEY

from MĀNOA

On a long walk over the mountain you'd hear
them first, the pang and chorus
of their jubilations, as though you'd strayed
out of Hawthorne into Cotton Mather—
such joyous remorse, such cranky raptures.

And you'd love their fundamental squawking,
little Pentecostal magpies, diminutive
raven priests. You'd walk into their circle
like a drag queen into a Texas truck stop—
silence first, then the caterwauls, the righteous gacks.

Someone's gutted out a deer is all.
In the late autumn snow you'd see the deacons'
tracks—ursine, feline, canine—sweet eucharist of luck
and opportunity for them all. Take and eat,
clank the birds, but not too much. It might be a while.

You'd wonder, yes you would,
and maybe nudge with the toe of your boot
the seeming rigidity of the severed esophagus.
It's gently belled, like a deaf man's antique horn.
Breathless, the lungs subside to carnate blood.

You'd want to go, but you'd want to stay;
you'd want a way to say your part in the service
going on: through high windows
the nothing light, the fourteen stations
of the clouds, the offertory of the snow.

Imagine the brethren returned, comical,
hopping in surplice and cassock, muttering,
made dyspeptic by your presence there, but hopeful too,
that something might yet come and open
your coarse, inexplicable soul to their sight.

Nominated by Claire Davis, Linda Bierds, Christopher Buckley, Jean Thompson, Mānoa

HOUSE OF STONE AND SONG

by MARGARET GIBSON

from GETTYSBURG REVIEW

for David

I

To lie very still, held at the dark margin of the morning,
　　　　dwelling nowhere—
who is not glad to be alone like this? More bare than

any prayer can pray me. Or to wake first, in just light
　　　　as one by one the birds
raise their cadenzas and solos, chips of song

da capo, delicato, con fuoco—far off and near, random
　　　　layers of song in my ear,
bringing withindoors stubble field and swamp oak,

mist in the hollows and wooded ridges. Spires of dark cedar.
　　　　The shadblow, the yellow
blur of the willow by the shallows. Bringing withindoors

cantabile, acciaccatura, hermit brown, red-winged
　　　　or hooded, green-throated
or blue, burnt sienna, rose-breasted or bronzed,

the pure wild sound of the world.

By the window the lilac, not yet full out, slants
            to a thicket of shadows
thrown on the bedroom wall. On a shadow branch

the tiny shadow of a bird, lilac the tremor of its throat,
            lilac the scent of its song,
and the roof of this house hovers over me like wings.

Now I know, without having to see it, how the pond fills
            with milk, with saffron,
with the whole sky's intimate incandescence.

II

Chip, chip, chip—now a sound of metal on stone,
            not a bird, it's Barry Patch,
stonemason, lover of stones and the uses of stone
            for the dead, for the living.

Goonies, potatoes, bones my husband calls the stuff
            of the walls he builds at the margins
we've cleared from the woods. He tells me
            not to steal the words,

so I give them back to him here as *field stone, blue stone*
            the granite and gritrock
we'll walk on when Barry finishes his work—
            which now resembles, in the early

stages of labor, ruin—dug trenches and red string, rubble
            that's maybe useful, maybe not,
all the markings of a dig, as at Xochicalco. In the ruins
            one sees plainly

the power of the unfinished. The stones whisper, *Know
            what we aspired to know, do what we dared
and couldn't, complete us*, the fierce glyphs burning into
            sky, a smudge of bougainvillea.

Chip, chip, chip—Barry's squaring one stone to fit
        close on another, each one
finding its place in what we might call *patio, terrace,*
        moon-watching pavilion,

a room whose roof is air. Barry builds it on shelf rock,
        on sand and stone dust,
keeping us part of the broad ledge of cedars and laurel—
        anchoring us, much as the house

we love on Bear Run, Fallingwater, is moored over
        impermanence and falling asunder.
And I think, moving now into a morning of tasks
        I can and cannot finish with,

how *soul* must be something unfinished, or never begun,
        or lapsed. Must be *no thing* at all,
at best *attentive*, a flowing attempt to form walls
        around a small glint of light,

that hint of abundance momentarily flashing, rarely
        up close, barely sensed—
if sensed at all, so likely misapprehended one keeps on
        inquiring—if only into the next room,

        where the secret is, hidden behind
stone walls, disclosed within undivided light and air.

III

Because we live in a country where no one I know
sings to God in the streets,
I'm given to wandering past margins of fern and wild honeysuckle,

following the burr of the tanager, that lazy, drowsy,
dozy buzz of triple notes
tied close together. I'm tethered and led, *legato,*

deeper in, beyond cedar field and hardscrabble, through
grapevine, bull brier,
globes of rhododendron and laurel lamp-lighting my way

156

over Indian graves and wetland, hellebore and hummock,
into the tall trees where
that flash of pure fire finds its high-branch summer niche.

Perhaps I want to be the crazy woman
who lives on roots and berries
in the only woods abandoned to her, perhaps a woman

inhabited, immersed, left open to the rain, a lit fleck
in the black eyes of the doe
who does not startle at the sight of me, a praise song

composed by the tail of a snake as it slithers into the rocks,
by the scattering of raw light
through the oak leaves—a generous rubble—

by the coyote's treble and the wild turkey's guttural call
taken in, this earthy music
dowsed for in the deep well of the woods, tasted,

taken into my body, alone and full, wind and stream.

IV

But yours, wise sojourner, is the art of recollection—
after home-leaving,
                    homecoming,
bringing with you "something perfect for the kitchen,"
for the table a blue bowl, for the mantel a Tibetan
oil lamp cast as the body of a bird.

You rescued once a weathered piece of a push broom
from along a railroad track,
the bristles gone—
                    but the pattern of absence
ground in there, and the patina of the seasoned wood . . .

It takes a quiet eye to see, a single heart to love.
*Blessed are the single ones . . . for you shall find
the Kingdom. You came from it,
you shall go there again.*

And so you put a road to nowhere through these woods
that were once abandoned fields
                                        and built this house.
You dowsed for the well, and when we married
in the living room, after the few words we'd planned,
you took my face into your hands and looked

and looked, in your eyes such a shining it startled me.
To be so recognized.
                      To be found.

As when wind catches up the sun and billows it
across dark water—such a shining
that we are held and sent forth at once.

Something flashes out—who can say what it is?
In its wake
              a net of light to catch our words,
and the words still holding us here.

V

When by accident he struck the stone, and it fell open,
as a book will,
                  half by half,

Barry saw the stones were a pair of wings, matched
exactly, and he set them
                          soaring, in.

Nominated by Eamon Grennan, Gettysburg Review

THE PASS

fiction by STEVE ALMOND

from NEW ENGLAND REVIEW

A MAN IN A BAR makes a pass at a woman. It's not a good era for passes, but he's giving it his all. His eyebrows have been laying groundwork for hours. His voice—a nice voice he's been told, a *radio* voice—lingers on her name. She's on her third drink and she's here, isn't she, with him, and not somewhere else and she's finally removed the purse from her lap, on which it had sat like a small guard dog.

They're downtown someplace, some downtown, some place, the skyscrapers blazing like exorbitant lamps, subway trains hurling their human cargo past, lake wind breathing concrete and car exhaust, dusk punching out.

He's Bill or Mike or Chuck. She's Rachel, Liz, Michele with one *l*. She has a beautiful name. He's told her so and now leans in, close enough to smell the Clamato on her breath. He hopes to appear smooth and audacious. Like Brando, or Valentino. She stirs her Bloody Mary with an odd precision, as if being evaluated.

He touches her arm with just his fingertips. Will she consent to the pleasure they might take in all this: the lifting of their bodies, the lying of them down, the pale revelations, wetness dispatched outward, all of it? With his hand and mouth, both, he asks her to share in the complicated electricity of the moment.

They have met before, these two—or two very much like them—at a costume party several years ago. She was dressed as Salome, with seven veils and a wispy black bra. He was a caveman. She lowered her painted eyes and spoke in the way of a Biblical moll. He said *unga-bunga-bunga*. She swung her hips and made her veils flutter. He dragged her by the hair to a dark back room; wishes he had.

❋

But why a bad era for the pass?

Because the pass is what semioticians would call a *lapsed signifier.* That which once defined the act—an attempted breach of the culture's sexual mores—has been overrun by the horny course of human affairs. It is not that nothing is sacred anymore. On the contrary. More is sacred than ever before, because more of the self is hidden away than ever before. But the pass no longer aims in the direction of anything hidden. It has become overt, incurably so.

❋

A woman awaits her flight to Denver; efficiently rouged, screwed into a stylish black pantsuit. But thunderheads have kicked up and those ninnies at the FAA have the incomings circling and God knows how long this will take, so she repairs to the eager banter of the terminal bar. She is a woman slightly older than her initial impression, shrewd in the matter of lighting. She settles in at the dim end of the teakwood bar, next to a man in a rumpled suit, another captive, and orders a screwdriver.

They are not drinkers, but they have time on their hands, and now, the communion of ill tempers. Judgment is passed on the vagaries of their airline, the bartender's matted chest hair, the focus-group decor. Intolerances line up nicely. Together, they listen to a New York matron bellow into a pay phone, sounding like a motherless calf. He makes a gentle observation about the indolence of the janitorial staff.

On the wall above them: a poster of *Casablanca*, Bogie and Ingrid on that backlot tarmac, draped in pink fog, doing their utmost to dignify lurid hope. And outside, in the crowded bay beyond the x-ray machines: couples trapped in farewell holding patterns, wearing travel outfits and travel hairdos and lip gloss, the women smudgy, the men guarding goodbye erections.

He has a certain gangster handsomeness, Mr. Rumpled Suit, his broad face pressed back, a nose she imagines has been broken, clear brown eyes. His hands are large and pleasantly scarred. Around his ring finger, not a ring, but a pale band. She orders another screwdriver. He hurries off in search of information about departure times. (He has a deposition to oversee in Pittsburgh.)

160

She finds that she misses him. Odd. Yet there can be no other way to explain the elation she feels when she spots him edging past the luggage cart-return rack, his rumpled trousers and, inside them, his thick legs.

"Bad news," he says. "I have a wife."

Or: "We will only hurt one another."

Or, just possibly: "No more outgoing flights." In this third case, her hand will slip onto his thigh for the joy of feeling astonished movement under her fingers, flesh awaiting further instruction.

✿

But these are strangers and the possibilities of the pass tempt them with no afterthought.

At a party in a suburb renowned for its outdoor sculpture, a group of coworkers shares red wine and veggie dip. They know one another in the way modern workers do, a forced animation of concern. Some are married and others single and each group covets the other. A life too full of choices has rendered them indecisive. They are prosperous on the scale of their parents, but lack the rootedness that might fortify their hopes. They live in apartments and spend hours on the phone, deciding things. Where to eat. What movie to see. They enter into relationships that feel, as much as anything, like arrangements. They are poorly versed in the mechanics of regret.

In this domain, the pass acquires something of a darkling's charm. The man about to make the pass, Geoff, is seated at the center of a comfy living room. The woman, Elena, is on the couch above him. She has the face of a Modigliani, exotically crooked, long and pale, cow-eyed. There has been speculation about her breasts in the office—they sit suspiciously high—but he is more taken by her backside, which is plump, cupidinous.

Elena's boyfriend is in the kitchen. He is a nice fellow with a large mole on his chin. He sometimes makes the mistakes of his small-town rearing, a certain misguided exuberance in dressing or off-color jokes. Geoff's girlfriend, on the stairs, is a sophisticate, versed in city tropes, an unembarrassed practitioner of seduction. When Geoff first started sleeping with her, her fierce scatology, the way she demanded to be slapped, thrilled him. More recently, he finds her vehemence frightening. They are a happy couple, Geoff supposes, as happy as couples tend to be.

But there is an innocence about Elena that pricks his vanity, makes him jumpy for what he doesn't have. She is tipsy and agreeable and words are his allies. He steers the conversation toward intimate topics: massages, body piercing, sensual ambition.

I think you know some things, he tells her. I watch you move through the office and I think you know some things that most people wouldn't think you know.

She rolls her eyes.

So many guys talk about your chest. I'm sorry. I don't mean to embarrass you. Please don't be embarrassed. There's a loveliness there that makes them curious. That's all. You can't blame them for that. But I think they're missing it, Elena. I think with you it's the lower body, the *nalgas*. I've been meaning to tell you this for a while. I know it's not right, but I watch you walk through the office, the way you move, and I think: I'm not sure I can go through my life without knowing.

❋

And there are provinces in which everyone does go about finding out, clusters of college graduates knotted at the bottom of tall cities, trying to invent community. Everyone has slept with everyone and they all drink together, hoping the alcohol and the music will restore some previously eluded glamour, or obscure its dissipation. Those few who haven't coupled operate at a disadvantage, edgy and prideful, untrammeled by ease. They watch the others sweat and sway, and imagine a daisy chain of limbs, themselves missing out. In this stewing lies the seed of future passes.

But what lies ahead is not our concern. Our concern is present, the glorious now, the moment of erotic transfer—isotopic, dangling, a question mark awaiting exclamation.

❋

In a rundown Stuttgart nightclub, two privates in the U.S. Army have arrived to hear jazz, arrived separately. They are from different divisions, have never met. The club is in the historic district, miles from the biergartens where their comrades fill themselves with liters of pale pilsner and oily sausage, counting colored bills for later descent on the hookers of this drizzled ashen city.

Technically, it's not even jazz on display in this blue-lit club. It's cabaret, the music of campy self-announcement, feather boas and top hats and tulle stockings and whorish makeup, and each of the privates drinks in the burly innuendo, sipping at sophisticated drinks, sneaking glances at each other, wondering. Between acts, the one named Shane spots the other leaning against the bar, uniform neatly tucked, back curving gracefully, the muscles under his shirt shifting like dunes.

Shane bites a piece of ice, moves to join him. They talk about where they are stationed, what their hitch is—awkward, beginning things. The lights vanish and another round of drinks gets drunk and another set of skits begins, more good-time tunes set against a black velvet curtain, a tall tenor with pasted-on mustache and a chanteuse treated rather sadly by the years (though, they agree, surely lovely as a maiden.)

The hours roll by and the drinks loosen them and soon they are confessing which high school shows they were in, bursting into stagy refrains. The hour is close to curfew, but the closing spectacle is more than either private could have expected. The old singer is up on the bar flashing her fallen thighs and the tenor is leaping from table to table in patent leather wingtips and the two privates are suddenly at the center of a spotlight with a microphone under their chins, thrown together in voice, led laughing through a wobbly chorus of *Auf Wiedersehen* by the older patrons.

Shane turns to his new companion and breathes the hot breath of want and with nothing so much as this asks to be folded into this stranger's body and kept there for the night.

✿

This is what the whole business is about, night. Without night, its hungering canvas, its needy musk and daring sediments, without all this, the amorous among us would fold our tents and, like Longfellow's Arabs, as silently steal away.

✿

He met her through a mutual friend and now she is in his home and he is cooking for her, chopping mushrooms and boiling water for pasta, washing the cupboard dust off his wine glasses. He has learned

163

to cook a few meals from TV chefs, and has knit these into the tight circle of his life. His business—consulting—sucks him through airports and phones and flights and conferences and beepers and burgers and sour suits and occasionally he suspects he is missing something. Not daughters or wives or azaleas, but the sense of his body as experienced against another. Night illuminates this need, tenders it, demands a dividend.

This woman in his apartment, she is—what? A nurse or a stenographer. A piano teacher. She exhibits patience worthy of a bygone era. He sees her traveling the Oregon Trail in a long plain dress, mending things. Her fingers are strong, able-looking. There is something steadying just in the way she holds her Chardonnay, cupped in both hands. She leans against the fridge carefully. Her eyes seem to want to dip beneath the surface of his words, to more telling information.

She is not someone he thinks of as pretty. There are flaws, which his life surrounded by advertising draws out, distorts. Slight underbite. Flat bottom. Saggy arms. The defects are not small. But then, there is him. Sometimes, before bed, he catches sight of himself in the bathroom mirror and sees his father.

They are here because he invited her. Night fell around him, his first one home after a cross-country trip, and something in the yellowing of the street lamps outside his building left him bereft. He remembered his friend pressing this woman's number onto him, how he had avoided calling her, thinking: *she must be desperate.* When he finally got her on the phone, two nights later, he was the one who felt desperate, trying to play the idea off as an impulse.

He continues to chop and she pours herself more wine and moves around his apartment, inspecting. He knows about her: she has been married before, she has a child who is away for the week, she is the same age he is. He knows *about* her. She glances at his stack of unopened mail, as if she would like to sort through it, as if she doesn't quite trust him to separate the junk from the significant.

He puts the knife down and tilts up his wine, stopping when he feels a slight burn against his gums. He slips out of his shoes and approaches her from behind and her neck is there, warm. He knows this could only happen from behind, that he is sneaking up on himself as much as her. He closes his eyes and hopes.

✿

Or a wedding. Sure. Why not? They still hold them. Big distracted churchy affairs glittering with pearls or earnest runty ones on damp lawns. The nudnik photographer, the sweaty caterers, weeping mothers and black sheep beckoned back, the bow-tied band and the bride and groom helpless with goodwill. It still goes on in all these places, San Leandro and Mount Kisco and Wallingford, and, at the fringe of it, behind the rectory or out near the pool, a bridesmaid stares ardently at a groomsman. They have had much to drink, as weddings recommend.

She is so proud of her friend, she says, and the groomsman agrees. It is something to be proud of. She is so beautiful. Yes. Never seen her so radiant. Yes. Beautiful. And him, too. He didn't look so tall in the photos. How tall is he? Six-foot-three. Wow.

He is thinking about the bachelor party, about the stripper called Danielle, between whose breasts his nose spent a brief and thrilling span, shocked at the scent (shoe leather and cinnamon) and the firmness of whatever held them aloft. This moony bridesmaid—with her wedge of a face and colored contacts, her peach chiffon dress and matching pumps—she is no Danielle. She is a creature in sad real time. Her nakedness cannot be anything men would pay to see, though men, if protected by payment, will look at almost anything.

And anyway, she is here before him, full of crab ravioli and champagne, swallowing back burps and twisting her bangs between her fingers. She hasn't the will to execute the pass. She can only display her markings, touch her body in ways that might induce in him a mimetic response.

He is at his leisure to consider this, to ease back on his ankles and assess the pros and cons. She is homely; there is that. But her homeliness weighs on him favorably, accents his moderate beauty. This is a wedding and there is drink and hopes run deep on such occasions, but not so expectations. All pageantry inspires fantasy, no matter how shabby. And besides, she is wearing these prim peach pumps, shoes that will never be used again, that almost demand to be torn off, bitten at in mock depravity.

He is not certain about kissing, though, not just yet. And so he lowers his hand down the front of her dress and lifts her breast so that it puddles on his palm and so that he can hear his name on her tongue.

❉

165

In every life, such deciding places must be reached. Especially in this era of frantic indecision, with its impatient sun and hammering moon, with its pathological ulteriority, when it seems a wonder that two people might ever agree to anything like terms. Day after fallen day, these odd delicious moments on which so much depends; unwrapped like papered pears, held close to the nose, sniffed, tasted.

✿

In the downtown bar, where Bill or Mike or Chuck has pinned his hopes on the sleeve of Rachel, Liz, Michele: a failure he could not have foreseen. (For if he had, why should he have invited her here and spent his money and time and dwindling predator energy?) She looks at his hand on her arm and smiles politely. She sighs and in her sigh invokes the nearest cliché: nothing personal a bad time still recovering just met someone.

He envisions her dressed as Salome, the dance of her veils. If this were physical trauma, the endorphins would come sloshing in to spare him. He would not hear the chant of looming humiliation, or feel suffused by brittle hate for this woman, who is no longer a woman, only something he will never have. The electricity in his arm, with which he had hoped to jolt her into panting collaboration, shuts down. The bartender freezes. The skyscrapers go dark. The set is struck.

✿

The airport pair have no such trouble. The airlines, after all, have arranged passage to a nearby hotel. Inside his room, the man who looks like a gangster shucks his suit, steps into the shower, pleased at the water's scalding pulse, emerging pink, soapy. On his bed: the woman who missed her flight to Denver. She is in towels, one around her chest, one twirled on her head. Older with her makeup scrubbed, her flesh unbundled. Nothing like Ingrid Bergman, with her slender white nose and her shadows. Nothing like his wife for that matter, who drinks protein shakes and runs half-marathons. Nothing like anyone he could have ever seen himself lying beside in a hotel room near the airport. And for this reason, an object of intense fascination to his body, which responds along predictable lines. They are not graceful, or pretty. He lunges, she groans. They press

166

together. The entire project fills no more than a few minutes. But when he reaches for one of her cast-away towels, she grabs his wrist. "Wait," she says. "I like to let it dry."

This, more than anything, more than his refusal to bestow upon her a goodnight kiss, more than his stiff retreat from her mouth, more than the silent next-morning shuttle ride, will haunt him. He has always worried that he looked like a thug, ever since his nose was broken by a bully in high school. The sight of his ejaculate spattered on her belly jolts loose a memory, this bully staring hard at a pornographic photo in a mildewy gym, now thirty years ago, announcing: *That broad is a waste of good sperm.*

❖

And what of Geoff, at the center of the warm suburban home unspooling his patter to Elena, who looks like a Modigliani? He too has misjudged. And he too will suffer a mortification, though not of the flesh. He reaches for her ankle and she pulls away and his chest stumbles. She stands quickly and moves to join her boyfriend in the kitchen. Soon, it will be announced to those assembled that the couple are engaged. And still later he will see the two of them outside, nuzzling against a car.

Closer to morning, with his own girlfriend curled away from him, Geoff will see things as they are: that he coveted Elena's innocence not as a thing to defile, but as a remedy. Beneath the fantasy of ravaging her was the fantasy that she would rescue him, stroke his brow and somehow cure him of his tired contempt for everything. With her, he might have become the sort of man who desires purely, rather than the sort who seeks betrayal at the center of a foolish party. He will never feel quite sure of himself again.

❖

The old torch singer is surprised and pleased by the presence of two young American soldiers. She dispatches the proprietor of the club to invite them backstage: the madame would like to say hello after she has changed. PFC Shane and his companion are led to a small room and seated on an old love seat. The light is soft, roseate. There is the pleasant, cherryish smell of pipe tobacco. Their thighs brush.

But now Shane wonders if this might not be an elaborate setup.

He has heard tell of such things, MPs descending with billyclubs. And then, too, there is the ambiguity of his new friend's responses: a fluttery hug in the shadows, that lopsided grin which could mean anything. When you are a soldier like PFC Shane, you learn to love quickly, to grasp and gulp and be done with it. Besides, there is the curfew to be considered.

Now the diva makes her appearance, shorter than she seemed on the bar, modestly wrapped in a chenille robe. French cigarettes in a silver case. A cocktail in a tall goblet. She lived for a number of years in Houston, Texas. Do they know the place? An oil baron kept her as his mistress. All quite scandalous. She was terribly lonely in her glass and marble flat on Carr Street, like a princess in her tower. This *awl* baron—her imitation makes them giggle—used to come and pounce on her. Fat and hairy as a woodchuck, with a prick like a jackass. When you are young, she says, it all seems enough. But love is the most important thing of all, don't you agree? How old are you boys? Really, that young? Well it's time you learned the first rule of love: Never hide. Love must be acknowledged by the touch of days. And here, she makes her exit, leaving them her dressing room and the time to decide for themselves.

What a trip, Shane says.

Yeah, says his new friend. Pretty amazing. The boy's arm falls across Shane's shoulders. His mouth is a wet red arrow.

Yeah.

✿

The consultant has placed his lips to her neck and she has responded with the consent of her body, turning against him, lifting her face. She is there and ready. But now he is unsure. The pass sits wrong with him, plunging dread where the flutter should be. All he can imagine is the moment after physical release, when the soul, the patient soul, reasserts sovereignty. This is the war that never ends: the body's simple needs set against the soul's byzantine wants, each accusing the other of insufficient grace.

No. No pass should suffer such sad scrutiny. She senses the slackening of his muscles and slumps onto the couch. It is called a pass because there is a movement of one desire past another. But the desires of this couple sit still as stone and stare down on both of them and the best they can manage is a kind of dour need.

We should do this again, the consultant says.

Sure, the piano teacher says. I'd like that.

There is a long pause. He doesn't know what to do with this. In his off-site seminars, they tell him to attack the lulls, tell a joke, make a comment about the weather. But listening to the sad uncertain timbre of her voice ruins his focus.

Anyway, he says.

Right, she says. Sure.

*

The young couple at the wedding, the bridesmaid and the groomsman, they have no such difficulties. Not yet. For the moment, they are tongues and tails and hips and hands. The arm of night lowers itself over the rectory, turns the swimming pool into a small blue jewel. They have pressed themselves against the side of a building, tumbled into the shallow end, staggered to the nearest flat surface; her peach chiffon dress is bunched around her thighs, his rented gray suit has split down the middle.

The body, the body, the body. And the dizzy players that spin across this smooth field. They are all of them to be applauded. Nights *are* long. An entire lifetime of long. And the pass, here, now, a merciful lantern which lights the way, softly dims, and drags us toward dream.

Nominated by Tom Paine

LINE

memoir by JOHN HALES

from THE GEORGIA REVIEW

A STRAIGHT LINE GOES WHERE IT GOES. This is the essence of the government surveyor's work, the source of hard consequences for both the surveyor and the landscape that is surveyed. Hikers, road builders, even infantry soldiers, knowing that a straight line is not always the shortest distance between two points, can negotiate with the terrain, accommodate its impositions and irregularities when necessary or convenient, but after the bearing is calculated and the correct angle is turned, the scope of the surveyor's transit points the only direction it can, and the crosshairs don't equivocate. They tell only one simple truth, and that truth is straight, narrow, and uncompromising.

I worked summers as a government surveyor through most of the 1970's, an employee of the Utah office of the Cadastral Survey, the arm of the federal government responsible for maintaining and extending the rectangular subdivision of America. Our mandate had been spelled out in Thomas Jefferson's Land Ordinance of 1785, legislation which (among other things) determined that settlement of the vast American West would take place amid ranks of perfect square-mile squares called sections, bounded by straight lines that ran according to the four points of the compass.

In specifying the means by which this mandate would be carried out, the Ordinance transformed the simple job of surveying a straight line into a 200-year project representing perhaps the most aggressive imposition of human will on natural landscape seen in the history of the world. Although land had been parceled out along straight lines for millennia—surveyors like to call theirs the second oldest profes-

170

sion—never before had those lines been extended with so little regard for natural landscape, nor on so continental a scale. Before 1785, land surveys were generally carried out according to the practice of metes and bounds, an approach which limited surveyors to running crooked lines that followed natural contours and avoided the obstacles inevitably served up by the landscape, establishing boundaries that outlined tracts of land that were topographically logical. A typical surveyor might run a necessarily contorted line that followed the twisting bank of a river, extend it straight for a distance until fertile bottom land met less economically useful cliffs, and then designate an immovable boulder or sizable tree (the "witness tree" of Robert Frost's New England) to serve as a boundary marker upon which ownership would depend. Because such a survey was based on relatively permanent physical points of reference, the orientation of the compass bearing and the straightness of the line were less important than general agreement concerning the objects and markers that determined the boundary of one's property.

Although it would be overstating things to argue that surveyors running metes and bounds surveys worked in harmony with the natural world, the basic theory embodied a healthy respect for nature as it stood. Even when boundaries were surveyed in advance of settlement, and in grids—as in the venerable New England township surveys—the grids were oriented in deference to the lay of the land, and rectangles were preferred because the math was easier, not because linearity was next to godliness.

To Jefferson, and others of like mind on the committee of the Continental Congress he chaired, metes and bounds surveys represented abject surrender to the caprice of topographical nature. His plan was to straighten up the dangerous clutter of wilderness by surveying the West into a grid that connected the nascent American empire with the mathematical equations and underlying linearity that defined true, universal, capital-N Nature, while at the same time inscribing an actual grid on the American landscape, a net of intersecting straight lines that would partition the wilderness into orderly square-mile sections. These lines and squares would be established well in advance of settlement, giving the first settlers the assistance they required in keeping the degenerating influence of wilderness at bay long enough to inscribe their own straight lines of private ownership—lines that would parallel and reinforce the section lines that in turn connected with adjacent sections to form lines that connected the Alleghenies to the Pacific. Jefferson's goal—of his many plans for America, perhaps the one that has remained most faithful to his intention—was a continent perfectly squared, gridded, and aligned: north-south lines running straight from pole to pole, east-west lines stacked in pure alignment with the equator, creating the squared and abstracted landscape of America one sees best from the window of an airliner flying from coast to coast.

Achieving Jefferson's ambitious scheme became the job of generations of obscure government surveyors. As descendants of this long, hardworking, and little-acknowledged line, my crew and I had to resurvey and restore old township and section lines, and run new ones. Put another way, our job was to follow line where it went and make that line tangible and material, to translate the pure language of mathematics into the vernacular of actual landscape, to carve straight lines into the slopes and curves of nature, and to mark with an iron pipe and a rock mound each point where lines intersected, ultimately creating a formal garden the size of a continent. Through the eight summers I worked for the Cadastral Survey—summers that didn't quite mesh with my nonsummer life as a college student and English teacher—I learned the equations and practices that define the theory and application of linearity, witnessed over and over again the intersection of mathematical order and topographical randomness, and came to understand that this was an uneven contest: line, undistracted by the conflicting agendas of the natural world, always prevailed.

My first few weeks as a surveyor can best be understood as a crash course in linearity. My crew had been assigned a township just north of Vernal, a small oil and ranching town in eastern Utah. This thirty-six-square-mile concentration of chaotic desert landscape straddled the geological boundary where the rise of that vast monolith of granite called the Uinta Mountains begins to disturb rock formations reclining comfortably to the south; for miles in each direction, layers and layers of sandstone, shale, limestone, and some ugly black rock I never could identify were pushed skyward, their backsides levered into ramps and cliffs that ran all over the map.

Although this township served as a pretty good geology textbook, what I needed was a text in elementary *surveying*, and this daunting collision of order and chaos, of desert and swamp, of ramps and domes and deep canyons, included far too few bunny slopes for the

172

beginning surveyor, far too many opportunities for incompetence and embarrassment—a learning curve as steep and rocky as the terrain. This was after all my first summer, long before I'd begun to understand what Jefferson and the Enlightenment had to do with all this. What I needed to understand that summer—and quickly—was simply *line*.

The first thing I learned was that government surveyors drop the article when talking about line. We didn't say, "Where does the line hit that cliff?" or "Now we'll project a line across that canyon." It was just "line." At some point in the Old Testament, the Lord God becomes simply God, and like Moses I learned that there was only one true line, and that government surveyors would have no other lines before them.

This was because our line was different from the lines of other surveyors. Our line followed its mathematical imperative, not the wishes of a client, or the legalisms of a deed, or the whim of a river's meander. Our line arose from calculations derived through observations of the sun and distant stars, ran not just according to the cardinal points of the compass but according to those cardinal directions made perfect, North-South and East-West bearings more exact than the trembling pointer of any earthbound compass could hope to deliver. Line was literally handed down from the sky: line running north aimed straight at Polaris, the North Star, and drew its identity from this otherworldly connection; at least once a week we'd spend a couple of hours checking the accuracy of line by nailing Polaris in the crosshairs of the transit—not the easiest thing to do in the bright sunshine of the desert—and recalculating our exact position in the great scheme of things. Line was real, at the same time transcendent and tangible, the Enlightenment's most visible and enduring legacy to the landscapes of America.

I spent my first week, assigned the lowly job of flagman, completely lost. They'd tell me: line goes across that ridge; hike over there, tie a couple of feet of red flagging around a four-foot lath (a splintery rough-sawn stake flat and skinny as a yardstick), sharpen its end with your ax, and hammer in the flag exactly where we tell you to. Of course, I'd see where Jerry, my party chief, was pointing, I'd nod my head, and I'd hike off in the general direction, appearing finally on a ridge a half-mile north of where I was supposed to be, waving hopefully with my T-shirt—we had no radios that summer— until they saw where I'd wound up, waved me over and over and

173

over until I'd hiked back the errant half mile and finally appeared alongside the transit's crosshairs, ready to pound in the lath. That spot I now knew was line, but how did it get from there to here?

I took weeks to learn the practices of lineation, and then a few weeks more to understand—and many more weeks to feel instinctively—how it all fit the insistent reality of the Utah landscape. I was learning the theory, even the meaning. What I wasn't learning was *line*. I wasn't getting what every good surveyor needs, more important than theory or even context: I wasn't getting the *feel*, the sense of *lineness*. My duty as a flagman was to pound in a flag on line. Problems involving direction were up to the guy who looked through the transit and measured the angles, and questions involving distance were up to the crew members who pulled the long measuring chain. But my job involved a great deal of hiking to the next ridge, or up a mountainside, or into the depths of a canyon, to pound in a lath on line. I needed to be where the others were looking before they could fine-tune my position, line me in on the exact bearing.

Here is what they did to make something useful of me, to transform me into a surveyor. Dan, the transit operator, would take me aside—protecting me whenever he could from Jerry's impatience—and point out the ridge he wanted me on. He'd suggest a way for me to get there; it wasn't necessary for the flagman to walk exactly on line, which is nearly impossible anyway once you're in the forest or the rockslide or the arroyo. He'd focus my task: put a flag *there*, he'd say, pointing toward a specific spot on a distant ridge. Then he'd have me look through the transit, pick out a foresight, a rock or tree that I'd recognize when I got up close. I'd find a tree with a bent trunk or a lightning scar, a feature that distinguished that tree from every other tree on the ridge. Then I'd carefully plan my route, figure out which path to descend, and where to begin my climb to the top of the ridge where the tree I'd picked out awaited me.

I'd have two things in mind: I'd focus on where line went, that ideal vector running straight and pure above my head; and I'd focus on where I needed to place my boots, one after the other, to arrive at the exact place where line crossed a particular ridge. The problem was that things look very different up close. In the desert landscape of eastern Utah, what looks like a plausible trail turns out to be an extended detour among rocks the size of boxcars, and those carefully differentiated clearings, clearly triangular or circular or the shape of a duck when seen from a distance, look pretty much alike—or don't

174

seem like clearings at all—when you're finally tramping through them. Even a ridgeline, a dimensionless outline from a mile away, might be as wide as a football field when you're walking along it, looking for that one tall cedar tree with the lightning scar that twists just so.

But after a week or two of complete incompetence, I began to understand how it worked. I learned the way a tree or a cliff changes as you shift your perspective. I did this at first by keeping my eye constantly on my foresight, noticing the change as it happened gradually, keeping track of its evolution from distant blur to an individual piece of topography next to which I could stand securely within the bright magnified circle of Dan's transit. I slowly developed an ability to see how terrain changes, to visualize how a ridgeline might look from a vastly elevated point of view, from a position alongside that transcendent ideal of a mathematically perfect landscape. I was finally able to picture myself as if from a distance, a person who was simultaneously an employee of the federal government and a point of mathematical definition, descending one ridge to ascend another, departing momentarily from line when the terrain forced him to, reattaching himself to line in order to place that necessary flag.

It's difficult to explain the profound change that took place in me during those first few humiliating weeks, when I'd gotten lost routinely enough to change the look on Jerry's face from amusement to resignation to disgust: How can a person be so lost, his face would say. How can you head off in the direction we send you, and then land a mile up the wrong mountain, facing the wrong direction?

My disorientation had to do with placement—my own, the rocks and trees, even the stars and the movement of the sun. I was learning to locate myself in natural terrain; I was learning to discover my place, to keep track of my position as it changed in response to the angle of a hillside or the turn of a tree's shadow. As a child growing up in a familiar landscape, I had found this to be easy: there had always been the customary rock faces of the Wasatch Front to the east, the distinctive islands of the Great Salt Lake to the west. But in unfamiliar landscapes, you discover other ways to orient yourself. For some, instinct serves: a sense of sun and shadow, a feel for the wind-bent arc of salt grass or the growth patterns of lichen—a sense you'd cultivated since you were born, an intuitive understanding of nature that is at least as cultural as it is personal. For me, a white boy raised in Eisenhower's America, the tepid flowering of Western civilization—a nation for whom intuition was suspect, circles indecisive, an unmowed lawn evidence of flawed character—that other way was line. Ultimately, I knew where I stood in relation to the landscape I surveyed because I understood where line ran.

I learned these truths about surveying slowly, within the set of circumstances that defined the danger and difficulty of our work: Utah contains some of the most rugged, untraversable, fractured-into-chaos landscape to be found on the well-wrinkled face of the earth. The work of a surveyor involves inscribing civilization's most prized invention—the straight line—into the landscape regardless of the degree to which that landscape rejects linearity, refutes mathematics, and mocks the idea of order. Combine this inevitable collision with the rule that has governed national survey practice since the Ordinance of 1785—that these lines must *actually be run*—and you understand something of the challenge faced by the employees of the Cadastral Survey.

Perhaps that goes without saying: of course you have to run line. How else does line get there? But most land surveyors—almost all of those who don't work for the government—don't always run the actual line. As inheritors of the metes and bounds tradition, they are allowed to substitute math for linearity. If a surveyor's job is to establish two points and to determine the bearing and distance of the boundary line that spans those two points, he'll run line directly if it's convenient. But if it's not convenient, and it often is not, he can run a traverse; that is, he can survey a crooked line that takes him around inconvenient rock outcrops, alongside difficult forests, and then back to the next corner. The miracle of trigonometry then allows this canny surveyor to compute all the angles and distances of his traverse—his crooked line between the two points, a neat sequence of triangles—and create a fictional straight line that on paper at least connects the points that are important, the corners of the boundary line he's responsible for establishing. This line will have a correct bearing, and it will have a specific and accurate distance, and it will go straight through impossible cliffs and pierce tree trunks three feet thick, and this line will constitute a legal boundary. And the surveyor, a person fortunate enough to be employed by a private surveying company, will not have broken a sweat.

But surveyors who worked through the 1970's for the US Cadastral Survey were still required both by custom and by the imperatives of the canonical *Manual of Surveying Instructions* to literally *run* line: to go where the transit directs up that mountainside, to physically occupy the crumbling edge of that cliff. It was allowable to triangulate a distance if it couldn't be measured directly—for example, if line shot out into space across a canyon so vast and deep that the front chainman would be swallowed up before he could hold a tight measurement for the rear chainman to record. In such extreme cases, surveyors were granted permission to lay out a baseline along the canyon's rim, and the instrument operator could turn angles to the flag the flagman planted across the gap, and the party chief could calculate the distance. But line must be followed exactly; the lath lined in across the canyon must be a direct reflection of the exact bearing line actually follows. If that one spot on the ridgeline across the canyon is occupied by a tree, the tree must be cut down, or at least trimmed until the transit operator can see clearly to a spot that can be physically occupied by the transit's tripod. For Cadastral surveyors, there is no traversing. There are no crooked lines.

There are a number of reasons for this, a few of them practical, the others philosophical and cultural. Basically, the fact that we continued to run the actual line is testimony to the enormous momentum of the Enlightenment. The intention of the men who conceived the rectangular survey was as straightforward as it was arrogant: the United States would be the first nation in the history of the world to be surveyed *reasonably*, a utopia where the hidden order of nature would be recognized and revealed, brought to the surface and then physically inscribed into the disorderly costume of rocks and trees that constituted the great unsettled West. In the same way that the bleeding, thorn-bound Sacred Heart of Jesus is displayed outside his ribcage in Renaissance paintings and inexpensive plaster statues for the purpose of bearing witness to the otherwise invisible truth of Christ's Passion, the invisible truths of the Enlightenment—the earth's mathematical essence, its clock-driven movement, its perfect sphericity—would be made visible by means of the exacting lines of latitude and longitude, of equator and poles, of meridians, parallels, azimuths, and tangents which cross and recross to form the web of intersecting lines that threatens to obscure everything else on eighteenth-century maps of the world. This national mission would assure that the perfection of true nature would be made manifest through the inscription of the square-mile grid upon as much of North America as Manifest Destiny could corral.

According to this vision, the United States would be more than a nation: it would become the actual meeting place of the ideal and the real. Just as its citizens' unruly passions would be ruled by the triangulated stability of the three branches of government, the unruliness of its wilderness would be ruled by the actual inscription of the straight line. (It's not for nothing they call a certain instrument a *ruler*.) In order to ensure that these lines would be drawn on the ground just as literally as they would be traced on maps, the Land Ordinance of 1785, and the several ordinances and instructions that followed, required that as surveyors established each line, they were to make it real, to actually carve line into the landscape, to blaze the trunks of those trees whose branches brushed line, to dig trenches, mound rocks, and otherwise chisel linearity into the very face of America.

The plan worked. Those markers and blazes eventually became fencelines, windrows, county roads; over time, the rocks and mounds that marked the meeting of section lines became fence corners, crossroads, and intersections of state highways that continue today to model the straight and narrow for dozens, sometimes hundreds, of undeviating miles. Those survey lines were made manifest as irrigation canals and county lines, and as freshly plowed furrows and rows of ripe corn—precise parallel echoes of century-old surveys run according to the cardinal points of the compass, an endlessly replicated grid that has given us the checkerboard aspect of America our astronauts can trace from outer space.

In following these first-generation surveyors in order to reestablish their lines and replace their rock markers with more permanent monuments, it made sense—both genealogically and practically—to replicate their methods, to follow their practices as precisely as possible; to run the actual line, just as they did. But the practices of these first surveyors were also determined by something more immediate than Jeffersonian utopianism. Simply put, their instruments were not capable of maintaining the integrity of a long traverse and still achieving the accuracy Jefferson's vision required. They knew the mathematical equations—the traverse is simply a sequence of math problems, a series of triangles to be calculated and solved—but their magnetic compasses and short measuring chains weren't sufficiently accurate to yield useful numbers. They could read angles only to within a degree or so, and chaining a mile meant at least eighty different pulls, each pull fraught with overlaps or gaps; to plug these

178

numbers into a complex trigonometric equation would only magnify the already considerable error. These surveyors could survey a *straight* line, however; they could pick out a foresight and chain their way to it, cutting a reasonably straight line in the process, and after they'd measured a mile, they could manage a ninety-degree angle to the east or west, check it against their compasses (and, when more precise instruments became available, the position of the sun), and carve out another straight line. Basically, they surveyed the actual line because they had to.

But we *didn't* have to. Even by the standards of the more evolved instruments that made their appearance through the 1970's—theodolites that could measure an angle to less than a second, and laser-powered distance meters—our transits and 500-foot measuring tapes were certainly accurate enough to traverse with, which is why most land surveyors not working for the government traversed routinely. The occasional surveyor who found his way onto a government survey crew with the significant disadvantage of having studied surveying in college was invariably shocked that we weren't using the traverse, that we stayed with the actual line in the face of swamps, trees, and dangerous rock faces. They spent their first weeks on the job asking, "Why don't we traverse here?" Or, "Wouldn't it be better to traverse *around* this cliff?" Eventually they'd stop asking and accept the practice, if not really understand the reason.

Not burdened by preconceptions or even the barest understanding of how surveying was done in what we called the "private sector," and assisted by the reading I did during my school months in psychology, anthropology, and literary theory, I eventually figured out some of the reasons. I slowly came to understand that we continued to run the actual line for reasons that were cultural and philosophical, perhaps even religious. Line itself was sacred. Line was what we followed, what we spent our days honoring, what we cleared safe passage for, what we left engraved into the face of the planet. We did it because it *was* difficult and inconvenient. We did it because we were human beings operating in the world of the Enlightenment, the uncompromising and cruel world of applied perfection.

Much of Utah's landscape cannot be physically occupied by a human being. Sometimes the space is already taken by a century-old ponderosa pine, sometimes by a forty-five-degree hillside of shale fragments slippery as marbles. Sometimes it's a perfectly flat spot, wide

179

enough for a tent, but atop a sandstone tower tall as a city skyscraper. Line projected by a survey crew inevitably grazes or intersects such difficult landscape, and our measurements often required that we occupy some of it. At minimum, we needed a spot to pound in a flag on line, with room for the transit operator to erect the transit and to stand while he extended line or measured an angle.

Nevertheless, I can't remember more than a few points on line that couldn't actually be occupied somehow. I *thought* I had found such a spot one afternoon early in my career, when we were surveying that rugged township north of Vernal. Our last line of the day shot from Dan's transit across a shallow wash, over a broad loaf of sandstone ridge, beyond a deep but hikable gap, finally bisecting a rock fin, a thin blade of sandstone nearly two miles away. Jerry wanted a flag placed on each high point, three flags in all; he wanted the last flag, the one from which we could eventually shoot line directly to where the map showed the section corner to be, on the relatively flat spread of sagebrush just the other side of the fin. That's where Jerry wanted the last flag: on a narrow uplift of sandstone that looked from a distance like the highest blade on the backbone of a half-buried stegosaurus. I said, as I always did now that I'd gotten past those first weeks of total confusion and had developed a provisional sense of where line went and how to get there, "Sure."

Jerry loved these shots, for reasons of elegance as well as accuracy. The more mileage you could cover, the more flags you could line in from one point—especially if the transit operator had a good foresight on the horizon (for example, a distant peak that stood in the crosshairs)—the more perfect would be line. The worst place was a jungle, where you shot only a few dozen feet at a time from flag to flag, forced to depend on the accuracy of the bronze bearings that held the scope true as you flipped it from the flag behind you to line in the next one. The collimation—the inevitable blip in the instrument as it flipped 180 degrees from back to front—added up to measurable inaccuracy. The best situation was what we faced today: the transit operator sat at one point with miles of visibility and a great foresight while the flagman, me, set up a row of flags, close to where each corner would be found and reestablished, on line for as many miles away as possible.

The first couple of flags were no problem. I hauled myself to the high points, found myself close to line each time, and mounded in flags—this was bare sandstone, so I stacked rocks around each lath until it was solid. But the fin was another matter. I was able to climb without too much trouble onto its crest, which was a couple of yards wide, and although the drop was significant on each side, it seemed possible at first to get in a flag. I waved to Dan to tell him I was ready to be lined in, and he started waving back, waving me with his white T-shirt farther and farther to the west.

It was like one of those jokes one inevitably hears at Grand Canyon overlooks: a photographer says to his wife, "a little to the left, a little more to the left . . ." Dan waved me farther along the fin than I'd hoped, farther west as the slope steepened and the sandy surface of the eroding sandstone felt increasingly unsteady under my boots. The fin grew steeper and steeper as I walked west until I was certain I couldn't go any farther. Line, I believed, ran where human beings couldn't go. Dan gestured; without a radio, I gestured back. I had pretty good eyes then, so I could see Jerry and Dan confer. I knew that my getting a flag in there would save us a lot of time and hard work, but if it couldn't be done, I hope they were saying, it couldn't be done.

I hiked back, met them at the truck, and Jerry seemed to accept my judgment: We'll figure out something else, he said. The next day, however, after we hiked to the base of the fin and looked it over from below, Jerry carried the transit up the gully to the head of the fin, and I watched humiliated as he walked down the crest and set up the transit, shifting it around until he could line up the flags I'd set yesterday with the foresight he could still make out on the horizon. He'd not only walked casually to the spot I'd been afraid to approach on my hands and knees the day before; he'd done it balancing a tripod over his shoulder, he'd set up the transit over the spot, and he'd lined us in to the north where we found the old rock marker we were aiming for.

Even today I feel the need to point out that by then I'd climbed some difficult mountains. Although I was still a beginner, I'd proven on peaks in the Tetons and the Wasatch that I was capable of some pretty good moves on rock. I wasn't especially coordinated or agile, but I had balance and what I thought was a good sense of friction, a sensitivity to just how sticky my boot's grip was on a specific piece of rock. I remember thinking the day before that I'd probably go a little farther down this spine of sandstone if I had a rope belay. What I

181

learned watching Jerry was that I'd have probably gone there if somebody had shown me that it was possible. Or if I'd known how necessary, how important, it was.

I had plenty of time to reflect on my failure. Jerry had a habit of only rubbing it in on minor screwups; he'd quickly learned that I was harder on myself than he could ever be, and he let me stew in my own juices the rest of the day. I made no excuses. I did resolve, however, from then on to go wherever line went—unless Jerry told me it was impossible. I resolved to think of establishing line as something profoundly different from what I did for sport: I was willing when climbing a mountain recreationally to say no to a pitch that was beyond my competence, but I'd let the party chief make that call for me as a surveyor. I worried that I might get hurt someday thinking like this, but I knew that rather than come back to the crew again saying it can't be done, I'd push myself as far as I needed to go.

The area of mountain-driven uplift contained within the borders of our township was made even more chaotic by Ashley Creek, a large stream that flowed south from the Uintas and wandered through the township according to gravity and geology, splitting the rock when necessary to pass through angled ramps of hard cap rock. In the intervals between these narrow canyons the stream slowed and spread, meandering through the swampy flood plains that were lush, overgrown counterpoints to all that dry, ordered chaos thrown up by the distant rise of the Uintas.

We eventually found ourselves surveying line that ran right up the bottom of the flattest and swampiest of these openings. This was an unusual line for us to survey: the southwest boundary of a long-defunct but still legally significant military reservation, the enduring legacy of a fort that had been established in the 1870's to address what Americans referred to then as the "Indian Question." The terrain was awful: mosquitoes, tangled underbrush, swamps everywhere, and we had to cross and recross the cold knee-deep stream over and over again. It was bad enough that we had to clear line through all this muck; chaining for distance would be a nightmare, and because the flood plain was both flat and wooded, there seemed to be no way to get the clear shot we needed to triangulate.

We knew we weren't fighting our way through a Vietnamese jungle only because we could see through the trees pinkish glimpses of the canyon walls that confined the flat swamps and willows of the flood plain: high sandstone ramparts stood to the east and west, and on one perfectly flat wall someone had lowered himself on ropes to paint a huge war memorial, a red, white, and blue American flag the size of a troop transport with—we counted—forty-seven stars; and beneath, in six-foot-high black letters, REMEMBER THE MAINE.

This kind of display wasn't unusual. The Utah landscape has always been regarded by its colonizers as an insufficiently stretched canvas upon which to paint the outlines of the New Jerusalem, and every mountainside above every Utah town is still marked with an oversized capital letter representing the local high school. The Wasatch Front has become one long billboard proclaiming the civic identities of the citizens who have lived in its shadow, and if a local Mormon imperialist had chosen to stir up Spanish-American War fervor—after routinely fighting wars *against* the US government for a half century, this was after all the first opportunity for Mormon boys to fight *alongside* the feds—who would stop him? The canyon walls were already crowded with pictographs painted and chiseled by the long-departed Fremont culture, themselves probably not the first inhabitants of our township, markings that in addition to representing the sun and moon might well be translated as some kind of Neolithic call to arms, an indigenous version of the stars and stripes, a pre-Columbian statement of nationalistic fervor, perhaps even the prehistoric equivalent of a survey marker. The porous sandstone walls had allowed the natural pigments as well as America's best lead-based paint to establish their messages for perpetuity; pictographs and the American flag were there for keeps, and I knew that archaeologists a thousand years in the future would ponder with equivalent curiosity the ambiguous markings left by the ancient Fremont, nineteenth-century American imperialists, and US government surveyors.

Jerry came up with a plan to get us through the swamp without chaining. First, we cut an eight-chain path (about two hundred yards) on line through the brush, measured the distance, and measured it again—whatever Jerry's idea was, it required an especially accurate initial measurement. Jerry then had Dan pick a specific star on the flag painted half a mile away on the sandstone face, move his transit to the lath at the end of the segment we'd just chained, and turn a second angle to the star. Using this side of the triangle as a base, Jerry then calculated the measurement for another side, the line between the star and our first lath. This line, at the same time

183

imaginary and serviceable, became the base from which we'd triangulate our distance, measuring our progress through the next difficult mile and a half without chaining another inch.

It was at least as accurate as trying to pull a chain through all that wilderness, and it was elegant. I was so impressed I could hardly stand it, and at the end of the day, back at the motel, as I pulled off my wet boots and wrung my soggy socks, I asked Dan to explain how it had worked: how, I asked, did Jerry create a baseline in the air, a transparent, intangible line measured by calculation alone, by turning only one base angle and directly measuring only one side of the triangle? How did he keep track of where we were? Wasn't it a little like pulling yourself up by your bootstraps?

It was, he explained, and it wasn't. Basically, as long as Dan had a clear view of the American flag and could read the angle that defined his relationship to the star he'd picked, Jerry could calculate the distance we'd run from each flag I'd pounded in, and to make sure line remained absolutely straight from flag to flag, we'd stopped halfway to recheck our line with a quick shot of the North Star, refining the line's accuracy by locating ourselves in this broadest of contexts. As Dan talked, I was able to picture in my mind a series of triangles connected like links in a tight length of chain, angles and distances anchored on one end by the American flag, connected on the other to line that ran unimpeded through the narrow corridor we'd clearcut through the trees and underbrush with axes and chain saws and marked with our own flags, me serving as a kind of guidon bearer.

Looking back over our shoulders at the stars and stripes that waved inertly above our heads, and renewing our alignment with the North Star—creating a neat web that somehow connected the Spanish-American War, a star on the American flag, a less metaphorical star that burned white with nuclear fuel a thousand light-years away, and a defunct but persistent cavalry outpost established a century ago—we forced our march with axes and machetes the distance necessary to reinforce the military boundary, to run line where it led.

I surveyed for seven more summers and didn't get killed; I put in flags that risked the transit operator's life, and I lived to see Jerry back down before I would. Once. But none of this prepared me for the experience I encountered eight years later, the last summer of my surveying career. I was working then with Ed Reynolds, a tall, skinny man in his early forties with an incongruously full beer gut and a blond redneck flattop. When I'd first met him a few years earlier, he was a happy crew chief, a full-time career surveyor, not overly burdened with responsibility for the accuracy of the survey nor accountable for the crew's rate of progress. He neither signed the notes as party chief nor filled out paperwork for the state office. Instead, he operated the transit with quiet skill, dug holes efficiently and happily, and chain sawed line across a cedar-choked plateau quicker than anybody.

By the time I'd been assigned to Ed's crew, I'd progressed from flagman to crew chief/instrument operator, and he'd advanced— against his deepest wishes—to the position of party chief. Ed had been promoted during a time surveying was changing dramatically, requiring a lot more book knowledge and technological training than he'd been exposed to in his fifteen years of no-longer-valuable experience; he looked at his fancy new Hewlett-Packard programmable calculator with suspicion and fear, and held it as if it would bite him, never quite trusting, and not always recognizing, the numbers that blinked red in its readout. He'd been surveying all these years because he'd loved it, and surveying had loved him; now he looked worried, even mournful, worn down by a year of party chief responsibilities, drinking less beer than he'd like each evening because of all the calculations he'd need a clear head to complete.

We were surveying a particularly precipitous section of the Wasatch Front above Provo. We'd been provided with a helicopter, but it didn't help much in these mountains. There was literally no place level enough for the helicopter to land between the line of peaks at 11,000 feet and the base of the mountains 6,000 feet below, which meant that workdays typically involved being dropped off on a summit or high ridge, hiking several thousand feet down, getting in a few hours of surveying, then hiking down the rest of the way either to a residential street where we'd parked a truck that morning, or to a foothill clearing where the helicopter would give us a quick ride back to the Provo airport. It was brutal work, not any less dangerous for being within a few miles of a sprawling city; we were working only the downhill muscles in our legs and ruining our knees in the process. We spent that summer struggling through thick oak brush, climbing down fierce rock outcroppings, shooting line up and down impossibly steep talis slopes—and averaging less than half a mile a day.

There was a corner of the township we'd been putting off all summer. On the USGS map it was called Deep Creek Canyon, but we'd renamed it Deep Shit the day we first flew over it and checked what we saw with our eyes against the ominous preview the map had provided. The map's contour lines ran so closely together in describing the near vertical steepness of the canyon that it looked like a dark ominous amoebic splotch, a black hole. Even the elements feared this chasm: an intermittent blue line on the map indicated that a seasonal stream (presumably Deep Creek) entered from above, but the map showed no stream emerging below, even seasonally. The notes recorded by the surveyor who had run the original survey a hundred years before claimed that a rock quarter corner would be found at the very bottom, which meant that there was no way of avoiding Deep Shit Canyon, and sure enough, when we finally ran line, followed it right to the brink, and peered over the edge into the place line went, we understood that our procrastination had been justified. It was an ugly hole, choked with rockslides and ledges sharp as teeth, metamorphic rock tortured and cracked beyond the possibility of any apparent trail or place to put your feet without being twisted and thrown; but we couldn't just shoot line over the canyon because there was a corner to be established, a specific intersection that we needed to tie into our survey, a point we'd have to monument with an iron pipe and a rock mound.

The original survey had been completed by a man motivated more by self-preservation than courage or honesty; we'd learned by now that he simply hadn't gone into many of the places he'd claimed to have gone. He had done a pretty good job of leaving well-marked corners where the surveying had been easy, but we never did find one of his markers on a steep rock face or deep in a ravine, and we knew we wouldn't be finding one at the bottom of Deep Shit Canyon, where he'd claimed to have been a hundred years ago. We understood that he'd observed the same combination of steepness, narrowness, and rock ledges that could tear your body apart, and had said, *No way.* Our job was to rectify this act of cowardice, to plunge literally into the breach, to plug this gap in the line that separated order from chaos, to reinforce the invisible wall that kept nature from hindering the advance of American civilization.

The cleft was so narrow that we couldn't see to the very bottom, which meant that we'd have a hard time shooting line exactly where it needed to go. The only way we figured we could get line in there was to carry a transit into the maw of all this rock. We settled on this plan: the flagman and I would climb down the cliff, passing the transit and tripod, and the pipe and ax, to each other from ledge to ledge. Ed would line us in from the edge of the canyon with the theodolite, and then I'd use the transit to extend the survey into the part of the canyon we couldn't see from above, a shaded rockslide where we figured the marker would go, and where we'd look for, but knew we wouldn't find, the old rock corner. After setting the pipe, we'd hike toward the narrow exit through which even water feared to run, go down one more ledged face, and meet up with Ed, who would have clambered down the hillside with the theodolite and found his way to the truck.

By then I'd learned a lot about biting the bullet and doing what had to be done. I was apprehensive, but mostly I just wanted to get it over with, to do a good job of running line and placing the corner, and come out without injuring myself. Then Ed said something to me I've never heard a surveyor say to another: he took me aside just as I was about to go over the edge and said quietly, almost whispering, "If it's too rough down there, just chuck the pipe and get the hell out. It's only surveying."

I can't tell you how Ed's words moved me. There was an aspect of the professionalism of surveying that I both admired and worried about: the complete inability of any of us to say no. Perhaps professionalism isn't the word, but macho isn't the word either. After all, we were surveyors, not mountain climbers or big game hunters or gunfighters. We never used words like *courage* or called each other pussies, as did some of the guys I climbed with on weekends; we were driven by trigonometry, not testosterone. And some days it was fun. We'd hike for miles, leaving newly marked section corners in our wake, rejoicing in the blue Utah sky and taking in all the beauty and sublimity that part of the world has to offer. We were being paid to spend our days in the same landscape national parks were built to celebrate.

But many other days involved some of the hardest, most dangerous work human beings are called upon to do, and it was never okay to just stop, to take more than a minute's rest, or to say *I can't do this.* There were a lot of things we couldn't say. For example, we couldn't say to each other, "Are you crazy? Carry a transit up there? *No way.*" "Cross this river without a rope? *Forget it.*" "Cut our way with axes through all this timber? Get *real!*" Those words would never escape our lips. Occasionally over the years we'd get a summer worker who would complain or goldbrick, but he'd never last through June. My first summer, the day I decided I couldn't plant a flag on the sandstone spur, was the one and only time I said *I can't do it.*

This assumption about surveying left me no alternative but to descend into Deep Shit Canyon. We slowly crawled our way downward through the ramparts of ledges, and after a search that left us scrambling up and down a rockslide that made it pretty clear the original surveyor had only observed this spot from afar, we calculated where our marker should go—based on the rock corners we'd already found along this north-south line—and mounded the pipe with rocks, of which there were plenty, and pulled our way out, suffering scratches and bruises but no lasting damage either to ourselves or (more important) the transit. As we stumbled out of the narrow divide and through the last set of rock ledges, finally sliding down the first actual dirt we'd encountered all day, Ed was there with the truck and a cold Coors and an actual handshake, the kind of gesture I'd grown accustomed to going without for just doing what the job required.

As I said, by then I'd come to accept the motivation for our work, our routine belief in the ultimate importance of line. But I hadn't realized just how *heartless* was the unexamined obligation of going everywhere line went, until that day when Ed told me, "It's only surveying." His words were so unexpected, so unprecedented in all the years I'd been a surveyor, that I felt a little jolted, even disoriented. Ed was telling me that I was more important than line. It felt a little like love.

Conventional wisdom has it that Americans have gone through some profound changes since the 1700's in the way we perceive nature. Just as the Enlightenment determined that the crooked lines and irregular lots of the metes and bounds survey would be replaced by the arrogance of the straight line and the squared grid, the Romantic revolution ushered in a new sensitivity to the integrity of natural landscape, which (as the Romantics relentlessly pointed out) seldom carves *itself* into squares. Frustrated by the tunnel vision of linearity, the Romantics encouraged us to search for correspondences with nature, to find ourselves in what pure nature presents to the eye, not what humans have placed there for us to find. They taught us that ultimate truth is accessible through intuition, not mathematics; in what

Emerson called "untaught sallies of the spirit," not the narrow calculus of science and reason.

The procession of what one college text calls the "Environmentalist Tradition" describes a steady march into increasingly respectful attitudes toward nature: from Thoreau and Emerson through John Muir and Teddy Roosevelt to David Brower and Edward Abbey; from Thoreau's groundbreaking *Walden* to Al Gore's ho-hum *Earth in the Balance*. It's supposed to *mean* something that we live in an America informed by such institutions as the National Park Service, the Sierra Club, and the American suburb, whose avenues curve gracefully according to the metes-and-bounds conventions of the English countryside. An evolutionary progression of legislation ever friendlier to the environment, including the American Antiquities Act of 1906, the Wilderness Act of 1964, even the routine national recognition of Earth Day, would seem to have rendered the tight-ass linearity of the Ordinance of 1785 not only quaint, but moot.

Nevertheless, as if occupying some kind of parallel universe that exists in blissful ignorance of all this cultural and ideological progress, the straight lines of Jefferson's vision have quietly extended themselves for over two hundred years. As artists, writers, and philosophers labored to revise and expand our attitudes toward nature—to lead us beyond the failed experiment that was the Enlightenment—government surveyors have worked quietly in the background, reinforcing the old lines and scratching brand-new ones into those few remaining islands of unsurveyed American terrain, constructing a squared and gridded landscape that is so pervasive as to be considered unremarkable. The Ordinance of 1785 has had the effect of keeping Americans trapped in the smug assumptions of the Age of Reason, and as a result post-Enlightenment insights sit uneasily on the American countryside: the square-mile section that serves as the starting point for all property boundaries, public and private; the state highway that runs due north until it disappears into the horizon; the rigid checkerboard expanse of the Midwest we observe from 40,000 feet—all these intersecting lines subtly direct our thoughts toward the mathematical equations of the Enlightenment, not the spiritual correspondences of Transcendentalism. In spite of Earth Day celebrations and new national parks, we continue to orient ourselves in a lined and squared landscape that inevitably frames our relationship with the natural world.

What does it mean for a nation to assume its identity amid all these straight lines? Bigger thinkers than I am can take that one on. I only know what it meant for me: chronic ideological confusion, occasional disorientation, and an unaccountable and unseemly pride. Working summers for the Cadastral Survey had the effect of bouncing me back and forth between paradigms, my summers committed to imposing straight lines on nature, the rest of the year in eco-rehab, backpacking and cross-country skiing and basking in the innocent glow of the modern environmental movement's golden years. Even so, my awareness of the vast disconnect in my life between my gentler inclinations and the work I did each summer didn't prevent me from reaping the psychological benefits of ruling the world. Through each long summer I watched myself getting better and better at my job, eating and breathing linearity until it became part of me, until line became *personal*. On those days when my equations came out right and the North Star confirmed my place in the universe, when line ran straight and true the only direction it could, Jefferson's vision became my own.

Nominated by Stephen Corey, The Georgia Review

THE BEAUTIES OF NATURE

by MARY JO BANG

from PLOUGHSHARES

She'd grown tired, she admitted,
of the picturesque—
pretty pipers piped

against a backdrape of pineapple yellow.
She closed her eyes
to it and it went away.

In this sight heaven she trilled her right hand
in the water-lilied water
and wondered at the weather.

Twenty starlings twittered.
The day had been
dieted down to twelve hours of light

and cushioned between two storms.
She thought
she could see through

the muggy dusk a balloon
bobbing in the distance, dripping
an empty basket.

What is Reason but a lid?
she asked herself.
What is Death but the end

of a season.
Like smoke her last thought
rose in the lead

air and hovered
above her head. Her head
swam in the glittery

pool of all the gone beloveds.
One by one
she held them under.

Nominated by Molly Bendall, Rachel Loden, Laurie Sheck, Ploughshares

ODE TO THE AIR TRAFFIC CONTROLLER

by JOSHUA BECKMAN

from SOMETHING I EXPECTED TO BE DIFFERENT (Verse Press)

Melbourne, Perth, Darwin, Townsville,
Belém, Durban, Lima, Xai-Xai planes
with wingspans big as high schools
eight hundred nine hundred tons a piece
gone like pollen, cumulus cirrus
altostratus nimbostratus people getting skinny
just trying to lose weight and the sky
the biggest thing anyone ever thought of
Acceptance, Vancouver, Tehran, Maui
school children balloons light blue nothing
one goes away not forever, in fact
most people, at least if you are flying
Delta, come down in Salt Lake City
Fairbanks, Kobe, Aukland, Anchorage
from Cleveland a hundred Hawaii-bound Germans
are coming in low, not to say too low
just low pull up Amsterdam pull up Miami
historically a very high-strung bunch
smokers eaters tiny planes must circle
we have bigger problems on our hands
New York, Tokyo, Hong Kong, Paris
the boy who has been ignoring dinner
throws thirteen paper planes out the window

does it look like this? Tashkent, Nome, Rio,
Hobart, yes yes it looks just like that
now do your homework Capetown Capetown
lots of rain good on one good on two
go three go four go five go six
Mau, Brak, Zella, Ghat, an African parade
good on two good on three
please speak English please speak English
good on five good on six gentlemen:
the world will let us down many times
but it will never run out of coffee
hooray! for Lagos, Accra, Freetown, Dakar
your son is on the telephone the Germans
landed safely Seattle off to Istanbul
tiny planes please circle oh tiny planes
do please please circle

Nominated by David Rivard, Verse Press

THE LIVES OF STRANGERS

fiction by CHITRA BANERJEE DIVAKARUNI

from AGNI

THE SEEPAGE OF RAINWATER has formed a tapestry against the peeling walls of the Nataraj Yatri House dining hall, but no one except Leela notices this. The other members of the pilgrimage party jostle around the fire that sputters in a corner and shout at the pahari boy to hurry with the tea. Aunt Seema sits at one of the scratched wooden tables with a group of women, all of them swaddled in the bright shawls they bought for this trip. From time to time they look down at their laps with a startled expression, like sparrows who have awakened to find themselves plumaged in cockatoo feathers.

Aunt beckons to Leela to come sit by her. "Baap re," she says, "I can't believe how cold it is here in Kashmir. It's quite delightful, actually. Just think, in Calcutta right now people are bathing in sweat, even with the fans on full speed!"

The women smile, pleased at having had the foresight to leave sweaty Calcutta behind at the height of summer for a journey which is going to earn them comfort on earth and goodwill in heaven. They hold their chins high and elongate their necks as classical dancers might. Plump, middle-aged women who sleepily read love stories in *Desh* magazine through the interminable train journey from Howrah Station, already they are metamorphosed into handmaidens of Shiva, adventure-bound toward his holy shrine in Amarnath. Their eyes sparkle with zeal as they discuss how remote the shrine is. How they will have to walk across treacherous glaciers for three whole days to

195

reach it. Contemplating them, Leela wonders if this is the true lure of travel, this hope of a transformed self. Will her own journey, begun when she left America a month ago, bring her this coveted change?

Tea arrives, sweet and steaming in huge aluminum kettles, along with dinner: buttery wheat parathas, fatly stuffed with spicy potatoes. When they have eaten, the guide advises them to get their rest. This is no touristy excursion, he reminds them sternly. It is a serious and sacred yatra, and dangerous, too. He talks awhile of the laws to be observed while on pilgrimage: no non-vegetarian food, no sex. Any menstruating women should not proceed beyond this point. There is a lot more, but his Bengali is full of long, formal words that Leela does not know, and her attention wanders. He ends by saying something about sin and expiation, which seems to her terribly complex and thus very Indian.

Later in bed, Leela will think of Mrs. Das. At dinner Mrs. Das sat by herself at a table that was more rickety than the others. In a room filled with nervous laughter (for the headman had frightened them all a bit, though no one would admit it) she held herself with an absorbed stillness, her elbows pulled close as though she had been taught early in life not to take up too much space in the world. She did not speak to anyone. Under her frizzy pepper-colored hair, her face was angular and ascetic.

Leela has not met Mrs. Das, but she knows a great deal about her because Aunt Seema's friends discuss her frequently. Mostly they marvel at her bad luck.

"Can you imagine!" the doctor's wife says, "her husband died just two years after her marriage, and right away her in-laws, who hated her because it had been a love-match, claimed that the marriage wasn't legal. They were filthy rich—the Dases of Tollygunge, you understand—they hired the shrewdest lawyers. She lost everything—the money, the house, even the wedding jewelry."

"No justice in this world," Aunt says, clicking her tongue sympathetically.

"She had to go to work in an office," someone else adds. "Think of it, a woman of good family, forced to work with low-caste peons and clerks! That's how she put her son through college and got him married."

"And now the daughter-in-law refuses to live with her," Aunt says.

"So she's had to move into a women's hostel. A women's hostel! At her age!"

The doctor's wife shakes her head mournfully. "Some people are like that, born under an unlucky star. They bring bad luck to themselves and everyone close to them."

Leela studies the kaleidoscope of emotions flitting across the women's faces. Excitement, pity, cheerful outrage. Can it be true, that part about an unlucky star? In America she would have dealt with such superstition with fluent, dismissive ease, but India is complicated. Like entering a murky, primal lake, in India she has to watch her step.

◆ ◆ ◆

Leela's happiest childhood memories were of aloneness: reading in her room with the door closed, playing chess on the computer, embarking on long bike rides through the city, going to the movies by herself. You saw more that way, she explained to her parents. You didn't miss crucial bits of dialogue because your companion was busy making inane remarks. Her parents, themselves solitary individuals, didn't object. People—except for a select handful—were noisy and messy. They knew that. Which was why, early in their lives, they had escaped India to take up research positions in America. Ever since Leela could remember, they had encouraged her taste for privacy. When Leela became a computer programmer, they applauded the fact that she could do most of her work from home. When she became involved with Dexter, another programmer she had met at one of the rare conferences she attended, they applauded that too, though more cautiously.

Her relationship with Dexter was a brief affair, perhaps inevitably so. Looking back in search of incidents to remember it by, Leela would only be able to recall a general feeling, something like being wound tightly in a blanket on a cold day, comforting yet restrictive. Even when things were at their best, they never moved in together. Leela preferred it that way. She preferred, too, to sleep alone, and often moved after lovemaking to the spare bed in her apartment. When you slept, you were too vulnerable. Another person's essence could invade you. She had explained it once to Dexter. He had stroked her hair with fingers she thought of as sensitive and artistic, and had seemed to understand. But apparently he hadn't. It was one of the facts he dwelt on at some bitter length before he left.

"You're like one of those spiny creatures that live at the bottom of the ocean," he said. "Everything just slides off of that watertight shell of yours. You don't need me—you don't need *anyone*."

He wasn't totally right about that. A week after he left, Leela ended up in the emergency ward, having swallowed a bottle of sleeping pills.

An encounter with death—even an aborted one (Leela had called 911 as soon as she finished taking the pills)—alters one in unaccountable ways. After having to deal with the hospital, the police, and the mandatory counselor assigned to her, Leela should have heaved a sigh of relief when she returned to her quiet, tidy apartment. Instead, for the first time, she found her own company inadequate. Alone, there seemed no point in opening the drapes or cleaning up the TV dinner containers stacked up on the coffee table. The place took on a green, underwater dimness. Her computer gathered dust as she wandered from room to room, sometimes with her eyes closed, trailing her fingers as though they were fins across the furniture, testing the truth of Dexter's accusation.

She didn't know when it was that she started thinking about India, which she had never visited. The idea attached itself to the underneath of her mind and grew like a barnacle. In her imagination the country was vast and vague. Talismanic. For some reason she associated it with rain, scavenger crows, the clanging of orange trams and the purplish green of elephant ears. Were these items from some story her parents had told in her childhood? No. Though her parents' stories had spanned many topics—from the lives of famous scientists to the legends of Greece and Rome—they never discussed their homeland, a country they seemed to have shed as easily and completely as a lizard drops its tail.

When she called her parents to inform them she was going, she did not tell them why. Perhaps she herself did not know. Nor did she speak of the suicide attempt, which filled her with a rush of mortification whenever it intruded on her thoughts. As always with her decisions, they did not venture advice, though she thought she heard her mother suppress a sigh. They waited to see if she had more to say, and when she didn't, they told her how to contact Aunt Seema, who was her mother's cousin.

"Try to stay away from the crowds," her father said.

"That's impossible," said her mother. "Just be sure to take your shots before you go, drink boiled water at all times, and don't get involved in the lives of strangers."

◆ ◆ ◆

What did Leela expect from India? The banalities of heat and dust, poverty and squalor, yes. The elated confusion of city streets where the beetle-black Ambassador cars of the rich inched their way, honking, between sweating rickshaw-pullers and cows who stood unmoving, as dignified as dowagers. But she had not thought Calcutta would vanquish her so easily with its melancholy poetry of old cotton saris hung out to dry on rooftops. With low-ceilinged groceries filled with odors she did not recognize but knew to be indispensable. In the evenings, the shopkeeper waved a lamp in front of a vividly colored calendar depicting Rama's coronation. His waiting customers did not seem to mind. Sometimes at dawn she stood at her bedroom window and heard, cutting through the roar of buses, the cool, astonishing voice of a young man in a neighboring house practicing a morning raag.

At the airport, Aunt Seema had been large, untidy, and moist—the exact opposite of Leela's mother. She launched herself at Leela with a delighted cry, kissing her on both cheeks, pulling her into her ample, talcum-powder-scented bosom, exclaiming how overjoyed she was to meet her. In America Leela would have been repelled by such effusion, especially from a woman she had never seen in her life. Here it seemed as right—and as welcome—as the too-sweet glass of orange squash the maid brought her as soon as she reached the house.

Aunt dressed Leela in her starched cotton saris, put matching bindis on her forehead, and lined her eyes with kajal. She forced her to increase her rudimentary Bengali vocabulary by refusing to speak to her in English. She cooked her rui fish sautéed with black jeera, and moglai parathas stuffed with eggs and onions, which had to be flipped over deftly at a crucial moment—food Leela loved though it gave her heartburn. She took her to the Kalighat temple for a blessing, to night-long music concerts, and to the homes of her friends, all of whom wanted to arrange a marriage for her. Leela went unprotestingly. Like a child acting in her first play, she was thrilled by the vibrant unreality of the life she was living. At night she lay in the

199

big bed beside Aunt (Uncle having been banished to a cot down-stairs) and watched the soft white swaying of the mosquito net in the breeze from the ceiling fan. She pondered the unexpected pleasure she took in every disorganized aspect of the day. India was a Mardi Gras that never ended. Who would have thought she'd feel so at home here?

So when Aunt Seema said, "You want to see the real India, the spiritual India? Let's go on a pilgrimage," she agreed without hesitation.

The talk starts at the end of the first day's trek. In one of the women's tents, where Leela lies among pilgrims who huddle in blankets and nurse aching muscles, a voice rises from the dark.

"Do you know, Mrs. Das's bedroll didn't get to the camp. They can't figure out what happened—the guides swear they tied it onto a mule this morning—"

"That's right," responds another voice. "I heard them complaining because they had to scrounge around in their own packs to find her some blankets."

In the anonymous darkness, the voices take on cruel, choric tones. They release suspicion into the close air like bacteria, ready to multiply wherever they touch down.

"It's like that time on the train, remember, when she was the only one who got food poisoning—"

"Yes, yes—"

"I wonder what will happen next—"

"As long as it doesn't affect us—"

"How can you be sure? Maybe next time it will—"

"I hate to be selfish, but I wish she wasn't here with us at all—"

"Me, too—"

Leela wonders about the tent in which Mrs. Das is spending her night. She wonders what people are saying in there. What they are thinking. An image comes to her with a brief, harsh clarity: the older woman's body curled into a lean comma under her borrowed blankets. In the whispery dark, her thin, veined lids squeezed shut in a semblance of sleep.

Struggling up the trail through the morning mist, the line of pilgrims in gay woolen clothes looks like a bright garland. Soon the light will grow brutal and blinding, but at this hour it is sleepy, diffuse. A woman pauses to chant. Om Namah Shivaya, Salutations to the Auspicious One. The notes tremble in the air, Leela thinks, like silver bubbles. The pilgrims are quiet—there's something about the snowy crags that discourages gossip. The head guide has suggested that walking time be utilized for reflection and repentance. Leela finds herself thinking, instead, of accidents.

She remembers the first one most clearly. It must have been a special occasion, maybe a birthday or an out-of-town visitor, because her mother was cooking. She rarely made Indian food from scratch, and Leela remembers that she was snappish and distracted. Wanting to help, the four-year-old Leela had pulled at a pot and seen the steaming dal come at her in a yellow rush. It struck her arm with a slapping sound. She screamed and raced around the kitchen—as though agony could be outrun. Long after her mother immersed her arm in ice-water and gave her Tylenol to reduce the pain, she continued to sob—tears of rage at being tricked, Leela realizes now. She'd had no intimations, until then, that good intentions were no match for the forces of the physical world.

More accidents followed, in spite of the fact that she was not a particularly physical child. They blur together in Leela's memory like the landscape outside the window of a speeding car. She fell from her bike in front of a moving car—luckily the driver had good reflexes, and she only needed a few stitches on her chin. She sat in the passenger seat of her mother's van, and a stone—from who knows where—shattered the windshield, filling Leela's lap with jagged silver. A defective electrical wire caught fire at night in her bedroom while she slept. Her mother, up for a drink of water, smelled the smoke and ran to the bedroom to discover the carpet smoldering around the sleeping Leela's bed. Do all these close escapes mean that Leela is lucky? Or is her unlucky star, thwarted all this time by some imbalance in the stratosphere, waiting for its opportunity?

She thinks finally of the suicide attempt, which, since arriving in India, she has quarantined in a part of her mind she seldom visits. Can it be classified as an accident, an accident she did to herself? She remembers the magnetic red gleam of the round pills in the hollow of her palm, how unexpectedly solid they had felt, like metal pellets. The shriek of the ambulance outside her window. The old man

201

who lived across the hall peering from a crack in his door, grim and unsurprised. The acidic ache in her throat when they pumped her stomach. Leela had kept her eyes on the wall of the emergency room afterwards, too ashamed to look at the paramedic who was telling her something. Something cautionary and crucial which might help her now, as she steps warily along this beautiful glacial trail, watching for crevasses. But for the life of her she cannot recall what it was.

◆ ◆ ◆

Each night the pilgrims are assigned to different tents by the head guide, according to some complicated logic Leela has failed to decipher. But tonight, when she finds herself in Mrs. Das's tent, her bedroll set down next to the older woman's makeshift one, she wonders if it is destiny that has brought her here.

All her life, like her parents, Leela has been a believer in individual responsibility. But lately she finds herself wondering. When she asked Aunt Seema yesterday, she touched Leela's cheek in a gesture of amused affection. "Ah, my dear—to believe that you control everything in your life! How absurdly American!"

Destiny is a seductive concept. Ruminating on it, Leela feels the events of her life turn weightless and pass through her like clouds. The simplistic, sublunary words she assigned to them—pride, shame, guilt, folly—no longer seem to apply.

"Please," Mrs. Das whispers in Bengali, startling Leela from thought. She sits on the tarpaulin floor of the tent, propped against her bedroll, her legs splayed out crookedly from under her sari. "Could you ask one of the attendants to bring some warm water? My feet hurt a lot."

"Of course," Leela says, jumping up. An odd gladness fills her as she performs this small service. Aunt, who was less than happy about Leela's tent assignment tonight, had whispered to her to be sure to stay away from Mrs. Das. But Aunt is at the other end of the camp, while destiny has placed Leela here.

When the water comes in a bucket, Mrs. Das surreptitiously removes her shoes. They are made of rough leather, cheap and unlovely. They make Leela feel guilty about her fleece-lined American boots, even though the fleece is fake. Then she sucks in a horrified breath.

Freed of shoes and socks, Mrs. Das's feet are in bad shape, swollen all the way to the calves. The toes are blistered and bluish with frost-bite. The heels weep yellowish pus. Mrs. Das looks concerned but not surprised—this has obviously been going on for a couple of days. She grits her teeth, lurches to her feet, and tries to lift the bucket. Leela takes it from her and follows her to the opening of the tent, and when Mrs. Das has difficulty bending over to wash her feet, she kneels and does it for her. She feels no disgust as she cleans off the odorous pus. This intrigues her. Usually she doesn't like touching people. Even with her parents, she seldom went beyond the light press of lips to cheek, the hurried pat on the shoulder. In her Dexter days, if he put his arm around her, she'd find an excuse to move away after a few minutes. Yet here she is, tearing strips from an old sari and bandaging Mrs. Das's feet, her fingers moving with a deft intelligence she did not suspect they possessed, brown against the matching brown of Mrs. Das's skin. This is the first time, she thinks, that she has known such intimacy. How amazing that it should be a stranger who has opened her like a dictionary and brought to light this word whose definition had escaped her until now.

◆ ◆ ◆

Someone in the tent must have talked, for here through the night comes the party's doctor, his flashlight making a ragged circle of brightness on the tent floor as he enters. "Now what's the problem?" he asks Mrs. Das, who attempts a look of innocence. What problem could he be referring to? The doctor sighs, hands Leela his torch, removes the sari strips, and clicks his tongue gravely as he examines Mrs. Das's feet. There's evidence of infection, he says. She needs a tetanus shot immediately, and even then the blisters might get septic. How could she have been so foolish as to keep this a secret from him? He pulls a thick syringe from his bag and administers an injection. "But you still have to get down to the hospital at Pahelgaon as soon as possible," he ends. "I'll ask the guide to find some way of sending you back tomorrow."

Mrs. Das clutches the doctor's arm. In the flashlight's erratic beam, her eyes, magnified behind thick glasses, glint desperately. She doesn't care about her feet, she says. It's more important for her to complete the pilgrimage—she's waited so long to do it. They're only a day or so away from Shiva's shrine. If she had to turn back now, it would kill her much more surely than a septic blister.

The doctor's walrus mustache droops unhappily. He takes a deep breath and says that two extra days of hard walking could cause gangrene to set in, though a brief uncertainty flits over his face as he speaks. He repeats that Mrs. Das must go back tomorrow, then hurries off before she can plead further.

The darkness left behind is streaked with faint cobwebs of moonlight. Leela glances at the body prone on the bedding next to her. Mrs. Das is completely quiet, and this frightens Leela more than any fit of hysterics. She hears shufflings from the other end of the tent, whispered comments sibilant with relief. Angrily, she thinks that had the patient been anyone else, the doctor would not have been so adamant about sending her back. The moon goes behind a cloud; around her, darkness packs itself tightly, like black wool. She pushes her hand through it to where she thinks Mrs. Das's arm might be. Against her fingers Mrs. Das's skin feels brittle and stiff, like cheap waterproof fabric. Leela holds Mrs. Das's wrist awkwardly, not knowing what to do. In the context of Indian etiquette, would patting be considered a condescending gesture? She regrets her impetuosity.

Then Mrs. Das turns her wrist—it is the swift movement of a night animal who knows its survival depends on mastering such economies of action—and clasps Leela's fingers tightly in her own.

◆　◆　◆

Late that night Mrs. Das tries to continue up the trail on her own, is spotted by the lookout guide, apprehended and brought back. It happens quickly and quietly, and Leela sleeps through it all.

By the time she wakes, the tent is washed in calm mountain light and abuzz with women and gossip.

"There she was, in the dark on her own, without any supplies, not even an electric torch, can you imagine?"

"Luckily the guide saw her before she went beyond the bend in the mountain. Otherwise she'd be in a ravine by now—"

"Or frozen to death—"

"Crazy woman! They say when they caught her, she fought them tooth and nail—I'm telling you, she actually drew blood! Like someone possessed by an evil spirit—"

Leela stares at Mrs. Das's bedroll, two dark, hairy blankets topped by a sheet. It looks like the peeled skin of an animal turned inside out. The women's excitement crackles through the air, sends little shocks up her arms. Are people in India harder to understand because they've had so many extra centuries to formulate their beliefs? She recalls the expression on Dexter's face before he slammed the door, the simple incandescence of his anger. In some way, she had expected it all along. But Mrs. Das—? She curls her fingers, remembering the way the older woman had clasped them in her dry, birdlike grip.

"Did she really think she could get to the shrine all by herself!" someone exclaims.

Leela spots Aunt Seema and tugs at her sari. "Where is Mrs. Das now?"

"The guides have put her in a separate tent where they can keep an eye on her until they can send her back," Aunt says, shaking her head sadly. "Poor thing—I really feel sorry for her. Still, I must confess I'm glad she's leaving." Then a suspicious frown takes over her face. "Why do you want to know? Did you talk to her last night? Leela, stop, where are you going?"

◆ ◆ ◆

Mrs. Das, whom Leela finds in a small tent outside of which a guide keeps watch, does not look like a woman who has recently battled several men tooth and nail. Cowled in a faded green shawl, she dozes peacefully against the tent pole, though this could be due to the Calmpose tablets the doctor has made her take. Or perhaps there's not much outside her head that she's interested in at this point. She has lost her glasses in her night's adventuring, and when Leela touches her shoulder, she looks up, blinking with dignity.

Leela opens her mouth to say she is sorry about how Mrs. Das has been treated. But she hears herself saying, "I'm going back with you." The dazed expression on Mrs. Das's face mirrors her own inner state. When after a moment Mrs. Das warily asks her why, all she can do is shrug her shoulders. She is uncertain of her motives. Is it her desire to prove (but to whom?) that she is somehow superior to the others? Is it pity, an emotion she has always distrusted? Is it some inchoate affinity she feels toward this stranger? But if you believe in destiny, no one can be a stranger, can they? There's always a connection, a reason because of which people enter your orbit, bristling with dark energy like a meteor intent on collision.

◆ ◆ ◆

Traveling down a mountain trail fringed by thick, seeded grasses the same gray as the sky, Leela wants to ask Mrs. Das about destiny. Whether she believes in it, what she understands it to encompass. But Mrs. Das grips the saddle of the mule she is sitting on, her body rigid with the single-minded terror of a person who has never ridden an animal. Ahead, the guide's young, scraggly bearded son whistles a movie tune Leela remembers having heard in another world, during an excursion with Aunt Seema to some Calcutta market.

Aunt Seema was terribly upset with Leela's decision to accompany Mrs. Das—no, even with that intense adverb, upset is too simple a word to describe the change in her urbane aunt, who had taken such gay control of Leela's life in the city. The new Aunt Seema wrung her hands and lamented, "But what would your mother say if she knew that I let you go off alone with some stranger?" (Did she really believe Leela's mother would hold her responsible? The thought made Leela smile.) Aunt's face was full of awful conviction as she begged Leela to reconsider. Breaking off a pilgrimage like this, for no good reason, would rouse the wrath of Shiva. When Leela said that the occurrences of her life were surely of no interest to a deity, Aunt gripped her shoulders with trembling hands.

"Stop!" she cried, her nostrils flaring. "You don't know what you're saying! That bad-luck woman, she's bewitched you!"

How many unguessed layers there were to people, skins that came loose at an unexpected tug, revealing raw, fearful flesh. Amazing, that folks could love one another in the face of such unreliability! It made Leela at once sad and hopeful.

◆ ◆ ◆

Walking downhill, Leela has drifted into a fantasy. In it, she lives in a small roof-top flat on the outskirts of Calcutta. Mrs. Das, whom she has rescued from the women's hostel, lives with her. They have a maid who shops and runs their errands, so the women rarely need to leave the flat. Each evening they sit on the terrace beside the potted roses and chrysanthemums (Mrs. Das has turned out to be a skilful gardener) and listen to music—a tape of Bengali folk songs (Mrs. Das looks like a person who would enjoy that), or maybe one of Leela's jazz CDs, to which Mrs. Das listens with bemused attention. When they wish each other good-night, she touches Leela's arm. "Thank you," she says, her eyes deep as a forest.

They have come to a riverbed. There isn't much water, but the boulders on which they step are slippery with moss. It's starting to rain, and the guide eyes the sky nervously. He pulls at the balking mule, which stumbles. Mrs. Das gives a harsh, crow-like cry and flings out her hand. Leela grasps it and holds on until they reach the other side.

"Thank you," says Mrs. Das. It is the first time she has smiled, and Leela sees that her eyes are, indeed, deep as a forest.

◆ ◆ ◆

"But Madam!" the proprietor at the Nataraja Inn cries to Leela in an English made shaky by distress. "You people are not to be coming back for two more days! Already I am giving your rooms to other pilgrim party. Whole hotel is full. This is middle of pilgrim season— other hotels are also being full." He gives Leela and Mrs. Das, who are shivering in their wet clothes, an accusing look. "How is it you two are returned so soon?"

The guide, who has brought in the bedrolls, says something in a rapid pahari dialect that Leela cannot follow. The clerk pulls back his head in a swift, turtle-like motion and gives Mrs. Das a glance full of misgiving.

"Please," Leela says. "We're very tired, and it's raining. Can't you find us something?"

"Sorry, Madams. Maybe Mughal Gardens in marketplace is having space—"

Leela can feel Mrs. Das's placid eyes on her. It is obvious that she trusts the younger woman to handle the situation. Leela sighs. Being a savior in real life has drawbacks she never imagined in her rooftop fantasy. Recalling something Aunt Seema said earlier, she digs in the waistband of her sari and comes up with a handful of rupee notes which she lays on the counter.

The clerk rocks back on his heels, torn between avarice and superstition. Then his hand darts out and covers the notes. "We are having a small storeroom on top of hotel. Big enough for one person only."

He parts his lips in an ingenuous smile. "Maybe older madam can try Mughal Gardens?"

Leela gives the clerk a reprimanding look. "We'll manage," she says.

◆ ◆ ◆

The clerk has not exaggerated. The room, filled with discarded furniture, is about as big as Leela's queen-size bed in America. Even after the sweeper carries all the junk out into the corridor, there isn't enough space to open the two bedrolls without their edges overlapping. Leela tries to hide her dismay. It strikes her that since she arrived in India, she has not been alone even once. With sudden homesickness, she longs for her wide, flat bedroom, its uncomplicated vanilla walls, its window from which she had looked out onto nothing more demanding than a clump of geraniums.

"I've caused you a lot of inconvenience."

Mrs. Das's voice is small but not apologetic. (Leela rather likes this.) "You shouldn't have come back with me," she adds matter-of-factly. "What if I *am* bad luck, like people believe?"

"Do you believe that?" Leela asks. She strains to hear Mrs. Das's answer above the crash of thunder.

"Belief, disbelief," Mrs. Das shrugs. "So many things I believed to be one way turned out otherwise. I believed my son's marriage wouldn't change things between us. I believed I would get to Shiva's shrine, and all my problems would disappear. Last night on the mountain I believed the best thing for me would be to fall into a crevasse and die." She smiles with unexpected sweetness as she says this. "But now—here we are together."

Together. When Mrs. Das says it in Bengali, eksangay, the word opens inside Leela with a faint, ringing sound, like a distant temple bell.

"I have something I want to give you," Mrs. Das says.

"No, no," says Leela, embarrassed. "Please, I'd rather you didn't."

"He who gives," says Mrs. Das, "must be prepared to receive." Is this an ancient Indian saying, or one that she has made up herself? And what exactly does it mean? Is giving then a privilege, in return for which you must allow others the opportunity to do the same? Mrs. Das unclasps a thin gold chain she is wearing. She leans forward and Leela feels her fingers fumbling for a moment on the nape

208

of her neck. She wants to protest, to explain to Mrs. Das that she has always hated jewelry, all that metal clamped around you. But she is caught in a web of unfamiliar ideas. Is giving the touchstone by which the lives of strangers become your own? The expression on Mrs. Das's face is secretive, prayerful. And then the skin-warm, almost weightless chain is around Leela's throat.

Mrs. Das switches off the naked bulb that hangs on a bit of wire from the ceiling. The two of them lie down, each on her blanket, and listen to the wind, which moans and rattles the shutters like a madwoman wanting to be let in. Leela hopes Aunt Seema is safe, that the storm has not hit the mountain the way it has Pahelgaon. But the world outside this square, contained room has receded so far that she is unable to feel anxiety. Rain falls all around her, insulating as a lullaby. If she were to stretch out her arm, she would touch Mrs. Das's face.

She says, softly, "Once I tried to kill myself."

Mrs. Das says nothing. Perhaps she is asleep.

Leela finds herself speaking of the pills, the ambulance, the scraped-out space inside her afterwards. Perhaps it had always been there, and she had not known? She talks about her father and mother, their unbearable courtesy, which she sees only this moment as having been unbearable. She asks questions about togetherness, about being alone. What the value of each might be. She sends her words into the night, and does not need a reply.

She has never spoken so much in her life. In the middle of a sentence, she falls asleep.

◆ ◆ ◆

Leela is dreaming. In the dream, the glacial trails have been washed away by rain. She takes a false step, sinks into slush. Ice presses against her chest. She opens her mouth to cry for help, and it too fills with ice. With a thunderous crack, blackness opens above her, a brilliant and brutal absence of light. She knows it has found her finally, her unlucky star.

Leela wakes, her heart clenched painfully like an arthritic fist. How real the dream was. Even now she feels the freezing weight on her chest, hears the ricochet of the cracked-open sky. But no, it is not just a dream. Her blanket is soaked through, and the floor is awash with water. She scrambles for the light switch and sees, in the dim

209

glare, a corner of the roof hanging down, swinging drunkenly. In the midst of all this, Mrs. Das sleeps on, covers pulled over her head. Leela is visited by a crazy wish to lie down beside her.

"Quick, quick!" she cries, shaking her. "We have to get out of here before that roof comes down."

Mrs. Das doesn't seem to understand what Leela wants from her. Another gust of wind hits the roof, which gives an ominous creak. Her eyes widen, but she makes no move to sit up.

"Come on," shouts Leela. She starts to drag her to the door. Mrs. Das offers neither resistance nor help. A long time back Leela had taken a CPR course, she has forgotten why. Mrs. Das's body, slack and rubbery, reminds her of the dummy on whose chest she had pounded with earnest energy. The thought depresses her, and this depression is the last emotion she registers before something hits her head.

◆ ◆ ◆

Leela lies on a lumpy mattress. Even with her eyes closed, she knows that the clothes she is wearing—a baggy blouse, a limp cotton sari which swathes her loosely—are not hers. Her head feels stuffed with steel shavings. Is she in heaven, having died a heroic death? But surely celestial bedding would be more comfortable, celestial clothing more elegant—even in India? She is ashamed of having thought that last phrase. She moves her head a little. The jab of pain is like disappointed lightning.

"Doctor, doctor, she's waking up," Aunt Seema says from somewhere, her voice damp and wobbly like a biscuit that's been dunked in tea. But why is Leela thinking like this? She knows she should appreciate her aunt's loving concern and say something to reassure her. But it is so private, so comfortable, behind her closed eyes.

"Finally," says the doctor's voice. "I was getting worried." Leela can smell his breath—it's cigarettes, a brand she does not know. It smells of cloves. When she has forgotten everything else, she thinks, she will remember the odors of this journey.

"Can you hear me, Leela?" the doctor asks. "Can you open your eyes?" He taps on her cheek with maddening persistence until she gives up and glares at him.

"You're lucky, young lady," he says as he changes the bandage around her head. "You should be thankful you were hit by a piece of wood. Now if that had been a sheet of rusted metal—"

Lucky. Thankful. Leela doesn't trust such words. They change their meaning as they swoop, sharp-clawed, about her head. The room is full of women; they wring their hands in gestures that echo her aunt's. She closes her eyes again. There's a question she must ask, an important one—but when she tries to catch it in a net of words, it dissolves into red fog.

"It's all my fault," Aunt Seema says in a broken voice that baffles Leela. Why should Aunt feel so much distress at problems which are, after all, hers alone? "Leela doesn't understand these things—how can she?—but I should have made her stay away from that accursed woman—"

"Do try to be quiet." The doctor's voice is testy, as though he has heard this lament many times already. "Give her the medicine and let her rest."

Someone holds Leela's head, brings a cup to her lips. The medicine is thick and vile. She forces it down her throat with harsh satisfaction. Aunt sobs softly, in deference to the doctor's orders. Her friends murmur consolations. From time to time, phrases rise like a refrain from their crooning: *the poor girl, Shiva have mercy, that bad-luck woman, oh, what will I tell your mother.*

A commotion at the door.

"I've got to see her, just for a minute, just to make sure she's all right—"

There's a heaving inside Leela.

"No," says one of the women. "Daktar-babu said no excitement."

"Please, I won't talk to her—I'll just take a look."

"Over my dead body you will," Aunt Seema bursts out. "Haven't you done her enough harm already? Go away. Leela, you tell her yourself—"

Leela doesn't want to tell anyone anything. She wants only to sleep. Is that too much to ask for? A line comes to her from a poem, *Death's second self which seals up all in rest.* She imagines snow, great fluffy quilts of it, packed around her. But the voices scrape at her, *Leela, Leela, Leela . . .*

The room is full of evening. Leela sees Mrs. Das at the door, trying to push her way past the determined bulk of the doctor's wife. Her disheveled hair radiates from her head like crinkly white wires, giving her, for a moment, the look of an alien in a *Star Trek* movie. When she sees that Leela's eyes are open, she stops struggling and reaches out toward her.

Why does Leela do what she does next? Is it the medication, which makes her lightheaded? The pain, which won't let her think? Or is it some dark, genetic strain which, unknown to her, has pierced her pragmatic, American upbringing with its sharp, knotted root? At times, later, she will tell herself, *I didn't know what I was doing.* At other times, she'll say, *liar.* For doesn't her response to Mrs. Das come from the intrinsic and fearful depths of who she is? The part of her that knows she is no savior?

Leela sits up in bed. "Aunt's right," she says. Her teeth chatter as though she is fevered. "All of them are right. You *are* cursed. Go away. Leave me alone."

"No," says Mrs. Das. But it is a pale sound, without conviction.

"Yes!" says Leela. "Yes!" She grasps the chain Mrs. Das has given her and yanks at it. The worn gold gives easily. Falling, it makes a small, skittery sound on the wood floor.

Darkness is bursting open around Seema like black chrysanthemums.

Mrs. Das stares at the chain, then turns and stumbles from the room. Her shadow, long and misshapen, touches Leela once. Then it, too, is gone.

◆ ◆ ◆

The pilgrimage party makes much of Leela as she lies recovering. The women bring her little gifts from their forays into town—an embroidered purse, a bunch of Kashmiri grapes, a lacquered jewelry box. When they hold out the presents, Leela burrows her hands into her blanket. But the women merely nod to each other. They whisper words like *shock* and *been through so much.* They hand the gifts to Aunt, who promises to keep them safely until Leela is better. When they leave, she feels like a petulant child.

From the doorway, the men ask Aunt Seema how Leela is coming along. Their voices are gruff and hushed, their eyes furtive with awe—as though she were a martyr-saint who took upon herself the bad luck that would have otherwise fallen on them. Is it cynical to think this? There is no one anymore whom Leela can ask.

212

◆ ◆ ◆

On the way back to Srinagar, where the party will catch the train to Calcutta, by unspoken consent Leela is given the best seat on the bus, up front near the big double windows.

"It's a fine view, and it won't joggle you so much," says one of the women, plumping up a pillow for her. Another places a footrest near her legs. Aunt Seema unscrews a thermos and pours her a glass of pomegranate juice—to replace all the blood Leela lost, she says. The juice is the color of blood. Its thin tartness makes Leela's mouth pucker up, and Aunt says, in a disappointed voice, "Oh dear, is it not so sweet then? Why, that Bahadur at the hotel swore to me—"

Leela feels ungracious, boorish. She feels angry for feeling this way. "I have a headache," she says and turns to the window where, hidden behind her sunglasses, she watches the rest of the party get on the bus. Amid shouts and laughter, the bus begins to move.

She waits until the bus has lurched its way around three hairpin bends. Then she says, "Aunt—?" She tries to make her voice casual, but the words come out in a croak.

"Yes, dear? A little more juice?" Aunt asks hopefully.

"Where is Mrs. Das? Why didn't she get on the bus?"

Aunt fiddles with the catch of her purse. Her face indicates her discomfort at the baldness of Leela's questions. A real Indian woman would have known to approach the matter delicately, sideways.

But the doctor's wife, who is sitting behind them, leans forward to say, "Oh, her! She went off somewhere on her own, when was it, three, no, four nights ago, right after she created that ruckus in your sickroom. She didn't take her bedroll with her, or even her suitcase. Strange, no? Personally, I think she's a little bit touched up here." She taps her head emphatically.

Misery swirls, acidic, through Leela's insides. She raises her hand with great effort to cover her mouth, so it will not spill out.

"Are you okay, dear?" Aunt asks.

"She looks terribly pale," the doctor's wife says. "It's all these winding roads—enough to make anyone vomity."

"I might have some lemon drops," says Aunt, rummaging in her handbag.

Leela accepts the sour candy and turns again to the window. Behind her she hears the doctor's wife's carrying whisper, "If I were you, I'd get a puja done for your niece once you get to Calcutta. You know, to avert the evil eye—"

Outside the bus, mountains and waterfalls are speeding past Leela. Sunlight slides like opportunity from the narrow green leaves of debdaru trees and is lost in the underbrush. What had the guide said, at the start of the trip, about expiation? Leela cannot remember. And even if she did, would she be capable of executing those gestures, delicate and filled with power, like the movements of a Bharatnatyam dancer, which connect humans to the gods and to each other? Back in America, her life waits to claim her, unchanged, impervious, smelling like floor polish. In the dusty window, her reflection is a blank oval. She takes off her dark glasses to see better, but the features which peer back at her are unfamiliar, as though they belong to someone she has never met.

Nominated by Katherine Min, Agni

TRAVELING WITH MOTHER

memoir by KATHERINE TAYLOR

from ZYZZYVA

THERE ARE NO FEMALE GYNECOLOGISTS on my family's medical plan. I didn't see a doctor for six years, because I refused to be examined by one of my father's golf partners. When the dog had cancer, Daddy Taylor flew it from Fresno to UC-Davis for special treatment. When my hair was falling out, he sent me to see a man who told me, "Eat more protein. See a psychiatrist. Your father has a fine swing."

My mother didn't think I needed a psychiatrist. She thought I needed a leisurely mother-daughter drive across America.

That summer people in the Midwest were dying from the heat. I had never thought about the Midwest except as space on the map between California and New York. That summer my brother ran an unmarked cop car off the road on the 99 between Stockton and Sacramento and was charged with assault with a deadly weapon. My grandmother was moved out of her house and into The Home. My obese Auntie Petra lost 75 pounds by having a shake for breakfast, a shake for lunch, and a sensible dinner.

My hair came out in clumps. In New York, I was worried and nervous and couldn't concentrate. I had moved there the previous autumn to act and write, but found myself too homesick to do anything but cry and socialize. I threw enormous parties to make myself feel less lonesome, and my neighbors left nasty notes threatening to tear me asunder. A man wearing roller blades molested me on 68th St. I had the screens removed from my windows in case I decided to jump out. Instead, I decided to fly home to California.

In Los Angeles, I called my hairdresser. His name is Armando and I roll the R. I said, "I don't care how busy you are. I have an emergency. My hair is falling out." He said, "First you come, we cut it all off. Then you stop worrying about whatever you worry." He rolls his Rs too. Armando knows all my secrets.

In Los Angeles, I met with a producer who had written a part for me in a film financed by rich Germans. I told him, "I'm not an actress anymore. I won't prostitute my emotions." Afterwards I felt ridiculous. Afterwards I wondered why I seemed to have no control over the things that came out of my mouth.

The dog died the day I arrived at my parents' house in Fresno. The bionic dog, the three-thousand-dollar chemotherapy dog. Cancer ate his ears off. Daddy Taylor had brought that mutt dog home after he ran over my Dalmatian with his truck on my tenth birthday. My brothers and I had marked the Dalmatian's grave in the backyard with a cross and stones. After the mutt dog died of cancer, I suggested we bury it in the pet cemetery outside. Daddy said, "What cemetery?"

I said, "Where you buried Buttons after you smashed her."

He said, "Katherine, I scraped that dog off the driveway and threw it in the garbage."

I said, "That's against sanitation laws."

My mother agreed. She got wild-eyed and said, "Your father yells at me when I break the speed limit."

In Fresno, the internist I saw for my hair asked if I were anorexic. I told him no. He told me I was probably anorexic whether I realized it or not. His nurse took my blood and stuck me with a needle three or four times before she found my vein.

The dermatologist looked at my scalp and told me I could be having a nervous breakdown. I told him I felt too bored to be having a nervous breakdown. He told me my hair would grow back.

The gynecologist was a family friend. He said, "Your father has a full head of hair. Your reproductive organs are all in order. I'll see you at brunch on Sunday."

My mother waited for me outside each doctor's office in her car listening to news on the radio. When I returned after an unenlightening examination, she would say, "Those doctors don't know what

216

they're talking about. You and I need to go see Mount Rushmore." I told her I had no interest in Mount Rushmore. I told her I could not possibly enjoy Mount Rushmore while I was dealing with the trauma of hair loss. I said, "Mother, I have no time in my life to go driving about with you all summer." She said, "You'll be sorry when I'm dead."

She called AAA to map out our trip. Mother began to see Mount Rushmore as the promised land, the solution to our suffering. We packed the car full of bottled water and rice cakes. We bought packages of red licorice and vitamin C. Mother bought dozens of Peppermint Patties and locked them in the glove compartment. She told me, "These are for me and you can't eat them. Let me have only one a day." My father bought me books on tape: *The Prince*, Oliver Sacks, the complete works of Kant. I brought along language tapes and thought I might spend the trip learning to speak Hebrew.

The first day we drove as far as Portland, where Mother was upset with the hotel accommodations. She refused to get out of the car at the Holiday Inn. "I don't like the looks of this place," she said. "There's no one out here to help us with our luggage."

I told her, "Mother, this is a road trip. You cannot have fancy room service and concierge on a road trip."

In our room she found a toothpick on the floor and refused to take off her shoes. She wouldn't use the bathroom or touch the phone without a tissue. In the morning we drove seven miles out of Portland to find an IHOP, because Mother craved Cream of Wheat pancakes. She complained about the service. We were bored by downtown Portland and left early for Washington.

We stopped at a gas station where Mother bought an aerosol can full of bleach. "For the toilets," she said.

"You never sit on the toilets anyway," I said.

"You never know what could happen," she warned me.

I didn't know you could buy aerosol cans full of bleach.

At the Seattle Sheraton we changed rooms four times. The first room had an acceptable view, but construction eight floors down which Mother thought might disturb her napping. The second room was quiet, but hadn't as nice a view as the first. The third room was quiet and had a nice view, but wasn't as large as the first or second. When we arrived at the fourth room, Mother told the bellhop, "This will be fine. Leave our bags here and thank you very much." The

217

bellhop refused to leave, suggesting we sit in the room a while and try it out before we made our final decision. Mother waited a moment. We all stood still without speaking. Eventually she said, "No, this room won't do either. I hear a buzzing sound." I heard no buzzing sound. The woman at the desk said it might have been the air conditioner. The hotel moved us once more and sent up a bottle of champagne.

We ate dinner at a fish restaurant on the pier. Mother disapproved of where we had been seated. "I don't understand why we cannot sit by the window," she said. She protested to the hostess, the waitress, the bus boy and finally the manager, who brought us free oysters and told us the window seats were all reserved. I had a martini.

Mother tired quickly of Seattle. She tired of latte and people in combat boots. We tried a trip to British Columbia; we thought we might see the gardens there, but Mother tired of that, too, after bad sandwiches and a quick argument with the people at the desk of the Empress Hotel. Less than 24 hours after our arrival in Seattle, we began heading east.

In the car Mother insisted on listening to Christmas music. Through Washington and half of Idaho, I slept and Mother sang along to "Feliz Navidad." She drove 100 miles per hour.

At dawn in small-town Idaho, she turned off the freeway. We had driven all night, unable to find a hotel to suit Mother's standards. Idaho smelled like pine trees and wet dirt. I needed to brush my teeth.

"Would you like me to drive?" I asked.

She pulled into an empty IHOP parking lot. "I'm stopping here."

"I'll drive."

"No, we're going to eat here."

"I think they're closed."

"I want my Cream of Wheat pancakes."

"Mother, they're not open."

"We'll just wait here until it's time."

We waited two hours. At precisely 7:30, when the doors to the pancake house should have opened, Mother banged on the locked front door. "Let us in! You have hungry travelers waiting!"

"Don't be so disagreeable," I told her.

"I'm not disagreeable," she said. "They're late opening." She banged again until an ordinary blonde girl in braids and white nurse shoes unlocked the door. "I'm terribly hungry," Mother said to her. "I don't mean to be disagreeable." The blonde girl seated us by the window.

I smiled to cheer myself up and drank a pot of coffee.

Through Montana, Mother slept and I learned Hebrew from tapes. She snored and yelled at me, even while dreaming, if she sensed I was driving faster than 80 miles per hour. Outside of Bozeman, she woke up. "I need a shower," she said. "I need some room service and a bed and toothpaste."

"There's a Best Western in Bozeman."

"No! I cannot tolerate Best Western! No Holiday Inns, no Quality Inns. Let's listen to Rush Limbaugh."

"No," I told her. "Don't you want me to be bilingual?"

"I need some soap." She picked up the cell phone and dialed the American Express travel office. "Hello, this is Elizabeth Taylor. Not that Elizabeth Taylor. I'm in the middle of Montana and where is the closest Four Seasons?"

"You're making my hair fall out."

"How far is that from Montana?" She turned to me, "The closest Four Seasons is in Minnesota." She spoke into the phone, "Well, I can't drive that far! I need something immediately. Thank you very much." She hung up.

"You're *rofef*," I told her. I had learned that from my tape. It meant "crazy," and I was excited to say it.

"There's a hotel inside Yellowstone Park," she said. "We can turn around and drive there." She navigated from an AAA map.

We arrived at the Yellowstone's gate early in the evening. The woman at the entrance booth told us all accommodations within the park were booked and, in order to exit the park before it closed, we would have to drive through without stopping. Mother looked as if the news quite devastated her. I told her not to worry.

We drove through the park slowly, stopping frequently to look at deer, buffalo, hot springs. Mother wasn't impressed. "We've been here 15 minutes and I haven't seen one bar yet!" she exclaimed. "I'm going to get our money back."

"There are not supposed to be bars in national parks, Mother."

"There are, too. What do you know?! Davy Crockett killed him a bar when he was only three."

The parking lot was full at the Old Faithful Inn. I told Mother to wait outside. I took her credit card and went in to the desk. "Do you have an available room for Elizabeth Taylor?" I imagined myself quite together and beautiful and tried to forget I hadn't showered in two days.

"Pardon?" The receptionist was a college boy whose name tag said, "BOB Oregon."

"Elizabeth Taylor would like to stay at the hotel tonight." I spoke quietly and in my best Hollywood lockjaw.

"Elizabeth Taylor?"

"Yes, thank you." I handed him my mother's credit card.

He read the name on the card and smiled excitedly. "Just a moment." He left and came back a moment later with the manager and a key. "The hotel would be honored to have Ms. Taylor stay with us," the manager said.

"Oh, she'll be very pleased."

I collected my mother outside and shuffled her in past the desk beneath a hooded raincoat.

That night we ate grilled-cheese sandwiches I bought at the Old Faithful Diner and drank bottled iced tea from the Old Faithful Market. We tried to sleep early, but the beds were hard. We tossed about, each pretending to be asleep.

In the dark Mother said, "Is your hair falling out?"

"Not so much anymore," I told her. We listened to the awake people in rooms around us. "I'm sleeping," I told her.

She paused a moment, sighing. "Are you sad, really?"

"I'm not sad." I said it as if she had asked a ridiculous question.

"Are you?" She was whispering now.

"Yes, Mother. I am sad. My hair is falling out."

She lingered a moment in the space between speaking and not. "Daddy's friends think you need a psychiatrist."

"They're all bored Fresno doctors. They're afraid of me." I whispered, too, now. "I don't want to be on those drugs."

"I don't, either," she said. "I want your hair to stop falling out."

"Me, too."

"Maybe if you were happy."

"I don't have to always feel like being happy, Mother." I turned to the wall, away from her.

"Neither do I," she whispered, still facing me.

"Those doctors are rofef."

"Daddy's friends are idiots."

"Be quiet, I'm sleeping."

The next day we drove about Yellowstone. We saw buffalo and moose, deer and volcanic activity. We walked off the paths and park rangers yelled at us. We were too impatient to wait around for Old Faithful to erupt.

We missed the heat in South Dakota. The day we found Mount Rushmore, the rain came down in hurricane volume. Tourists took refuge in the gift shop or snack bar. Mother and I stood outside in the lightning, drenched but not cold, staring at the carved faces.

I said, "This isn't as climactic as it was supposed to be."

"I should have seen this a long time ago," she said.

We had an argument just outside of South Dakota. I didn't give her enough warning for a turn-off, and we had to drive an extra 32 miles to get back on our route. She shouted at me with all her might. Neither of us apologized. By the time we arrived in Minneapolis that night, we had not exchanged a word all day. She finally said, "If you don't want to travel with me, I'll leave you off at the airport and you can just fly back to New York by yourself."

"That's fine," I said.

"Roll down the window and ask someone where the airport is."

"Find a gas station."

"Just roll down the window!"

"I hear you Mother, don't shout."

"I'm taking you to the airport."

"Fine."

"I don't know how we're going to find the airport."

"I'm sure there will be a sign."

We never saw a sign. Instead, we found the Four Seasons and stayed there overnight. Mother's mood improved considerably. We did not change rooms. Still, she refused to take off her socks and told me twice not to sit on the bedspreads. "People have sat on those with their dirty bottoms," she warned me. We ordered hot chocolate and sandwiches from room service.

My hair had stopped falling out by the time my mother left me in New York. The doormen were happy to see her. She tips them every time they open the door. Normally she likes to visit for weeks on end, but this time she didn't stay long.

221

"I have to go to your little brother's felony hearing."

"He'll be happy to see you there."

She bought me new towels, dusted the bookshelves, and put all my books in alphabetical order.

She continued down the southern route, alone, to California.

Nominated by David St. John

PRAYER AGAINST THE EXPERTS AND THEIR WAYS

fiction by PAUL MALISZEWSKI

from COLORADO REVIEW

THE ARMY OF EXPERTS has advanced roughly halfway across the plains heading east. Late last year the experts' elite brigades, a highly trained force numbering in the hundreds at least, landed at six strategic points along the Eastern Seaboard. The elite brigades came ashore under cover of darkness. They wore wet suits, which they peeled each other out of upon landing. Underneath they wore suits, ties, shoes. They made no fires and no fuss. They hardly made any noise. They ate their food out of cans, washed the cans in the ocean, and separated their garbage into piles of that which can be recycled and that which cannot. On their persons they carried briefcases and binders stuffed with papers. It was plain to see that the papers were of a statistical and columnar nature—that much was clear. They possessed supporting graphics, a series of illustrative models, various pedagogical devices, and some unverified number of laser pointers. Certainly pie charts were on the premises somewhere. According to several independent witnesses who have recently come forward, the experts mimed and gestured their way through their memorized public speeches and presentations after eating. Our very best guess is that the experts undertook the performances on the beach as a final preparation before invading, simply to smooth over any minute rough spots remaining in their body language, their efficacy, and their overall likability when expressed as a percentage. The laser pointers are of particular concern because they are thought to be so impressive, so coolly efficient.

According to our intelligence, the locations of the landing of their numbers have now, for our purposes, been irretrievably lost to the experts. Those cities have fallen to their control. Our map is turning blue, gradually, as the experts make their way across the country. As our pins come out their blue pins go in. It's a miserable business, updating the map with the pins.

Our best forward reports indicate that they, the elite brigades, are busy, working their way west. According to sources close to the administration, the brigades traveled in a southerly direction before, but that's all changed, overnight almost. Now they're working their way west, toward us, working to make the conventional wisdom more conventional, or, in some cases, working to change the conventional wisdom. However it suits them. It hardly matters which, really. What matters is that everything and every person they touch, they reduce to evidence, example, indicator.

For example, take Samantha Wilson, age twenty-six, lifelong resident of Jamestown, New York, currently residing at 1405 East Avenue, Apartment 3. Wilson is a mother of three children, ages four, two, and six months. Wilson works in a dentist's office, doing the insurance paperwork. She enjoys making desserts, watching television, and going to the park. Wilson, or whatever is left of her now, may be best remembered as a component in certain published reports on life expectancy, infant mortality, family income as it correlates to education, etc., etc. The experts are turning us into brittle things, is the point, brittle and thin. By the summer solstice their brigades will join the main army, combine forces, rally and whatnot, and have their way with us. Presently they will meet at 40° north latitude, 120° 35' west longitude. Such is their plan as I know it.

We lie between the two approaching camps.

I know all this because I was an expert, or I should say I believed myself expert in certain areas, specifically virtual mathematics and various applied manipulations of infinity as they relate to various stock market indices. As some of you may know, I've since repudiated that period in my life, however, and so stand before you today a new man, decidedly and vigorously inexpert—joyously inexpert, in fact. And I stand before you to warn you and to say that this army of experts must be stopped. Now, I could stand up here and show you certain bar graphs and line charts that would horrify you, possibly anger you, perhaps even incite violence, but instead let me say this: I will help you. If you allow me to do so. Let me. Let me help you. I will do what I can. We all must. If you choose. For our effort will require your total cooperation, of course. If you should be willing. Dedication, devotion, and commitment—you are, I trust, familiar with all these qualities? But let any one of you be unsure or even momentarily waver in the slightest and we will most assuredly fail. How bad would that be? It would be bad, let me tell you. But don't think of that, not now. Put it out of your minds. It's all just too depressing. Look, if we work together we will succeed. Surely we will succeed. Listen, how could we not succeed? In the end, I mean.

Now, this is what we will do.

Nominated by Michael Martone

THE PART OF THE BEE'S BODY EMBEDDED IN THE FLESH

by CAROL FROST

from LYRIC

The bee-boy, *merops apiater*, on sultry thundery days
filled his bosom between his coarse shirt and his skin
with bees—his every meal wild honey.
He had no apprehension of their stings or didn't mind
and gave himself—his palate, the soft tissues of his throat—
what Rubens gave to the sun's illumination
stealing like fingers across a woman's thigh
and Van Gogh's brushwork heightened.
Whatever it means, why not say it hurts—
the mind's raw, gold coiling whirled against
air currents, want, and beauty? I *will* say beauty.

Nominated by Michael Waters, Elizabeth Spires

I DEMAND TO KNOW WHERE YOU'RE TAKING ME

fiction by DAN CHAON

from EPOCH

C HERYL WOKE IN THE MIDDLE OF THE NIGHT and she could hear the macaw talking to himself—or laughing, rather, as if he had just heard a good joke. "Haw haw haw!" he went. "Haw haw haw!" A perfect imitation of her brother-in-law, Wendell, that forced, ironic guffaw.

She sat up in bed and the sound stopped. Perhaps she had imagined it? Her husband, Tobe, was still soundly asleep next to her, but this didn't mean anything. He had always been an abnormally heavy sleeper, a snorer, and lately he had been drinking more before bed— he'd been upset ever since Wendell had gone to prison.

And she, too, was upset, anxious. She sat there, silent, her heart quickened, listening. Had the children been awakened by it? She waited, in the way she did when they were infants. Back then, her brain would jump awake. Was that a baby crying?

No, there was nothing. The house was quiet.

The bird, the macaw, was named Wild Bill. She had never especially liked animals, had never wanted one in her home, but what could be done? Wild Bill had arrived on the same day that Tobe and his other brothers, Carlin and Randy, had pulled into the driveway

227

with a moving van full of Wendell's possessions. She'd stood there, watching as item after item was carried into the house, where it would remain, in temporary but indefinite storage. In the basement, shrouded in tarps, was Wendell's furniture: couch, kitchen set, bed, piano. There were his boxes of books and miscellaneous items, she didn't know what. She hadn't asked. The only thing that she wouldn't allow were Wendell's shotguns. These were being kept at Carlin's place.

It might not have bothered her so much if it had not been for Wild Bill, who remained a constant reminder of Wendell's presence in her home. As she suspected, the bird's day-to-day care had fallen to her. It was she who made sure that Wild Bill had food and water, and it was she who cleaned away the excrement-splashed newspaper at the bottom of his cage.

But despite the fact that she was his primary caretaker, Wild Bill didn't seem to like her very much. Mostly, he ignored her—as if she were some kind of *wife*, a negligible figure whom he expected to serve him. He seemed to like the children best, and of course they were very attached to him as well. They liked to show him off to their friends, and to repeat his funny sayings. He liked to ride on their shoulders, edging sideways, lifting his wings lightly, for balance. Occasionally, as they walked around with him, he would laugh in that horrible way. "Haw, haw, haw!" he would squawk, and the children loved it.

But she herself was often uncomfortable with the things Wild Bill said. For example, he frequently said, "Hello, Sexy," to their eight-year-old daughter, Jodie. There was something lewd in the macaw's voice, Cheryl felt, a suggestiveness she found troubling. She didn't think it was appropriate for a child to hear herself called "sexy," especially since Jodie seemed to respond, blushing—flattered.

"Hello, Sexy," was, of course, one of Wendell's sayings, along with "Good God, Baby!" and "Smell my feet!" both of which were also part of Wild Bill's main repertoire. They had subsequently become catch-phrases for her children. She'd hear Evan, their six-year-old, out in the yard, shouting "Good God, Baby!" and then mimicking that laugh. And even Tobe had picked up on the sophomoric retort "Smell my feet!" It bothered her more than she could explain. It was silly, but it sickened her, conjuring up a morbid fascination with human stink, something vulgar and tiring. They repeated it and repeated it until finally, one night at dinner, she'd actually slammed her hand down on the table. "Stop it!" she cried. "I can't stand it any-more. It's ruining my appetite!"

And they sat there, suppressing guilty grins. Looking down at their plates.

How delicate she was! How lady-like! How prudish!

But there was something else about the phrase, something she couldn't mention. It was a detail from the series of rapes that had oc-curred in their part of the state. The assaulted women had been at-tacked in their homes, blindfolded, a knife pressed against their skin. The first thing the attacker did was to force the women to kneel down and lick his bare feet. Then he moved on to more brutal things.

These were the crimes that Wendell had been convicted of, three months before. He had been convicted of only three of the six rapes he was accused of, but it was generally assumed that they had all been perpetrated by the same person. He was serving a sentence of no less than twenty-five years in prison, though his case was now be-ginning the process of appeals. He swore that he was innocent.

And they believed him—his family, all of them. They were all de-termined that Wendell would be exonerated, but it was especially important to Tobe, for Tobe had been Wendell's lawyer. Wendell had insisted upon it—"Who else could defend me better than my brother?" he'd said—and Tobe had finally given in, had defended Wendell in court, despite the fact that he was a specialist in family law, despite the fact that he had no experience as a criminal attorney. It was a "no-brainer," Tobe had said at the time, "No jury would be-lieve it for a second." She had listened, nodding, as Tobe called the case flimsy, "A travesty," he said, "a bumbled investigation."

And so it was a blow when the jury, after deliberating for over a week, returned a guilty verdict. Tobe had actually let out a small cry, had put his hands over his face, and he was still in a kind of dizzied state. He believed now that if he had only recused himself, Wendell would have been acquitted. It had affected him, it had made him strange and moody and distant. It frightened her—this new, filmy look in his eyes, the drinking, the way he would wander around the house, muttering to himself.

She felt a sort of hitch in her throat, a hitch in her brain. Here he was, laughing with Jodie and Evan, his eyes bright with amusement as she slammed her hand down. She didn't understand it. When the bird croaked, "Smell my feet," didn't Tobe make the same associations that she did? Didn't he cringe? Didn't he have the same doubts?

Apparently not. She tried to make eye contact with him, to plead her case in an exchange of gazes, but he would have none of it. He smirked into his hand, as if he was one of the children.

And maybe she was over-reacting. A parrot! It was such a minor thing, wasn't it? Perhaps not worth bringing up, not worth its potential for argument. He stretched out in bed beside her and she continued to read her book, aware of the heaviness emanating from him, aware that his mind was going over and over some detail once again, retracing it; pacing around its circumference. In the past few months, it had become increasingly difficult to read him—his mood shifts, his reactions, his silences.

Once, shortly after the trial had concluded, she had tried to talk to him about it. "It's not your fault," she had told him. "You did the best you could."

She had been surprised at the way his eyes had narrowed, by the flare of anger, of pure scorn, which had never before been directed at her. "Oh, really?" he said acidly. "Whose fault is it, then? That an innocent man went to prison?" He glared at her, witheringly, and she took a step back. "Listen, Cheryl," he'd said. "You might not understand this, but this is my brother we're talking about. My little brother. Greeting card sentiments are not a fucking comfort to me." And he'd turned and walked away from her.

He'd later apologized, of course. "Don't ever talk to me that way again," she'd said, "I won't stand for it." And he agreed, nodding vigorously, he had been out of line, he was under a lot of stress and had taken it out on her. But in truth, an unspoken rift had remained between them in the months since. There was something about him, she thought, that she didn't recognize, something she hadn't seen before.

Cheryl had always tried to avoid the subject of Tobe's brothers. He was close to them, and she respected that. Both of Tobe's parents had died before Cheryl met him—the mother of breast cancer when Tobe was sixteen, the father a little more than a decade later, of cirrhosis—and this had knit them together. They were close in an old-fashioned way, like brothers in westerns or gangster films, touching in a way, though when she had first met them she never imagined what it would be like once they became fixtures in her life.

In the beginning, she had liked the idea of moving back to Cheyenne, Wyoming, where Tobe had grown up. The state, and the way Tobe had described it, had seemed romantic to her. He had come back to set up a small law office, with his specialty in family court. She had a degree in educational administration, and was able, without much trouble, to find a job as a guidance counselor at a local high school.

It had seemed like a good plan at the time. Her own family was scattered: a sister in Vancouver; a half-sister in Chicago, where Cheryl had grown up. Her father, in Florida, was remarried to a woman about Cheryl's age, and had a four-year-old son, whom she could hardly think of as a brother; her mother, now divorced for a third time, lived alone on a houseboat near San Diego. She rarely saw or spoke to any of them, and the truth was that when they'd first moved to Cheyenne she had been captivated by the notion of a kind of homely happiness—family and neighbors and garden, all the mundane middle-class clichés, she knew, but it had secretly thrilled her. They had been happy for quite a while. It was true that she found Tobe's family a little backward. But at the time, they had seemed like mere curiosities, who made sweet, smart Tobe even sweeter and smarter, to have grown up in such an environment.

She thought of this again as the usual Friday night family gathering convened at their house, now sans Wendell, now weighed with gloom and concern, but still willing to drink beer and play cards or Monopoly and talk drunkenly into the night. She thought back because almost ten years had now passed, and she still felt like a stranger among them. When the children had been younger, it was easier to ignore, but now it seemed more and more obvious. She didn't belong.

She had never had any major disagreements with Tobe's family, but there had developed, she felt, a kind of unspoken animosity, perhaps simple indifference. To Carlin, the second-oldest, Cheryl was, and would always remain, merely his brother's wife. Carlin was a policeman, crew-cut, ruddy, with the face of a bully, and Cheryl couldn't ever remember having much of a conversation with him. To Carlin, she imagined, she was just another of the women-folk, like

231

his wife, Karissa, with whom she was often left alone. Karissa was a horrid little mouse of a woman with small, judgmental eyes. She hovered over the brothers as they ate and didn't sit down until she was certain everyone was served; then she hopped up quickly to offer a second helping or clear a soiled plate. There were times, when Karissa was performing her duties, that she regarded Cheryl with a glare of pure, self-righteous hatred. Though of course, Karissa was always "nice"—they would talk about children, or food, and Karissa would sometimes offer compliments. "I see you've lost weight," she'd say, or: "Your hair looks much better, now that you've got it cut!"

Cheryl might have liked Tobe's next brother, Randy—he was a gentle soul, she thought, but he was also a rather heavy drinker, probably an alcoholic. She'd had several conversations with Randy which had ended with him weeping, brushing his hand "accidentally" across the small of her back or her thigh; wanting to hug. She had long ago stopped participating in the Friday night card games, but Randy still sought her out, wherever she was trying to be unobtrusive. "Hey, Cheryl," he said, earnestly pressing his shoulder against the door frame. "Why don't you come and drink a beer with us?" He gave her his sad grin. "Are you being anti-social again?"

"I'm just enjoying my book," she said. She lifted it so he could see the cover, and he read aloud in a kind of dramatized way.

The House of Mirth," he pronounced. "What is it? Jokes?" he said hopefully.

"Not really," she said. "It's about society life in old turn-of-the-century New York."

"Ah," he said. "You and Wendell could probably have a conversation about that. He always hated New York!"

She nodded. No doubt Wendell would have read *House of Mirth*, and would have an opinion of it which he would offer to her in his squinting, lop-sided way. He had surprised her, at first, with his intelligence, which he masked behind a kind of exaggerated folksiness and that haw-hawing laugh. But the truth was, Wendell read widely, and he could talk seriously about any number of subjects if he wanted. She and Wendell had shared a love of books and music—he had once stunned her by sitting down at his piano and playing Debussy, then Gershwin, then an old Hank Williams song, which he sang along with in a modest, reedy tenor. There were times when it had seemed as if they could have been friends—and then, without warning, he would turn on her. He would tell her a racist joke, just to offend her; he would call her "politically correct" and would goad her with his far-right opinions, the usual stuff—gun-control, feminism, welfare. He would get a certain look in his eyes, sometimes right in the middle of talking, a calculating, shuttered expression would flicker across his face. It gave her the creeps, perhaps even more now than before, and she put her hand to her mouth as Randy stood, still wavering, briefly unsteady, in the doorway. In the living room, Tobe and Carlin suddenly burst into laughter, and Randy's eyes shifted.

"I miss him," Randy said, after they had both been silently thoughtful for what seemed like a long while; he looked at her softly, as if she too had been having fond memories of Wendell. "I really miss him bad. I mean, it's like this family is cursed or something. You know?"

"No," she said, but not so gently that Randy would want to be patted or otherwise physically comforted. "It will be all right," she said firmly. "I honestly believe everything will turn out for the best."

She gave Randy a hopeful smile, but she couldn't help but think of the way Wendell would roll his eyes when Randy left the room to get another beer. "He's pathetic, isn't he?" Wendell had said, a few weeks before he was arrested. And he'd lowered his eyes, giving her that look. "I'll bet you didn't know you were marrying into white trash, did you?" he said, grinning in a way that made her uncomfortable. "Poor Cheryl!" he said. "Tobe fakes it really well, but he's still a stinky-footed redneck at heart. You know that, don't you?"

What was there to say? She was not, as Wendell seemed to think, from a background of privilege—her father had owned a dry-cleaning store. But at the same time, she had been comfortably sheltered. None of her relatives lived in squalor, or went to prison, or drank themselves daily into oblivion. She'd never known a man who got into fistfights at bars, as Tobe's father apparently had. She had never been inside a home as filthy as the one in which Randy lived.

But it struck her now that the trial was over, now that Randy stood, teary and boozy in her bedroom doorway. These men had been her husband's childhood companions—his brothers. He loved them. He *loved* them, more deeply than she could imagine. When they were together, laughing and drinking, she could feel an ache opening inside her. If he had to make a choice, who would he pick? Them or her?

In private, Tobe used to laugh about them. They were "characters," he said. He said, "You're so patient, putting up with all of their bullshit." And he kissed her, thankfully.

At the same time, he told her other stories. He spoke of a time when he was being abused by a group of high school bullies. Randy and Carlin had caught the boys after school, one by one, and "beat the living shit out of them." They had never bothered Tobe again.

He talked about Randy throwing himself into their mother's grave, as the casket was lowered, screaming "Mommy! Mommy!" and how the other brothers had to haul him out of the ground. He talked about how, at eleven or twelve, he was feeding the infant Wendell out of baby-food jars, changing his diapers. "After Mom got cancer, I practically raised Wendell," he told her once, proudly. "She was so depressed—I just remember her laying on the couch and telling me what to do. She wanted to do it herself, but she couldn't. It wasn't easy, you know. I was in high school, and I wanted to be out partying with the other kids, but I had to watch out for Wendell. He was a sickly kid. That's what I remember most. Taking care of him. He was only six when mom finally died. It's weird. I probably wouldn't have even gone to college if I hadn't had to spend all that time at home. I didn't have anything to do but study."

The story had touched her, when they'd first started dating. Tobe was not—had never been—a very emotional or forthcoming person, and she'd felt she discovered a secret part of him.

Was it vain to feel a kind of claim over these feelings of Tobe's? To take a proprietary interest in his inner life, to think: "I am the only one he can really talk to?" Perhaps it was, but they'd had what she thought of as a rather successful marriage, up until the time of Wendell's conviction. There had been an easy, friendly camaraderie between them; they made love often enough; they both loved their children. They were normally happy.

But now—what? What was it? She didn't know. She couldn't tell what was going on in his head.

Winter was coming. It was late October, and all the forecasts predicted cold, months of ice and darkness. Having grown up in Chicago, she knew that this shouldn't bother her, but it did. She dreaded it, for it always brought her into a constant state of pre-depressive gloom, something Scandinavian and lugubrious, which she had never liked about herself. Already, she could feel the edges of it. She sat in her office in the high school, and she could see the distant mountains out the window, growing paler and less majestic until they looked almost translucent, like oddly shaped thunderheads fading into the colorless sky. A haze settled over the city. College Placement Exam scores were lower than usual. A heavy snow was expected.

And Tobe was gone more than usual now, working late at night, preparing for Wendell's appeal. They had hired a new lawyer, one more experienced as a defense attorney, but there were still things Tobe needed to do. He would come home very late at night.

She hoped that he wasn't drinking too much but she suspected that he was. She had been trying not to pay attention, but she smelled alcohol on him nearly every night he came to bed; she saw the progress of the cases of beer in the refrigerator, the way they were depleted and replaced.

"What's wrong?" she thought, waiting up for him, waiting for the sound of his car in the driveway. She was alone in the kitchen, making herself some tea, thinking, when Wild Bill spoke from his cage.

"Stupid cunt," he said.

She turned abruptly. She was certain that she heard the words distinctly. She froze, with the kettle in her hand over the burner, and when she faced him, Wild Bill cocked his head at her, fixing her with his bird eye. The skin around his eye was bare, whitish wrinkled flesh, which reminded her of an old alcoholic. He watched her warily, clicking his claws along the perch. Then he said, thoughtfully: "Hello, Sexy."

She reached into the cage and extracted Wild Bill's food bowl. He was watching, and she very slowly walked to the trash can. "Bad Bird!" she said. She dumped it out—the peanuts and pumpkin seeds and bits of fruit that she'd prepared for him. "Bad!" she said again. Then she put the empty food bowl back into the cage. "There," she said. "See how you like that!" And she closed the cage with a snap, aware that she was trembly with anger.

It was Wendell's voice, of course: his words. The bird was merely mimicking, merely a conduit. It was Wendell, she thought, and she thought of telling Tobe; she was wide awake when he finally came home and slid into bed, her heart was beating heavily, but she just lay there as he slipped under the covers—he smelled of liquor, whiskey, she thought. He was already asleep when she touched him.

Maybe it didn't mean anything: filthy words didn't make someone a rapist. After all, Tobe was a lawyer, and he believed that Wendell was innocent. Carlin was a policeman, and he believed it too. Were they so blinded by love that they couldn't see it?

Or was she jumping to conclusions? She had always felt that there was something immoral about criticizing someone's relatives, dividing them from those they loved, asking them to take sides. Such a person was her father's second wife, a woman of infinite nastiness and suspicion, full of mean, insidious comments about her stepdaughters. Cheryl had seen the evil in this, the damage it could do.

And so she had chosen to say nothing as Wendell's possessions were loaded into her house, she had chosen to say nothing about the macaw, even as she grew to loathe it. How would it look, demanding that they get rid of Wendell's beloved pet, suggesting that the bird somehow implicated Wendell's guilt? No one else seemed to have heard Wild Bill's foul sayings, and perhaps the bird wouldn't repeat them, now that she'd punished him. She had a sense of her own tenuous standing as a member of the family. They were still cautious of her. In a few brief moves, she could easily isolate herself—the bitchy city girl, the snob, the troublemaker. Even if Tobe didn't think this, his family would. She could imagine the way Karissa would use such stuff against her, that perky martyr smile as Wild Bill was remanded to her care, even though she was allergic to bird feathers. "I'll make do," Karissa would say. And she would cough, pointedly, daintily, into her hand.

Cheryl could see clearly where that road would lead.

But she couldn't help thinking about it. Wendell was everywhere—not only in the sayings of Wild Bill, but in the notes and papers Tobe brought home with him from the office, in the broody melancholy he trailed behind him when he was up late, pacing the house. In the various duties she found herself performing for Wendell's sake—reviewing her own brief testimony at the trial, at Tobe's request; going with Tobe to the new lawyer's office on a Saturday morning.

Sitting in the office, she didn't know why she had agreed to come along. The lawyer who Tobe had chosen to replace him, Jerry Wasserman, was a transplanted Chicagoan who seemed even more out of place in Cheyenne than she did, despite the fact that he wore cowboy boots. He had a lilting, iambic voice, and was ready to discuss detail after detail. She frowned, touching her finger to her mouth as Tobe and his brothers leaned forward intently. What was she doing here?

"I'm extremely pleased by the way the appeal is shaping up," Wasserman was saying. "It's clear that the case had some setbacks, but to my mind the evidence is stronger than ever in your brother's favor." He cleared his throat. "I'd like to outline three main points for the judge, which I think will be quite—quite!—convincing."

Cheryl looked over at Karissa, who was sitting very upright in her chair, with her hands folded and her eyes wide, as if she were about to be interrogated. Carlin shifted irritably.

"I know we've talked about this before," Carlin said gruffly. "But I still can't get over the fact that the jury that convicted him was seventy-five percent female. I mean, that's something we ought to be talking about. It's just—it's just wrong, that's my feeling."

"Well," said Wasserman. "The jury selection is something we need to discuss, but it's not at the forefront of the agenda. We have to get through the appeals process first." He shuffled some papers in front of him, guiltily. "Let me turn your attention to the first page of the document I've given you, here. . ."

How dull he was, Cheryl thought, looking down at the first page, which had been photocopied from a law book. How could he possibly be more passionate or convincing than Tobe had been, in the first trial? Tobe had been so fervent, she thought, so certain of Wendell's innocence. But perhaps that had not been the best thing.

Maybe his confidence had worked against him. She remembered the way he had declared himself to the jury, folding his arms. "This is a case without evidence," he said. "Without *any* physical evidence!" And he had said it with such certainty that it had seemed true. The crime scenes had yielded nothing that had connected Wendell to the crimes; the attacker, whoever he was, had been extremely careful. There was no hair, no blood, no semen. The victims had been made to kneel in the bathtub as the attacker forced them to perform various degrading acts, and afterwards, the attacker had left them there, turning the shower on them as he dusted and vacuumed. There wasn't a single fingerprint.

But there was this: In three of the cases, witnesses claimed to have seen Wendell's pickup parked on a street nearby. A man matching Wendell's description had been seen hurrying down the fire escape behind the apartment of one of the women.

And this: The final victim, Jenni Martinez, had been a former girlfriend of Wendell. Once, after they'd broken up, Wendell got drunk and sang loud love songs beneath her window. He'd left peaceably when the police came.

"Peaceably!" Tobe noted. These were the actions of a romantic, not a rapist! Besides which, Wendell had an alibi for the night the Martinez girl was raped. He'd been at Cheryl and Tobe's house, playing cards, and he'd slept that night on their sofa. In order for him to have committed the crime, he'd have had to feign sleep, sneaking out from under the bedding Cheryl had arranged for him on the living room sofa, without being noticed. Then, he'd have had to sneak back into the house, returning in the early morning so that Cheryl would discover him when she woke up. She had testified: he was on the couch, the blankets twisted around him, snoring softly. She was easily awakened; she felt sure that she would have heard if he'd left in the middle of the night. It was, Tobe told the jury, "a highly improbable, almost fantastical version of events."

But the jury had believed Jenni Martinez, who was certain that she'd recognized his voice. His laugh. They had believed the prosecutor, who had pointed out that there had been no more such rapes since Jenni Martinez had identified Wendell. After Wendell's arrest, the string of assaults had ceased.

After a moment, she tried to tune back in to what Wasserman was saying. She ought to be paying attention. For Tobe's sake, she ought to be trying to examine the possibility of Wendell's innocence more rationally, without bias. She read the words carefully, one by one. But what she saw was Wendell's face, the way he'd looked as one of the assaulted women had testified: bored, passive, even vaguely amused as the woman had tremulously, with great emotion, recounted her tale.

Whatever.

That night, Tobe was once again in his study, working as she sat on the couch, watching television. He came out a couple of times, waving to her vaguely as he walked through the living room, toward the kitchen, toward the refrigerator, another beer.

She waited up. But when he finally came into the bedroom he seemed annoyed that she was still awake, and he took off his clothes silently, turning off the light before he slipped into bed, a distance emanating from him. She pressed her breasts against his back, her arms wrapped around him, but he was still. She rubbed her feet against his, and he let out a slow, uninterested breath.

"What are you thinking about," she said, and he shifted his legs.

"I don't know," he said. "Thinking about Wendell again, I suppose."

"It will be all right," she said, though she felt the weight of her own dishonesty settle over her. "I know it." She smoothed her hand across his hair.

"You're not a lawyer," he said. "You don't know how badly flawed the legal system is."

"Well," she said.

"It's a joke," he said. "I mean, the prosecutor didn't prove his case. All he did was parade a bunch of victims across the stage. How can you compete with that? It's all drama."

"Yes," she said. She kissed the back of his neck, but he was already drifting into sleep, or pretending to. He shrugged against her arms, nuzzling into his pillow.

One of the things that had always secretly bothered her about Wendell was his resemblance to Tobe. He was a younger, and—yes, admit it—sexier version of her husband. The shoulders, the legs; the small hardness of her husband's mouth that she had loved was even better on Wendell's face, that sly shift of his grey eyes, which Wendell knew was attractive, while Tobe did not. Tobe tended toward pudginess, while Wendell was lean. Wendell exercised on mail-order machines, which brought out the muscles of his stomach. In the summer, coming in from playing basketball with Tobe in the driveway, Wendell had almost stunned her, and she recalled her high school infatuation with a certain athletic shape of the male body. She watched as he bent his naked torso toward the open refrigerator, looking for something to drink. He looked up at her, his eyes slanted cautiously as he lifted a can of grape soda to his lips.

Stupid Cunt. It gave her a nasty jolt, because that was what his look said—a brief but steady look that was so full of leering scorn that her shy fascination with his muscled stomach seemed suddenly dirty, even dangerous. She had felt herself blushing with embarrassment.

She had not said anything to Tobe about it. There was nothing to say, really. Wendell hadn't *done* anything, and in fact he was always

239

polite when he spoke to her, even when he was confronting her with his "beliefs." He would go into some tirade about some issue that he held dear—gun control, or affirmative action, etc., and then he would turn to Cheryl, smiling: "Of course, I suppose there are differences of opinion," he would say, almost courtly. She remembered him looking at her once, during one of these discussions, his eyes glinting with some withheld emotion. "I wish I could think like you, Cheryl," he said. "I guess I'm just a cynic, but I don't believe that people are good, deep down. Maybe that's my problem." Later, Tobe told her not to take him seriously. "He's young," Tobe would say, rolling his eyes. "I don't know where he comes up with this asinine stuff. But he's got a good heart, you know."

Could she disagree? Could she say, no, he's actually a deeply hateful person?

But the feeling didn't go away. Instead, as the first snow came in early November, she was aware of a growing unease. With Daylight Savings Time, she woke in darkness, and when she went downstairs to make coffee, she could sense Wild Bill's silent, malevolent presence. He ruffled his feathers when she turned on the light, cocking his head so he could stare at her with the dark bead of his eye. By that time, she and Tobe had visited Wendell in prison, once, and Tobe was making regular weekly phone calls to him. On Jodie's birthday, Wendell had sent a handmade card, a striking pen-and-ink drawing of a spotted leopard in a jungle, the twisted vines above him spelling out, "Happy Birthday, Sweet Jodie." It was, she had to admit, quite beautiful, and must have taken him a long time. But why a leopard? Why was it crouched as if hunting, its tail a snake-like whip? There was a moment, going through the mail, when she'd seen Jodie's name written in Wendell's careful, spiked cursive, that she'd almost thrown the letter away.

There was another small incident that week. They were sitting at dinner. She had just finished serving up a casserole she'd made, which reminded her, nostalgically, of her childhood. She set Evan's plate in front of him and he sniffed at the steam that rose from it.

"Mmmm," he said. "Smells like pussy."

"Evan!" she said. Her heart shrank, and she flinched again when she glanced at Tobe, who had his hand over his mouth, trying to hold back a laugh. He widened his eyes at her.

"Evan, where on earth did you hear something like that?" she said, and she knew that her voice was too confrontational, because the boy looked around guiltily.

"That's what Wild Bill says, when I give him his food," Evan said. He shrugged, uncertainly. "Wild Bill says it."

"Well, son," Tobe said. He had recovered his composure and gave Evan a serious face. "That's not a nice thing to say. That's not something that Wild Bill should be saying, either."

"Why not?" Evan said. And Cheryl had opened her mouth to speak, but then thought better of it. She would do more damage than good, she thought.

"It's just something that sounds rude," she said at last.

"Dad," Evan said. "What does 'pussy' mean?"

Cheryl and Tobe exchanged glances.

"It means a cat," Tobe said, and Evan's face creased with puzzlement for a moment.

"Oh," Evan said at last. Tobe looked over at her, and shrugged.

Later, after the children were asleep, Tobe said, "I'm really sorry, Honey."

"Yes," she said. She was in bed, trying hard to read a novel, though she felt too unsettled. She watched as he chuckled, shaking his head. "Good God!" he said with amused exasperation. "Wendell can be such an asshole. I thought I would die when Evan said that." After a moment, he sat down on the bed and put his fingers through his hair. "That stupid Playboy stuff," he said. "We're lucky the bird didn't testify."

He meant this as a joke, and so she smiled. Oh, Tobe, she thought, for she could feel, even then, his affection for his younger brother. He was already making an anecdote to tell to Carlin and Randy, who would find it hilarious. She closed her eyes as Tobe put the back of his fingers to her earlobe, stroking.

"Poor baby," he said. "What's wrong? You seem really depressed lately."

After a moment, she shrugged. "I don't know," she said. "I guess I am."

"I'm sorry," he said. "I know I've been really distracted, with Wendell and everything." She watched as he sipped thoughtfully from the glass of beer he'd brought with him. Soon, he would disappear into his office, with the papers he had to prepare for tomorrow.

"It's not you," she said, after a moment. "Maybe it's the weather," she said.

"Yeah," Tobe said. He gave her a puzzled look. For he knew that there was a time when she would have told him, she would have plunged ahead, carefully but deliberately, until she had made her points. That was what he had expected.

But now she didn't elaborate. Something—she couldn't say what—made her withdraw, and instead she smiled for him. "It's okay," she said.

Wild Bill had begun to molt. He would pull out his own feathers, distractedly, and soon his grey, naked flesh was prominently visible in patches. His body was similar to the Cornish game hens she occasionally prepared, only different in that he was alive, and not fully plucked. The molting, or something else, made him cranky, and as Thanksgiving approached, he was sullen and almost wholly silent, at least to her. There were times, alone with him in the kitchen, that she would try to make believe that he was just a bird, that nothing was wrong. She would turn on the television to distract her, and Wild Bill would listen, absorbing every line of dialogue.

They were alone again together, she and Wild Bill, when Wendell telephoned. It was the second day in less than two weeks that she'd called in sick to work, that she'd stayed in bed, dozing, until well past eleven. She was sitting at the kitchen table, brooding over a cup of tea, a little guilty because she was not really ill. Wild Bill had been peaceful, half-asleep, but he ruffled his feathers and clicked his beak as she answered the phone.

At first, when he spoke, there was simply an unnerving sense of dislocation. He used to call her from time to time, especially when she and Tobe were first married. "Hey," he'd say, "how's it going?" and then a long silence would unravel after she said, "Fine," the sound of Wendell thinking, moistening his lips, shaping unspoken words with his tongue. He was young back then, barely twenty when she was pregnant with Jodie, and she used to expect his calls, even look forward to them, listening as he hesitantly began to tell her about a book he'd read, or asking her to listen as he played the piano, the tiny sound blurred through the phone line.

This was what she thought of at first, this long ago time when he was still just a kid, a boy with, she suspected, a kind of crush on her. This was what she thought of when he said, "Cheryl?" hesitantly, and it took her a moment to calibrate her mind, to span the time and events of the last eight years and realize that here he was now, a convicted rapist, calling her from prison. "Cheryl?" he said, and she stood over the dirty dishes in the sink, a single Lucky Charm stuck to the side of one of the children's cereal bowls.

"Wendell?" she said, and she was aware of a kind of watery dread filling her up—her mouth, her nose, her eyes. "Where are you?" she said, and he let out a short laugh.

"I'm in jail," he said. "Where did you think?"

"Oh," she said, and she heard his breath through the phone line, could picture the booth where he was sitting, the little room that they'd sat in when they'd visited, the elementary school colors, the mural of a rearing mustang with mountains and lightning behind it.

"So," he said. "How's it going?"

"It's going fine," she said—perhaps a bit too stiffly. "Are you calling for Tobe? Because he's at his office . . ."

"No," Wendell said, and he was silent for a moment, maybe offended at her tone. She could sense his expression tightening, and when he spoke again there was something hooded in his voice. "Actually," he said, "I was calling for you."

"For me?" she said, and her insides contracted. She couldn't imagine how this would be allowed—that he'd have such freedom with the phone—and it alarmed her. "Why would you want to talk to me?" she said, and her voice was both artificially breezy and strained. "I . . . I can't do anything for you."

Silence again. She put her hand into the soapy water of the sink and began to rub the silverware with her sponge, her hands working as his presence descended into her kitchen.

"I've just been thinking about you," he said, in the same hooded, almost sinuous way. "I was . . . thinking about how we used to talk, you know, when you and Tobe first moved back to Cheyenne. I used to think that you knew me better than anybody else. Did you know that? Because you're smart. You're a lot smarter than Tobe, you know, and the rest of them—Randy, Carlin, that stupid . . . moron, Karissa. Jesus! I used to think, *What is she doing here? What is she doing in this family?* I guess that's why I've always felt weirdly close to you. You were the one person—" he said, and she waited for him to finish his sentence, but he didn't. He seemed to loom close, a voice from nearby, floating above her, and she could feel her throat constricting. What? she thought, and she had an image of Jenni Mar-

243

tinez, her wrists bound, tears leaking from her blindfold. He would have spoken to her this way, soft, insidious, as if he were regretfully blaming her for his own emotions.

"Wendell," she said, and tried to think of what to say. "I think . . . it must be very hard for you right now. But I don't know that . . . I'm really the person. I certainly don't think that I'm the *one* person, as you say. Maybe you should talk to Tobe?"

"*No*," he said, suddenly and insistently. "You just don't understand, Cheryl. You don't know what it's like—in a place like this. It doesn't take you long to sort out what's real and what's not, and to know—the right person to talk to. Good God!" he said, and it made her stiffen because he sounded so much like Wild Bill. "I remember so much," he said. "I keep thinking about how I used to give you shit all the time, teasing you, and you were just so . . . calm, you know. Beautiful and calm. I remember you said once that you thought the difference between us was that you really believed that people were good at heart, and I didn't. Do you remember? And I think about that. It was something I needed to listen to, and I didn't listen."

She drew breath—because she *did* remember—and she saw now clearly the way he had paused, the stern, shuttered stare as he looked at her, the way he would seek her out on those Friday party nights, watching and grinning, hoping to get her angry. Her hands clenched as she thought of the long, intense way he would listen when she argued with him. She worked with high school boys who behaved this way all the time—why hadn't she seen? "Wendell," she said. "I'm sorry, but . . ." And she thought of the way she used to gently turn away certain boys—*I don't like you in that way. I just want to be friends. . . .* It was ridiculous, she thought, and wondered if she should just hang up the phone. How was it possible that they could let him call her like this, unmonitored? She was free to hang up, of course, that's what the authorities assumed. But she didn't. "I'm sorry," she said again. "Wendell, I think . . . I think . . ."

"No," he said. "Don't say anything. I know I shouldn't say this stuff to you. Because Tobe's my brother, and I *do* love him, even if he's a shitty lawyer. But I just wanted to hear your voice. I mean, I never would have said anything to you if it wasn't for being here and thinking—I can't help it—thinking that things would be different for me if we'd . . . If something had happened, and you weren't married. It could have been really different for me."

"No," she said, and felt vaguely nauseous, a surreal wave passing through the room. A bank of clouds uncovered the sun for a moment, and the light altered. Wild Bill edged his clawed toes along his perch. "Listen, Wendell. You shouldn't do this. You were right to keep this to yourself, these feelings. People think these things all the time, it's natural. But we don't act on them, do you see? We don't—"

She paused, pursing her lips, and he let out another short laugh. There was a raggedness in his voice that sent a shudder across her.

"Act!" he said. "Jesus Christ, Cheryl, there's no *acting* on anything. You don't think I'm fooling myself into thinking this appeal is going to amount to anything, do you? I'm stuck here, you know that. For all intents and purposes, I'm not going to see you again for twenty years—if I even live that long. I just—I wanted to talk to you. I guess I was wondering if, considering the situation, if I called you sometimes. Just to talk. We can set . . . boundaries, you know, if you want. But I just wanted to hear your voice. I think about you all the time," he said. "Day and night."

She had been silent for a long time while he spoke, recoiling in her mind from the urgency of his voice and yet listening steadily. Now that he had paused she knew that she should say something. She could summon up the part of herself that was like a guidance counselor at school, quick and steady, explaining to students that they had been expelled, that their behavior was inappropriate, that their SAT scores did not recommend college, that thoughts of suicide were often a natural part of adolescence but should not be dwelled upon. She opened her mouth, but this calm voice did not come to her, and instead she merely held the phone, limp and damp against her ear.

"I'll call you again," he said. "I love you," he said, and she heard him hang up.

In the silence of her kitchen, she could hear the sound of her pulse in her ears. It was surreal, she thought, and she crossed her hands over her breasts, holding herself. For a moment, she considered picking up the phone and calling Tobe at his office. But she didn't. She had to get her thoughts together.

She gazed out the window uncertainly. It was snowing hard now; thick white flakes drifted along with the last leaves of the trees. Something about Wendell's voice, she thought restlessly, and the fuzzy lights of distant cars seemed to shudder in the blur of steady snow. Her hands were shaking, and after a time, she got up and turned on the television, flicking through some channels: a game show, a talk show, an old black and white movie.

She could see him now very clearly, as a young man, the years after they'd first moved back to Wyoming—the way he would come over to their house, lolling around on the couch in his stocking feet, entertaining the infant Jodie as Cheryl made dinner, his eyes following her. And the stupid debates they used to have, the calculated nastiness of his attacks on her, the way his gaze would settle on her when he would play piano and sing. Wasn't that the way boys acted when they were trying not to be in love? Could she really have been so unaware, and yet have still played into it? *What is she doing in this family?* Wendell had said. She tried to think again, but something hard and knuckled had settled itself in her stomach. "My God," she said. "What am I going to do?" Wild Bill turned his head from the television, cocking his head thoughtfully, his eyes sharp and observant.

"Well?" she said to him. "What *am* I going to do?"

He said nothing. He looked at her for a little longer, then lifted his pathetic, molting wings, giving them a shake. "What a world, what a world," he said, mournfully.

This made her smile. It was not something she'd heard him say before, but she recognized it as a quote from *The Wizard of Oz*, which Wendell used to recite sometimes. It was what the Wicked Witch of the West said when she melted away, and a heaviness settled over her as she remembered him reciting it, clowning around during one of the times when they were just making conversation—when he wasn't trying to goad her. There were those times, she thought. Times when they might have been friends. "Yes," she said to Wild Bill. "What a world."

"Whatever," Wild Bill said; but he seemed to respond to her voice, or to the words that she spoke, because he gave a sudden flutter and dropped from his perch onto the table—which he would sometimes do for the children, but never for her, not even when she was eating fruit. She watched as he waddled cautiously toward her, his claws clicking lightly. She would have scolded the children: *Don't let that bird on the table, don't feed him from the table*, but she held out a bit of toast crust, and he edged forward.

"It's not going to work," she told Wild Bill, as he nipped the piece of toast from her fingers. "It's not," she said, and Wild Bill observed

246

her sternly, swallowing her bread. He opened his beak, his small black tongue working.

"What?" she said, as if he could advise her, but he merely cocked his head.

"Stupid cunt," he said gently, decisively, and her hand froze over her piece of toast, recoiling from the bit of crust that she'd been breaking off for him. She watched the bird's mouth open again, the black tongue, and a shudder ran through her.

"No!" she said. "No! Bad!" She felt her heart contract, the weight hanging over her suddenly breaking, and she caught Wild Bill in her hands. She meant to put him back in his cage, to throw him in, without food or water, but when her hands closed over his body he bit her, hard. His beak closed over the flesh of her finger and he held on when she screamed; he clutched at her forearm with his claws when she tried to pull back, and she struck at him as he flapped his wings, her finger still clutched hard in his beak.

"You piece of filth!" she cried. Tears came to her eyes as she tried to shake loose, but he kept his beak clenched, and his claws raked her arm. He was squawking angrily, small feathers flying off him, still molting as he beat his wings against her, the soundtrack of some old movie swelling melodramatically from the television. She slapped his body against the frame of the kitchen door, and he let loose for a moment before biting down again on her other hand. "Bastard!" she screamed, and she didn't even remember opening the door until the cold air hit her. She struck him hard with the flat of her hand, flailing at him, and he fell to the snow-dusted cement of the back porch, fluttering. "Smell my feet!" he rasped, and she watched as he stumbled through the air, wavering upward until he lit upon the bare branch of an elm tree in their backyard. His bright colors stood out against the grey sky, and he looked down on her vindictively. He lifted his back feathers and let a dollop of shit fall to the ground. After a moment, she closed the back door on him.

It took a long time for him to die. She didn't know what she was thinking as she sat there at the kitchen table, her hands tightened against one another. She couldn't hear what he was saying, but he flew repeatedly against the window, his wings beating thickly against the glass. She could hear his body thump softly, like a snowball, the tap of his beak. She didn't know how many times. It became simply a kind of emphasis to the rattle of the wind, to the sound of the television that she was trying to stare at.

She was trying to think, and even as Wild Bill tapped against the glass, she felt that some decision was coming to her—that some firm resolve was closing its grip over her even as Wild Bill grew quiet. He tapped his beak against the glass, and when she looked she could see him cocking his eye at her, a blank black bead peering in at her—she couldn't tell whether he was pleading or filled with hatred. He said nothing, just stared as she folded her arms tightly in front of her, pressing her forearms against her breasts. She was trying to think, trying to imagine Tobe's face as he came home from work, the way he would smile at her and she would of course smile back, the way he would look into her eyes, long and hard, inscrutably, the way Wild Bill was staring at her now. Are you okay, he would say, and he wouldn't notice that Wild Bill was gone, not until later. I don't know, she would say. I don't know what happened to him.

The rich lady on television was being kidnapped as Wild Bill slapped his wings once more, weakly, against the window. Cheryl watched intently, though the action on the screen seemed meaningless. "How dare you!" the rich lady cried as she was hustled along a corridor. Cheryl stared at the screen as a thuggish actor pushed the elegant woman forward.

"I demand to know where you're taking me," the elegant woman said desperately, and when Cheryl looked up Wild Bill had fallen away from his grip on the windowsill.

"You'll know soon enough, Lady," the thug said. "You'll know soon enough."

Nominated by Martha Collins, Epoch

GINKGO TREE

by TOM CRAWFORD

from THE TEMPLE ON MONDAY (Eastern Washington University Press)

The knee-high juvenile smile
in the slender trunk of the little ginkgo tree
planted between the curb and the sidewalk
won't tell you anything
about what happened here
in Kwangju at this intersection a year ago
when our bus smashed into the blue pickup.
It raised up on its right side
the little truck did
almost turning over
then settled back down
in an animal gentleness
in a shower of tempered glass
driverless, the door flung open
going now in a whole new direction
coasting, as it were, toward the little ginkgo tree
rolling ever so slowly
dragging its chrome trim along the street
while one of its silver hubcaps rolled
in the opposite direction,
toward us, pointing an accusing finger, I thought.
But if one discounts the dead driver
lying next to the curb
then the little truck, its black tires
carrying it away down the block
took on a certain charm,

the blue door waving back as it rolled
ever so slowly toward the curb
where it bounced softly like a beach ball
then struck the young tree, not such a hard blow,
but enough to ring all of its bell-shaped, green leaves
causing two or three to fall,
one landing on the hood
the other two on the blue cab.

Nominated by Eastern Washington University Press

THE MASTER OF DELFT

essay by ALEKSANDR KUSHNER

from ANTIOCH REVIEW

(translated by Dinara Georgeoliani and Mark Halperin)

> *"And won't you," she had ventured, "come just once and have tea with me?" He had pleaded pressure of work, an essay—which, in reality, he had abandoned years ago—on Vermeer of Delft.*
>
> M. Proust

LET ME ASK THOSE who love Vermeer if they have noted in his paintings the other canvases decorating the rooms he painted? I'm not sure everyone will answer affirmatively, but those who noticed are unlikely to recall what they depict. I said Vermeer's "paintings" and "canvases" in his paintings because compared to the intimate, domestic subjects of Vermeer's work, the "canvases" on the walls of his rooms almost always depict something massive, serious, and thematically distant from his style: a stormy landscape with a cloudy sky and boiling leaves (*The Concert*), a reserved, formal portrait of a man in black (*The Coquette*), the Last Judgment (*The Woman Weighing a Pearl*), an ancient mythological scene with nude figures on a sea shore (*The Letter*), and so forth. Finally, there are maps (*The Officer and The Smiling Girl, The Artist's Studio*). Sometimes it is almost impossible to discern what is painted on the "canvas." In the painting *The Sleeping Girl*, the edge of such a canvas appears—what is depicted on it? It seems to be a chopped-off head. Or is it a tragic mask?

The artist seems to pay tribute to an art preceding his, although he himself has moved far from it.

This second perspective meant much to the artist, but does not to us. We almost fail to notice it, though there must be some patch there, and so there is. For us it is just another pattern, arabesque, resembling inscriptions on the purple tiles of Persian temples and mosques; we don't attempt to read them, we just admire them. Remove them—and the picture will fade, lose part of its charm, but why bother deciphering?

The woman weighing a pearl on a little hand scale is shown against a background of a painting depicting the Last Judgment: the righteous on the left, with hands raised to God's throne, will be taken up to heaven; the sinners on the right, wringing their hands, expect nothing good. The woman's swollen belly shows through the dark purple velvet cloak. It's not a pearl that lies on the scales, but the fate of her unborn child.

But, while scrutinizing this woman, we ignore the allegorical sense. It almost fails to reach us: her sweet, gentle, meek face, the buoyant hands, the green wrinkled tablecloth, brown skirt, white fur trim of a cloak, the silk, homemade hood on her head—these are what attract and captivate us. I say: green, white, brown, purple, but none of these words has anything to do with the genuine color, for it's a shade that decides everything, even if it can't be named and there are no words for it.

By using an approximate, poor substitute, I feel like saying: scram, out of here, we are not wanted here, as unwanted as the allegory on the mind of the artist. "All the rest is literature." It's as if the artist didn't trust himself completely or the traits of his art, and sought a justification for the painting in a word, an idea. He could have accompanied his painting with an explanatory emblem, an edifying reference, with an explanation or musical phrase with the same result. Let's imagine that we go up to the picture—and as we do, music begins to pour from a speaker built into the frame (after all, clavichords, lutes, guitars, are found in his canvases now and then; somewhere, it seems, even a double-bass lies on the floor). I'm afraid that such fraternization between the painting and music would be imposing (isn't that fraternization what the most sentimental, symbolically ardent daydreamers sigh for?) or resemble a mournful farewell ceremony.

The soul of the artist connects with us directly via color: such a blue (the apron on his milkmaid), such a scarlet (the officer's caftan), such a yellow one can't find anywhere (the piece of yellow wall in his *A View of Delft*—while deciphering the mystery of this yellow at an exhibit, the writer Bergotte, in Proust's novel, dies.

You and I stood in front of his milkmaid in Amsterdam. This twisted thread of milk, streaming from jug to bowl, is an absolute miracle. It speaks of the mystery of life of the artist himself, who did not leave behind any authentic biography, not an iota less than Holy Scripture; for me, in any case, it stands in the same line, and one can say that he embodied himself in everything he painted including this thread of milk.

And when we walked away from *The Milkmaid* and looked back at it again, left the hall and returned again—the hall was stuffed with wonderful paintings (only Terborch's is worth a lot!), everything faded and looked drained by comparison with the blue apron of the milkmaid. Let me say it again: no one else has such a blue. It can be found neither in painting nor in life; it's extracted from the soul of the artist, manifested to us as its brightest, and, indeed, immortal incarnation.

What I have just said is no exaggeration. Doubters are welcome to visit the Amsterdam museum when they have a chance. I am speaking about a color, but not only about that. Not only about the combination of blue with green and yellow: about the texture of the cloth, creases, the peasant arms of the milkmaid, the concentrated expression on her face, shadows in the left corner of the room. . . .

Kandinsky got rid of all of that, retaining only color; color and whimsical configurations of geometric, spiroid, amoeba-like abstractions—it seems to me that Vermeer would have liked them; he didn't know that this was possible. All the same, how fortunate that the Delft Master lived, not in the twentieth century, but in the seventeenth!

—You don't understand a thing about painting, a professional would say.

But I never said I did. I love it. Nonetheless, I favor understanding. I understand poetry. I'm annoyed by the conversations of amateurs. Maybe when I speak about Vermeer, I also speak not about painting, but about poetry.

I saw his *A View of Delft* first in The Hague, and then, a day or two later, saw Delft itself. To me, this is one of the world's best spots:

253

there's no need to compare it with the Delft on the canvas. One can recognize several towers, maybe a few roofs—all the rest looks different. No, it is in no way worse, because the main sources of joy for the newcomer are the narrow green canals, sometimes on a level with the roadway, with water lilies afloat on their flat, green dishes. The city resembles a clean, whimsical, sparkling magical theater in which water, air, an idle crowd, bicycles chained to the iron railings of bridges, workshops, and the cathedrals stage the same engaging, plotless play about earthly joy and merriment—I am speaking thus because I could have been happy there had I visited not the three times I actually did, but thirty-three times. "Merriment," "joy"— what are they after all? Isn't it a shame to use such words? It is a shame. But Vermeer, whom I have been fond of since youth, taught me a thing or two during those years, including the knack of giving up excuses, of living my way. Tragedy has been taken advantage of more than enough in art. As I have come to believe, lovers of tragedy in art are often prudent and cold people, besides being great gourmets. Vermeer's life wasn't easy; neither was Pushkin's, ". . . full of merry and pleasant thoughts, / He will pass you in the dark of night / And will remember me."

In 1902, in The Hague, Proust saw Vermeer's *A View of Delft* for the first time, and in 1921, a year before his death, wrote to his friend, "When I saw 'A View of Delft,' in The Hague, I realized that I had seen the most beautiful painting in the world."

This is the largest painting by Vermeer (98cm × 118cm), and his only landscape (not counting *The Backstreets*, in which there is little landscape, and so much interior). Dutch miniaturists are famous for their narrow specialization: one would paint cathedrals all his life, another the sea and sails, a third, rural landscapes with cows and windmills, a fourth, scenes from peasant life, a fifth, still-lives, and not just still-lives in general, but only, for example, "breakfasts."

As for "breakfasts," it's worth writing about them separately: this genre bloomed in a circle of Haarlem painters. The best of them were Willem Claesz Heda and Pieter Claesz. How many times in the Hermitage would I pause before these overturned goblets, crumpled tablecloths, half-peeled lemons, each with a sparkling spiral of dangling rind. . . . In Haarlem, they knew how to breakfast. The things on the table speak of a host who has left the room, his way of life, his taste, of the seventeenth-century Dutch "dandyism" no less than portrait painting. Such a still-life is a terrific, intimate portrait. Isn't the ability to breakfast alone truly a trait rare and worthy of respect? No, joking aside, at breakfast conversations go poorly. A person who has slept well is full of hope, untapped energy he will surely need; it's a shame to spend it on friendly jabber, intimate dialogue. On the other hand, supper is better with a companion.

It really seems Pieter Claesz, Willem Claesz Heda, Williem Kalff (oh, what a marvelous Kalff I saw at the Harvard University Museum!) could easily have become close and concurred about the Pelam of Bulverovski, the Pelimov of Pushkin, his Onegin, Proust's Swann. . . . But how surprised I would have been to find a landscape carried out by any of them!

Perhaps one more reason Vermeer's *A View of Delft* produces such a stunning impression is that this is the last thing you expect from a master of intimate, domestic scenes and interiors; it's as if we suddenly came across a poem of Tutchev or Mandelstam.

In the foreground, a voluptuous (what kind? what kind?), a voluptuous, golden-nacreous city panorama, with its mirror-smooth, river-like surface, as if seen in a dream—and an uneven, bright, disturbing sky over it, as if agitated by unanticipated news. And, perhaps, most remarkable, is a smoke-gray, "unattractive," brown, dark-umber cloud drifting into this world from no-one-knows-where. But I do know where it came from. Such clouds swirl up in the middle of September in Saint Petersburg, which had to wait fifty to sixty years to be built.

And if no reproduction is able to convey the genuine charm of the painting seen in reality, then it goes without saying that this cloud can't be conveyed through the medium of printer's ink.

How do people live in today's Delft and what are their interests? Could we live here among these antique surroundings and prosperous times, safe and sound—in the direct sense of this set-phrase— and that's what we talked about, climbing little bridges, leaning over water, sitting on steps, dropping into cathedrals. In the Old Cathedral, we fell silent over a stone slab embedded in the floor: JOHANNES VERMEER 1632–1675. Right beside it were flowers in a white, ceramic pitcher: yellow carnations, golden marigolds; also, in a glass jar, there was a bundle of pink cyclamen someone, not us, had thought to bring.

The slab was placed there only in 1975, on the three-hundredth anniversary of the artist's death, but there were no remains of Vermeer under it: at some time, due to a depression in the earth and the threat of collapse, almost all the burial-remains from the Old Cathedral were transferred.

Vermeer lived so quietly, so inconspicuously, was so entirely forgotten by subsequent generations, that it occurred to them far too late, although it's a well-known fact that books, paintings, music are more enduring than stone—"taller than pyramids." The same holds for church records. This is precisely why we know the exact date of his death: 16 December 1675. It's also known that he died from a heart attack, depressed by his extreme poverty (he lost much during the war with France, which had broken out at that time, and during the French occupation), by the threat of utter pauperism and ruin, by the drop in demand for paintings (his and others, which he traded, having inherited from his father this troublesome business), by fear for the future of his children.

In accordance with custom, after someone's death, representatives of a charitable organization would appear in the home: it was expected that they would be given the best outer fur clothing of the deceased for the city poor. And so, in the record book of this organization is noted that they left Vermeer's house empty-handed: "there was nothing to take."

One may ask, but where are all those ladies' attire, tapestry tablecloths, chandeliers and clavichords, the armchairs that moved from painting to painting on their four, anthropodian extremities, decorated by a pair of either dogs' or lions' bronze heads on each side? Where are the goblets and dishes, embroidered pillows and silk curtains, the paintings in oak and gilded frames, the wrought-iron cases, the pearl necklaces?

We know them by heart: the stone floor, laid out in black and yellow marble slabs, the dish of blue china with apples and lemons, the white pitcher with a blue glass stopper, migrating from one theme to another: here it stands on a table before a drowsing girl, who sleeps leaning her elbows on the table; here, a cavalier in a wide-brimmed, black hat holds it in his right hand, while treating a young girl to wine; later the same pitcher stands on a freshly ironed, silk tablecloth, only in this painting the young girl is already in the company of two cavaliers; then it appears anew on a tray, and the hostess plays for her guest on the clavier. This time, it is without a lid: has it perhaps been broken? I look more closely: no, this is a different pitcher, similar to the first, but nonetheless different. Which means the other broke. You see the artist walking time and again around the same things all his life—and they don't bore him. This is how poems should be written. Imagine you wrote a poem "Carafe" and after a year or two another "Carafe," and some years later, a third one.

"What is the point of looking for themes for poems," said Fet to Polonskij, "themes are all around you—toss a woman's dress on a chair or take a look at two crows sitting on a fence; look here are your themes. . . ."

We know them by heart, all these objects in his paintings, know by sight all the sweet, female inhabitants of this spacious, clean, cordial, hospitable, open to music and love, to romantic fascinations and paintings, we'd like to believe, this prosperous home.

Four of the fifteen children Vermeer and his wife had died in infancy. Still, it's difficult to link, in one's imagination, the festive and relaxed atmosphere of his paintings with eleven, to say nothing of fifteen children! Children mean eternal illnesses, care, and concern. "I love it when there are children in a home / And when they cry at night." But so many, hungry or crying at once. . . .

And now I will name his daughters: Maria, Aleda, Gertrude, Catherine, Elizabeth, Beatrice, Joanne. . . . It seems to me that these daughters of his look out at us from some of his later paintings: one embroiders, another plays the guitar, a third writes a letter—they're similar: it's easy to confuse them, to take one for the other; the one in a red, fluffy beret appeals to me most; her mouth half open. Her eyes glitter as if she had a cold, a scarlet reflection on her cheek. Who are you: Gertrude, Elizabeth?

And one more, very young, a teenager, resembling a mouse: round, bulging eyes in a sharp little face, a gray cape on her shoulders. When I arrived in New York for Brodsky's funeral I was depressed. So I went to the Metropolitan Museum—and this young girl helped me cope with my grief.

As for the objects I've enumerated, many of them can be found in the archival documents; the inventory of the deceased painter's possessions is preserved. The pictures he used in his own works are also mentioned there: still life with fruit, small lake, seascape, crucified Christ—and seven panels made of gilded leather, a knight's armor, furniture, a helmet, a Turkish coat—evidently people from the charitable committee found them too exotic—two easels, six stretchers, ten canvases, three sets of pigments, a pestle for their grinding, three brushes, even a cane, encrusted with ivory, the same one that appears in one of his paintings, blending in with a sumptuous tablecloth lying next to the fruit on the table.

And, moreover, there are family portraits, the painting *Marsyas and Apollo,* a painting "with a skull and 'cello," a stone table for grinding pigments. It surely is of no use to the city poor.

Vermeer's widow gave two of her late husband's paintings to the baker to pay off a debt (*The Girl with a Guitar* and *The Girl Writing a Letter*); later, they were bought back and restored to her by Vermeer's executor, the noted naturalist Leeuwenhoek. (As Zabolotsky says: "Through the magical apparatus of Leeuwenhoek / The drops of water on the surface are seen. . . .") In general, he played a large role in supporting the orphaned family of the artist, and it is pleasant to think how the fates of a painter and a naturalist who looked on the world with the same attentive and enraptured eyes were interwoven.

The seven panels of gilded leather mentioned in the inventory. . . . Couldn't these be the maps that moved from painting to painting in Vermeer? Let's have a closer look at them. They are stretched on two horizontal black lacquered poles, the latter crowned by black, round, wooden spiked helmets. (But what else can we call these pieces? There should be some word that we have forgotten—cantilevers? No. Cornice brackets? No. I called a hardware store: "Do you have wooden devices on which curtains on rings can be hung?" They answered me: "Fasteners? Sometimes we have them, but not now.")

Let me look closely at these maps. Searching for the familiar outlines of the earth's continents would be pointless. What's this—Europe? Africa? Maybe it's America, discovered recently, a hundred years ago. It seems a different, better, an unearthly geography, where flocks of moth-ships stretch along the shoreline (*The Officer and the Smiling Girl*).

Then that very map on the very black stretchers appears in the painting *The Woman in the Blue Cloak with a Letter.* Only here everything's smeared, drowned in a brownish yellow darkness,—the Gobi Desert, Tien Shan, Tibet are colored such hues.

And in the painting *The Woman with the Pitcher,* the map also looks as if it were sprinkled with sand, smeared with clay—it's impossible to recognize actual continental outlines.

And in *The Artist's Studio*, a girl, posing for the artist, is placed against a map, which does not look like one at all, but rather resembles a gilded tapestry, puckered and gathered in creases.

The only painting behind which a map hangs is the one called *The Girl with a Lute*, (1664); it is a map in greenish-gray tones, on which clearly emerges the shoreline of Western Europe, Gibraltar, the Mediterranean Sea. . . .

What you absolutely can't find on these maps are Russia, Moskovy.

The second half of the seventeenth century. The reign of Alexi Mikhailovich. Falconry. Floor-length sleeves on Boyar caftans. Church law consolidating serfdom. Yet another suppression of uprisings in Novgorod and Pskov. The patriarch Nikon. The Schism. The exile of the "Proto-pope" Avvakum to Mezen' (1664), and later to Pustozerik. Stepan Razin. What is scientific microscopy, lenses with three hundred-power magnification, spermatozoa, bacteria, erythrocytes and their movement in the capillaries compared to this!

The main sources of biographical data for a man who lived in Holland in the seventeenth century can be found in the Civil Registrar's office, extracts from church books, and archivist documents. So, perhaps, our complaints that we know little about Vermeer are groundless? No, they're not groundless. Yes, we do know of his debts, and we do know his wife's name (Katarina Bolnes) and that she was a Catholic while he was a Protestant, and that her mother at first opposed this marriage, but then helped her son-in-law and daughter, to whom she bequeathed her fortune. We know that Vermeer's father had a hotel (after his death it passed to his son) and traded in art objects, that Vermeer was twenty-one when he was accepted into the guild of Saint Luke as an artist, and that later, from 1662 through 1671, he was the vice-president of this guild.

But we could have obtained the same or even more information about any Delft burgher who lived then.

There's a belief that he went to Amsterdam and stayed at Rembrandt's. Alas, it's only a belief, proceeding from the understandable and ardent desire of a researcher to acquaint the two artists three hundred years later.

Not a single statement of Vermeer has reached us! And in his self-portrait (*The Artist's Workshop*) he sits with his back to us. Thick, red hair sticking out from under a velvet beret, a solid figure in a black blouse with white stripes on the back, sumptuous black trousers, red hose—that's actually all. On the other hand, the girl with the wreath on her head, wearing an absurd, blue shift and holding a heavy book and trumpet, looks as if she stepped out of a twentieth-century film, a movie by Fellini. Juliet Mazin would have posed just so for the artist.

This is what is called the absence of biography.

Archivist documents won't tell us anything about Vermeer's teachers, about his contacts with other painters, or his artistic tastes.

But in 1652 Carel Fabritius painted *A View of Delft* (not at all resembling Vermeer's 1660 *View of Delft*), and Vermeer surely knew this work and one can suppose that it meant a lot to him. (By the way, Fabritius did study in Rembrandt's studio.)

There was yet another Dutch artist whose name is worth mentioning here: Pieter de Hooch. Speaking about a musical phrase from Vinteuil's sonata, Proust, in his novel, recalls this artist: "He began, always, with the sustained tremolos of the violin part which for several bars was heard alone, filling the whole foreground; until suddenly it seemed to draw aside, and—as in those interiors by Pieter de Hooch which are deepened by the narrow frame of a half-opened door, in the far distance, of a different color, velvety with the radiance of some intervening light—the little phrase appeared, dancing, pastoral, interpolated, episodic, belonging to another world."

Pieter de Hooch, who arrived in Delft around 1654 when Vermeer was twenty, was a major influence on the young artist. The house in which he lived is located at the end of Oude Delft Street; it can still be found today; though the narrow door leading to the interior little courtyard is gone, it is preserved forever on his canvases. One of them (*The Landlady and the Maid*) hangs in the Hermitage. Looking at it, you understand better both Vermeer and Proust with his Vinteuil; there, beyond an open, narrow door leading from the little courtyard to the street, one can see a tree, a canal, and a house on the opposite side of the canal, apparently, with a similar little courtyard and similar inhabitants—but since all this is so far away, it seems even more enchanting, as if really from another world.

Ten years later, Pieter de Hooch left for Amsterdam—and in the noisy capital lost the best qualities of his art. Another Delft artist,

Emanuel de Witte, who painted cathedral interiors and stony groves filled with light, committed suicide after moving to Amsterdam. Better not to move to the capital, stay faithful to Delft, and live there unto one's death like Vermeer.

A writer asks his favorite character to write a study of the artist. But the latter has no time: he falls in love with a woman and suffers because of her. Besides, the man, a member of high society, is in great demand. He is expected at the salons of the Verdurins, at the Duchesse de Guermantes—and so the study is not written. You can't help but regret it.

However, it's not exactly so, for the author, on his own, tells us what's most important: "Certainly, experiments in spiritualism offer us no more proof than the dogmas of religion that the soul survives death. All that we can say is that everything is arranged in this life as though we entered it carrying a burden of obligations contracted in a former life; there is no reason inherent in the conditions of life on this earth that can make us consider ourselves obliged to do good, to be kind and thoughtful, even to be polite, nor for an atheist artist to consider himself obliged to begin over again a score of times a piece of work the admiration of which will matter little to his worm-eaten body, like the patch of yellow wall painted with so much skill and refinement by an artist destined to be forever unknown and barely identified under the name Vermeer."

The burden of obligations contracted in a former life, in a pre-life environment, from which we appeared and to which we will return after death. . . .

Somewhere, at the end of the sixties, about twenty years before *The Captive* was translated into Russian, I recall how I translated this passage from the novel with the help of a dictionary, just to check; I went to Lydia Ginzburg and we spoke about the above argument in favor of the immortality of the soul.

She objected to one word in the text: why did Proust call the artist "an atheist" (l'artiste athée)?

And, in fact, doubtlessly Vermeer was a believer. As is known from church records, he was baptized on October 31, 1632 in the New Church, the very one that emerges from behind the houses in his *View of Delft*.

In one of his last (but not best) works, *The Allegory of Faith* (allegories rarely succeed), a semiconscious woman in an exalted pose is depicted (in the same familiar room with the marble floor and arm-chair on which lies the same familiar cushion), only this time there's a huge picture of the crucified Savior and a mourning Mary at the base of the cross in the background. The painting is strained, artificial, but doubtlessly speaks of the artist's religious convictions.

So when Vermeer "redid a part of the picture twenty times," he did so for the same reason an unknown gothic sculptor did, bringing a saint's statue somewhere under the domes of a cathedral to an inconceivable state of perfection, a statue no one would ever see except for some future restorer, climbing a scaffold two or three hundred years later.

Once, on coastal sand, I also saw a deep-sea creature in convulsions, glittering and growing numb, with drops of moisture on each hair—its faceted body seemed sculptural, chiseled by a nameless underwater artist on the sly, secreted away from human eyes.

There is an artistic instinct that compels the artist to achieve perfection.

As for faith, its excess, if one may use this expression, is capable of not only strengthening, but also impeding an artist: one recalls the catastrophe that overtook Botticelli, who was enchanted by the sermons of Savonarola, or the story behind the second volume of "Dead Souls." We don't want to think that something similar threatened Vermeer toward the end of his short life. Yet he felt he was being a guild-master, vice-president of the artists' guild—but not a teacher or a prophet.

Creative labor, that is the very prayer of the artist, irrespective of his being a believer or not. "Talent," as a poet said, "is mission."

And in this sense, "the twisted thread of milk" pouring from the pitcher may be more eloquent than the "allegory of faith" and of the Crucifixion, depicted too rationally and didactically behind the back of the lady, posing, her eyes fixed on the ceiling.

What a pleasure it is to sit in a café in Delft, right on the street under a colored awning! A middle-aged woman at a neighboring table spots us for Russians—I am able to explain myself to her in French. It turns out she lives here, in Delft. What does she busy herself with?—flowers. She's a horticulturist. Primarily, she deals with the flowers that decorate the city window boxes, cornices, restaurant borders, and front garden-plots. She has a husband, and grown children who live on their own in another city. She loves Russia very, very much.

She has been to Russia several times, visited Petersburg. And once, together with her husband, she took the train as far as Vladivostok. Across all Siberia! (As for me, I've never gotten further than Krasnoyarsk in Siberia. I've never seen the Pacific Ocean.)

She asked for our address in Petersburg and wrote it down (just as people do, i.e., in Yalta on vacation); in the fall she plans to be in Russia again, and if she happens to be in Petersburg, she will certainly call. A very sweet, simple-hearted, inquisitive, trusting woman. . . .

It was as if a multi-paned window swung open and from a narrow Delft street we glimpsed the room of a Dutch home.

How do people live in this place? "A bit boringly—and hygienically?" I'm not sure this line from Kuzmin is appropriate here.

Or is it after all? The reason they take on Russia is that each trip is like a heroic enterprise. It's something like Alpine deeds or a skiing expedition to the North Pole. You return home and you feel like you've really done something.

Just think, there exists a bewitching, pristine, well taken care of Delft, while the earth somewhere near Tymen is half-rotted, half-charred, torn up by caterpillar tractors, mutilated by drilling towers, poisoned by factory effluents.

It seemed that fate deliberately invented this meeting, brought us to this café (we could just as easily have chosen another). How would we live here? Like this: you would breed flowers (or be occupied with prosody—is that any worse than horticulture?); we would travel to Russia. . . .

Do you know what Russia means to this resident of Delft who sat at the neighboring table? I'll tell you: just the same as the scenes of the Last Judgment or maps behind the backs of Vermeer's landladies and maids!

In 1716, under Peter, 120 Dutch paintings were delivered to Russia en masse, as if they were not paintings, but cows or sheep, and immediately after the first herd came a second, of yet another 117 items. The headcount grew from year to year. Rembrandt's painting *David's Farewell from Jonathan* was the first in Peter's collection. On close examination, Jonathan bears the features of Rembrandt himself, while David, sobbing on his breast, resembles a woman with loosened, curling, flaxen hair. "Does the artist's farewell from Saskia come to life in this painting?" asks a contemporary researcher (Yu. I. Kuznetsov). No matter what—this is one of the most sorrowful and mysterious of his works.

It's unlikely that anyone in Peter's Russia could properly evaluate this masterpiece of the great artist (paintings were purchased "by size"), and besides, the Czar's favorite themes in painting were scenes from the lives of "Dutch peasantry," as Peter's biographer, Jacob Shtelin, informs us. The phrase sounds more than modern, and really, didn't Rubens's paintings, imported in large quantities at the same time, fit this definition: his *Adam and Eve,* or *Bacchus*—depict the same "Dutch peasantry," and in their birthday suits to boot!

But one way or another, in Russia, where, before Peter, there were no social paintings nor sculptures nor public gardens nor fountains, certain things, to put it mildly and cautiously, have changed for the better.

A tyrant (however, we have no right to call Peter a tyrant: according to the Greeks, a tyrant is a ruler who seizes power illegally), "an autocratic ruler," importing Rembrandt, Rubens, Van Dyke, Breughel, Wouwerman, Jan Steen, and van Ostade into the country, is preferable to a tyrant, that is, a usurper, who destroys artists in gulags and, with resolutions from the Central Committee, exports paintings from the country to increase industrial production.

How Delft differs from what we see before our eyes, in Russia, even today! We don't have to go as far as Nizhnevartovsk or Cherepovets. We don't even have to step outside. Let's stop at the staircase. To open a foreigner's eyes to Russia, it's sufficient to show him an ordinary staircase in a Petersburg apartment house: the stink, the filth, smashed mailboxes, the latrine in the entrance, the pearls of public, obscene creativity on the walls of the elevator. . . .

We're left with the consolation that compared with the seventeenth century, we have come, nonetheless, closer to Holland. Since I don't have a book at hand about everyday life in Russia during the seventeenth century, I'll cite an extract from the book *The Petersburg of Anna Joannova as described by foreigners*: "The peasant huts in the Russian Karelia, and as reported, in the northern part of the Great Kingdom of Finland, are earthly Purgatories: there are small openings instead of windows and no chimney pipes. Thus, the smoke leaving a stove and for some time floating along a room seeps out at last through a porous roof, and all those present are unable to live through this without floods of tears. . . . A traveler must carry both food and drink with him, for nowhere will he find any suitable food to eat but in large cities. He must also take bedding and usually travel lying down in a sleeping carriage or sleigh, covered with a small rug or hide, for there are no beds in peasant homes and it is so smoky there that you can't stay long."

Well, this was written by the Swedish scholar Karl Reinhold Berk—why should we trust a foreign scholar? In Radishchev's "The Travels" the description of the hut is the same and even more frightful: "There are cracks throughout the floor, at least an inch and a half of filth," etc.

Let's leave huts and open *War and Peace*: 1806, the year of Nikolai Rostov's return from the army to Moscow. "Finally, the sled managed to take to the right in the direction of the entrance; over his head, Rostov saw a familiar cornice with broken plaster, a porch, a sidewalk column. . . . 'My God! Is everything okay?'—Rostov thought . . . starting to run further along the passageway and familiar crooked steps. The same doorknob, whose dirtiness would anger the Countess, opened with the same difficulty. In the entranceway one tallow candle burned. . . . The old man, Mikhaelo, slept on the chest. Prokofij, the carriage servant . . . sat and knitted bast sandals."

Reading the novel, we don't pay much attention to these pieces of fluff; we rush toward love and great thoughts, like young Rostov. But the broken off plaster, the crooked steps, and even the doorknob, not only dirty, but which "opened with the same difficulty," the utter darkness in the entrance way, the old servant sleeping on that chest. . . .

It's clear that according to Tolstoy's design, all these things are meant to speak in favor of his beloved Rostovs and of old-Moscow upper-crust lifestyle, as opposed to Petersburg's high-society and bureaucratic polish, as is justly stated in school textbooks. But sometimes it is interesting to liberate oneself from the author's hypnotic suggestion and look at this given description from another point of view, void of morality.

One can't but marvel at little, provincial Holland, where already in the sixteenth to seventeenth centuries townspeople undressed to sleep on starched sheets and featherbeds with fringes (Rembrandt's *Danae*, Van Mieris the Elder's *Morning of a Young Lady*), where doorknobs and window handles glittered, parquet floors and stained-glass windows shone, the rooms were flooded with light or, on the contrary, shaded with reliable, dense shades (P. Jansens Elinga,

Room in a Dutch House; Gabriel Metsu, *Breakfast*). Most of all, I am touched by a broom in one of Vermeer's paintings—not our twig-broom or worn-down ship's mop, but some rational, thought-out invention with a long, black lacquered handle and flexible sweeping part along the periphery. Is this conversation about painting? I am burning with shame.

When S. A. Tolstaya arrived for the first time in Yasnaya Polyana, she was amazed that in Tolstoy's house the pillows didn't have pillowslips. Some would say: you don't need pillowslips; had he slept on pillowslips he would not have written *Childhood, Adolescence, Youth* or *The Morning of the Squire*. But why not? Later, when pillowslips were in use, he nevertheless wrote something—namely, *War and Peace*.

In his country sketches, Fet says the following: "No matter where fate tosses you for a night's lodging, unless it's a landlord's house, you're a martyr anywhere you go. Everywhere it's the same thing: it's stuffy air, a murderous stink of the most various nature, flies, fleas, bedbugs, mosquitoes, no human bedding at all, filth to the point of greatness; no amount of money could purchase anything clean. It blows and flows everywhere, and nothing is done about it. There's white heat there, but no desire to plant a sapling under the window. . . . You will say: it's poverty. But why then in provincial cities do well-off people, who drain several samovars a day, live in the same way? There's the same striking smell of rancid oil and an uncleaned pickling barrel, and the same lack of clean crockery or food. . . . No,—you think,—it will take another thousand years. . . ."

It's unlikely that anyone would dare to call Fet a foreign malingerer, although before he was granted nobility, he had to sign documents, "the foreigner Fet put his hand to this."

Perhaps all the horror of revolutions and civil wars, including the war in Chechnya, all the torturing nightmares of prisons and camps, obvious lies and humiliations of man are connected with this filth, with the fact that there was and is no need "to plant a sapling under the window." There, where saplings are planted and the pavements washed with a brush, life is valued and rejoiced in.

Oh, of course, "I love your strict, slender look," of course "it rose up in splendor and pride," of course we had Pushkin and Batyushkov and Baratinskij and Annenskij. . . . Not thanks to this filth, but rather in spite of it. "Before dusk, I went to the English Club, where a most unusual event befell me," writes Pushkin from Petersburg to his wife in Moscow. "Three hundred and fifty rubles were stolen from me in the club, stolen not while playing tinter or whist, but stolen as they steal on the streets. How do you like our club? We have outdone even the one in Moscow!"

In Leningrad lived Aleksandr Khazin, a poet. During the war he was at the front and landed in a hospital. He returned to Leningrad and published poems in a magazine. In the 1946 speech in which Comrade Zhdanov, politburo member and cultural commissar, came down on Akhmatova and Zoshchenko, he also "baited" Khazin in passing—I use the word from bear hunting—for his parody of "Onegin's Return." Someone on a Leningrad tram steps on Onegin's foot and calls him an "idiot."

> Recalling the ancient ways,
> he resolved to end the dispute by a duel,
> dug in his pocket. . . . But someone had swiped
> his gloves long ago
> and for lack of them
> Onegin held his tongue and quieted down.

"That's how the vulgar Khazin presented Leningrad and its people." How about that? Vulgar indeed. Pushkin's purse was stolen—it was nothing! "You think that I got angry—not at all. I am angry at Petersburg and rejoice in its every dirty trick."

Aleksandr Abramovich Khazin, sweet and sad like all humorists (though you can become sad even without a talent for humor), wrote in the fifties and sixties monologues and sketches for A. Raikin. I met him two or three times in his life—the last time in the Metro, not long before his death. He told me that his dacha in the Leningrad suburbs had been burned down.

Private property in Russia is a major ordeal. You can't keep a TV, a bicycle, or any decent crockery, chairs, armchairs at a dacha—everything will be ripped off and carted away.

I certainly don't keep anything at my dacha. I have to admit such Spartan simplicity actually suits me. When my father retired, he became a passionate orchardist; we had fine apple trees with lots of apples: "shtrifel," cinnamon striped (I'm not sure I remember the name correctly and there's no one to ask), yellow transparents. . . . Strawberries, currants, gooseberries. . . .

Now, my two-tenths of a hectare are in utter ruin. The apple trees froze, withered, and had to be cut down. The gooseberries failed. Instead, the wild rose spread and glows all summer, a pleasure for the eye. As Baratinsky says in "Neglect": "You are still lovely, failed Elysium." Coming from the orchard, we track grass inside and have to sweep its silver threads from the rooms now and again. I could say that I cultivate another orchard—and there I am a most hardworking, zealous landlord, as they would say in olden days. But this phrase is high-flown, vulgar, and a worthless excuse. In fact, there is no excuse. That's why I live in Russia, don't and can't live in another country; perhaps the reason I love Vermeer so much is that I'm built not like the Dutch, but differently.

"A person needs not three 'arshins' of land, not an estate, but the whole wide world, all nature, where in vast open space he could manifest all the qualities and peculiarities of his free spirit." I'm afraid that we in Russia manifested these "capabilities and particularities of our spirit in vast open space" in a way no one else on earth has ever dreamed of. And it is Chekhov who writes this! Chekhov, who was neither ideologue nor maximalist, who at his place in Melikhov planted trees and flowers and then built a house in Yalta in the "style Moderne" according to the most civilized, European standards (the fireplace really was built in such a way that smoke, for some reason, blew into the room and it was so cold in winter that the host slept in felt slippers—but these are mere trifles and quibbles after all).

Is that good? That is, to sleep in felt slippers. It goes without saying that it isn't good or comfortable. But I have something else in mind: do we need to go into such details when speaking about a remarkable person? Details always expose inasmuch as they bring the object of our attention closer to us—actually, tour guides do exactly this (so do memoirists in part), otherwise who would believe or listen to them? Chekhov had no luck—Vermeer had: no memoirs are written about him and the house he lived in is not a museum; he was supposed to have lived in several houses, but all of them are so completely reconstructed in such a way, both inside and out, that the owner himself would be confused and couldn't recognize them as his own.

Let's return to the Russian theme. The Russian spirit is in anyone living in Russia. Even in Chekhov. Even in Akhmatova. As a memoirist recalls, with either tenderness or compassion, in Akhmatova's room in the House on the Fontanka, the armchair had only three legs; a brick was used to replace the fourth. The brick has traveled there from her youthful verses, so convincing in their seemingly unnecessary details: "On the bushes the gooseberries begin to bloom, / And bricks are carried past the cemetery fence. . . ." A brick falls from the carriage and is pressed into domestic use.

Dutch cities are built of brick. Not only buildings, but pavements as well. Therefore, both yards and streets seem the continuation of interiors: the same adjustment, orderliness, cleanliness. A Dutch mason in the seventeenth century was well-paid. In 1671, after the death of his sister, Vermeer received an inheritance of 648 florins. As it turned out, this sum was two year's pay for a mason and so the artist became well-off. Twenty years after his death, his painting *The Woman Weighing a Pearl* was sold at an Amsterdam auction for 155 florins, while *The Artist's Studio* went for 45.

A *View of Delft* with its tiled roofs, flaming-crimson walls, *A Small Street,* all ochre and brick—I am not carried away—a brick bears as direct a connection to Vermeer as armchairs and brocaded table-cloths, goblets and pitchers, and in that regard does not yield to a pearl so far as beauty is concerned.

My narration also bears a direct connection to a certain detail in an article by Pushkin: "The widow of an old professor, hearing that the conversation concerned the famous educator, scientist, and writer Lomonosov, asked: 'Which Lomonosov are you talking about? Could it be Mikhail Vasilevich? What a shallow person he was! Since he didn't have a coffeepot, rather than buy one, they used to fetch one from us!' "

What if I start here probing the factors that have influenced the Russian character? The Tartar-Mongolian yoke, serfdom. . . . Personally, I always feel like explaining history through geography: huge territories and severe winters. Probably Vermeer would agree with me: he has a painting, *The Geographer.* A scholar in a blue robe, dividers in hand, a globe on a bookcase. And also some rolled-up papers on the table. Neither beakers, nor flasks, nor coiled tubing, nor medical scalpels and knives, nor lenses, nor a lit alcohol lamp . . . a casual, simplified science. What is the shallowest subject, the one nobody ever studied or feared in school? Geography. And in Vermeer's painting, the geographer is also unconvincing. The crumpled, heavy, patterned tablecloth looks best of all.

Pushkin concluded that Russian misfortunes resulted from the fact that "the schism" (ecclesiastic separation) isolated us from the rest of Europe, and that the nature of Christianity in Russia differed from that of the West. "Modern history is the history of Christianity. Woe betide the country outside the European system." He calls Russia such a country. At the same time, he probably has in view the same things that the Englishwoman Elizabeth Justice noticed visiting Russia in 1734: "The Russians go to Church both in the evening and during the day. When they perform rituals, they cross themselves, bow and beat their heads against the floor, while repeating as often and fast as possible the words 'Lord pardon us.' And those who utter the fastest are considered the most pious."

Recognition of works as the most important side of communication with God and service to Him is almost unknown to us.

However, in speaking of Vermeer, we hardly need to emphasize industriousness; rather, we need to insist on the exuberance of his art and the feeling of neatness, festivity, and spiritual purity inspired by it. The works indisputably attributed to Vermeer are few—thirty-five. How little he painted compared to Rembrandt, Rubens, Cézanne, or Degas. How I dreamed of seeing the originals, not reproductions. In 1984 the Hermitage exhibited paintings from Dresden—and there, for the first time, we saw his *The Girl Reading a Letter by an Open Window*. I hurried to it as to a tryst. I'm not exaggerating in the least—I even wrote a poem about it at the time:

> I can't believe I'll see today
> this girl on the foreign golden canvas.
> Could a precious blue thread reach us,
> could we turn it in our hands, hold it?
>
> Could a pearly light gush, filling my eyes,
> with a Dutch maritime and hazy moisture?
> Could a fabulous tablecloth and a stool with tacks around it;
> or an armchair fill my eyes? The girl, immobile, a letter in her
>   hands.

And the poem ended this way:

270

To live in the seventeenth century, and not to suspect
how life would change two or three centuries later,
and be charmed and gladdened by this stained glass,
by this warm air, like honeysuckle racemes. . .
(December 1984)

I would not introduce my poetry into a prose text, but how else
can I explain what Vermeer meant to me? These lines are not summoned here to serve as decoration of the text, but rather as material
evidence. Maybe the reason biographies disappoint and fail is that
meetings with a book, with a painting, with a musical work, sea
waves, with a mountain path are no less meaningful than knowing a
remarkable person, invading Prague with tanks, or getting a new job.

My God, prowling around the world to see, wherever possible, one
more piece by a beloved artist—that kind of collecting exists too! For
example, how well I understand A. D. Chegodaev, who traveled the
globe in order to publish, in 1985, a book about *Edouard Manet*!
How I envied him!—in the Louvre there are *Olympia* and *Red-
bearded Man with an Eel*; in Avignon, *Still-life*; in Zurich, *The Harbor of Bordeaux*; and in New York, well. . . . Later, in New York, I
saw for myself *The Woman with a Parrot*, and *The Boy with a Foil*,
and *Victorina Mauran in a Matador's Suit*. . . .

"This is happiness! These are rights. . . ." My time had come; I
used these rights after 1987, when I was allowed to travel abroad.
The Metropolitan Museum and the Frick Collection in New York.
The National Gallery in Washington. The Gardner Museum in
Boston. Amsterdam, the Hague, Berlin, London, Paris. . . . I have
not been to Vienna—and so I've never seen *The Artist's Studio*
(known as *The Allegory of Painting*). Somewhere in Ireland, in Bless-
ington (I have never heard of such a city), there is one Vermeer (*The
Letter*).

Probably Vermeer's interaction of colors, the warm overtones and
coloristic achievements, and the problem of light should be mentioned. Light is the leading character in his paintings and means as
much as Rembrandt's swirling red-smoky-brown or swampy-green-
golden haze. In Vermeer's paintings light creates color harmony; it
lights up the sash of a dress with sun-like fire, strengthens the whiteness of a light-bluish mantle on the head of a woman—such a bluish-
pink can only be found on fresh March snow. Not without reason,
the woman with the pitcher, the one with the necklace, the one with

271

the lute and the one with the letter, all face one and the same window; sometimes it is open (*The Officer and the Laughing Girl*). And then you don't know why her smile is so radiant—is it chatting with the suitor she likes, or the light, pouring through the window. Here, involuntarily, I fall into the pompous style used in art history studies; the way musicologists paraphrase music when writing program notes. Avoiding the special terminology of glazes or pastosity (you can't find it in Vermeer)—is the same as ignoring rhythm and metaphors, let alone dactylic rhythms, *pyrrhics*, and spondees while talking about verse. . . . Alas, such talk is beyond my powers. God help me from making obvious errors or mistakes. Even Goethe, who called Rembrandt a thinker, and Ruysdael a poet, stumbled over Terborch and named one of his paintings *The Paternal Admonition*, whereas it depicts the exact opposite. Even an expert of the stature of Alexandr Benois had no luck with Terborch and made the same gaffe. He explained the noted *Goblet of Lemonade* thus: "The joke of the painting is the most ordinary. A suitor prepares lemonade for a young lady, who does not feel well, while her respectable mother looks on sympathetically." But the fact is that *The Goblet of Lemonade* is a typical scene at a matchmaker's, a favorite subject of cheerful, Dutch painters.

I am examining last summer's photographs. You are standing with your back to a canal, under a slim trunked, slender leafed acacia somewhat thinned out and "softly-blown," as Tyuchev would have put it—in the background, there's an old redbrick Dutch house with huge tall windows and white casings, a scarlet geranium in the second-story window; and here you are again, leaning over a bicycle chained to the white handrail of a fence—here again, a canal, houses rising from the water as in Venice. Light haired, in a green suit, smiling—you could have easily passed for a Dutchwoman.

Here I am; seeing yourself in a snapshot is as unpleasant as listening to your own taped voice. (I skip. . . .)

Here you are again; how bright yellow, red, blue are the awnings that shade local shop windows, how peaceful the passers-by, in no hurry, cautiously going around you so as not to enter the photoframe, not to bother these two tourists—from where? maybe from Austria, France? no, probably from Eastern Europe—and, since they dawdled at the last instant, are still seen in the snapshot, on its periphery—smiling, obliging, polite extras.

You are outlined against the statue of Justice on the multi-towered, magnificent town hall, which is decorated with red shutters; the statue appears to have climbed the roof with its bulky symbols: scale and sword. Vermeer used to come here. As was the customary practice at the time, here, on the 5th of April 1653, the announcement of his future wedding to Katarina Bolnes took place. I copy out this information from a French version of a Delft guidebook, *Sur les traces de Johannes Vermeer*, which reminds me of the novel *Remembrance of Things Past*—a favorite translation in its Russian edition of 1936, strange, absurd, but nonetheless, dear to my heart.

And we are together only in one, final snapshot. Do you remember? A Dutch woman passing by smiled and offered her help: we took seats on the steps of a high, steep, stone bridge, which resembled a grotto, and she snapped us. That happened in the evening, on one of the quietest and most deserted streets of the city, as we turned toward the station. Had we shown him, The Master of Delft, how snapshots are taken, he would have been delighted, and then, probably, frustrated realizing what a threat this magic apparatus posed to great art.

—Novij Mir, 8, 1997

Nominated by Antioch Review

COCK ROBIN

by MIRANDA FIELD

from POST ROAD

Not eat the thing you took. Not pluck its feathers, peel its skin.
Not kiss your own face on the mouth, imagining
the tasting. Nor bury the thing you bring down from the sky.

Not interpret the meaning of its cry. Not clothe the cooling thing
in woollens. Not reel it in. Not wind it while it writhes.
Not breathe hard while you work, not speak of it, not burrow in.

But barely look upon the garden where the weight fell, sudden.
Where the falling broke it open, the plummet stopped.
Where rain falls down in dying angles and damage blooms.

Not touch the entry wound. Not stitch it up. Nor enter.
Not with a finger. Not the Viking eye. Not wonder.
But leave be what you took. But let what spills congeal.

And wager everything you own the grass grows over it in time.
It will not rise again. The sky assists this with its rain.
And the garden, and the mind.

Nominated by Post Road

AMAZING GRACE

fiction by BRADFORD MORROW

from CONJUNCTIONS

Whereas I was blind, now I see.
—John 9:25

T HE MIRACLE THAT RESTORED MY SIGHT, one wicked winter morning, was a miracle which led to many desperate others. Who could
have foreseen the catastrophes that followed this moment I had
dreamed of for over a decade? The only blessing that accompanied
the sudden, unexpected reversal of my blindness was this: I was
alone when it happened. My wife was away shopping; the two children were out. Myself, I was in my humble study, listening to an old
recording of Sviatoslav Richter playing Schubert's Sonata in G Major.
Thanks to Sarah, a fire crackled in the wood-burning stove, making
my sanctum warm and dry—the room where I worked was an unin-
sulated extension added to the house in the months after my accident. A pot of nice fragrant cinnamon tea was on my desk, along with
my Braille Bible, some reference books also in Braille, and my computer loaded with voice-synthesizing software I used to draft the
many motivational speeches I gave touring the country. It has always
struck me as ironic, although naturally I never mentioned it in my
uplifting talks, that I made a far better living after the accident than
when I was among the sighted. No one would have paid a plug nickel
to hear me speak before tragedy struck me down. Now I filled rented
auditoriums and motel convention halls, and my talks on surviving
personal crises were well-received wherever I went. Not that my phi-

275

losophy about adversity management was more informed or refined than the next survivor's—not a vain bone in *this* body—it's just my story had all the necessary elements. The perfect life, the great disabling affliction, the season of despair, the awakening of hope, and the long road of spiritual renewal that rewards the steadfast pilgrim with a life far richer than what seemed so perfect before. Sarah, I must say, deftly supervised this unanticipated chautauqua career of mine, from bookings to billings, and oversaw with the help of our dedicated manager every detail of our burgeoning mission. And with seldom—no, never a complaint. She was nothing less than a stoic saint, an altruistic martyr, with just enough savvy to hold our shattered lives together, not only keeping her eye on our spiritual needs, but making sure there was always bread on the table.

One reason I have been so successful on the circuit is because I believed every word I said, or at least *most every word.* To the sort of individual who attends such seminars, unwavering personal conviction on the part of the speaker is nine-tenths the victory. I have often felt that if I held up an egg in the palm of my hand and proclaimed with firm faith that it was not an egg, but a flower or a shoe, say, the right audience of seekers would cry out in agreement, *So it is!* With conviction and what might be called a *winning idiosyncrasy in the presenter*—in my case, blindness—one can bring people around to anything. That I never used my powers of persuasion to ends other than kindly inspiration, positive role-modeling, carrying the simple message of hope to souls willing to listen, pleases me. The temptation to deceive was always there, somehow, but it was a human weakness never acted upon. Not that I'd have known what to deceive my acolytes about, nor that I ever made the logical next step to consider the possibility that some of them entertained deceptive thoughts regarding me. No one, I convinced myself, would want to victimize this victim: Hadn't I suffered enough? The answer is *I had not even begun my real suffering.*

Not born blind, indeed I had 20/20 vision for thirty years. A robust, confident young man, I met my Sarah at a church bazaar—we were always active members at St. Francis Episcopal—and it was love at first sight. Her thick auburn hair drifting in gentle waves down the back of her white dress, her quick blue eyes, the exquisite mole above her lip, the strong warm hands that shook mine when we were introduced, her smile as radiant as dawn. How many times since my world fell into shadow have I conjured up the visual memory of that day. After a succinct courtship, we married and started a family. Rebecca was born first, and then the twins, Emma and Luke. Emma survived only a few weeks, poor little bird. My grief over the loss was so great that to this day I indulge in fantasizing about her, what her interests would have been, how her voice might have sounded. I would like to think she'd have turned out a trustworthy Milton's daughter. In my mind's eye, I always pictured her as a young Sarah, slender as a willow and sturdy as an oak, along those lines. But we all know how ingenious imagination can be, how it sometimes finds *a shining berth* in the rankest mound of dung.

Time passed, our young family thrived. My job at the utilities company was going well enough; the benefits were good and hours such that I could spend quality time with my children. I worked the graveyard shift at the local power plant as a maintenance technician troubleshooting outages, servicing customer emergencies, getting people back on line when an ice storm or high wind brought down wires or blew out a transformer. In the Northeast, where we live just a mile from my own childhood home, our crew had more to do during the night than one might imagine. Always something going wrong, always some problem to remedy. I very much enjoyed the challenge, as I've told my rapt audiences, and learned a lot meeting people from all walks of life under trying circumstances. So long as I live, I will never forget the courage of the little girl—her name was Belinda, if I'm not mistaken—who, during a severe nor'easter that crippled not just Gloucester but the whole corridor from the Carolinas up to Maine, offered her mommy her teddy bear to feed to the flames in the fireplace that heated their home while our crew worked through the night to restore power. A bunch of us later pooled together to buy her a new bear, bigger and fuzzier than the one she sacrificed. *Duress* brings out the *best* in us—so I often advised my Ramada listeners. In a file somewhere there is a newspaper clipping with a photograph of Belinda surrounded by her benefactors and our stuffed bear. Sarah had it up on the refrigerator for months. She thought it was a flattering shot. I must have looked pleased with myself, because in those days I was. Life was a river awash with proverbial milk and honey.

A stifling, muggy midsummer night changed all that. I wasn't even supposed to work the shift, but a massive brownout across our regional grid forced the company to call upon every available hand. My memory of that night is selective at best. I whispered goodbye to

Sarah, kissed the children where they lay asleep in their bedrooms. The streets were eerily dim. Thick steamy amber haze hung in the wilted trees. Cicadas had burrowed up from the earth to mate that year, dogday locusts we called them, and were lustily clicking and buzzing away outside the open windows of our utility van, their boisterous droning sounding like bandsaws underwater. We were at work on a central routing transformer, using the headlights of the van to see by, when I must have made the simplest error, crossing two clusters of wire in such a way that I sparked a high-voltage explosion. Knocked unconscious, I have no recollection of what happened in the hours that followed. My first perceptions had only to do with a searing, bludgeoning pain in my neck and around the base of my hot skull. My face was burned and my eyes felt as if they were molten.

Recuperation swallowed up days and weeks of time, all of which remains vague even now. What stands out from the miasma of my slow recovery was the ophthalmologist's concern that the many lesions on the corneas of both eyes were healing, as he'd expected them to, but my vision still hadn't returned. Yet one should have resulted in the other. I could make out uneasy shapes at a distance of a foot or so in front of me, but had no strong sense of day or night, of whether the lights were on or off. The doctors performed tests to determine ocular blood flow, ran an MRI against the possibility of brain damage, but found nothing that would explain the blindness. My 20/20 vision was now 20/400 at best and when I was released from the hospital my condition was not only unimproved, but worsening. They continued to chart my progress but there wasn't much more that could be done medically.

Summer faded into fall. The once steady stream of colleagues and friends who dropped in to visit, read me the Bible, listen to music with me, dwindled. I couldn't in fairness expect otherwise. Sarah's considerate idea of building an extension onto the house, thus to spare me the trouble and danger of walking up and down stairs I couldn't see, kept me busy for a while. Not that I was able to help. But my wife and the contractor did consult with me about construction specs. Ever the *clever one in our family*, Sarah suggested we might save money by forgoing windows in my modest wing—they could be added later, when and if my sight returned—and used the balance of the home improvement loan to carpet the whole house. I thought it an extravagance, but she insisted it would cushion any falls

I happened to take. Although my equilibrium hadn't been a problem, I commended her ingenuity.

Around Thanksgiving I lost my job. My supervisor was kind enough to give me the bad news in person. They'd held out as long as they could, he said, sitting with me in my den over some chowder Sarah served us in mugs. Damn bad luck, he told me, his voice gooey from the thick soup *if not the tacky sentiment*. I nodded, trying to form an understanding smile on my lips, though I'd already begun to forget what I looked like before the accident, and had no clear concept what such a smile might look like now. Vivid silence clouded the room before I heard him shift in his seat and rise to leave. Your workman's comp is all in order, he said, taking my free hand into his, which was clammy. I thanked him, climbing to my feet. I wanted to touch his face but hadn't the nerve to ask. As I recall, he had a dense, large nose, the by-product of a long-standing love affair with cheap scotch chased by cheaper ale. Balls and beer, the boys used to call it at work, a thousand years ago. Off the top of my head I couldn't tell you his or any of their names now.

Then came the truly dark days. Days that added up to months, a year of miserable months that vanished like voices murmuring in an empty room. Learning Braille was a necessary but grim admission that my blindness was not the temporary setback my ophthalmologist had diagnosed. A second sightless Christmas came and went. Luke and Becca seemed happy with their presents, none of which I could see any more than I could their presumptive beaming faces. Sarah thanked me for the nightgown I bought her with the help of a salesperson who was kind enough to describe it to me over the telephone—rayon, beige, a few flounces edged in lace. We tried to act celebratory, to make the best of the situation, and I even indulged in a little champagne which gave me a migraine that lasted a week. Sitting alone in my personal black hole on New Year's Eve, I urged Sarah to go without me to a party down the street, hire a sitter, *enjoy herself a little*. It hardly seemed fair for her, who looked after me day and night, to stay home reading to me from Isaiah, or Job, while I followed along with my fingers. Even as I sat wallowing in my misfortune that evening, listening to Mahler and eating a bowl of popcorn my wife had placed on the side table, I guessed the busybodies were talking about none other than me and what a shame all this was for poor Sarah, who was still so young and vibrant. I drowned myself in the choral voices of the Ninth Symphony, then fell asleep in my chair. Later, Sarah woke me and led me by the arm upstairs to bed, which smelled of roses and sage. My melancholy delirium lifted for a moment, for these fragrances reminded me of the careless, caring nights we used to enjoy, the nights of intimacy that resulted in the birth of our babies. Half-awake, I kissed her and thanked her for all she had done to help me through this tragedy. I promised her—though she might not have heard, since I could tell by her breathing she was asleep—that I would try harder, would overcome the doldrums that made life so tough this past year and a half. That I would do something with myself, defeat my disability in some way, learn to see anew, like blind Bartimaeus whom Jesus cured in Jericho with nothing more than a few words of encouragement.

True to my promise, the next morning I glued Braille tabs to the keys of my old typewriter and sat myself down to outline everything that conspired to bring me to my present predicament, and what I believed as I began my long journey back to life. Sarah set me up with a fresh ream of paper. The work was slow. It took a while to get a feel for producing words and phrases through the clumsy machinery of the typewriter. Not being able to review what I'd just written, I had to visualize the sentences fore and aft in my head. Initially, Sarah read me back what I'd sketched, but even she had reasonable limits as to how much time she could devote to my little project. The children weren't getting younger. She had even taken a part-time position with that contractor who built the extension, in order to supplement my benefits. He was called Jim James, a name whose triumph of redundancy might have intimated the ways matters were drifting but did not. We were grateful for the income.

At first I thought to write an article for the St. Francis newsletter about how faith in God is essential to our surviving crises, or some such, but as I got the ideas down on paper, I realized it was one cliché after another and of no use to anybody. I had to *delve deeper into my reservoir of pain* so turned some of my ideas around backwards and found they came out much better. Faith alone, in other words, was not enough to carry us through. Rather, it was one oar we could use to pull our fragile ship through the turbulent waters of doubt and despair, the other oar being hope. Like that. I spent hours on end working out my thoughts, quoting passages from my King James whenever the reference seemed apropos, or sometimes—if the pretty image struck my fancy—when it wasn't. Not only did the newsletter publish my first effort but, thanks to someone in the congregation who showed it to an editor at the local paper, reminding him who I was—*the man blinded while trying to bring light to others,* as he put it—I was commissioned to write a human interest article detailing the aftermath of that horrifying night. I missed the deadline and Sarah asked for an extension, which they granted. When I did turn in my manuscript I explained in an apologetic cover letter that typing on an old Royal rigged with Braille tabs that kept falling off made for perhaps not the best working conditions. I hoped nevertheless that they would find the final product worthy of their esteemed pages.

The memoir was a success. Letters came in from around the state, the most gushing of which were published in the newspaper over the days that followed. Sarah knocked on my door soon after, announcing that the editor himself had dropped by the house with something that might make me very happy. Indeed, I was floored by Mr. Harrison's kindness. On behalf of everyone at the paper, he presented me with a used computer preloaded with software for the blind. Little Luke, who was eight then and computer savvy, taught me how to use this gift, and within a matter of months I was contributing regularly to various periodicals distributed in the area. From this print exposure came my first invitations to speak before the public. My wife's *inherent Christian strength of spirit* was aroused by what she saw happening before her eyes. The love, empathy, and compassion she witnessed flowing toward her husband from these strangers, common workaday people who listened intently to what insights I was able to give them, overwhelmed dear Sarah. That Mr. Harrison offered to assist us financially, lift the burden of her having to work for the contractor, so she could devote more time to helping answer every request to address this crowd or that, constituted another blessing on our household. I, who had come to abide misfortune, was now in the pulpit of Everyman, as it were. *Many are called but few are chosen,* the Bible tells us, and I—an unfledged beggar by the waters of Siloam—was called.

Sarah was never more attentive, more heedful than during the heady times that followed. Invite followed invite, obliging us to be away from home for days, even weeks, at a time. When my wife told me that we'd begun to charge sponsors a nominal fee to offset expenses of travel, lodging, meals, not to mention the live-in housekeeper who also looked after Luke and Becca, I didn't object, though deep down I would have preferred offering my inspirational views without money attached. Harrison advised her on the best ways to proceed, and acted on my behalf as an agent, placing my lectures in various journals and anthologies, *building the rep*, as he put it. They were right, of course, telling me that if we wanted to get my message out there, we needed assistance, and who better than the listeners and readers themselves to assist? The venture was worthy, we all knew. There were many who wanted, needed, to hear my story of hardship and hope. I told Sarah that, if she didn't mind, she should be the one who managed the practicalities with Harrison's help. Back in the halcyon days before the world went dark I wore the financial pants in the house, if you will. Given that now I couldn't tell a one-dollar check from another of a thousand made our positions clear. Sarah agreed with all my requests, *bless her heart*. Both my muse and protector, she was brilliant in her role.

What possible point would there be in reproducing a transcript of the speeches I made? Often I was introduced by a local priest or minister. My wife would then lead me to the podium. Applause. I launched straightaway into my backstory, guided my auditors from the shadowy valley of pain and grief to the mountain of renewal and joy. Self-pity was just that: a *pit* from which we must rise and shine. I told them about my New Year's Eve revelation, mentioning how I had come to believe that the marvelous scent of sage and roses in the bedroom that night was an auspicious sign from God, the soulstruck breath of my guardian angel. My favorite concluding exhortation was *Don't be afraid of miracles*. Applause. Then a few questions and answers. Do you think that God will restore your sight one day? was the perennial query I could count on being asked. My response was, in this life or the next, I know He will let me see my wife and children again, for *He's a good and generous God*. A reception would follow during which the voices around me brimmed with appreciative respect that made me understand just how attached each member of the human family is to another. My calling as a missionary of faith suited me well and as the years elapsed the uneasy peace I'd made with my blindness deepened. Never would I have touched so many lives had I not been stricken. I like to think that I was always a good man, but so many have proclaimed there's a genuine spark of greatness in me that at times I have to believe there may be. If so, all credit goes to our Savior, as such blessings flow only from Him, and so forth.

Home, now, from nine weeks on the road, after a restless night in my bed in the study—Sarah and I agreed to sleep in separate quarters after such long trips on the circuit because when I was particularly fatigued I tossed and turned—I awoke feeling not quite myself. True, I had been working harder than ever. Our schedule had been nonstop for months, so perhaps this explained my sensation of unbalance. Along with prayer, music has always been my remedy for any illness, and so it was I'd put on Schubert's Opus 78 for piano, whose divine opening chords would, I was sure, bring me around. Martita, the housekeeper, served cinnamon tea and tended my fire. Not wanting to bother her—and besides, the monumental Richter seemed to be working his magic—I said nothing about my disposition.

Some minutes after she closed my door, abrupt pain erupted in my temples. Beset by wild dizziness, by violent nausea, by spasms that stabbed like long needles through my skull, I shrieked, though no noise left my throat. Gasping, I rolled from my chair onto the floor, hitting my head as I did. I tried to call out for Sarah but couldn't. Then, as suddenly as the pain began it was replaced by numbness. I could hear the piano music very distantly, as if it were coming from the far end of a long tunnel. Light engulfed my eyes—a cascade, a flood, a torrent of *unblinding light*. As I grabbed at the arms of my chair to stand, I found myself staring into what appeared to be flames dancing behind the grate of the potbellied stove. My eyes agonizingly darted around the room and there, in this dim place on whose walls firelight flickered—more like Plato's cave than a Christian's den—were all the things I'd come to know only by touch. My table, my books, my computer, my cot, my chair. No embellishments, nothing on the walls, all very minimal, even dreary to my naive eyes. But of course, I thought. Why decorate? Why wallpaper a blind man's cell? Standing now, a bit shaky, admiring *my wife's wise Christian expediency*, I walked around placing my hands on everything, still not quite sure what was happening. My vision was blurry but with each new moment I became more reassured this wasn't a dream, a taunting nightmare. The radical pain having largely subsided, I remained a little numb, whether from excitement or physiological impulse, I didn't know or care. I wanted to climb to the roof and cry out to the world that my miracle had finally come. My feet carried me to the door that led to the main house, and I who rarely left my sanctum—why should I have?—opened it.

Bright white light poured through the living room windows, sun reflected off the snow. But for the ticking of a clock, in Franz Schubert's wake, the house was silent. I took a few tentative steps and gazed, blinking hard while heavily tearing, in wonder. What had happened to our simple home? If you will, I couldn't believe my eyes. The walls were gilded and the windows dressed with billowing chiffon sashes. In an alcove stood a gargantuan breakfront on whose glassed shelves were countless porcelain figurines. I stumbled ahead toward facing sofas and stuffed chairs upholstered in striped silks of chartreuse and gold. Here was a commode with a marble top and a vase of orchids above the marquetry. There were two reclining brass deer on a prayer rug by the hearth. An antique grandfather clock clad in luminous mahogany stood haughty in a corner. Oriental carpets of red, blue, yellow, and green lay atop the white wall-to-wall. Fine old portraits of men and women dressed in the garb of another century hung everywhere, staring out at me from canvases black as lacquer. A chandelier centered it all, its prisms reflecting hundreds of tiny rainbows on the ceiling, which was done up with decorative plaster moldings. Though I examined each piece of furniture, horrified and fascinated, and though what I saw was as tangible as truth itself, my heart sank, because I knew this couldn't be so. I pinched myself, closed my eyes, reopened them. But the room didn't change. If anything, it became more lavish as my sore eyes adjusted to the light.

A familiar sound came from upstairs. It seemed to be Harrison, softly whistling to himself some random tune, as he often did when he accompanied us on the road. I thought to call out his name, tell him the astonishing news, ask him to come down, fall to his knees with me and *pray Lord God thanks for this deliverance,* but didn't. Who knows how or wherefrom inner voices speak to us, or in what mysterious ways they confide to us involuntary prophecies that save us from harm, disillusion, even doom? The whistling stopped and when it did, I took a couple of steps back, bumping into a side table and knocking a crystal lamp to the floor. I was startled to hear Harrison say, *Bunny?* And hearing him ask the question again, this time in a deeper, softer, more melodiously concerned voice, I looked around for a place to hide, *an Adam's fig leaf as it were,* suddenly frightened, frightened even beyond the terror of finding myself among the sighted, standing there agog, a dumb novitiate, a stranger in my own house. He glided down the carpeted stairs, silent as a proverbial ghost, and seemed relieved to find me, half-crouching behind one of the big plush sofas. You all right? asked Harrison. Instinctively, I stared forward and said I was. What did I break? I wanted to know. Out of the corner of my eye I saw him inspecting the damage, dressed to the nines in a deep blue silk robe, the same color I remembered Sarah's irises as being. His hair, which I'd always pictured black and short, was silver and stylishly long. His unshaven face was taut and handsome. Averting my eyes when he glanced at me, I noticed that he, like Sarah, had a mole, though his was on the cheek. What bothered me most was that his robe was open in the front. If my wife or children were to walk into the room just then, what an eyeful they'd get. Think how embarrassed everyone would be. Stay here, he calmly requested, his voice sweet but the look on his suntanned face as annoyed as a pet owner scolding a naughty puppy. Taking me by the arm, he sat me by the gold wall in a chair appointed with fine overstuffed upholstery. I could have sworn he cursed under his breath as he left, but at that moment I didn't trust my ears any more than my eyes. At least while he retreated toward the kitchen he tied his winsome dressing gown. I had caught a subtle glimpse of what hung there, haloed by white hair. It was nothing anyone should want to see, let alone someone who'd been denied the privilege of seeing anything whatever for a decade.

Other astonishments appeared. The more I saw, the more I understood it was important, somehow, that those around me thought I saw nothing. Conspicuous among my discoveries was how wrong I'd imagined everyone and everything. I who had begun truly to believe my fervent homilies, urging my followers to keep the faith first by trusting themselves, their convictions, their own views—*be thee blind or seeing with lucid eyes*—slowly understood how utterly I'd erred. If that morning returned to me my sight, the rest of the day brought my insights, as I have come to think of them. Harrison in his baronial robe waltzing through our kinky nouveau riche living room was merely the first verse in my New Apocrypha. Martita, who came to clean up the broken lamp, was someone whose voice, again, I recognized but whose appearance struck me as incongruous with the life I'd believed my family was leading. Not that she, poor Cayman immigrant and clearly a good if very illegal girl, behaved in any way that could be perceived as unChristian. No, it was that they had her in a black uniform with white starched trim and in a state of *quasipenal subservience*. Harrison wondered if I wouldn't like to go back to my room, said I looked exhausted, Lord knows no one would blame me for wanting a little more rest, given the grueling schedule

I had just endured. Again I asked what I'd broken and he answered that it was nothing, just a glass one of the kids left on an end table, not to worry. The maid crossed herself and, having finished cleaning, left the room. Where is Sarah? I asked, my hands shaking although I anchored them between my thighs. Out, he said, shopping. When I inquired when she was expected back, he muttered something and, excusing himself, flew upstairs, ever silently, no doubt to change into some clothes.

Time passed—twenty-three minutes to be exact, now that I could watch the clock—then Sarah unlocked the grand front door. Making her way to the kitchen, she failed to notice her husband seated in an unwonted corner, escapee from his holy cage. The years had not been kind. My once-wholesome Sarah had acquired, I must admit, a gaunt sophistication. Though elegant and drily beautiful, her face was as if invaded by knives—angular, hewn, deblooded. It was all I could do to maintain on my own face the blankest possible expression. This was only the beginning. What I saw next *I wouldn't wish on the Prince of Darkness himself.* Harrison floated back downstairs, gathered my wife in his arms and kissed her, put his forefinger to his lips, and pointed in my direction. I would like to believe she might have fainted, standing there in the arms of this man, staring at her blind husband not thirty feet away. To the contrary, she sweetly called my name, breaking from Harrison's embrace, and asked me the same question he had, patting my head, offering to help me get back to my room. I needed more rest, she cooed. After all, we had only a week before we were committed to going to Louisville for the Christian Recovery Convention, at which I was one of the headliners. Bed did seem a desirable destination at the moment. Yes, bed, I answered, and allowed her to take me by the arm, as she had countless times over the last decade, and lead me into my hermitage. I fell asleep immediately.

Seeing the world, I had not yet come to know how to reckon it. That was, I always felt, God's distinct purview, His task. Yet in the days that followed, seeing what I saw was judgment enough and though Job was my cherished Old Testament hero, I would prove to be no Job. Seeing, like my original blinding, was an unexpected trauma, a crossroads. The more I reflect upon what has happened, whether from a vantage of darkness or light, the more I see life as an investigation into just this: how much pain we can tolerate before we either (1) turn ourselves humbly over to our God, that His will be done, or (2) turn against the sadistic Bastard *with every fiber of our being.* Just how He found the fortitude, tenacity, and nerve to look down on me from on high these ten long suffering years, knowing all the while that every word of encouragement I offered to the far-flung members of His miscellaneous flock was fouled by the adultery and avarice of those who pretended to sustain His wretched servant, I cannot pretend to know. The ways of the Almighty are, it has been often recorded, mysterious. We mere mortals who fail to know our own hearts can't begin to fathom what motivates His. Not that my poor wife's weakness of the flesh, her infidelity, and materialist lust are in any way the fault of the Precious Savior. Nor that my benefactor and proponent, Harrison, without whose support I might never have found my audience, all those hungry souls who have dined—I hope nutritiously—at my inspirational banquets, was guided by the hand, if not the hoof, of the Lamb. As I lay in the equally dark but somehow less blurry shadows of my new world, as deeply dejected as I ever was when I first lost my sight, I decided to follow my instincts and *see what there was to see.* My life became a blindman's bluff.

Sarah checked in on me sometime later that same day, concerned why I'd been stumbling around the living room. Was I feeling all right? she wanted to know. I was fine, I assured her, and testing the waters asked if I couldn't sleep upstairs with her tonight. We generally had separate bedrooms on the road, and so often slept apart at home. I said; surely the Lord would want a wife to abide some snoring now and then, if only *for the sake of Old Testament conjugal duty.* Though I stared at the wall behind her, the look of dismay that shrouded her face, like Beelzebub's specter, was unmistakable. Her voice smilingly assured me that we need to take it easy during this week off, while the frown on her lips mutely bespoke another message. I wanted to say, how could I have been so blind to her true feelings all this time? but kept my own counsel and meekly agreed. That seemed to brighten her mood. Her face relaxed as she brushed back her frosted hair and asked what kind of soup I wanted Martita to bring me for lunch. Barley, I said, and watched my estranged wife's hips pitch softly back and forth as she left the sanctum.

The children were my only hope. My wonderful babies, my joys, bounty of my loins. They, I assured myself, had not veered from the path of righteousness like their mother. Persisting with my charade the next morning, I once more entered the main house. Rather than loiter in the garish living room, I joined Martita in the kitchen, which was also extensively renovated, shiny chrome and glass everywhere, and a tile-work splashback depicting urns choked with flowers and French farm scenes. Though she was at first surprised by my appearing in her domain, Martita helped me to a chair at the long table and got me my morning tea. It was quite early, I saw by the wall clock, too early for Sarah, but maybe not for the kids, who I assumed would come down first, on their way to class. Becca was in her last year of high school, and Luke a junior. As Martita busied herself, chatting amiably about this and that, I furtively studied her, wondering just how much she knew about the goings-on around here. Her black hair combed into a chignon, her handsome concise form moving lithely in her uniform, her dark eyes, her pretty hands—she cut a finer figure than I had imagined. Some obvious questions came to mind to ask her, but I thought the better of it. Ease up, I reminded myself. As St. Paul advised in his Epistle to the Hebrews, *Let us run with patience the race that is set before us.*

Luke entered the kitchen first. That is, a young man whom Martita referred to as Luke. Rather than coming downstairs, however, to have his breakfast, he ducked through the back door having apparently spent the night elsewhere. Abstracted, with eyes glazed, he noticed me as he opened the refrigerator door and drank long and hard from an orange juice carton, but said nothing. His hair was every bit as orange as the juice he consumed, and rose in numerous spikes off the top of his head. His mascara was smudged—little Luke wore mascara? Great chunks of silver graced each of his fingers. He was skinny as a broomstick and looked the warlock part he affected. I sat in stunned silence, maintaining my own vacant glazed-over stare which matched my son's. I didn't know they made boots that big. What's *he* doing here? Luke asked Martita. I interrupted, How are you doing this morning, Luke? Awright, I guess, he answered. You're up with the roosters, I pressed, at the same time wondering if he oughtn't be nervous that the coffin lids were all supposed to be down by this time, and then saw him give Martita a look that could only be described as threatening. Sure am, he said, taking a fat green apple from the bowl of fruit on the table and politely excusing himself with a sneer. After he left the kitchen, I said, Luke's a fine young man, isn't he.

If both Sarah and Luke had gone the way of Judas, and Harrison with them, it seemed improbable Rebecca had managed to resist the tide of treachery. For having *betrayed my credulous innocence with vizor'd falsehood, and base forgery*, as blind Milton himself once wrote, *the pillared firmament is rottenness, and the earth's base is built on stubble.* I fled to my cave.

A pestilence had swept through my household, like the very dog-day locusts which prophesied the onset of my blindness that summer night a decade ago. I lay on my cot, hands over my forehead and face, unable to move, loath to think, as sweat broke out across the length of my body and a range of black emotions chased through me. Above all, I wanted never to leave my room again. They could bring me my filthy barley soup and vile cinnamon tea whenever they found time between the commission of sins, and to hell with the rest of it. Indeed, when Sarah ventured by later, reeking of sage and roses, and found me prostrate, she let out a little cry of fear. Perhaps I should be ashamed to admit it, but that cry was like sweet music to me— even better than the opening strains of Stravinsky's *Apollon Musagète*, though it sounded more like Honegger's Symphony No. 2, the *molto moderato*, so very crushingly ominous, as performed by von Karajan and the Berliner Philharmoniker. Not because I was deluded enough to think it meant she was concerned, as such, for my sake, or that my heart melted with sudden forgiveness. No, no— rather because *it gave me my idea.* Whereas before I couldn't see her face if she voiced distress on my behalf, now I did, and Sarah's look was that of a caretaker grown weary of her role, disgusted, in fact, by it. Humanitarian that I strove to be, and *many had seen fit to call me*, I reluctantly sympathized with my wife. I understood her failings and well-knew how many persons of good intent and a hopeful heart nevertheless plant the earnest seeds of their goodness and optimism in *the yielding muck of ambition.* Look at Harrison. He probably didn't have designs on my wife, my home, my finances, my very self, when he first got me into print and onto a podium. How do I know? Because by the same reasoning one might say that I never intended for him to succeed so assiduously in ruining me, even as he saved the souls of thousands by helping me to save my own. Having noted that, inspiration took hold of me and would not give way to any alternative from that day forward, until it had fulfilled itself like the competent beast it was.

The idea began simply. I didn't feel up to Louisville. We would have to cancel. Sarah thought we should pray for guidance, and we went through the gesture of prayer. I still didn't feel like going. Harrison suggested that a doctor ought to be brought in to look me over.

Louisville was, after all, *awfully darned important to the furtherance of the crusade*—the Christian Recovery Convention was, if I didn't mind his saying so, the Holy Grail, a motivational orator's Valhalla. It was a dream come true for me, for Sarah, for everyone who believed in my message of hope. A doctor wouldn't find anything wrong with me, I said, staring right through him. What then? he asked, before underscoring again the importance of keeping this engagement, reminding me it was the kickoff to our big tour through the South, saying something about another book deal in the works. I appreciated how much work Sarah and he had put into Louisville, the tour, all the rest, but couldn't do it. The problem was this. Somehow I lost my calling. Sarah's pale face drained of all color as she looked at Harrison, who was also ashen. You still believe in God, of course, my wife whispered. I told her I suppose I did, it wasn't that. Well, what is it, man? Harrison asked, noiselessly taking my wife's hand in his. Not sure, I said. My message of hope seemed stale, banal, for some reason, and the more I thought about it the more I'd come to believe it was one better repudiated than preached. Likewise, God seemed more complicated than I'd believed Him to be. I didn't understand Him or His ways, certainly not well enough to speak His cause before others whom, by the way, I also did not understand. Sarah withdrew her hand, stepped toward me, placed it on my head, which made me wince a little, and she said, You're tired, dear, is all . . . your audiences need you, your family needs you, *all of us need you* to go to Louisville and shine the light of truth into the darkest corners of people's souls and help them find their way back into the sun.

Sarah, it would appear, had been listening to my patent drivel these past years so perfectly was she able to quote me to myself. God in heaven, I almost laughed, but the idea had nothing to do with mirth. Instead, allow me to admit, it ran more along the lines of St. Paul's Epistle to the Romans 12:19. Look it up for yourself.

Over the days that followed my initial confession of apostasy came many wearying pleas and petitions from my wife, my manager, even the children. My prediction regarding Rebecca was not wrong. She had become what the kids call a Goth. The dyed black hair, the black fingernails, the black dress and black boots even bigger than Luke's, *if that was possible*, and a girlfriend in tow dressed in the same uniform. Becca, I should say, did seem the least egregious of the lot of heretics my family had become. She at least didn't seem to care as much as the others whether the income from my missionary work

290

continued or not. She styled herself, I'm guessing, as a bit of an anarchist, though we all know anarchy is best proselytized by the disaffected well-to-do. Be that as it may, Rebecca was no more able to budge me from my den than the others, and Louisville soon came and went, absent its blind featured speaker. Harrison told me we received hundreds of cards and letters from well-wishers.

Which brought me to the second phase of the idea. The revenue stream must be stopped. This was not as simple as merely dropping off the lecture circuit since, clearly, Harrison had invested wisely and, despite myself, money still flowed in with those letters. An anonymous tip to the Internal Revenue Service informing them that my family and closest advisor were bilking our religious foundation of tens of thousands of dollars, maybe more, for personal gain, rather than funding programs for the blind and other disableds, got the job done. It all went rather quickly. The lien on our home and bank accounts, the removal of the furniture and frippery in the living room and everywhere else in this house—yes, things moved irrevocably, decisively. Sarah spent a lot of time crying, I can report. When she wasn't doing that she was arguing with Harrison. Luke simply disappeared off the scene. And Rebecca, I gathered, was spending more and more time over at her girlfriend's place. Harrison's indictment for fraud and income tax evasion was bittersweet for me though my residual sentimentality toward him, the former him, I should say, the man who did help me in the beginning, faded away to nothing when I learned how much we had earned over those fruitful years, and how much he had stolen from his gullible mistress. They broke up. And once my lawyer—a former devotee who volunteered his time— cleared me of any collaboration in my handlers' schemes, I filed for divorce from the lovely Sarah, who, seeing there was nothing to salvage, didn't contest the action. The foundation was dismantled. The media was ruthless. An insightful if scathing article about *my amazing fall from grace* was published in the very newspaper that gave me my computer and printed my own first efforts. Fond memories. Now I was left with the house and enough money to live modestly, having such comforts as society thinks are due a poor blind fellow who'd been bruised a bit in the proverbial school of hard knocks.

While I sometimes feel a numbness in the pit of my stomach when pondering the arc of my brilliant life, I still have my Sviatoslav Richter disc of Schubert's Sonata in G Major to comfort me. I still indulge in fantasizing how my daughter Emma, had she lived, would have saved me from my hapless enemies if not myself. But the past has passed. The sole question that remains is whether or not to feign a sudden miraculous recovery of my sight after Martita becomes my new bride. God knows, there's much to be said for blindness, especially when one can see. Either way, I'm sure she and I will be quite happy living here together once we get this damn gilt off the walls.

Nominated by Joyce Carol Oates

HEAT WAVES IN WINTER DISTANCE

by JAMES GALVIN

from DENVER QUARTERLY

Cloud brow over the swaying Medicine Bow,
These thoughts of mine—they're yours.
Pray for me as I pray
For you to turn tacit,
To cauterize me in a searing kiss.
You know—I know you know—
Just how much blood is out there,
Most of it in circulation,
Enough to make a single drop worthless.
Mark my words.
Imagine an anorexic mosquito,
Euphemistic as the number two,
Hot all over.
Dried blood is not worth anything either,
Except to the awful law
That turns against
Its former mirror image ripped in waves,
Electrified by heat in distance.
My mother waved good-bye
Every single day I left for school.
Heat waves, particle waves, tidal waves—
You know.

Nominated by Katrina Roberts, Marvin Bell, Denver Quarterly

293

THE ROAD TO ROME, AND BACK AGAIN

Memoir by MICHAEL PALMA

from QUADERNI DI YIP (YIP: YALE ITALIAN POETRY)

IN THE CONSCIOUSNESS of most people who pick up a work of literature in translation, the translator exists, at best, only for a moment as a name looking somewhat out of place on the title page. Even translators, when we manage to get our often battered egos under control, would acknowledge that this is largely as it should be. The dedicated translator desires to be a transparent medium between author and audience. I was highly gratified when a poet friend recently told me that my translations of six Italian poets in the current issue of *Chelsea* spoke in six individual voices. But the impersonal translator is, of course, a fiction. One does not shed one's experiences, motives, tastes, and style, and turn into a giant, walking Captain Marvel decoder ring, in the act of translation. And while translation is a much scrutinized process, translators themselves are relatively undocumented phenomena. In what follows, I wish to present some of my own experiences, motives, and tastes—I'll let the style take care of itself—to try to explain how and why I got mixed up in the translation racket, such as it is, in the first place, and what, in turn, the practice of translation has done for, and perhaps to, my own practice and sense of myself as a poet.

Since at least the age of thirteen, I have known, without ever knowing why, that poetry would be of central importance in my life. But I do not recall that I ever wanted to be a poet, in the usual sense of choosing a career. As far as I could tell, I already was a poet: all that remained to do was to write some poems. And I certainly never wanted, back then, to be a translator of poetry. Without presuming to speak for anyone else, I would guess that sixteen-year-old prospective translators are about as rare as six-year-olds who want to be accountants when they grow up. Adolescents, after all, aspire to remake poetry in their own image, not to remake themselves in the image of another poet. And there was in those days another, much greater obstacle to my ever becoming a translator: I had no competence in any language but my own.

My parents were born in New York, to parents who had been born in Italy. My mother and father were fluent in both English and Italian, but they made no effort to teach their children the language of their parents. In fact, the only times they used Italian when their parents were not present was when they did not want us children to know what they were saying. The notion thus conveyed, that Italian was none of my business, was reinforced by the surrounding culture. The 1950s were the high point of the melting-pot era. Unlike Europe, America was a place free from the burdens of history, a land that offered endless prospects for reinvention. To become real Americans, we packed away our ethnic identities with the quaint clothing that our ancestors had worn when they came here. Thus, both in and out of the house, circumstances created a state of affairs that I later tried to capture in one stanza of a poem called "Coming of Age":

> How Italian was I then? A handful of words—
> Counting to ten, hello, goodbye, *fangul*—
> What everybody knew. My grandmother
> Sent me to buy a jar of parmigian,
> I asked the man for a brand called Farmer John.

In high school and especially in college, one of the many things I rebelled against was, I am sorry to say, my own Italian heritage. Being Italian, in my experience in the Bronx and southern Westchester, meant gaudiness and coarseness and overexcitability, an unquestioning adherence to tradition, and an often active anti-intellectualism. Off school grounds, I did not know anyone who had ever read a book, let alone written one. In my experience, poetry, which was an escape from everything that comprised the rest of my experience, existed only on the campus. The poet who meant most to me then, and in many ways still does, was Eliot—then for the seeming priestlike purity of his commitment to poetry, now for the struggle with personal torment that informs his most passionate lines. The European poets who mattered to me were Apollinaire, whose originals I could parse with William Meredith's translations on the facing pages, and Mayakovsky, whose own words are still inaccessible to me. The translations I attempted in those days, which were stiff and slavishly literal, smothering the artistry of the originals, were from the French. Then and for several years thereafter, the only modern Italian poets I had any acquaintance with—all in translation, of course—were the usual trio of Montale, Quasimodo, and Ungaretti, the last of whom appealed instantly because of his concentration and his clean phrasing. I had also discovered a volume by a more contemporary poet whose intensity struck me almost physically—Alfredo de Palchi's *Sessions with My Analyst*.

In my late twenties, in the early 1970s, like many others at that time, I began to feel a curious internal sensation, which I came to identify as the itching of my long-buried roots. The first symptom was a surprising sense of annoyance—at Chico Marx, at the "Macaronic" verses of T. A. Daly, at the witty observations of friends regarding the degree to which I had or had not managed to escape my origins. (And while I am as amazed and disgusted as anyone by the sudden appearance of a new, extra-Constitutional guarantee that supersedes all other rights, including that of free speech—namely, the right not to be offended—I nonetheless sense the lingering acceptability of anti-Italian prejudice even in these hypersensitive times. For example, there was a cartoon series a few years ago based on the film *Bill and Ted's Excellent Adventure.* In a segment dealing with Marco Polo's expedition, all the Chinese characters, from Kublai Khan on down, spoke perfect English, while Polo and his companions waved their arms like berserk windmills and expressed themselves in variations on "Datsa some spicy meataball!") At that time, I drew up a short, eclectic mental list of goals for my life. These ambitions have had differing degrees of fulfillment: I have briefly owned a house, I still have not learned to play the piano, I no longer want a Rolls Royce. But the item on the list to which I turned my readiest attention was to learn the language of my ancestors, the only language, until a century ago, that anyone of my blood had ever used.

I decided that the best way to soak myself in the language was to turn up, with a view toward doing my own translations, some appealing, manageable Italian poet who hadn't yet registered on the Anglophone radar screen. I kept my eyes skinned for some time, until, at the end of 1975, I came across a recent bilingual anthology of twentieth-century Italian poetry. Toward the front of the book I found a long poem called "La signorina Felicita," and even in my linguistic darkness I could see that what was going on on the left-hand pages was infinitely more interesting than anything on the right. When I researched the tiny bit of information on Guido Gozzano available in English, and saw that the poet to whom he was most frequently compared was T. S. Eliot, I knew I had found my man. Within the week, I went down to Rizzoli's in Manhattan, which was then still a real Italian bookstore, scooped up a volume of Gozzano and a shopping bag full of dictionaries and grammars, and never looked back.

So, in terms of my original motivation to learn the language and to connect with my origins, I became a translator in order to become more fully myself. And yet the Gozzano project served also, as have all subsequent translations, as a means of escape from myself. I have always been particularly drawn to the literature and culture of the first few decades of this century, especially to the Modernist period. (I find it fascinating that Gozzano, on the eve of Modernism, was afflicted by the same sense of diminished ambitions that seems to enervate our culture today, the same feeling that the great ones have gone from us and that everything has already been done. May we then presume to hope that we too are on the verge of a creative explosion?) I could not literally become an early twentieth-century poet, but in the process of translation I could put on a dead man's clothes and grope my way along the roads that he had walked. I had more than Gozzano's thematic preoccupations in mind when I titled my translation of his poetry *The Man I Pretend to Be.*

Some might argue that my pretenses are far more outrageous than anything I have admitted to thus far. Where do I get the face, as my ancestors might have phrased it, to translate poetry from a language that I cannot speak at all and that I still cannot read easily without a dictionary at my side? Well, for one thing, I am guided always by a respect for the original text that prevents me from using it as a mere platform for a poem of my own or even a hybrid adaptation. This respect requires me to get to know that original as thoroughly as I can, which, in light of my limitations, is an often laborious process. I have taken apart, cleaned, and reassembled many a poetic carburetor in my time. Of course I make mistakes. Every translator does. But at least I avoid the kinds of mistakes customarily produced by haste and overconfidence. And in my respect for the original poem, I respect it in its entirety, in its rhythms and sounds and structures, not merely the one-to-one dictionary equivalents of its component words. And just as I feel that an Italian poet with some English can better respond to a poem by, say, Wallace Stevens than can a native speaker of English who has no feeling for the imaginative and sensuous richness of language, I believe that I have something of my own to bring to the exchange. I may not speak Italian, but I speak poetry.

And how has my fluency in that language been affected by my work as a translator? For the most part, I would say, favorably. My encounters with Italian poems have involved a closeness of examination and study that I am compelled only rarely to give to other individual texts, and this study has enriched my own understanding of the wide range of organizational strategies and expressive possibilities available to poets in any language. On a more directly practical level, translation has seen me through many of those endless fallow periods that are the terror of almost every poet (and I expect that every poet has shared my response on a first reading of Yeats's "The Circus Animals' Desertion": "He's bitching because he hasn't written a poem in *six weeks*?"). Thanks to Gozzano and others, I have managed to keep my poetic engine running through many a below-zero "night of the soul." And translation has given me the opportunity to try on a wide range of disguises, from a man in his late eighties to a girl still in her teens, as well as to experiment with styles and subjects that I never would have turned to on my own. Interestingly, however, I find that it is when I am translating an avant-garde poet that my own work tends to become most formal, as if it is the function of translation not to reinforce particular poetic impulses in me, but to siphon them off so that their opposites may rise to the surface.

Translation, especially to the extent that I engage in it, presents potential risks as well. One obvious one is dependence. In those times when inspiration lags, I begin to worry whether I will ever be able to write another poem that someone else has not first written for me in Italian. And then there is the issue of how I am perceived, to the degree that I perceive myself to be perceived at all. Through time, I developed a mantra to console myself over not becoming more securely established as a poet (at my current rate of one chapbook every twenty-five years, I should get all my poetry into print in just under two centuries). Part of the problem, I told myself, was that

I was "white in the '60s, male in the '70s, and straight in the '80s." Now I worry about an opposite and equally dangerous problem—being ethnic in the '90s. Every poet wishes to be identified first and foremost by that one simple word. To be identified solely as a translator, or even as a translator-poet, is cause enough for concern, but even more worrisome is the idea that my involvement with Italian poetry will label me ethnically in ways that my own concerns as a poet, for the most part, do not. I no more want to be known as an "Italian-American poet" than I wish to contribute to an anthology devoted exclusively to the poetry of middle-aged bald men who wear glasses.

And yet, whatever the risks may be, I would not have missed it. Through translation, I have discovered, and continue to discover, a wonderful body of literature that I am eager to share with those of my country and my language. Through translation, I have made many friends and have had many opportunities that would never have come to me otherwise. *Traduttore, traditore*, the Italians say: "Translator, traitor." The phrase itself presents a rare, felicitous instance of the poetry being carried over with the sense. It's a neat phrase, but I do not believe it is true. It certainly does not have to be. But, if this be treason, I certainly have tried to make the most of it, and I have discovered, along with Delilah, Benedict Arnold, and others too numerous to mention, that it has its compensations.

Nominated by Daniel Hoffman

THE LEAST YOU NEED TO KNOW ABOUT RADIO

fiction by BEN MARCUS

from PARKETT

Bʏ ᴛᴜɴɪɴɢ ᴀ ʀᴀᴅɪᴏ, you control the amount of wind in your house and, to a lesser degree, the language spoken there. You dial in the wind and regulate which rooms it will enter, how hard it will blow, and the form it will take: shouting, singing, silence, breath, whispering, aroma. The antenna on radios is long, thin, and retractable because it measures the level and style of breathing people do near the radio. When too many people gather near a radio, one of them will feel short of breath, clutch her throat, wobble, swoon to the floor. She is referred to as Julie. Often she carries her own antenna, which looks like a key and opens the front door of her house. If a family collectively holds its breath, known as "getting ready for bed," no sound will be possible in their house. A father loses his temper if his family does not breathe fast enough, if they are dull and seem exhausted when their breathing is shallow. He fears his house will collapse, so he frightens his children, to quicken their breathing, by striking the furniture with a long, flat stick. His anger operates as a bellow inside his children's chests and is referred to as a "radio-driven mood." This is why he claws and growls outside their doors in the morning. This is why they hear noises in their sleep and wake up feeling uneasy.

Children are resistant to the strangled sounds of radio because they have not yet shed their windproof layer, referred to in Indiana as baby fat. When adults practice their knife work at waist-high countertops, chopping, slicing, and shredding objects they will later warm in clear fat and present to the regard of their families, children hiss at each other in radio static, their mouths gaping. Children's teeth are small because the flow of radio static chisels them down and keeps them from growing into hard, square bones. This is why they cannot dismantle entire animals with their mouths. After repose, when adults maneuver from their beds to an upright position and align their heads next to radios tuned to static, they are able to remember the first wind of their childhoods: its height and color and sound, what part of their bodies it targeted, and how weak it made them feel. If you held a microphone to your father's neck, you would hear a muted, crackling static: the sound of a lifetime of wind that has flowed over his body. Wrapping his neck in a scarf will briefly mute the sound, allowing for short conversations to occur.

Most speech that occurs in the home can be attributed to one or another call sign on a radio. The numbers are old American words used to procure food, express alarm, and soothe frightened animals. A store-bought radio with a digital tuner can dial in many of the conversations of today's American homes. If Mother controls the radio, she determines what will be discussed in the kitchen, the living room, and the den. Of special note is her remote control: a long, slender fin with hinged digits called a "hand." On holidays she colors the nails on her hand, dips it in ointment, wraps it in gauze, then pounds it against the table to neutralize it. It expresses a milky color and blends in with the rest of her body, appearing to extend from her arm. She waves her hand, buries it in her pocket, collides it against the faces of her children, and the speech in the room comes quietly under her command. When Mother is alone at her window, she can be overheard muttering numbers, which is her way of planning the moods her family will have throughout the day and week. She confines herself to the lower, monosyllabic numbers, to prevent the occurrence of actual fires in her home, a physical reaction at the far end of the mood scale.

Different radio stations collect different kinds of wind, then break it up and slow it down until it sounds like a song or a man talking. This kind of wind does not blow under its own power; instead, it must be broadcast weekly in the evenings when houses have surrendered their father-free shields, when their listening block is lifted.

The term "broadcast" was first used to describe a special muscle in the face that gave propulsion to sound generated in the mouth; mostly words, but also yelling and singing. Men and women inspect their broadcast muscles by pushing a fist into each other's mouths and opening up their hands once inside. With their free hand, they grasp the back of their partner's head and impale their hands further into their faces so that the head is worn in the manner of a glove. A strong and healthy broadcast muscle relaxes, letting the hand massage the face from the inside. When a child's broadcast muscle is snipped with a scissors, his words cannot leave his mouth, which becomes fat and overstuffed, leading to large, moist lips and a slack, lazy face. He sits by the window and rocks in his chair, a suction tube dangling from his mouth. At night his mother digs into his mouth with a spoon, assisting him with the discharge. Sometimes she pretends to pat his head and read him a story.

The English language was first overheard in a wind that circled an old Ohio radio operated by a Jane Dark representative. Words from the language were carefully picked out of this clear wind over the next thirty years and inscribed on pieces of linen handed out at farmer's markets. When the entire vocabulary of words had been recovered from the old radio, it was destroyed and the pieces of linen were sewn together into a long, thin flag that was then loaned out to various cities and towns, where it was mounted over houses. Once the fabric was hoisted on a flagpole, the language was easily taught to the people inside of their homes, who had only to tune into the call sign of the flag station, extract and aim their freshly-oiled antennas, and position their faces in the air steaming from the grill of their radios. When their faces became flushed and hot, they could retreat to other rooms and say entirely new things to the children who were sleeping there.

If you speed up a song or the sound of a man talking and you broadcast this sound outside your house through speakers affixed to your roof, the trees will quiver as if bent by a western wind and the birds of the yard will be grounded below the speech wires that connect the houses. By grounding birds, the air is kept clear of surveillance in case an important message is scheduled. Windows on the upper floors of houses are left open for language projection and sometimes boys are seen scrambling from them, slipping down the roofs, falling to the ground, often reciting cries for help known as sentences.

The weather outside your house can be captured and preserved, then played back later through a simple AM radio. These radios can be taken on picnics to the lake, for customized weather and simple wind performances, benefiting the other families parked there to eat sandwiches and cast pebbles into the water. If several families stationed on blankets along the shore play their AM radios in a simulcast, calibrating the tilt of their antennas to focus their broadcast just over the water, the sky will appear stronger, the children's words will be clearly enunciated, and the currents in the water will ripple more realistically. Every family has a favorite weather style and a radio that will play it back for them. Sometimes it sounds like the shortest words of the American language, in particular the first names that are used to summon people up from sleep, to groom their heads with a softly blowing oil, preparing them to be addressed by the largest person in the house, often the mother or father.

A radio was once referred to as a "weather bottle." People said, "Turn on the bottle, listen to this," and the bottle was shaken until air fizzed out of it and everyone laughed and enjoyed themselves. People bought bottles of old weather at farmer's markets and co-ops and poured them over their roofs, hoping to immunize their houses from special re-broadcasts of famous storms and Father's repetitive speech. Most storms could be had for a nickel, with a deposit on the bottle. Radios can't be turned off. They have four settings: man, woman, child, and low. Just like people, if too much happens, they fill up, burst and die. A dead radio is treated similarly to a pet. It is burned and the antenna is planted in a field. When children clutch a detached antenna, they are gathering strength to go home, when they are afraid to enter their rooms.

You can have a party and everyone will come to sit around your radio, which sometimes looks like an old, trampled flower. People pour water or milk on it and wait for something to happen, but the radio only gets older and produces a wind known as disappointment. At a party, people stand perfectly still and wring their hands, and the liquid is collected in a vial. In Ohio, when people meet, they smell each other's small radios, unscrew the cases, touch the tuning needle, shake the speakers next to their ears until the sound erodes into the words they most require to hear. Some people cry when they re-

303

member the first time they felt wind on their faces. Crying is a weakness of the face that can be corrected with a strong FM blast from a radio, tuned to a call sign in the high nineties. An emotion-prevention wind should occur in the home and last for some time after that. A family can then move freely from room to room, with only minor adjustments of the dial when their feelings grow too strong.

Nominated by David Plante, Parkett

CORD

by LINDA GREGERSON

from THE KENYON REVIEW

O. T. G. 1912–1994

Dearest, we filled up the woodroom
        this week,
           Karen and Steven and I and Peter's

truck. You would have been amused
        to see us in our
           woodsman's mode. It's your wood still.

You know those homely cruxes where the odd piece,
        split
           near the fork for instance, has to be turned

till it's made to fit and another
        lame one
           found for the gap? Sap

just yesterday, smoke in the end, this
        clubfoot
           marking the meantime. I came

to one of them, one of the numberless
                    justnesses
            a life of stacking wood affords (had you even

broken rhythm?) and for just that instant
                    had you back.
            I know. I know. It wasn't the last, despite

the strangled heaving of your chest, despite
                    the rattled
            exhalation and the leavened, livid, meat-

borne smell, it wasn't the last till afterward, I've
                    made that
            my excuse. But Mother was sleeping not five

feet away, she'd scarcely slept in weeks, I could
                    have
            waked her. I (sweet darling, the morphine

under your tongue) am much (your quiet
                    hands)
            to blame. And when we had dismantled this last-

but-one of the provident stores you'd
                    left—
            a winter's worth of warmth in each—

and hauled it in, we split and stacked the new
                    oak Peter
            felled last spring. We took a day off in

between, we wrapped ourselves in virtue, we
                    can be
            good children yet. The gingkos

have come back from their near
                    poisoning, have
            I told you that? Our tenant's

remorseful, he's sworn off new insecticides. My
hour with you (one
breath, one more) was theft.

Nominated by Bob Hicok

ON THE NATURE OF HUMAN ROMANTIC INTERACTION

fiction by KARL IAGNEMMA

from THE PARIS REVIEW

WHEN STUDENTS HERE can't stand another minute they get drunk and hurl themselves off the top floor of the Gehring Building, the shortest building on campus. The windows were tamper-proofed in August, so the last student forced open the roof access door and screamed *Pussy!* and dove spread-eagled into the night sky. From the TechInfo office I watched his body rip a silent trace through the immense snow dunes that ring the Gehring Building. A moment later he poked his head from the dune, dazed and grinning, and his four nervous frat brothers whooped and dusted him off and carried him on their shoulders to O'Dooley's, where they bought him shots of Jaegermeister until he was so drunk he slid off his stool and cracked his teeth against the stained oak bar.

In May a freshwoman named Deborah Dailey heaved a chair through a plate-glass window on the fifth floor of the Gray Building, then followed the chair down to the snowless parking lot, shattering both ankles and fracturing her skull. Later we learned—unsurprisingly—that her act had something to do with love: false love, failed love, mistimed or misunderstood or miscarried love. For no one here, I'm convinced, is truly happy in love. This is the Institute: a windswept quadrangle edged by charm-proofed concrete buildings.

The sun disappears in October and temperatures drop low enough to flash-freeze saliva; spit crackles against the pavement like hail. In January whiteouts shut down the highways, and the outside world takes on a quality very much like oxygen: we know it exists all around us, but we can't see it. It's a disturbing thing to be part of. My ex-PhD advisor, who's been here longer than any of us, claims that the dormitory walls are abuzz with frustration, and if you press your ear against the heating ducts at night you can hear the jangling bed-springs and desperate whimpers of masturbators. Some nights my ex-advisor wanders the sub-basement hallways of the Gray Building and screams obscenities until he feels refreshed and relatively tranquil.

I used to be a PhD student, but now my job is to sit all night at a government-issue desk in the TechInfo office, staring at a red Tech-Hotline telephone. The TechHotline rings at three and four A.M., and I listen to distraught graduate students stammer about corrupted file allocation tables and SCSI controller failures. I tell them to close their eyes and take a deep breath; I tell them everything will be all right. The TechInfo office looks onto the quadrangle and, just before dawn, when the sky has mellowed to the color of a deep bruise, the Institute looks almost peaceful. At those rare moments I love my job and I love this town and I love this institute. This is an indisputable fact: there are many, many people around here who love things that will never love them back.

A Venn diagram of my love for Alexandra looks like this:

My inventory of love is almost completely consumed by Alexandra, while hers is shared by myself and others (or, more precisely: $|A|>|M|$; $\exists\, x$ s.t. $x\in (A\cap M)$; $\exists\, y$ s.t. $y\in A$, $y\notin M$; $\exists\, z$ s.t. $z\notin A$, $z\notin M$). We live in a cabin next to the Owahee River and the Institute's research-grade nuclear power plant. Steam curls off the hyperboloidal cooling tower and settles in an icy mist on our roof, and some nights I swear I can see the reactor building glowing. Alexandra has hair the color of maple syrup, and she is sixteen years younger than me; she is twenty-five. She sips tea every morning in the front room of our cabin, and when I turn into the driveway and see her hair through the window I feel a deep, troubling urge.

Alexandra is the daughter of my ex-advisor, who has never claimed to be happy in love. On Wednesdays at noon he meets a sophomore named Larissa in the Applied Optics Laboratory and scoots her onto the vibration isolation table and bangs her until the air pistons sigh. Every morning my ex-advisor straps on snowshoes and clomps past our cabin on his way to the Institute, gliding atop the frozen crust like a Nordic vision of Jesus. I have given Alexandra an ultimatum: she has until commencement day to decide if she wants to marry me. If she does not want to marry me, I will pack my textbooks and electronic diagnostic equipment and move to Huntsville, Alabama.

When students jump off the Gehring Building, they curse and scream as though their hands are on fire. I can't say I blame them. This is the set of words I use when I talk about the Institute: hunger, numbness, fatigue, yearning, anger. Old photographs of this town show a cathedral of pines standing in place of the bare quadrangle, and a sawmill on the Owahee in place of the nuclear plant. People in the pictures stare at the camera with an unmistakable air of melancholy, and looking at them I wonder if there was ever a happy season on this peninsula.

Alexandra tells me I'm ungenerous toward the Institute; she tells me the cold has freeze-dried my kindness. Here is a fact I cannot refute: on nights when the TechHotline is quiet and snow is settling in swells around the Gehring Building, the silence is pure enough to make you want to weep. Windows in the Walsh Residence Hall blink off, one by one, until the quadrangle is lit only by moonlight. Icicles the size of children work loose and disappear into snowdrifts. Bark-colored hares hop lazily toward the Owahee. In the early-morning dark, before the sun climbs over the Gray Building and the Institute begins to stretch, you can wade into a drift and lie back like an angel and let snow sift down onto you, and the only sound you hear is the slow churn of your own unwilling heart.

Slaney is the name of this town: a few thousand houses and shops crushed up against the Institute like groupies. Slaney has a short but tragic history: founded in 1906 by a Swede as a company town for the Michigan Land and Lumber Company; within a year there were four hundred inhabitants, six boardinghouses, two general stores, a meat market, an icehouse, a whorehouse, seven saloons. The Swede, his heart full to bursting with pride, felled the tallest white pine in the county and propped it in the middle of Slaney's main drag as a monument to the town's greatness. By 1925 there was nothing left around Slaney except birch and tamarack and scrub poplar, and if tumbleweeds existed up here they'd have blown through the abandoned streets with a lonely rustle. The monumental white pine was dragged off to the sawmill in the middle of the night by timber thieves. The Swede drank himself into a stupor in Dan Dunn's empty saloon, then passed out during the twelve-block walk to his house and nearly froze to death.

That spring the hills hiccuped with dynamite blasts from prospectors looking for iron ore, and the Michigan state legislature chose Slaney as the location for a new institute of mining engineering. Every year in Slaney someone loses grip and commits an unspeakably self-destructive act. Here is something my ex-advisor does not think I know: seven years ago, when his ex-wife still lived in Slaney, he followed her to her house on Huron Street for eleven straight days, and one night as he crouched outside her kitchen window was knocked unconscious by a blow from a policeman's nightstick. When he woke he was shackled to a stainless-steel toilet. Ontonagon County, I've heard, has the toughest anti-stalking laws in the state.

On Friday nights the TechHotline is quiet. Dormitory windows are dark as graves, and the quadrangle echoes with shouts of horny undergraduates. I lock the TechInfo office, and Alexandra meets me on Mill Street outside the Caribou Lounge, where a six-piece band called Chicken Little plays Benny Goodman and Cab Calloway and Nat King Cole. Twenty-one year olds wearing circle skirts and two-tone shoes jam the dance floor and Charleston like they're scaring off demons. Rusty, the bandleader, wears a white silk suit and by eleven is drenched with sweat. I lindy until my knees ache, but Alexandra's just getting started: she climbs onto the stage and whispers into Rusty's ear. He says, *We're gonna do one for the spitfire in the pretty pink blouse.* I sit at the bar and watch Alexandra press up against strange men, and think about how miserable it is to be alone.

On Saturday nights students throng to the Newett Ice Arena to watch the hockey team lose to future NHLers from Houghton and Escanaba. Bartenders on Middle Street stockpile pint glasses and rub their hands together, waiting for the post-game crush. My ex-advisor locks his office door and drinks a half-bottle of sherry, then

311

calls his ex-wife in Sturgeon Falls. He waits until she says *Hello?*
Who is this? John, please—then hangs up. Afterwards he dials the
TechHotline, stammering, and I tell him to close his eyes and take a
deep breath; I tell him everything will be all right. He says, *I'm sorry,*
Joseph, good Christ, and begins to sniffle. Snow ambles down outside
the TechInfo window. One Saturday, drunk, my ex-advisor called and
managed to say, *Listen, I'm not going to repeat this: my daughter can*
be somewhat difficult, and I frankly don't know if you're up to the
challenge.

The Swede kept a leather-bound journal detailing the events of his
life from the day he arrived in Slaney until the day he died. *Town has*
grown faster than even my most incautious estimates, he wrote in
1911. *Andrew Street now one-quarter mile long. Irish, Finns, Cousin*
Jacks have come, and for some reason a band of Sicilians. No chicken
for eight months. When Slaney was booming in the 1910s, lumberjacks from as far as Bruce Crossing would descend on the town on
weekends and get knee-walking drunk on Yellow Dog whiskey, then
smash pub stools to splinters with their peaveys. Their steel-calked
boots punched holes in Slaney's plank sidewalks. A tenderloin sprang
up along the eastern edge of town, and the Swede met a young prostitute named Lotta Scott at Hugh Logan's place on Thomas Street;
she charged him two dollars. *Disarmingly frank*, he wrote. *Eyes dark*
as bituminous coal. Slim ankles. Short patience.

Before I leave for the TechInfo office in the evening, Alexandra
walks from room to room shedding her prim librarian's turtleneck
and knee-length skirt and woolen tights, then lies back on the
kitchen table, naked, ravenous. Her eyes follow my hands, nervous as
squirrels, as I unbuckle myself. She tugs at the seam of my jeans.
Outside, snow movers pound down the ice-packed street, their
carbon-steel blades gouging the curb. Alexandra smells archival—
glue and musty paper and indelible ink—and she loves sex as much
as a snowman loves cold. This is what I do: I say a small prayer just
before I begin, even though I am not religious. By her own count,
Alexandra has had sex with more than thirty-five men.

Alexandra called the TechHotline one night and said, *Sometimes I*
wish you'd cool it a little bit. I mean, I love you, I love all the nerdy
things you do, I just don't understand why you feel the need to
control me. We can love each other and still lead normal, semi-
independent lives. I could hear the soft rush of her breathing, a
sound that made me dizzy. Alexandra is stingy with love; she is afraid

of ending up like her parents, who squandered their love like drunks at a craps table. *I don't want to control you,* I explained, *I'm just a little uncomfortable with the idea of you having sex with strange men.*

The Swede in his journal described the deep silence of the woods, which seemed to him a cruel and beautiful sound. *Streets filled with sweet smell of pitch. Pine as far as I can see. Have fallen in love with that dissolute woman, Lotta Scott. Consumed by thoughts of her.* His spindly, frugal hand filled the journal pages. On May third he recorded the purchase of a new frock coat, for four dollars, tailored by *a clever Polander from Detroit,* and a set of linens *of surpassing quality.* Then on the tenth of May, 1919, the Swede in deliriously shaky script wrote that he and Lotta Scott were married in Burke's Saloon by the justice of the peace with forty-four witnesses present. *I feel as the first French explorers must have felt,* he wrote, *when they gazed for the first time upon the vast forests of this wondrous peninsula. Glorious, glorious chicken.*

I have tried to convince myself that Alexandra is not a tramp, that she simply suffers from too much love—that she loves too much for her own good. My ex-advisor knocks on the TechInfo office door when he's too lonely to go home. One Saturday night, his shirt unbuttoned and a styrofoam cup of sherry balanced on his knee, he told me I am too particular when it comes to love, that I should accept love no matter how it appears and be grateful. He sipped sherry in a languid, pensive manner. *There's a certain kind of imperfection that acts as a reference point, that gives a sense of perspective. Understand? The pockmark on the perfect cheek. The small, tragic flaw, like a beauty mark, but deeper.* He squinted out at the forlorn quadrangle. *I don't trust perfection. Alexandra's mother was so wonderfully, perfectly imperfect.* I once snuck into an auditorium in the Gray Building and watched my ex-advisor deliver a Physics 125 lecture on kinetic and potential energy. As he lectured he smiled at a pair of sleepy-eyed sophomore girls, showing his artificially whitened teeth.

The harder I pull Alexandra toward me the harder she pushes away. It's heartbreaking. Every third Saturday in February the people of Slaney hold Winter Carnival, where they flood the Kmart parking lot and ice skate under a mosaic of stars. Teenaged boys in Red Wings jerseys skate backward and play crack-the-whip to show off. My ex-advisor dons a black beret and circles the rink in long, fluid strides. Last February Alexandra and I skated couples, and in the chilly night her skin was as smooth and luminous as a glass of milk. *What a world!* I found myself thinking, *where a failed engineer with a crooked nose can skate couples with a syrup-haired woman who smells archival.* On Andrew Street, we ate elephant ears and watched a muscular young townie lift people in his arms to guess their weight. Alexandra gave him a dollar, and he hoisted her up with one meaty arm and hugged her to his chest. Alexandra shouted *Whoa, hey! Wow!* and kicked her legs girlishly. When the townie put her down, she kissed him on the cheek, and when she came back and saw my face she said, *Oh, for God's sake, Joseph. Grow up.*

That night at three A.M. I turned on the bedroom light and knelt over Alexandra and asked her to be my wife. I felt tearful, exultant; I felt as vast and weightless as a raft of clouds; I felt all of Lake Superior welled inside my bursting chest. Sweat seeped from my trembling hands and dampened Alexandra's nightdress. *Joseph,* she said, *Joseph, Joseph, Joseph. Oh, God.* She kissed my cheek, the same way she'd kissed the townie. *I just don't know, honey. I just don't know.*

This town: everywhere I look I see equations. Ice floes tumbling in the Owahee, snowflakes skidding past the TechInfo window: everywhere I look I see fractals and tensors and nonlinear differential equations. Some mornings when my TechInfo shift is over I stand in front of the Bradford Student Center and hand out pamphlets entitled, "Proof of God's Existence by Series Expansion," and, "The Combinatorics of Ancient Roman Orgies." Undergraduates walk broad circles around me. They're bundled in scarves and wool hats; only their eyes show. Alexandra tells me I make people uneasy, that not everything can be described by mathematics, and I tell her she's probably wrong.

I have considered admitting to Alexandra that I hate dancing but worry that she'll find another partner. One night at the Caribou Lounge I ducked out for fresh air, and on a whim wandered into the meager woods; there were no lights in sight but the moonlit snow glowed bright enough to count change by. I laid down and stared up at the muddy streak of our galaxy. I thought—how to explain?—about the nature of imperfection. My ex-advisor every September stands before his Physics 125 class with his arms spread wide, like a preacher, and says, *Listen sharp, this is important: Nature. Hates. Perfection.* Alexandra says I sometimes remind her of her father, and this bothers her more than she can say.

314

In 1919 Slaney sent three million board feet of pine down the Owahee, and the sawmill howled from morning to dusk. Lumberjacks, tired of two-dollar whores on Thomas Street, sent agonized letters to *Heart and Hand* matrimonial newspaper and convinced scared young women to pack their lives into trunks and board the train north. The Swede on May seventeenth—one week after his wedding—walked deep into the thinning woods and realized the pine would not last forever, that in four or five years it would be *cut out*, and Slaney would be *all caught up. Jacks will move westward, toward Ontonagon and Silver City,* he wrote. *Saloons will empty, sawmill will fall idle. Lotta departed for Hurley this morning at dawn to visit her mother. Declined my offer to accompany her.* Lotta Scott, before she left, borrowed two hundred dollars and a gold-plated pocketwatch from the Swede.

I like my ex-advisor but worry that he cares too much about the wrong things. Larissa, the sophomore he bangs on Wednesdays in the Applied Optics Laboratory, has told him he'd better stop worrying about ancient history and start focusing on the here and now. *For Christ's sake,* my ex-advisor said, *She's nineteen years old—a child— telling me this. I love Larissa, but it's not the kind of love she thinks it is.* Alexandra does not remember the names of some of the men she has slept with. *It was just sex,* she explains, *it wasn't this huge colossal thing.* The first time we made love, she stroked my hair afterwards and explained that I was not supposed to cry, that it was not supposed to be that way.

The tombstones in Slaney's cemetery have Finnish and Polish and Swedish names; they say COOPER and SAWYER and LUMBERJACK. Women who came to town, it seems, took a dismayed look around then headed back south. The lumberjacks died alone. The Swede, two weeks after Lotta left for Hurley, wrote, *Met a man Masters from Sault Ste. Marie, who claims the entire eastern half of the peninsula is cut out, not a stick of white pine standing. Martinville, Maynard, Bartlow he claims are empty, the houses deserted and mill torn down for scrap. Queer fellow. Says land looks "naked and embarrassed" without the pine. No word from Lotta.*

The tenderloin was razed in a fit of prohibition righteousness in 1931 and lay vacant and weed-choked for twenty years. A Methodist church now stands where Dan Dunn's saloon used to be. Hugh Logan's whorehouse has been replaced by an electronics store called Circuit Shack. The Swede wrote nothing in his journal for two weeks, then, *Took train to Hurley to find no trace of Lotta. Walked all up and down the dusty streets. Back in Slaney, heard from John Davidson that Lotta was seen on the Sault St. Marie train as far along as Allouez. Davidson was drunk and perhaps not being truthful. Nevertheless I fear she is gone completely.* This is a fact: I live with a woman with syrup-colored hair who loves me in a hard, unknowable way. My ex-advisor one Sunday in the TechInfo office, his feet propped on my desk and a cup of sherry balanced on his knee, smiled cryptically and said, *I believe I can solve your problem with my daughter. I have an idea. A theory.*

Alexandra left to visit her mother in Sturgeon Falls two weeks after Winter Carnival. At the station I blinked back a swell of longing as her train dragged slowly north. Alexandra leaned out the window and blew me a kiss, then tossed a small white bundle into the snow. She was supposed to stay one week in Sturgeon Falls; she was supposed to tell me *yes* or *no* when she returned. I searched for almost two hours but never did find the bundle she threw out the window.

My ex-advisor that night, sprawled in front of the TechInfo radiator like a housecat, told me I cannot expect to understand Alexandra with mathematics alone, and that my view of love is analytical whereas his is romantic. My ex-advisor as he thawed smelled stale, like cooked cabbage. I set my mug of Seagrams down and on a wrinkled envelope wrote:

$$\frac{dJ}{dt} = \alpha J - \beta JA$$
$$\frac{dA}{dt} = \chi JA - \delta A$$

Where J is my love, A is Alexandra's. The predator-prey equations—simple, but very elegant. My words were cold clouds of Canadian whiskey. I rattled the ice cubes in my glass like dice. *You should trust mathematics*, I told him. *Nothing is too complex to describe with mathematics.* Alexandra called early the next morning to tell me she'd decided to stay an extra week in Sturgeon Falls. I closed my eyes and listened to her syrup-colored voice. *I'm going to sit in my mother's sauna and think about everything. Have you ever been in a sauna, honey? It's incredible. First you feel like you're going to die, then you pass a certain point and feel like you're going to live forever.*

316

She sighed. *And I'm helping my mother plan her wedding—she's getting re-married. Don't tell my father.*

I can build you a sauna. I can build it in the backyard, next to the big poplar.

His name is Harold. He breeds minks. There's hundreds of minks running around up here, honey. Her voice dropped to a whisper. *It makes me horny, in a weird way.*

I didn't say anything.

Joseph, I have never cheated on you, she said suddenly. Her voice held a thin edge of desperation. *I want you to understand that.* Alexandra, before she hung up, said that the bundle she threw out the train window contained a peach pit, nothing more.

My dissertation, which I never finished, was entitled "Nonlinear Control of Biomimetic Systems." The first chapter, which I finished, was entitled "On the Nature of Human Romantic Interaction." It begins: *Consider a third-order system with three states corresponding to three distinct people, A, B, and C. A is attracted to both B and C. B and C are both attracted to A but not to each other. We would like to describe the behavior of this system over time.*

One night while Alexandra was in Sturgeon Falls I sat staring into the darkened quadrangle for a long time. Finally I called her and said, *I can't wait forever. I can give you until commencement day, but then I'm moving to Huntsville, Alabama.* Alexandra was stunned, silent. *I don't know what else to do.* My ex-advisor convinced me to give Alexandra the Huntsville ultimatum. I had four handwritten pages of equations contradicting his advice, but he took the pencil from my hand and said, *Joseph, my friend, it's extremely simple: the only reason my daughter will not marry you is if she does not, in fact, love you.* Huntsville, Alabama. I chose Huntsville randomly off the map; I don't know what I'd do in a January without snow.

In my dissertation I proved analytically that it's possible to design a control system such that A's attraction to B grew exponentially, while A's attraction to C diminished exponentially. In the concluding paragraph, however, there is a caveat: *In practice the coupling factors are highly nonlinear and difficult to predict, and depend on phenomena such as shyness, boredom, desire, desperation, and self-knowledge, as well as numerous local conditions: the feeling of self-confidence gained from wearing a favorite pair of socks, the unexpected sorrow of seeing the season's first flock of geese flying south, etc.*

Alexandra returned from Sturgeon Falls five weeks before commencement day wearing a white muff, a gift from her mother's mink-breeder fiancé. She walked from the front door to the bedroom and dropped her suitcase on the bed, then walked back into the kitchen and gripped my shoulders and said, *Listen to me, Joseph: I love you. I love the shit out of you. But I'll never belong to you.*

That night I waited until Alexandra was asleep then pulled on boots and a parka and walked the half-mile to the Institute. The Gehring Building was quiet except for a dull chorus of electronic devices. The TechInfo office was silent as a prayer. Suddenly I had an idea: I ran across the quadrangle to the Olssen Building, the tallest building on campus, and sprinted from classroom to empty classroom, turning on lights. I formed a three-story lit-up A, then an L, then an E, then part of an X—then I ran out of classrooms. The Olssen Building wasn't wide enough. Back in the TechInfo office, I threw open the window, breathless, and looked out across the quadrangle. ALE. The lights spelled ALE. A group of fraternity brothers had gathered and when I appeared as a silhouette in the TechInfo window they shouted, *Yo, hotline man! Ale! Fuckin' A!*

I closed the office door and turned off the lights, picked up the telephone and dialed. The phone rang three times, four times, five—and then Alexandra answered. Her voice was husky and irritable, the voice of a confident young woman disturbed from sleep. She said, *Hello? Who the hell is this—Joseph?*

I hung up.

They found ore in the hills around Slaney in 1926—not the glittery hematite they were seeing in Ishpeming, but a muddy blue sludge that assayed at sixty percent iron. Overnight, Slaney was reborn: the front glass of Dan Dunn's saloon was replaced and the floor re-planked; Hugh Logan's place on Thomas Street was scrubbed down and re-opened. The Swede awoke from a month-long bender, his handwriting looser and less optimistic. *Strange to see trains unloading again. Excitement even at the meatmarket; ore, they say, is everywhere. No chicken for nine months.* My ex-advisor, one chilly April Sunday in the TechInfo office, explained that his ex-wife had taken out a restraining order, and if he called her one more time he would be arrested. It took me two months to realize that *chicken* was the Swede's code word for intercourse.

Alexandra's mother, my ex-advisor said, *has the sort of posture you see in Victorian portraiture. Ivory skin, fingers that are almost im-*

318

possibly delicate, yet strong. Beautifully strong, and that noble Victorian posture. He stroked his stubbled chin and nodded, agreeing with himself. *And I treated her like shit on a heel.* My ex-advisor, one month before commencement day, somehow learned about his ex-wife's impending wedding, and he wandered into the quadrangle and slumped down in the dingy snow and refused to budge.

Alexandra was asked by her mother to be maid of honor. She sipped tea in the front room of our cabin, tearing pages from *Bride* magazine and acting like everything was okay. Alexandra does not understand the urgency that grips you at thirty; she does not understand the desperation that settles in at forty. I began staying late at work, wandering the Gehring Building's damp sub-basement tunnels. Down in the tunnels, I walked for hours without seeing a hint of the morning sky, and I felt how I imagined the old ore miners must have felt. One morning I told Alexandra that if she marries me she does not necessarily have to stop seeing other men, and she looked at me with confusion and deep pity and slapped my face.

The Institute graduated its first class of engineers in 1930, but the residents of Slaney had no use for book-taught miners. The Swede, caught up in the excitement, paid thirty dollars for a claim on fifteen acres he'd never seen, and his first week out found a nugget of what he thought was solid gold. He squatted in the snow outside his lean-to and threw his head back and shouted at the moon. He was sixty-two years old. *As much as I can haul out,* he wrote. *Nuggets size of fists. Rapture.*

The Slaney Mountain was a wet hole of a mine with a safety record that made the sawmill look like a nursery. A 1931 cave-in sent pressurized air pounding through the shaft, and thirteen miners were punched into the air then flung down, uninjured. A moment later the creaking support timbers fell silent, and a blanket of rock crushed the breath from their lungs. All thirteen died. In 1932 an Italian accidentally stubbed his cigar into a tub of freshly thawed dynamite, and the blast rattled windows as far away as Andrew Street. The Swede on March 13, 1933, convinced he'd hit a mother lode, sold his house and hocked his gold family ring for three hundred acres and a pair of mules. He sat all night atop his tiny hill, staring at the forest draped in darkness and dreaming of Pierce-Arrow automobiles and English leather gloves, and when the sun broke over the frozen valley he began to dig.

Two weeks before commencement day I woke to find Alexandra

319

sitting at the foot of the bed, teary-eyed. *Bride* magazine lay tattered on her lap. She climbed beneath the comforter, sniffling, and said, *I wish you'd quit doing what you're doing. I wish you'd let things keep going the way they're going.* It's crushing to remember the years before Alexandra: partial differential equations, cold beef pasties, the smell of melting solder and the heartless glow of a fluorescent lamp. I pulled Alexandra close and told her to close her eyes and take a deep breath, I told her everything would be all right, and she looked at me with confusion and deep pity and said, *Cut it out.*

The Swede stockpiled gold for five months, then one morning hitched his mules to a rented sledge and paraded his mound of nuggets down Slaney's main drag. Old broken prospectors with hematite in their hair and an alcoholic's tremble stared out through Dan Dunn's front window and muttered softly at the sight. *Celebrated with sirloin steak and Yellow Dog whisky, then strolled over to Thomas Street. Feasted on chicken.*

One week before commencement day the snow in the quadrangle began to shrink; then as if by sleight of hand the sun appeared where there had been only clouds. Physical plant workers tucked geraniums into planter boxes and for the first time in months students unwrapped their scarves and looked around. One night I stayed sixteen hours at the TechInfo office. When I got home I packed my books into milk crates and stacked them next to the door; Alexandra waited until I was asleep then unpacked them and placed them neatly back on the bookshelf. The nuggets the Swede had spent everything to pull from the ground were not pure gold, he discovered, but copper spiked with fatty veins of pyrite. The rock he'd spent five months hauling from his plot was worth nine dollars and sixty-three cents.

The day before commencement day I purchased a non-refundable ticket to Huntsville. I had not showered, and the TechInfo office reflected what must be my own human smell: lemon and sour milk and powdered cumin. That night, his feet resting on the TechInfo desk, my ex-advisor said, *You should not let yourself go like this, Joseph. It's undignified.* After he left, two Slaney policemen knocked on the door. Their furry snow hats were pulled low on their foreheads. They were looking for my ex-advisor. When I asked them what they wanted the smaller policeman pursed his lips and said, *We can't divulge that information.* When I asked them if my ex-advisor was in trouble he said, *We can't divulge that information.*

The police, I learned eventually, were searching for a man who'd climbed into the heating ducts of the Benson Dormitory and watched an unnamed freshwoman apply lotion to her calves. The police had swept the Gray Building and sat for hours watching the Student Center, but no one had seen my ex-advisor. I told them I had no idea where he was. I told them it's not easy to hide in a town this small.

The ore around Slaney, it turned out, was not a single wide vein but pockety and impossible to follow. The D & C, Silver Lake and Petersen mines stopped drilling in 1937. The Slaney Mountain mine—the first mine—stayed stubbornly open, and in 1939 engineers thought they'd hit a million-ton ore body. But two months later the ore was gone. The mountain shut down. The last miners boarded the train west, for Houghton or Ishpeming. Dan Dunn nailed planks across the front window of his saloon and left Slaney for good. The Swede, penniless and without a home, took a bottle of Yellow Dog whiskey into the cut-out woods and sat down in the snow and put a .45 pistol in his mouth and pulled the trigger.

The pine around Slaney is gone. The ore is gone. The shaft house stands crumbling and windowless a half-mile from the Institute, and on Friday nights high-schoolers sneak inside and drink Boone's Farm Strawberry Hill and grope one another. My ex-advisor says that men never dig for iron or copper or coal; secretly, in their heart's heart, they're digging for gold. The Swede before he shot himself in 1940 wrote: *Heard from a man Jonsson that Lotta is in Grand Rapids and married to a furniture magnate. Said he saw them two months ago in church, Lotta dressed in silk and singing a beautiful soprano. Not certain Jonsson was being truthful; told of Lotta only after securing a loan of thirty dollars. So be it. Wherever Lotta is I wish her happiness. I write these words without regret.*

On the morning of commencement day the air smelled salty, like trouble, and from nowhere a milk-gray sheet fell over the sky and the temperature dropped twenty degrees in twenty minutes. By eight A.M. snow was swirling in the late-May breeze, and by nine there were four inches on the highway and the radio was saying it looked like we were going to get socked but good. Alexandra and I stayed in bed. I rolled her into a position we called the log drive, and she told me—she shouted—that she loves me, goddamnit, *yes*, and she wants to be with me forever. I stopped. Outside, the wind sobbed. Alexandra, her face flushed the color of ripe rhubarb, stumbled from the bedroom and closed the door. Forty minutes later, when it was clear she wasn't coming back, I bundled myself in a parka and thermal snow pants and set off for the Institute.

From outside the TechInfo office I heard a floorboard creak, then a moist sniffle. I opened the door: Alexandra was sitting in the Tech-Hotline chair in front of the window, staring into the quadrangle. She looked at me; she looked back out the window; she shrugged awkwardly and said, *So, this is it. The famous office.*

In the quadrangle a stage had been erected near the Gray Building, and on the lawn an assembly of crimson-gowned seniors squirmed and hooted in the driving snow. Behind them, underdressed parents shivered in their seats, wondering what kind of people could live in a place like this. At the edge of the quadrangle the Caribou Brass Band sent up a frozen-lipped Sousa march. I drew the window shade, momentarily nostalgic at the sight of so much unbridled optimism, and as I did the crowd quieted and the provost took the podium and cleared her throat. *Students, parents, distinguished guests, fellow alumni and alumnae: welcome. Today is a joyous day.*

Alexandra scooted onto the desk, her snow-booted feet not touching the floor, and pulled me down to her. *Just lie here*, she said. *Don't get funny.* Her breathing was loud in my ear: a seashore, a multitude. I kissed her smooth neck, and let myself believe that we were two strangers pressed together, shivering with possibility. Alexandra stroked my back, but when I began to stir she gripped my shoulders with heartbreaking finality. *Just don't*, she said. *Okay? Please. Just stay.*

From the quadrangle, the voice of the Institute's first female graduate drifted into the office. *I remember that my bedroom was in the infirmary, and boys would stand outside arguing over who would walk me to chemistry class. I remember walking to class and wondering how in the world a girl like myself ended up at a place with so many wonderful, wonderful boys.* Alexandra shifted beneath me. Suddenly there was a ripple of applause, and the microphone reverberated as if it had been dropped, then the tinny, shouted voice of my ex-advisor announced that he was having an immoral relationship with an undergraduate.

Alexandra struggled to her feet. The crowd hushed. Alexandra shoved aside the window shade and said, *Jesus Christ, fuck, Dad—* then grabbed her parka and threw open the TechInfo door and clattered down the Gehring Building stairs.

Outside, the crowd had fractured into a jumble of bewildered voices. The provost stood at the podium, saying, *Okay, let's just be calm, people*—then a woman screamed and two people stood and pointed: I followed their gaze to the roof of the Gray Building, where my ex-advisor stood in full academic regalia, looking like an Arthurian pimp. His arms were hugged against his chest in a way that struck me as tremendously fragile. He shifted his weight from foot to foot, his crimson robes billowing in the snowy breeze; then I spotted Alexandra, a red-jacketed streak across the quadrangle. She sprinted past the brass band, past the podium, and burst through the Gray Building's tall front doors.

I threw open the window, half-expecting the TechHotline to ring, as a distant wail went up from the Slaney firehouse. Atop the Gray building, my ex-advisor tugged off his eight-cornered hat and tossed it limply over the edge. It fluttered down, down, down, then landed on the sidewalk, flopped once and laid flat. An anxious moan rose from the crowd. He climbed the safety railing and leaned over the roof edge, his wispy hair whipping in the breeze, and the provost over the loudspeaker said, *Please, please: please.*

Then Alexandra appeared behind her father. She approached him slowly. He turned to her and spread his arms wide, his face a mask of nervous relief, then seemed to slip on the icy roof: he took a quick step backward and froze, arms thrown up to heaven, and then he was airborne. Down he went, his crimson robes rippling as he bicycled in the frozen air then disappeared without a sound into a steep snow bank.

A chorus of screams rose up, and the provost whispered, *Sweet Jesus* into the microphone and covered her face. Alexandra rushed to the roof edge. A quartet of Slaney firemen jogged into the courtyard with a folded-up safety net and looked around, confused. I made a quick calculation: a 180-pound man, falling thirty feet at 32.2 feet per second squared—I drew the shade and turned away from the window and closed my eyes.

Wind howled past the TechInfo window. A baby broke into a restless wail. After what seemed like a long time I heard a hopeful shout, and I peeked around the shade: my ex-advisor was struggling out of the snow bank, clutching his left shoulder, surrounded by shocked firemen. I closed my eyes. I looked again: Alexandra, red parka gone and hair whipped into a cloud, rushed hip-deep into the snow bank and threw her arms around her father's neck. She touched his cheek, as if to make sure he was real and not some snow-blown mirage. My ex-advisor, eyes squeezed shut with pain, slumped down in the drifting snow and hugged his daughter with his good arm and began to weep.

The Detroit train left at eleven thirteen P.M., and from there it was two connections and twenty-one hours to Huntsville. I sat in the TechInfo office until it was time to leave for the station, and when the TechHotline rang I didn't pick up. The CALL light threw jagged shadows against the dark office walls. I knew there were equations describing the contour of the shadows, the luminescent intensity of the CALL light, the heat distribution in my hands as I clasped them together, the stress distribution in my eyelids as I pressed my eyes shut. In the quadrangle, snow drifted down with perfect indifferent randomness. In thousands of dormitory bedrooms, young men and women were asleep and dreaming of numbers.

I would begin a new line of research in Alabama, I decided. I would throw away my textbooks and Institute notepads and start fresh. What effect does geography have on love? What effect does weather have on love? There are events in nature, I've noticed, that cannot be explained or reproduced, that simply *are*. It's enough to give a person hope.

Nominated by Elizabeth Gaffney

NIGHT TRAIN

by TED GENOWAYS

from BULLROARER (Northeastern University Press)

Theodore Thompson Genoways, December 28, 1916

He stirs before dawn, tucks a lantern in his pack,
and leans out into the cold. Half-dark, chimney smoke
feathers and molts, circling the frozen window glass,

fading across drifted fields. He wades through snowbanks,
windblown to the eaves of an abandoned milk shed,
and across the barnyard, where leaf-bare cottonwoods

and evergreens stretch from the farm to deeper woods.
His skates curl like a promise in his canvas pack.
At the river's edge, he builds a small fire and sheds

his overshoes, while gusts send a thick rope of smoke
and cherry sparks, swirling toward the distant bank.
Late last August, he honed his father's reading glass

on a knot of bluestem and dried cobs, till the glass
shimmered, grass curled and burned. He piled on scrubwood,
then whole logs. Together, the boys walked the ditch bank,

touching torches to each row, but Ted trailed the pack,
blinking as his brothers—one by one—passed into smoke.
He kindles his lantern. The little light it sheds

casts his legs in wide shadow, down the watershed
and across the river, stretched below like frosted glass.
He buckles his skates, watching the gray thread of smoke

from his chimney stitch across the sheltering woods,
firs straight and green as soldiers. He shoulders his pack
and takes a long, gliding step from the near bank,

buoyed on a scalpel blade of steel, toward the bank
on the far shore. For a moment, the valley—washed
in moonlight, the sky-blue glow of ice and snowpack—

speeds and scrolls by him, as if passing through the glass
of a Pullman car. Boys fresh from the backwoods
crowded the platform that summer morning, coal smoke

dotting girls' dresses with soot as the train left, smoke
clinging to their tear-streaked cheeks. He curls on the bank
under the bridge, waiting for thunder from the woods

to jar ashes, bitternut, bur-oak till they shed
their brittle leaves. Its hiss echoes like breaking glass
or a snake in tall reeds. He braces for impact.

From the bone-black woods, the night train rockets past, packed
with sleeping recruits. It banks through the plume of smoke
it sheds like a skin and slithers on tracks of glass.

Nominated by Northeastern University Press

FIELDS OF MERCY

memoir by LADETTE RANDOLPH

from FOURTH GENRE

I FIRST HEARD THE STORY of Armageddon from my best friend's
stepfather. A Southerner with a Southerner's sense of drama and
elaboration, he told us about the book of *Revelation* without equivo-
cation. This *was* going to happen, every bit of it, just the way St. John
had seen it in his vision on the Island of Patmos. The graves would
open, the dead would rise. A hellish cast of characters would cause
the world endless suffering: the dragon, the beast, the Antichrist.

At fourteen I was primarily concerned with the suffering described in the story and did not take much note of the promises for
eternal peace and bliss that would follow the years of tribulation.
Though deeply impressed, I wasn't certain at first if I believed the
story. At home I asked my parents about it. They were obviously dis-
pleased, but they confirmed that what I had heard was all there in
the book of *Revelation*. They too believed in a literal interpretation
of the book, though they never talked about it, and seemed to feel it
wasn't a fit subject for children's ears or for discussion with other
church people.

With an adolescent's preoccupation with the grotesque, I became
fascinated. I was drawn to the details of the prophesied end of time
in much the way I was drawn to horror movies. The delicious sensation of being scared out of my wits fit in perfectly with the intensity
of emotion I was experiencing in other areas of my life in those years.
My church friends and I obsessed about the spectacular end we
imagined. We recounted the gruesome details. It wasn't only us,
however, for the early seventies marked an increased fascination with
predictions of the apocalypse. David Wilkerson, famous for his book

The Cross and the Switchblade, wrote a book detailing his own vision for the end times, aptly titled *The Vision*. He claimed he had seen a vision that indicated the end was very near at hand. There were other books written by conservative believers, one more graphic and wondrously detailed than the next. I bought them all, and I loved them. I was waiting for the inevitable end, hoping, as the *pre-millenialists* prophesied, that believers would be taken up—raptured—before the seven years of tribulation began. But just in case I had to suffer through the tribulation, I also read Richard Wormbrand's *Tortured for Christ*, a graphic testimony of his ordeal behind bars in a communist block country; Corrie Ten Boom's *The Hiding Place*, an account of her years in a Nazi concentration camp because of her family's role in hiding Jews (which they saw as their Christian duty); and a book by a female doctor (the title escapes me now), a missionary in the Congo, who was raped and driven from her camp by the "heathen natives." I was riveted by these accounts of faith and endurance in light of the quickly approaching end of time, and I was consumed with religious fervor, set to become a martyr for Christ.

Conversion stories fascinated me as well. They were the stories I gathered from the adults I knew, from testimonials at church camp and revival meetings. I collected these stories and retold them to friends. It was inevitable that I began to evangelize, bringing numerous friends into the church because of my influence. (To my amazement, all of those converts have stayed in the church twenty-five years later while I, the evangelist, have left.)

⌐⌐

I was a precocious believer. By five I was singing solos in church, and at six I was baptized by immersion. Because the individual must choose to receive this form of baptism, which in my church (Christian Church) was believed essential for salvation, there were at first doubts that my six-year-old mind had grasped the enormity of that step. Mine was a farm family. We lived near the great Sandhills of Nebraska, a stark landscape. There were no neighbor children. No parks. No museums. It was an austere place where I grew up, and I was a child who wanted to sing and dance, to play the piano, to make up stories and plays, to draw elaborate pictures of mythical worlds. Where else in that environment but the church would I have found the beauty I craved? Only the church provided music and color and words. Such beautiful words. I still hear the words I first heard with chills at a Christmas pageant when I was very young, "And lo, this night in the city of David a son is born, Christ the Lord." And there were the Old Testament stories too: such passion and commitment. Such spectacular human folly and sin. Sin. I understood well the salvation I was receiving by going under the baptismal waters at age six. I was making a choice for a grander life.

In many ways I was not disappointed. I had a grand interior life. Perhaps I would have my faith yet today if I had been born into a church tradition that hadn't demanded such literalness of belief, if I had been exposed to the silent ritual of liturgical worship. (Instead, I was privy to the sermon, to the Sunday School lesson where no story was valued or recognized for its symbolic content.) Or a Pentecostal faith with its emphasis on the gifts of the spirit, allowing for a quirky individual vision, might have been enduring for me. Even as I seem to mourn my lost faith, I know it is irrational. Still, there are things I miss.

I miss my fundamentalist friends. The camaraderie of shared assumptions, the likes of which I'll never find again, is worth a moment of affectionate nostalgia now and then. There was a real community with those friends. Every weekend we met to cook meals together, to take long walks, watch movies. And we talked. We talked long into the night. If through the years my ideas became more and more abstract and mystical, even dangerously ecumenical, and if now and then I alarmed my friends with these ideas, I was still one of the gang, and my house a central meeting place. Those conversations I now recall spiraled and billowed. Ideas blossomed and stacked gloriously, airy and high. Such conversations reflected an intense search for the truth that I no longer pursue. The truth I found took me straight out of the very group that had provided such fertile ground for thought.

I remember one night shortly before I left the church telling one of these friends that I wanted to know myself so well that I would be perfectly distilled, like a drop of water, know exactly who I was in any circumstance, while at the same time be so big, so capable of understanding anything human that like an ocean I could find room for everyone and every idea. "You want to be God?" my friend said that night critically. I hadn't thought of it that way, that paradox a perfect description for what some might call God. "Why not?" I answered.

And then I read Blake, "Everything that lives is holy." And the

Tao-Te Ching, and Jung. This was no crisis of faith, but rather an ever-expanding acceptance of broader truths.

It was at about this time I had a dream. In the dream I came into an old-fashioned college classroom. I was late for class and everyone else had left. There had been a test that day, and the professor, an old white-haired man, who showed no impatience with my tardiness, pointed to where I should start. The test involved a number of booths at which some mathematical principle was enacted. My task was to name the principle or the theory behind the illustration. This was *not* a math class, and as I went from booth to booth, my test paper blank, I grew angrier and angrier. Finally, in complete frustration I at last put the unfinished test on the professor's desk and began to cry. The professor and I seemed to have a friendly, or familiar relationship, and he came from behind his desk to hug me in a fatherly way. He seemed genuinely concerned as he tried to comfort me. I said to him in anger then, "If I fail, you fail too." The meaning is apparent. I was telling the God that I had created—a kindly, delusional, and ultimately cruel God—goodbye. I sometimes miss him, too.

⌐┐

When I left the church, I also left my husband of twelve years, and I think in the minds of many of my fundamentalist friends, I went insane. My ex-husband certainly contributed to this idea. He told people that a demon had gotten hold of me, and he meant it. Friends I had lost track of since high school wrote to say they'd received letters from him telling them about my insanity and how I'd made off with the children, endangering their souls with my harebrained ideas. He said he was raising money for a custody fight, would they please help? There were a series of these letters. My own family members, all still in the church themselves, received the letters. "He's saying horrible things about you," one of my sisters-in-law told me. "How can you stand it?"

I shrugged, "I knew I would have to take the blame," I said. "It's worth it."

After weekend visits with their father, my children tell me about their activities: A pro-life march, a chastity conference, a revival meeting, a Christian rock concert, a missionary talk, an anti-abortion film, a movie about Armageddon. My friends outside the fundamentalist Christian community are horrified by these reports. "You have

330

to tell them . . ." they say, suggesting any number of counter-activities, counterarguments, as though the minds of my children are like seesaws and need to be balanced with more weight on my end. But I don't see it that way, even though I, too, am deeply disturbed by the things they are being exposed to, all of it in a frantic attempt to save their souls from my influence. The balance I had provided while still living with their father is gone, for I would never have permitted all of this excess, and their father, now terrified by his loss, has become a caricature of fundamentalist belief—on his dining room wall hangs a huge bulletin board with missionary newsletters and appeals, Christian music plays on the stereo all day, and the activities mentioned above occupy the three weekends a month he has visitation with the children. When he doesn't see the children, he writes them letters filled with Scriptural admonitions. He warns them against the "spirit of the age," and reminds them to read their Bibles. He'll quiz them later to be sure they've read the assigned passages. So, just as I gained freedom from fundamentalism and their father, my children have become more imprisoned by both. No, I could not set up counterarguments or counter-activities. Instead of creating balance, I felt it would tear their psyches to bits. I felt that their father's energy, his fanaticism, could not be matched, that in fact it would not be healthy for me to try to match it.

For those who sometimes wonder why I've stayed in the same city, why I didn't move to avoid these problems, I have to say this is a progressive city where I have supportive friends, good work, a rich life beyond my past.

⌐⌐

These days, I often feel suffocated by a world that seems to be filled with a saccharine, commercialized belief. Television programs like *Seventh Heaven* and *Touched by an Angel* are not only popular among viewers but sympathetically reviewed. Evangelistic Christian music and books now constitute a huge economy. Young people, including my three teenagers, flock to Christian rock concerts where the music is not only derivative, but the look is mainstream rock. Audio Adrenalin, DC Talk. Their music flirts with the edges, defining "cool" by how far they can go toward "worldliness" without crossing over. Each time I'm confronted by this commercialized Christianity I'm reminded of the story of Jesus' rage in the temple, clearing the money changers out (still the heart of the zealot in me). I find this industry far from benign. On the front door of the local Christian bookstore is the cartoonish depiction of an apocalyptic world. It's the advertisement for a new book by Tim LaHaye, a fictional account of the end of time. LaHaye is familiar from my own days of fevered reading in the early seventies. What is new now is the dominance of the industry and the evolution from prediction (a form of fiction) to an open fictionalization of events.

In the ten years since I left the church not only has this commercialized Christianity gained a strong foothold in the economy and in mainstream American thought, but it has gained tremendous influence politically. I was disturbed by the rumblings of the Christian Right as it began to emerge in the five years before I left the church, but I could never have predicted that in 1994 the U.S. Congress would support Newt Gingrich's Contract with America, and that that year's election would seat several freshman senators with openly fundamentalist agendas. I could not have predicted that within the public schools, talk of religion in the classroom would become such an impassioned subject that support for a Christian-based curriculum would have enough backing to support legislative initiatives. I could not have predicted that these political/academic shifts would lead my beloved brother-in-law, a conservative politician involved in the grassroots of the Christian Coalition, to tell me in 1994—when I said I couldn't live in this country if Newt Gingrich had his way—"And we'll want you to leave." The chilling first person plural suggested far more of a plan than my paranoia had even seen coming. I was beginning to have apocalyptic flashbacks. The glee with which the wars and skirmishes in Iraq were met by some in the Christian Fundamentalist community—convinced the long awaited prophesies for the end of time had been fulfilled—signaled a dangerous collective thinking, a wish fulfillment of destruction. Jerry Falwell's glib announcement that the Antichrist would be a Jewish male in his thirties, who was most likely walking the earth now, was not as singular a notion as many people wanted to think.

⌐⌐

I feel less burdened now, having laid my faith aside, but I feel life is less magical, less intensely personal, too. While I still had faith, I felt I was the center of a meaningful drama, part of the fight for my soul. The universe had a specific beginning and a prescribed end. There was a definite plot—a battle between good and evil that would inevitably end in a violent and glorious battle, with the good guaranteed to win. No action film could compete with my own psychodrama. Trumpets would sound. Every knee would bow. All tears would be dried and there would be peace between all things. Beautiful words. "There will be no more crying, no more tears. . . ."

I had a dream once about the Rapture. I dreamt I was walking downtown in a large city. No city I recognized, though it vaguely resembled the mythical Gotham City. It was a gray day, very dreary, and I was on the sidewalk between stores when suddenly the wind came up and whipped around the crowds of shoppers. The weather was frightening enough, but suddenly the sky above us was filled with black helicopters. The sound was deafening. Without warning I was pulled hard, as if by magnetic force, to my knees. I saw that everyone else around me had been pulled to their knees as well. We covered our ears against the noise of the helicopters. I exchanged a glance with a woman beside me on the sidewalk, and I said, "I wonder if this is the Rapture." The woman nodded in agreement. I shudder now in recounting this menacing dream, but the feeling during the dream and for weeks afterward was one of both terror and euphoria, for I had known without a doubt as I shivered and cowered there on my knees that I would be allowed to board one of those black helicopters, like my sister-in-law's story of being airlifted out of Vietnam right before the fall of Saigon. I would be spared all sorts of horrors, literally saved by my faith.

Such drama is hard to leave. My faith was like a thick curtain, like a flat-earth theory of the world. I felt safe and knowing within its parameters. If I ventured close to the edge, or reached out to pull back the curtain, I always retreated to the safe known world. The sense of safety, of clear margins, allowed me freedom of range. I had a sense of knowing where I was in the world. Now, with all sorts of intellectual freedom, I often find my world is strangely prescribed. Paradoxically, though the world seems more vast I opt not to explore as much. There is now nothing at stake. While my faith had certain limits, those very limits became the site of great intellectual work, defining, defying. My fundamentalist friends were smart and interesting, educated, well-read. I would still find certain conversations with them stimulating, I believe, but I gave up my passport to that world. I had to. And even as I miss that sense of belonging, it is in much the same way that I miss childhood. There is no going back.

It was not easy to leave. I'd been warned most of my conscious life about "out there," "the darkness," "the ignorant," "Satan's sphere of influence." The books that might have introduced reason into my life when all of this fervor began in adolescence were somehow never available. They weren't on the bookshelves at home, and in my school's curriculum the archaic reading material somehow never cut through the bulwark of my already captive imagination.

I'd like to say I was looking for something in my adolescence and never found it but, truthfully, I had a resistant arrogance. It was I who was privy to information others needed; I knew the truth; I had the key to salvation. What could penetrate such suspicious, over-confident armor as that? The changes had to come slowly from within myself.

By the time I graduated from high school those changes had begun. I was no longer quite so certain. Church ritual annoyed me. My father's ministry was in turmoil, and the church people had revealed themselves to be more cruel than any adults I had previously known. The seeds were there, but nothing had quite taken root, and I made a bad decision to go to Bible College, to the dismay of some of my high school teachers. Though I turned a deaf ear to their protests, I was miserable both the summer before I left and the year I spent at Bible College. How could it have been called a college? One hundred and sixty students. Course offerings such as: Personal Evangelism, Life of Christ, Sunday School Education. The bald-faced indoctrination hastened my realization that organized religion was foolishness. Being forced to attend daily chapel services and nightly devotions only added to my rebellion in ways that might never have happened had I not been forced to take part.

My frustration did not signal a loss of faith. I was still an adamant believer. The problem was that the church was hypocritical. I couldn't stand the inconsistency between what was claimed and what was practiced. I wanted the integrity of Richard Wormbrand's experience, the refining test of faith. I'd lost respect for the pedestrian nature of the church. On some deep level I was a fanatic. My faith was still intact, but I wished to leave the church; however, some strange inertia held me back. I knew of nothing else, no other life, and my vague yearnings had no specific goal. I wanted the challenge of a beautiful life, but kept feeling myself restrained by a squalid reality. My contacts were so restricted that I knew no one I admired outside the church. I had been trained not to want things, trained by my reading material, my church doctrine, my own passivity, my loyalty to friends and family to want only the familiar, but there in the midst of the faithful, I was miserable and wanted out. And then I fell in love.

That should have perhaps been the end of the story, the beginning of my adult life, a life still of faith though perhaps a more reasonable faith. I visit that time now and again as we do all ruptures and wonder what if. . . . It is unavoidably a turning point in my life, for I married the young man I fell in love with. My life of faith, though, had not prepared me for his sudden death six weeks after we were married. And if I trace my loss of faith to the fissure that resulted from my grief over his death, it is also the site of my momentary return to the church, my blind, headlong, free fall back into organized religion, into a wrong-headed second marriage. I found again, desperate to define a life that had suddenly gone to sea, my old familiar fervency, my passionate zealous religiosity. I went mad in my own peculiar way.

Funny, how years later when after hard work and careful thought I finally regained my sanity, I would be considered mentally disturbed by my fundamentalist friends and acquaintances. In a way, I was absurdly amused. I was so happy to be back to some semblance of myself that it didn't matter what anyone said, how they criticized. It didn't matter that some of my friends not only abandoned but betrayed me. How could such little things matter?

There were all those years to be accounted for, though. They seemed wasted, wasteful. I remember two distinct images of my second marriage: one, the feeling that I was on the wrong path, that I was living the wrong life; and two, how time and again in the midst of the most mundane tasks, I would think in these words exactly, "these are my years in the wilderness." And like the Israelites, forced to wander, the promised land glimpsed but ultimately denied them because they had sinned, I felt I was paying a penance. I had made my bed, and now I had to lie in it. My harsh world view, the strict demands I made of myself were only what many others had suffered before me who believed in a strict, moralistic God. Such a God is in some ways easier to leave than the gentlemanly, slightly doddering God of those "fuzzy headed Methodists," the God I finally adopted before leaving my faith altogether.

What I retain of my lost faith is a respect still for the abstract tenets of Scripture: love, mercy, grace, forgiveness. In the end it was not scorn that enabled me to leave the church, but these tenets. Another story altogether. While I agonized in that awkward juncture before leaving, I unexpectedly felt no condemnation, only fields and fields of mercy, a sense that as humans we are destined to be both absurd and lovely. Eventually, I understood there was no God judging me. There was no religious faith that was not in some way of our own making. What I decided to make for myself, instead, was mercy. So I did.

Nominated by Nancy McCabe, Fourth Genre

THE WOMAN WHO HATED VALENTINE'S DAY

by SUSAN HAHN

from CHELSEA

A quiver of arrows, a quiver of eros,
she cannot hold bow or beau—
both intent on a massacre
of the heart where each obliterates
the other—no thing left to stitch up.
Cat gut has become as weak
as lace. Martyred

Saints beatified and canonized—
it's they whom she idealizes,
as she repeats the rites of purity, the right
tasks. Desperate Psyche on her knees

attempting to serve the myth—
Venus, Please, she cries,
I need to find Him—meaning

Cupid. Instead, in the bent and the dead
forest, the archdemons await:
Lucifer, Mammon, Asmodeus,
Satan, Beelzebub, Leviathan
are tempting her, again.

Nominated by Mark Irwin, William Olsen, Richard Burgin, Chelsea

THE WORST DEGREE OF UNFORGIVABLE

fiction by NICHOLAS MONTEMARANO

from THE ANTIOCH REVIEW

THE BEDROOM DRAPES MUST TOUCH; we must beat dust from the drapes; we must wave our hands through the airborne dust; if the dust makes us sneeze we must use a tissue from the tissue box on the nightstand; we must place the used tissue in the small garbage pail beside the toilet; if the garbage bag is filled, or almost filled, we must tie the bag, remove it from inside the pail (making sure to re-cover any stray garbage found in the pail under the bag), and place it inside a larger bag under the kitchen sink; if the bag under the kitchen sink is filled, or almost filled, we must tie that bag, remove it from under the sink, and place it in one of two garbage pails in the back yard; if both garbage pails are filled, or almost filled, or if it is Tuesday or Friday—garbage pickup days—we must wheel the pails to the front of the house and place them close to the curb; we must make sure the pails' lids are secured tightly enough that raccoons or stray dogs cannot easily knock the lids off and rip open the bags and scatter garbage along the sidewalk; we must position the pails close enough to the street so that sanitation workers may carry them the shortest possible distance from curbside to the back of the sanitation truck (thereby decreasing the chance that garbage might fall from the pails), but not so close to the street that the sanitation truck, when it passes, can possibly knock over and damage the pails; we must sweep any leaves and pollynoses that have collected in the spot in the yard where the garbage pails have been; before we step back

338

into the house, we must wipe the bottoms of our shoes on the welcome mat outside the back door; we must place a fresh medium-sized garbage bag under the kitchen sink; we must place a fresh smallest-size garbage bag in the bathroom pail; we must make sure the tissue box on the nightstand beside the bed is in its proper place at the proper angle with exactly one tissue extending up through the hole in the top of the box; if while sneezing or while blowing our noses we sit or lean on the bed, we must smooth the bedspread so that there are no creases, so that the design embroidered onto the bedspread is symmetrical so that there are an equal number of butterflies and an equal number of flowers on each side of what we estimate is the center of the bed; if while smoothing and aligning the bedspread one or more of our fingers should touch the headboard, we must use the furniture polish and the furniture polish rag stored under the bathroom sink to wipe away our fingerprints; we must rub the polish onto the headboard thoroughly so that there are no streaks; after using the rag to wipe any fingerprints from the furniture polish can, and using the rag as a buffer between our hands and the can, we must place the can and the rag in their proper positions under the bathroom sink; if when we sneeze we spray the bedroom mirror, we must use the glass cleaner and the glass cleaner rag stored under the bathroom sink (next to the furniture polish and furniture polish rag) to wipe away any moisture; we must rub the glass cleaner thoroughly onto the mirror to prevent streaks; we must wipe away any fingerprints from the plastic glass cleaner bottle and place the bottle in its proper place under the sink; we must fold the rag and place it in front of but not touching the bottle; (if we forgot to fold the furniture polish rag and place it in front of but not touching the furniture polish can, we must do so now); if thoroughly rubbing glass cleaner on the mirror causes any earrings or pins or framed photographs on the dresser below and attached to the mirror to shift, we must move these items to their proper places; if our fingers leave any marks on these items when we move them to their proper places, we must use the glass cleaner and glass cleaner rag to clean the smudged glass fronts of picture frames, and the furniture polish and furniture polish rag to clean any wood frames; we must place the furniture polish can and the glass cleaner bottle in their proper places under the bathroom sink, making sure the rags are folded and placed in front of but not touching the appropriate bottle or can; if we touch the top of the dresser while making sure the items on the dresser are in their proper places, or while polishing or cleaning these finger-printed items, we must use the furniture polish and furniture polish rag to wipe away any smudges, making sure to rub in the polish thoroughly, and making sure to place the can and the rag in their proper positions under the sink; if at any point we notice that the furniture polish can or the glass cleaner bottle are empty, or close to empty, we must look in the hallway closet for an unopened bottle or can and place it under the sink; we must wrap the empty or almost-empty bottle or can in the rag that goes with it and place bottle or can and rag in the small garbage pail at the side of the toilet; we must take from the fresh rags pile in the hallway closet a fresh rag and place it in front of but not touching the unopened bottle or can; we must return to the bedroom to shake the blankets; we must fold the blankets so that all the edges are aligned; if while shaking and folding the blankets we scatter lint and dust on top of the dresser or on the bed's headboard or on the glass fronts or wood frames of the picture frames, we must use furniture polish and glass cleaner to wipe everything clean, making sure to rub thoroughly and making sure to return the bottle, the can, and the rags to their proper places; we must secure each pillow in its pillow case (so that the tagged side of each pillow cannot be seen) and smooth each pillow case so that there are no creases; we must pluck lint from the pillow cases; we must place the blankets in their proper order inside the pillow-and-blankets storage alcove in the hallway, and place on top of the blankets, in their proper order, every pillow; we must balance the pillows on top of the blankets so that there is no chance of their toppling if someone opens the storage alcove; the storage alcove door must be closed and the door's handle wiped clean; every drawer of every dresser must be closed and every drawer handle wiped clean; every piece of clothing must be folded neatly inside a dresser drawer or hanging inside a closet; pants must be clipped onto pants hangers, skirts onto skirt hangers; shirts must be hung from wire shirt hangers, jackets and coats from wood jacket-and-coat hangers; there must be the same amount of space between hangers so that each article of clothing touches the next, but not so that the removal of one article of clothing disturbs the symmetry of articles hanging nearby; belts must hang from the metal hooks on the inside of the closet door; shoes and sneakers must be arranged in their proper order on the closet floor (laces inside; left shoe or sneaker to the left of the right shoe or sneaker); the top of every dresser in every room must be wiped with

340

furniture polish and furniture polish rag; every mirror and every glass front of every picture frame in every room must be wiped with glass cleaner and glass cleaner rag; every framed picture or certificate on every wall in every room must hang straight; every light in every bedroom must be turned off; before cleaning the bathroom the bathroom light must be turned on; the bathroom floor must be dry; the rim and sides and faucets of the tub and sink must be wiped with tub-and-sink cleaner (found under the sink) and tub-and-sink sponge (found next to but not touching the soap in the soap holder on the inside rim of the tub), and then rinsed with warm water, and then dried with a fresh towel (found in the fresh towels pile in the hallway closet); if any water spills onto the floor while washing the tub and the sink, the floor must be dried with a fresh towel (never with a used towel, which may have picked up stray hairs and soap scum); every used towel must be placed in the washing machine in the basement (making sure not to drip any water onto any part of the floor in any part of the house); the television in the living room must remain off (so that if someone touches the back of the television it will not be warm); the front door must remain double-locked; if someone knocks at the door the door is never to be opened; we are never to look through the small triangular stained glass window in the wood door; if by mistake we look through the window in the wood door, we must use the glass cleaner and glass cleaner rag to wipe away any nose or finger smudges, and then we must return the glass cleaner bottle and rag to their proper places; the living room drapes must touch; we must never part the drapes to look outside to see who is knocking at the door, or to see who is leaving a flyer in the mailbox; we must never answer the phone; if by mistake we answer the phone we must say politely that our mother is busy at the moment and that if the person at the other end of the line would care to leave his number our mother would be happy to return the call; we may sit on the living room couch, but we must never lie on the couch or place our feet (and certainly never our sneakers or shoes, which are never to be worn in any part of the house, not even in the basement where the floor is cold) on the coffee table in front of the couch; if by mistake we lie on the couch, we must realize our mistake and stand up; we must make sure all couch pillows are in their proper places, symmetrically spaced against the couch's long back cushion; we must smooth the covers of the couch's bottom cushions until no creases remain; if by mistake we place our feet (or God forbid our shoes or

341

sneakers) on the coffee table, we must use the furniture polish and furniture polish rag to wipe away any dirt and smudges (rubbing thoroughly) and return furniture polish can and rag to the storage cabinet under the upstairs bathroom sink; we must never eat or drink on the couch; we must never eat or drink anywhere in the house but at the kitchen table, and always with plastic serving mats under our plates and coasters under our glasses; if by mistake we eat or drink anywhere in the house but at the kitchen table, we must make sure never to spill; if we spill dry food we must make sure to recover all crumbs or whole pieces of food, even taking the extra few minutes it takes to check under the couch and under the coffee table and around the entire room, even going so far as to vacuum the rug (making sure to wipe away with a damp rag any finger smudges on the handle of the vacuum, or sometimes using a damp rag as a buffer between the handle and our hands, and certainly making sure to return the vacuum to its proper place in the back of the dining room closet, and while returning the vacuum making sure not to disturb the symmetry of the clothes hanging in the closet); if by an act of the worst carelessness we spill a drink on the rug of any room, we must immediately wipe the spot with a damp rag with all the strength we have, even sometimes taking turns to maintain the maximum amount of pressure on the wet spot, for as long as it takes to eliminate any evidence that a drink has been spilled in a place a drink never should have been; if we rub the spot until the rag breaks apart we must dampen another fresh rag and begin again; if we rub the spot until all four of our arms are sore to the point of unbearable pain, we must throw away the used rags (first making sure to wrap them in paper towels or aluminum foil or anything else that will prevent them from being seen should she glance into the kitchen garbage bag) and we must vacuum any remains of the rags from the rug (carefully returning the vacuum to its proper place in the dining room closet); if we discover, after sitting on the rug (holding hands) and watching the spot dry, that the spot has become a stain, we must do our best to stand up, compose ourselves, and move through the rest of our day without thinking too much about how carrying a drink where a drink never should be carried is one of the worst acts of carelessness; we must try not to hate ourselves; we carried a drink where a drink should never be carried; we lost our concentration for a fraction of a second; we committed an irreversible act of supreme carelessness; still, we must try not to hate ourselves; we must remember that as

342

terrible and unforgivable as one act of supreme carelessness is, two or three or twenty acts of carelessness can be worse, can be more unforgivable (if indeed there are degrees of unforgivable, as we believe there are); we must recover enough to remember to wipe the plastic serving mats with a fresh damp rag and dry them with a fresh dry rag and place them in their proper places in the kitchen pantry; we must wipe the insides and bottoms of the coasters and place them inside the cabinet above the stove; we must stand on a chair to reach the cabinet above the stove; we must remember to wipe our fingerprints from the handle of the cabinet; we must remember to wipe from the leather cushions of the kitchen chairs any dirt and smudges caused by our feet (or, if we have not learned from past moments of carelessness, by our shoes or sneakers); the chairs must be placed in their proper places around the kitchen table; while arranging the chairs we must use every bit of our strength to lift rather than slide, so as to prevent the bottoms of the legs of the chairs from scratching the floor; there is no recovery from scratching the floor; if by the worst sin of carelessness we scratch the floor we must try immediately to forget about the scratches and not to concern ourselves with how the sun shining through the kitchen window may illuminate the scratches; we must close our eyes, breathe in through our noses, out through our mouths, concentrate every bit of our mental energy on slowing the beating of our hearts, count to five after every breath out and before every breath in, tense our fingers, turn our hands into fists, dig our nails into our palms until the skin turns white, relax our hands for a moment, pinch the skin on our thighs or on the undersides of our arms, clench our toes inside our socks, release, breathe, open our eyes, and remember: there are degrees of unforgivable; we must compose ourselves enough to remember to wash any utensils, plates, and drinking glasses we may have used; when walking slowly from table to sink we must remember to cup our free hands under utensils, plates, and drinking glasses to prevent any morsels or condiments from falling or dripping onto the floor; should a fluid drop of anything fall or drip onto the floor we must use a fresh damp rag to wipe away any evidence that one of us has committed an act of supreme carelessness; we must dry the wet spot on the floor with a dry rag; we must throw both used rags into the kitchen garbage bag; we must use hot water when washing utensils, plates, and drinking glasses; we must use a dab of dish soap when washing plates, making sure to wipe away with the soft side of the dish-washing sponge any traces of food (and remembering to wash the bottoms of the plates, which may have picked up crumbs); if any morsels of food are stuck to the plate we must use the rough side of the dish-washing sponge; if these hardened morsels remain stuck to the plate we must scrape them away with our fingernails; we must rinse each plate thoroughly with hot water; we must hold each plate up to the ceiling light (or, on sunny days, up to the sunlight coming through the window above and behind the sink) to make sure every hardened morsel is gone, every dish soap streak gone; when washing forks we must make sure never to forget the food that sometimes gets caught between a fork's teeth; we must not forget the back of a spoon; we must be careful when washing the serrated edges of knives to avoid slicing the dish-washing sponge; if by an unforgivable lapse of concentration we slice the dish-washing sponge we must wrap the sponge in aluminum foil and place it at the bottom of the kitchen garbage bag; we must find in the cabinet below the sink a fresh dish-washing sponge and place it in its proper place on the rim of the sink; we must remember to rinse the dish soap from the used dish-washing sponge and squeeze it dry before placing it on the rim of the sink; we must use only a dab of special glass-cleaning soap for each used drinking glass; we must use the drinking glass sponge to scrub the inside of each glass, pushing the sponge into the glass vigorously enough to remove any remains of juice from the bottom and sides of the inside of the glass; we must fill each scrubbed drinking glass with the hottest water the kitchen sink can produce, and allow this water to remove any remains of juice even our most vigorous scrubbing cannot remove; while the hot water is acting on the insides of the drinking glasses we must use the dish-drying towel to dry the plates and utensils, making sure never to forget the handles of spoons or between the teeth of forks, making sure to concentrate when slowly drying the serrated edges of knives; we must place the sharp knives with the other sharp knives in the drawer between sink and stove; we must place large spoons with large spoons and small with small (making sure the back of each spoon rests inside the bowl of the spoon below); we must place the forks symmetrically with the other forks; we must place the plates on top of similar plates in the cabinet above the stove; we must pour the now warm water from the drinking glasses and hold the glasses up to the ceiling light (or up to the sun on sunny days); we must wrap the dish-drying towel around our fingers and do our best to squeeze our fingers deep into each drinking glass to dry every inch of the bottom and sides; we must stand each dried drinking glass alongside other drinking glasses of its kind; we must use the sink-cleaning sponge and a dab of dish soap to clean the bottom and sides of the sink (remembering to clean the drain and to remove with a paper towel, or with our fingers, any pieces of food too large to pass through the holes in the drain); we must remember to clean the rim of the sink, making sure never to spill soapy water over the rim and onto the floor; we must rinse the inside of the sink with the hottest water from the sink's spray hose; if one of us burns the other (and in the process sprays water onto the floor), we must try our best not to retaliate; we must not point fingers; we must not swear; we must not spit; we must not slam our hands on the kitchen counter; we must not smack or kick; we must not pull hair; we must not scratch the other's eye; we must not pull the other's lip or bend back the other's fingers; we must believe when the other says sorry sorry sorry, the spraying from the spray hose the hottest water the sink can produce must have been an accident, must not have been meant to harm; we must compose ourselves; we must close our eyes and take deep breaths; we must remember the degrees of unforgivable; we must forgive; we must work together; we must dry the faucet, the hot and cold knobs, the inside of the sink, the rim; we must dry the floor; if at any point, while drying the kitchen floor, or while dusting the basement coffee table and the top and sides of the basement television set and credenza (making sure not to disturb the glass knickknacks on the shelves inside the credenza) and stereo and bookcase (remembering the tops and bottoms of the four shelves of the bookcase), or while making sure the books on the basement bookcase are arranged in the proper order (the spine of each book dusted and any dust that falls dusted from where it falls), or while cleaning with a damp rag between the numbered buttons of the basement television remote control, or while making sure the pillows are symmetrically placed on the basement couch, or while making sure the zippered sides of the couch's bottom cushions cannot be seen, or while vacuuming the basement rug (remembering that the rug continues up the stairs to the main floor), or while cleaning the basement television screen and the glass front of the stereo and the glass front of the wall clock and the glass fronts of all picture frames, hanging or standing, with glass cleaner and glass cleaner rag, or while returning glass cleaner bottle and rag to their proper places, if at any point, while making sure the decorative towels hanging from the towel bar in the basement bathroom are not damp from use, or while drying any carelessly dampened decorative towels with the blow dryer stored in the upstairs hallway closet (making sure never to hold the blow dryer close enough to damage the towels), or while draping the dried towels symmetrically over the towel bar, or while returning the blow dryer (first wiping away any fingerprints with a damp rag) to its proper place in the upstairs hallway closet, or while making sure all dirty clothes and used towels are spread out evenly inside the washing machine (remembering, after closing the lid of the washing machine, to wipe away any fingerprints), or while making sure the drapes hanging from the three small basement windows touch, or while beating dust from the drapes, or while waving our hands through the airborne dust, if at any point, while cleaning the basement, or while waiting quietly in the living room, going through the mental checklist of all that must be done, if at any point our anger returns upon remembering the pain of the hottest water from the kitchen sink spray hose being sprayed on our face or neck or in our eyes, we must resist the urge to retaliate; we must resist the urge to point fingers or swear or spit or slam or smack or kick or bend fingers or scratch or pull hair; we must remember sorry; we must remember forgive; we must resist the temptation to threaten; if we cannot resist the temptation to threaten, and if upon threatening we see the familiar repulsive look of fear on the other's face, we must resist the urge to hate the other more than we already do; we must recognize that threatening one threatens both; we must use every bit of our mental energy to resist following through with our threat; we must not remove used tissues from the garbage and scatter them on the bedroom floor; we must not press our fingers against the bed's headboard and against the bathroom mirror and against every window in every room; we must not spray the mirrors with furniture cleaner and spray the tops of the coffee tables with glass cleaner; we must not place the furniture cleaner rag in front of but not touching the glass cleaner bottle and the glass cleaner rag in front of but not touching the furniture polish can; we must not use the decorative towels hanging from the towel bar in the basement bathroom as rags; we must not hang pants from shirt hangers and skirts from jacket-and-coat hangers; we must resist the temptation to place shoe next to sneaker, left to the right of right; we must not eat or drink in the back of the pillow-and-blankets storage alcove; we must not rip open the outside garbage bags and scatter garbage on the street or roll around in the garbage for all the neighbors to see; we must not pull apart or tear down the drapes; we must not pull off the bedspread or burn the bedspread or throw the earrings and pins from the top of the bedroom dresser into the toilet; we must resist the urge to break the glass fronts of every picture frame or slam the blow dryer into the upstairs bathroom mirror; we must resist the growing urge to pull out our own hair, to pull out each other's hair, to place those hairs in the bathroom and kitchen sinks and along the rim of the tub; we must not stomp on the soap; we must not close the tub's drain and turn the hot water knob and allow the water to run over the sides of the tub and onto the floor, nor must we allow the water to drip from the downstairs ceiling, nor must we allow the water to pool on the downstairs rug, nor must we allow the water to drip from the basement ceiling onto the basement rug; we must remember there is no turning back from the worst degree of unforgivable; we must not turn the kitchen chairs on their sides; we must not scratch the kitchen floor with unwashed knives; we must not tear open the rugs; we must resist the most powerful urge to rig the kitchen sink spray hose with a rubber band so that when she turns the hot water knob her face will be sprayed with the hottest water the kitchen sink can produce; if we cannot resist the temptation to follow through with our threat, we must begin again; we must close our eyes and breathe deeply; we must compose ourselves; we must try to slow our hearts; we must tell ourselves that there is enough time, the day is only beginning, certainly there must be enough time before we hear a key in the front door, before we hear the doorknob turn, before we hear footsteps moving from one room to the next, before we wait, eyes closed, for the sound of her voice.

Nominated by Paul Maliszewski, Kevin Prufer, Antioch Review

THE HICKEYS ON SALLY PALERMO'S NECK: SOME THOUGHTS ON BEAUTY AND THE CREATIVE LIFE

memoir by ANDREA HOLLANDER BUDY

from CREATIVE NONFICTION

1

SAM, MY GRANDFATHER, was a womanizer. After 12 years of marriage, he finally left my grandmother to marry a younger woman. My father, who was 11 at the time and the eldest of five, had to get a job to help support the family. None of them ever saw my grandfather again, but they heard that he eventually divorced again to marry yet another, *much* younger woman.

When my grandmother was in her 90s, she told me how Sam's turning away had made her feel. "I let my hair grow again," she said. "It had been cut in a bob for years. But when I was 16 it was long, and Sam used to like to braid and unbraid it. I thought maybe if he saw me again with hair like that, he'd *really* see me and come back." As she told me this, her hair was almost white, and cut short.

2

My father was stationed in Japan during the last year of his military obligation. Since my mother and I couldn't accompany him, we lived with my father's brother and his family—Uncle Joe and Aunt Kitty and their two children, Ron and Brenda.

A few months after we moved in, Brenda and I were invited to the birthday party of another 7-year-old girl who lived a few blocks away. My cousin and I took a bath together, dressed ourselves in the identical dresses our mothers had made for the occasion, and—feeling a little more grown up than we actually were—asked and were given permission to walk to the party by ourselves. I kissed my mother goodbye, and as I turned to leave, party gift in hand, I watched Brenda as she stepped away from her mother.

She looked beautiful—so much so that as I admired her, I felt suddenly inadequate and homely. Though my own dress was identical, the particular shade of yellow seemed to make me look jaundiced. I was thinner than Brenda, too—*skinny*, in fact. And my knees, which I've always thought were oddly shaped, stuck out from just below the dress's hemline. To make matters worse, under a Band-Aid on one of them were the last unpicked remains of a scab.

Then there was the problem of my hair. "Mouse brown" is the way I'd heard it described by my mother, who was always honest. She'd taken me to the beauty parlor that morning to have it trimmed and shaped. When I emerged I was wearing not a mouse on my head but a giant rat. My hair had been teased out with a comb to make it appear thicker, and the hairdresser had sprayed it with an awful-smelling, glue-like substance (the odor of which still depresses me and has kept me away from "beauty" parlors ever since).

I stood on the steps of Brenda's house, my eyes brimming.

"What's wrong?" my mother wanted to know.

"Brenda's prettier than I am," I said in barely a whisper, and I began to cry.

Parents—I now know because I have become one—are put to the trickiest tests. They're asked the most impossible questions, and their answers, even when right, are wrong. Or inappropriate. "Why is the sky blue?" is an easy one. "Why is Brenda prettier than I am?" is something else. But that afternoon, as I stood not looking into my mother's face, as I concentrated instead on my right index finger as it ran up and down, up and down the white ribbon that she'd helped me secure around the neatly wrapped birthday package only a few hours before, my mother said something I never forgot.

Brenda and I had thrived happily together until this moment. An only child, I'd been given the pleasure of an instant sister, a comrade my own age who shared so much with me—her house, her parents, her dolls, her coloring books. We taught each other songs, stayed up for hours telling one another stories in the twin beds we'd pushed together in her room. There was nothing I wouldn't give her, nothing, I believed, that could ever make me regret a single day of that wonderful year. At that moment, however, my sudden awareness of Brenda's unstoppable beauty and my apparent plainness became relevant and permanent. I felt dumb. Why hadn't I noticed before? Why had we seemed so equal, so like twins?

My mother knelt down to me so that we would be eye to eye. She seemed to be ignorant of both Aunt Kitty, who was standing next to her and perhaps feeling a little sad and embarrassed for me, and Brenda, who remained radiant at the other end of the front walkway. Instead of denying the obvious, instead of telling me that I was as attractive as Brenda, or saying that *to her* I was pretty, or even that I was going to be a late bloomer, she said without the least hesitation, "Your beauty is *inside*, Andrea, where all the important things are."

3

In Latin class Sally Palermo sat at the desk one row in front of me and a seat to my right. Miss Blake, a Quaker woman who every day wore one of what we surmised to be the same two brown or navy shirtwaist dresses, insisted that even though Latin was largely an unspoken language, the only way we were going to learn it was to drill. "*Amo, amas, amat, amamus, amatis, amant,*" we chanted together as a class. "*Hic, haec, hoc, hujus, hujus, hujus, huic, huic, huic,*" we sang. During these drills I liked to glance over at Sally Palermo. She wore no makeup, her shoulder-length, chestnut-colored hair was consistently combed in a loose but always-in-place pageboy (though she never seemed to have it styled), and she dressed differently from the rest of us. It was 1962, and while we had discovered plaid, pleated skirts and solid-colored sweaters, Sally wore virtually see-through white or pastel blouses, under which it was easy to spot full-length slips or camisoles. Her skirts were always straight and dark, as though she were already a professional in the work force. She seemed older than the rest of us, and she was smart and kind but a little aloof, too.

One day Sally wore a paisley scarf around her neck. She looked relaxed, comfortable, sensual (a word I apply only in retrospect, as it was beyond my vocabulary or understanding at the time). And I'd seen other students looking at her, too, girls as well as boys. But the staring never seemed to lead any of us to say anything much to Sally. We would walk down the hall near her between Latin and English; we might even make small talk—"Did you understand what Miss Blake meant about the nominative?" or "Why aren't there cases like that in English?"—but small talk with Sally was always school-centered or, more specifically, knowledge-centered. None of us ever ventured into her personal life. I could not have imagined asking even so harmless a question as "Do you have any brothers or sisters?"

I don't know why Sally Palermo was unapproachable. She may not have set out to maintain such separateness, but that is how it was. She was without a doubt the brightest among us—she'd moved the previous year from Chicago to our suburban town in New Jersey—and we blamed her overall sophistication, her stylishness, and what we determined as her slightly superior attitude to having been born and raised in that city. The fact was, we liked her, but we were in awe, too, and a little bit jealous, which prevented any of us from truly befriending her. As far as we knew, none of the boys ever asked her out, either. But rumor had it that she was seeing a college guy.

The next day there was no scarf, but she was wearing, I noticed, a little makeup for the first time. Her face was more striking than ever. She hadn't overdone anything—just a little light-green shadow on her eyelids, some mascara, foundation and light powder, coral-colored lipstick that seemed to echo the sheen in her hair, and barely noticeable rouge. But on her neck, nearly invisible beneath a layer of liquid foundation, was a series of blue-and-purple, inky marks I'd never noticed before. Perhaps she'd applied the makeup so that our eyes would be drawn to her face and not her neck. But I was not the only one who saw the marks, because a few hours later, as a few of us lingered at our lockers after gym class, one girl asked if we'd noticed the hickeys on Sally Palermo's neck. "Hickeys?" I asked, knowing just which marks she meant but never having heard the word before.

"You know—love bites," she said. "She got them from her college boyfriend."

"I wonder if she's got them anywhere else on her body," someone else said. Then there was some condescending giggling, and the bell rang.

For the rest of that week, I found myself unable to keep from glancing over at Sally during Latin. She sat a little straighter in her chair, it seemed to me, or maybe it was that I was slouching in order to examine her neck. As I watched the blues and purples fade to gray and ocher, I felt somehow betrayed for her. And I wondered, when the hickeys disappeared altogether, whether more would material-ize—or whether Sally had stopped her boyfriend from kissing her like that.

Later I came to understand that the hickeys were a kind of brand. A man—or woman—claimed a lover by bringing the loved one's blood to the surface in a deep, sucking kiss and continued to do so until a mark was sustained. It was a signature of sorts, a sexual seal that lasted up to a week or more.

The other girls, and I sensed, the boys as well, behaved differently toward Sally after that. To them, her hickeys meant that she was cheap; they marked her as a slut, a teen-ager who was surely having sex, an "easy lay," a "bad" girl. Those were the days when huge dis-tances lay between true beauty and the corrupted kind. At the time, we were reading "The Scarlet Letter" in English class and, no matter what Hawthorne or our open-minded teacher wanted us to believe, we reasoned that Hester Prynne had deserved what she got.

But I never truly felt that way. Sally Palermo remained beautiful to me. Those hickeys, too, were beautiful. They seemed to be medals earned through great sacrifice. They signified an inner beauty that could be expressed only by committing one's whole body. They said: "I am not only beautiful, I am capable of passion. I am loved." To me it was wonderful that love—that coveted, impossible, extraordinary quality, as important as it was invisible—could be made tangible.

4

Writing for the New Yorker in the fall of 1995, essayist Lawrence Weschler reflected on the initial showing of 21 works by Vermeer (all the extant paintings of the 35 known to have been created by him) exhibited at the Mauritshuis Museum in Den Hague, in Vermeer's home country, the Netherlands. The exhibit was simultaneous with and only a short walk from the building that housed the hearings of the Yugoslav War Crimes Tribunal. Weschler discovered that Antonio Cassese, head of the international panel of judges, was spending much of his break time at the museum. Cassese said he was there because he *needed* the Vermeers. He explained that the stories he was forced to listen to every day at the trials were horrific. For example:

> A soccer player, a famous guy, a Muslim. When he was captured, they said, "Aren't you So-and-So?" He admitted he was. So they broke both his legs, handcuffed him to a radiator, and forced him to watch as they repeatedly raped his wife and two daughters and then slit their throats. After that, he begged to be killed himself, but his tormentors must have realized that the cruelest thing they could possibly do to him now would simply be to set him free, which they did. Somehow, this man was able to make his way to some U.N. investigators, and told them about his ordeal—a few days after which he committed suicide.

While he himself shifted back and forth between the preliminary hearings of the Tribunal and the Vermeer collection, Weschler remembered a comment made 25 years before by a professor visiting his history class, upon observing that the class had gotten caught up in the fervor of a political crisis. The professor, citing the story in the Gospel of Matthew of Jesus on the waters, pointed out that "in moments of crisis one mustn't allow the storm to enter oneself but should, instead, find peace inside oneself and then breathe it out."

As Weschler sat among the paintings of the Master of Delft that afternoon, he understood that that was exactly what the great artist had been doing. In Vermeer's lifetime there was much—often bloody—upheaval in the Netherlands. The Spanish had only recently left, and both France and England posed continual threats. Yet while this relentless turmoil persisted, the artist created a separate peace within himself and breathed it out onto his canvases. But the paintings answer more than the artist's own need to find peace; 300 years later they lend solace and grace to at least two men confronted by the horrors disclosed at the War Crimes Tribunal.

5

In 1988 I traveled through Europe for six weeks with my husband and son. One night at 2 a.m., my husband woke to find me still writing in my journal. "It's curious," he said, "that you seem always to be up late writing, while Brooke and I are able to summarize the highlights of the day so much more quickly."

"I don't know what it is," I said, "but I can't simply summarize. Perhaps I'm just wordier than the two of you. But I know that if I don't write it now—all of it—I'll lose it. I can't quite experience what I experience until I write about it." That was my 2 a.m. answer, and it may still sound like one. But even now, more than a decade later, I understand what I was getting at.

I can't quite experience what I experience until I write about it. Even our most vivid experience is in danger of transience if we don't learn how to hold onto it. Writing is one approach. Rilke understood this. In "Second Duino Elegy," he says (via Stephen Mitchell's translation):

> But we, when moved by deep feeling, evaporate; we
> breathe ourselves out and away; from moment to moment
> our emotion grows fainter, like a perfume. Though someone
>   may tell us:
> "Yes, you've entered my bloodstream, the room, the whole
>   springtime
> is filled with you . . ."—what does it matter? he can't contain us,
> we vanish inside him and around him.

Rilke's poem—all art, in fact—is an attempt to call us out of ourselves or, rather, to call us into the deepest places in ourselves. In this way, art is an argument against our ordinary lives—or it is at least a curtain drawn long enough against the commonplace to remind us as penetratingly as possible that we are alive.

6

Because the family was poor, my father wore hand-me-down clothes. One pair of shoes, he remembers, had belonged to a girl in the neighborhood. He didn't mind the other clothes, but he hated those shoes. On one of his daily walks home from school during that time, a group of older boys who hung out together in front of the nearby dry cleaner stopped him. "You're a Jew-boy," they sneered, "and Jew-boys have lots of money." He tried to pull away, show them he had none. Then one of the boys spotted his shoes. "You're not a

354

Jew-boy at all," he shouted at close range. "You're a girl, a Jewess." When my father told the story, he always made a hissing sound at the *ess* in *Jewess*. And then the boys tore at his trousers, trying to get his fly down, wanting to see whether he was a girl or a boy.

From the time he was 16 until his mid-20s, my father worked at the fur factory not far from his house in Newark, N.J. His job was to remove the fur from the carcasses of minks, foxes and badgers that were shipped in daily. He became quite skilled at it, he told me, but the smell was sometimes asphyxiating. After high school, he began more and more to consider doing something else. He was not stupid, but he had nearly flunked out of high school because he rarely had time to study or complete his homework. By the time he was 21, he decided that he had to get an education. It was the only way he'd ever be able to get rid of the smell.

His youngest sister was 11 years old when he was accepted on probation to New York University, and because his brothers contributed to the family income, too, such an education became affordable as long as my father kept his full-time, graveyard-shift position at the fur factory during those four years.

At NYU he majored in chemistry—he would eventually become a pediatrician—but each year, along with the required science classes, he took a course in English, often in poetry. "Why poetry?" I asked him one night when I was still in high school.

I'm sure he told me about the balance necessary in one's education. No doubt he also explained that literature was a refreshing change from the kind of reading and study required of a science student and that reading poetry was a special kind of human luxury. But all I remember him saying, finally, is, "Why poetry? Because I remember what it felt like to wear girls' shoes."

7

In 1987 I met Mary Steenburgen. She was complaining at the time about the difficulty of dating. She was divorced from her first husband, actor Malcolm McDowell, and it would be nine years before Ted Danson would become her second. All the men she went out with seemed nice, she told me. "But I'm never sure," she said, "whether it's me they're dating or some version of me they've invented from the screen."

The problem with being beautiful on the inside is obvious: You have to let people in to see it, and that is scary. I was a shy child, which made matters worse. In high school I was not likely to be the first one to raise my hand in class, and in college I had to sit in the front row, directly in front of the professor, so that when I felt brave enough to take part in class discussion, I saw only him or her and not the other students, whom I feared, certain they would ridicule me.

When I was 23, my first serious relationship with a man ended abruptly; then, just as abruptly and unexpectedly, my mother died. Working and living alone in Cambridge, Mass., I began reading poems, poems that seemed to me to have been written directly from someone else's heart for mine. When I read a truly good poem, my whole body became charged. It was not unlike the experience of falling in love: I felt lifted out of myself almost electrically—every cell tingled—and when I settled back into my body again, I was aware that I had somehow splendidly changed. If this is what other people's poems could do, I wanted to write poems that would do it, too.

9

Like my father I was right to keep literature in my life. It is a way of reminding ourselves that we matter, that what you see and what I am are often not the same. It is a way of honoring beauty.

But beauty is, of course, paradoxical. We behave on one hand as though it were an inherent trait—people are either born with it or not. On the other hand, we know that beauty, as the clichés articulate it, is in the eye of the beholder and only skin deep. To complicate the matter further, beauty is unreliable (it fades, for example, or it doesn't tell the beholder the whole story). And beauty can also be misleading—even interior beauty.

Six years ago at the San Francisco Airport, I was in line to board a flight to Little Rock when I observed a small, attractive, tailored young woman bidding a reluctant and tearful goodbye to an overweight, somewhat sloppy-looking man about the same age, which I guessed to be about 30. Not only were they physically and stylistically different, but the pair appeared to be living different kinds of lives;

thus, I deduced that they were deeply caring siblings. However, when the young woman sat next to me on the plane, I learned otherwise. The tearful parting I'd observed was from the man she'd been in love with for four months but whom she'd never before met. Never before met *in person,* she explained. "I met him on the Internet," she said.

At the time, I was a novice to such terminology, but she carefully explained how one could buy something called a modem, attach it to a personal computer, and—she snapped her fingers—communicate with millions of people. The woman, who told me her name was Dorothy, went on to explain that she'd "met" Rick in what she referred to as a "chat room."

"I mentioned having been born in East San Francisco," she said, "and suddenly Rick described his view of the bay from his bedroom in that very part of the city. Well, we began talking right away, got a private on-line chat room, and my life changed." I had to remind myself that Dorothy and Rick's liaison that first night—and every night for the four months preceding her trip to San Francisco—took place *not* in person but via computer screen.

"How did it feel to finally meet Rick face to face?" I asked.

"I was scared, of course. I was afraid he wouldn't like the way I look"—I couldn't imagine any man not liking the way Dorothy looked—"or that maybe we wouldn't have anything to talk about when we were finally together." Then she explained that this hadn't been the case at all, that they had spoken on the telephone several times before she flew to California—"just to get used to the actual sound of one another's voices, as a kind of warm-up"—and that actually meeting one another had not deterred either of them.

"It was the best four days of my life," she said and got teary-eyed. Then we read our airline magazines for a while, ate our peanuts, drank our ginger ales. Just before our plane landed in Little Rock, Dorothy said, "You know, I never would have met him in *real* life. I mean, I would never even have *looked* at a guy that looked like Rick—you know, kind of nerdy and, well, kinda chunky. He doesn't look like a guy I'd have even noticed. You know?"

I nodded.

"That's the beauty of it," she said.

I asked her what she meant.

"I mean that I *know* I love him. I know it. Because I fell in love

357

with who he really is, not what he looks like." I told her I understood, and when we left one another at the baggage claim area, I wished her luck and happiness.

I still wonder what happened when Dorothy and Rick began living together, as she assured me was their plan. Did they continue to care as deeply for one another as they had for four months on the Internet? Would they tire of one another's physical presence—not in the sexual sense of the term, but in the literal sense—as opposed to the merely *virtual* presence each had created for the lure and capture of the other? For that is how it is, isn't it?

Writers understand this. We write, in part, because we want the reader to fall in love with us. If he does not, of course, that is the end of everything. The book stays closed, is not recommended, has no hope of ever again being examined. For this reason we use language with great care. Every word is a long-stemmed red rose, every sentence an implement of courtship, every book we write our essential selves—body and spirit packaged inseparably with both integrity and beauty. Always we must put the best words in the best order (to quote Coleridge). We want not only to charm the reader; we need to seduce him. We crave more than anything to be desired by him. And hope that he will maintain this desire until at least our next poem, our next story or our next novel. Our next work must be as engrossing as our last. It is love we are after, a lasting relationship—not lust, not an easy lay, a one-night stand. We understand very well that we must reveal from the inside out whatever beauty we are capable of creating. No writer can afford to be just a pretty face. And neither—I admit with a kind of sad, reluctant recognition—can Rick or Dorothy or the potentially millions of other Internet users who may not be who they pretend to be on their chatty message boards.

10

In 1994 I attended my 30-year high school reunion. When I caught sight of Sally Palermo, whom I'd not seen since graduation, my heart jumped. She scarcely looked different. Her hair had hardly grayed, she had remained slim, and she looked elegant in an understated, black crepe dress and single string of pearls. Most of the other women wore bright colors and enough makeup to cover smile lines and crow's-feet. Things don't change much, I thought.

After the "gala" dinner, the hired photographer called "alumni only" together for a group shot. "What? Only the men?" I complained, mostly to myself.

From behind me a voice answered. "*Alumnae* is pronounced the same way as *alumni*," Sally said. "But don't worry, he means us as well. The masculine term includes both men and women. Remember?" We hadn't left Miss Blake's Latin class.

"You're right," I said. "How could I have forgotten?"

In a few sentences, we traded 30-year synopses. Sally told me that she was not married, that she lived in California, and that she worked as a researcher in an alternative health laboratory.

"When we were in high school, I really admired you," I confessed.

"Me?" she said. "Why, for heaven's sake?"

"Because you were the brightest and the most beautiful," I said.

"Not me," she said.

Nominated by Stephen Corey, David Jauss, Creative Nonfiction

TWO VARIATIONS ON A THEME BY STEVENS

by SARAH MANGUSO

from THE IOWA REVIEW

First there is the thing and then there is
the account of the thing, bent into new
alphabets. Living your life twice is no feat.
Or there is what happens to you, as if
to you only, the yes of no comparison,
until finally, or secretly, the yes
repeats. So a vine with grapes enough
to persuade it to the ground may be a line
with one grape repeated. All love's sighs
are this, simply: an inhalation, an
exhalation, something in between that
is imagined. The final word is the first word
reiterated with gray hair.

Much like mine, your delight.
No discrete evidence of the new
is invented. For the other suns are
our sun surrounded similarly and not seen
together. Some uncertain planet is
what one wants it to be, until found,
when it is the earth. The documents

of genius are nightmares with the sentences
rearranged. Your aspirations
to magnificence are already done
and recorded as the memoirs of sad kings.

Nominated by The Iowa Review

PILGRIMS

fiction by JULIE ORRINGER

from PLOUGHSHARES

It was Thanksgiving Day and hot, because this was New Orleans; they were driving uptown to have dinner with strangers. Ella pushed at her loose tooth with the tip of her tongue and fanned her legs with the hem of her velvet dress. On the seat beside her, Benjamin fidgeted with his shirt buttons. He had worn his pilgrim costume, brown shorts and a white shirt and yellow paper buckles taped to his shoes. In the front seat their father drove without a word, while their mother dozed against the window glass. She wore a blue dress and a strand of jade beads and a knit cotton hat beneath which she was bald.

Three months earlier Ella's father had explained what chemotherapy was, and how it would make her mother better. He had even taken Ella to the hospital once when her mother had a treatment. She remembered it like a filmstrip from school, a series of connected images she wished she didn't have to watch: her mother with an IV needle in her arm, the steady drip from the bag of orange liquid, her father speaking softly to himself as he paced the room, her mother shaking so hard she had to be tied down.

At night Ella and her brother tapped a secret code against the wall that separated their rooms: one knock, I'm afraid; two knocks, don't worry; three knocks, are you still awake?; four, come quick. And then there was the Emergency Signal, a stream of knocks that kept on coming, which meant her brother could hear their mother and father crying in their bedroom. If it went on for more than a minute, Ella would give four knocks, and her brother would run to her room and crawl under the covers.

There were changes in the house, healing rituals which required Ella's mother to go outside and embrace trees or lie facedown on the grass. Sometimes she did a kind of Asian dance that looked like karate. She ate bean paste and Japanese vegetables, or sticky brown rice wrapped in seaweed. And now they were going to have dinner with people they had never met, people who ate seaweed and brown rice every day of their lives.

They drove through the Garden District, where Spanish moss hung like beards from the trees. Once during Mardi Gras, Ella had ridden a trolley here with her brother and grandmother, down to the French Quarter, where they'd eaten beignets at Café du Monde. She wished she were sitting in one of those wrought-iron chairs and shaking powdered sugar onto a beignet. How much better than to be surrounded by strangers, eating food that tasted like the bottom of the sea.

They turned onto a side street, and her father studied the directions. "It should be at the end of this block," he said.

Ella's mother shifted in her seat. "Where are we?" she asked, her voice dreamy with painkillers.

"Almost there," said Ella's father.

They pulled to the curb in front of a white house with sagging porches and a trampled lawn. Vines covered the walls and moss grew thick and green between the roof slates. Under the portecochère stood a beat-up Honda and a Volkswagen with mismatched side panels. A faded Big Wheel lay on its side on the walk.

"Come on," their father said, and gave them a tired smile. "Time for fun." He got out of the car and opened the doors for Ella and her mother, sweeping his arm chauffeur-like as they climbed out.

Beside the front door was a tarnished doorbell in the shape of a lion's head. "Push it," her father said. Ella pushed. A sound like church bells echoed inside the house.

Then the door swung open, and there was Mr. Kaplan, a tall man with wiry orange hair and big dry-looking teeth. He shook hands with Ella's parents, so long and vigorously it seemed to Ella he might as well say *congratulations*.

"And you must be Ben and Ella," he said, bending down.

Ella gave a mute nod. Her brother kicked at the doorjamb.

"Well, come on in," he said. "I have a tree castle out back."

Benjamin's face came up, twisted with skepticism. "A what?"

"The kids are back there. They'll show you," he said.

"What an interesting foyer," their mother said. She bent down to look at the brass animals on the floor, a turtle and a jackal and a llama. Next to the animals stood a blue vase full of rusty metal flowers. A crystal chandelier dangled from the ceiling, its arms hung with dozens of God's-eyes and tiny plastic babies from Mardi Gras king cakes. On a low wooden shelf against the wall, pair after pair of canvas sandals and sneakers and Birkenstocks were piled in a heap. A crayoned sign above it said SHOES OFF NOW!

Ella looked down at her feet. She was wearing her new patent-leather Mary Janes.

"Your socks are nice, too," her father said, and touched her shoulder. He stepped out of his own brown loafers and set them on top of the pile. Then he knelt before Ella's mother and removed her pumps. "Shoes off," he said to Ella and Ben.

"Even me?" Ben said. He looked down at his paper buckles.

Their father took off Ben's shoes and removed the paper buckles, tape intact. Then he pressed one buckle onto each of Ben's socks. "There," he said.

Ben looked as if he might cry.

"Everyone's in the kitchen," Mr. Kaplan said. "We're all cooking."

"Marvelous," said Ella's mother. "We love to cook."

They followed him down a cavern of a hall, its walls decorated with sepia-toned photographs of children and parents, all of them staring stone-faced from their gilt frames. They passed a sweep of stairs, and a room with nothing in it but straw mats and pictures of blue Indian goddesses sitting on beds of cloud.

"What's that room?" Benjamin said.

"Meditation room," Mr. Kaplan said, as if it were as commonplace as a den.

The kitchen smelled of roasting squash and baked apples and spices. There was an old brick oven and a stove with so many burners it looked as if it had been stolen from a restaurant. At the kitchen table, men and women with long hair and loose clothes sliced vegetables or stirred things into bowls. Some of them wore knitted hats like her mother, their skin dull-gray, their eyes purple-shaded underneath. To Ella it seemed they could be relatives of her mother's, shameful cousins recently discovered.

A tall woman with a green scarf around her waist came over and embraced Ella's mother, then bent down to hug Ella and Benjamin. She smelled of smoky perfume. Her wide eyes skewed in different directions, as if she were watching two movies projected into opposite corners of the room. Ella did not know how to look at her.

"We're so happy you decided to come," the woman said. "I'm Delilah, Eddy's sister."

"Who's Eddy?" said Ben.

"Mr. Kaplan," their father said.

"We use our real names here," Delilah said. "No one is a mister."

She led their parents over to the long table and put utensils into their hands. Their mother was to mix oats into a pastry crust, and their father to chop carrots, something Ella had never seen him do. He looked around in panic, then hunched over and began cutting a carrot into clumsy pieces. He kept glancing at the man to his left, a bearded man with a shaved head, as if to make sure he was doing it right.

Delilah gave Ella and Benjamin hard cookies that tasted like burnt rice. It seemed Ella would have to chew forever. Her loose tooth waggled in its socket.

"The kids are all out back," Delilah said. "There's plenty of time to play before dinner."

"What kids?" Benjamin asked.

"You'll see," said Delilah. She tilted her head at Ella, one of her eyes moving over Ella's velvet dress. "Here's a little trick I learned when I was a girl," she said. In one swift movement she took the back hem of the dress, brought it up between Ella's knees, and tucked it into the sash. "Now you're wearing shorts," she said.

Ella didn't feel like she was wearing shorts. As soon as Delilah turned away, she pulled her skirt out of her sash and let it fall around her legs.

The wooden deck outside was cluttered with Tinkertoys and clay flowerpots and Little Golden Books. Ella heard children screaming and laughing nearby. As she and Benjamin moved to the edge of the deck, there was a rustle in the bushes, and a skinny boy leaped out and pointed a suction-cup arrow at them. He stood there breathing hard, his hair full of leaves, his chest bare. "You're on duty," he said.

"Me?" Benjamin said.

"Yes, you," the boy said. "Both of you." He motioned them off the porch with his arrow and took them around the side of the house. There, built into the side of a sprawling oak, was the biggest, most sophisticated treehouse Ella had ever seen. There were tiny rooms of sagging plywood, and rope ladders hanging down from doors, and a telescope and a fireman's pole and a red net full of leaves. From one wide platform—almost as high as the top of the house—it seemed you could jump down onto a huge trampoline. Even higher was a kind of crow's-nest, a little circular platform built around the trunk. A red-painted sign on the railing read "DAGNER!" Ella could hear the other children screaming, but she couldn't see them. A collie dog barked crazily, staring up at the tree.

"Take off your socks! That's an order," the skinny boy said.

Benjamin glanced at Ella as if to ask if this were okay. Ella shrugged. It seemed ridiculous to walk around outside in socks. She bent and peeled off her anklets. Benjamin carefully removed his pilgrim buckles and put them in his pocket, then sat down and took off his socks. The skinny boy grabbed the socks from their hands and tucked them into the waistband of his shorts.

The mud was thick and cold between Ella's toes, and pecan shells bit her feet as the boy herded them toward the treehouse. He prodded Ella toward a ladder of prickly-looking rope. When she stepped onto the first rung, the ladder swung toward the tree and her toes banged against the trunk. The skinny boy laughed.

"Go on," he said. "Hurry up. And no whining."

The rope burned her hands and feet as she ascended. The ladder seemed to go on forever. Ben followed below, making the rope buck and sway as they climbed. At the top there was a small square opening, and Ella thrust both her arms inside and pulled herself into a dark coop. As she stood, her head knocked against something dangling from the ceiling on a length of string. It was a bird's skull, no bigger than a walnut. Dozens of others hung from the ceiling around her. Benjamin huddled at her side.

"Sick," he said.

"Don't look," Ella said.

The suction-cup arrow came up through the hole in the floor.

"Keep going," said the boy. "You're not there yet."

"Go where?" Ella said.

"Through the wall."

Ella brushed the skulls out of her way and leveled her shoulder against one of the walls. It creaked open like a door. Outside, a tree limb as thick as her torso extended up to another plywood box, this one much larger than the first. Ella dropped to her knees and crawled upward. Benjamin followed.

Apparently this was the hostage room. Four kids stood in the semi-darkness, wide-eyed and still as sculptures, each bound at the ankles and wrists with vine handcuffs. Two of the kids, a boy and a girl, were so skinny that Ella could see the outlines of bones in their arms and legs. Their hair was patchy and ragged, their eyes black and almond-shaped. In the corner, a white-haired boy in purple overalls whimpered softly to himself. And at the center of the room a girl Benjamin's age stood tied to the tree trunk with brown string. She had the same wild gray eyes and leafy hair as the boy with the arrows.

"It's mine, it's *my* treehouse," she said as Ella stared at her.

"Is Mr. Kaplan your dad?" Benjamin said.

"My dat-*tee*," the girl corrected him.

"Where's your mom?"

"She died," said the girl, and looked him fiercely in the eye.

Benjamin sucked in his breath and glanced at Ella.

Ella wanted to hit this girl. She bent down close to the girl's face, making her eyes small and mean. "If this is so your treehouse," Ella said, "then how come you're tied up?"

"It's *jail*," the girl spat. "In jail you get tied up."

"We could untie you," said Benjamin. He tugged at one of her bonds.

The girl opened her mouth and let out a scream so shrill Ella's eardrums buzzed. Once, as her father had pulled into the driveway at night, he had trapped a rabbit by the leg beneath the wheel of his car; the rabbit had made a sound like that. Benjamin dropped the string and moved against Ella, and the children with ragged hair laughed and jumped on the platform until it crackled and groaned. The boy in purple overalls cried in his corner.

Benjamin put his lips to Ella's ear. "I don't understand it here," he whispered.

There was a scuffle at the door, and the skinny boy stepped into the hostage room. "All right," he said. "Who gets killed?"

"Kill those kids, Peter," the girl said, pointing to Benjamin and Ella.

"Us?" Benjamin said.

"Who do you think?" said the boy.

He poked them in the back with his suction-cup arrow and moved them toward the tree trunk, where rough boards formed a ladder to the next level. Ella and Benjamin climbed until they had reached a narrow platform, and then Peter pushed them to the edge. Ella looked down at the trampoline. It was a longer drop than the high

367

dive at the public pool. She looked over her shoulder, and Peter glared at her. Down below the collie barked and barked, his black nose pointed up at them.

Benjamin took Ella's hand and closed his eyes. Then Peter shoved them from behind, and they stumbled forward into space.

There was a moment of terrifying emptiness, nothing but air beneath Ella's feet. She could hear the collie's bark getting closer as she fell. She slammed into the trampoline knees first, then flew, shrieking, back up into the air. When she hit the trampoline a second time, Benjamin's head knocked against her chin. He stood up rubbing his head, and Ella tasted salt in her mouth. Her loose tooth had slipped its roots. She spit it into her palm and studied its jagged edge.

"Move," Peter called from above. The boy in purple overalls was just climbing up onto the platform. Peter pulled him forward until his toes curled over the edge.

"I lost my tooth!" Ella yelled.

"Get off!"

Benjamin scrambled off the trampoline. Ella crawled to the edge, the tooth gleaming and red-rimmed between her fingers, and then the trampoline lurched with the weight of the boy in purple overalls. The tooth flew from her hand and into the bushes, too small to make a sound when it hit.

When she burst into the house crying, blood streaming from her mouth, the long-haired men and women dropped their mixing spoons and went to her. She twisted away from them, looking frantically for her mother and father, but they were nowhere to be seen. Her throat ached with crying. There was no way to explain that she wasn't hurt, that she was upset because her tooth was gone, and because everything about that house made her want to run away and hide. The adults, their faces creased with worry, pulled her to the sink and held her mouth open. The woman with skewed eyes, Delilah, pressed a tissue against the space where her tooth had been. Ella could smell onion and apples on her hands.

"The time was right," she said. "The new tooth's already coming in."

"Whose is she?" one of the men asked.

Delilah told him the names of Ella's parents. It was strange to hear those familiar words, *Ann* and *Gary*, in the mouths of these long-haired strangers.

"Your mother is upstairs," Delilah said, her eyes swiveling toward some distant hidden room. "She felt a little swimmy-headed. Your dad just brought her some special tea. Maybe we should let her rest, hm?"

Ella slipped out from beneath Delilah's hand and ran to the hall, remembering the stairway she'd seen earlier. There it was before her, a curve of glossy steps leading to nowhere she knew. Her mother's cough drifted down from one of the bedroom doors. Ella put a foot onto the first stair, feeling the eyes of the adults on her back. No one said anything to stop her. After a moment, she began to climb.

In the upstairs hallway, toys and kids' shoes lay strewn across the floor, and crumpled pants and shirts and dresses lay in a musty-smelling heap. Two naked Barbies sprawled in a frying pan. A record player sat in the middle of the hall, its vacant turntable spinning. Ella stepped over the cord and went into the first room, a small room with a sleeping bag on the bare mattress ticking. In a cage on the nightstand, a white rat scrabbled at a cardboard tube. A finger-painted sign above the bed said CLARIES ROOM. Her mother's cough rose again from down the hall, and she turned and ran toward the sound.

In a room whose blue walls and curtains made everything look as if it were underwater, her mother lay pale and coughing on a bed piled high with pillows. Her father sat on the edge of the bed, his hands raised in the air, thumbs hooked together and palms spread wide. For a moment Ella had no idea what he was doing. Then she saw the shadow of her father's hands against the wall, in the light of a blue-shaded lamp. A shock of relief went through her.

"Tweet, tweet," Ella said.

"Right," her father said. "A birdie."

Ella's mother turned toward her and smiled, more awake, more like her real self than earlier. "Do another one, Gary," she said.

Ella's father twisted his hands into a new shape in the air.

"A dog?" Ella said.

"A fish!" said her mother.

"No," he said, and adjusted his hands. "It's a horsie, see?"

"A horsie?" said Ella's mother. "With fins?"

That made Ella laugh a little.

"Hey," her mother said. "Come here, you. Smile again."

Ella did as she was told.

"What's that? You lost your tooth!"

369

"It's gone," Ella said. She climbed onto the bed to explain, but as she flopped down on the mattress her mother's face contracted with pain.

"Please don't bounce," her mother said. She touched the place where her surgery had been.

Ella's father gave her a stern look and lifted her off the bed. "Your mom's sleepy," he said. "You should run back downstairs now."

"She's always sleepy," Ella said, looking down at her muddy feet. She thought of her tooth lying out in the weeds, and how she'd have nothing to put under her pillow for the tooth fairy.

Her mother began to cry.

Ella's father went to the window and stared down into the yard, his breath fogging the glass. "Go ahead, Ella," he said. "We just need a few minutes."

"My tooth," Ella said. She knew she should leave, but couldn't.

"It'll grow back bigger and stronger," her father said.

She could see he didn't understand what had happened. If only her mother would stop crying, she could explain everything. In the blue light her mother looked cold and far away, pressed under the weight of tons of water.

"I'll be down soon," her mother said, sniffling. "Go out and play."

Ella opened her mouth to form some protest, but no words came out.

"Go on, now," her father said.

"It fell in a bush!" she wailed, then turned and ran downstairs.

The other children had come in by then. Her brother stood in line at the downstairs bathroom to wash before dinner, comparing fingernail dirt with the boy in purple overalls. Hands deep in the pockets of her velvet dress, Ella wandered through the echoing hall into a room lined from floor to ceiling with books. Many of the titles were in other languages, some even written in different alphabets. She recognized *D'Aulaire's Book of Greek Myths* and *The Riverside Shakespeare* and *Grimm's Fairy Tales*. Scattered around on small tables and decorative stands were tiny human figurines with animal heads—horse-man, giraffe-man, panther-man. On one table sat an Egyptian beetle made of milky-green stone, and beside him a real beetle, shiny as metal, who flew at Ella's face when she reached to touch his shell. She batted him away with the back of her hand.

And then, just above where the beetle had fallen, Ella saw a shelf without any books at all. It was low, the height of her knees, with a frayed blue scarf pinned against its back wall. Burnt-down candles stood on either side of a black lacquer box, and on top of this box stood a glass filled with red water.

Ella reached for the glass, and someone behind her screamed.

She turned around. Clarie stood in the doorway, dress unbuttoned at one shoulder, face smeared with mud.

"Don't touch that," she said.

Ella took a step back. "I wasn't going to."

Clarie's eyes seemed to ignite as she bent down and took the glass in both hands. She held it near a lamp, so the light shone through it and cast a red oval upon the wall.

"It's my mother," she said.

For dinner there was a roasted dome of something that looked like meat but wasn't. It was springy and steaming, and when Mr. Kaplan cut it open, Ella could see that it was stuffed with rice and yams. Benjamin tried to hide under the table, but their father pulled him up by the arms and set him in his place. He prodded his wedge of roast until it slid onto the tablecloth. Then he began to cry quietly.

"The kids aren't vegetarian," their father said, in apology to the men and women at the table. He picked up the slice of roast with his fingers and put it back on Ben's plate. The other men and women held their forks motionless above their own plates, looking at Ella's mother and father with pity.

"Look, Ben," said Delilah. "It's called seitan. Wheat gluten. The other kids love it."

The boy and girl with almond-shaped eyes and ragged hair stopped in mid-chew. The girl looked at Benjamin and narrowed her eyes.

"I don't eat gluten," Benjamin said.

"Come on, now," their father said. "It's great."

Ella's mother pressed her fingers against her temples. She hadn't touched her own dinner. Ella, sitting beside her, took a bite of wheat gluten. It was almost like meat, firm and savory, and the stuffing was flavored with forest-smelling spices. As she glanced around the table, she thought of the picture of the First Thanksgiving on the bulletin board at school: the smiling Pilgrims eating turkey and squash, the stern-faced Native Americans looking as if they knew the worst was yet to come. Who among them that night were the Native Americans? Who were the Pilgrims? The dark old house was like a wilderness around them, the wind sighing through its rooms.

"I jumped on the trampoline," said the boy with ragged hair, pulling on the sleeve of the woman next to him. "That boy did a flip." He pointed at Peter, who was smashing rice against his plate with his thumb. "He tied his sister to the tree."

Mr. Kaplan set down his fork. He looked sideways at Peter, his mouth pressed into a stern line. "I told you never to do that again," he said. He sounded angry, but his voice was quiet, almost a whisper.

"She made me!" Peter said, and plunged a spoon into his baked squash.

Mr. Kaplan's eyes went glossy and faraway. He stared off at the blank wall above Ella's mother's head, drifting away from the noise and chatter of the dinner table. Next to him Delilah shuttled her mismatched eyes back and forth. Ella's mother straightened in her chair.

"Ed," she called softly.

Mr. Kaplan blinked hard and looked at her.

"Tell us about your tai chi class."

"What," he said.

"Your tai chi class."

"You know, I don't really want to talk right now," he said. He pushed back his chair and went into the kitchen. There was the sound of water, and then the clink of dishes in the sink. Delilah shook her head. The other adults looked down at their plates. Ella's mother wiped the corners of her mouth with her napkin and crossed her arms over her chest.

"Does anyone want more rice?" Ella's father asked.

"I think we're all thinking about Lena," said the man with the shaved head.

"I know I am," said Delilah.

"Infinity to infinity," said the man. "Dust into star."

The men and women looked at each other, their eyes carrying some message Ella couldn't understand. They clasped each other's hands and bent their heads. "Infinity to infinity," they repeated. "Dust into star."

"Matter into energy," said the man. "Identity into oneness."

"Matter into energy," everyone said. Ella glanced at her father, whose jaw was set hard, unmoving. Her mother's lips formed the

372

words, but no sound came out. Ella thought of the usual Thanksgivings at her uncle Ben's, where everyone talked and laughed at the table and they ate turkey and dressing and sweet potatoes with marshmallows melted on top. She closed her eyes and held her breath, filling her chest with a tightness that felt like magic power. If she tried hard enough could she transport them all, her mother and father, Benjamin and herself, to that other time? She held her breath until it seemed she would explode, then let it out in a rush. She opened her eyes. Nothing had changed. Peter kicked the table leg, and the collie, crouched beside Clarie's chair, whimpered his unease. Ella could see Clarie's hand on his collar, her knuckles bloodless as stones.

Mr. Kaplan returned with a platter of baked apples. He cleared his throat, and everyone turned to look at him. "Guess what we forgot," he said. "I spent nearly an hour peeling these things." He held the platter aloft, waiting.

"Who wants some nice baked apples?" he said. "Baked apples. I peeled them."

No one said a word.

After dinner the adults drifted into the room with the straw mats and Indian goddesses. Ella understood that the children were not invited, but she lingered in the doorway to see what would happen. Mr. Kaplan bent over a tiny brass dish and held a match to a black cone. A wisp of smoke curled toward the ceiling, and after a moment Ella smelled a dusty, flowery scent. Her mother and father and the rest of the adults sat cross-legged on the floor, not touching each other. A low hum began to fill the room like something with weight and substance. Ella saw her father raise an eyebrow at her mother, as if to ask if these people were serious. But her mother's shoulders were bent in meditation, her mouth open with the drone of the mantra, and Ella's father sighed and let his head fall forward.

Someone pinched Ella's shoulder, and she turned around. Peter stood behind her, his eyes narrow. "Come on," he said. "You're supposed to help clean up."

In the kitchen the children stacked dirty dishes on the counter and ran water in the sink. The boy and girl with almond eyes climbed up onto a wide wooden stepstool and began to scrub dishes. Peter scraped all the scraps into an aluminum pan and gave it to Clarie, who set it on the floor near the dog's water dish. The collie fell at the leftover food with sounds that made Ella sick to her stomach. Clarie stood next to him and stroked his tail.

Then Benjamin came into the kitchen carrying the glass of red water. "Somebody forgot this under the table," he said.

Again there was the dying-rabbit screech. Clarie batted her palms against the sides of her head. "No!" she shrieked. "Put it down!"

Benjamin's eyes went wide, and he set the glass on the kitchen counter. "I don't want it," he said.

The boy in purple overalls squinted at the glass. "Looks like Kool-Aid," he said.

"She gets all crazy," said Peter. "Watch." Peter lifted the glass high into the air, and Clarie ran toward him. "You can't have it," he said.

Clarie jumped up and down in fury, her hands flapping like limp rags. Her mouth opened, but no sound came out. Then she curled her fingers into claws and scratched at Peter's arms and chest until he twisted away. He ran across the kitchen and onto the deck, holding the glass in the air, and Clarie followed him, screaming.

The ragged-haired brother and sister looked at each other, arms gloved in white bubbles. In one quick movement they were off the stool, shaking suds around the kitchen. "Come on!" said the boy. "Let's go watch!"

Benjamin grabbed Ella's hand and pulled her toward the screen door. The children pushed out onto the deck and then ran toward the tree castle, where Clarie and her brother were climbing the first rope ladder. It was dark now, and floodlights on the roof of the house illuminated the entire castle, its rooms silver-gray and ghostly, its ropes and nets swaying in a rising breeze. The children gathered on the grass near the trampoline.

Peter held the glass as he climbed, the red water sloshing against its sides. "Come and get it," he crooned. He reached the first room, and they heard the wall-door scrape against the trunk as he pushed it open. Then he moved out onto the oak limb, agile as the siamang monkeys Ella had seen at the zoo. He might as well have had a tail.

Clarie crawled behind him, her hands scrabbling at the bark. Peter howled at the sky as he reached the hostage room.

Benjamin moved toward Ella and pressed his head against her arm. "I want to go home," he said.

"Shh," Ella said. "We can't."

High above, Peter climbed onto the platform from which they had

374

jumped earlier. Still holding the glass, he pulled himself up the tree trunk to the crow's-nest. High up on that small, railed platform, where the tree branches became thin and sparse, he stopped. Below him Clarie scrambled onto the jumping platform. She looked out across the yard as if unsure of where he had gone. "Up here," Peter said, holding the glass high.

Ella could hear Clarie grunting as she pulled herself up into the crow's-nest. She stood and reached for the glass, her face a small moon in the dark. A few acorns scuttled off the crow's-nest platform.

"Give it!" she cried again.

Peter stood looking at her for a moment in the dark. "You really want it?"

"Peter!"

He swept the glass through the air. The water flew out in an arc, ruby-colored against the glare of the floodlights. Clarie leaned out as if to catch it between her fingers, and with a splintering crack she broke through the railing. Her dress fluttered silently as she fell, and her white hands grasped at the air. There was a quiet instant, the soft sound of water falling on grass. Then, with a shock Ella felt in the soles of her feet, Clarie hit the ground. The girl with the ragged hair screamed.

Clarie lay beside the trampoline, still as sleep, her neck bent at an impossible angle. Ella wanted to look away, but couldn't. The other children, even Benjamin, moved to where Clarie lay and circled around, some calling her name, some just looking. Peter slid down the fireman's pole and stumbled across the lawn toward his sister. He pushed Benjamin aside. With one toe he nudged Clarie's shoulder, then knelt and rolled her over. A bare bone glistened from her wrist. The boy in purple overalls threw up onto the grass.

Ella turned and ran toward the house. She banged the screen door open and skidded across the kitchen floor into the hall. At the door-way of the meditation room she stopped, breathing hard. The adults sat just as she had left them, eyes closed, mouths open slightly, their sound beating like a living thing, their thumbs and forefingers circled into perfect O's. She could smell the heat of them rising in the room and mingling with the scent of the incense. Her father's chin rested on his chest as if he had fallen asleep. Beside him her mother looked drained of blood, her skin so white she seemed almost holy.

"Mom," Ella whispered. "Mom."

Ella's mother turned slightly and opened her eyes. For a moment she seemed between two worlds, her eyes unfocused and distant. Then she blinked and looked at Ella. She shook her head no.

"Please," Ella said, but her mother closed her eyes again. Ella stood there for a long time watching her, but she didn't move or speak. Finally Ella turned and went back outside.

By the time she reached the tree castle, Peter had dragged Clarie halfway across the lawn. He turned his eyes on Ella, and she stared back at him. The sound of the mantra continued unbroken from the house. Peter hoisted Clarie again under the arms and dragged her to the bushes, her bare feet bumping over the grass. Then he rolled her over until she was hidden in shadow. He pulled her dress down so it covered her thighs, and turned her head toward the fence that bordered the backyard.

"Get some leaves and stuff," he said. "We have to cover her."

Ella would not move. She took Benjamin's hand, but he pulled away from her and wandered across the lawn, pulling up handfuls of grass. She watched the children pick up twigs, Spanish moss, leaves, anything they could find. The boy in purple overalls gathered cedar bark from a flower bed, and Peter dragged fallen branches out of the underbrush near the fence. They scattered everything they found over Clarie's body. In five minutes they had covered her entirely.

"Go back inside," Peter said. "If anyone cries or says anything, I'll kill them."

Ella turned to go, and that was when she saw her tooth, a tiny white pebble in the weeds. She picked it up and rubbed it clean. Then she knelt beside Clarie, clearing away moss and leaves until she found Clarie's hand. She dropped the tooth into the palm and closed the fingers around it. A shiver spread through her chest, and she covered the hand again. Then she put her arm around Benjamin, and they all went back inside. Drawn by the sound of the chanting, they wandered into the hall. All around them hung the yellow photographs, the stony men and women and children looking down at them with sad and knowing eyes. In an oval of black velvet, one girl in a white dress held the string of a wooden duck, her lips open as if she were about to speak. Her eyes had the wildness of Clarie's eyes, her legs the same bowed curve.

At last there was a rustle from the meditation room, and the adults drifted out into the hall. They blinked at the light and rubbed their elbows and knees. Ella's mother and father linked arms and moved toward their children. Benjamin gave a hiccup. His eyes looked

376

strange, the pupils huge, the whites flat and dry. Their mother noticed right away. "We'd better get going," she said to Ella's father. "Ben's tired."

She went into the foyer and pulled their shoes from the pile. Mr. Kaplan followed, looking around in bewilderment, as if he could not believe people were leaving. He patted Benjamin on the head and asked Ella's mother if she wanted to take some leftover food. Ella's mother shook her head no. Her father thanked Mr. Kaplan for his hospitality. Somewhere toward the back of the house, the dog began to bark, a crazy, high-pitched bark, as if the world were ending. Ella pulled Benjamin through the front door, barefoot, and her parents followed them to the car.

All the way past the rows of live oaks, past the cemetery where the little tombs stood like grounded boats, past the low flat shotgun houses with their flaking roofs, Benjamin sat rigid on the back seat and cried without a sound. Ella felt the sobs leaving his chest in waves of hot air. She closed her eyes and followed the car in her mind down the streets that led to their house, until it seemed they had driven past their house long ago and were moving on to a place where strange beds awaited them, where they would fall asleep thinking of dark forests and wake to the lives of strangers.

Nominated by Joy Williams, Ploughshares

RED BERRIES

by JANE HIRSHFIELD

from THE YALE REVIEW

Again the pyrocanthus berries redden in rain,
as if return were return.

It is not.

The familiar is not the thing it reminds of.
Today's *yes* is different from yesterday's *yes*.
Even *no*'s adamance alters.

From painting to painting,
century to century,
the tipped-over copper pot spills out different light;
the cut-open beeves,
their caged and muscled display,
are on one canvas radiant, pure; obscene on another.

In the end it is simple enough—

The woman of this morning's mirror
was a stranger
to the woman of last night's;
the passionate dreams of the one who slept
flit empty and thin
from the one who awakens.

One woman washes her face.
another picks up the boar-bristle hairbrush,
a third steps out of her slippers.
That each will die in the same bed means nothing to them.

Our one breath follows another like spotted horses, no two alike

Black manes and white manes, they gallop.
Piebald and skewbald, eyes flashing sorrow, they too will pass.

Nominated by Cyrus Cassells, Wesley McNair, The Yale Review

WHERE THE DOG IS BURIED

memoir by GARY GILDNER

from THE SOUTHERN REVIEW

In Prague, when Lizzie and I asked an official about taking the train to Prešov, she said, "I do not advise it. It is a filthy method. The only way to Slovakia, if one must go there, is by plane." She made a face like she'd just lost a filling.

I exchanged dollars for crowns. On the hundred-crown note a man and woman stood side by side, he wearing welder's gear, his shirt open, she in overalls, a babushka, a sheaf of wheat under her arm. In the background, industrial chimneys poured smoke into the sky. The pair gazed straight ahead, workers sharing the load. They might have been drawn by Norman Rockwell, except there was no humor, no irony, no surprise in their faces or anywhere else . . . unless you counted a kind of halo that hovered over their heads, constructed from a gear wheel, wheat berries, and coils of steel. Once upon a time they were the new saints, but who knew what they were now; this bank note was pre-Revolution (pre-1989) and would soon be replaced.

Prešov lay ten hours to the east, almost in Ukraine. Our compartment was clean and comfortable, and we saw much more than we could have from a plane: kids beating dust from rugs, geese in single file following an old woman across a field, tidy apple orchards whose cidery scent wafted our way. In small towns we passed through, the stationmasters stood at attention in their doorways, hats on, shoulders back, and saluted. We went between autumn hills, through tun-

380

nels into piney corridors, past streams, beside a lake that reflected our waving arms. I was fifty-four, Lizzie thirty-eight—the only time, she pointed out, when my age would match the year of her birth and vice versa. I thought about chance and how I was now a grandfather traveling to Slovakia and planning to walk in the Polish village that my grandfather, then a teenager, had walked away from, carrying his loaf of bread. I thought about how intently he gazed into the northern Michigan sky those summers he sat in his apple orchard while I, a boy in a tree, watched him and wondered, as I wondered on the train, what he was looking for.

Outside Prešov we were delivered to a huge housing estate called Sečov, named—we learned later—for a brook that the development had destroyed. We also learned that our street, Dumbierska, meant something like "ginger," that the road connecting us to Prešov was Sibirska—meaning "Siberia"—and that the 38 bus would carry us back and forth for two crowns. But the first time we went to Sečov was in Igor's Skoda, at night, and laughing, he said he was trying not to get lost.

After the lush, dreamy countryside we'd seen all day, Sečov was sobering. Prefab high-rises surrounded us. I tried to count them once, weeks later, and lost interest. They all looked alike, cement-colored, nine stories—dormitories plunked down in a raw, treeless setting. Ours was new, Igor told us: "You will be the first occupants of your flat!"

An elevator not much larger than a phone booth—basically a platform in a shaft—took us up six floors. You could touch the building's skeleton as you rose. Igor, squeezed in with us, said in his acquired British accent, "Is it all right then?" He'd asked the same thing about our mailbox down in the entryway. He was my chair at the university, a man who got up on the balls of his feet a lot and showed you the big gap between his front teeth, his eyes bulging. He'd met our train and brought us directly to what he called "the new digs," where he commenced to show us all our keys: building key, mailbox key, flat key, and the remaining six that—he demonstrated—would unlock the bedroom, living room, toilet, bath, kitchen, and a large foyer closet.

"Is it all right then?"

"Everything looks fine." I didn't know what else to say. The important business seemed to be that all the keys worked.

"Fine, then." He shook our hands, started to leave, stopped. "Oh, did you bring food? You're not hungry, I hope." We said we were fine. "Fine, then. Ah yes, Professor Grmela and his wife will call on you tomorrow with certain details. Cheerio!"

We turned on the TV in the living room. Young women paraded in evening gowns, bathing suits: a beauty contest. They all had long, gorgeous legs and exaggerated the swing in their hips as if in parody. They took turns caressing a new Skoda, falling onto new sofas, having their high, shiny cheekbones dusted with powders, modeling furs and leather motorcycle-jackets and jewelry; they held up glossy photos of cocktail lounges and swimming pools and airplanes. All these products and pictures were praised by a tux-clad, toothy master of ceremonies. When he paused, a voice off-camera sang, in English, "Only you can make my life complete." Almost every Saturday night, we discovered, we could turn on the TV and see a contest like this one.

In the middle of the night we were wakened by a wail from the flat above. It was a man's voice, and his long, melancholy cry seemed to say that no one, no one, could help him. But then we heard a woman's voice—from the same place—and its barklike syllables apparently came to his rescue. In moments the wail trailed into silence. This, too, seemed a regular weekend event.

Looking straight down from our living room-window, we could see what appeared to be a gigantic unfinished basement. It seemed long and wide as a soccer field, had partitions for rooms, and was full of water. This had been the start of a neighborhood bunker, but work came to a halt the day the Revolution arrived because the builders no longer knew who would pay them and walked off the job. It had sat three years now collecting rain, tossed stones, refuse, and rats.

Almost daily a small boy on a tricycle would appear down there and ram the bunker's outer wall, then back up a few yards, lower his head, and, pedaling hard, ram the wall again. He did this over and over until his mother arrived to lead him away. At first we feared for him: feared he would become bored and climb the wall—which was not much taller than he was—and maybe fall into the water. But he never got off his trike that we could see; he had a mission, somewhere to get to, a job to do—and this thing, this stupidity, was in his path. It made him mad, and ramming it was all he could do.

That first Sunday morning, Anita and Nicole, the daughters of Josef and Anna Grmela, arrived at our door with bread, fruit, tea. "Our parents wish to come at one o'clock and take you to lunch," said one. "They would have called, but you haven't a phone," said the other. Anita and Nicole were eighteen and seventeen, red-haired, freckled, cheerful, and curious.

"Are you glad you're here? I mean in Slovakia?" Nicole asked.

"Yes, we are," Lizzie said. "Aren't we, Dr. G.?"

"You call your husband by his title?" said Anita.

"It's a joke," Lizzie said. "I call him that, sometimes, because he's not a doctor."

"Weren't you a little afraid to come?" Nicole asked.

"What should we be afraid of?" Lizzie said.

"People here are afraid," said Anita. "They don't know what will happen after the separation."

"Even our parents are concerned," Nicole said.

"We're Czech, not Slovak," Anita said.

I asked where they lived. Through the window they pointed toward a small mountain in the distance.

"Šariš Castle is up there, or what remains."

"It resembles a cake."

"In fact, eggs were used in the mortar."

"And you live up there, on that mountain?" Lizzie asked.

"No, no," Anita laughed. "Below it. In Development Number Three."

"But there is no egg in the mortar," Nicole said.

"No, it is not a cake, I'm afraid," replied Anita.

At one their parents arrived, Anna vivacious as her daughters, Josef barrel-chested, red-bearded, freckled. They took us on the 38 bus to a hotel in town. Anna said, "I know in the West—especially in America, I think—that people invite you in, not out. Here it seems to be the reverse. But very soon, when things are calmer, you must come to our home." She consulted the menu. "Veal is their best dish. Is that all right?"

Josef said, "I for my part must try to avoid anything with flavor these days." He ordered carrots and soy croutons, and though he wanted coffee, Anna said, "Not today."

"I never contradict my wife," he said. "It's the only rule I faithfully keep."

"He is having an experience," she said.

"Yes, for fifty years my kidneys enjoyed themselves and their work and never complained. Now one of them, according to science, may be proposing a revolution. Very dull politics, believe me."

We liked the Grmelas. Words—conversation—seemed to make them spontaneously happy. Especially out in the open. If they'd pointed to a leafy branch where we all might sit and imitate bird calls, I would not have been surprised. In the halls of the university, later, they would sound more like their colleagues, who did not sing, certainly not foolishly in a tree in the year when Czechoslovakia was splitting apart and everything, at any moment, might topple. But on that first day, strolling cobbled streets almost nine hundred years old, there was nothing more dangerous around us than a Gothic church, the Renaissance town hall, the subtle perfumes of autumn, arches with lions' heads, and look, up there, on that chimney—a stork nest!

At a sweetshop we bought ice-cream cones—*zmrzlina*—and Lizzie pushed out her lips to try the word. "*Shmers*lina!"

"Do you like it as well as American ice cream?" Anna asked.

"Mmm, maybe better. And I *think* it's my first cone since our wedding."

"Since your wedding!" Anna said.

"We've only been married a little more than a year," Lizzie told her.

"You're practically on your honeymoon, then. Josef, we should have a party."

"If you will pardon me, I think honeymoons should be left entirely to the principals involved." He said this while keeping a careful eye on the small dip of vanilla he'd been allowed.

Anna said, "I meant of course a party to honor their anniversary. In my excitement I wasn't clear."

"Perhaps," Josef said. "Anniversaries early in a marriage are a very delicate matter."

"He always talks like this," Anna said to us. Josef made a mild grumble of protest. "I mean when you are having fun, dear Josef."

"I'm now reminded of my duty as a representative of the Philosophical Faculty to explain to our visiting Fulbright professor certain nuances, shall we say, in the academic system here."

"Please, Josef, we are enjoying our ice cream."

"The discussion about the quality of this food, in fact, reminded me of our grading methodology. Are you curious?"

"Shoot."

"Yes, shoot. We have three grades—Excellent, Very Good, and Good."

"No Fail?"

"If a student does not receive one of our three grades, he fails."

"So there are four grades."

"You could say so, but we only count the first three."

"Good must be the average grade, what we call C in the States."

"No. The most popular grade is Excellent, followed by Very Good. Almost no one receives Good, which is a disgraceful mark."

"Most of the students are above average?"

"Most are quite average. What I explained is what is done."

"Oh, Josef," Anna said, "look at the sky." He did. "Is it excellent?"

"Clearly."

"Is it complete and independent and pure, would you say?"

"I would say so."

"And beautiful?"

"That too, absolutely."

"Thank you."

Alphabets and Maps

The fall wind blew down all night from the Tatra Mountains, and sometimes we woke before dawn, smelling the pines it had come through, and told our dreams.

"I was studying Polish. Trying to carry the alphabet home across a field. I kept dropping letters in the tall grass."

"I was a girl again, walking along the Mississippi, searching for a little boat I'd lost."

Once, after a dream about my grandfather, I looked at the Polish map. His village, Ostrów, was reachable by bus, but we needed time. We didn't want to rush, and we wanted good weather. I also wanted to be ready, I told Lizzie, not exactly sure what I meant.

Often, those mornings, we went up the street to buy a round loaf of fresh-baked bread. I spoke broken Polish to the old woman, and she replied, laughing. She was always pleased that we preferred her specialty, rye made with potatoes. Most mornings after breakfast I stayed in the flat to write, and Lizzie took the 38 bus to my office, which was quiet and had excellent light from a large window facing north. She could make her pastels, with the radio on, and not disturb anyone. She could also play the office piano, which was in there,

Josef suspected, because no one knew where else to put it; the stacked marble tiles, stone planters, broken tables—all these were there for the same reason, he supposed. "Really, you have a large closet," he said, "with one wonderful window." The inner wall had two small openings with removable covers—"not so wonderful"—that looked down into a lecture hall. "Originally," Josef said, "a camera was operated from in here; people were surreptitiously observed." My office was at the top of a stairway from the building's main foyer—a handsome, almost elegant stairway you'd sooner expect in a castle.

One day I went looking for Josef, but he wasn't around. Monika, the department's young, blond secretary, greeted me as she often did: "Oh, my English! No good!" On the bulletin board I noticed the results of a contest for the best student essay in English. The winner was from nearby Poprad. I looked at his picture—he was wearing a tuxedo—and then read his essay, which was printed underneath. He wrote, "Although the great majority of Slovaks wish to keep the Federation, they will do nothing about it. They will let the nationalist fanatics have their way." I asked Monika, "Have you read this? Is it true?"

"Yes, of course."

"But why is it true?"

She rolled her eyes. "For me, no politics. I like young people—for example this handsome boy in the picture—who I hope will continue to be handsome—and cooking and—how do you call it?—computers. Also psychology!"

Monika's bubbly friend Mary, a secretary in the geography department, on the floor below, came in. "Mary," I said, "can you help me find a map of Slovakia? None of the stores seems to have one."

"Slovakia? Oh, la-la, I wonder."

"Yes, yes, we can do that," Monika said, taking my hand. "Tomorrow. For now, join with us and enjoy a cigarette, yes?" She patted my hand. Her long nails were pearl-colored; Madonna's face was printed everywhere on her blouse. I thanked them, no. Monika let go of my hand to answer the telephone. She spoke rapidly in Slovak, set the phone on her desk, came back and seized my hand again. All this caused Mary to bubble more. "Yes," Monika said, "you must sit." Mary sat in a chair to show me how. They were flirting, we all knew it, and meanwhile the phone lay on the desk.

"Your call." I pointed.

Mary popped up, fired mock-serious-secretarial Slovak into the phone, then laid it down and returned to our little meeting. I had to laugh; they did too, Monika patting my hand, Mary showing me how to sit, the caller, perhaps a friend of theirs, perhaps also laughing, and why not? Who could imagine such silliness under the old system? But what about the young man from Poprad, his essay, his warning against apathy? Oh, him, yes. His English is very good! Very. And how nice he looks in his tuxedo, like on TV. Then Lizzie showed up in her baseball cap and aviator's scarf, and Monika said, "Here is your woman!" They greeted each other; the bubbly meeting was now larger. The phone was still on the desk, a tiny, tinny voice escaping, and Monika produced a Czech-English dictionary to find a good word that would help us continue—"Pages and pages! This book is so big!"

Josef and Anna's flat was basically like ours except the furniture was nicer and there were many books and pictures. "We have been here," Josef said, "seventeen years." He laughed. "I won't tell you where we lived before; I can't bear to remember it." Anna served soup made with fresh morels picked from the nearby woods. They gave us the best seats, so we could see the central yard—where grass and trees had been planted, years ago, to soften the near view—and then the woods beyond. The hardwoods were turning red and yellow.

Nicole was not there. She had got up at five that morning to dig carrots in the country for spending money. She would earn a hundred crowns for a full day, Josef said. "A grand sum," Anita smiled, letting us know she didn't think it worth the effort. She had recently returned from a year in Connecticut on a government scholarship—one of only three high-school students in Czechoslovakia to receive such a grant—and now she knew, even more than before, what things were worth. Her sweatshirt said OXFORD; she planned to be an academic like her parents.

Anna brought out a casserole of chicken breasts and paprikas and cheese. "Our lunch," she said. "But Josef will have vegetables and rice."

"I have three guardian angels watching everything I eat," he said.

"Nicole is the worst," Anna laughed, "and so sharp-tongued about it. She caught him drinking coffee at the university and practically made a speech."

"Yes, Nicole is my sharpest critic."

"As sharp as any you've had." Anna shook her head.

Josef laughed. "I was thinking recently about those Kennedy books that got me in Dutch."

"What happened?" Lizzie asked.

"Typical nonsense," he said. "A boring story. But humorous in a way. I had library duty in those days, in addition to my teaching. Six copies of *Profiles in Courage* arrived—the U.S. Embassy in Prague sent them—and I put them in the library. A young colleague, who was in the Party, saw them and at his monthly meeting stood up and said to the Party chief, a man whose IQ I don't believe could be measured, it was so low—a real, well, a real *dumb* man. . . . Anyway, this colleague—"

"Who is still on the faculty," Anna broke in.

"Yes, yes, that's right," Josef said. "Anyway, he said to his chief that copies of a book by the imperialist John Kennedy were in the library, and he wondered if faculty member Grmela was ideologically ripe enough to be responsible . . ."

"Ideologically rigid enough, you mean," Anna corrected.

"What did I say?"

"You said 'ripe.'"

"Oh, well," he laughed, "I must be reaching for something. In any case, this Party boss decided to freeze my salary and take away my specialty course, American literature." He sighed. "But you know, Anna, we all compromised ourselves to one degree or another. No one was untouched."

"He is too generous," she told us. "Even as a student he paid."

"No, no," he protested, "that's too far back; it's ancient history."

"You should tell them."

"I've said enough. I will sound like a crybaby, if I don't already."

Anna said, "When Josef was at the School of Economics in Prague, he got caught listening to Radio Free Europe. They expelled him. Made him work for six years as a clerk before he could enroll again."

"A lucky thing," he sighed. "I would have made a lousy economist—the country would be even worse off than now."

Anita pointed out that the sun had left the yard but was still brilliant in the woods beyond.

"Yes, a walk," Josef declared. "Under the common trees with us!"

Outside, Anna said he should have been a forester. "I will use my next life with great pleasure," he said, "perhaps sampling one of those lookout towers in the American West—pondering such expressions as 'pardner' and wearing a ten-gallon hat."

Anita smiled. "My father has been to Pittsburgh."

"Yes," he said, "I was there in '89, during the Revolution. But you see the kind of luck I have? Every time I go away, something nice happens," he joked.

"They only let you go, finally," Anna said, "because they knew something bad was about to happen, and they wanted to be on your good side."

"The truth is we do not know why they let me go abroad. My guess is a bureaucratic blunder. By the way," he said to me, "I am suddenly reminded that you are having a bureaucratic experience regarding residence cards. Let me just say—then we can enjoy our walk—that it is not necessary to possess such cards. It is only necessary to apply for them. As long as you make an application you are within the law, even if the process takes forever. All you need is to be strong when matters become absurd."

"We should go to the castle," Anita said. "For some romance."

I walked beside her. "You must have deer in these woods," I said.

"We used to have a lot, but now there are none. The Communists shot one whenever they liked. My girlfriend ate deer tongue so often she got bored with it."

Fog clung to the castle ruins. We climbed a stone stairway, dodged trees growing through walls, and stopped on a grassy plateau in the lee of a leaning turret. "The former cake," I said.

"Yes," Anita smiled, opening her backpack. "But I have real cake, apple cake made from an old Moravian peasant recipe."

I thought of my Polish grandmother and of sitting with my chin on the oilcloth covering her kitchen table, with its waxy, leathery, vine-gary smell, and then smelling the fresh coffee cake she brought from the oven, an aroma that changed everything.

Lizzie took pictures of us in the fog, and then we started down a path to Šariš village. We heard a rifle shot. Maybe, I said to Anita, there was one deer left. She said no, it was probably a rabbit. Josef pointed toward a cluster of Gypsy shanties in the trees. I thought of the fluid earth-colored drawings in a children's book Lizzie brought home in which trees might be animals and animals might be people and people might be trees again, but you had to look close.

Expression

I went to meet my requalifiers, the former teachers of Russian. Using English, especially in front of their peers, was difficult for them. "We don't want to sound stupid," Xenia said. "After all, we are teachers." I kept praising their efforts and challenging them, and in the way, more or less, that a rusty nut can be unbound with oil and a wrench, they began to loosen up.

Drahomira Dragonova ("Call me Dada, maybe is easier for you") was an exception. She was a professor of philosophy, and married to the former Dean of Ideology, whom the students, in the first heady days of revolution, demanded be canned. The position was canned, too. Dada remained. She sat in the first row and needed no invitation to speak. (She put me in mind of Yogi Berra, not for her dipsy-doodle syntax—there was no accidental poetry in it—but for the shape of her jaw.) If she got stuck in English, she'd fire off what she meant in Slovak and snap her fingers for a translation. Someone always provided it. No matter whom we discussed—Hawthorne, Twain, Dickinson, Welty—Dada wanted to nail his or her "philosophy," summarize it in a sentence. When I called for further comments, other ways of describing Hawthorne's or Welty's view of humanity, Dada's eyes would narrow and her jaw clench. It was hard for her to entertain the notion that writers, or the characters and dramas they created, were larger or more complex than a simple declarative sentence, especially if the sentence had just come from her. I became fond of the Slovak expression *za'hada*, which means "a mystery." For example, why was Dada—who did not conduct her courses in English—taking my class? When I asked, she threw me an interesting curve. "Kde je pes zakopaný," she said. It meant, literally, "Where the dog is buried": or, as Slovak friends would tell me, "Where the truth begins."

Josef was standing outside his office, having just returned from Bohemia and a special treatment for his kidney. I told him I was happy to see him back.

"As a man pommeled by science, I share your happiness."

"But you look fine, you really do."

"If I'm left alone I feel normal, though I am told I should feel otherwise. How is Elizabeth? How are you? Have the police given you your residence cards yet?"

"We're fine . . . and the cards, well, that's a story-in-progress."

He invited me in and closed the door. "The police," he said. "You know, last summer Anna, running across the street, in the rain, to catch a bus, is struck by a car. Her collarbone is knocked out of line,

390

ribs are bruised, nylon stockings ruined—but please, please, she mumbles, it is her fault, not the driver's; she simply wasn't paying attention under her umbrella." He pulled at his beard. "She visits the police station as required and gives her report, absolving the driver. Yet months later, they are still investigating. Today, at an early hour, they took Anna to the scene of the accident, stopped all traffic downtown, made chalk lines, occupied their stations, gave the signal, and sent her back across the street, at a run, to reenact the moment before the car struck her. The police held stopwatches, were timing her for some reason known only to themselves. Over and over they sent this unathletic, middle-aged professor of British literature running across the street, timing her, refining their art, I suppose, until at length she fell and ruined another pair of stockings. She also bloodied her elbows and knees. We can't help but feel she is under suspicion, but for what?"

The sunniest member of the English faculty was Slavka. "How are things going, Gary?" I told her I was in pursuit of residence cards and having some trouble, but otherwise all was well. "Really? No other problems?"

"Well, my fourth-year students and I seem to have lost our lecture room. We meet in the courtyard."

"What will you do when it snows in earnest?"

"A question raised—timidly—by one or two. I said we could get close and recite Whitman. 'Smile O voluptuous cool-breath'd earth! Smile, for your lover comes.' "

"Your American humor. But tell me, seriously, what is the situation with regard to the residence cards?"

I showed her the last form to be filled out.

"It seems," she said, "they are requesting physical examinations."

I explained that Lizzie and I had complete physicals just before leaving the States—as required by the Fulbright office. "I have Xeroxes of the reports," I said.

"Good," Slavka replied. "I will go with you to the police."

The official who handled residence cards had dyed hair that made me think of purple Easter-basket grass. Grape Hair and Slavka had two very long exchanges, the clerk dominating. The gist of the first was that the police *might* accept the U.S. health reports. The question was whether the exam had been complete or only partial; partial

391

was unacceptable. And, too, the reports were too old; thirty days seemed to be the limit, but ours were dated almost exactly three months ago. So Grape Hair needed to phone someone in the ministry to obtain special approval, but the person who could grant such approval was not, she knew, available at this hour. The second long exchange concerned any criminal acts Lizzie or I may have committed since arriving in Czechoslovakia. Grape Hair gave me a form that I needed to take downstairs to the police-station coffee shop and buy a special stamp for. Then we were to fill it out with our personal histories—and then, third, mail it to the Division of Criminal Investigation in Bratislava. If this form came back showing that Lizzie and I were clean, I could bring it to Grape Hair's office for *her* stamp. At that time, she assured Slavka, her call to the ministry regarding the acceptance or refusal of the medical reports should have been completed.

As Slavka translated, I kept my mouth shut. It wasn't easy. I wanted especially to point out that the medical reports had aged because of Grape Hair's sending me home with a new form to complete every time I came to call. Even Slavka's usual sunny aspect was darkened. But in the coffee shop she brightened again. "Well"—smiling bravely—"everything will turn out fine. Would you care for a snack?"

The café was filling with clerks and liver-faced cops on their midmorning breaks. We bought the special stamp I needed from the same woman who sold us coffee. Slavka guided me through the personal-history form—except for an item or two in different locations, it was identical to all the others. As I sat there keeping my mouth shut about that and about the need to be declared innocent, I saw Grape Hair come in. She bought three hot dogs. No bread, just the sausages. She sat at a nearby table and dipped her dogs, bite by bite, into a great pool of mustard.

A tall, slender woman in her thirties was waiting for me outside the requalifiers' classroom. "I missed your fall lectures because I was promised work in Canada. But now is no work. So I am here. I have everything. The big book, your assignments." Her voice seemed thinned by distance, like some I picked up on shortwave radio. She had blond hair waxed in a kind of rooster comb, red-painted lips more vertical than horizontal—bright as a valentine—and light blue-gray eyes so still they seemed fake. Over a white turtleneck sweater she wore a black T-shirt that said in glittering green: KING OF THE DESERT.

"You are a Russian teacher?"

"Finished."

I told Luba Baranova the fall lectures were not quite over and invited her in. She went to the back row, produced a notebook and pen, sat up straight, and fixed her eyes on me. Not once during class did her expression or position seem to change; she might have been posing for a long camera exposure. At one point I asked if she was following OK, and her eyes turned even flatter, as if I were trying to get more information out of her than she was willing to give. The next week her T-shirt said U.S.A. YANKEE WINNER. The hairdo, the lips, the pen in hand, the stare—all the same. I tried another question—what, in her opinion, was the biggest lesson Huck Finn learned? The blue-gray eyes seemed to say: Please, I am here, isn't that enough?

On the day before midyear break, Luba approached me in the hall. HELLO HOLLYWOOD, read this week's shirt. She held up her gradebook, which resembled a passport; all students carried them. "I request your signature," she said. "For my first-semester credit. Or I will lose everything. I must have it today. I pray you."

"Don't pray me. Explain. Why today?"

The eyes didn't move. "I must," she said.

"Look, Luba, I am happy to help you. But why today?"

"My credit. I pray you."

"OK, look. The day is young. We will meet later."

I went to the English department to see what anyone knew about this woman. In Igor's office, Monika was helping him count books for a private bookshop he ran on campus. They were into it like thieves. I knocked on Josef's door; no response. I found Slavka in, eating a cucumber: "My breakfast. I have been rushing all morning wondering where I am." She had the warmest smile of anyone I'd met in Slovakia, but now, hearing Luba Baranova's request, she turned almost grim. "Yes, I know this situation. You may give her an exam or ask her to write an essay for the first-semester credit."

"But why does she need a signature today?"

"Her problem is not your problem," Slavka said. "Do what you think is best."

At the lecture Luba fixed her look on me as always. I tried to gather up a few threads: a sense of place, the times they are a-changing, who am I? Near the end I went to the padded door and whacked it with my palm, quoting Whitman: "Unscrew the locks from the doors!/Unscrew the doors themselves from their jambs!" It opened. There stood Igor, smiling, up on the balls of his feet. He had the former Russian teachers now, for Didactic, his specialty.

I left. In the hall Luba was suddenly beside me. "Relax," I said. "Don't you want to go to Igor's class?"

"My credit," she said.

"OK. Five o'clock, in my office?" Meanwhile, I suggested, she might go somewhere quiet, perhaps the library, and prepare.

She shook her head. "No examination can be necessary, because look"—she showed me two pages of exquisite calligraphy detailing the basic facts of Stephen Crane's life, information copied from her text.

"That's fine," I said, "but can you talk about something he wrote?"

"I pray you."

"Please, no praying. Go read. Something *by* Crane, anything, and we'll talk about it. Also anything by Thoreau.

"Thoreau avoided the capitalists."

"Good start. At five o'clock . . ."

"No five o'clock." She was beside me on the stairway to my office. My back was aching. I needed a swim. The pool was open for faculty from four to five. It was quarter to four. I could hear her breathing.

"OK," I said, stopping, "who is Huck Finn?"

"A little boy."

"Do you like him?"

"I pray you."

"Please, Luba, go read something."

" 'Song of Myself' is a poem by Walt Whitman." She looked at me as if the light had stunned her, maybe even hurt her, then held up her gradebook again. I took it. At the front was a photo taken when she first entered the university, at eighteen or so. Her eyes were regular eyes, youthful, bright, and her lips almost smiled, not yet frozen into the neon heart she walked around with now.

"Listen," I said. "I *will* help you." Her expression softened; she even glanced away and sighed. "Good," I said. "So go to the library and read some passages you can tell me about at five o'clock." I made to return the gradebook, but she didn't want it; she wanted me to take her pen.

"Please, you can sign it now."

My neck was heating up. "Luba, are you listening?"

"Understand me."

"Understand you. Jesus. Where is the dog buried?"

I continued up the ornate handsome lousy stairs and opened my door. She was right beside me. She glanced at Lizzie's new pastels on the walls, then walked to the piano. "Do you play?" I shook my head. "But you have this nice instrument."

"It was just in here."

Suddenly she was heated, playing. Beautifully. Rachmaninoff. The room filled with gorgeous, round, passionate sound. What could be more important?

A Kind of Fable

Lizzie and I settle into our compartment on the Budapest Express, going to Bratislava. A six-hour ride in the new year—the year the Slovaks and Czechs are officially divorced. We are happy to be leaving Prešov for a while. I open my copy of *Tess of the D'Urbervilles*, and there is Thomas Hardy quoting Whitman: "Crowds of men and women attired in the usual costumes, / How curious you are to me!"

A young couple enters. "Dobrýden," we all say. *Good day.* The newcomers each carry a large bottle of Coke; their jackets say LOS ANGELES on the back. They sit side by side. The man opens a book; the woman slings a leg over one of his and watches him read.

Lizzie and I sit across from each other by the window. I try to follow Angel falling in love with Tess, but I'm distracted by the woman beside me stroking her companion's inner thigh. Finally he tells her to sit across from him. She sighs theatrically, feigning great disappointment, but moves away, taking a magazine from her tote bag. On its cover Madonna is almost bare-breasted, her hair, like Luba Baranova's, twisted in a rooster comb.

The train, brakes shrieking, stops in Ružomberok, and in step four young women with big red Nike duffel bags. The Madonna fan quickly moves next to her man. The tallest newcomer sits beside me, the others beside Lizzie. I say, "Basketball," and they all smile and say, "Basketball!" I introduce myself and Lizzie and explain that we're spending a year in Slovakia.

They are Sylvia, Nora, Bibi, and Susan. Sylvia, the shortest, most talkative one, says, "We make our names easy for you." Then she announces, "I am the playmaker."

"You bring the ball downcourt," I say, and she nods. "Who is the shooter? You?" I say to Susan beside me.

"They all score!" Sylvia laughs. "I feed them."

Unlike my students, they warm up fast. They are in high school in Ružomberok; they study English, economics, geography, literature; their team is sponsored by a local club that sends them to Italy, Spain, Poland; they're a junior team, but next year they can play senior ball if they're good enough. Susan, they say, has played in several senior games already. Sylvia proudly says that two years ago, at sixteen, Susan was recruited for Ružomberok, brought there from Stara Tura, given an apartment, money to live on. "Susan will be big!" Sylvia promises.

Susan is at least six feet tall and, I'm guessing, not easily pushed around. Last week, says Sylvia, they were in Valencia. Susan's brother, a student there, came to watch them play. Susan says, "Maybe I will study in Valencia, too, if I don't sign with a professional team."

"A professional team in Slovakia?" Lizzie asks.

Of course, they all say. In Ružomberok they draw three hundred people a game! Better than in the capital, Bratislava, where maybe only fifty come.

When I ask why that is, they laugh. Maybe there is nothing else to do in Ružomberok! All four women are relaxed and at ease with us, confident. In Bratislava tomorrow they will play an exhibition against an Austrian team, and they expect to win; afterward they will enjoy a hot shower, a good meal, and maybe—why not?—some dancing. I am for them, with them, and though I can't watch tomorrow because I will be giving a poetry reading at Comenius University, I will be closer to them, I think, than to any of their countrymen. I ask if the Czech-Slovak split will change things much for them. They shrug. I ask if it's better in Slovakia now than three years ago, and Sylvia says maybe.

"Could you travel to Italy and Spain before the Revolution?"

"Me? I was too young. But my father—of course." Her father is manager of their club. Before becoming manager, he too was an athlete and could travel. "But he is not a businessman," she wants to make clear. This is a delicate point, because "manager" in her part of the world is a complex word: Formerly it meant "important Party functionary"; now it describes, more often than not, an ex-Communist who emerged from the revolution with money from a strongbox or a secret Swiss account, money he could invest, hence a capitalist, a mover and shaker, perhaps a quick-change artist. (I think of Igor and his private bookshop.) But this is messy territory, nothing like a basketball court, where the lines are clearly drawn and everything is in the open, so we turn our attention to the window, and we're passing the town where the delicious Figaro chocolate is made—have we tried it?

Then we pass another town, where the players say a nuclear reactor sits, boiling away—"the dirtiest anywhere." We pass Stara Tura, where Susan grew up. All these connections are suddenly bouncing around the compartment like so many loose basketballs: revolution, candy, poison, home. Talk about messy. Well, we don't. We change the subject, focus on Bratislava. We are all eager to arrive and be hosted, honored, distracted by the capital. And, too, Bratislava is only a short hop from Vienna, gateway to the fabulous West.

Yes, Slovakia is difficult to talk about, but so is a rainbow, so is a fish. Maybe that's why none of my colleagues except the Grmelas— who scarcely count because they are Czech and never joined the Party—have invited us into their homes. Things are too much right now—too hopeful, too slippery, too messy. Meeting at the police station is one thing; where one sleeps and perhaps dreams is another. They say, "We must get together and really talk . . . soon"—then look at their watches—"but not today, unfortunately"—and rush to class. It is a refrain, a tic, a speech for a play that doesn't have much development. But the locked-in is everywhere: from the glum silence on city buses to—ironically—the best essay in English (despite its content, it won, I was told, because it had no grammatical errors and was therefore declared perfect) to my perpetually worried fourth-year students. When I handed out questions at the start of the year and explained we would look for different ways to respond, they said, "Ways? But there is only one way." No ambiguity for them. A poem, a story, or a novel is not a work of imagination reflecting the richness and complexity of the human condition but a document of almost legal shape, a treatise, a blueprint demonstrating something black and something white, and it all means *this* in a sentence or two.

"But why?" I burst out. "I mean, why *now*?" They gaze at their hands.

I think of Luba Baranova's remark, "You know, we are used to behaving. Under the Nazis, under the Communists, we were good." I think of Katarina Fetkova, who chairs the English department at the

University of Mateja Bela, the school where Party members once went for seminars to keep rigid. She invited me to give a poetry reading: "You will have an attentive audience. We are a rural people—like everywhere in Slovakia—trained not to make noise." Later she said, "Allow me to tell you a fable. There are all these young children who receive very nice treatment, warm attention; even their schools seem cleaner and brighter than schools for older kids. As they grow up, less personal attention is paid to them; they are divided into two basic groups, the clever and the dull, and given their lessons in earnest. The clever will go to university, the dull to trade school, but in either case they will want the same things. It is no accident," Katarina Fetkova said, "that we live as we do."

But once a beautiful moment: I said to my fourth-year students, "When I appear to be angry with you, I'm really not. I'm only pretending—it's a ruse, an attempt to get you to *talk*." A little voice among them said, "It's like us. When we appear to be quiet, we're really not. We're only pretending to be quiet."

The train makes one more stop before Bratislava. The Madonna fan and her man depart, and we're joined by a woman wearing a new leather jacket and carrying a big cardboard box that Sylvia helps her settle on the floor. The woman, about forty, is all smiles when she hears English being spoken. She tells Sylvia to tell us that she gets English on her TV every day now because she has a dish. We all acknowledge her good fortune.

Now she wants to open her box and show the Americans something. *Here! Look!* She takes out a handful of dolls—each maybe three inches tall—made from cornhusks. At first I think they are little girls wearing some festive Slovak head-wrap, but no, they are Jesus dolls, two hundred of them, and the yellow head-wrap is a halo. She, her husband, and their son spent all week constructing them. The son helped because he wishes to buy a motorcycle with his share, the mother says, smiling, proud of his ambition. She is taking the dolls to Bratislava for the tourists. Are we tourists? Sylvia explains that I am a visiting professor, and the woman says, "Ano, ano," *yes, yes*, and puts away her dolls.

I ask how long she has been making them. She holds up three fingers: three years. And every week she can travel to the city and trade them for designer jeans, leather jackets, a satellite dish, even a motorcycle. She sinks back in her seat. "Life," she sings in English, "is A-OK." I catch Sylvia's eye. She who has three hundred Ružomberok fans come watch her dribble a ball, she whose father manages a club that sponsors a team that can travel to Italy or Spain—that has been able to travel outside the country for years—she shrugs and gives me a grin that says, I think, *So what else is new?*

Where To?

On the bus that would take us into Poland there were five other passengers, all smugglers. They'd come down to Slovakia early that morning, loaded up with vodka and hair-coloring in Prešov, and as we rode north four of them were busy working to hide the stuff, to avoid paying Polish import tax. Lizzie and I watched.

The one who wasn't fussing was feeling good. He stood in the aisle combing his black cowlick and sang a song about swans. The young woman who resembled Ingrid Bergman fixed a pillow under her sweater to look pregnant, then got out needles and a partially finished rug; she spread her knitting over the sackful of hair-coloring boxes in the seat beside her, a wary expression in her eyes but otherwise the picture of serene budding motherhood.

The other three Poles were jittery as squirrels. The thin one had packaged his hair-coloring in a crate that resembled an air-conditioning unit and placed it under a rear seat. Though he sat near the front, after every bump or sharp turn he would hustle back to check on the crate, nudge it with his foot to line it up just so.

The heavy woman in the first seat, catty-corner from the driver, had both vodka and hair dye. She spent much of the journey to the border telling the driver how good the coloring was, holding a box for him to see. Look, she said, beautiful red tint, very natural—and at such a good price! She regretted now the vodka—it took up too much room. Look, she said, didn't the driver agree the coloring was beautiful? He said, "Tak, tak," *Yes, yes,* but kept his eyes on the road. She had her vodka in a suitcase and the hair-coloring in two duffels piled atop it, everything snug beside her, and she patted the luggage and cooed as if she had a pet in there that needed comforting.

Finally, the man with the mustache—the least organized of all—stood in the aisle as if in despair over his two jumbo suitcases of vodka. An hour out of Prešov he was still debating whether to leave them in their separate seats or to push them under. Too full, too full, he kept telling the man who was feeling good. His eyes drooped like a basset hound's.

Back in Prešov he'd helped me out. I approached the driver to buy my tickets. "Dokad," the driver said. *Where to?* He told me how much to Krosno in zlotys. I offered crowns. "Polish bus, Polish money," he said. I didn't have any. He shrugged. "Szkoda." *Too bad.*

I knew the exchange rate, more or less, and offered extra crowns. He shook his head; he couldn't be bothered. He was waiting, I reckoned, for dollars. I was about to pull some out when the man with the mustache said, "Here." He handed me 100,000 zlotys and asked for 200 crowns. I was happy to let him make a good commission so I could save my dollars for Poland.

On the bus, he asked if I could carry two bottles across the border. I said sure. Why were we going to Krosno? I explained we were going beyond it, to Rzeszów, spending the night, then going to a small village, Ostrów, where my *dziadek*, Stefan Szostak, was born.

When the man who was feeling good heard I was a Polish grandson, he immediately brought me a plastic glass filled with vodka and orange pop. He was Marek, he said. We told him our names. He said, "No Gary, no Elizabeth. Gariego, Elzbieta." Then—beaming— "Chicago!" We told him no, Iowa. But next year Idaho. "Idaho? Idaho? Dlaczego?" *Why?* For the mountains, we told him.

He smiled, and said Elzbieta needed vodka. I told him no, only me, and put my hand on Lizzie's stomach. *Dziecko*, child.

He slapped me on the back and insisted we toast the child, Elzbieta, grandfather Szostak, Chicago, the mountains, the USA, Poland, and finally this good Polish bus. "Not bad," he said, "is life."

The man with the mustache, who'd eased away during all this, now returned. He had two more bottles he wished me to carry over: "You can do it, no problem." I said OK. Then he showed me a bus ticket to Rzeszów, saying I would need forty thousand zlotys for it. I counted out enough crowns to trade, plus a tip. He shook his head sadly; he had no more zlotys. I handed back the two bottles. He looked shocked: Marek roared, then said, "Greedy boy." He waved Mustache away and produced the zlotys I needed.

As the bus slowed for the border crossing, the driver barked, "Pivo! Pivo!" Marek got two bottles of Czech pilsner from his bag and handed them up. When the Polish guard came to the driver's window, the bottles were stealthily slipped out. He returned to his shed; the five smugglers sat up straight and kept their eyes dead ahead, as if to show how good they could be. He came back with a clipboard and had the driver step out and open the storage area. Then the guard boarded the bus. He walked slowly to the rear, saying nothing. The heavy woman looked in a small mirror and put on fresh lipstick, watching him; as he passed, the knitter belched, patting her stomach, clacking her needles; the thin man bent to tie his shoelace and looked back along the aisle to see how his fake air-conditioner would fare; Marek produced a small black book and a thoughtful expression; Mustache sat with his feet on the two enormous suitcases that he'd finally decided to push to the floor. The guard only glanced at us. He finished his stroll and waved us on. After the driver crossed into Poland, just out of sight of the border station, he pulled over, and the smugglers scrambled out as if the bus were on fire. Cigarettes were lit and glasses filled. By God, they'd done it! For only two bottles of Czech beer and a presentation of respect.

The next day a bus delivered Lizzie and me to a country crossroads. "Ostrów," the driver said. In a circle of speckled shade made by a single oak, a dozen mares and colts stood muzzle to muzzle while a man measured bellies, examined teeth. Other men watched. Judging from the shapes of jaws and noses and full, unbroken eyebrows, I reckoned they were all kin to me. They took us in, briefly, shyly. A breeze came and pushed over green hay in the field beside us, and then the grass sprung up straight again. I could have hung around that tree for as long as I did my grandfather's orchard and creek and forge, unconcerned with time, simply waiting for the next thing, but after a while we walked up the road in the spring air toward a lone house.

It was a café. We ate bean soup and bread. I asked the teenaged girl serving us if any Szostaks lived in Ostrów. She shrugged. Then, leading us outside, she pointed to a wooden steeple rising above a cluster of trees. The village center. I asked about a *cmentarz*. She said, "Tak," and pointed to a rise just up the road.

We started for the cemetery. Lizzie sighed when a stork flew over, flapping and clacking. She said, "I'm sorry, Dr. G, it's almost too damn much." Beans and wheat grew in fields on either side of us, and in the distance, across from the cemetery, a white horse, a plow, and a man—the reins looped around his neck—cut fresh furrows, like waves, in a soft brown, almost perfectly round hill.

The treeless graveyard seemed far too big, too populous, for such a small village. Months before, in a reference book on patronymic surnames, I found Szostak and Szostek, good Polish names. I also found Shostack, Shustak, Shustek, Shostag (East German), and Šesták (Czech). All were derived, the book said, from the Belorussian Shostakovich. There was conjecture that the names were connected to the word *shast*, six, possibly denoting a person with six fingers on one hand. Still I was finding no Szostaks or anything close. When I looked up to stretch my back, the farmer and his beautiful white horse continued to cut their wavelike furrows in the brown hill. I wanted to go ask his name, and his horse's. Then Lizzie, in a far row, said she'd found one. Maria Szostak Something, who died in 1933 or 1938. We found more, pressing our fingers against the fading letters and numbers as if tracing them into the soft stone.

The village center consisted of a simple, bark-colored wooden church, a few shade trees, and a packed-dirt area where horse carts could park. We approached a man lying in his empty grain cart under a tree, having a smoke. Waving my arm around, I asked, "Szostak?" He sat up, looked at the sky, then smiled and pointed down a lane to a barn. There, Lizzie and I found a pink-cheeked old man searching his tool bench. I asked him, "Szostak?" He glanced at our bags twice, then took off on a hard dirt path.

"Are we supposed to follow him?" Lizzie asked. I guessed we were.

We met a man on a bicycle, at whom our guide fired some Polish. The man got off his bike, let it fall; now the two of them led us. We came to a stream and walked beside it. We were in a forest, though here and there a weathered house abruptly revealed itself. I thought of the Gypsy settlement below Šariš Castle. Our guides stopped at a little house held up, it appeared, by cherry and apple trees. The cyclist knocked; a man came out and said he was Andrzej, grandson of Maria Szostak. He looked so much like my uncle Joe I had trouble making verbs, the possessive. Reduced to nouns and pointing, I got across that I too was grandson of a Szostak.

"Moment." He went back in and returned with a handsome carved chair, one clearly intended for special occasions. He set it under a cherry tree for Lizzie. He then brought out three more like it: one for me, one for himself, and one that our two guides shared by sitting sideways with their elbows on their knees. Then Andrzej and I, using American placenames and mainly Polish nouns (my plunge into pidgin had infected him), struggled and thought and slapped our foreheads and clapped our hands. "Moment!" He brought out an envelope, very old, bearing a Chicago return address. Everyone studied the writing, the stamps, licked by my great-uncle Jacob—brother of Maria and Stefan. The bicyclist grabbed the sides of his head and exclaimed, in English, "Fantastic!" Andrzej gazed into the canopy of limbs shading us and could not stop smiling.

That night Lizzie and I stayed in the Hotel *Cukrownia* ("Sugar"), which sat beside a sugar-beet factory five kilometers from Ostrów. It was a workers' hotel. We paid 110,000 zlotys, about six dollars. I recorded this in my notebook, along with the detail that next to our room a worker fried eggs in a communal kitchen for his dinner.

I couldn't remember asking my mother much about Grandpa when I was growing up. Not that I wasn't curious; but almost always there seemed to be this response in my family when I asked a question: "Just watch—and see." I was instructed by people who used their hands, who laid down a level and followed the bubble, who wiped a knife blade in the up position, not the down—so you won't hurt yourself, see? But once I heard words that were better than usual, words that didn't end when my mother stopped saying them: "He came from the old country, a handsome, educated young man—oh, yes, very smart—and strong as a bull; he had to be, because of all the troubles he went through. They were always fighting over there, those Polish kings, those Russian Cossacks. On horses, with swords!" I'd seen Grandpa drape complicated harnesses on his big-shouldered Belgians, seen him lift red-tipped pokers from the forge, and I believed everything she told me. I still believed her, collecting my facts, my details.

I knew the dangers of facts, their insistence on making a straight line, a balanced weight, an answer the teacher will give you a star for and that you can tuck away in the place where you store your answers and stars. And maybe forget about. I did not want that. I did not want the exact number of clacking bones in a skeleton—I wanted what Joseph Conrad wanted, the questions, the mysteries, the imperfections and contradictions of the human heart. "A man's real life," he wrote, "is that accorded to him in the thoughts of other men by reason of respect or natural love." I respected my grandfather, but did I love him? Or did I love those images of him in his blacksmith shop, gazing at the sky in his bee-sweetened orchard, opening his book in the honeyed glow of a kerosene lamp at a table we all moved away from? "The dead," Conrad said, "can live only with the exact intensity and quality of life imparted to them by the living."

My mother was old enough to remember the day he came home

from Ford's foundry, splashed on by molten steel. He took his family north from Detroit and became a farmer. The summers I was eight, nine, and ten I followed him around. We never exchanged a word. Then one summer I elected to stay in Flint and play baseball. That August he died and was buried on my eleventh birthday. Almost two decades later Grandma told me, "Korzeniowski, always reading this Korzeniowski, even on his last day." Trembling, I asked if I could see that last book. She said no, because just before Mr. Savage, the undertaker, closed the coffin, she put it under Grandpa's arm. All those years Steve Szostak had read Joseph Conrad, in Polish—even on his last day. But how would I know that? I knew other things. That he stood in a driving rain and raised his fist at the heavens for drowning his beans. That he sat me on the hay wagon, between his knees, and gave me the reins. Up and down the field we raced until Grandma rushed out, *her* fist, her skirts, and the Polish flying, afraid I would be hurt . . . and he, his hands over mine, helped me steer the wagon around and around her. He called my grandmother Nelly. He had a mare of the same name, and waded into the creek with her, took off his shirt, bathed his scarred shoulders and back while she waited. In 1902, the year of their marriage, Grandma wears a rose in her hair. She is sixteen, looking out at the world like a young woman who's spent the afternoon in her flower garden, alone, thinking how lovely everything is, how temporary, and just at that moment when happiness and melancholy compete most for her heart, the photographer snaps her. And later, in his studio, applies to her full and youthful cheeks a subtle blush.

In the Hotel Sugar, I stood at the window seeing stars, their random toss. I also saw a circle of sun-freckled farmers, a plowman and his beautiful white horse cutting furrows in a round hill. A stork flew over our heads, speaking. "How do you feel?" I asked. "At the beginning," Lizzie said. We sat in special chairs under apple and cherry trees planted by a man with whom I shared a name we found on some fading stones. He couldn't stop shaking his head in wonder. I wondered, before we went away from those trees making speckled shadows in my wife's hair, if I would ever again see such bright shade. We had spent only a short while there, a blink in time; it was enough and not nearly enough.

Nominated by Paul Zimmer, The Southern Review

BOOK

by ROBERT PINSKY

from THREEPENNY REVIEW

Its leaves flutter, they thrive or wither, its outspread
Signatures like wings open to form the gutter.

The pages riffling brush my fingertips with their edges:
Whispering, erotic touch this hand knows from ages back.

What progress we have made, they are burning my books, not
Me, as once they would have done, said Freud in 1933.

A little later, the laugh was on him, on the Jews,
On his sisters. O people of the book, wanderers, *anderes*.

When we have wandered all our ways, said Raleigh, Time
Shuts up the story of our days—beheaded, his life like a story.

The sound *bk*: lips then palate, outward plosive to interior stop.
Bk, bch: the beech tree, pale wood incised with Germanic runes.

Enchanted wood. Glyphs and characters between boards.
The reader's dread of finishing a book, that loss of a world,

And also the reader's dread of beginning a book, becoming
Hostage to a new world, to some spirit or spirits unknown.

Look! What thy mind cannot contain you can commit
To these waste blanks. The jacket ripped, the spine cracked,

Still it arouses me, torn crippled god like Loki the schemer
As the book of Lancelot aroused Paolo and Francesca

Who cling together even in Hell, O passionate, so we read.
Love that turns or torments or comforts me, love of the need

Of love, need for need, columns of characters that sting
Sometimes deeper than any music or movie or picture,

Deeper sometimes even than a body touching another.
And the passion to make a book—passion of the writer

Smelling glue and ink, sensuous. The writer's dread of making
Another tombstone, my marker orderly in its place in the stacks.

Or to infiltrate and inhabit another soul, as a splinter of spirit
Pressed between pages like a wildflower, odorless, brittle.

Nominated by Threepenny Review

CANDACE COUNTS COUP

fiction by NANCY LORD

from THE MAN WHO SWAM WITH BEAVERS (Coffee House Press)

In a crowd, you would notice Candace. She wore a large gold nose ring. Her hair, in front and on top, was purple. Neither the nose ring nor the purple hair would be remarkable on a teenager, but you would notice them on a fifty-five-year-old head that was otherwise unadorned and capped by gray, largely straight and somewhat thinning hair. Because Candace's face tended to be very large and her eyes very small, she somewhat resembled a buffalo. The nose ring was something she had chosen, perhaps for effect. The purple hair had just happened. Somehow, painting, purple paint had come to be all through the bangs and crown of Candace's hair, and there it stayed.

As it stayed on her clothes, which tended to be shifts made from enormous expanses of fabric. Some were tie-dyed. Some just looked that way. Some were fluorescent. In all of them, Candace's massive, generally unrestricted breasts bulged at the front, the fat at her waist stretched the seams so that the stitches and the space between stitches showed, her meaty knees and long-haired calves protruded. When she walked, her thighs rubbed with a sound like pieces of vinyl mating. Her feet scuffed on the floor, on the broken pavement, *shh-shh-shh*, her sandals taking little tiny, crepe-soled steps.

She would never think of herself as brave. She was just Candace. It was the rest of us who came to call her Brave Woman.

Candace was an artist. Not an ordinary artist, not what you think. She didn't do sketches or paintings or etchings, not carvings or ceramics or quilts. She didn't do the kinds of things that could go into a gallery, or on an art lover's wall. Her art wasn't the kind anyone, no matter how avant-garde or unreasonably rich and hip or poor in taste, would, or could, *buy*.

Candace called herself an installation artist, which meant that her pieces were constructed to go into particular venues. They were conceived as parts of places and assembled for those places, and when the time was up, they were removed from those places, usually, for lack of space in Candace's life, to the dump. They were by their nature, ephemeral. It was hard to get even the government to pay for something here today and gone tomorrow.

For example, one of Candace's recent uncommissioned installations was for an outdoor pavilion. She had sewn a wonderful parachute-like thing out of, well, parachutes and road fabric, and painted it to look like flames. Hanging there from the roof, it had billowed in the wind, looking in fact very much like flickering fire. She'd outfitted the entire student body of the neighboring grade school to look like little brown roasting nuts, and placed them under the pavilion, and she had sat in the center, dressed as a marshmallow. People—mostly the parents of the students, who thought what-the-heck-now—showed up to look at her installation, and then, because the hanging-down fabric truly was a fire hazard, or so the fire marshall said, the whole work of art, minus its human component, was torn down and trucked off to the dump, where some said the parachute and road fabric materials were meant to go to directly, or perhaps had come from.

Candace's commitment to her nonrenumerative art meant that, among artists, she was the poorest of the poor.

But still, somehow she found rent money, food, materials for her work. It helped that her father was still living and that he, despite being a capitalist enslaver, had always had a fondness for his daughter, if not for her art. Maybe it was guilt he felt. Who knows?

❦

That morning, when Candace awoke in her low-rent basement apartment, it was to the screams of a woman overhead and a sound like *clunk-a-clunk-a-clunk*, someone smashing that woman's head against the bare floor. The noise had entered Candace's dreams as buzzards screeching over a nearly dead African animal of some hoof-stomping kind, but as soon as she was awake, she lost no time in wrapping herself in a large paint-covered sheet and running—well, rushing, faster than you might think—up the flight of stairs, where she pounded on the paneled door and then, using a stepladder someone had left in the hall, broke through the door.

It was hard for her to both hold onto her sheet and to do something about the man who was holding a weeping woman by the hair, so when she let go of the sheet, the man was so stunned that he instantly put his hands up in front of him. Candace nonetheless pushed him back and then sat on him, while the woman, clutching her bruised neck, crawled away.

"Call 9-1-1," Candace said. The woman hesitated a moment and then, as though she found Candace too frightening to not obey, did as she was told.

The man underneath Candace bellowed and twisted and swore. "Please," he begged. "They'll put me in jail. What is this shit? I don't deserve this! Please! Get off me! I can't breathe!"

Candace did not know either of her upstairs neighbors from Adam and Eve, though she thought she might have seen the woman a time or two going in and out of the building. She said, "You think I like this? You woke me up, *and* I haven't even had time to wash the sleep out of my eyes. I've had zero cups of coffee and my mouth tastes like snakebite. I've got no clothes. You think I want to have to explain this situation to pistol-packing, flagrantly abusive peace officers at this hour of the pre-dawn morning? I don't even know what time it is. What time is it?"

The man wouldn't tell her and the woman didn't seem to know. There was no clock in the room that Candace could see, though she did see the big-screen TV, the metal legs of a kitchen table, a painting on the wall of cats with a ball of yarn. These people had no taste at all. She began to sing something she'd heard on the radio the night before, an old sad Billie Holiday song about bad luck and trouble. She didn't have much of a voice, but the song, you could say, was called for under the circumstances.

"Cut the crap!" the man shouted.

Candace shifted her weight and heard something crack. Something in the floor, maybe, something in the man's pocket, something in the man. He groaned, and she thought, *maybe a rib*. She placed her marsupial feet firmly over the man's wrists and said to the woman, "Could you please hand me my cape?" As best she could, she wrapped herself up again. She thought but did not say, *so shall ye reap*, and she meant both the man and the woman. She suspected they deserved one another, though nobody deserved to get their head smashed on the floor. She thought she herself deserved to reap a little more artistic recognition, but she was not complaining. She did not look for earthly rewards.

Later, there was a little trouble about the man's medical bills, the broken door, rudeness to officers who also apparently had not had their morning coffee, and Candace's removal of the offending painting. Candace was informed that it was very dangerous to involve herself in domestic violence situations and that next time she should call the police and wait for them to handle the situation professionally. To which she said, "Right. Like I'm going to listen to someone get killed." That morning, she had only done what anyone in her position would do. Or should do. She did not consider herself heroic, only human.

⁂

That morning, still before seven A.M., Candace returned to her apartment, where she washed, dressed, drank coffee, blew the insides out of six dozen white-shelled eggs she needed for her work, ate two eggs scrambled, and put five dozen and ten eggs down the toilet because the neighborhood soup kitchen would not accept eggs outside of their shells and would not blow eggs themselves, even if she donated them. She ate toast with jam and experimented on white bread slices with a blowtorch to create pieces that, together, formed a mosaic portrait of someone looking very much like Richard Nixon in his better days.

On her way to her installation site in a warehouse just a few blocks away, *shh-shh-shhing* in her sandals over the paving stones, the grates, the dirt and broken glass, she stopped numerous times with her box of blown egg shells packed in popcorn. The box was not heavy, only awkward. As she rested it on steps, railings, the bumpers of cars, she studied the life around her. A hawkish bird soared overhead. Someone shouted in a language she didn't know, something that sounded like *car-luffle-lay*. A delivery truck with squeaky brakes rolled past her. She examined a stained, cushionless settee poised at the curb and left it, regretfully, though she thought she might come back with her little chainsaw and take the hardwood legs. She glanced into the shopping cart of a raggedy man going through a dumpster.

"You got any polka dots or pantyhose?" she asked the man. "I'm looking for anything polka-dotted, and any color pantyhose or stockings but especially fishnet. And sneakers, especially the old cloth or canvas kind." She had an idea, just that morning, for a few hundred painted sneakers on a wire, all dancing in the wind. Or the wire could be connected to a motor that gave it a good, constant jiggle, and she wouldn't need wind.

The man shook his head and tossed two aluminum cans into the cart. "Sorry. But if you got some change you could spare, I could get something to eat and not get another bellyache from the spoiled cakes."

Candace set down her box and unzipped the leather purse she wore belted around her middle. She handed the man a crumpled dollar bill and some change. She knew she wasn't supposed to. Everyone said to give to charities instead, if you wanted to help, but to her it made sense to give directly to people who needed it. She would want them—anyone—to do the same for her. What was the point of money, anyway? This was a discussion she had had many times with her father and many other accumulative people.

"God bless you," the man said.

What social agency ever thanked her like that? What institutional face looked as grateful as that one, cavernous and yellow-eyed as it might necessarily be?

Candace walked another half-block, looking at the facades of buildings, their faded inscriptions and gargoyles, and thinking what she could do with them with a little dynamite and reassembly, a little wire and paint. She was dreaming this—building walls of Roman numerals and angels with facial hair and pink private parts—when a car, an old blue Mercury, ran up on the sidewalk and into the iron gate across a liquor store doorway, missing Candace by ten feet. It was an easy calculation for Candace to see that if she had not been asked for change by the man in the dumpster and had not fished around in her waist purse for precisely the minute that she had, she would have found herself square in the car's path.

Candace set her box down again. The car had not been going fast, and she had watched the people's heads, when the car came to its abrupt stop, fling forward and back, together. She had seen the bigness of their eyes and the way their arms thrust out in front of them. It was a dramatic moment that impressed her, even without inflating airbags, with its artistic potential. What luck besides! The car, going over the curb, had kicked off a hubcap, which now spun in the street like a wavering, unbalanced top, and the muffler. Candace helped

411

the two stunned people—an older, church-dressed couple—from the car, and after ascertaining their physical well-being, she asked if she might have the hubcap and the muffler, which they said she could. She went off again with her box of egg shells topped with the warm muffler set inside the hubcap like a leg of lamb on a platter. It was amazing to her, always, that the very things she needed had a way of appearing in her path as agreeably as that.

❦

When Candace reached the warehouse, she only dropped off her materials and took a look at the shape of what she had so far: a collection of shiny metallic car parts, egg shells (some of them glued to painted cardboard), pairs of pantyhose stretched from ceiling to floor and anchored with bricks, paving stones, and blocks of crumbled cement, which she'd fed down the legs and into the toes (causing numerous runs), the polka-dotted clothing she had yet to tear into strips and integrate into the background. The piece had to do with chaos theory, the way molecules organized themselves, and technology as organized chaos; it was still coming to her—the patterns of randomness, the beauty of repetitions and waves, the way things would finally fit together within her artistic vision.

She had more to think about, so she took the subway across town to the botanical garden, where she wandered through the misty humidity and various exotic ecosystems, searching for lilies, carnivorous flycatchers, cacti, the baby sequoia trees. She went around leaning over the rails to sniff one flower and another. She wanted an olfactory element to her work, and she had to meditate on what to include, what effect she would get from apple blossom, tiger lily, the tropical hibiscus. She let her nose draw her around the walkways, *shuffle-shuffle-sniff*. She closed her eyes. The scents were like colors, not the colors of blossoms, but something more—more peaches, more pastels, more and deeper blues and purples. She let her nose sort out the differences, the singular shades and strands; she thought how she would paint the dots of scents, the waves of stripey smells, how she could get the essences into sprays that were not stinky perfumes or piney room fresheners, but themselves, one scent and sense blending to another.

She was thinking these things, and about taste, too, and why the smell and taste of some things, like vanilla, were not quite the same.

When she reached the prickly pear cactus and found it in full, luscious red fruit, she reached across the rail and broke off a piece. It tasted good, like honeyed water, like a juicier plum. It was not until she was leaving that a woman in charge looked at her strangely and said, "What's that on your face? Are you bleeding?" and she wiped away a part of the cactus fruit that had stuck there.

"Just cactus fruit," she said.

The woman looked at her with even more concern. "*Our* cactus fruit? You weren't eating from the plants in the greenhouse, were you?"

Candace knew the correct answer would be *no*. But, like little George Washington and unlike another president she could name, she could not tell a lie. "Just a taste," she said. "I never tasted one before."

The woman looked as stern as a nun, and like she'd use a ruler on Candace's knuckles, if she had one. "The plants here belong to *everyone*. They're not for any one person's personal use. Plus," she said, "we are not liable for poisoning. Many of our plants are extremely toxic."

But Candace knew that plants liked to be eaten. There was an old Indian belief she'd learned from an old Indian boyfriend, that plants gave themselves for people to use, and if you didn't use them, didn't eat them and make your baskets from them, they would quit offering themselves. Which was maybe one of the principal problems in the modern world and why we were stuck with iceberg lettuce.

Candace put her hand on the woman's wrist. At first she felt the woman draw back, but then she felt the transfer of energy between them. The cactus fruit had entered her, was at that moment being transformed into a part of her, and the molecules were tripping right through her, down her arm, across her fingertips, to a person who needed to lighten up and who now, surely, in Candace's cosmogonic belief, would.

❧

Outside the botanical garden, Candace immediately came upon a man walking a very thin, dispirited-looking spaniel-style dog.

"Your dog is way too thin," Candace said to him. "You're either starving the poor animal or it has worms."

"Thank you for your expert opinion," the man said.

413

Candace stooped beside the dog and rubbed its head and bony back. The dog wagged its tail. "Yes, you're a nice doggy," she said, "and your master is a sorry piece of shit."

"I should kick your fat ass across the street," the man said.

Candace stood up. She was a little taller than the man and outweighed him by at least one hundred pounds. She tapped him on the chest, on the front of his alligator shirt. "Just try it," she said. She blew from her bottom lip, so that the gray and mostly purple hair hanging over her eyes fluttered. She stared down the man, who seemed to withdraw behind the surprise, then the fear, in his eyes, until his face was a blank. "So take this dog home and make him a doctor's appointment, or the next time I see you, you will become horsemeat yourself. *Do you understand?*" She pressed her finger into his chest and felt him lean away.

"I'm not looking for any trouble," the man said.

"Good. I'm sure you love your dog. Everybody loves dogs. I'd have one myself except I can't in the apartment I'm in. I'd have ten. But a city's no place for a dog, anyway. It's not natural." Candace walked next to the man and his wagging dog, a way down the sidewalk. She told him about dogs needing room to run and bark and do their business without being stared at, and the man was entirely agreeable. He didn't say a word.

※

After that, except for her nap and a sandwich, Candace worked all day at the warehouse. She sorted eggs by size and pointedness of end and glued them to cardboard, cleaned and polished car parts, painted other car parts. She ran the industrial warehouse fan at different speeds to determine the best undulations of pantyhose, and she rearranged some of those legs and their anchors for improved wave effects. She cut polka-dot cloth and stapled it to walls, and she pinned sheaths of it around her bodice and her head to make a sort of multilayered, multicolored, multidotted gown. Outside, she posted painted cardboard signs announcing her work-in-progress and inviting participation, and when people did wander in, she offered them round bologna sandwiches and Cheerios and put them to work painting or reclining behind the undulating waves of pantyhose while holding different combinations of polka-dot fabrics. She laid out an array of Salvation Army polka-dot dresses and had people

414

choose and model them and tell her, into her tape recorder, what they thought about Chaos.

~

It was after dark when Candace cleaned her last brush and collected her signs and leftover bologna. On her way home, *shh-shh-shhing* along the street with her bag of foods in need of refrigeration, she was accosted by an agitated young man who demanded her money, watch, and jewelry.

"Are you crazy?" Candace said. "Jewelry?" In the poor light she thought that perhaps he'd mistaken the paint splatters around her neck and on her tunic as necklaces and brooches. She was definitely not parting with her nose ring. "Scat on out of here before I make you sorry. *And*, by the way, don't you know it's rude to pick on impoverished ladies with veins in their legs? Why don't you go rob a Brink's truck or something *manly*?"

The man backed up a couple of steps and moved his finger inside his shirt, trying to make her think he had a gun. "You do what I say or you'll be sorry," he said. "Put down that bag and cane and give me that money belt."

It wasn't a cane, exactly, that Candace was carrying. It was a buffalo penis bone made to be a cane, but she carried it more for these kinds of occasions. People with good sense didn't tend to bother her, but now and then she'd run into a hoodlum like tonight's, or she'd be called upon to help someone else in a situation, though certainly, despite what you might think, she didn't go around looking for situations. They just sometimes happened around her. She had taken to carrying her buffalo penis bone like someone else might carry a folded umbrella, just in case.

"Take that!" Candace yelled, banshee-like, as she swung the bone into the man's midsection. He fell back and she stepped forward, and she pounded him again, on one shoulder, then in the legs.

He dropped a gun, then cried out like he was choking and ran.

Candace picked up the gun. *Gosh-darn*, she thought. It was the real thing. She thought about keeping it, but then decided guns were more trouble than they were worth. One less in the world would have to be an improvement. She dropped it through a sewer grate.

She knew she had not really hurt the young man, though she thought maybe she should have. The head of her buffalo penis bone, the part she had hit him with, was well-padded with mink fur. She had only, mostly, scared him.

~

At home, when Candace only wanted to have some chamomile tea, toast, frozen lasagna, and Cheese Doodles with a movie channel, she found she had company. Her husband was in her bed.

He was her husband, technically. They were married, and they'd been married for four years. Bob was Algerian and had needed her help to stay in this country. She'd obliged.

"Wake up," she said. "What are you doing here?" She had changed the lock the last time she'd thrown him out, but now she was regretting leaving the key to the new lock on the little nail next to the molding. It did not take a genius, which Bob was not, to let himself in. She was also, at this moment, regretting dropping that gun into the sewer.

"Darling Candy," Bob said, sitting up. His dreadlocks, the front ones, fell over his face. "I was wondering where you were. I was worrying about you out there in the jungle, in this terrible dangerous neighborhood. Why don't you let me take you away from here?"

"Take me where?"

Bob shrugged. Of course he had nowhere to take her, and no money. If he had a place to stay or food to eat, he wouldn't have come to Candace's. He didn't like her that much to put himself in her presence outside of a more-or-less emergency. "It's the thought that counts. Is it not?"

Candace went to the stove and made tea and toast, which she brought to Bob in bed. "One night," she said. "Then you go."

He fell back asleep almost immediately. He did not look good, Candace, sitting there on the edge of the bed, thought. The man was exhausted from whatever. She didn't know what he did. As brave as she was, she didn't want to know. She looked at the mahogany mask of his face and thought how beautiful he was, even in the folds of skin around his closed eyes, especially in the little laugh wrinkles beside his mouth. If she could make a face like that . . . She turned down the covers and looked at his hairless sculpted chest, the hollow at the breastbone, the nipples like perfect dark, pimpled circles. His chest moved with his breathing, with the pulse of his heart. She had two, not quite revelations, but serious, clear thoughts: A human, even an ugly one, is a work of art. And life, even a vague, underac-

416

complished one, is art, and the highest form of art/life is just getting through without causing harm.

Candace put her hand on her husband's chest, the pads of her four fingers over his heart. She felt his heart beat, regular, regular, skip-murmur, regular again, thump, thump. A chaotic behavior. She would have an audio portion to her installation. People talking about chaos, and then chaos, the arrhythmic beating of her husband's heart, while the pantyhose waves flowed, while the dots dotted, while the flower smells smelled. The whole work was coming together now in her mind. She would need heart-monitoring equipment, Bob hooked up in a chair, other people too, listening to their own and each other's hearts and learning something about order and disorder, persistence, goodwill. There was still something misty in the conceptualization, but Candace was getting there, to what, when it was done, we might all see had to do not only with beauty and strength but with grace.

Nominated by David Romtvedt

[MY LOT TO SPIN THE PURPLE: THAT THE TABERNACLE SHOULD BE MADE]

by D.A. POWELL

from CHELSEA

(a song of Mary)

my lot to spin the purple: that the tabernacle should be made

with ten curtains of fine twined linen and scarlet.   and the silk

and the hyacinthine.   even woven with the gold and the undefiled
which is white.   having the true purple for its veil.

when the lot fell to me I took up my pitcher and filled it
took the purple upon my fingers and drew out the thread

in shag and floss: in coarse bottoms and in tight glossy skeins
the thrum did wind itself away from me

for a word had entered my womb and leapt inside me

I make the dark pillow where the moon lays its opaque head
I am the handmaid: pricked upon the spindle

the fine seric from the east was brought to me
soft and unfinished.   dyed in the tyrian manner

of purpura and janthina the violet snail.   cowrie and woodcock shell
the spiny hedgehog murex and the slender comb of venus

from betwixt my limbs arachnine the twisting issue I pulled forth

purple the night I felt the stab of the godhead in my side
purple the rot of the silk: its muscardine.   its plague

a raw tuft dwindles beneath me: I feel the tug of a day ravelling
even as such gloom as this winds tight around the wooden reel

would that a potion could blot out the host inside me
grove of oak, chestnut, willow.   a place of skulls.   succubi

a necropolis in me rises. its colors mingle in the dark: aurora

spinster to throwster: purple my loom spread with the placenta cloth
I put a fine pattern to it: damascene sheaved and lilied

threads thrown in acute manner so that the bee rises on the border
the rose of sharon the cedar the camphire.   calamus and pleasant
    fruits

and these even dotted with locusts caddis flies and polyphemus moths
a fountain: a garden wattled with reeds upon the weaving

garden to be betrayed in?   a shadow against the breast of the tree

so the flox did luster in mine eye: in the cloth I beheld a fine water
as one might arduously with calander produce: the weft

a wave offering in my hands.   pin that pierces the body

over my lap a spreading wound of purple: purple that puckers and
    gathers
cloaking my folds of purple.   the swollen vein of a young boy's
    manhood

purple deep and hopeful.   a scar under the frenum.   a heavy
    prepuce

a caul.   an umbilical cord.   a wet sluice.   an angry fist.   a
    broken vessel
a bruise.   a blemish.   a raincloud.   a lesion.   a fissure.   tissue

the ends I took up and selvaged.   this veil shall not fray

and vast the warp of the cloth.   sea of galilee.   tigris euphrates
    and jordan
flow not as wide as my great bounty: undulant sky above my loom

the shuttle through me: a lance in my side.   a heave in my
    bowels
how will the temple receive my gift: scab of purple.   pustule.
    genitalia

[and a future who? unfurls above the altar]   the thread the thread
    the thread

Nominated by Chelsea

SISTER CARRIE AT 101

essay by JOSEPH EPSTEIN

from THE HUDSON REVIEW

THE ENGLISH CRITIC Cyril Connolly, he who, in Edmund Wilson's light verse, "behaves rather fonnily / Whether folks are at peace or fighting / He complains it keeps him from writing," this same Cyril Connolly, in *Enemies of Promise*, his book of 1938, began what he called "a didactic enquiry into the problem of how to write a book which lasts ten years." Writing an introduction to a reissue of this book in 1948, Connolly thought he had brought it off—and I suppose he had, *barely*. I happen to be an admirer of Connolly's lush and hypercivilized prose, but it is a paradox of paradoxes that this man, son of Eton and of Balliol College, Oxford, his mind stocked with vast quantities of learning, wide reading in many languages, and an experience of the world in its most exotic corners and subtlest aspects, couldn't write anything whose interest would be felt outside the most rarefied of circles. Meanwhile, a fellow named Theodore Dreiser, one year of Indiana University under his belt, a man who sometimes seems to write with a meat cleaver, an inelegant, often literarily deeply inept man—a yokel, a rube, really—could write a first novel before he was thirty years old that still vibrates with life a century after he wrote it.

"After forty years," announced William Maxwell, the novelist and longtime fiction editor at *The New Yorker*, "what I came to care about most was not style, but breath of life." *Breath of life*—that was what Theodore Dreiser was able to bring to his fiction, and without it, no amount of sophistication, cleverness, or grandeur of style will suffice to keep literary work alive. Theodore Dreiser's fiction had the

421

magic; it lived when he wrote it, and much of it lives now, decades and decades after he wrote it.

A friend of mine, a research oncologist and a reading man, recently asked me whose work among current novelists I thought would live fifty years from now. My answer, I knew as I gave it, was less than satisfactory. I said I thought the novels of the narcissistic crew, those virtuosi who don't tell stories but tell only of themselves, would not be long-lived. Style can be a preservative of literature, but only up to a point, and I suspected that those novels best known for their style would, after a certain number of decades, turn and go bad. The sex-ridden writers, I thought, didn't have much of a shot, either, for fifty years from now human beings will doubtless have some sort of Internet-organ-transplant-pill-induced-open-heart sex, and so not much about our current sex lives seems likely to hold their interest, let alone shock them. I told my friend that I thought the solid storytellers among contemporary writers had the best chance to survive, but the sad fact was that I really hadn't a clue who they might be.

A few examples of the guttering of once glittering literary stars will make more vivid how extraordinary an accomplishment it is to have a book live for a century. The novels of Dreiser's supporter Sinclair Lewis haven't really made it. Neither, alas, have those of John Dos Passos. With the single exception of *The Great Gatsby*, I suspect the same could be said of those of F. Scott Fitzgerald. Ernest Hemingway, I believe, is also on the casualty list, though many of his early stories carry an almost poem-like lyrical beauty that keeps them alive. A decade or so ago, I tried to reread *The Sun Also Rises*, the book that I found most scintillating of all novels when I first read it at twenty years old, and found myself bored blue by it, to the point of making a small tick in the back of the book for each drink knocked back by any of its fairly large cast of characters, quitting somewhere, as I recall, around seventy-six drinks at page 139.

Fitzgerald and Hemingway have both, I suspect, had their literary lives prolonged by the internal dramas of their extraliterary lives. Fitzgerald is well-served in this wise, if in no other, by his early death. The death of a young, handsome, bountifully talented man at forty-four has its own literary poignance: all that waste, all that sadness, all those lingering questions, all that might have been and never will be. Still, the lure of Fitzgerald's elegance remains, as witness all those boys and now grown men walking the streets of America with the first name Scott.

Hemingway's allure is less but far from inconsequential. It was of course most powerful when he was alive, and could play Papa—not, I think, the best of his characters, although the attraction of Hemingway refuses to die out even now. Other writers needed to be on the premises to keep their reputations intact and books readable: one thinks of Mary McCarthy here or Robert Lowell, the interest in whose writing melted almost instantly upon their deaths.

Some writers have had their work prolonged, of course, for political reasons. Black and women's studies have kept alive—at least in the classroom—certain books that would otherwise have naturally languished and died. Willa Cather, almost all of whose books continue to live majestically for me, has gained renewed academic currency through women's and gay studies, which, given her strong feelings about her privacy, would have been, for her, far from a cause for giddy delight.

But Theodore Dreiser makes no such claims, biographical or extra-literary. Quite the reverse. In answer to an effusive fan letter, Dreiser once responded: "And I give you one kindly piece of advice. Never bother to know me personally. Remain illusioned, if you can." Anyone who has had even a brief soak in the biographies written about Theodore Dreiser will conclude that this was probably sound advice. One has to scratch around to find anything attractive said about him. John Dos Passos, who went to Harlan County, Kentucky, with Dreiser to investigate the conditions under which the coal miners there worked, said that there "was a sort of massive humaneness about him, a self-dedicated disregard of consequences, a sly sort of dignity that earned him the respect of friend and foe alike."

But there was also the Dreiser whom Earl Browder kept out of the Communist Party in 1930, saying that "he did not seem quite adult. . . ." There was the Dreiser of whom H. L. Mencken said "the concept of gratitude was simply not available." There was the Dreiser whom, such was his reputation as a skirt-chaser, a notorious heterosexual, one would have been foolish to leave alone in a room with one's great-grandmother. There was the Dreiser who thought Hitler, on balance, a pretty decent fellow, and approved the signing of the Soviet-Nazi Pact. There was the Dreiser whose public pronouncements took on an anti-Semitic cast, at one point suspecting that his publishers, Simon & Schuster, were involved in a plot to suppress his work and who also suspected that Hitler might have been on target in thinking Franklin Delano Roosevelt was Jewish.

Perhaps the most charitable view of Dreiser the man is John Updike's. Much to Updike's credit, he, the leading hedonist of prose style of our day, shows great regard for Dreiser, and especially for *Sister Carrie*. But Updike sees Dreiser's mind as a powerful muddle. "His bewilderment," he writes, "enabled him to enter without condescension or any slighting of nuance into the bewilderment of his characters." Mencken, too, is of the Dreiserian muddle school, noting, with characteristic flair, that Dreiser had "an insatiable appetite for the obviously not true." Updike, though, trumps Mencken, writing: "Yet it was Dreiser's embrace of muddle that made him an artist and Mencken something less."

It is beyond a commonplace to say that no one would ever be drawn to Dreiser for his style. Mencken, in yet another altogether too deft phrase, noted Dreiser's "incurable antipathy for the *mot juste.*" In the late 1920s, Thomas K. Whipple summed up Theodore Dreiser the stylist when he wrote: "His style is atrocious, his sentences are chaotic, his grammar and syntax faulty; he has no feeling for words, no sense of diction. His wordiness and his repetitions are unbearable, his cacophonies incredible." That is a statement, I should say, true only in its particulars.

One could stage a rousing contest among people who care about style for the very worst sentence in all of Dreiser. Herewith I offer a few candidates from *Sister Carrie*: Consider this, from the mind of Carrie Meeber, observing the theatergoing crowd in Chicago: "If ever there was dressiness it was here. It was the personification of the term 'spic and span.' " For people with a taste for the tone-deaf combined with awkward phrasing, the following is not easily beaten: "When he [Hurstwood] rode downtown in the cars of a morning, he had the satisfaction of brushing elbows with numerous plethoric-pursed merchants and of answering solicitations concerning his wife and children which were made in that perfunctory manner common to Americans of the money-making variety." For misfired lyricism, there is this: "The sparrows were twittering merrily in joyous chorus." For tinniest ear in the short sentence category, the winner is: "These events [Hurstwood's not returning home to Carrie for dinner] were months apart, each." Here is the drummer Charles Drouet after visiting the now successful Carrie at her apartment in the Waldorf: "The merry frou frou of the place spoke all of her." But my own personal favorite occurs on page 109 of the Pennsylvania Edition and runs: " 'Um huh,' he returned pleasantly," which seems to me right up there with Ring Lardner's great comical sentence, " 'Shut up,' he explained."

There are two kinds of writer, it has been said, bad writers and neurotic writers. Theodore Dreiser was in some sense both; the complicating factor is that he also happens to have been, despite all that may be said against him, and I think I have just now recapitulated a fair amount of it, a great writer. When I said that Thomas K. Whipple's animadversions upon Dreiser's style are true only in their particulars, I meant to imply that in a general, and more important way, these particulars finally don't signify. Easy enough though it is to mock Dreiser's prose, the fact is, when careful, even perfect, words were required, Dreiser always managed to find them. In his novels, he never muffed a key scene. Where the greatest delicacy was required, he had it. And for sustained powerful writing, few things in literature, American or Continental, can top the perfectly persuasive, inexorable fall of George Hurstwood, down on his uppers in New York City.

I do not know the true significance of memorability in literature—by which I mean the peculiar way that certain things one has read stay with one decades after one has read them—but Dreiser ranks very high on my own memorability meter. Shaving, I often think of Hurstwood's slovenliness on this point of personal hygiene as part of his degradation in *Sister Carrie*. "I satisfy myself," says Frank Cowperwood, and so, in parody, sometimes do I say, reaching out for a second piece of cake or helping of ice cream in the kitchen of my own apartment. The scene of the lobster slowly but relentlessly devouring the squid at the beginning of *The Financier* has never left me, nor I suspect anyone else who has read it. Nor have a great many other touches, little and large, in Dreiser's fiction. This past August I was at a place called Lake Quinault, in one of the rain forests of the state of Washington, gazing upon a tranquil lake surrounded by a deep lushness of vast coniferous trees, when I realized the scene was not yet complete; something was missing. What it was, I realized, was the cry of the screech owl accompanying the end of the life of poor Roberta Alden in a physically similar setting in *An American Tragedy*. Dreiser has imprinted such things, many such things, indelibly on my mind.

Still, if literary elegance be the name of your desire, Theodore

Dreiser cannot be the name of your novelist. The same holds for humor. Has there ever been a more deeply humorless novelist than Dreiser? I haven't of late reread vast quantities of Dreiser, yet I cannot recall a single bit of humor, wit, or even ironical utterance in all his novels.

Not that this deep, utter, and abiding humorlessness need disqualify a writer. Tolstoy didn't rely on irony as a literary method—the method, that is, of saying one thing and meaning another—neither did Balzac; and even Proust wasn't as heavy a user as all that. Writers may be divided between those who depend upon irony and those who don't, and—even though I cannot myself get dressed in the morning without irony—I'm not sure but that those writers who don't depend on it may, somehow, be better than those who do.

"People in general attach too much importance to words . . . ," Dreiser writes apropos of the current of feeling flowing between Carrie Meeber and George Hurstwood in the early pages of *Sister Carrie*. "They but dimly represent the great surging feelings and desires which lie behind. When the distraction of the tongue is removed, the heart listens." There's something to this—a great deal, in fact, if your subject is the one Theodore Dreiser chose to explore, at a depth and with a persuasive realism greater than anyone before or since.

I take that subject, Dreiser's great subject, to be the destinies of the less than sapient up against the hard facts of life. Dreiser once told an interviewer that he dealt with "life as it is, the facts as they exist, the game as it is played." The primary hard fact, I believe, is that men and women are small, trembling animals padding around in a world they can't hope to understand, while awaiting decay and attempting to put off the knowledge that the mortality rate, at least at last report—and here I hope I don't shock any of my readers—was still one hundred percent. Flesh-covered bags of needs, desires, and hopes, ridiculous self-dramatizers, impressive over-self-estimaters, such are the less than sapient. I am sorry to have to add that I don't know anyone who, whatever his or her protective coloration of culture, isn't, in some sense, among them, myself of course included.

When I say that Theodore Dreiser's subject is the lives of the less than sapient, I don't mean to imply that he is—at least as a novelist— the great champion of the unwashed, the underdog, the People (with a capital P and several sets of quotation marks around it). I emphasize this because the most telling shot taken at Dreiser was the one

426

made by Lionel Trilling, who, in "Reality in America," an essay of the 1940s, launched an attack on Dreiser from which his reputation has never quite fully recovered. "Reality in America" has pride of place as the first essay in *The Liberal Imagination*, the best book of critical essays by the writer many deem the most thoughtful, sophisticated, and sensitive figure in twentieth-century American literary criticism.

Trilling's essay is divided into two parts: the first was published in 1940 in *Partisan Review*, the second in *The Nation* in 1946. The essay is really a defense of Henry James, a writer not then so solidly set in the firmament of Anglo-American literature as he has long since become. Trilling shows the insipidity, not to say stupidity, of the critics who didn't understand the subtlety of James; and didn't moreover have a clue that, in rejecting the novels of Henry James because they were thought to lack a connection with the reality of life, they were rejecting nothing less than mind and art itself.

All this is fair enough, but what I think is less fair is that in this essay Theodore Dreiser became for Trilling the nail upon which he beat down to lock up his point about James. Trilling cites the critics—V. S. Parrington, Granville Hicks, F. O. Matthiessen, and others—who have taken up the cause of Dreiser as an artist. These critics, he argues, set aside all Dreiser's profound defects—the artificiality of his style, his anti-Semitism, the general coarseness of his thought—because they believe Dreiser's ideas serve their cause. At bottom, "Reality in America" is an argument, and a sensible and historically useful one, against the Communist Party's attempt to shape and direct literature in America.

On his essay's final page, Trilling quotes Robert Elias, Dreiser's early biographer, arguing for the congruence of Dreiser's last novel, *The Bulwark*, and his joining the Communist Party: "When he supported left-wing movements and finally, last year, joined the Communist Party [Elias writes], he did so not because he had examined the details of the party line and found them satisfactory, but because he agreed with a general program that represented a means for establishing his cherished goal of greater equality among men." Dreiser's dreamy, not to say dopey, politics almost makes Trilling's attack on him justified.

Almost but not quite. At no point in this essay does Lionel Trilling really engage Dreiser's fiction. *Jennie Gerhardt* and *An American Tragedy* are mentioned in the most glancing way; *Sister Carrie* isn't mentioned at all. Instead a false choice is offered, Henry James for those of the higher sensibility, Theodore Dreiser for those with coarse left-wing politics. At the close of "Reality in America," Trilling sets up another opposing pair, that of ideals versus ideas. "But ideals are different from ideas," Trilling writes; "in the liberal criticism which descends from Parrington ideals consort happily with reality and they urge us to deal impatiently with ideas. . . ." The liberal critics are excoriated by Trilling for not taking ideas seriously, but instead treating them as "mere details" that only have the effect of "diminishing reality."

Yet, one has to ask, what has Henry James, Lionel Trilling's hero—and, let me add, mine also—to do with ideas? Not much, I think. Recall T. S. Eliot saying of James that he had "a mind so fine no idea could violate it." What Eliot meant by this, I believe, is not that Henry James was incapable of grasping or mastering ideas, but instead that he operated above the level of ideas. He was interested not in the perishable truths of ideas—all those grisly little isms—but in the enduring truths of the heart. T. S. Eliot never wrote about Theodore Dreiser, but had he done so, he might have written that Dreiser had a mind so crude no idea could violate it. Of Dreiser, Trilling writes: "He *meant* his ideas, at least so far as a man can mean ideas who is incapable of following them to their consequences." And a bloody good thing he couldn't, I say. Because those of us who value Dreiser do so not for his ideas but instead for the same thing for which we value the very different Henry James: his insight into the truths of the heart.

I don't know with any certainty the standing of Theodore Dreiser in the university today. Is he still much taught? He must be something of an embarrassment, what with all that is politically incorrect about him, including his insistent and not always complimentary views about the nature and psychology of women. He thought, poor benighted fellow, that women were both better *and* worse than men. He flunks cold on Jews; I'm not sure he would pass on race. I'm told someone has tried to slip him on the wrack of current-day literary theory, doing the new critical dipsy-do on him, the results of which—a Dreiser-Derrida cocktail—must be highly intoxicating and laugh-making. But unless some enterprising academic begins a course—a department? a field?—called Lecher Literature, I'm not sure Dreiser quite fits in anywhere these days in the contemporary university.

Yet, as with all important writers, Theodore Dreiser doesn't disappear. His name continues to pop up in odd places. In *The New Yorker* of May 26, 2000, the movie critic David Denby, writing about his own adventures in the stock market, remarks on what is for him "a new enthusiasm, *The Financier,* by Theodore Dreiser, whose capitalist hero Frank Cowperwood possesses all the qualities of coolness that I lack. . . ." Susan Sontag, America's official advanced thinker, a writer who can be likened to the minor character in *The Man Without Qualities* whom Robert Musil describes as "one of those practicing the profession of being the next generation," Susan Sontag, *mirabile dictu*, in the *Los Angeles Times Book Review* not long ago cited Dreiser's *Jennie Gerhardt* as one of the forgotten classics of the twentieth century.

In Philip Roth's recent novel *American Pastoral*, there is a lengthy, almost stitch-by-stitch account of the hero's business of glove manufacturing that is not only intrinsically interesting but clearly owes something to Dreiser's own interest in a detailed presentation of the work his characters do. Dreiser's interest in details is easily mocked—one recalls Robert Benchley's parody, titled "Compiling An American Tragedy," with its various notes to the printer: *"Run attached: Fifteen Midsummer Menus for Cole Slaw Lovers."* Yet, as Robert Penn Warren rightly noted: Dreiser "had the gift of observation when the facts observed had some fundamental relation to human feeling."

Serious writers such as Penn Warren have always understood that, though Dreiser had the most strenuous shortcomings, he nonetheless also had, as the Greeks said of true artists, the divine spark. Saul Bellow has often spoken of his deep respect for the power of Dreiser's fiction. Jorge Luis Borges, whose own lapidary art might almost be regarded as the very antonym of Dreiser's, wrote, "Dreiser's art is no different from his tragic face: it is as torpid as the mountains or the deserts, but like them it is important in an elemental and inarticulate way." Tom Wolfe recently allowed that only now, approaching the age of seventy, had he read *Sister Carrie* and found himself blown away by it. Edward Shils, that most well-read of modern social scientists, once told me that the difference between Theodore Dreiser and E. M. Forster was that Dreiser had gravity of a kind that the more educated and subtle Forster lacked. I suppose one could say that this gravity derives, inevitably, from the circumstances of Dreiser's life.

Twice I have myself attempted to teach novels by Theodore Dreiser, first *Sister Carrie*, then the lengthier *An American Tragedy*. On both occasions I was teaching freshman university students, and each time I felt I had not really succeeded. I had not done the books proper honor by setting them out in all their odd, awkward but utterly genuine complexity, thereby conveying the true weight of their seriousness. In frustration, I wanted to say to these eighteen-year-old kids: "Look, all this discussion may be beside the point. All you need to know is this: Theodore Dreiser was born dirt poor and hopelessly homely in an atmosphere of heightened religious ignorance; he grew up hungry and with as intense a sense of being an outsider and as keen a craving for love and ease and self-betterment as anyone ever born in this country. Please write this down. After you have done so, go home and reread the novel, because, you see, it's freakin' great."

What makes *Sister Carrie* great, I believe, is that Dreiser, in his late twenties, took on a powerful subject and proved worthy of it. The subject can be formulated in any of a number of different ways. In a letter pitching his novel to Walter Hines Page, the second man at the firm of Doubleday, Page & Co., Dreiser formulated it thus: "I feel and know . . . that the world is greedy for details of men's rise and fall. In the presence of a story which deals with the firm insistence of law, the elements of chance and subconscience [*sic*] direction, men will not, I have heart to feel, stand unanimously indifferent."

Ernest Becker, a cultural anthropologist, in a book called *The Denial of Death*, which never mentions Dreiser, nonetheless states the novel's theme perfectly when he writes that man "doesn't know who he is, why he was born, what he is doing on the planet, what he is supposed to do, what he can expect. His own existence is incomprehensible to him, a miracle just like the rest of Creation, closer to him, right near his pounding heart, but for that reason all the more strange."

The terror of the chaos of the cosmos, every man and woman's position of absolute aloneness in it, comes through brilliantly, one is inclined also to say brutally, in *Sister Carrie*. All one has on one's side in the struggle are one's instincts and one's will, which I hesitate to call one's free will. "We see man," writes Dreiser in an early philosophical aside in the novel, "far removed out of the lairs of the jungles, his innate instincts dulled by too near an approach to free will, his free will scarcely sufficiently developed to replace his instincts and afford him perfect guidance." May this struggle be said to have changed in any serious way over the past century? I once heard someone ask Isaac Bashevis Singer, after a reading at a university, if he believed in free will. "Of course I believe in free will," Singer replied, "what choice have I?"

Over the large canvas that is *Sister Carrie*, Dreiser provides pretty much the same answer, for his characters and finally for himself. "We are, after all," he writes, "more passive than active, more mirrors than engines, and the origin of human action has neither been measured nor calculated." Freud, who thought he had measured and calculated it, used to say that he learned everything he knew from the poets. One is left today to wonder if he learned it well enough. (When asked what he thought of Freudianism, the English essayist Max Beerbohm replied, "A tense and peculiar family the Oedipuses, were they not?") If we want help divining any of these mysteries, it is to poets, the tellers of tales, to whom we must return. Which means to, among others, Theodore Dreiser.

If I am correct about the largeness of Dreiser's theme in *Sister Carrie*, perhaps the first question to ask is, Are the book's characters grand enough to see the theme through; do they, in other words— the words, actually, of T. S. Eliot—provide a proper objective correlative to the action set out in the novel? Two characters, Carolyn Meeber, an eighteen-year-old girl with "only an average little conscience," from the sticks; and George Hurstwood, the manager (not even the owner) of a bar and grill and a man of what turns out to be flimsy dignity, predominate; toss in a third, to include Charlie Drouet, a traveling salesman and a masher, in Dreiser's old-fashioned word for a ladies' man. Can such a slender cast, slender in almost every sense of the word, carry the weight of their author's large ambitions?

Note, please, how Dreiser sets things up in *Sister Carrie*. Religion simply doesn't exist in the novel. "The voice of the people," Dreiser notes, "was truly the voice of God," adverting to Carrie's conformity early in the story, and God is never mentioned again in the novel: never prayed to for balm, invoked for aid, cried out to for forgiveness. God cannot be said to be dead in this novel, for he never comes alive.

One recalls here the lecture of Professor Godfrey St. Peter, in Willa Cather's *The Professor's House*, about how men and women were happier when they had the drama of religion, with the salvation

431

of their souls at its center. Science hasn't replaced this drama, St. Peter insists, "hasn't given us any new amazements, except of the superficial kind we get from witnessing dexterity and sleight of hand. It hasn't given us any richer pleasures, as the Renaissance did, nor any new sins—not one!" St. Peter continues: "Art and religion (and they are the same thing in the end, of course) have given man the only happiness he has ever had."

Dreiser's characters in *Sister Carrie* live without both art and religion. Family, far from existing as a consolation, is for them chiefly an obstacle. Upon her arrival in Chicago from Columbia City, Wisconsin, Carrie stays with her sister and brother-in-law, but everything about their frugal lives she finds grey and discouraging. Hurstwood's family is a source of little beside bickering and anger. When he is quit of them, he never, really, looks back. Carrie is no different. Her own parents in the novel are rarer than God—that is, they are not mentioned at all. Of Charlie Drouet, that averagely sensual man with patent leather shoes added, he seems to come out of nowhere, which also appears to be his destination. Without resources in religion, family, art, or philosophy, these are people working, as they say of certain circus trapeze acts, quite without a net.

Circus is to the point here. If other novelists are sometimes guilty of anthropomorphizing animals, Dreiser, in *Sister Carrie*, indulges in zoologizing human beings. People in this novel move about one another with the same fatal attraction as "the moth to the flame." Mrs. Hurstwood, who will later be likened to a python, senses change in her husband, "as animals sense danger, afar off." Hurstwood, holing up in his and Carrie's apartment in New York, loses, like the common canary in its "gilded cage," the power to shift for himself. Earlier in the novel, pursued by his wife's lawyers, he is "like a fly caught in a web, wearying itself by beating its wings," for his wife "has the reins in her hands and could drive him," like a horse. When a man slips in the snow, a minor character viewing the scene from a window remarks, "How sheepish men look when they fall, don't they?" Dreiser doesn't let us for long forget that men and women are a species of animal. And when human beings aren't being compared to animals, they are compared to one or another kind of plant, troping this way or that, reacting to heat and cold. Theodore Dreiser, you might say, is the anti-Disney.

In *Sister Carrie*, he presents us with something not done before or since in literature—he presents a love triangle absent the love. Each

432

of the triangle's three members has what we nowadays would call his or her own agenda. In Carrie, Drouet is looking for, and has temporarily found, what is known as a new squeeze. Hurstwood's attraction to Carrie is, as Dreiser tells us, "the ancient attraction of the stale for the fresh." As for Carrie, she is the great wanderer in the vast desert of unformulated desire. She cannot be said to have cared much for Drouet, despite living with him; nor, once she discovers he is married, does she ever regain such feelings as she had for Hurstwood, feelings that, after they hie off together to New York, turn out to be dutiful at best.

Of these three characters, it is most difficult to draw a clear bead on Dreiser's view of Carrie. Does he, as Thomas K. Whipple thinks, have nothing but "contemptuous pity" for this young girl, who may qualify as one of those "weaklings who are bound by moral scruples"? It's not so simple. Dreiser seems to go back and forth in his opinions about Carrie. On the one hand, she regularly feels shame: at one point for expressing anger at the already defeated Hurstwood, at another at the prospect of his having to go out in stormy weather as a strike breaker, and, finally, at moving out on him. Once her theatrical success arrives, she is incapable of *hauteur*, yet she has accurately taken her own social measure, understands adulation, accepting it, as Dreiser notes, with "coolness and indifference." On the other hand, she is often shown quite the woman in business for herself: keeping bits of her raises in salary from her acting for herself and dreaming of keeping all of it, imagining how free life would be without the drag of Hurstwood. Carrie, according to the character Bob Ames who emerges late in the novel, is said to suffer gloominess, to be "melancholic," "lonely in [her] disposition." She represents, in its purest form, what Dreiser calls the "blind strivings of the human heart."

Dreiser neither glorifies nor attacks Carrie, treating her without sentimentality or disgust. He shows none of the hot anger that, say, Tolstoy feels for Anna Karenina, or the cold contempt that Flaubert feels for Emma Bovary. In *Two Dreisers*, Ellen Moers wrote that "Dreiser set himself the task of making Carrie sufficiently null to skirt moral criteria, but vital enough to personify the creative force. . . ." She reminds us how little Dreiser actually allows Carrie to talk or even to think in the novel. Yet Carrie nonetheless comes alive and fills the page the way, as an actress, she filled the stage—always a presence, always riveting. There is great art in this.

In *Sister Carrie* Dreiser was writing what Ellen Moers called "inarticulate fiction," by which she meant fiction about people who aren't able to express their own deepest feelings. In such fiction, the novelist must find a way to do it for them. Carrie Meeber is a model of this art, which can finally only be cited—if not quite explained—as the working of an imagination fired by empathy of a kind so strong that it makes moral judgment at best a secondary consideration and gives first place to understanding.

Vladimir Nabokov claims that only dull readers identify with—which is to say put themselves in the place of and root for—characters in fiction. I tend to agree. If identify we must, let us identify with the author, poor fellow, and worry about how he is going to get himself out of the tight spots in his stories into which his imagination has put him.

Yet exceptions to this rule have to be made. No one—certainly no man—can long remain aloof from the chronicle of the decline and fall of "the ex-manager," as Dreiser frequently calls George Hurstwood. So strong is this chronicle that it threatens to take over the novel. Mencken, in 1911, wrote to Dreiser: "You strained (or perhaps even broke) the back of 'Sister Carrie' when you let Hurstwood lead you away from Carrie." James West, in *A Sister Carrie Portfolio*, notes that, in the abridged edition of the novel done for the English firm of William Heinemann, in which Dreiser was asked to condense the first 195 pages into roughly 90, but to keep intact the Hurstwood pages, *Sister Carrie* became "Hurstwood's book, and his tragedy dominates the narrative." Dreiser may have felt something of this himself, when he added what Thomas Riggio nicely calls "the ameliorative apostrophe to Carrie" that ends the 1900 edition of the novel, giving the last scene to Carrie rocking and thinking, instead of closing on Hurstwood's whispered cry from the heart.

The real slide begins when Hurstwood loses the saloon in New York in which he has had a one-third ownership. A cycle now begins in which depression joins with inertia, and pride invoked too late meets with the hardship of a national economic crisis. It begins with Hurstwood's finding the job-hunt painful, and ducking into hotel lobbies to take respite from it to read his newspaper. Soon he begins going out less, doing errands around the apartment instead. He claims winter is a bad time to look for a job. He wears old clothes around the house; gets a shave only once a week, guaranteeing his seediness. He ceases to share a bed with Carrie, who begins to question whether he is really looking for work at all. He begins to sense that he is out of the game. He bestirs himself to work as a scab during a trolley-car strike, but tells himself that it's "a dog's life and a tough thing to have to come to." Walking about the streets in which he knows no one, he begins hallucinating about the plush old days in Chicago.

After Carrie leaves him, Hurstwood's fall is more precipitate. Friendless in a great city, he knows himself outside the walls where gaiety and self-confidence reside and certain of never being allowed in. His money dribbles away, reducing him to sleeping in 15-cent-a-night rooms. He begins talking to himself in the streets, grows thin, crashes with pneumonia. After a stay at Bellevue, he becomes a beggar soldier in Coxey's Army. Life is reduced to getting something to eat, finding somewhere warm to sleep: his is now existence lived at the animal level. He walks the wintry street, as Dreiser writes, "begging, crying, losing track of his thoughts . . . as a mind decayed and disjointed is wont to do." It's this way, we now all sense, to the gas. "What's the use?" are his last words, and he's right—there is no use, because he no longer has any use, to himself or to anyone else. One is further brought up by this powerful scene when one recalls that, when he allows the gas to leak into his room, insuring his death, George Hurstwood is only forty-three years old.

Dreiser's portrait of Hurstwood on the way down provokes thoughts of the irrelevance, if not the complete negligibility, of a man when his economic power is gone. One thinks here of Pa Joad in Steinbeck's *The Grapes of Wrath*, who, out of work and out of luck, is a figure without force of significance in that novel, a novel whose hero is his wife. Hurstwood's fall in the world is paralleled by his fall in Carrie's opinion of him. Dreiser writes: "When a man, however passively, becomes an obstacle to the fulfillment of a woman's desires, he becomes an odious thing in her eyes,—or will, given enough time." This sounds at first blush a Marxian, or—if your taste favors a different sort of blatancy—a sexist, notion. But I suspect it is a truth of a deeper sort: a truth of human nature.

I say "suspect" because we have all been rendered nervous when it comes to talking about human nature. "The great characteristic of our time," wrote Ernest Becker, whom I cited earlier, "is that we know everything important about human nature that there is to know. Yet never has there been an age in which so little knowledge is securely possessed, so little a part of the common understanding. The reason is precisely the advance of specialization, the impossibility of making safe general statements, which has led to a general imbecility."

When one speaks of human nature one is of course speaking about human beings under the aspect of eternity, *sub specie aeternitatis*. Dreiser, we know, admired Balzac; in *Sister Carrie*, he has his stand-in Bob Ames suggest to Carrie that she read Balzac. Balzac's accomplishment was greater, more comprehensive, than Dreiser's. Balzac was much the smarter, the more savvy, man. Yet of the two novelists, Dreiser was the deeper. Balzac's underlying message is that Society wears a mask, which is to say, so, too, ought anyone who hopes to succeed in it. Dreiser came later in life to understand a fair amount about the wearing of public masks, but his deeper message was that in the human struggle . . . no message was to be found. True, the vaporous Bob Ames—Dreiser's one unconvincing character in this lengthy novel—tells Carrie that she must find a way to get outside herself as an artist, that she "can preserve and increase [her powers] longer by using them for others. The moment you forget their value to the world, and they cease to represent your own aspirations, they will begin to fade." But as messages go, that ain't much—if you want messages, better, as Samuel Goldwyn once suggested, go to Western Union.

Luck has dealt the characters in *Sister Carrie* difficult hands. They play them with what cunning is at their disposal. But, as Dreiser at one point says about Charlie Drouet, he (along with Dreiser's other characters) for the most part "bobbed about." The picture is that of human flotsam, bobbing upon a vast ocean of confused and unreflected-upon experience. Julian Markels, otherwise a generous critic of Dreiser's fiction, writes that his method works successfully only when the characters "are, so to speak, below the threshold of consciousness." I wonder. I prefer to think myself above that threshold, but here allow me to insert a brief personal anecdote that for me has long carried a heavy Dreiserian feel of my own destiny being quite out of my hands.

When I was an enlisted man in the U.S. Army at Fort Hood, Texas, in the late 1950s, I applied for a transfer, which I was pleased to discover went through. At headquarters a master-sergeant, whose long suits did not seem to be either patience or delicate repartee, announced with a scowl that I had a choice of going to either Shreveport, Louisiana, or Little Rock, Arkansas. "Which you want?" he asked, in a tone of voice two stages beyond the peremptory. I had, I realized, fewer than ten seconds to answer. Shreveport, being in Louisiana, suggested more in the way of enticing sin and rich food; Little Rock, not long before the scene of national racial tumult, was a few hundred miles closer to my home in Chicago, which finally seemed a compelling point. "Little Rock, Sergeant," I heard my voice say, and Little Rock it was.

Talk, as Dreiser does in connection with Carrie, about "unfolding fate." Attend, please, to mine. In Little Rock I met and married my first wife—of two—with whom I had two sons. I returned there after my military service, and made various connections, which, through the unpredictable concatenation of events, has led me to be writing this essay about the novel of a man for whom human destiny was perhaps the only interesting question. But what, I ask you, as I have asked myself till I have turned a Matisse-like blue in the cheeks, what if I had instead said, "Shreveport, Sergeant." Might I have had daughters instead of sons, or been killed in a honky-tonk bar in Plaquemines Parish, or gone to law school, or ended up Vice-President of the United States, or be writing an article on the importance of NATO?

"Dreiser's facts, which are our facts," as Julian Markels writes, "are still inscrutable," and then he adds that, since Dreiser's time, other writers have picked up "where Dreiser left off, trying to discover by their art the point at which emerges from the amoral drift of experience conditions under which we might honestly assume our responsibilities." I wonder yet again, for it seems to me that, over the past century, other novelists haven't advanced the ball all that far down the field. "The valuelessness of speculation in the face of certain patent facts," Dreiser writes in one of his authorly interjections in *Sister Carrie*, "is often one of the humorous phases of life. It has the quality of futility which is a fine ingredient of humor. . . . Many frequently imagine, when a change for the better takes place, that his reasoning has done it. As a matter of fact all such complications are largely modified by the inherent qualities of the things themselves. They change, and by exposing new phases give the watchful a chance. The strain of thinking has done little except keep the interested one in touch."

Toward the end of the novel, Bob Ames says to Carrie: "You and I, what are we? We don't know where we came from nor where we are going to. Tomorrow you might die and dissolve and I could search high and low in all the winds and waters and not find you." He ends by telling her that she has power as an actress, adding that its source, too, is without explanation, but that she must make the most of it. "Oh blind strivings of the human heart . . . ," writes Dreiser, in the penultimate chapter of the novel that gives us his final view of Carrie.

Brilliant achievement though Carrie Meeber is—she ranks, I think, with Emma Bovary and Anna Karenina and Isabel Archer, among the great heroines of literature—she is finally an unfinished character, and one wonders why Dreiser never thought to write a sequel to *Sister Carrie*, a subject with such great literary promise. Perhaps the disastrous commercial failure of the novel was too discouraging for him ever to think of returning to it, this piece of unfinished magnificent business. Henry James still had sixteen years to live when *Sister Carrie* was published in 1900; perhaps it would have taken a novelist of his subtlety to have picked up the baton and written *Sister Carrie, Part Two*. Such a novel might seem excruciatingly long, but not to all of us. Some of us, contemplating the prospect of such a book, might say, as Edith Wharton's friend Walter Berry reported to Proust he said whenever anyone asked him if he read Proust's novels, "Yes, but they have a grave defect; they are so short."

Marcel Proust, a novelist who may seem as far from Dreiser—in subject, sensibility, method—as anyone might conceive, in *The Guermantes Way*, the third volume to *The Search for Lost Time*, wrote: "By art alone we get out of ourselves, find out what another person sees of this universe which is not the same as ours. . . . Thanks to art, instead of seeing only one world, we see it multiplied, and we have as many different worlds at our disposal as there are original artists." Later in the same volume, Proust adds: "The greatness of true art . . . was to find, grasp, and bring out that reality which we live at a great distance from . . . that reality which we run the risk of dying without having known, and which is quite simply our own life. True life, life finally discovered and illuminated, is literature; that life which, in a sense, at every moment inhabits all men [and women] as well as the artist." *Sister Carrie* lives today, more than a hundred years after its first, far from properly appreciated appearance in the world, because Theodore Dreiser qualifies as one of Proust's "original artists" and because, through literature, he, too, "discovered and illuminated" true life in a way that still rings significantly, absolutely, dead-on true.

Nominated by The Hudson Review

HE WRITES TO THE SOUL

by CHRISTOPHER HOWELL

from NEW ORLEANS REVIEW

I'm just jotting this note so you won't forget
that though life is blue behind me and stony
in the instances I pause for, I have beads and shells
enough to hold back a sidelong toppling. Anyway,
at every crossing I kneel and say "excelsior"
and light a little fire in a jar and and drink it down,
hoping if fire's a prayer no one will answer it just yet.
But I guess that's clear. At first I thought I'd write you
about the hemp-trap roses that grow by collapsing
and bringing home whatever's trying to sniff them
at the time, about what that means. Then I thought
that's just peering at the innards of luck and no good
comes of such haruspicy. So I guess I'll give you
the news about the lake dark which is growing, too,
and just yesterday began working up into the sky
among softball and badminton of the angels.
Lucky they were already wearing headlamps
to bedazzle the fish up there! Lucky their suede rings
keep their hands afloat, otherwise who knows
how they'd copy down the braille God keeps sending
like flocks of perforated swans. Some good news is
the apple tornadoes are out of blossom now
and have become zinc, which as you know
says very little and requires practically no disaster.
That's what Mom says, anyway, and she should know.
She says she knows about you, too. She says

you are the shade of something folded and alone
on a long leash of red pearls. And that God
put you there because he couldn't help it.
But I don't know, I think you're somehow related
to this lake . . . like its language maybe, or like the idea
of swimming, which I've always enjoyed. Well, that's it,
I guess. Don't fret about my safety. If the weather
doesn't suck its trigger finger while it hunts for time,
or if something huge and golden lets me have its keys,
I'll be okay. Lake or no lake, some days I feel
perfectly disguised in front of you, like intention
around an iceberg or sunlight on the skin of the rain.
And I'm happy now, happy as a jungle, happy as a wisp
of dreaming melon, and I cry only on your days off.

Nominated by Henry Carlile, Michael Heffernan, Vern Rutsala

DANGEROUS DISCOVERIES

essay by MELANIE RAE THON

from FUGUE

Jᴜɴᴇ 29, 1999, Mother's birthday, and I am on my way to prison. For five years, I have been trying to understand the passion of a violent, tender boy—now this is where he leads me.

Norman Maclean is one of my heroes. At the age of 74, he devoted himself to the story of *Young Men and Fire*. His words guide me: "Unless we are willing to escape into sentimentality or fantasy, often the best we can do with catastrophes, even our own, is to find out exactly what happened and restore some of the missing parts."

My desire to restore the missing parts of Flint Zimmer's short and troubled life has compelled me to climb alone in the Black Hills of South Dakota and the Absaroka Mountains of Montana. I have visited nine Indian Reservations: Rosebud, Pine Ridge, Colville, Coeur d'Alene, Cheyenne, Flathead, Blackfeet, Nez Perce, Crow. Like Flint and his Métis ancestors, I have wandered, hungry. I've been charged by a buffalo bull, chased by mountain goats, and visited in my cabin by an auburn bear too starved to hibernate. Every vision of the journey brings revelation and a lost piece of the story: a mahogany piano crackles in flame; a rusted Pontiac Torpedo soars; five gray union suits fat with wind blow like headless men on a clothesline.

One cold March day in Indianapolis, I learn to shoot a Taurus 85 revolver and a 9 mm pistol. If sixteen-year-old Flint and his ten-year-old sister Cecile are going to handle these weapons, I believe I need to know them. Gary, my teacher, is a paraplegic in a wheelchair, a man wounded in a robbery when he was seventeen and working nights at a gas station. I fire his .357 Magnum, battering the chest of

441

the paper target. The noise scares me as much as the recoil. "What's to fear?" Gary says. "You just fired one of the baddest guns on the market, and nobody's dead or even wounded."

He speaks without irony. There is mystery at the center of every life, what cannot be explained or rendered in human language.

When Norman Maclean died at the age of 87, he believed his manuscript was unfinished—not because it was inadequate, but because its mysteries sustained his compassion and curiosity. On August 5, 1949, fifteen of the United States Forest Service's elite air-borne firefighters, the Smokejumpers, leaped from their small plane and parachuted to the edge of a remote blaze in Montana. They thought they were invincible. One hour later, twelve were dead or mortally burned.

White crosses on the hillside of Mann Gulch in the Gates of the Mountains north of Helena mark the places where each firefighter fell. The day Norman Maclean climbed the steep slope of Mann Gulch, he was almost 80 years old, and the heat at the bottom peaked at 130 degrees. Not a day of fire, just an ordinarily brutal day in August. Breathless and dehydrated, the old man felt his legs and lungs and heart failing him. He grabbed fistfuls of grass to pull himself to the top. He needed to follow each firefighter's path, to contemplate and imagine each one's separate suffering. He would not leave his young Smokejumpers until he was able to say: "If now the dead of this fire should awaken and I should be stopped beside a cross, I would no longer be nervous if asked the first and last question of life, How did it happen?"

I am not nearly so brave or noble. I want to be done with my novel, *Sweet Hearts*. I am ready to let Flint Zimmer and his family go: the deaf aunt who signs his story, the little sister who becomes his victim and accomplice. Like Flint's own mother, I am relieved whenever he is gone. With Flint locked up, we both feel safer.

I hope the visit to Montana State Prison in Deer Lodge is my last piece of research. I seek only physical details: walls and toilets and wires and rivers, cows and horses on the prison ranch, snow glittering high on distant mountains. Hawks, Kestrels, Pileated Woodpeckers, Dark-eyed Juncos, Warbling Vireos, and a hundred thieving Magpies will make Flint's arrival real.

In the High Security Unit, the chained man who is removed from his cage so that I can enter is not much older than the child in my story. He has stuffed his air vents with spitballs of toilet paper to

442

keep from freezing. The guard removes each tiny wad. I measure the white cinderblock cell, 12-foot lengths by 7. I read the graffiti: *Be Not Afraid. Jesus Rules.* I stare at the window that is not a window but a four-inch wide translucent slat.

In the Minimum Security Unit Library, I see the tiny prisons within the prison, a birdcage and aquarium. Three yellow-headed cockatiels are free for the day, one happy pair, and one recently widowed male. I'm told he cried constantly in the days after his partner died, until someone had the brilliant idea of giving him a mirror. He thinks his reflection is his mate. Now he sings and pecks at the glass. It is a metaphor too perfect to use in a novel.

Along every walkway, flowers bloom: poppies and columbines, bleeding hearts and petunias. The man who has planted them once kidnaped a female athlete. He wanted a strong wife for his son. Now, he is a gardener.

Inmates here do 45% of the state's Recording for the Blind and Dyslexic. Together, they have painted huge canvases of Montana's four seasons—not from sight, but from memory, and from their teacher's inspired descriptions. If they have not earned their high school diplomas, they go to class three hours a day. A teenager who murdered his teacher has become a model student. Felons wear caps and gowns. Some weep at graduation.

I think, Yes, there is hope for Flint here. There is the possibility that he will survive long enough to find solace for himself and begin to feel tenderness and sorrow for his victims. This is what we all need: long days of mercy in our own lives, hope, and freedom from pain, so that we have space in our hearts and minds to imagine another person's anguish.

But Flint's redemption and my own escape will not be this easy. Linda Moodry, my guide for the day, tells me that during the 1991 riot in Maximum Security, five Protective Custody inmates were murdered by other prisoners.

Norman Maclean is so close I hear him whisper: "If the storyteller thinks enough of storytelling to regard it as a calling, unlike a historian, he cannot turn from the sufferings of his characters. A storyteller, unlike a historian, must follow compassion wherever it leads him. He must be able to accompany his characters, even into smoke and fire, and bear witness to what they thought and felt even when they themselves no longer knew."

I have copied these words at least a dozen times in my own hand.

They are my prayer. They give me courage when I feel my own strength leave me. I consider the young men who risked their lives to fight a fire, and I envision the old man who climbed, weak and parched, risking his own life to tell their story. And though fidelity to the people of our fictions may seem less sacred than devotion to the quick and the dead, I believe every storyteller bears the same burden of responsibility. We make a covenant with the people we invent to serve and love them as honestly as possible, to bear witness to their lives without sentimentality or prejudice.

September 22, 1991, just one year after the boy I had come to know as Flint Zimmer entered Montana State Prison, the inmates held in Maximum Security broke through the cyclone fencing with their bare hands, shattered the plate glass glazing of the officers' cage, set mattresses and trash and clothes on fire to melt a hole in the Lexan shield, and gained access to every cell in the unit.

Four hours later, the Prison's Disturbance Control Team entered a maze of fire and fumes they described as hell. They meant it literally. Sprinklers worked, but the smoke evacuation system didn't. Electrical wiring fell into standing water. Any misstep here might mean death by electrocution. One Protective Custody inmate, anticipating the riot, had mixed a bucket of blood-red paint to splatter himself. While fellow prisoners beat him with their fists and prodded him with a broken mop handle, he held his breath and lay motionless. He was one of the lucky ones. In five other cells, the blood on the walls and floors and ceilings was real.

Norman Maclean is not my only teacher. Kate Braverman says that a writer needs the stamina of a channel swimmer and the faith of a fanatic. Mikal Gilmore must have thought he'd reached the limits of both during the years he explored *Shot in the Heart* and chose to expose himself to the ghosts and demons that had destroyed his parents and three older brothers. Long before I was fortunate enough to know Andre Dubus and learn from him as a person, his stories reminded me that everyone has his grief: the murderer knows despair; the rapist has been wounded. Goethe said, "There is no crime of which I cannot conceive myself guilty." In Frank Bidart's poem, "The War of Vaslav Nijinsky," the dancer confesses: "I know people's faults / because in my soul, / I HAVE COMMITTED THEM." I believe Andre Dubus was a man who understood this kind of intimate turmoil, the fear that his own impulses made him both vulnerable and dangerous, the conviction that a man who witnesses an act of violence

444

and does nothing is as much to blame as the one who commits it. Yet even he recalled a time when empathy eluded him.

Decades before Andre Dubus lost the use of his legs, he pushed a friend in a wheelchair to the crest of a hill. The man was agile and strong despite his paralysis. Later, when Andre thought of people in chairs, he conjured men like his friend: "Stouthearted folk wheeling fast on sidewalks, climbing curbs, and of course sometimes falling backward."

He didn't fully understand what that meant until a day over 20 years later when he fell backward in his own wheelchair, and his head slammed the floor, and he lay hurt and helpless. In "Song of Pity," he says: "I lacked the compassion and courage to imagine someone else's suffering." He never dared to think of his friend "making his bed, sitting on a toilet, sitting in a shower, dressing himself, preparing breakfast."

Sometimes the smallest details of another person's daily struggle threaten to destroy us. We avert our gaze because sympathy forces us to recognize the fragility of our human bodies and our human spirits.

When I learned of the riot, Norman Maclean's prayer to follow my people into smoke and fire became an exhortation. On my way to Deer Lodge, I thought I faced four weeks of revision. Returning to Kalispell, I realized I stood on the brink of six more months of immersion.

It was, I suppose, unnecessary work. Flint did not live in Maximum Security. He was not among the dead; he was not a killer. But I believed I could not know this boy, I could not love him fully, unless I too confronted the terror he must have felt when he learned what had happened. I needed to see the naked, barefoot prisoners beaten by guards as they ran a gauntlet of broken glass. I needed to learn how they lay facedown in No Man's Land for seven hours. Fierce with panic and perilously outnumbered, the guards could not determine who might be a victim and who a perpetrator. The sun blazed that day, and the night was cold, and still the prisoners lay, burned raw, but freezing.

In the novel, my description of the riot spans less than three pages, but should I meet Norman Maclean walking in the woods today, I will be able to answer him if he asks the most important question: *How did it happen?*

Andre Dubus once told me he prayed for me every day, and that when he did, an angel came and sat on my shoulder. The day he died, I was afraid of what might happen to me, how I would live without his faith and his protection. But Andre had more faith than even he fathomed. When he comes to me now, I am pushing his chair up a long hill on a cold, bright day in early winter. We will never reach the top. He speaks into the wind as we go—my friend, my fiery angel. If I try to go too fast, if he senses my impatience, he laughs. *Look at me,* he says. *I am your proof: there is no swift or easy way to gain the courage for compassion.*

Nominated by Michael Martone, Kim Barnes

IN THE CAFÉ

by GRACE SCHULMAN

from BARROW STREET and SHEEP MEADOW PRESS

Blue notes like words cry out to one another.
Harsh trumpet phrases, open-horn—like rage
dug into earth, then risen to huge tones—

vault the night air, and, muted, fall.
At bedtime, Father read a poem in Polish,
lines memorized and chanted. There were trumpets

and bells in his voice that held back the night
with wizard-talk I never understood,
words that told secrets, padlocks to pry open,

spells against the dark. My father learned them
from his brother, Jan, who cursed hunger in song,
and who was found at last on a dirt road

beaten, frozen, dead. Father fled Poland
and seldom spoke of Jan, but still I heard,
under his satin tones, Jan's mockery,

blue trumpet notes that sang to one another,
secrets that unfurled like silver waves
far out at sea. Then traveled closer, closer.

Nominated by Arthur Smith, Marilyn Hacker, Marianne Boruch, Jim Barnes

YANGBAN

fiction by JUNSE KIM

from ONTARIO REVIEW

M RS. CHA'S HUSBAND joked that it was her cooking that brought
the raccoon into their lives. In the spring she threw a Korean ban-
quet dinner party to celebrate her husband's retirement. All of Dr.
Cha's friends and co-workers came to the event, including their only
child, Bum-Jin, who brought a dark-skinned girl that Mrs. Cha and
her husband had never seen before and instantly disliked. It was
raining that night, hard as the early summer monsoons Mrs. Cha
grew up with in Korea. After the guests had left, she hand-washed
the dishes—Dr. Cha thought it a waste of money to buy a machine
for what could easily be done by a person—and went to throw away
the trash. Tiny pins of rain slanted into the lit circle from the garage's
floodlight as Mrs. Cha lifted the top off one of the two squat garbage
cans. She heard claws scraping against bark from the old elm tree behind her and turned. A raccoon was hunched down on all fours atop
a low hanging branch, its eyes brightly reflecting back at her through
the rain. Mrs. Cha was momentarily surprised but not scared; she
was fond of raccoons and their reputation for cleverness. More than
anything, she felt concern. The alley became a swift creek from the
storm's runoff and Mrs. Cha imagined the raccoon being swept away
by the rising current. She was about to tell the raccoon to stay in the
tree where it was safer, but then thought it a ridiculous thing to do
and silently returned to the house.

It was still lightly drizzling the next morning when Mrs. Cha went
to put the linens in the laundry and found the basement flooded. It
was the first time that it had ever happened. All of the Chas' boxed-
up keepsakes were immersed. Mrs. Cha began to scoop up the flood

water with an old, dented bucket she had refused to throw away through the many moves to new houses they had made, and dumped the water into the utility sink next to the washer. Dr. Cha went through the boxes, trying to salvage what he could. Most of the ruined items should have been discarded years ago, except for one, a shoe box of letters Mrs. Cha received from her family in Taegu when she first moved to Chicago. Surprisingly, she felt no remorse when she told her husband to place them in the garbage pile.

They put the casualties of the flood into trash bags and carried them out, but in the alley they found their rusty trash cans knocked over, bags ripped open. On the muddied asphalt were sparerib bones stripped clean, translucent noodles that were once chap chae, and napa cabbage chewed to the stem from what was a hunk of kimchee. Mrs. Cha knew the raccoon was the culprit and told her husband. The next morning, they found white fish skeletons ripped apart and the skin of a rotten persimmon on display in the alley. Dr. Cha said it was a compliment to her culinary skills—even as garbage her food was delicious. From then on, a variety of other dishes were scattered about, depending on what Mrs. Cha had cooked the previous evening.

In the beginning, it was Dr. Cha who cleaned up the mess. Mrs. Cha would often see his stocky torso through the kitchen window bent over as he tidied the area. Mrs. Cha thought perhaps in his retirement he wanted to show that he could help her do housework like he never did while making a living, show that he could pitch in like his American colleagues would do at home. For whatever his reason, it pleased her. She took it as a sign of appreciation. But as the weeks went by and the raccoon continued to enjoy the meals that she had made, Dr. Cha began cursing the raccoon while cleaning up the eggshells, soup bones, and orange rinds it had left, loud enough for Mrs. Cha to hear inside the house. Then he would storm back into the kitchen. As he washed his meaty fingers streaked with dirt and food, he would yell out how undignified that he, not just a doctor but a man whose traced pedigree to the Koryo dynasty put him into the aristocratic class of Yangban, had to clean up after an American rodent. Mrs. Cha heard the same over and over, *Yangban* this, *Yangban* that, always culminating in his disgust at having his Yangban ancestors watch him perform this lowly work.

Lowly work? The phrase stayed with Mrs. Cha and it came back to her every time she wiped down the counter in the corner of the kitchen.

Weeks later, after a few loud minutes in the alley, he stomped back into the house, said he didn't feel well, and asked her to collect the trash. Eventually he didn't bother to begin the cleaning that he knew she would finish, and he would lie down on the couch or get into the car and go to the driving range.

Though it was an annoyance to add another item to Mrs. Cha's long list of chores, she knew that she did not have the right to complain. If Mrs. Cha had written her parents and told them how she felt, she could hear them say how her husband was entitled to leisure in his retirement after working so hard all these years to support the family. So she kept her mouth shut and let these feelings collect and rise inside of her, wondering if she would become so full that one day they would eventually spill out of her mouth.

In the early autumn, the tree next to the garage succumbed to Dutch elm disease. Around that time Mrs. Cha had become as fed up with the raccoon as her husband had been. What made it worse was the fact that Dr. Cha was rarely at home. She couldn't tell the difference between life before his retirement and after. Every time she went to the alley to pick up the trash, she grew angrier knowing that he was off playing golf or attending another meeting at the Midwest Radiology Forum, a medical association that he recently joined. Why he wanted to continue the life he had retired from was a mystery to Mrs. Cha. She thought that they would be spending more time together, but nothing had changed. She continued to dust, vacuum, crush garlic, and wait and wait and wait until her husband returned home.

It had been such a long time since she felt like a wife. She needed two hands to count the months since the last time he touched places on her body that were only offered to him. Maybe these were things that she should tell him, she thought. Then she decided not to. He was her husband, he should know how she felt. He should know.

Mrs. Cha decided to take action on the raccoon problem by herself and bought a metal garbage can. It was large enough to hold a week's worth of garbage and it had a sturdy screw top lid. Since Dr. Cha was such a frugal man, she did not tell him of its very expensive price until it was too late to return it.

From then on, a metal clang could be heard late in the evening; and the following morning, the trash can would be found knocked over with its lid secured tight. Eventually, the garbage can was left undisturbed by the nightly visitor. No longer bothered by the raccoon's presence, Mrs. Cha busied herself with anything she could. She watched cooking shows and prepared meals that were more complex than ever before; she re-organized the eleven family photo albums and wrote accompanying captions for each picture; and she began to wipe down every surface in the house on a daily schedule instead of weekly. It didn't matter how elaborate the chore or project, just as long as it helped pass the time during her husband's growing absence.

It was now October and the first frost had come. Mrs. Cha sat with her husband on their large heated mat. Their wide-screen TV was, as usual, set to the Korean station. This was the first time in a month that she spent a relaxing afternoon with him, and though she enjoyed just being together, she wanted to say something about her increasing unhappiness. But who was she to tell him that she was unhappy? She thought of the ceaseless praise and envy she received from friends and family in the letters from Korea that were ruined in the flood months earlier. Mrs. Cha always understood that to them, her life in America was a dream come true. She married a successful radiologist who grew up in Seoul; they had a grown son who lived close by; and they owned a four-bedroom, interior-decorated house more luxurious than any of the homes her family members lived in. From these facts, Mrs. Cha's parents and sister had gauged her a success. Yet, how could she tell them that this wasn't what she wanted when she came to America? That her life was not a great journey across an ocean but one immersed within it, the water's pull forever preventing her from taking breath.

The TV program showed a grown son leaving his parents at the airport gate and walking down the runway smiling, excited at his job posting in Los Angeles. She too remembered how she was full of excitement when she first came to the States. She had defied her parents and accepted a fellowship to a small liberal arts college in Chicago, borrowing money from aunts and uncles for the plane ticket. She left because she didn't want her married sister's life, one where the most challenging weekly task was to haggle at the vegetable market. She thought herself above that. The arrogance she once had! Then a year passed and she still hadn't improved speaking the new language that she could easily read and write. She had been known as the class clown back in Korea, but without the ability to communicate, she couldn't even crack a joke. She desperately wanted to join the other girls in their circle of laughter before each class started. One time she approached them in the cafeteria and made a quip about the food. The girls responded by tilting their heads and giving courteous and confused smiles. She didn't bother repeating the joke and walked out of the cafeteria.

On her twenty-third birthday she went to study in the library alone after finding her mailbox empty. She tried not to think of how alone she felt as she sat down amidst the students at the long oak table, but it was hopeless. She broke down and cried in front of everyone. People came over to her, asking if she was all right. She couldn't even find the words to express her loneliness. Hopefully the young man on the television wouldn't have to experience what she had. How happy he now looked. She hoped the show would let him meet someone soon after his arrival.

When Mrs. Cha first met her husband, it had been a year and a half since she had arrived in the States. She was waiting for the El at the Addison Street station when an Asian man walked up to her. It was a wet April morning, and at first she could only see his polished black shoes and brown wool slacks from underneath her umbrella. He asked her in Korean if she was from Seoul. She felt comforted in the simple act of speaking her own language. They went out for dinner the following evening, and she became enamored with him—it was the first time anyone had ever bought her flowers. And though she would never admit it, for her, speaking Korean with him felt better than receiving the flowers. She was almost beginning to feel like herself again.

Like her own father, he was a man of tradition. Over dinner, he talked about his family background as if it were more important than himself. He was the type of man that she never would have married back in Korea—full of pride and touting the importance of familial roles—yet in America she found this familiarity surprisingly comforting. Against her expectations, they were wed. Now she sees in the years that have passed—after moving several times to larger and larger houses, after giving birth to their son and watching him grow up, after waiting for her husband to finally retire—she had been slowly sinking back to the loneliness she had felt when she first arrived. Would the young man on the television have a similar fate? She hoped not. As the scene on the television changed to the young man's parents crying in the airport, a soft patter of claws came down

452

from above. The sound skittered back and forth and the thump thump thump of tiny feet resonated in the room like an irregular heartbeat.

Dr. Cha poked his head through the attic trapdoor and then called Bum-Jin. Mrs. Cha heard the flat cadence of authority in her husband's voice when he told Bum-Jin to drive the twenty minutes from where he lived in the city to their house. She immediately began to prepare more food for dinner.

Bum-Jin, who preferred to be called B.J., would always listen to his father. Mrs. Cha knew that. With all of the Confucian ideology instilled in him from his upbringing—the filial piety, the Yangban integrity—B.J. had little choice but to obey. And how B.J. tried to rebel! Usually directing his rage at her. As a child, he threw tantrums when he didn't want to eat the Korean meal she had made for dinner; as a teenager, he cruelly mimicked back her reprimands for piercing his ear, or striping his hair, or coming home too late. He wasn't a bad-natured boy, he just found it difficult when life didn't go his way. She knew this part of his personality came from her, so she tried to be lenient with her punishment: five minutes facing the corner when he was young, a day's grounding when he was too old for the corner. But no matter how old her son was, it always took her husband's intervention for B.J. to accept her discipline. It seemed the men in her family were the only ones who had voices that could be heard.

Dr. Cha had already set a ladder under the attic's trapdoor by the time B.J. arrived. B.J. ran upstairs and almost bumped into Mrs. Cha at the top where she was on all fours with the dented bucket and a damp rag—the only way to get *all* the dust and dirt off the floor. Mrs. Cha looked up, feeling perspiration on her face and down her thin neck. Her son nodded a greeting. She silently pointed at her husband next to the ladder and resumed cleaning the floor.

"Check up there," Dr. Cha said to B.J.

Mrs. Cha saw her son pull himself up through the trapdoor, his legs dangling for a second before he disappeared above. A switch clicked and then light shone down on her husband and the ladder. Mrs. Cha kneeled on the outskirts of the light and dreamily dunked the rag into the bucket. She pictured the attic bulb shining over the boxes of expensive toys they had bought for B.J. as a child and never

453

thrown away. Save them for his children, Dr. Cha insisted to her. At fifty-eight she always imagined herself to have at least one grandchild. She was supposed to be like her husband and wish for a grandson in order to carry on the Yangban line. For Mrs. Cha, a girl would be preferable. This wishing was useless, though, since B.J. refused to come to her church and meet the young women in the congregation. They were all Korean-Americans, just like him, except they spoke the language.

"Ya, Bum-Jin," called his father.

"There's no raccoon up here," yelled their son. "Only a small hole in the corner."

B.J. made a temporary repair with nails and a piece of plywood that Dr. Cha had saved from a remodeling done to the house twelve years before. Mrs. Cha went to the kitchen to check on dinner. She dwelled on how she could get B.J. to church. Thanksgiving wasn't that far away, and she knew she could convince her husband that they should go as a family. Once his mind was set, B.J. would be obliged. As B.J. went to the basement to put away the ladder, she pondered on which girl she would introduce to him first.

"Dinner is ready," called out Mrs. Cha as B.J. came back up.

"Sorry, Mom. Can't stay. I have other plans," said B.J. He walked to the coat closet.

"*Muh-heh?*"

"I'm going out. A date."

"*Day-te?*" Mrs. Cha stood rigid in a directed silence. She breathed deep and loud through her nostrils. B.J. put on his brown leather jacket and zipped it up, seemingly oblivious to his mother. "With *that girl.*"

Mrs. Cha knew her son would go out with girls, but never before had he been with the same one for so long. It sparked an anger within that she didn't know existed. The bile in her voice brought her husband out from the living room.

"*Muh?*" said Dr. Cha.

"It's nothing, Dad. I just told Mom I had plans. I'm cooking dinner for Anisa tonight," said B.J.

"*The Mexican?*" said Dr. Cha.

"Dad, she's Persian. And please don't speak as if attacking her," said B.J. in an exemplary civil tone. He wrapped a cashmere scarf around his neck.

"She looks Mexican."

"And what if she was from Mexico? You and Mom and me could pass as Japanese and Chinese to other people. It doesn't affect who we are." Mrs. Cha was surprised to hear B.J. speak back to his father.

"Pah! You know nothing," muttered Dr. Cha. Mrs. Cha could hear her husband's nationalism in his voice. She began predicting his often heard diatribe before the words left his mouth. "We do not look like *those* people. We are Korean, and more so, we are Yangban. *Jungmal Yangban.*" Yangban, Yangban, always something with Yangban. "If you understood this, you would know that *we* do not look like others. You would know that a Yangban does not cook, or do any other women's work." Women's work? She did not expect that phrase.

B.J. stood as quiet as before with his mother, but now paying attention to his father. Dr. Cha took B.J.'s arm and gently guided him to the living room.

"Dad, I have to go."

"Come and sit. Just listen." Dr. Cha's voice was soft and easy and held the same weight as an order, so B.J. obeyed.

Mrs. Cha followed them. She was even more upset now. Never before had her son defended a girl he went out with. And it was bad enough to endure her presence at the retirement party, but to hear about their *friendly* outings every week made Mrs. Cha afraid. She wanted this dark-skinned girl to disappear. Mrs. Cha never thought she would care who her son dated, as long as she was a nice girl. Then as she grew older, she saw things more like her husband, but for different reasons. She didn't share her husband's sense of lineage purity; she wanted B.J. to marry a Korean because of a fear of being forgotten. She pictured her grandchildren, half-Korean, then her great grandchildren, then their children, from quarter to eighth to sixteenth until inevitably the Korean part of her descendants would be diminished to a point where no trace of her could be found.

B.J. and Dr. Cha sat down on the couch and Mrs. Cha took the ottoman.

"How long have you been seeing this girl?" asked Dr. Cha.

"She has a name, you know." Mrs. Cha was shocked that B.J. continued to speak to his father this way. What had gotten into him?

"How long?"

"Six months."

"That is a long time. Do you want to marry her?"

"Dad, we're just dating. It's no big deal. Jesus, all I'm doing tonight is cooking dinner, not proposing."

"Don't use the Lord's name in vain," interjected Mrs. Cha.

"*You* are cooking dinner? Not her?" asked Dr. Cha.

"Yes."

"Bum-Jin, you have to understand that the American saying is true: It's a man's world." Dr. Cha nodded in agreement with himself. "It's a man's world."

"Actually, Dad, I think that's exactly what's wrong with it."

"It *is* a man's world, and you always must remember that. It is the man who passes down the family name. When you meet someone you like, you should think of who would be a good mother and wife, see what her family history is like. I know you're young, and it's fun for you to be with girls who you think are pretty or interesting. But for marriage, think about someone who understands and appreciates how hard you work to support her. Then she will happily cook and clean for the family. Think about your children. How nice it would be for them to look like you and your parents. It's better that way. Your mother and I know. We were once like you."

Mrs. Cha quietly sat, listening to her husband's speech, looking out the window at the emptiness of night where she thought she heard God's creatures rustling tree limbs as if a storm were brewing somewhere. Man's world? Those words and the tone in which her husband spoke them brought back a memory. Soon after they were married, her husband's father visited from Seoul, and one day she heard them talking in hushed tones while she prepared dinner. Her curiosity led her to the living room doorway. She didn't think what she was doing was wrong; she could still watch the simmering pot of kimchee jigae from across the kitchen, she reasoned. She couldn't hear well through the door, but she believes herself certain that they were talking about the wedding. Her husband's father lectured that marriage is for companionship, affairs are for love.

"I'll think about it, Dad," said B.J.

The next week the Chas hired a professional roofing company to repair the hole in the eaves properly. Sometimes, when coming home from an errand during the day and walking from the garage to the house, Mrs. Cha would see the raccoon hanging over the roof, scratching at the repaired hole. From a distance, she thought the raccoon looked cute, a child-bandit trying to gain entry to a safe haven, and whenever she saw it she would stick her index finger in the air, shake it side to side and say, as if to an infant, "No no no, you can't come in." But like her son, the raccoon didn't listen to her.

On the first Friday in November, while Mrs. Cha was wiping the floor next to her neglected bucket, she heard wood cracking from somewhere in the house. Or maybe it was outside? She put on her son's old Wisconsin Badgers windbreaker and went out into the gray autumn afternoon. She circled the house, looking under the eaves. The red coat blew against her like an oversized house dress, and she wondered if there was any part of her that could be found in her son's thick body that resembled his father's so much. She rounded the last corner and at the end, right next to where she started, she saw a new hole, larger than the last.

Her husband swore at the American rodent for the extra repair fee he would have to pay. Since his son was away for a long weekend with *his friend*, he told Mrs. Cha to call the town's animal control department to get rid of the raccoon.

"We don't handle any animals when they're in your house. It's a city ordinance," said the voice to Mrs. Cha through the cordless phone. "It's your responsibility. What we can do is rent you a trap for a hundred forty-five dollars and then you would have to deal with the creature. Just catch it, then drive five miles out and release it. Or pay us fifty bucks and we'll drive it out. I'd like to help, but like I said, it's not our job."

When she told her husband what they had said, he cursed the raccoon again and called the roofers; they could chase it out before repairing the damage if it was still there, though Dr. Cha failed to mention it to them over the phone.

Her husband had left to speak at a doctor's conference in Minnesota the day after the roofing company repaired the hole in the water damaged eaves for a second time. Three hundred fifty dollars, same price as before. Dr. Cha was livid at the expense incurred because of the raccoon while Mrs. Cha quietly wrung her rag into the bucket, relieved to have her house free from the intruder. Relief was not what she felt this day, though, as she attempted to take a nap on the couch. Her son had called that morning and explained how Anisa had won two tickets to Paris in a raffle and that he would not be coming home for Thanksgiving dinner. She didn't say anything back to

457

him over the phone, letting the gap in conversation voice her disappointment, but he quickly said good-bye and hung up before the silence could speak her words. Two days until Thanksgiving and this coal-eyed girl was taking her son away from the family dinner and probably making him touch her the way only a husband should a wife. She grew angrier at this thought and shut her eyes tighter. She hoped that B.J. at least felt some sort of love for this girl and she for him, that there was some meaning behind their actions. Then she thought, if she had followed this advice herself, perhaps she would not have married nor had a child. And what if this girl had true feelings for her son? Was that such a bad thing? Why would a mother deny her son that? To love out of attraction instead of necessity. She knew that if her husband were here, he wouldn't have let their son go. But where was he? Again, away for work. And he doesn't even have a job anymore! She didn't understand why he wanted to be away. A clean house and a warm meal were always waiting for him, but why clean or cook if he is rarely home? A man's world, he had said, and it made her feel helpless. A *man's* world.

Mrs. Cha turned onto her side and opened her eyes. She sensed a scattering of dust particles on the floor, imperceptible to her eyes, but they were there, they were always there. Her husband was arriving the next day and she knew she should fetch the pail and begin cleaning the house again—rag in hand, dunked over and over, her fingers puckered for hours from the water. Something sank within Mrs. Cha and she remained lying on the couch. She turned on the television and watched a family gossip about relatives. They were eating a meal similar to what she had served for her husband's retirement party. Mrs. Cha found comfort in the fact that this took place in the country that she once called home, spoken in a language that had never become foreign to her.

A slow creak from above brought Mrs. Cha out of her nostalgia. Then she heard the snapping of wood. Mrs. Cha ignored the noise and turned up the volume on the TV. The sound of scratching clawed steps on the wooden rafters traveled down the chimney and out from the fireplace next to the television. Mrs. Cha raised the volume higher, hoping the family gossip could drown out the proof that the creature had, once again, broken into her home.

Dr. Cha usually came back from business trips in good cheer and an overabundance of affection, but there was no affection of any sort

458

after Mrs. Cha told him of the raccoon's return and his son's departure. He immediately called the animal control department himself. That night, the eve of Thanksgiving, Mrs. Cha watched her husband climb up into the attic and set the trap.

They decided not to cook the turkey the next day. Thanksgiving was more for their son than for themselves, and it seemed wrong for an incomplete family to eat a traditional family meal. What was there to be thankful for in that?

Instead, Mrs. Cha warmed up leftover kimchee jigae. The phone rang as they sat down to eat. Dr. Cha began eating from his bowl, so Mrs. Cha got up and answered. It was B.J. calling from Paris. Mrs. Cha cheerfully greeted him. He wished them a happy Thanksgiving, and she listened to his light, smooth voice, similar to her own. She was in the middle of asking about his trip when Dr. Cha snatched the phone from her. She tried to grab it back but he shooed her away sweeping the air with his hand. He raised his index finger as if telling her to wait, and then she saw him say, "Ya, Bum-Jin. What is more important, your family or an affair? You should know the difference." Then he hung up on their son.

Without saying a word he returned to the table, but in her mind's eye, her husband's finger still hung in the air, pointing at her to keep away, denying her wish to speak to her son. Her own son! She walked back to the table and slowly sat down. She picked up the spoon and her fingertips turned red from squeezing it so hard. She wanted to speak out against her husband, say something, at least one word to voice herself.

Just then the sound of grating metal came down upon them.

The raccoon was now caught.

Dr. Cha carries the cage down from the attic. The cage is made of thin metal bars that are spaced wide enough for the raccoon to bite Dr. Cha, but the raccoon sits stiff and unmoving. Mrs. Cha believes it is frozen from fright. The raccoon is on its hind legs and Mrs. Cha says that it looks like a baby in a costume. Dr. Cha ignores his wife's comment, tells her to get a bucket and follow him, and quickly takes the cage outside and to the garage. *Eight hundred forty-five dollars wasted on this animal*, is what Dr. Cha calls out in Korean to her as he puts down the trapped raccoon. He opens the garage door. *Eight hundred forty-five dollars and no more.* He pulls the car out onto the driveway and then carries the huge trash can into the garage.

Mrs. Cha is behind him, empty bucket in hand. Through the garage door, she sees dusk turning into night and smells a faint smoldering scent, somewhere between burning leaves and melting rubber. Her husband slams the metal can on the cement floor, unscrews the top, and throws the garbage bags out of it. *What are you doing?* she asks her husband. He is silent as he places the cage inside the garbage can and takes the bucket from her. Into the darkness of the yard he disappears. She hears the splash of water from the garden spigot as it hits the bucket. He enters the garage, walks straight to the garbage can, and splashes the water into it. The raccoon cries, a high-pitched squeal. Mrs. Cha stands against the wall and sees the garbage can shimmy, then jerk, and she hears the raccoon panting beneath the sounds of the rattling cage and scraping cement. She hasn't noticed her husband has left until he returns with another full bucket.

Yoboh, she calls out, spouse, wanting to stop him. He ignores her and turns the bucket upside down over the garbage can. The water drops down and the raccoon screams louder. He walks out again before she can say anything.

She steps towards the can and sees the raccoon standing on its hind legs, thigh high in water, its body hunched forward, its arms crossed in front like a scared child. Her husband returns and the water sloshes through the metal bars as he empties the bucket again. The raccoon's fur is now completely matted down, revealing the frail body beneath its luxurious coat. Its shrill cries turn into deep, helpless moans. She no longer thinks the raccoon looks like a child, it must be older for it to make such a sorrowful noise. She turns to say something to her husband but he is already outside. The water level is at the raccoon's chest. She fears the next bucket will raise the level above the raccoon's head.

Yoboh, she says as her husband returns with the bucket dripping from the sides. *We should stop this. We have to drive it away.*

What! Drive it away? I have to pay money for it to come into my home uninvited, and now you want me to drive it around town so it can return again? he says, his voice rising above the raccoon's moans. He brings the spilling bucket up. *That is foolish.* He throws the water down into the can. *And a Yangban is never a fool.*

The raccoon goes under but the top of the cage is still above the water. Two claws, like little hands, reach out, grab the cage's narrow bars and pull the raccoon up. The raccoon crushes its wet, furred face against the bars, its nose barely poking above the water level. The moans are even louder, the sound wavering in the raccoon's quick, sharp breaths.

For almost a thousand dollars, he continues in the stern tone often used with their son, *I want to make sure this is done right.* She opens her mouth and tries to say something to make him stop, but falls silent as his posture turns stiff and challenging. He pushes the bucket out to her and says, *Fill this up.*

The bucket hangs from his hand between them and she turns to look at the raccoon. The image is too disturbing for her. She stares into the empty bucket for a moment before taking it from her husband.

She walks outside to the spigot. The water swirls inside the pail and she becomes dizzy wondering what kind of person could kill a defenseless animal. Her arms strain under the weight of the bucket as it fills with more than enough water to drown the raccoon. She turns off the spigot and returns to the garage as she was told.

The moans become louder the closer she gets to the garage. She wonders if the community can hear this. What are they thinking? Will they call the police? Come out and investigate? Or keep their eyes averted and mouths shut as she has? She walks in and sets the pail next to him.

He stands motionless, watching the animal struggle. She thinks that his face no longer holds the anger it did moments ago, perhaps he's moved by the raccoon's pain. She tries to reach him and again says, *Yoboh*. He turns, irritated, and shushes her. She shuts her mouth as he reaches down and picks up the old pail—older than their son, she suddenly thinks. She watches him tentatively hold it over the raccoon. What kind of *man* would kill a defenseless animal? What would that man's world be like? The raccoon is now softly whimpering, the sounds come gurgling out as small bubbles at the water's surface from the corners of its mouth. As she thinks he is about to pour, he pulls the bucket back. He puts it down.

She exhales deeply.

Let's go, he says.

Let's go? Her heart feels trapped in a small box. She watches the raccoon's claws slide off the bars and quickly regrip. Its face bobs under for a moment; then is pulled up. An open eye presses against the grate and a tiny pink tongue sticks out, panting.

Leave it alone, he tells her as he picks up the screw top lid.

Why?

It will be over by tomorrow. We don't have to watch.

We can't leave the raccoon like this, it's torture, she says, her voice becoming as loud as his. *If you can't do it, then pay the animal control people to take it away.*

Do you think I'm a fool? he yells back. *Do you think we could live this well if I paid everyone to do things I can do myself? All you women don't know the value of money, think that I can spend it like water for whatever you want.* She listens and understands, finally accepting what a man's world means to her husband. He holds the garbage can lid out to her. *Put this on the can and go inside the house.* She hears him, but instead she listens to the cries of the raccoon calling for release.

Let's go, he says again, as if she has no option.

Then she feels it in her throat, the thing she wants to say to her husband, and she feels her mouth open again. *You,* she says, drawing the word out as long as she can, her voice strong and direct, and she knows the one word she could never think of before and yells it out as if mocking a coward, *Yangban?*

He stands shocked for a moment, and then begins to shout at her, his free hand chopping the air in front of her face. She ignores him. All she can hear is the raccoon pleading for freedom. She reaches down. Her arms are tired from carrying the bucket across the yard, but she finds enough strength in bitterness to lift the load. She looks down at the trapped creature and whispers a quick prayer.

She pours.

The water level slowly begins to rise, from the bottom of the raccoon's mouth, then up the length of its nose. Gradually it envelops the entire snout and the raccoon begins to thrash out at the bars above, slow motion in water. Her husband attempts to stop her, but she blocks his reach with her back. *Stop,* he yells. *Stop it!* Even from under the surface, the raccoon's cry seems louder than her husband's; and soon the last bubbles of air from the raccoon's lungs come floating up; yet still, the water level continues to rise, higher, higher, until the bucket finally drips empty.

Nominated by H. E. Francis, Ontario Review

from THE LIGHTNING FIELD

by CAROL MOLDAW

from CHICAGO REVIEW

5.

Your mind unkinks itself like carded wool
as one foot steps in front of the other, circling
the five-foot figure-eight infinity loop,
painted on tarmac at the beach's edge
in Bolinas. Soon, like a Himalayan ascetic,
you've walked yourself into a waking trance,
not breaking pace for any passerby
who cuts into your path, only asking a man
to move his motorcycle when he begins
to park it where one end of the eight loops back.
You've heard that if you soften a silkworm's cocoon
with water, a continuous thread of silk
will unravel for a thousand yards, and think
the spool a spider draws from must be endlessly
self-renewing, her many spinnerets
producing thread as her design requires.
You keep walking. With each successive loop,
you are being unwound and reconfigured,
a skein of slub silk crisscrossed between thumb
and little finger of an outstretched palm.
Weavers call this bundling a butterfly.

On your way home, a brood of Monarchs hovers
over a field of purple milkweed, roosting.
But one moment you could put your finger on?
There were no omens, only unread signs.

8.

I had thought the rectangle of steel shafts
would feel imposed upon the pristine landscape,
an arbitrary post-modern conceit
spoiling the view. But once inside the matrix,
surrounded by the austere expanse, the sleek
sparsely planted forest of tempered poles
fanning out and lofting above me, I found
that the field's exactingly strict geometry
yielded not just jackrabbits, lizards,
blue-winged moths, gilia, and grasshoppers
flinging themselves against my face, but also
a sense of seemingly endless possibility.
Pacing the distance between adjacent poles,
from one vertex to the next we stopped to plot
a makeshift constellation's coordinates,
our footsteps connecting points like dashes to dots
in a child's draw-by-number book of stars.
That no pole stands at the rectangle's center
makes mathematical sense (it's not a square)
but came as a surprise. I kept count
under my breath, though the farther in we got
the more they blurred together at the far verge.
Midway between the two most central poles
was only a scuffed clod of desert scrub—
an omphalos among the obelisks.

14.

Walking back, as if an axis had gone slack,
we didn't feel that geometric pull
on where we stood and which way we proceeded;
let loose, we were free to cut across the field,
to circumvent the poles, to stop counting.

The meticulously placed pre-fabricated poles
had come to seem as natural as the cholla
and locoweed the wind sowed here and there.
We barely noticed them, as we wandered out,
we'd grown so used to their enigmatic presence,
and reaching the field's edge we stepped beyond it
without a twinge, before we even knew.
Then, on the porch landing, we turned to look.
It must have been the angle of the sun
that made them practically invisible,
consumed by light the way an echo will
consume a sound, and silence consume an echo,
and yet in the air they reverberated still,
a soundless echo of their solid selves,
staves of a faded score—not wholly lost,
not like one of Bach's cantatas being wrapped
around the roots of a transplanted sapling,
or greased and folded up to hold a measure
of grain, the paper scarcer, of more worth
to his widow sold as paper than as song.

15.

Indelible as the potter's smudged thumbprint
on a carbon-dated thousand-year-old shard;
as the silk route traced back to a shred of silk
plaited in an Egyptian mummy's hair;
as a leaf-shaped lime burn scarring a left wrist;
as Cossack hooves heard from inside a cold oven—
while to someone else the rain brings back nights
of caged silkworms chewing on mulberry leaves,
and for me, walking the city's gridded blocks,
tears that didn't fall but never stopped
sounding inside me. Until all at once they did
stop, leaving an exquisite quiet,
and the air clear. As after a lightning storm,
when the sky's electrical balance is restored,
billions upon billions of electrons having swarmed
earthward, through a channel five times as hot
as the sun. As my friend described the bodiless voice

it could not have been more emphatic or distinct:
"Not one breath, not one heartbeat, is your own."
After that, he never took psilocybin again,
and began keeping his Covenant with God.
Before searching the sky for Hyakutake,
first I trained my binoculars on you.
In the desert, your eyes must be strong as stone.
But come, close them now, rest them in this dark.

Nominated by Jacqueline Osherow, Martha Collins, Chicago Review

JINX

fiction by AIMEE BENDER

from BRIDGE

TWO TEENAGERS WERE STANDING on a street corner. They were both wearing the hot new pants and both had great new butts, discovered on their bodies, a gift from the god of time, boom, a butt. Shiny and nice.

They did not like their butts.

One was complaining to the other that she thought her butt was more heart than bubble and that she wanted bubble and her friend said she thought heart was the best and they stood there on the street corner pressing the little silver nub that changed the mean red hand to the friendly walking man and the light did not change.

One friend had breasts, the other was waiting.

When the light changed, they both walked to the poster store where the cute boy worked. He was growing so fast he slept fourteen hours a day and when he came to work he had a stooped look like he'd been lifting large objects for hours and in fact there was some truth in that, he'd been unfurling his body up through his spine, up through itself. Each day people looked shorter and today these two cute girls—the one he liked with the ponytail bobbing, the other one that touched his elbow which he liked too—they were there again looking in the glass case at the skull rings and joking.

The boy showed them a new poster of a rock-and-roll star in a ripped shirt on a stage with a big wide open mouth that you could fall into. The girls, at the same time, said they thought it was gross. Jinx! They laughed endlessly. Too much tonsil, said one and she grunted in such a way that made them laugh for another ten minutes. It was that sixteen year old laugh that is like a stream of bubbles but makes

467

everyone else feel stupid and left out. Which is part of its point. The boy got a break halfway through the time they were there and one girl said she wanted to look at the posters one by one, flipping those big plastic lined poster holders, because she liked to stare at her own pace, and the other girl, ponytail, went out back with the growing boy, rapidly notching out another vertebrae right as they spoke, straightening higher like a snake head rising from an egg. They went out back so he could smoke a cigarette and she smoked it with him and when touchy girl finished flipping through the leather pants women and the leather pants men and looked for her friend, she couldn't find her and wandered out of the store by herself.

Ponytail girl leaned over and she and the tall boy kissed and it was carcinogen gums and magical.

She liked to kiss in public, so that if someone had a movie camera she could show people. See.

The other girl, now called Cathy, was on the street alone, looking for her friend who was out back with ash on her lips pushing lips against ash, using her tongue in all the different interesting ways she could think of, her breasts rising.

Cathy, teenager, out on the street alone.

This is so rare. This moment is rare. This teenage girl out on the shopping street alone: rare. She walked by herself, eyes swooping side to side, looking for the bobbing blur of her friend, Tina's, pony-tail, but Tina was not to be seen, not even in the dressing room of the cute clothes store next door where they'd recently tried on skirts made of almost plastic that were so short they reminded you of wrist bands.

Tina now had his hands on her waist, thinking of that exact skirt right as Cathy walked by it, thinking how it had held in her butt and if she was wearing that plastic skirt now, and he held her butt, it would remind him of a bubble, not a heart. I do not want guys to feel my butt and think of hearts, she said to herself, that is too weird.

Cathy walked to the corner. She thought did Tina leave? She thought she'd head back to the poster store but she sat down on a bench instead and when the bus came she just took it. She looked at the people on the bus and no one was looking at her except some creepy old man at the front with those weird deep cuffs on his pants and the seat was cold and Tina was somewhere left out in the stores and would they miss each other? Did she miss Tina? Oh, she thought, probably not. And this was her stop and she got off and

468

walked home, and it was hours too early, they were supposed to be at a movie and when she went inside her mother was sitting there on the couch looking at the backyard. It was like the whole afternoon had got a haircut that was too short. She sat with her mom, making sure the backyard stayed put, which it did, and when her mom fell asleep it all seemed disgusting and this was what happened in the afternoon and she went and looked at herself in the mirror for an hour and felt terrible even though she liked the pose of her left profile best.

And Tina, done with kissing, done with skull rings—the boy settled back behind the counter after waiting two minutes, counting, to tame his erection—Tina was walking the streets and asking people if they'd seen a girl with a great yellow shirt on. No one had, they thought she meant some older woman but Tina said no no, and she started to cry on the street because she thought the worst thing, but when she called on the phone just to see, just in case, the most familiar numbers in the world, Cathy answered. Hello? Tina forgot how to talk for a second, she was so surprised, and then she just said Oh. Oh? Hi. Cathy? Tina? Hi? The two girls bumped around the conversation for a few minutes, but for the first time in life, they didn't know what to say to each other. After awhile they just said goodbye and hung up. From then on at school they tended to be friendly but distant and awkwardly found other people to sit with at lunch. By graduation day, three years later, they had forgotten each other's phone numbers completely, even though they hugged in their caps and gowns and tassels for old times sake and said good luck, keep in touch, have a hot summer, later.

Nominated by Bernard Cooper, Bridge

AUTUMN IN THE YARD WE PLANTED

by ELLEN BRYANT VOIGT

from PLOUGHSHARES

Whoever said that I should count on mind?
Think it through, think it up—now that I know so much,
what's left to think is the unthinkable.

And the will has grown too tired to stamp its foot.
It sings a vapid song, it dithers and mopes,
it takes its basket to the marketplace,
like a schoolgirl in her best dress, and watches
others ask outright for what they want—
how do they know what they want?—and haul it away,
the sweet, the dull, the useless, and the dear.

A maudlin, whimpering song: in which I lament
my own children, scything their separate paths
into the field, one with steady strokes,
one in a rage. We taught them that. And,
not to look back: at the apple tree, first
to shatter its petals onto the clipped grass,
or the blowsy heads of the russet peonies,

or even that late-to-arrive pastel, all stalk
with a few staggered blossoms, meadow rue—
though surely they could see it from where they are.

Nominated by C.E. Poverman, Linda Bierds, Andrew Hudgins, Marianne Boruch

THE INSTRUCTOR

fiction by JOYCE CAROL OATES

from SALMAGUNDI

1.

SHE WOULD LONG REMEMBER: she'd taken no notice of him at first.

Kethy, Arno C. One of thirty-two names on the computer print-out. After the name was an asterisk and at the bottom of the page the asterisk was decoded: Special Student, Night Division. But most of the students enrolled in Composition 101 were in the Night Division of the university. They were all adults; some were conspicuously older than their twenty-seven-year-old instructor E. Schegloff who was a petite, smiling, tense woman looking much younger than her age. Her voice was husky and tremulous. "I realize that my name—Schegloff—" she pronounced it slowly, as a spondee, "—is difficult to pronounce and yet more difficult to spell, but please try. Any reasonable approximation will do." Was this meant to be humor? A few of the more alert, sociable students in the class laughed appreciatively while the rest sat staring at her.

Erma Schegloff would wonder afterward, with a stab of chagrin, if *Kethy, Arno C.* had been one of those staring at her in silence.

I am not what I appear to be! I am so much more.

To be a young woman of hardly more than five feet in height, weighing less than one hundred pounds, is a disadvantage like disfigurement. Erma Schegloff's size had always seemed to her a rebuke to her ambitions and pretensions. Hadn't her parents reproached her years ago when she'd told them she hoped to teach? *You! You're not strong enough! Too shy! Used to stammer!* She wore leather boots

471

with a medium heel to give her a little height and a little authority. Temporary height and spurious authority, but wasn't that often the case, in civilization? Her face was a striking, sculpted face like a cameo; plain and fierce as that likeness of Emily Dickinson, waif-woman with a secret, implacable will. Erma parted her fine dark wavy hair severely in the center of her head, Dickinson-style, and brushed it back and plaited it into a single thick bristling braid like a pony's mane thumping between her delicate shoulder blades. Her eyes were large and intelligent and inclined, when she was excited or nervous, to mist over. In the early morning, walking in the cold to the university swimming pool a quarter-mile from her rented apartment, Erma brushed repeatedly at her eyes, which wept without her volition; tears threatened to freeze on her cheeks. She wore no makeup and there were times when her pale skin glowed, or glared, as if she'd been scrubbing it with steel wool to abrade its predominant, feminine features. She had a dread of her male students gazing upon her with sexual interest, or indeed with any interest other than the academic.

Please respect me! I must succeed with you, I can't fail.

Erma Schegloff was a poet, though not writing poetry at the present time, an emotionally complicated time in her life; she was, more practicably, a Renaissance scholar, completing a Ph.D. with a dissertation on seventeenth-century visionary poetry (John Donne, Richard Crashaw, Henry Vaughan, George Herbert) at the elite main campus of the state university sixty miles away. She'd applied for this modestly paying teaching position because, she told her friends, she needed the money: she was helping to support her aging, ailing parents back in Pennsylvania. She'd wanted to test herself outside the rarified atmosphere of a graduate program of seminars and endless research projects. She'd wanted to become *adult*.

That first evening, her voice quavering with drama, Erma read the class list for Composition 101, enunciating the names (and what unusual names) with care; as if she were reading not a miscellany of sounds but a mysterious surrealist poem. She was young and romantic enough to believe it must mean something that these strangers, enrolled seemingly by chance in a remedial writing course, had been assigned to her, E. Schegloff, and would be in her care for twelve weeks. She meant to teach them everything she knew! *Brielli, Joseph. DeVega, Alban. Hampas, Felice. Eldridge, E.G. Hasty, Lorett V.* As she read off these names she glanced about the room, smiling and nodding as individuals murmured "Here" or "Yes, ma'am" or shyly raised their hands in silence. The classroom was oddly proportioned, wider than it was deep, with a high ceiling of hammered tin peeling pale green paint; antiquated fluorescent tubing hummed, as in a clinical setting; there was a faint hollow echo. *Inglas, Sylvan. Jabovli, Nada. Kethy, Arno C. Marmon, Andre. Poak, Simon. Portas, Marta. Prinzler, Carole.* And so to the end of the alphabetized list. An incantatory poem! But she'd taken no special notice of *Kethy, Arno C.*

Except, several hours later, in her apartment, restless still from the excitement of her first class, Erma began to read through the papers her students had written in response to an impromptu assignment— "Who Am I? A Self-Portrait in Words"—and was stunned by the unknown Kethy's composition.

WHO AM I

First thing is when your on Death Row long enough you dont ask WHO AM I becuse you have learnt nobody would be there anyway. And not seeing any face in the mirrer (because there is no mirrer trusted to you) you accept not having a face and so could be anybody.

I would say I saw you before tonight. Not knowing your name till now. INSTRUCTOR E. SCHEGLOFF. You were a beacon to me. You were shinning all that time.

On Death Row where Id been condemned like an animal I swear the face I would see was yours. Not that long ago—5 weeks, 16 days. You were a sign MISS SCHEG-LOFF that my luck would change. There was a lockup thru the facility (Edgarstown) becuse thered been trouble earlier. (Not on Death Row I mean, we were in our cells.) 1 hour of 24 for outdoor exercise.

Next day a guard took me to Visitors. Hed handcuffed my wrists tight to give pain. They hope for you to beg but I never did. He took me to Visitors. My lawyer was there I had not seen in a long time. Your conviction is overturned

473

he says. I am not even sitting down yet, I tell him God damn I knew I was innocent. I tried to tell you all *eight years.*

It was your face E. SCHEGLOFF I beleive I saw in my cell that day. You knew me though I did not (yet) know you. You were saying, Arno dont give up hope. Arno, I am awaiting you. Never give up hope thats a sin.

But, I did not die. Its absolute truth I was innocent all those years. That was my plea.

Erma read and reread this composition. Indeed, it didn't seem like a composition, composed, but a plea from the heart; as if Arno Kethy were in the room with her, speaking to her. She'd begun to breathe quickly. She tried to recall Kethy from class: a smiling youngish black man with a pencil-thin mustache, at the back of the room? Or a blunt-faced Caucasian, in his late thirties, in black T-shirt and soiled work pants, hair in a pony-tail? In the last row, by a window? She seemed to recall how when she'd called his name, this man had raised his hand furtively, only a few inches, and quickly lowered it, wordless.

Kethy had written his self-portrait in a tight, cramped hand on a single sheet of lined tablet paper. His sentences ran out to the edges of the paper. The letters of his words were clearly formed and yet the words were so crowded together, the effect was claustrophobic, crazed. That voice! Erma set the paper aside, shaken.

How different Kethy was from his fellow students:

Hello! My name is Carole Prinzler and I am 32 years old. Returning to school now that my youngest is started school (at last) and I have a chance to breath now and then! My hope is to improve my writing skills and acquire work in Public Relations.

My name is Dave Spanos, 29 years old. I am a Post Office employee (downtown branch). I am a born resident of this city. I am also enrolled in Intro. to Computers (Wed. night). I am hoping to improve my skills to "upgrade" my

474

statis at the P.O. where I have been selling stamps for 7 years at the counter. Though I enjoy such work, for I like people . . .

There was Eldridge, E.G., a round gleaming butterball of a black man in his fifties who wore a suit and tie and gave off a powerful fragrance of cologne. Turning his self-portrait in to Erma, he'd shaken her hand vigorously.

> May I itroduce myself, I am the REVEREND E.G. EL-DRIDGE of the Disciples of Jesus Christ. I am a proud resident of this city and of the City of God. I am a father of nine children and eleven grandchildren and a husband of many years. I am blessed with good health and a desire to improve my fellow man. Already you have given us faith, Miss Schegloff, with your opening words that we will write, write, and write like pratising a musical instrument—PRACTISE MAKES PREFERT.

Erma set these aside, and reread Arno C. Kethy's composition. What did he mean, he'd seen her face? In his cell? She smiled nervously. But it wasn't funny, of course. Kethy was serious. (She didn't want to consider he might be mentally unbalanced.) Why not interpret such extravagant thinking as poetry of a kind? Poetry in prose. A stranger's anguished yet intimate voice.

I seem to know him, too.

She smiled. Her heart was beating quickly. For the spring term she'd rented the cramped, austerely furnished upstairs of a rundown Victorian house near the university hospital grounds; the sound of sirens frequently filled the air, a wild, yearning cry that grew louder and louder and ceased abruptly, like lovers' cries. To hear, as a neutral observer, is to feel both involved and excluded. Erma wondered at the prospect before her. An unwilling witness to crises she couldn't control. But her landlady had assured Erma that she'd get used to the sirens—"We all have."

That night, she woke repeatedly hearing a man's yearning voice mixed with the sound of sirens real or imagined. Sitting up, not knowing at first where she was, Erma was panicked that someone might have broken into the apartment. But there was silence. Not even a siren.

On the door to her three-room apartment, as on the downstairs front door to the house, there was a reassuring Yale lock. And she could bolt her door, too, when she was inside.

Thursday evening, her second class, E. Schegloff resisted the impulse to look for *Kethy, Arno C.*

E. Schegloff, Instructor. What a mystery that, as soon as she stepped inside the classroom, her nervousness began to lift. Since Tuesday night she'd been anticipating this moment. *Too shy! Used to stammer! Remember how you'd cry!* But now, in the busyness of the classroom, so many faces, all that faded. Erma knew she had helpful information to impart and she knew, from their self-portraits, that these adults were motivated to learn. They were not adolescents of the kind enrolled as undergraduates in the daytime university. These were adults with responsibilities. They had full-time jobs, and families; some were divorced with children; some were newly naturalized American citizens; a few were retired; a few were mysteriously afflicted (a woman with multiple sclerosis in remission, an ex-Marine "legally blind" in one eye). Their common hope was that Composition 101 taught by E. Schegloff would somehow improve their lives. Erma's Ph.D. advisor had expressed concern that such elementary teaching would exhaust her and delay the completion of her dissertation; her intelligence and her sensibility were too refined, he feared, for remedial English; she was destined to be a university professor and a poet. Erma had been flattered but unswayed. She'd risked the man's disapproval by pressing ahead anyway and taking the job, without apology. Years before, Erma's parents had tried to discourage her from moving to the Midwest, a thousand miles from home, as if such a move were a personal betrayal. (Which possibly, in the secrecy of Erma's heart, it was.) But Erma was a young woman with a quiet, implacable will. *My life is my own. You'll see!*

Midway in the class Erma handed back the students' self-portraits and asked for volunteers to read their work aloud, which induced a flurry of excitement and drama. On their papers she'd commented in detail, but without grading. (She dreaded the prospect of grading! How do you grade adult men and women who've spilled their guts to you, in utter trust?) When she handed back Arno Kethy's paper she was shocked to see, rising stiffly from his seat at the rear of the room, coming reluctantly forward, a scowling man in his late thirties with a sunken, shadowed face and downturned eyes. His face was mysteriously ruined as if stitched-together, a mass of scars. Razor scars, acne? His voice was an embarrassed mumble—"Thank you, ma'am." In his self-portrait he'd spoken of Erma Schegloff's face as a beacon of light and it seemed now he might be blinded by her, approaching her, refusing to meet her gaze, even as Erma smiled forcefully, determined to behave as normally as possible. She'd rehearsed this moment but Kethy took the paper from her fingers with no further acknowledgment, folding it at once, turning away and lurching back to his desk like an agitated child. So this was *Kethy, Arno C.* Not the handsome black man with the thin moustache who smiled at her so readily during class, but the Caucasian with the slovenly ponytail straggling down his back. He was tall but limp-boned like a snake gliding on its tail. His greasy hair was receding at the crown of his head, a coarse gingery-gray. His jaws had a steely unshaven glint. His eyes were evasive, in bruised, hollowed sockets. Yet he wore a cheaply stylish sport coat of simulated suede, fawn-colored, that gave him an incongruous sexy swagger; beneath it a black T-shirt with the logo of an obscene grinning skull out of whose mouth a floppy pink tongue protruded. A man who'd spent eight years of his life on Death Row, and might have been executed . . .

Erma wondered if others could sense the intensity of emotion, the tension, in Kethy's body. It seemed to radiate from his pallid skin like waves of electricity.

Kethy returned to his seat without having looked the instructor in the face. His mouth was twitching. Erma steadfastly looked away. She'd planned to say to him Mr. *Kethy . . . Arno? . . . this is very strong, compelling writing . . . If you'd like to speak with me after class . . .* but the words stuck in her throat.

At the end of the class, as a number of students gathered around the instructor wanting to talk to her, Arno Kethy left quickly by a rear exit. Erma saw that he didn't glance back at her, nor was he walking with any of the others. A loner. A very strange man. Erma was light-headed with exhaustion after the lengthy class but determined to speak with the students as if she were delighted they wanted to speak with her. Later she would wonder if she'd been disappointed in the ex-convict's eccentric behavior, or relieved that he'd kept his distance from her.

Erma had made a photocopy of Kethy's self-portrait, and her detailed comments on it, for safe-keeping. She was eager to see what he might write next. (Or did she halfway hope he might drop the course?) When a friend from graduate school called to ask how her first week of teaching had gone, Erma said vehemently, "I love it. I mean—I've never had such an experience before." She could not have said what these tremulous words meant.

You were a beacon to me. E. SCHEGLOFF.
Your face I beleive I saw.

In her office on the third floor of Greer Hall, at a temporarily assigned desk, Erma glanced up at a hesitant knock on the opened door, or a murmured approximation of her name. But, through the remainder of January, it was never Arno Kethy.

Because she was only an adjunct instructor with a single-term contract, Erma Schegloff had no permanent office. She shared a battered aluminum desk, large and vaguely military in appearance, like a tank, with two or three other instructors who taught at other times, and whom she never saw. The desk drawers were stuffed with old, yellowed papers by students long since vanished, syllabi and memos and university print-outs. She'd neatly taped to a water-stained wall a reproduction of a beautifully austere painting by Georgia O'Keeffe— a steer's skull floating in a pellucid-blue sky. *Only just a coincidence, its resemblance to Kethy's ugly T-shirt.* On sagging bookshelves in the office, crammed and untidy, were aged books abandoned by their owners; hardcovers, paperbacks, textbooks, outdated dictionaries and university directories. On the uneven floor was a grimy carpet faded to the color of dishwater by the sun which, on clear days, flooded the office through a ceiling-high, ill-fitting window. The room smelled of dust, mouse droppings, forlorn desires. Lost or worn-out hope. Above the door, confronting Erma as she sat at the desk, was an old-fashioned clock that was not only no longer functioning but had somehow lost its minute hand.

Except that Erma's office was three steep flights up from her classroom in the basement of Greer Hall, and therefore discouraging to visitors, she liked it very much. *My first office! Until I'm expelled.* She hadn't had a particularly happy childhood back in Erie, Pennsylvania amid a family of older brothers but she often recalled random moments when she'd stepped into an unexpected, magical space, indoors or out, but usually in, a space mysteriously waiting for her; for her alone; warm and dazzling with light. And even if the space was small, she felt a sense of amplitude. And this office was large, even cavernous; especially at night, when the windowpanes reflected only the interior.

Instructors in the Night Division were required to keep two office hours a week, preferably before each class, and Erma's was 6 PM to 7 PM Tuesdays and Thursdays; but she'd added an extra hour each evening, following class, for she wanted to give her students every opportunity to meet with her. "Come see me, please. I'll be in my office upstairs." After her initial euphoria over their self-portraits, Erma had come to a more realistic assessment of their writing skills. Two-thirds of the class performed at about the eighth-grade level, a few were virtually illiterate. And there were two or three, in addition to Arno Kethy, who weren't turning in any work at all, for what motive Erma didn't know.

Yet she was feeling optimistic. Reckless!

A mysterious strength suffused her days and even her nights. She rose, in the dark, at 6:30 A.M. to swim in the university pool, amid strangers; she spent hours each day at her scholarly work in the university library and in her apartment; she prepared diligently for Composition 101, choosing exemplary essays from their text to teach and scanning newspapers and magazines for clippings to bring to her students of good, forceful writing. She loved her solitude. She was never lonely. *So physically lonely! Of that, I can't speak.* In fact she'd come to this aging post-industrial city on a famously polluted river partly to put distance between herself and a man for whom she'd felt a complex of emotions and she was discovering (contrary to what poetic sentiment might suggest) that the blunt fact of distance, sixty snowswept miles of interstate highway and monotonous, level countryside, was a remedy. Far from the intellectual and cultural center of the state, at the university's main campus, Erma felt like a renegade from a proper, approved life. She felt illicit, and renewed.

Not a man to be pushed, obviously. He's suffered.

Arno Kethy had not handed in the next two assignments ("description of a setting," "description of an action or process") and he'd offered Erma no excuse. She was determined not to call him to account, just yet. She would wait another week or so, before asking to speak with him privately.

Am I afraid of him?

479

I am not!

Those eyes. Wounded, haunted. Ever-shifting. Fixed upon the instructor covertly, hidden behind his raised, big-knuckled hands.

Often in the library, in the midst of researching the myriad religious schisms of the vanished seventeenth century, Erma found herself thinking of *Kethy, Arno C.* His deformed-seeming yet swaggering body. His ravaged face. And those eyes. He was standing in the cheap stylish coat and black T-shirt, not before her, but at the periphery of her vision, like an imperfectly recalled dream. His behavior was a riddle she would one day solve.

In the meantime she'd become a true teacher. An instructor. She was discovering the very real satisfactions of teaching motivated adults who yearn to know skills elemental to the lives they envision leading; not luxury skills of an affluent civilization, but skills of necessity. How impassioned Erma Schegloff felt, speaking to her students: "Many of you have these skills by instinct, and now you'll be formalizing them. You'll be revising your papers for me which means you'll be steadily improving. That's our goal!" Strange and wonderful, Erma's students seemed to believe her. They seemed to like her. They must have forgiven her her youth and inexperience and were beginning to appreciate her oblique sense of humor. (Did Arno Kethy smile at her jokes? Erma didn't dare look.) Other adjuncts in the Night Division warned Erma not to spend too much time on her course, these were low-paying, dead-end jobs in the university, but Erma thought stubbornly what was too much time when you were crucially involved with others? "They need me. Someone like me. Who will help them, and not judge harshly."

Since she'd become an instructor, it seemed to her that the flaws of her personality, as she saw them—shyness, self-consciousness, insecurity, an excessive concern with detail and precision—evaporated as soon as she stepped into the classroom. As soon as her students saw her. As if the humming flickering fluorescent lights of the undistinguished room had the power to magically transform her.

She was determined that Arno Kethy would not distract her. No one would have guessed (Kethy himself could not have guessed) that she was aware of him at all. The fact that he slouched in his seat at the back of the room, staring fixedly at her. She told herself *That man is on my side.* In three weeks Kethy hadn't missed a single class but he never participated in the frequently lively discussion. So far as

Erma could gather he shunned all contact with his fellow students. (As they shunned contact with him.) Often, as Erma spoke, he began to scribble rapidly in his notebook. He was left-handed, and writing involved some contortion of his body. *A man imprisoned in a tight space.* Her heart welled with pity for him.

She meant to commiserate with Arno Kethy when at last he spoke with her. She rehearsed her words, even her facial expressions. She would be quietly sympathetic, she would urge him to speak. If he wanted to speak. She would say nothing (of course) about his fantasy of her; his conviction that he'd somehow known her before meeting her. *Arno don't give up hope. Arno I am awaiting you.* She couldn't help but wonder how close he'd come to being executed. Months, weeks? She believed that, in time, he would tell her.

And she wondered what he'd done, or had been wrongly convicted of doing, to warrant a death sentence. It could only have been murder. Murders. In this Midwestern state executions had been rare for decades but were being reinstated under a Republican governor and legislature. Erma had made inquiries and learned that the state no longer electrocuted men but killed them by lethal injection.

Yet when class ended at 8:15 PM, Arno Kethy left abruptly. He didn't drift forward to speak with her, nor even to say goodnight like the others. There he was gathering up his duffel bag, shrugging on an overcoat that looked too large for him, and with a practiced gesture flicking his gingery-gray hair over his collar. He departed swiftly by the rear exit. Erma saw how others moved out of his way.

He can't be judged by ordinary standards. A man who has survived Death Row.

One night in early February, Erma was in her office after her last student left. It was nearly 9:30 PM. Greer Hall felt deserted as a mausoleum. She'd had conferences with several students, one of them the ebullient charmer Reverend Eldridge, and now she was alone, and realized that the corridor outside her office was unlighted. She felt the first tinge of concern, preparing to leave. During the preceding hour a custodian had been working in the main corridor, perpendicular to this corridor; when he'd finished he had evidently switched out all the lights on the floor, assuming everyone had left for the night.

So Erma stood hesitantly in her office doorway. The overhead light in her office was still on; the switch was near the door. Some distance away, perhaps fifty feet, was a dimly-lighted stairwell that led off the main corridor of Greer Hall. This was the stairwell she would take when she left; her car was parked close by, just behind the building. Heavy double doors with inserted windows divided the stairway from the corridor so that light falling back into the corridor was murky; between Erma's office and the stairwell was an alarming darkness. Erma could barely make out the walls. There were office doors, bulletin boards, a drinking fountain, a custodian's closet, all lost in darkness. Erma swallowed hard. She didn't know Greer Hall well enough yet to remember where the light switch for her corridor was, though she assumed it must be near the double doors. On this large urban campus there were frequent assaults and attempted assaults against students, especially lone women; Erma knew this was a risky situation. She could telephone one of the university proctors, as they were called, to come escort her to her car . . . "God damn! I won't be intimidated." Asking for help when there was no discernible danger would only underscore a woman's weakness. Erma Schegloff's weakness.

What Erma might do: leave her office door open so that she could see into the corridor for a few yards, make her way quickly to the light switch (if she could locate it); turn on the lights, and return to her office to darken it and lock the door, behaving with caution, though if anyone were waiting to attack her it wouldn't make much difference except of course she could see her assailant, and could scream, and screaming might scare him off . . . But yes, it would make a difference: lights would discourage an assailant even if no one else was in Greer Hall. A sane, reasonable assailant.

Erma's mind was racing. She heard her own quickened breath.

She decided against such over-scrupulosity. The building was absolutely silent. There could be no one here. She switched off her office light and shut the door, acting as if the corridor were adequately lighted, not pitch-black, and she wasn't terrified. She could see the stairwell ahead, dimly. She had only to get there. She wouldn't run, for she might collide with something and hurt herself. She walked like a blind woman, groping one hand against the wall. *Breathe naturally. Like swimming. Inhale on a stroke, exhale in the water. Don't inhale water!* She was reminded of the numerous times her brother Lyle had lain in wait for her . . . She pushed away all thoughts of Lyle, they were inappropriate here, never did she think of Lyle any longer, or the others, she was no longer the trapped girl who'd had to

482

think of Lyle, and of her family. By the time she got to the stairwell her heart was beating so rapidly she felt faint. But she got there, safely. Clearly no one was waiting for her. Erma pushed through the double doors with a smile of relief, and there, squatting on the stairway landing, smoking a cigarette, like a nightmare figure calmly coming to life, was the stitched-faced, pony-tailed Arno Kethy.

Erma screamed. She'd never been so frightened in her life.

Stammering, "W-What—what do you want—" knowing Kethy was there for her, unable to pretend in the crisis of the moment that he was not; that this was an accidental encounter. Kethy rose out of his crouch at once. How tall he was, towering over Erma. He was a nocturnal creature blinded by light. He muttered something Erma couldn't decipher, turning away from her and running down the stairs.

She was faint with shock. She leaned against the railing weakly. Listening to a man's footsteps echoing in the dim-lit stairwell until he was out of the building, and gone.

2.

"He's mad."

But was it so simple? Could she dismiss him, and what he represented, with a blunt, ugly term?

ASSIGNMENT #2: DESCREPTION

Descreption of Edgarstown Death Row.
The cell measures 6 feet 11 inches by 9 feet.
There is the cot. The toliet. The locked door.
There is the air which you have breathed and fouled
and must breath again. Or suffocate.

There is the concrete-block wall which is
one wall on three sides.

First, you are in the cell. Then, the cell
is in you. If I shut my eyes (like now)
I am there. When sleeping, I am there.
But every time words are put to it,
they are not the exact words.

483

This descreption has been writen so many times.
I would say that I have failed.

They say that there are grounds for suing,
for false incarceration. But to recall that other time
(before Edgarstown Death Row) you would have to be
that other person again. But he is gone.

I confessed to what they said was done,
for I did not know certainly that I had not done it.
Later it was known to me, I was INNOCENT.
I was 31 yrs old when put like an animal in a cage.

He was #DY4889- But that person is gone.
They sliced his face with a razor.
He could not look to see the wounds. But,
he could feel with his fingers.
What you try to descrebe, a long time later,
the words are false.

E. SCHEGLOFF your name is please understand
I was not born a beast. I said I was INNOCENT
and they laughed. Thats what a beast
always says they told me.

If I hurt those people I was said to hurt,
there would be a memory of their blood,
I believe. But it is my own blood I remember.
Your face told me, always have hope.
I had no knowledge of how you would be waiting.

Descreption of Room #417 Greer Hall.

It is three times larger than a cell on Death Row.
There is a smell of mildue and time here.
The window is very high, to the cieling.
The panes do not fit well. There is leakage.
The desk is a large one, and old.
There are bookshelfs with many books looking
    old and used.

There is a swivil chair behind the desk.
The Instructor E. SCHEGLOFF is seated in this chair.
The Instructor E. SCHEGLOFF shares this desk with
    other instructors.
There is a skull in a blue sky on the wall!
The Instructor E. SCHEGLOFF put this picture
    the wall. Reaching to above her head, and
    her hands trembled with the strain.
I did not have a tape to measure the room but believe
    it is maybe 20 feet by 30.
And the cieling maybe 12 feet high.
There is an overhead light and a light on the
    desk.
The clock above the door is broken, the hour hand gone.
It is strang to see a clock broken in that way.
You look at it a long time wondering, what is wrong.
When the Instructor remains here late the windowpanes
    darken. You cant see outside.
When the Instructor remains here late there is danger.
A woman by herself is in danger. In danger of beasts.

I would protect E. SCHEGLOFF I promise.
I believe I am summoned for that purpose.
Her face I could not see in my cell clearly.
It is a very beautiful face like an angels.

Seeing you then at your desk when you did not see
me (and your hair like mine!) I wanted to say
I would protect you I promise forever.
I wanted to say I am not a beast
for if even my hands did what they said,
which I believe was not so,
I did not give up HOPE.

Erma read Arno Kethy's "Descreption" several times. She was in a
haze of alarm and sympathy. Surely the man was mentally unbalanced, and yet . . . "He's speaking from the heart. He isn't stopping to
think how it must sound." She was alone in the bedroom of her small
apartment, it was midnight. That morning in the pool she'd gotten
chlorine in her eyes and through the long day her eyes had been

485

stinging and watering and it was difficult for her to read Kethy's small cramped words, crowded and urgent, on a lined sheet of tablet paper without margins.

Erma was upset, that Kethy had somehow watched her at her desk in Greer Hall. He'd certainly been waiting for her in the stairwell. To protect her? *Summoned for that purpose.*

She knew she should show Kethy's compositions to someone else. The program director in the Night Division. "But he trusts me. I can't betray him."

Erma was agitated, on her feet to stare at herself in the oval mirror of her bureau beside the bed. *Your hair like mine!* She plucked at the braid, quickly unraveling strands of hair. From now on, she would wear her hair loose. Better yet, she would get it cut. How could Kethy imagine her hair resembled his! Her cheeks burned with the insult.

Beutiful face like an angels.

Arno Kethy was in love with Erma Schegloff. Was that it?

"But he doesn't know me. It's his delusion."

Arno Kethy was stalking her. In the guise of protecting her.

Yet truly he believed he was protecting her. He would not wish (Erma was certain) to harm her.

(Or was this, Erma wondered, a delusion of her own? To be so convinced.)

He'd known that evening that Greer Hall was deserted and Erma's corridor was darkened and he'd remained after their class, to protect her. In case there was danger, she needed him.

Seeing herself as in a hallucinatory flash pushing again through the double doors into the stairwell and there was that figure of nightmare Arno Kethy with his stitched-looking face and staring eyes, squatting on the landing and smoking a cigarette. *I beleive I am summoned.*

"He might have hurt me then, if he wanted. We were alone."

The incident had happened on a Tuesday night. On Thursday, Kethy handed in the second assignment, "Descreption." It was weeks late. He'd passed it up to the instructor, several times folded, by way of another student. When Erma received it, she saw Kethy slouched in his seat, as if hiding; his ropey-muscled forearms lifted to shield his face. Since the other night, they were known to each other. There was the connection between them, irrevocable. He'd seen her face, her terror of him she'd tried to hide. She'd seen his face, the shock and adoration in his eyes. During class, as she taught, Erma was aware of Kethy as she hadn't been previously. While speaking she lost the train of her thought several times and noticed students looking at her quizzically.

It was midwinter malaise on the campus. Many students had flu. She was disheartened, a little. Seven students of thirty-two were absent that night.

When class ended, Erma didn't go upstairs to her office. She could not. She remained in the classroom to speak with those several students who'd arranged for conferences with her. "This will save us all a hike up those stairs. Those steep stairs." When she left the building in the company of another student, a woman, she had the idea that Kethy might be close by, watching.

You see? I don't need you to protect me.

But that night, in her apartment, the door locked and bolted and the telephone off the hook (in case her former lover should call, for he'd been calling, late, several times that week) and no sirens to interrupt her solitude, Erma read and reread Arno Kethy's "Descreption" and could not decide: was it a voice of madness, or a voice of radiant insight? Might the two be conjoined?

Nor could she decide if it was a declaration of love, or a subtle threat.

A woman by herself is in danger. In danger of beasts.

She wondered what would happen if her former lover drove to see her. As she'd forbidden him. If Arno Kethy saw them together.

She went to bed, turned off the light, at 2 AM. Though knowing she couldn't sleep. In this unfamiliar bed, in this unfamiliar place. She shut her eyes. There was Kethy, squatting. Gazing at her with hurt, hopeful eyes. And in the swimming pool. Was that why her eyes had been bleeding all day? *Glimmering of a pony-tailed man in the pool's choppy aqua water in the instant before Erma Schegloff drew breath, to dive in.*

These were snowy blinding-bright Midwestern days. Flat land, enormous sky. Erma's eyes wept behind dark glasses.

She was remembering (she hated remembering!) how back in Erie, Pennsylvania, in the squat ugly asphalt-sided house near the railroad tracks where she'd lived a captive for eighteen years, her parents, sullen and demoralized by life, debilitated by physical ailments and alcohol, had ignored her brothers' relentless teasing of her. *Erma! Er-ma where're you hiding! Little bitch.* There was Judd,

487

six years older than Erma; there was Tommy, three years older; and there was Lyle, eighteen months older. Who'd most resembled Erma. Lyle with dark features, thick-lashed intelligent eyes glistening with hatred. Lyle with a speech impediment he'd exaggerated out of spite. *Little bitch. C-c-cunnnt. You in here?* Kicking at the bathroom door with its notoriously loose lock. Giggling when the door flew open and Erma was revealed, frightened, embarrassed, rising from the toilet and trying to adjust her clothing. Lyle who chased her, tickled and pinched her, one Halloween night in a Batman mask squeezing, squeezing, squeezing his fingers around her neck until Erma fell unconscious to the floor.

"You kids. What're you kids doing, God damn you."

Much of it, the "teasing," had been in or near the bathroom. At the top of the stairs. A single poorly heated bathroom for the six of them. Filthy toilet, filthy sink and tub. There'd been a year when Erma's mother, recovering from a gall bladder operation, hadn't done any housework. Erma's father was often gone from the house. Downstairs, watching her daytime TV, Erma's mother had been indifferent to cries and thuds overhead. Once, aged thirteen, Erma had desperately slapped Lyle as Judd and Tommy looked on laughing and Lyle had flown into a rage and punched her in the back so hard she fell stunned, unable to breathe. Their mother yelled at them hoarsely, up the stairs, "Shut up! I'll get your father to beat the shit out of you! You kids make me *sick*."

Arno Kethy would have protected her from Lyle. From all her brothers.

Unless (she didn't want to consider this!) Arno Kethy was one of her brothers.

Now, a decade later, Erma was gone from Erie, Pennsylvania and guiltily plotted never to return. Not for her father's angina and alarming weight loss, not for her mother's swollen joints, blackouts and "nerves." Not for Judd's wedding, and his fatal car crash barely a year later. Not for Lyle's mysterious "trouble with the police." Speaking two or three times a month on the phone with her parents, she liked it that the line crackled with distance. You could hear the howling cleansing wind of the prairies. You could hear stinging particles of snow. Before each of her calls home Erma was nervous, anxious, but she called dutifully, and she put a smile into her voice. For, now they were older, seriously ailing and their meanness as curtailed as vicious dogs on leashes. "When am I coming home, I'm not sure, Mom. My term doesn't end until . . . After that, I have a summer research grant . . ." But she sent them checks. Considering her poverty, generous checks.

She was a captive paying her kidnappers ransom in order to remain free.

Oh, gratefully! That was why she smiled.

ASSIGNMENT #3: ARGUEMENT

Sometimes its just simple, you want to improve
your Life to where it is worthwhile as a citizen.
Its hard to argue what would be my exact hope
as I did not gratuate from high school.
I had trouble with all my subjects especially
English where the teacher hated me. Even gym,
I failed. The coach hated me!
They think if you are quiet, you are hating them.
You are thinking of ways to hurt them.

My arguement would be, what does the US expect
if you treat us like shit? Eight years, on
Death Row and saying they are sorry afterward,
sorry I am alive they mean. That the appeal
went so slow. (A man in the block, his appeal
went faster and was rejected, and so he was
put to death, and the new law applied to me,
that would have saved him, was not on the books
yet. A laugh on him.)

I drive my car at night, for I am lonely.
There are so many houses in this city.
Sometimes, you don't pull your shades
to the window sill, Im thinking.
Could toss a bomb through any lighted window.
People watching TV, or having supper.
What about us out here in the Night.

489

I quit Mayflower movers. Its not a life
to plan for. I cant believe—I am 39 yrs old.
Where is my life taken from me, I dont know.
My arguement is to return to schooling, where
I took a wrong turn. If I had sertain skills
as with computers. I started Accounting
too but have not done too good. My mind is fixed on
sertain issues. There is the wrongness of putting
a man to death, if he is innocent or even if
he is not. I would wish to marry one day
but at Edgarstown I was injured in sertain ways
and (I beleive) contacted diseases, but
the insurance will not cover it. They said
it was before I went in, in another State.
There records but no records (they say) of this.

My conviction was overturned and so I was free,
still I would wish sometimes to murder ~~you~~ them all.
I was not born a beast, that is my arguement.

3.

It's time. It can't be avoided. Erma went to consult with the program director. Mr. Falworth was an earnest, harassed-looking old-
young man of about forty who didn't seem to recognize her until she
told him her name twice. "My hair," she said apologetically. "I've cut
my hair." Her long braid had vanished. Her hair was wavy and insub-
stantial as feathers, framing a winter-pale, scrubbed-looking face.
Falworth smiled a quick but vague social smile, saying his hair, too,
had departed in the service of remedial composition; he made a fluttering gesture with his fingers across the dome of his near bald head.
Such a gesture meant simply *I like you, I'm a decent guy. But don't
bring me trouble.* Erma had brought with her a number of student
compositions to show Falworth, a sampling of the range of her
grades; among them were Arno Kethy's three ungraded compositions
which she intended to show him matter-of-factly, as if Kethy were an
academic problem merely, and not a personal problem. As they conferred, Erma began to doubt the wisdom of what she'd planned. She
had rehearsed saying to Falworth *What do you make of these, I can't*

490

grade them by any standards I know, it's like prose poetry isn't it, or is it just illiterate, unacceptable, this student isn't following the guidelines is he, what do you advise, Mr. Falworth? She supposed the program director would be shocked. But possibly he wouldn't be shocked. The Night Division, Erma had been told by other, more experienced instructors, accepted virtually all applicants who were residents of the state. The legislature looked at numbers, not academic records. No doubt there were mentally disturbed patients among the Night Division's clientele, even criminals. No doubt there were frequently problems for new instructors, especially women. Falworth might have just the answer. He might call in Arno Kethy to see him. He might speak severely with Kethy, he might suggest that Kethy drop out of school. Since Kethy's third composition seemed to contain a threat of violence, Falworth might report him to authorities.

Or, what was equally likely, he might be annoyed with the inexperienced young woman instructor who'd come to him with such a problem. Would a male instructor have had this problem? As they conferred, through most of an hour, Erma realized that she couldn't betray Arno Kethy; he was emotionally disturbed, but he trusted her; he would never hurt her. *I would protect you. I promise.* Erma slipped Kethy's handwritten papers into her brief case; if Falworth noticed them, he wasn't about to ask for more compositions to examine. He said briskly, "You appear to be doing very well, Erma. This is good work." This was meant sincerely and Erma felt a wave of relief. Some guilt, but mostly relief. The consultation was ending on a positive note. Falworth saw her to the door of his office, a gesture she guessed he didn't ordinarily make with visitors. He asked if she would like to teach in the program in the fall, possibly two courses, for more than double her current salary, and Erma heard herself say yes, possibly she would. "I've never had an experience like this before."

"Our most successful instructors always say that," Falworth said with a smile. "It's the others, the ones with problems . . ." His voice trailed off into disapproving silence.

Erma Schegloff had said the right thing.

Next day, she made inquiries after *Kethy, Arno C.* in the registrar's office. But Kethy had no transcripts predating that semester when he'd enrolled, as a special student in the Night Division, in Composition 101 and Accounting 101. No high school transcripts or letters of recommendation seem to have been required. Erma went to the office of the dean of the Night Division and was allowed to look through a similarly meager file for Kethy there. (Aluminum filing cabinets filled most of a room, containing thousands of students' files, since 1947! It was a daunting vision, like looking into a vast mortuary.) Here there was a poorly photocopied letter dated September 1989 from a county parole officer attesting vaguely to Arno C. Kethy's punctuality, willingness to cooperate with authorities and "adoptive nature," which Erma supposed must mean "adaptive nature." Yet the letter was only a form letter addressed to To Whom It May Concern; it concluded with a disclaimer—

> Arno C. Kethy is of above average intelligence it is believed, but not easy to communicate with. The report of the court psychiatrist is that he is a "borderline" personality capable of knowing right from wrong and therefore sane under the law. He has always claimed total innocence for his actions even those of which he has been found guilty on the testimony of witnesses and circumstantial evidence.

Whatever Kethy had done, or had been convicted of doing, in this instance, had been before 1989. And 1989 was a long time ago.

Erma saw that Kethy's address was 81 Bridge Street.

But how is he borderline? Dangerous?
He reveals himself in words like a poet.

Maybe (Erma conceded!) she'd regret it. But she showed Kethy's most recent, most disturbing composition to no one. She lay the single, much-folded sheet of tablet paper on top of the bureau in her bedroom, a primitive piece of Shaker furniture painted robin's egg blue and decorated with tiny pink rosebuds, a girl's bureau with a romantically fogged oval mirror in which Erma's own face, girlish, rather pale, somber yet often smiling, floated; and after a week she'd read and reread it so many times, it no longer seemed threatening. It was a poem in prose. She could hear Kethy's anguished voice reciting it. And it was written for her, Kethy's instructor. *I was not born a beast, that is my arguement.* Erma thought of Shakeseare's Caliban.

492

Milton's rebellious Satan in *Paradise Lost*. She still hadn't attempted to grade him, for how could she grade a man's soul?

He reveals himself to me. Alone.

There came Thursday evening, their next class. When Erma hurried into the room breathless and invigorated from the cold, already Kethy was hidden in his corner, remote and downlooking. Among so many other individuals, Kethy might be ignored even as the instructor was sharply aware of him, his searching eyes. She knew he would be struck by her hair. The thick braid between her shoulder blades, suddenly missing.

Now it was late February in this snowswept Midwestern city and the winter term was beginning to wear. Flu was locally rampant; nine students were absent. Erma had looked forward to teaching Zora Neale Hurston's self-portrait "How It Feels to be Colored Me"—a choice she assumed would meet with enthusiasm since it was zestfully written yet a serious glimpse into the soul of a brilliant black woman writer; but to her surprise and chagrin, Reverend E.G. Eldridge loudly objected on the grounds of Hurston's "mocking tone" and "ignorance of the place of Jesus Christ" in the lives of black Americans. In turn, others objected to the reverend's bold, blustery statements. Students who'd been silent all term joined in. But Eldridge dominated, clearly accustomed to being the authority in any gathering. Erma found herself in the instructor's perilous position of disagreeing strongly with a student yet wanting to respect his opinion and wishing to be, or to appear to be, neutral. As others, mostly women, black and Caucasian, defended Hurston, and the Reverend and a few others attacked her, Erma stood uncertainly before them, no longer in control. She might have been observing, from a few yards away, a suddenly raging brushfire. When a black woman said to Eldridge with withering scorn, "This Hurston a genius, man, and you a sorry asshole," Erma was shocked, stammering, "Oh, Lorett! That isn't very—polite." Eldridge shot back, baring his teeth in fury, "You, woman, are just plain *ig-nor-ant.*" Erma said, trying to regain their attention, "Mr. Eldridge, please—." Eldridge turned to the young woman instructor to whom, for weeks, he'd been excessively courteous, his usually benign face creased with disdain, "Ma'am! Ex-cuse me! You are not qualified to speak on this subject!" Erma flinched as if she'd been slapped.

The instructor's nightmare epiphany. *This has all been a game. He doesn't respect me at all. Do any of them . . . ?*

493

Erma's face burned. She must have looked like a slapped, publicly humiliated child. Eldridge, having gone too far, realized his blunder and began to make amends. Others, who hadn't taken part in the noisy discussion, looked on like observers at an auto wreck. Some were shocked, a few hid smiles and smirks. Arno Kethy had risen partway from his desk, peering over heads. His stitched-looking Caucasian face shone with indignation. Eldridge was apologizing profusely, having reverted to his usual benevolence. Erma said, smiling, "It's quite all right, Reverend Eldridge. I stand corrected." She meant to turn the unpleasant confrontation into a good-natured joke, though Eldridge's hard round face gleamed with oily beads of sweat, and Erma was still trembling. Lorett said with pursed, pouty lips, "See, Miz S'heg'off, what we women got to contend with? The black male ego revealed." Eldridge managed to laugh at this remark, barely, dabbing at his face with a handkerchief. Erma guided the class onto another, safer essay. She didn't glance back at Arno Kethy. Everyone would be on good behavior for the remainder of the class and, of course, at the end, Reverend Eldridge would hurry forward to further apologize. *He's worried. He showed me his true face. He'd been hoping for a high grade.* Erma was disillusioned, but behaved graciously with Eldridge. She wasn't upset with him in the least, she said; in fact, she was pleased that their discussion had been so animated. "That's the aim of strong writing, isn't it? To provoke thought."

By this time Kethy had vanished by the rear exit. Erma had wanted to hand back his "Arguement" and ask him to speak with her about it, but when she looked up, exhausted and demoralized, Kethy was gone.

Next class meeting, and the next, E.G. Eldridge was absent. Erma felt the sting of a public rebuke. She wondered if Eldridge had dropped the course, or was just staying away temporarily to punish her. She wanted the man back, to make amends; though she'd been disgusted with him, she couldn't bear it that he might be disgusted with her. She made inquiries in the dean's office and was told only that Eldridge's wife had called to say he was hospitalized, and would probably not be returning to school. Erma was astonished. "But he seemed to be in good health. He's a strong, vigorous man . . ."

She wondered guiltily if, in any way, she was to blame.

ASSIGNMENT # 4: OBSEVATION AND ANYLSIS

The house is two floors, brown shinglewood with a
look of soft rotted wood. There is a front porch
and a side porch. The roof is black tarpaper.
It is just an ordinary house you would think
from the outside. It is near the hospital.

Her place she lives in, is on the second floor.
The stairs are squeezed in. There is a smell
of cooking from the downstairs. There is linolum
tile on the floor. The mailboxes are downstairs.
The lock on the front door is not a serious lock.

Her skin was very white even in the shadow.
There was radio music playing, very soft.
She has wrapped a white towel around her hair.
When she brushes it out, it is strange to her,
it has become shorter. It makes her younger.
There is a swatch of bush-hair, a lighter color
between her legs. It is curly and if you
sallowed a hair, it would tickle!

There are only three rooms in the apartment,
this is a surprise. Not what a college teacher
deserves. Except for the blue ~~buear~~ bureau
and some pictures of trees she has taped to her walls
there is not enough beauty in this place.

The blinds are drawn but you can see through.
Maybe they are not drawn to the window ledge.
The lock on the door is the same lock as downstairs.
From the hospital, there are sirens.

She came out from the steamed bathroom drying
her hair, and another towel wrapped around her.
His hands helped her. He was holding the big towel,
she felt his hands through the clothe and shivered.
She would look up though she did not SEE him then.
Yet she smiled. For she knew he was there.

Hed painted the bueau for her. A little wood bueau
with pink rosebuds and the knobs made of glass.
He explained to her he would like to marry
and have children except they have tired to discorage
him. Its their hope to discorage you from life.
They laugh if you try to hang yourself, they provide
the clothes. They pretend they dont see spoons,
for you to sharpen. They hope for the lower class
to die out like dogs.

Before he knew her name ERMA SCHEGLOFF
he was granted knowledge of her face.
If you love somebody that is all there is.
If you anylise it you will fail.
You knew each other before it happened.
Always he would recall her face that brought him hope.
For you cant live without hope.
He would protect her from all enemies.
He would cut away their faces and their hearts.
To protect her he would not be afraid
to use all his strength,

He would not live without her, he felt.

" 'Borderline.' But 'borderline' to *what*?"
She had a vision of a single, isolated nation-state floating in darkness, its borders touching upon nothing.

In the all-but-deserted reference room of the downtown public library there was Erma Schegloff scrolling through back editions of the city newspaper on microfilm. Anxious, dreading what she might find in these rows upon rows of shimmering print. Headlines of national and international crisis juxtaposed with area news and all of it reduced to history. Time past. The extraordinary set beside the commonplace. It was *County News* she focussed upon, the second section of the paper. Scrolling through weeks of campaign and election coverage, photos of smiling politicians, town meetings, sewer bond issues, school board debates, schoolbus safety, fires, arson, arrests for robbery, theft, drunken driving, armed assault. Ladies' charity bazaars, church news, archbishop dies, scholarship winners, lottery winners, arson suspected, arson-suspect arrested, embezzlement of bank funds, school superintendent dies, dean of business school at the university retires, honorary degrees conferred upon, arrests in drug raids, and suddenly there was

EDGARSTOWN DEATH ROW PRISONER, 39
FREED AFTER 8-YEAR ORDEAL

The date was December 2 of the previous year. She'd been staring at a photo of Arno Kethy aged thirty-one, young-looking, with hurt narrowed eyes and the shadow of a beard and brutally short-trimmed hair, without recognizing him.

Kethy had been convicted of raping and murdering a woman and her thirteen-year-old daughter in a state park in July 1990; he'd been identified by witnesses as being near the scene of the crime, there was "evidence" linking him to the crime site, he'd made a confession to police, a police informant testified at his trial he'd boasted of committing the crimes. Kethy had subsequently recanted the confession, alleging he'd been beaten by police. He had a "drug history." He'd spent time in rehabilitation, in Iowa. He'd also spent time in Iowa State Penitentiary on a charge of armed robbery. At his trial he'd taken the witness stand but became "catatonic" and could not testify. During his two-week trial he became violent and had to be placed under restraint in the courtroom. A jury found him guilty of two counts of murder and two counts of rape, and he was sentenced to death by lethal injection. His case was automatically appealed. His conviction was overturned when a county man, arrested by police for drug dealing, told police that the rape-murders had been committed by another man, not Kethy; subsequent DNA evidence proved that Kethy had not been the rapist, and linked the other suspect to the crimes. When Kethy was released after eight years on Death Row TV reporters had asked him to comment on his ordeal but Kethy "shook his head wordlessly and walked away."

Erma wiped at her eyes. *Shook his head, walked away.* What more manly gesture!

It was when Erma was returning the rolls of microfilm to the librarian that she happened to see, on a table, scattered pages of the city paper. Immediately her eye leapt to a photo of a familiar face. Reverend E.G. Eldridge. And the headline MINISTER BRUTALLY ATTACKED IN ROBBERY ATTEMPT.

Appalled, Erma read that E.G. Eldridge, fifty-one years old, had been attacked with a razor while getting into his car in the parking lot behind his church, the Disciples of Christ, on Friday of the previous week. The attack had occurred at 7 PM, after dark but in a lighted area. Eldridge had not seen his assailant. He'd been severely lacerated in the face and hands and was in stable condition in the hospital. The unknown assailant had removed Eldridge's wallet from his coat pocket but dropped it near him without taking money or credit cards. Police believed he'd been frightened off by someone on the street, but no witnesses to the crime had yet come forward.

"For me. He did it for me."

For several minutes she sat stunned. Then she folded up the newspaper carefully, inserting pages in their proper order, and returned it to the librarian's desk where current issues of the local paper were kept.

She lifted the telephone receiver. She would call the police, she would say carefully: "I think I know who might have assaulted Reverend Eldridge. His name is . . ."

So long she held the receiver in her sweaty hand, the dial tone turned to an irritated mechanical squawking in her ear. Somewhere close by, a siren wailed. It had begun to snow again, windborne sleet. Not yet March, this winter of Erma's life seemed to have gone on forever with the fascination of one of those mad works of adoration, *The Faery Queen, The Romance of the Rose* . . . By the time she replaced the receiver the mechanical squawking had ceased. There was no dial tone, no sound, as if the line had been cut.

This can't be happening can it? I am not truly here.

Through the ice-stippled side window of her car Erma saw the dimly-lighted windows of 81 Bridge Street. A shabby red-brick townhouse in a neighborhood of similar rundown rowhouses near the ramp of the enormous bridge. Human life was dwarfed here, human habitations like caves, hives. Though close by, the polluted river was invisible.

She wondered if Kethy was home. If he was alone.

I can't love you. You mustn't love me. You don't know me: my face is not me.

You must not hurt others on my account . . .

498

Yet their connection was forged too deep for such words, now.

No words Erma uttered would matter to Kethy, no words could deflect his adoration.

He'd stayed away from class. He wouldn't come again, Erma understood. So she must go to him, if they were ever to meet again. He would injure and even kill on her account but he believed himself unworthy of her.

Uncertain what to do, Erma drove on. She was morbidly excited, exhilarated. She'd brought Kethy's last composition with her, to give to him personally. What madness! Yet she would do it, if she could force herself. She'd become, she believed, a stronger person: willful, resolute. Like the man who adored her, reckless.

The last time she'd called home, for instance. The duty-bound daughter. Gentle all-forgiving never-judging daughter. Her mother was saying in a hurt whining voice why are you so far from us Erma, why have you left us in our old age, like your brothers, no better than your brothers, why do you imagine you can "teach," you're not the type, never were, you're shy, you used to stammer so badly remember how you came home crying, the other children teased you so— and Erma quietly hung up the receiver on her mother's voice. Smiling, thinking *The connection was broken. No one's fault.*

Within the hour she'd arranged for her telephone number to be changed, unlisted.

She would tell Kethy, maybe. They'd laugh together. She would tell Kethy such things she'd never told anyone in this raw new life of hers in the Midwest or in the old lost life back east. She would tell him *None of them ever knew me, I'm so lonely.*

Erma was circling the block, evidently. She perceived that that was what she was doing. One-way streets, and narrow. And vehicles were parked on the streets, some of them abandoned. There was trash dumped on the pavement, overturned trash cans. In this setting Kethy's "Obsevation and Anylsis" acquired a touching, comical significance. Remedial English, taught to inhabitants of such a world. The strategies of prose, persuasive prose, prose to save one's life, taught to death row prisoners. Erma hadn't graded Kethy's compositions, out of respect. Out of fear for him, yes; but out of respect, too. She would return the composition to him in person as an act of homage but she hadn't committed herself to any action beyond that. She was one who wished to believe that human motives precede actions, for she was (she had always been) a rational individual, yet clearly there were times (was this one of those times?) when actions might precede motives and even render them useless.

The one-way streets made this part of the city a maze. Erma had been forced to drive several blocks out of her way. *Go home! Continue on home, no one will ever know you've been here.* She passed beneath another ramp of the old ugly Victorian-era bridge. In warmer weather it would be dangerous for Erma to drive in this part of the city, a lone white woman in a compact car, but tonight no one was on the street. Though her heart was pounding, she knew the symptoms of anxiety. Exhilaration! She saw that she was driving again on Bridge Street, heading south. Street numbers were diminishing: 231, 184, 101 . . . She approached Kethy's house another time. She was fairly certain someone was home. That bluish undersea TV glimmering. She braked her car at the curb: a shadowy figure was passing by the window, behind the carelessly drawn shade. *I drive my car at night, for I am lonely. Could toss a bomb through any lighted window.* Erma turned off the ignition. She saw that, while the porches of other rowhouses on the street were cluttered with objects, chairs, bicycles, trash cans, the porch at 81 Bridge was empty except for a single trash can.

He lived alone. He was in there, alone.

Carefully, Erma walked up the icy sidewalk. Stepped onto the porch. Through the thin, cracked shade she had the impression of a male figure moving swiftly toward the door by the time she pressed the bell. The door was opened within seconds like an inhalation of breath: Arno Kethy stood there, staring at her.

He wore a clean black T-shirt. Work pants, hiker's boots. A long spidery blue tattoo covered much of his left forearm. His eyes were deep-set, shocked. As if he'd been expecting a visitor he'd shaved so recently that tiny beads of blood shone on the underside of his jaw. And he'd cut his hair with a scissors, now the gingery-graying hair fell just below his ears, newly washed, limp and thin.

Erma heard her prepared words. "Mr. Kethy, may I speak with you? Arno."

Nominated by Christina Zawadiwsky

CLOUD ATLAS

by DONALD PLATT

from THE PARIS REVIEW

How can there be a book that maps these continents
        of clouds that drift
apart, reshape their puzzle pieces, and coalesce into new

        geographies of air
within one windblown hour? No one can map the sky's quicksands.
        Open the atlas,

and you will see only color photographs of clouds, their Latin
  names,
        genus, species, features,
and then the place, day, month and year, even the hour

        and minute at which
some cloud fanatic, some paparazzo covering the cirrocumuli and
  other
        high society, snapped

their unposed pictures: "Scattered Cumulus Along a Squall Line,"
        a cirrus's coiffure
in serious disarray, the mother clouds, dust devils, halo

        phenomena, coronas,
glories, nacreous and noctilucent clouds, virga, fallstreaks of rain
        that evaporate before

they touch the ground, all these special effects alongside
            ordinary hazy days
through which the sun's bright shadow cuts, altostratus

            translucidus.
Underneath each plate are the photographer's initials and last name,
    and always
            what direction

he was facing. Isn't there an unintended poignancy in almost every
            caption? "A.J. Aalders,
Bussum, Netherlands, first of October, 1935, oh-six-hundred-

            fifty-seven hours,
towards the southeast: Stratus in Ragged Shreds." In his photo
            clouds blow like smoke

from heavy artillery fire above the outline of a few wind-shaken
            yew trees and someone's
roof with two chimneys. The risen sun is barely visible, the smudged

            period of a child's
first fountain pen in a copybook left out in the rain. The clouds are
            words that have bled

across the unlined page. Innocent of history, the meteorologist's
            caption reads,
"Disturbances were crossing Western Europe from east

            to west that day."
And what direction am I facing, sunning on my back deck, doing
    nothing
            but writing this one poem

and watching all summer long the clouds form
            and reform,
how a cumulus's beehive hairdo comes undone, airy acrobat

            to the prevailing wind's
least whim? Most mornings it's a chaotic sky, clouds at many levels,
            low broken combers of cumulus,

the rippled dunes of altocumulus undulatus, highflying
                cirrus vertebratus,
a fish skeleton picked clean by the northwest wind. Aren't we too

                a bare spine with ribs
of ice crystals and water vapor mixed, condensed around particles
                of dust? Don't we too

shine in the west? I am facing my fifth decade and the first year
                of our third millennium, pileup
of late afternoon's cumulonimbus coming at us out of the south,
    spikes

                of lightning driven
home from heaven to earth, God's Instamatic flash,
                where eternity opens

for one five-hundredth of a second, then darkness, the stammering
    thunder's
                aftermath. "That's the preacher
preaching, and he's not happy with us," says my Southern Baptist

                neighbor. But why
does almost no one look up at the clouds except when bad weather
                rips the sky in half?

Why are there so few poets of the clouds? Where are our odes to
                cirrus uncinus,
that octogenarian who clips his white, bristly eyebrows

                into the blue
washbowl and leaves the stray hairs there, forgetting
                to clean them up? We have only

a few lines by Hopkins, "what wind-walks! what lovely behaviors
                of silk-sack clouds!",
and one backlit, apocalyptic line by Apollinaire, poet of flying ma-
    chines

and jugglers on city streets
that smell of rain—*"Siècle ô siècle des nuages."* Look up, I say to all
    of us window-shoppers
            and passersby. I see

my mother's face in the wrinkled skein of cirrus fibratus veiling
            the west. She'll be
eighty-two by summer's end. How can the flesh I once swelled

            within, a blood-ripened watermelon,
turn to such wisps of cloud? And there's Apollinaire in the cumulus
    congestus,
            the turban of his white-bandaged

head trepanned under chloroform after the shrapnel hit him,
            only a few more months,
some more summer poems, left to live with Jacqueline, his sunset-
    headed

            girl. What does it mean
to be "true" to each other? Take that small, cotton boll cloud
            in the fire-shrouded

southwest. Doesn't it rise like an empty thought-balloon from some
    vast
            unknowable mind
in the last comic strip of molten daylight left

            along the charred
horizon? Watch it float the wind's way. Our lives are high clouds that
    still catch the sun
            although here the dark has already come.

Nominated by Marianne Boruch

LANDSCAPE WITH BEES

by DAVID YOUNG

from ORION

Santa Gíuliana, Umbria, 1995

Another morning on this mountain,
    goat bells, butter-colored broom,
a few clouds bunching in the south,
    milk-foam, silk mattress stuffing.

Someone is swimming in the horse pond,
    someone's exploring the hillside.
Like me, the lizards on the rocky wall
    are poleaxed by the sunshine.

To be able to read a page—say Virgil's *Georgics*—
    and then glance up
across a gulf of laundered air
    at a brother mountain, fifteen miles away . . .

❧

    Old age comes very softly on
like a door swung open, leading nowhere,
and a small wren lights on the rosemary bush,
    no heavier than a butterfly.

    In the bowl of fruit on the chipped
enamel table, peaches speak,

lemons hum, and the day
        is just a *borgo* we belong to.

                        ❦

The poem bounces down the slope,
        a rock
you tossed and lost
found
        and threw away.

A bee flies by.

Each poem's not exactly what
        you mean
because, of course,
you don't
        quite ever know—

A bee returns.

                        ❦

Nearing the solstice, noon looms large.
        Trees and shrubs
suck their own shadows in.

        A hawk
cruises the fat slope and disappears
        over the ridge-crest.

Arrow of jay-flight,
        arc of the honeybees
humming where there are blossoms.

        The monastery gongs twelve times.
Astounding pine-smell
        brandished in narrow shade.

                        ❦

Sometimes I hear the bees,
        sometimes I see them.

More and more I suspect
         our perception slows and flattens the world
to get it inside our heads.

Suppose you had a sense
         tuned in to magnetism?
And one that could pick up quarks
         as they blink in and out
of what we call existence?

Somebody says that bees
         dance on a flag manifold,
interacting with quantum fields,
         speaking a language we can't conceive of.
Inside the hive is better than my head.

❦

Rilke leans forward
to whisper a few
words to his Polish
translator, von Hulewicz.

Wir sind, he says,
able just for a moment
to think in six dimensions,
we are the bees of the invisible.

Bees are the bees
of the invisible, most likely.
But we are the ones
who get to think about it.

I'll take that home today,
high on this mountain,
high on the thoughts
that leave the words behind.

Bees on their patterned errands,
neutrinos on theirs,

pass right by and through us,
we, the big-brained dreamers.

❦

We bought a round flat *crema* cake
     shaped like a moon
     in Umbertide.
It looks like a phosphorescent frisbee.
We munch its wedges as the solstice turns.

The constellations wheel and quiver.
     All night, the small
     owls hoot and hunt,
skimming through pines,
and I slide down into the deeps and reefs

where humans go when they have lived too long—
     tangles of memory, imagination,
     animal faith and love,
the call of kin,
the missed and missing world.

❦

*These tootings at the weddings
of the soul?* Well, one good sleight-of-hand
deserves another.

Solstice to solstice to solstice,
the yo-yo game around the sun,
stitching a life . . .

*The great golden hive
of the invisible.* Raw honey
and goat-footed sunlight.

Nominated by Mark Irwin, Martha Collins

CABEZA

fiction by MONIQUE DE VARENNES

from CRACKING THE EARTH (Calyx Books)

NONE OF THEM, not even Barbara herself, quite understood why
she brought the pig's head home from the market. She had browsed
in the meat department's hooves-and-hearts section many times—
Variety Meats, it was euphemistically called—but she had never before been tempted to buy. For one thing, she had no idea how to
cook the innards and extremities whose red or pink or tannish flesh
jammed the display case. For another, she had always felt that looking was quite enough.

And she did look, nearly every time she visited the market. She
loved the colors and textures of the meat: the deep red coils of
spleen, the lacy tripe, the kidneys like weighty, dark bunches of
grapes. She liked to see the thick slabs of tongue, so surprisingly
large and muscular that she wondered how they fit in an animal's
mouth, and the pigs' feet, small and achingly dainty, like a society
matron's helpless, manicured hand.

The pig's head, though, was altogether different. It was the first
one Barbara had ever seen in Variety Meats, and it had her attention
from the moment she laid eyes on it. It had belonged to a young pig,
a piglet, she surmised, for it was not very big. Whitish, sightless, it
wore an expression of great seriousness, as if it fully recognized the
gravity of its situation. It seemed isolated there in the case, separated
by shrink-wrap from the neat neighboring packages of organs and
hocks, some of which were undoubtedly its own. It looked lonely
even, and impulsively Barbara popped it into her shopping cart.

Driving home, she smiled with pleasure at the thought of her purchase. No exile in the dark recesses of the meat keeper for this baby; she would make a place for it at the very center of things.

But even when she had settled the head front and center on the refrigerator's middle shelf, pushing jars and leftovers aside with rare abandon, she felt that something was missing. The pig looked as mournful of countenance and as forlorn as ever.

Barbara got busy. She brought out a white serving plate, and, stripping off the head's wrappings, set it carefully in the center. Some lettuce leaves gave color to the dish, and she accented the green with a sprinkling of cherry tomatoes. Briefly she considered stuffing an apple into the pig's mouth, but she discarded the idea: it would give the head far too rakish an air. Still, she could not resist draping one sprig of parsley over the pig's right ear.

She set the plate in the refrigerator and stepped back a few paces to contemplate the effect. The pig looked less gloomy now—almost cheerful, in fact. And if its gaiety seemed somewhat forced, well, at least she knew she had tried her best. Satisfied with the disposition of the head, she closed the refrigerator door and forgot about it entirely.

Two hours later, hearing the kitchen door slap shut behind her fourteen-year-old, Barbara remembered. No greeting, of course. No call of inquiry, drifting down to the basement where Barbara folded laundry; Carol had abandoned such pleasantries a good two years earlier. She now communicated rarely, except to express displeasure. Upstairs, kitchen cabinets slammed as she hunted for an after-school snack.

Barbara dropped the T-shirt she was smoothing out and rushed to the foot of the basement stairs. "Carol, honey, before you open the refrigerator, there's something I—"

But she was too late. Carol's shriek ripped through the air, a blade of sound. Barbara dashed upstairs. She found Carol standing squarely in front of the refrigerator, her eyes fixed on the closed metal door. Barbara put awkward arms around her daughter.

"What is that? Mom, what's in there?" Carol demanded, shaking free of her mother.

"It's a pig's head—a piglet's, really. I bought it at Ralphs."

The words sounded strange to Barbara. Clearly they sounded strange to Carol as well, for she gave her mother one brief, dark look and fled abruptly from the room. A moment later, Barbara heard a door slam in the far reaches of the house. She opened the refrigerator.

There sat the head, all innocence, clearly incapable of hurting even a fly. Really, she couldn't see why Carol was raising such a fuss. In any case, she had no time to contemplate the question now. There were piles of laundry still to fold, then there was dinner to be made. She thought pork chops would be nice, though she realized the choice showed a certain lack of sensitivity. She would serve them on a lovely bed of saffron rice.

It was not Barbara's habit to make the same mistake twice, and as five-thirty neared she kept alert for the sound of the garage door. Jed she did not have to worry about, at least not yet; he had soccer practice nearly every afternoon during the season and rarely made it home much before dinner. But she did not want Peter to be surprised. Her husband did not do well with surprises. She settled down distractedly for a look at the newspaper.

It was nearly six when she heard the sound of Peter's car. Barbara folded the paper neatly, taking care to smooth out the creases she had made, then wandered as casually as she could into the kitchen. Carol must have been listening for Peter too, for when Barbara entered, her daughter was already there, and Peter, briefcase in hand, was bending close to hear her whispered voice.

"A what?" he exclaimed. He did not seem to notice that Barbara had come into the room.

"A pig's head, Daddy—I swear. She got it at Ralphs. Check it out for yourself."

Peter opened the refrigerator impatiently, as if anticipating some particularly stupid prank. Then a small sound escaped him, something between a grunt and a groan, and his back slowly stiffened. He stood absolutely still. After eighteen years of marriage Barbara knew that silence, that utter stillness; he was busy rearranging the unpleasant into some form that suited him better.

After a moment he seemed to shake himself, and he reached in for the pitcher of whiskey sours that Barbara always had waiting for him when he came home from work. "Well, Carol," he said finally, "I don't see that this is anything to get excited about." His voice was bland. "Your mother is probably planning to make cabeza."

Carol's pointed, freckled face sharpened a bit in disappointment. Clearly she had hoped for a scene. "Cabeza?" she repeated sullenly. "What's that?"

"A traditional Spanish dish—a kind of stew, I believe."

"She's planning to cook it? To make us eat it?"

"I never said I was going to cook it. Never uttered a word about that," put in Barbara, who had begun chopping up a crisp napa cabbage. The pork was baking nicely. But they did not seem to hear her.

"Well, she can cook it any way she wants," Carol continued. "I'm not touching it."

"Touching what?" Jed banged in the kitchen door and swung his backpack to the floor.

"Look in the refrigerator for a preview of tomorrow's dinner. Mom's going Spanish on us."

Jed followed Carol's suggestion, gazing for a moment into the antiseptic brightness of the refrigerator. Then he reached behind the head for a bottle of Gatorade. "Weird," he murmured appreciatively. "When Mom's done, can I have the skull for my room?"

Not much more was said about the pig's head that evening; Peter effectively glowered them all into silence. But it was he who brought up the subject as Barbara was getting ready for bed. She knew what he planned to discuss from the moment he cleared his throat. Stretched out on the mattress, his reading glasses perched atop his head like a second set of ears, he had the same look of strained forbearance he'd worn the day he had dissuaded her from filing for divorce, three years earlier. His voice, when he spoke, was low and calm. "About the cow's head, honey—"

"Pig's head," Barbara corrected promptly. "It's a pig."

"About the pig's head. Are you planning to cook it or not? Because if you're planning to cook it, I personally will eat it and encourage the kids to do the same. But if you're not, I think you ought to consider—" and here he appeared to be sorting rather carefully through his words "—disposing of the thing."

Barbara received this suggestion in noncommittal silence, though her bones froze at the thought of throwing away her pig. She watched Peter's face grow increasingly intense, and she knew he was struggling with something. "Why did you buy it?" he blurted out at last.

Barbara considered this for the first time, rather surprised that it had not occurred to her to wonder until now. She did not dare tell him that the pig had looked lonely, and that was not, she guessed, the whole truth in any case. "I don't know," she said finally.

For a moment she thought, I should try to talk to him about it.

512

Who else, after all? The children were still too young, and no one outside the family could possibly understand. She looked at him, exposed on the bed, his rough, hairy legs poking out from smooth pajama bottoms, his stomach wearing the soft bulge of middle age. He looked vulnerable, approachable. Then his face hardened, and that was all she could see.

"Never mind why you bought it," he said gruffly. "I don't even know why I asked. Just deal with it, Barbara, won't you?" He flicked his glasses down from his forehead to cover his eyes again, as if closing himself to any further conversation. And that was that.

Next morning, Barbara noticed that the upstairs bathrooms needed cleaning, and she spent a couple of hours working on them. She was the sort of housekeeper who always let things get a little disreputable before she cleaned, so she could experience the small satisfaction of seeing her scrubbing and polishing make a difference.

Later, over a sandwich, Barbara paged through her cookbooks, looking for a recipe for cabeza. She was not quite sure that such a thing existed. She knew that the word meant head in Spanish. She also knew that Peter was quite capable of inventing a dish if it helped smooth over an awkward moment in his day. Certainly none of her foreign cookbooks—of which she had several, left over from the days when she had truly enjoyed her time in the kitchen—made reference to it. The *Larousse Gastronomique* came closest, with one recipe for brains, one for the snout, and no fewer than eight ways of fixing the ears.

The very thought of cutting into the pig's head aroused anxiety, and Barbara brought the platter out onto the kitchen table and sat down in front of it. Today it looked scoured and sere and somehow wise. Peter was right to ask: Why had she bought it?

She stared at it hard, trying to understand. Its presence seemed to overflow the kitchen. It was, for her, utterly there, more than her cookbooks or the salt shaker or the Pothos on the windowsill, whose small green life she had nursed for nearly fifteen years. She was aware that the head aroused in her a tangle of feelings, and that those feelings were quite strong. But when she tried to separate them so that she could name them—name even one—they eluded her, vanishing in wisps of emotional fog.

She looked at her watch—an entire hour gone. There would

513

barely be time to throw some caramel custard together before Carol got home from school. Barbara thought she would make a double batch; caramel custard was Carol's favorite.

By the time she heard her daughter's step on the driveway, Barbara was a bit apprehensive. But to her surprise Carol did not seem inclined to be hostile. "Did you cook the head yet?" she asked bluntly.

Barbara shook her head.

"Well, that's a relief." Carol sniffed the air avidly; she still had a child's unerring radar for sugar. "Hey, something smells sweet."

"Caramel custard. It's for dessert tonight, but there's extra, if you'd like a snack. In the refrigerator."

Barbara watched Carol's mouth tighten as she contemplated the refrigerator uneasily. She smiled a bit as her daughter pulled open the door and quickly withdrew a dish of custard. This Carol bore off, wordlessly, to her room.

That night neither Peter nor Jed mentioned the pig's head, though both of them asked, almost upon entering and with enormous wariness, what was for dinner.

"Chicken," Barbara answered primly, and each refrained from commenting on what she had not cooked.

The next morning, as soon as the last of her family had left the house, Barbara took out the head again. A faint odor had begun to emanate from it and its garnish was past its prime. Barbara removed the wilted greens (the tomatoes were still serviceable) and sprinkled a little Arm & Hammer on the plate before tenderly laying a new bed of fresh lettuce. She patted the top of its skull. "You might smell a little off, but you look just fine," she reassured the piglet, smiling at it warmly. Then she wrapped it in heavy layers of Saran Wrap and returned it to its shelf in the fridge.

She did not take it out again, but the knowledge that it was there eased her through the day. She greeted Carol that afternoon with a plate of freshly baked cookies.

"You're cooking a lot these days," her daughter commented as she filled a glass with tap water.

"For some reason I've just been in a kitchen mood." Barbara registered the water in her daughter's hand. "Don't you want some milk?" she asked solicitously. "I was thinking as I baked these cookies how tasty they'd be with a tall, foamy glass of milk."

"No, this'll be okay." Carol's eyes jerked nervously toward the refrigerator, and Barbara could see that she had no intention of opening that door. So, helpfully, she threw it open herself, revealing the gleaming shelves, the milk carton, the pig's head. "Come on, have a glass."

When Carol had retired—rather abruptly, Barbara thought—to her room, it occurred to her that no one had been visiting the refrigerator much, not since the head had come home. Last night, Jed hadn't made his usual late-night food raid. And Peter hadn't even gone for his nightly whiskey sour; she had found the pitcher untouched on its shelf this morning.

Her observation about the refrigerator was confirmed that evening at dinner, when it became clear that she had not set out horseradish for the pot roast. This combination was traditional in their family; Peter had been known to become quite irritable if they were out of the condiment on pot roast night. But tonight no one mentioned the missing horseradish. It was always, of course, possible that they did not notice, but somehow Barbara doubted it. She sat in quiet amazement, watching her uncomplaining family eat their pot roast unadorned.

The evening passed without incident. Only Peter mentioned the head, commenting in an offhand way that she might want to make that cabeza soon if she was planning to cook it at all; he didn't think that kind of meat had much of a shelf life. Barbara responded with an alert and agreeable nod.

She had noted with interest that the family was tiptoeing around her, humoring her. Peter was his usual reserved self, yet there was a guarded solicitude in his treatment of her that she had never noticed before. Jed, the charmer of the group, had begun to favor her with doses of his incredible smile. Even Carol had been almost polite. Barbara wandered through this atmosphere in a mild fog, curious as to what would happen next.

Three days passed. No one spoke to her about the head. One morning she got up early and, as always these days, went straight to the kitchen. Even before she opened the refrigerator, she could smell it. The odor was stronger now, and it was not pleasant. She pulled out the platter and, holding her breath just a bit, patted a thick layer of Arm & Hammer on every surface of the head. It gave the thing a ghostly look but seemed to tamp down the odor considerably.

Barbara had long ago abandoned the garnishes that surrounded it. The lettuce lay flat and black on the plate, the tomatoes were dimpled with softening dark spots, and the once jaunty parsley was little more than a smear along the piglet's cheek. Ignoring this, she doubled the sheath of Saran Wrap, masking the smell.

By the time Jed came in she had coffee going. A bowl of pancake batter was at the ready by the side of the stove. She could tell from a tightening around his eyes that he smelled the pig too, but still he offered her his rich smile. "So, Mom, you want to come to my soccer game this morning? Dad and Carol are coming, and we're thinking of going out to lunch after."

"Oh, I couldn't possibly. I'm making a terrine of veal for dinner and it takes forever. If I don't start early we won't eat till midnight. Besides, isn't this a school day?"

"No, Mom," Jed said gently, "it's Saturday. Come on—you haven't been to a game for ages. It'll do you good to sit out in the sun. We can have burgers for dinner, for all I care."

But Barbara demurred. She had too much to do here, she insisted; the dinner ingredients were bought already. Besides, she had seen him play a hundred games and would see a hundred more—she could miss just one. Finally, Jed was forced to relent.

Barbara enjoyed her day. When the kitchen had been cleared of breakfast things, she set a pot of spices simmering on the stove to freshen the air. With the cheerful bubbling in the background she made her stuffing, chopped and marinated her meat, lined her terrine with pork fat, and artfully filled it with layers of the stuffing and veal and ham. It was the first time in ages that she had taken real pleasure in cooking. She glazed oranges for dessert while the terrine baked, and while it cooled, made arranged salads and cold rice. It would be the perfect light supper for her family.

They all, however, displayed a striking lack of appetite for dinner. They talked loudly—with more animation than usual, Barbara thought—but they only picked sporadically at their food. Perhaps they had eaten too much, or too late, at lunchtime. It was fortunate that she'd decided on a cold dinner, one that would keep—for days, if necessary—in the refrigerator.

That night, Barbara went to bed early. But the sound of crying pierced her dreams, and with a mother's instinct she got up, stumbling across the darkened bedroom, to offer comfort. The light was on in Carol's room. Even from Barbara's doorway down the hall she could hear her daughter's voice, raised in weepy complaint. Was she babbling to someone on the phone at this hour? A small twist of annoyance infiltrated Barbara's concern.

As she approached the door, Carol's words came clearer. "It's just so weird. She spends all of this time cooking—cakes, cookies, fancy dinners. And there's that head, just rotting in the refrigerator. It scares me, Daddy." She sobbed loudly, her breath ratcheting.

Barbara felt excitement trickle through her, and was invigorated. Crouching in the dark hall just outside the doorway, she settled in to listen.

"I know it seems odd," Peter replied, his voice steeled to calmness, "but you have to look at this from your mother's perspective. She bought the head to cook it, naturally, and for some reason she just hasn't. Maybe she's embarrassed about that. And—"

"And what, Dad?" Jed broke in. So it was a full family conference. "And she just leaves it to rot? Face it, Dad, there's something wrong with this picture. Mom's gone over the edge."

There was silence for a moment; then Jed spoke again, his voice strained and determined. "I don't know about the two of you, but I'm not eating another thing that's been sitting in there with that head. And first thing tomorrow I'm going to talk to Mom. I'm going to find out what she's been thinking. This is crazy, going on like this, pretending nothing is wrong."

Carol began to cry again. This time, Barbara could hear real pain in her sobs. She knew that Carol's face would be red and slick with unwiped tears, that her shoulders would be heaving, that her hands, forgotten, would lie limp at her sides. It was the way she had always cried as a child. As far as Barbara knew, she had not cried that way for years. How nice that she could still feel things so deeply.

But Peter ignored Carol. "I think you're blowing things out of proportion," he told Jed. "And I don't want you bringing this up with your mom." An edge had come into his voice, and he paused for a moment. Barbara could see his back from where she crouched; it twitched almost imperceptibly. When Peter spoke again his tone was neutral. "Sometimes it's better just to let things pass, to let them resolve themselves on their own. If you talked to her you might—"

"Might what, Dad?" Jed demanded. "I don't understand. Might what?"

517

"Leave it alone, Jed," Peter said harshly. "You're too young to understand the damage you might do." He turned away abruptly and stared out into the hall. Barbara was sure he had sensed her presence—he was looking straight at her. She cringed a little farther into the darkness. Then she saw that his eyes were focused inward. As she watched, his facial muscles began to work crazily, convulsively, and for a moment it looked as if he were about to cry. Then his features congealed into a rictus of pain and woe.

Barbara knew that for this moment, at least, he saw it all—that with their life stripped for this brief time of all its custom he was forced to see it: the dry boneyard of their existence. Pleasure coursed through her like a river breaking onto a parched plain. It swelled her, and she luxuriated. And in this moment of fulfillment she knew: this was what she had wanted. This was what the pig was for.

Yet even as she exulted, Peter's expression was changing again. Fascinated, she watched him as slowly and with great effort he forced his features back into their normal aspect of impenetrable calm. He turned back to the children. "Listen to me, both of you. Carol, stop your crying now. We will have to be very kind to your mother." He spoke slowly, deliberately. "Very kind for a long, long time."

Sensing that the conference was close to an end, Barbara slipped down the dark hallway, back to her bed. She closed her eyes, feigning sleep, and it engulfed her, closing over her like the dark waters of the sea.

The next morning, the pig's head was gone. One by one the family ventured tentatively into the kitchen, to be greeted by the sight of Barbara on her knees, scrubbing out the refrigerator. Air freshener spread its artificial comfort; homemade Belgian waffles warmed in the oven.

Peter, concerned that the head might draw ants, slipped out to the trash bins behind the garage to see that it was properly wrapped. But there was no sign of the pig. It did not occur to him to search the yard. There, deep behind the rhododendrons that marked the farthest reaches of their property, he might have seen a mound of freshly turned earth, the *Larousse* laid upon it like a tombstone.

For a while, things improved. Barbara felt herself at the very center of her family, as she had been when the children were infants. There

518

was a strained quality to Peter's concern, and to the children's attempts to include her in their lives, but Barbara did not mind, knowing as she did how conscious effort could grow in time into habit.

But then, in the way that families have, they abandoned their efforts, drifting slowly back to the patterns they were accustomed to. Barbara could feel their relief as they reverted. She tried to insert herself into their conversations and their plans, but she had become invisible again, inaudible. And the triumph she had felt the night of the family conference was lost to her.

One afternoon Carol came home and found her mother absent. Everything else was as it should be, but it was disturbing that there was no note, no explanation. Barbara had not returned by the time Peter came home from work, nor when Jed banged his way in the back door. No smell of dinner rose to meet them, and they wandered the house edgily, murmuring to one another.

At last, around 7:30, Barbara's car pulled into the driveway. "I can't believe how late it is," she sang as she entered the kitchen. Her voice, unnaturally cheery, drew them into the room.

"Let me help you with those," Jed offered, indicating the collection of Ralphs' bags around her knees. They were jammed with food.

"Oh, that's all right. They're not that heavy." With a protective gesture, and grinning a little crazily, Barbara stepped in front of the bags. "Just look at the time! If everyone will clear out and give me some room, I'll get dinner going. It's something we haven't had for a while. Something Spanish."

Efficiently, Barbara lifted the bags to the counter. No one else moved. They watched as if hypnotized as Barbara unloaded groceries: bright tomatoes; smooth, golden onions; a green profusion of limes, cilantro, and jalapeno. Then, what they were waiting for—a large package wrapped in butcher paper.

She unwrapped it slowly, eyeing them provocatively, and lifting the bundle of whitish flesh to her nose, she inhaled deeply. "Lovely!" she exclaimed. "The freshest snapper Ralphs has had in ages. You all liked snapper soup the last time I made it, didn't you?"

And she began to laugh. Oh, it was a terrible sound—she knew it was terrible. Her family's faces, horror-struck, confirmed it. Still, she could not stop. Wave after wave of hysterics assailed her until at last her knees buckled and she dropped unceremoniously to the floor. This set her off even more. Her throat ached from howling and her ribs felt as if they might crack.

The children were backing away from her, aghast, but Peter edged in closer, the expression on his face, all twisted again as it had been that other time, too comical to bear. She choked a bit, recovered, and then, unexpectedly, hiccupped. The laughter that this inspired nearly did her in. She rocked back and forth on the linoleum, red-faced and tear-stained and heaving helplessly. And as she rocked she wondered, with that small part of her brain still rooted to consciousness, if she would ever be able to stop.

Nominated by Kristin King

FOR A CHINESE POET WRITING THROUGH THE NIGHT UP ON THE EDGE OF MT POLLUX

by DARA WIER

from JUBILAT

Now I could see I'd been stirring the pot
For almost ten thousand years.
I could see I'd be stirring forever.
So far nothing'd changed.
Nobody appeared.
I stirred myself into a bottomless sleep,
I was the smallest thing in the world.
Fragment of spit, rumor of mud.
Something that almost might have been.
I no longer had skin or fine hairs along
My arms for wind to chill or an ant to wander
Over. I no longer had friends.
No sister, no brother.
I hadn't cried when my father & my mother
Waved good-bye and their ship exited the harbor.
I hadn't asked them where they were going.
They left me no instructions.

Nominated by David Madden, Richard Jackson

AUTOCHTHONIC SONG

by REBECCA SEIFERLE

from BITTERS (Copper Canyon Press)

We knew the buffalo were dangerous, but, most of the time
as we drifted among them, longing to touch

the bright curls of one of the spring calves,
their coats the color of new pennies, they lowered

their heads to the wild grasses, and shied away
only when we drew too near. For months

we moved among them, circling
the sweet expressions of the calves,

as they kept circling that hill that seemed a ziggurat,
pointed at the summit, like that odd vision

of Columbus—off the coast of South America
"the earth was round and something rising

in the distance like a breast"—who thought
he had reached the beginning

of all creation, the nipple
of time and space. The hill glittered

with mica—flakes, the size and breadth
of a human hand—scattered

over its flanks. We tried many times to bevel by hand
the stones into a clear plane, an eyeglass

through which we could view the world,
but the crystals only split along the cleavage,

until, running among that shaggy tribe,
we forgot our mothers, our fathers, as if, running among

that remnant, we could save some part of ourselves
from extinction. Crazy with liberty,

I veered toward a calf, drew so close
that I could never remember

if I had touched it or not. But the mother,
her malevolence, one movement with her desire

to protect, wheeled in alarm,
and as she did so the herd wheeled with her, as a flock of sparrows

will turn in the sky to enfold a red-tailed hawk. A current
of rippling fear or anger, the buffalo

turned to charge us. We ran, the breath scattering
out of our child-lungs, barely able to keep ahead

of that rhythm that had always seemed like that of a choppy
rocking horse but which now seemed as fluid

as a flash flood churning down an arroyo.
We ran toward the hill, hoping the slope would save us

by wearing them down, the climb exhaust their fury,
and it did, but so slowly that by the time the buffalo stopped,

milling about halfway up, we were ourselves stampeding,
seized by a panic, so ancient, it kept our ribs

splintering in our chests all the way up the hill
until we crammed ourselves into the tiny cave

at its summit, clinging to ourselves
among the black widow spiders, the sloppy cobwebs

of fear, and it was only then that I understood—
the earth is not our mother but a wild music beyond the self.

Nominated by Copper Canyon Press

SONNET

by KAREN VOLKMAN

from NEW ENGLAND REVIEW

Lease of my leaving, heartfelt lack, what does
your plunge propose, its too-loose turning?
A deepfall trill, always-again returning
when Leaving, stepchild of Staying, is and was

always already going, condition, cause
of future's rapture—the baby always burning—
and present never present, always yearning
for plummet's pivot—articulate pause.

Lack lurks, blue and black. What acrid, airy sea
will give the whither anchor, heed the calling
for harbor, shore, to stall the listing lee

of always-motion, infant and appalling?
My infinite late, dark nascence: Tell me,
will there be an end to all this falling?

Nominated by Reginald Shepherd

HERON

by WILLIAM WENTHE

from THE SOUTHERN REVIEW

That drought summer the lake hung low.
Once-sunken stumps hugged
their shadows as we watched
a heron, across the water, articulate itself
in grave, measured strides, to where
a turtle slept on a log. The heron bowed
its fluent neck, its clever beak
nudged the turtle—slap into the lake!
In the story I wanted to tell,
the turtle was me, the water
that unreadable depth I feared,
and the heron, the heron was love.

Something underwater we couldn't see
moved the heron
to thrust—a frantic foot-long fish
speared on its beak. Lunging, splashing,
the heron bungled shoreward, flung the thing
on hard mud as if rejecting it,
then battered, batting and flipping it till
the beak raised skyward—
fish-head toward throat, fish-tail still writhing—
then a kind of backwards vomit, swelling
the long gullet. We watched, and wore
ourselves out with watching

the elegant wader reveal
an appetite so hideous—that heron,
that heron I had taken for love.

Nominated by Bruce Beasley, Jeffrey Harrison, Robert Cording

OFF ISLAND

fiction by MICHAEL PARKER

from FIVE POINTS

for Lee Zacharias

AFTER SO MANY STORMS hit the island the people started to move away. In the end it was only Henry Thornton on one side of the creek, Miss Maggie and Miss Whaley on the other. Sisters: Miss Maggie with her dirty same old skirt and Henry's old waders she used to slosh across the creek, Maggie hugging on him nights when she got into her rum and came swishing down to his place to hide out from her sister. Henry hid out from Miss Whaley himself, stuck close to his house down the creek where his family had stayed since anyone could remember. Three bodies left on the island and a Colored Town right on until the end. Every day Henry would cross the creek up to where his white women lived: sisters, but Miss Maggie had got married and could go by her first name instead of Whaley which her older sister by three years clung to like the three of them clung firm to their six square miles of sea oat and hummock afloat off the elbow of North Carolina.

Across the sound it got to be 1979. Henry's oldest boy Crawl gave up fishing menhaden out of Morehead to run a club. He wrote Henry that he'd purchased this disco ball. Miss Maggie read the letter out to Henry on the steps of the church one warm night. Henry told her, write Crawl tell him send one over, we'll run it off the generator in the church, hang it up above the old organ, have this disco dance. Henry made a list in his head of everybody he'd invite back, all of them who'd left out of there after Bertha blew through and took the power and the light. Crawl wrote how that ball spinning under special bulbs would glitter diamonds all up and down your partner. Miss Maggie snickered, said, I ain't about to take a letter and tell him that. Imagine what Whaley would do come some Saturday night when we're dancing in a light bound to suffer her a hot flash. Up under his breath Henry said, We? Ain't no we. In his head he was twirling his Sarah around in a waterspout of diamonds. Tell everybody come back for the disco, Crawl, he wrote in his head. All of his eleven children and Miss Maggie's son Curt the prison guard up in Raleigh. Hell, Crawl, invite back those Coast Guard boys and some of the summer people even. He was sealing up his letter when he looked out across the marsh to where night came rolling blueblack and final over the sound. He ripped that letter open and crossed it all out and said instead, No thank you son to some disco ball, we got stars.

Every morning Henry poled his skiff out into the shallows to fish for dinner. He stayed out in good weather to meet the O'Neal boys, fishermen from Ocracoke who met the Cedar Island ferry every day for mail. Be sure you give me all them flyers, he'd say every time and the O'Neals would hand him a sack of grocery store circulars sent over from the mainland advertising everything. Miss Whaley liked to call out the prices at night. "They got turkey breast 29 cent a pound." All it took to make Henry wonder how come he stayed was to sit around long enough to hear Whaley say this three times a night about a two-week-old manager's special one hundred miles up in Norfolk. Crawl was always after him to move off island, had come after him six times since Bertha. You don't got to stay here looking after the sisters daddy til they die or you one. Come on, get in the boat. Crawl showed up wearing his hair springy long and those widelegged pants made out of some rough something, looked like cardboard, to where your legs couldn't breathe. Boots don't ought to come with a zipper. Why would Henry want to climb in any boat with duded-up Crawl? He would keep quiet, watch his grandbabies poking around the beach and going in and out of the houses standing empty waiting on their owners to come back, sitting right up on brickbat haunches pouting like a dog will do you when you go off for awhile. He would watch his grandsons jerk crabs out the sound on a chicken liver he give them and having themselves some big easy time until they hit that eyecutting age. Look at Granddaddy fussing after his white women, what for? Henry would look at them not looking at him and hear the words out of Crawl's mouth all across the Pamlico Sound and all the way back. Your granddaddy don't want to change none. That island gonna blow and him with it one of these days.

What would Henry Thornton be across the sound? Now, who? This he could not say but it wasn't what they all thought: scared to find out. Maybe fear was what kept the sisters from leaving, though they had their other reasons. Maggie would do right much what her big sister said do when it came down to it. Miss Whaley stayed on partly for the state boys who came down from Raleigh every spring before the mosquitoes rode the landbreeze over. Every April a boat load of them, always this fat bearded one with his bird glasses and often a young white girl who asked most of the questions. They'd get the answers up on a tape machine, so Henry called them the Tape Recorders. Miss Whaley'd put on her high-tider talk the Tape Recorders loved to call an Old English brogue. They said Henry spoke it too, though how he could have come out talking like an Old English, they didn't tell him that. He didn't ask. He didn't care to talk for them, but it didn't matter much because Miss Whaley loved a tape recorder. Every year she'd tell them about her father's daddy got arrested in Elizabeth City because he favored the man shot Abraham Lincoln who was loose at the time. She didn't mention he was over there on a drunk. Sometimes Maggie would though, and cackle right crazy loud. Miss Whaley every time would tell about Henry's younger brother Al Louie Thornton who cooked for the guests over at the first lodge before it washed away and who was known all over the island for wearing bras and panties and shaved his chest hairs and plucked around his nipples and painted his toenails. Sometimes he'd cook in his apron and shirt and that's all. Babe Ruth came over to hunt, they took him back in the kitchen to meet Al Louie. Babe Ruth took Al Louie's autograph, though Miss Whaley left that part out too.

One year the tiny white girl pulled Henry aside, said, That lady's digging dirt all the way around your family tree Mister Henry, serves her right if you want to return the favor. Wanting Henry to tell it on a tape machine, Miss Whaley almost getting married three times and then falling all over Miss Maggie's, her own sister's, husband, the nofishingest man ever born on island and some said a thief. Henry could have taped that and more. He could have had Miss Whaley showing her white ass in some book right alongside Al Louie's black aproned ass. But he just gave that little girl a smile and said, I don't no more hear than the wind after seventy-some years on this island and last six with just us three.

The Tape Recorders were all the time trying to get Henry to act like he hadn't ever been off island much at all. He played them like they wanted, even though he'd spent two years at the Coast Guard base up in Weeksville and six years in the Norfolk shipyards. There he took up welding and did decent at it. Now his children reached right up the east coast to Troy, New York like stops on a train. Morehead, Elizabeth City, Norfolk, Baltimore, Philly, Newark, Brooklyn, up all the way to Kingston and Troy. He'd took that train many times when Sarah was alive. She loved it off island. All the time talking about moving, retiring she called it. But what was there to retire from? Wasn't any *after* to sit down from on this island. Henry came back to the island a damn good welder but what was it to weld? Can't weld conch shell, seaweed, fishbone. He bought some pigs and chickens off his brother and later on two milk cows from the O'Neals and got by selling crabs and flounder to O'Neal who turned right around sold to the wholesalers in Hatteras for what Henry knew was some serious profit.

Two storms before Bertha, the one that opened up a new inlet down on the southern tip of the island, Sarah bled to death on the kitchen floor. Henry had got caught over in Ocracoke on errands for the sisters and what it was was the wind. Henry'd tacked the kitchen on himself out of washed-up timber mostly and some he'd paid the ferryman to bring him from Belhaven, which wasn't much better grade than what the tide brung up. And Henry's hand-hammered kitchen falling, slashing a hole in his Sarah's forehead. Sarah lying on the floor in the rain, her blood running the brown boards black. Before he left he'd asked the sisters, y'all check up on Sarah while I'm gone. Sarah wasn't nearly as friendly with them as Henry. Maybe because they were women and it had got down to four of them, three women and one man to run man things. Sarah did not stomach Miss Whaley's attitude and as for Miss Maggie's mess when she took a drink and came right up close enough to Henry to blink crosseyed (maybe because at that particular nearness he wasn't even black, just blurry) well, Sarah knew it. She studied everything but didn't say one word to Henry about it even though he knew when she knew something, he could read her just like he could the wind and the sound and the sky. If Henry wasn't there to drag his wife across the creek nights she'd have stayed home singing those gospel songs Crawl's wife taped her off the radio. They had the lights then and Sarah favored this Al Green out of Memphis. Maybe she was singing her Al Green right up until Henry's kitchen came down on her and do you know the timber he cobbled that kitchen out of blew right off island? Ocean brung it to him, wind took it away. And left Sarah lying out on the floor holding a pair of scissors in her hand, what for? What was she fixing to cut? The sight of those scissors drove Henry crazy. He pried them out of her fist and flung them into the inlet and tried not to look at her head whichways upside the stove.

She wouldn't let me go after her, Miss Maggie told Henry, talking about Whaley, which Whaley herself was big enough to admit. Why lose two to save one? she said. Sarah bled to death and it turned up big-skied sunny like it will do after a storm to make you feel worse and the sun dried the blood on the floorboards until it looked like paint. Toting the wood down-island is how he discovered the new inlet. And in his mind it was Sarah cut the island in two. Sheared right through the marshland with her sewing scissors. Low tide he'd walk over to the good-for-nothing-but-birdshit southside. He'd crouch and smoke him an El Reeso Sweet if he could get one off the O'Neals. Wasn't one thing over there worth seeing but he knew Sarah was wanting him where the sisters weren't.

But he couldn't be hiding all day down island. They would be wanting their mail. Henry would pole out and the O'Neals would tie him up if they won't in a hurry and pass him a Miller's High Life. They liked to get him talking about the sisters. He knew they went right back to tell it all over Ocracoke and said how he was getting something off Miss Maggie and Miss Whaley liked to watch, he'd heard that, it got back to him. Brung back on the wind maybe. From his house down by the inlet you could see across to Ocracoke the winking lights of Silver Lake and the lighthouse tossing its milky beam around but neither Henry nor the sisters crossed over unless one got bad sick. The O'Neals brought groceries and supplies which Henry mostly paid for with his catch, Whaley being too tight to part with what money left the sisters from their daddy who even the Tape Recorders knew to have gotten filthy off a load of Irish whiskey washed ashore on Sheep Island in the twenties. Whaley when she paid him at all was so ill-mouthed about it Henry stopped asking. Sarah used to collect on it and because she knew Sarah was not scared of her, Whaley always paid her what she owed. Henry wasn't scared of neither of them but it seemed like with only three of them on the island and him keeping the two of them alive he could leave off acting the nigger and one way to do that was not go knocking on Whaley's door asking for anything he didn't leave over there the night before. Sometimes Maggie would pay him in dribbly change and yellow-smelling dollars she stole and hid God knows where on her person but it wasn't enough to make much of a difference.

Across the water Crawl wrote claiming it was 1980. He says you're seventy-five this year, Henry, Maggie said to him one night on the steps of the church. Miss Whaley sitting in her lawn chair had her flyers to go through, she wasn't listening. When she had her newspapers spread out across her lap on the church steps where the three of them would sit just like people in town will linger after supper to watch traffic and call out to neighbor women strolling babies, she was just not there. Would a two-storied green bus come chugging across the creek, she wouldn't have lifted her head to grace the sight through her reading glasses. Henry thought at first she was loosening her grip, preparing to go off island by teaching herself what to expect to pay for a pound of butter across the water in 1980. But after four or five years he figured the flyers were part of what kept her here. She'd spit the prices out like fruit seed. She'd get ill at a bunch of innocent bananas for costing highway robbery, she would read her prices like Maggie would read the letters to the editor, taking sides and arguing with every one of them, My Land the way people live in this world she'd say every night when it got too dark to read and she folded up her newspaper like the Coast Guard taught Henry to fold a flag, that careful, that slow, like a color guard was standing at attention waiting on her to finish.

Crawl don't know nothing about how old I am, Henry said to the water.

Old enough to know better, said Maggie. She tugged at his shoelace while her sister studied the paper above them. Henry always sat on the second to bottom step and Miss Maggie'd start out on the top step and slide down even with him as the evening settled though her sister would rustle prices to try to halt her.

Too old to change, what it is, said Miss Whaley.

Henry swatted the back of his neck loud, but he didn't come away with any bloody mosquito because it was a sea breeze and there wasn't any bite. His head was getting ready to switch around and stare out Miss Whaley over her paper and he backslapped himself to keep still. The slap rang out like a hammering. Miss Whaley cleared

533

her old throat. Miss Maggie to cover up got on with Crawl's letter but Henry didn't listen any more. In his head he started his own letter to the sisters, one he knew he'd never ever send them even if he could write. Y'all ought not to have done me like y'all done me, he wrote in the first line, and that was as far as he got.

That night he lay talking to Sarah in the dark. He told her what Miss Whaley said and he discussed it. How come she talking about me not changing when it's her sitting up in her throne reading out her numbers on and on. Why you let that white woman hurt you so, Henry, he heard Sarah say. He heard her words like he heard the surf frothing on the banks, making its claim and then receding, taking it back, offering more words. A conversation. Sarah used to say to him: You the strongest man I ever met, you can work all day and all night if you care to and not make a noise about it to nobody. I seen you sit outside shucking corn in a nor'easter and you ain't scared of anybody who'd pull a knife on you. How come you let what people say get away with you so much? And Henry never answered though he knew how bad people could hurt him with what they said. He just hurt. He'd been knowing that. Maybe that was why he stayed on this island so long after everybody left and there wasn't anyone to hurt him anymore but Miss Maggie who was too sweetly dizzy in the head to hurt much and Miss Whaley who he thought he knew every which way she had of hurting him but she was good for coming up with a new one. Sometimes it didn't take anybody saying anything to him to his face, he'd remember what one of the men he used to fish with said to him sixty years before when they were boys swimming naked in the inlet and he'd be out in his skiff all by himself and he'd want to put his head down on his knees and let all the crabs and oysters and mackerel and blues and tuna go on about their business. He didn't care about reeling in a thing. Hurt nearly bad enough to let everybody starve.

Henry had been this way ever since he was born on this island that the wind was taking away as he lay there not sleeping. Wondering how old he really was, he thought of the island as it used to be when he was a boy, the two stores stocking shoelaces and bolts of colored cloth, the old hospital and the post office with over fifty boxes in the walls, little glass windows Henry would peek through and pretend he was looking right inside something mysterious—the innards of some complicated machine, some smart so-and-so's brain—like he was being offered a sneak at the way things worked in this life. And then the wind took that life away before he could put what he saw to any good use, and then the wind took Sarah and now what it was him and the sisters holding out for the final storm to take them off island.

Because sleep would not come to Henry he got up and pulled on his waders and packed himself some bologna biscuits and a can of syrupy peaches like he liked and he boiled up last night's coffee and poured it in his thermos and took his flashlight out to search the weeds in front of the house for the stub of a Sweet he might have thought he'd finished one day when he was cigar flush. The beam sent sandcrabs sideways into their holes and Henry let the light play over the marsh wishing he could follow them down underneath the island where the wind could not get to them. Y'all be around way after I'm gone, he said to the crabs. Y'all wait, y'all still be here when this house is nothing but some rusty nails in the sand. He imagined his crabs crouched just below ground, ready to spring right back out once he switched his light off and give up on trying to find something to smoke himself awake good, imagined their big pop eyes staring right at him now, maybe their ears poked up listening to this sad old man out talking to the island like it cared to listen. He imagined the crabs calling to each other, hole to hole, old Henry Thornton won't never change.

What does it mean to change, Henry wondered as he cranked his outboard and throttled slow through the inlet towards the sound. What do I want over there across the water in nineteen-hundred and eighty bad enough to give up whatever it is they're wanting me to give up? He'd spent the late 60s in Norfolk and all around him everybody was carrying on, army off fighting someplace he'd never heard of before or since, white boys growing their hair out and putting all kinds of mess down their throats, black people, his own children, trying to act all African, bushing their hair out and taking new names. Then crazies popping out the windows of tall buildings shooting presidents and preachers and the whole country catching afire. Henry brought Sarah home to stay. She tried to tell him wasn't anywhere safe left in this world, but Henry said he favored wind over flame, he'd rather be blown out to sea than die choking inside some highsky building with a brick lawn and blue lights streaking the night instead of the sleepy sweep of the lighthouse which he'd long ago learned to set his breath to.

Checking on the first of his crab pots, Henry told himself that Whaley said all that mess about him too old to change but was really talking about herself. Her sister too. What had the two of them done to change but choose to remain on this island where there weren't any bananas on sale, nor 19 cent a pound fryers, buy one get half off the other? He knew Sarah, had she lived, would have left him sooner or later, would have given up trying to talk him off island and gotten fed up with Whaley's ill mouth and Miss Maggie drunkstumbling across the creek to interrupt her Al Green tapes with a whole bunch of Where's Henry at, I need to ask Henry something, call Henry for me. Henry let the rope slide slowly through his hands, watched the empty pot disappear into the deep and cut the engine. He knew he would have let Sarah go, would have stayed on just like he was doing, providing for the sisters, getting hurt over not much of nothing, spending half his days just waiting on that wind—the last one, the big one that would take the three of them out of this life where everybody was waiting on you to change.

Henry knew this too: if he went first, like they claimed men were likely to do, the sisters would have to leave. No way they could stay without him. Whaley could hurt him with her meanness, Miss Maggie could keep right on trying to get him to slip his hands somewhere they'd as soon not be, but neither of them could get on for more than a week without him. Without Henry there wasn't any island. Hell, I am that island, Henry said. Sarah when she passed cut me right in half. There's a side of me sits and smokes me a Sweet and just plain hurts, there's another part of me keeps the three of us and this island from blowing away.

Peering back on his island, Henry thought, This life ain't blowed away right yet. I can sit right here in the sound and let the wind take me wherever and still make a change. He could lie back and eat a bologna biscuit and talk to Sarah and let the change come on ahead, let the skiff drift right across the sound to Morehead where he'd call Crawl and tell him, Crawl, you ain't won, don't think you changed me, I'm just here because the wind brung me over here and I let it. He could sit outside Crawl's yard and mend nets for the boys who still pulled things out of the sea, and he could think while he mended about the sisters and about how he'd saved them. Made them change. He could sit outside on Crawl's porch and smoke on a Sweet and close his eyes and know he'd go before the sisters but that he would not leave them on that island because here he was taking the island with him, right across the water, him and the wind. He could close his eyes and see the sisters sitting right up front at his funeral,

536

sea-salty tears raining down on the Sunday dresses they had not worn for years. Hoarse preacher shouting out some Bible and Sarah whispering right over him how she could surely forgive Henry for not taking her off island before it was time for him to change. All eleven of his children and their children and the babies of his grandbabies looking up at the casket where Henry had laid down one day halfway through his crabpots, let the wind take him off island. Inside that casket Henry was sipping peach syrup and wishing he had one last Sweet. The sun was high and it was a mean sun. The church was crowded and so hot the air conditioning was sweating and coughing like some sick somebody. Preacher called out a hymn. Let it be Sarah's singer sending me off sweetly. The sun and the water blended in brightness, the casket drifted, the wind picked up, the whole church rose up in song. Then came a lady in white passing out fans only to the ones who were moaning: sisters, hurting like Henry hurt, but thankful to be spared the wind.

Nominated by Stuart Dischell, Five Points

KILLING SALMON

by MATT YURDANA

from NORTH AMERICAN REVIEW

After five weeks it's difficult to see them, each like a shadow with
   the same struggle and heft as the one it follows,

the swift, tapered moments nearly overlapping

as we wade into them, in pairs, after the net is pulled taut, one of us
   stooping to find the muscled groove above the tail that's made for
   the hand,

then twisting it up while sliding thumb and forefinger inside the
   gills, holding it out and away from the body, while the other

delivers two quick blows behind the eyes with a length of steel pipe,
   a shuddering, then a deep loosening

as it rides the conveyor up to the spawning room.

Those first days, their dramatic humps, the reds and bruised greens
   moving like a thunder storm across their bellies

kept us respectful and arrogant, believing we were an essential link
   in their life cycle,

but now, every third day or so, one of us slips into a rage; maybe it's
   a blunt snout ramming his shin, or the overgrown teeth snagging
   his waders

that makes him climb, as each of us has climbed, the cement bank
of the holding pond, dragging the salmon behind him with more
anger

than long hours, miserable pay, and the agony of our lower backs
should allow,

fifteen seconds where everything wrong in his life exists in the body
of this fish,

and he kneels, jaws clenched, ears gone red, swinging the steel pipe
again and again until it is unrecognizable;

and afterward, before his breathing slows, he tries to tell himself he
didn't enjoy it, that it wasn't satisfying, but back in the pond

he's a little embarrassed, a little afraid, and it lingers

like the nightmares he used to wake from on those quiet summer
nights from back home,

trembling in the bathroom, washing his face under the startling light
or catching the tail end of an old black and white late-night
movie,

where two lovers suffered over a whisper out of context, a letter in
the wrong hands, a message never delivered on which the entire
plot rests,

simple and reassuring, mistakes he'd made a dozen times, misunderstandings he could understand and carry with him back into
sleep.

Nominated by Robert Wrigley, Claire Davis, North American Review

A WORKING BOY'S WHITMAN

memoir by GEORGE EVANS

from SHEARSMAN

ONE SPRING DAY in the early 1960s, the dust of a final play swirling on the diamond, I exited a Pittsburgh Pirates' baseball game via the same break in the outfield wall at Forbes Field through which I entered. There were ways in the middle of that century to watch a game from the outside if you lacked ticket money (hanging from poles or trees, peering through gaps in the fence), and if you really wanted, with good timing you could sneak through various breaks in the patchwork walls and get a bleacher seat. The teams were not millionaire-boys' clubs then, Americans were less mean-spirited in general, money was not the game's Holy Grail, and guards were more interested in what was happening on the field than in gate-crashing kids.

A bronze statue of Honus Wagner, frozen in the afterswat of whacking a ball into eternity outside the left field fence, seemed to me the ultimate in modern art. But that was unmatched by the nearby bronze confection of favorite son Stephen Foster, which featured, as described in a local newspaper for its unveiling in 1900, "The poet seated, notebook in hand, catching the inspiration for his melodies from the fingers of an old darkie reclining at his feet strumming negro airs upon an old banjo." If it's true that Foster was no fan of minstrelsy and blackface, it's not something he would be proud of, regardless of the strained Southern black dialect in his lyrics. It was, and is, a double-figured statue with strong racist undertones, which if

540

proposed at this moment in history would cause brain lesions. Close by, there also stood a statue of be-knickered plough-boy poet Bobby Burns in a tam-o'-shanter, holding a mountain daisy like a potato chip.

I didn't realize then that public art with few exceptions is doomed to fail because art and consensus mix as poorly as the well-intentioned who raise money to erect such monuments mix socially with the rich who dole it out, or with the agenda-ridden municipalities and landlords who provide the space. Popular lore has it that the Stephen Foster bronze was funded with pennies raised by school-children, but my understanding of world history tells me that in those days only children of the wealthy would have had time to raise money for a statue, and it would not have been pennies they raised. The children of the poor (which many Pittsburghers either were or were becoming) would, on the other hand, have been working hard for their pennies, handing them over to parents who counted every copper drop as if it was a loaf of bread in famine.

As for Foster, although his songs were immensely popular, including the likes of "Oh! Susanna," after adding almost 300 works to America's songbook, he died alone and broken in 1864, a family man descended into alcoholism. In that era before recording and radio, there was no music industry to speak of, no legal system to protect musicians or songwriters, and he had signed away the rights to his music for next to nothing, a survival technique that would plague popular musicians far into the twentieth century. In his final days, he could have used some of those pennies collected for his statue. He had only thirty eight of them in his pocket, one for each of his years on earth, when he mortally injured himself in what must have been a drunken fall at a twenty-five cent per day hotel (reportedly and iron-ically the American Hotel) in New York's Bowery District in 1864. He fell so hard he broke a washbasin with his head, cut his throat on it, then died the next day of blood loss in the charity ward at Bellvue Hospital, occupation listed as laborer.

My paternal grandfather, an actual laborer and steel worker on bridges and smokestacks, grew up in the same cold world, and lost his legs in an industrial accident for which he was never compensated. Born in Virginia after the Civil War, he migrated north, more than likely for work, married a working class Pittsburgh girl, and settled in the neighborhood where I grew up. She died first, in the great influenza epidemic of 1920 at forty one, and he died a few years later in his mid-50s from the strain of having to continue working, even with his disability, to raise his four sons alone. They worked too, of course, but the oldest, my father, was only fifteen when they were orphaned, and though he'd dropped out of school years before to work full time (not uncommon in that world), he was forced to redouble his efforts so they could survive. He never talked much about what he went through in those years, because the working poor are more than willing to forget the horrors they survive, but he never stopped cursing and fighting the system that let it happen.

I was raised by parents without illusions, whose aspirations were limited to what they could earn to get through a week. My father was a Teamster who delivered ice and coal, and my mother a cleaning lady when she could squeeze in outside work between raising five children and keeping her own house. Her past was working class Boston, also orphaned, a life no more glamorous than my father's, but what they had in common held them together all of their lives, not always happily, but always.

That makes me a son of the fabled American working class, the one of mythic labor struggles and idealized social progress, a universe made up of wishful stories about heroic workers fighting the system and winning, a world that faded in relevance after World War II, and seemed to disappear completely during my youth. It was a brutal reality, and no amount of organizing, idealism, nostalgia or social proselytizing could save anyone in it from the backbreaking demands of daily life. Everyone worked, and I had some sort of job from the moment I could walk and think at the same time. But I was a dreamer. To me all statues were beautiful, no matter what they represented, regardless of the fact that none of them depicted anyone from our working class world or history.

It didn't matter. What I was admiring in my innocence was not exactly art, but eponymous commemorative knick-knacks I thought were art. That was before I eventually wandered into nearby Carnegie Museum to discover the extraordinary collections of plundered and otherwise amassed treasures from around the world, booty scooped up on the run by the moguls who built the city. In my neighborhood it was widely believed, when thought of at all, that Pittsburgh's museums contained only surplus examples (and not necessarily the best) of that which would not fit on the walls of the rich or in their safes. They were mediocre things displayed for the edification of working people, a peek into a world we could not be part of but were encouraged to appreciate in order to "improve ourselves," as it was phrased in public school. Improve ourselves for what we were not told in school, but our parents told us, explaining it was to improve our obedience to that which was so far above us even God Himself looked up to it. They said such things with funny accents, index fingers raising their noses into the air.

Scion of a labor intensive, union-driven world that existed in the belly of steel hogs and lace curtain Irish, as the rich were called, I was never led to believe that the art collections in those great museums were anything more than window dressing, candy for the masses, cynical displays of power and waste. My teeth were sharpened on the adage that all great fortunes hide great crimes, which perspective colored my view of all public attempts to lift the working class (made up of the only two available races in Pittsburgh at the time, blacks and whites) out of its sweaty morass, into a more cultured form of suffering. My father and his buddies would have choked on their boilermakers to hear it put that way, but would have appreciated the smartass tone.

Still, beauty has a way of surviving both sides of any argument. On occasion, those condescending displays of power and wealth had the unexpected result of igniting the imagination of a boy like me, who worked in coal yards, on trucks, on loading docks, and didn't go to school when he was supposed to, but instead went fishing, bridge climbing, train hopping, swimming in the rivers, and sometimes to museums, searching for amazement and relief from exhausting, boring labor.

At first, I spent most of my time in the great museums of Pittsburgh while playing hooky from school, mixing in with hordes of field trip students to hang around the dinosaur bone collection in continuous awe. I wondered what it would be like to have them fleshed out and walking the streets, same as the Godzilla I admired, not knowing even he (or she) was a political statement, the Japanese embodiment in celluloid of our country and its reptilian insensitivity to human life. But then again, I didn't so much care that I even lived in a country. I lived in Pittsburgh. What I was told about democracy, flags, history, and national pride, mostly went through my ears like water through a straw. I knew we were in a place called America, but didn't really care. All I could see was Pittsburgh, which I found fascinating, and that's what was important. Convincing me otherwise would have been like showing small children X-rays, trying to convince them, as they look back and forth through the light of the negatives to the glowing flesh of their bodies, that bones are what hold them together.

After I found the art in those museums (paintings and shocking nude sculptures, some with anatomically puzzling body parts), the importance of dinosaurs to my world changed forever. The fascination would remain, but in another context. It was a passage of sorts, like when a boy's voice begins to crack then deepens permanently. The collections may indeed have been surplus, whatever that actually meant, but for a boy raised without television, seeing a Van Gogh painting for the first time was akin to being hit in the head with a baseball bat and watching the stars turn into a dream, then a window into another world, then climbing through that window and getting lost.

That was it. I was going to be an artist. I couldn't afford paints or any other materials, so I started drawing on napkins, then on paper from a neighborhood printer's scraps left over when he trimmed his jobs, which he would sometimes, with amusement, bind into little notebooks. When my father found out what I was doing, he nearly disowned me. No son of his was going to make trinkets for the rich, and if I thought that drivel in the museums could afford anybody an honest living, I should just go get a gun and start robbing honest people outright like those sonsofbitches who built the museums. But my mother, who I then found out once held a job painting illustrations on greeting cards in Boston during her orphaned youth, confessed that she too had once wanted to be an artist, and encouraged me, somehow managing to settle my father's anger. Still, in the end, it did not go well because my father could not remember to be patient, and could not subdue his hatred of the rich, which my drawing in his house brought horribly to life at unexpected moments, so I quit trying to be an artist, to pursue instead something I could almost do in private and in secret, read and write.

We lived in Manchester, a neighborhood in a slummed out section of Pittsburgh originally known as Allegheny City, a town unto itself until gerrymandered by rigged elections into the great Steel City across the river early in the century, after which it was simply called the North Side. Gertrude Stein, on the front steps of whose nativity house I often sat with my droogies smoking cigarettes, playing with knives and singing doowop (her vestibule and the porch next door being perfect echo chambers), insisted she was born in Allegheny

544

City, not Pittsburgh, though boosters of Pittsburgh culture have always insisted otherwise, claiming not only Stein for their own, but my other 19th century-born, long gone Allegheny neighbors, Robinson Jeffers, Martha Graham, Mary Cassatt, and the transplant Willa Cather, who in 1901 became an English teacher at the school I eventually dropped out of—Allegheny High.

None of these celebrated individuals were much remembered or acknowledged on the North Side during my time. They were overshadowed by the likes of our resident rock & roll group, The Marcels of "Blue Moon" fame, the vocal bass refrain of which song, transcribed, would have been considered great literature by all who loitered at Gertrude's stoop: "Bom bababom ba bom ba bombom baba bom baba bom ba danga dang dang da dinga dong ding blue moon, moon moon blue moon, dip dadip dadip . . ."

But we had a marvelous library, the Allegheny Carnegie Library. Built in 1889, it was an island of calm in the center of urban disaster (snoring day residents notwithstanding), and the first free library Andrew Carnegie built in the US, close to Slabtown where he worked as a bobbin boy in a textile mill after arriving from Scotland in 1848. Meant to be a "working boys" library, it was the culmination of his dream to honor his mentor Colonel James Anderson, a pioneer iron manufacturer. Pittsburgh, famous as the Steel City, was actually once known as the "Iron City," due to the industry of Anderson and his fellow Ironmongers, but that moniker now exists only as the name of a popular local beer. In the mid-nineteenth century, Anderson opened the doors of his private library (a then staggering 400 volumes) to the working boys of Allegheny City so they could better themselves in the world. Carnegie always said Anderson had opened "the temple of knowledge" to him, changing his life forever, and it was that act that inspired his Carnegie Free Library system.

It must be noted, I was one of the only boys who hung out in that boys' library. At least ninety-nine percent of the patrons were girls. Those same girls, some of whom would eventually teach me to love, laugh, cry, would break my heart (sometimes my head), and one who destroyed a large part of my 45 record collection by hurling them out a window at me one by one, angry at some act of emotional idiocy on my part, taught me how to use that library long before they taught me how to dance. Hanging around the girls did not endear me to other boys at first, but neither did reading books, so I adapted to fighting my way back and forth through the streets, learning the various methods of using books as lethal weapons as I went. I had to maintain my image as one of the many North Side gang members for whom shooting pool, stealing cars for joy rides, rioting at Friday night dances, and waiting our turns to go to war (with each other or for the government), was the meaning of life.

Our library occupied the northeast corner of a busy intersection which, when it was built, marked the center of Allegheny City. In front stood a monument to Anderson designed by Daniel Chester French: a raised plaza with granite exedra, and at the zenith of the exedra curve sat a giant bronze statue of Labor, work shirt off, sledge hammer leaned next to him, reading a gigantic book upon which I used to sit in the sun. A bronze bust of Anderson rested solidly on a pedestal above Labor. It was a useful public space for soap box politicians and pre-airwave evangelists, but in local terms it was no more than a monument to a monument.

In my neighborhood, libraries fared no better than museums. It was understood (and resented) that Carnegie had spent a minuscule amount of what he gained exploiting working people in order to give them a gift they would eventually be taxed for the upkeep of, thereby creating a perpetual monument to himself to be swept and maintained by the very people who despised him most. To my parents' generation of working class North Siders (sons, daughters and grandchildren of those who felt most exploited by Carnegie), the monument and library served only to remind them of the long arm of an oppressive and impoverishing 19th century.

As a matter of fact, and most likely because of this well-known but unpublicized criticism of Carnegie by the poor he was supposed to have uplifted, it is widely and erroneously assumed in Pittsburgh that the actual first US Carnegie Library is the one located in the wealthier neighborhood of Oakland, near the University of Pittsburgh. That bit of mythology is simply the result of PR by those who wished to deny Carnegie would build his first library in a shithole neighborhood populated by ungrateful ineducabilia. When those same city fathers renovated North Side in the mid-1960s, they decided to dismantle the Anderson monument and destroy the exedra, wiping away the evidence, and the residents did not stop them. Poignantly, the bronze of Labor remains nearby.

In our neighborhood saloon, behind and above the revolving lamp of a boy urinating into a river with an ever increasing arch, was a sign painted in gold letters:

"A man who dies rich dies disgraced."
A. Carnegie—Liar, Philanthropist, Thief

Under it in red:

"You can't eat books."
A. Worker—Robbed & Cheated

But I didn't really care about any of that. I admired Carnegie for his nickname "King of the Vulcans," as well as for his rise from the factories. I went to the library every day to pore over the books, and took many home to read under blankets with a flashlight, concealing my interest from my father, only barely more tolerant of books than he was of art.

I found Walt Whitman's *Leaves of Grass* on a shelf sagging with the 19th Century American poetical tonnage of (to name an illustrious few) Edgar Fawcett, Richard Watson Gilder, Charles Fenno Hoffman, Emma Lazarus, Sidney Lanier, Celia Thaxter, and Cincinnatus Hiner Miller (better known as Joaquin Miller, a Whitman impersonator), Parnassian giants all, for the sake of whose yodeling countless acres of virgin forest had been pulped. Whitman was held upright by dog-eared volumes of Elizabeth Stuart Phelps Ward (renowned), and John Greenleaf Whittier (a voice humanely silenced "by the breeze, moaning through the graveyard trees" of his productions).

There were other editions of Whitman's book, but I recall pulling out the thinnest, the first edition, or a facsimile of it. It was probably the size that drew me (less than a hundred pages and tall like a picture book), as well as its striking design. It was green with a gold title, roots sprouting from the bottoms of the letters, leaves flowering from the tops, and the back cover was identical when you flipped the book over, implying the beginning and end were the same, or that there was no beginning or end, or that everything was somehow upside down. There was no author's name on the cover (though copyrighted inside by one Walter Whitman in tiny letters), but opposite the title page, was an engraved daguerreotype of a man who looked like a cowboy: hat, no suit, no tie, no flowing hair, no pencil poised like a dart, and no Victorian look of smug transcendence or self-indulgence.

I knew it was poetry because of where it was located in the library, but it had a wonderful absence of the tin-eared rhyming nailed into my head in English class. Thumbing through it, I thought it was some sort of mis-shelved bible because of the language, until I read the introduction, which told me the genius of America was its "common people," for which I read "working class poor." I believed it immediately and imagined the president doffing his hat to me at the construction site where I worked demolition on weekends, or at the Five & Ten where I washed dishes weekday afternoons, asking my advice on everything from the price of beans to pending wars, especially the one my friends and I were destined to be involved in— each working class generation had its own war, and we were waiting for ours.

The force of my experience with Whitman's introduction paled once I read the first poem, the untitled, unnumbered blasts of language and thought which in later editions would be tamed into numbered sections with the misleading title "Song of Myself." It was Whitman at his purest, untainted by later affectations and delusions of grandeur—a profound masterpiece resulting from some sort of pre-Civil War satori experience without the benefit of Buddhism or LSD. I didn't really know what he was talking about, but I couldn't put it down. The moment I picked it up, *Leaves of Grass* ignited in my hands. It expressed a view of the universe that was as like and unlike Pittsburgh as possible, and, if not cohesive or even comprehensible to me then, appeared to be all-inclusive. Its subject was not merely the world but the universe, and not only life but consideration of its opposite. The subject matter was no less than everything, or so it seemed.

In contrast to the tinkling dross that kept him company on the shelves, I was engulfed by Whitman's vatic tone, and, unlike the others, he energetically glorified and celebrated the kind of world I lived in. I was attracted by the attention, though skeptical. Beneath the stereotypical image of the noble worker (we forthright, positive citizens who could never afford to believe official descriptions) lay the truth. Our existence was hardly a subject for celebration. It was dominated by crippling accidents, violent struggles for improved conditions, corrupt labor unions, subsistence and mortgage worries, collapsing businesses, a sliding belief in government, hatred of taxes, and a violent desire to get drunk.

But I kept reading.

Whitman seemed to view industry as a force that could carry humanity forward to higher purposes, while I constantly brushed mill ash out of my hair and teeth, fished mutant creatures from factory polluted rivers, and squinted to see the sky through gaseous mist. The working people he so revered constantly punched one another in the head, worked overtime without wages, battered their wives and children, chewed up and spit out youth and beauty with bitterness, and could never work hard enough to make enough to drink and still keep food on the table.

The sane governments, insights, and human affections Whitman intimated were not present where I lived, but he caused me to imagine there was another world, a parallel world, a shadow world of sorts, the way our labor unions were a shadow government. Perhaps in that other world, if I could find it, I would discover the source of his optimism and philosophical certainty, colored with its odd, all-embracing skepticism: "Do I contradict myself? Very well then . . . I contradict myself; I am large . . . I contain multitudes."

But first I had to understand what he saw when he scanned the wage slave, wife beating, war-scarred motor humpers of the multi-racist working class I was part of, a world where you could be pounded with a bottle if you disagreed with someone, or smashed with a chair if you agreed. What did Whitman see? People with dreams but no money to accomplish them, I concluded, people who mistook work for freedom and poured everything into it, people who lived at the top of their lungs because they were used to being ignored, and people who lived in perpetual motion because they always had somewhere to go for someone else's sake.

What he praised was not so much our quotidian lives as our loyal industry, unabashed directness, and our impulse to move and change. Change into what? Into anything. In that world only a fool would want to remain the same, though most had no choice but to live out static lives interrupted only by childbirth, military service, layoffs, and death. Perhaps, I thought, Walt Whitman was trying to drum up compassion for our world, while trying to lift our spirits and encourage us to break loose—it struck me that way, and there was no one around to argue otherwise. For all I knew, his work represented the sort of political bombast my father was fond of pointing out, but I didn't want it to be so, and luckily it wasn't. Like any other adolescent, I cautiously wanted something pure to believe in, and while baseball and basketball won over many of my friends, I went for Whitman.

I never discovered the source of his optimism, but eventually, despite a lack of critical ability and historical understanding, began to appreciate his work for its sheer exuberance and energy, its resistance to conservative logic, and its almost total absence of Victorian prosody. It was his ineffable reality I came to accept most deeply, not his meaning, and certainly not what I initially misinterpreted as simple nationalism, though that was certainly part of it. It was poetry as powerful force of observation, mysterious vision, and insight, no matter how impossibly hopeful.

By extolling the virtues of human experience with such ostensible ease and unabashed ecstasy, he was, I thought, in a way inviting everyone to be a poet or an artist, to free books from their libraries, paintings from their museums, and to pry everything creative away from professionalism. The farther from institutions, the better, the more distance between art and hallowed halls, the more likely it was to evolve, or, at minimum, change importantly.

As it happens, North American poetry has emerged since his time as the most inclusive and malleable of arts, though not because it is plastic, but because from it the least is expected. It cannot be traded as commodity because it has no physical value, and cannot specifically belong to anyone—its virtue and curse. It cannot be defended from pretenders because it has no gate to guard, no public expectations exist for it, very few people read it seriously unless they intend to write it (or already do), and no one can defend its higher qualities comprehensively because none can agree upon what they are. In fact, no one understands exactly what it is, and it is protected from legislative censorship not by its failure to provoke consensus or dissent, but by the reality that most US politicians do not (or simply cannot) read it, including recent presidents.

One must, however, note an exception to that generalization, considering that Whitman's *Leaves of Grass* was drawn, along with cigar dildos, into the late twentieth century President Clinton-Intern Lewinsky debacle by virtue of the fact that the book was given as a gift by the sax blowing commander in chief to his kneeling beloved at the outset of their trysts. Until that information surfaced, Whitman had not been involved in a government scandal (albeit on a lesser level) since being fired from his job at the Bureau of Indian Affairs in 1865 by secretary of the interior James Harlan just after the Abraham Lincoln assassination. Harlan, a conservative, considered *Leaves of Grass* obscene, though he later denied that was the reason he fired

550

Whitman, which makes him a liar as well as a government censor, neither of which is rare. The more recent Whitman sighting is humorous, somewhat thrilling if one considers the romantic nature of the gesture, and, if anything, illustrates that Clinton did indeed have something in common with Lincoln: they both seemed to like Whitman, though there's no evidence that either actually read him.

For aspiring poets, there's still an important lesson to be learned from Whitman the artist, and the earlier the better (those already cynical and putrefied may relearn it if they wish): he was not doing a job. Poetry was not his profession, it was his life, a necessity, pure love, and when he wrote "I, me, my," he wasn't writing to draw attention to a suffering, unattended ego. He was reaching beyond the self, out into the living universe of things, ideas, and events—the world he was part of—as if through poetry the universe could rise up with a human voice.

In his case, it could. But in the end, I think he was mistaken (however ecstatically) about the realities of the working class, the common people, though his roots were those of a working man and commoner. He wanted their world to be something it never was, and transformed it into a platform from which to project idealized perceptions and imagined possibilities for a flawless democratic society, something quite impossible. Then again, the poet who would come to write one of the most moving of Civil War memoirs (embedded in his autobiography *Specimen Days*) could not foresee, or chose to ignore, the carnage poised to emerge from the intrinsic flaws of the virtuous society he extolled and glorified in that first masterpiece, "Song of Myself."

Hindsight may not be to the point, and his world lacked the mass communication syndicates that inform us of the most minuscule news items and social developments, but one must question how it could be that a man who lived with his eyes and heart wide open, could have so little to say about certain matters that truly contradicted his notions of liberty and freedom. He was, for example, sympathetic, but not very mindful of slavery, and was certainly not an abolitionist. Nor was he particularly attentive to the past and pending genocide wrought against native Americans by the original Euro-invasion and on-going US westward expansion, in spite of his employment at the Bureau of Indian Affairs.

In his work, there are no songs of labor about the severely abused transcontinental railroad and Gold Rush Chinese, no mellifluous observations of gandy dancing Irish pounding their brains out on the tracks, no Latinos to speak of, and only a passing mention of Jews. His was not an empty country (what we see now by way of human variety also existed then), but his expanse was confined by the fact that he was mainly an arm-chair traveler. Many of the missing may be found in works like the poem "Salut au Monde!," but from such catalogues we learn only that he knew his geography, had a vivid imagination, and was literally (merely) popping a salute from his "America" to the rest of the world, which he never saw.

For all his curiosity, he didn't travel much. He went to New Orleans as a young man, to parts of the south and Washington, DC during the Civil War, and later in life went west by train as far as Denver. He visited Canada briefly, made it to Boston, and settled in Camden, New Jersey near Philadelphia in old age, but he never crossed an ocean, or even the Rockies (a feat for someone who lived through the great California Gold Rush and not only claimed to be manly, adventurous, healthy, and universally curious about his country, but was also a working journalist at the time). As it turns out, he was not, in fact, caught up in the turbulence and sweep of things to the degree his readers tend to believe, and his vision of the larger world bordered on the romantic and imaginary.

He adored his America, but didn't see or experience much of it (his impressions from train windows aren't very convincing), and his poetry suffers from the fact. He was not particularly interested in the trademark evils of the brand of democracy practiced on his home court, and there is a bruising lack of criticism in his work regarding the life crushing exploitation of the poor and working classes by the wealthy and powerful. He was our first public poet, but as observer of society at large, his poetry generally ignores the limited prospects and impoverishing conditions that faced the common people he lionized. But that's no great surprise.

There are important exceptions (their number increases sharply mid-twentieth century), but avoiding social criticism and political content has long been endemic and symptomatic for a wide range of North American poetry, not that social indifference is confined to poetry by any means. This artistic silence (not unusually referred to as good taste) reflects a type of selective silence that flowed into our general social consciousness from the early Puritan tradition of colonial leaders never telling the British king the truth about the horrors of life in the colonies, lest he take away their power. Bad news was forbidden, and once the new Americans learned to be selective about reporting horrid social conditions, especially their disgraceful treatment of indigenous people, it became a trait to willfully ignore them, planting, perhaps, the seeds of the illiberal, intolerant conservatism that has dogged our history. In that context, it follows that even one of our most public of poets might tend to be (if not apolitical) uncritical of the country's deepest social faults in his poetry, adding to our image of Whitman the iconoclast intimations of one flirting with conventionalism.

Still, who Whitman really was remains unclear on a number of levels. For example, which of these sexes was he: heterosexual, homosexual, bisexual, or asexual? Based on his work and biographical details, and viewed through the lens of the present, he seemed to be all four at various points, sometimes all at once, and should probably be considered—if as a sexual being at all—humanly omnisexual in order to grasp the breadth of his implications. But even in those matters, touchy if not dangerous in Victorian North America, he avoids taking a distinct position, while managing to project a sexually liberated persona throughout his work. Politically speaking, he also remains in the closet, but comes off as more limited, though it's probably intentional.

He was very selective about his subject matter, and careful about its implications, but he absolutely believed in and promoted Democracy, which bears its own range of historical problems, leaving his work open to serious criticism. In his 1898 political essay "The Triumph of Caliban," Nicaraguan poet Rubén Darío (Whitman's Spanish language counterpart, and otherwise an admirer of his work), called him "a prophet of Democracy, Uncle Sam style," meaning Uncle Sam the imperialist, unwanted invader, cultural imposer.

Claiming to be the poet of the common people, Whitman's weakness, as I've been pointing out, is to have overlooked the darkest aspects of their lives in his poetry. One would not think to criticize him on that level if he had not projected his image and poetry as the voice and living body of the people en masse, but he did, and the facts of his neglect must be observed if we are to appreciate him fully, which also means considering the non-political context of most serious North American poetry. It's not that Whitman was unaware of social problems, he was very aware of them. Among other things, he published a clumsy temperance novel (about a sot named Evans, I'm sorry to note: *Franklin Evans; or The Inebriate*) thirteen years before the first edition of *Leaves of Grass*. But that book and a number of other didactic prose and poetry texts are so gratuitously pro-American and nationalistic in spirit that they seem disingenuous in retrospect, and he would have been dismissed as a minor pamphleteer had he written nothing else.

However, on a positive note, his overall work is too important for such a fate, and he was too impressive a figure in life to be dismissed, unless we dismiss the past completely. The seminal poet of North American literature, the best aspects of this work remain (acknowledged or not) an unshakable influence on all poetry written in English since his time.

When his poetry hit its stride in 1855 with the first edition of *Leaves of Grass*, it was destined to change just about everything there was to change about North American poetry, breaking linguistic, prosodic, and emotional barriers so successfully that one could no more go back to writing the sort of poetry that existed before him (not seriously at least) than one could go back to painting Rembrandts. Because of the concept and reality of time, forward progress seems actual, and as far as we know at present, nothing in the universe can return to the exact state it was in before moving forward (or in any direction we can perceive), and such is the case with all things, including poetry and other arts. Apparently, change is continuous, if not progressive, rendering Neo-movements (such as poetry's various and recurring stabs at producing classical verse, or Neo-formalism as it is sometimes called) flat and boring unless they incorporate intentional humor or self-conscious reference to the original models.

Mixing mediums to make the point, a successfully executed sonnet today (for that matter, any classical verse form) must be at least as inventive as a Komar and Melamid painting. They are the two Soviet artists who brought us the mid-1990s *Most Wanted* painting series by conducting a broad, ten country survey of what average people most want and expect from art, then painted the results, which are both disturbing and entertaining. What they created are and are not paintings—they are representations of paintings. More to the point on the subject of Neo-formalism is their series of at least fifty-nine 5" X 7", conventional looking (except for their size) romantic landscape oils attributed to a one-eyed Russian painter named Nikolai Buchomov, born near the end of the 19th Century. These paintings are part of a conceptual work, complete with a convincing photograph of Buchomov, eye patch in place, and biographical documentation, all compiled or created by the artists. The work is playful and attractive, sublime and absurd.

As pointed out by the lively art critic Arthur C. Danto, upon close examination, one comes to realize that a recurring geological detail in the paintings is actually the side of Buchomov's nose as he gazed out with his one eye, brush in hand, at the landscape. An engaging classical sonnet written now, if possible, would have to contain self-conscious references at least that clever and subtle. We have Whitman to thank for that in part.

Since his time, North American poetry (and the rest of the world seems not far behind at this point) has experienced many deaths, mainly by university and creative writing workshop executions, and by those who insist it is a job—a crude punching of the poetry clock. It has been frozen, ossified and manipulated over and over for reasons and prizes that have nothing to do with poetry, the results of which often have nothing to do with anything significant. But it has not been buried because one moment it might be stiff upon the floor with rigor mortis, rhyming couplets dribbling from a hole in its temple, but the next it is fully awake, running around the streets with its head on fire.

It's a duppy art. Art of the living dead.

Whitman might have added that nothing so intangible and difficult may be adequately taught at any rate, and that poetry is therefore in no danger of being taught to death. Inspiration is important, but if one is not a born genius or prodigy, the act of writing genuine poetry can only be learned, or awakened, through a life of patience, observation, omnivorous reading, and hard work. To continue doing so past middle age, it helps to view failure and success as relative, and to trick one's good sense into thinking obscurity is the equal of fame. One must also, as Whitman did, work always without a net or concern for unfriendly opinions, and upon hitting the ground continue to plummet willingly, through everything, until gravity reverses itself and you are falling upwards again.

That may sound like hard medicine, or optimistic hyperventilation if you're a poet on the downswing feeling dark and inconsolable, but in the United States (a now nearly post-book, post-literate society on the edge of finding out what dot commerce and the Internet will really do to the imagination, not to mention publishing, especially poetry books, which generally have a briefer shelf life than a butterfly's existence), odds are things can only become a more intensified version of the same, until unbearable, then far worse than imagined possible. It's best to brace oneself against the storm, though Whitman might have somehow managed to sweep even this grim reality into an optimistic poem. Then again, his accomplishments are completely native to his own time, rich as it was without airplanes, radios, televisions, computers, world wars, or atomic weapons.

§

Not long after that spring day I left Forbes Field to wander among the statues, I decided to run away from home. It took a year or so of staying away for longer and longer periods, but I finally left for good. I remained in Pittsburgh, memorizing every inch of it, and made some effort to continue going to school while living by my wits, exploring that world of rivers and ethnic neighborhoods cupped within a green circle of hills. My adventures, many and extreme, lasted until I finally dropped out of high school, and in 1966 became determined to go find the war I was raised to participate in.

My best friend since elementary school, who was not a dropout and lived in a different world than mine by then, came looking for me when he heard about my plans. He had somehow discovered the unvarnished truth about the horrors of a conflict on the verge of exploding into full-scale war in a place called Vietnam. How he unraveled the knot of media and government misrepresentations about Vietnam at such an early stage of open US involvement still puzzles me. I was oblivious, knew nothing about it, and was hardly alone in my ignorance. Like most military-age males (as the Army put it) I was a prime example, a fledgling member, of the brotherhood of benighted working class cannon fodder the US is so famous for.

Like the Korean War, the events in Vietnam were being referred to as a "Police Action," and that should have tipped us off. The most likely to serve, and with relatives who had survived what they only referred to as a war in Korea, we might have asked a simple question: If it's a police action, why tanks and bombers instead of squad cars and billy clubs? But of course there was no one to ask, and the question would have sounded silly. We remnants of the romanticized working class, along with an emerging underclass (nearly full-blown at the beginning of the twenty-first century), were a vital part of the now obvious poverty draft. For us, military service was the only way to get out of the streets and on track to a good job, the most promising means of securing enough dignity and money for an education. No books, no art, and nobody could change that reality.

My friend knew all that, but he wasn't merely afraid, he was troubled. He did not want to go to a place that had nothing to do with us, had serious moral compunctions about killing other people (in this case the Vietnamese), and did not want to die fighting for something that had nothing to do with Manchester, the North Side, or the whole country for that matter. I didn't want to die either, but it never crossed my mind that I could. I can't say for certain his thinking was as complex as I like to remember, but I knew him to be anything but a coward, so his arguments were not about simple fear, and because I was otherwise aimless, therefore open minded, I listened. He'd thought about things I hadn't imagined, and though there was never a question that any upstanding North Side boy would ever wait around to be drafted, he talked me out of joining the high-mortality-rate Army or Marines. Instead, he insisted we join the Air Force, where our chances for survival would be much improved, and where we innocently believed they would allow us to fly airplanes. We took the recruitment tests at the same time one sunny day, with the promise that we would be part of what they called a "buddy system," stationed together for the whole four years of our enlistment. The plan was for me to stick around until he graduated high school in a month or so, then we would take on the world from the wild blue yonder.

It was a good plan, but he failed the physical and I headed south for basic training in San Antonio without him, on a train during the great airline strike of 1966. I had traveled a lot on trains, they were a particular obsession of mine since the tracks were only a half block from my house, but I'd always traveled on the outside ladders or in empty box cars, and that trip to Texas was the first time I ever sat in the passenger section. I missed my friend, but felt like a king, serenading myself with every railroad song I could remember. It was a thrilling adventure, and the absurdity of going off to the Air Force on a train would not strike home until later when I realized no one in their right mind was going to strap a high school dropout into the pilot's seat of a multi-million dollar aircraft. Humans, on the other hand, were obviously more expendable because I qualified to be a medic, a sort of short order surgeon. But I took it very seriously,

557

putting my new skills to good use, especially during a brief exposure to the results of martial violence in Libya during the Six Day War of 1967, then at a hospital in Vietnam during the flat out hell of 1969.

In the end, I did not escape that war as my friend hoped, but had in fact volunteered to go to it because I wanted to see what was happening to my generation without relying on slanted details from the newspapers or television. I wanted firsthand knowledge. It was stupid and reckless, but I was not unlike my hero Whitman. Finally roused to action in the Civil War by news of the wounding and possible death of his brother George, who had disappeared at the battle of Fredericksburg, he went south to the war zones searching for him. Finding him alive, with a minor shrapnel wound to the face, Whitman stuck around to help nurse him back to battle, then hitched a ride to Washington, DC with a shipment of wounded soldiers. He could not bring himself to leave the hospitals after that.

For the rest of the war he tended the wounded, told them stories, eased their pain, wrote their letters, and held them as they died. He was finally in a position where he could not avoid what he already knew but had not written about: the true miseries of the poor, which are unmitigated in the reality of war. In my own way, by going to war, I wanted, like him, to be able to say: *I understand the large hearts of heroes . . . I am the man . . . I was there.* I came to understand nothing of the sort, and what I learned I could have lived without, but the experience made me admire Whitman even more. Understanding the world a little better than I did as a boy, having witnessed what humans can do to one another, I discovered a vital point rereading his work: it is not only possible but necessary to wring beauty and compassion out of horror, even if the results seem unthinkable. Otherwise, there can be no important art at all.

After the war, I went back to Pittsburgh to attend college for a few years, and though I finished, grew restless, discouraged by what was happening to my city, heart of labor that even I had managed to romanticize by then. Unemployment was touching everyone, and old friends were plunging back into the poverty they had worked so hard to escape. The money was leaving, especially the North Side where it never really took root. Steel mills began to disappear, and smaller factories everywhere were shutting down. For the time being I had my fill of tragedy, and left. No, actually I escaped.

Two decades later I returned again and wandered around North Side. The Manchester section, where I was born, was darkened with areas that appeared to be open-air crack dens sprawled through the streets like eviscerated guts of a once-animated body composed of houses, factories, and productive lives. Other sections were barely clinging to life. My best friend's house had become a derelict building.

I was a nascent airman marching around in the hot Texas sun when he managed to do something unheard of on the North Side. He lucked into a group of Quakers, or some other religious group, registered with the draft board as a conscientious objector, and was granted CO status, which meant he didn't have to go, and he really did not want to. He could not believe in war, and wanted to spend his life differently, which included going to college without having to do battle for the sake of someone else's blind political ambitions. But the combination of being hopelessly poor, bearing principles that aroused suspicions of homosexuality and cowardice (which must have cost him physically every day, though he was respected and feared as a street fighter, and famously in love with the girl he intended to marry), proved that ideas were no match for peer pressure in the working class, and after a year of struggle, he allowed himself to be drafted, easily passing a physical he could not pass for less demanding duty. He became an Army Medic, went to Vietnam near the beginning of 1968, and was killed in action six months later. He hated the war. He wrote from Vietnam and told me so. He warned me not to come. He said it would not be what I expected. It was not an adventure, he said, it was wrong, a crime against both sides. A few months later, I would be wincing as mortars fell, thinking of Whitman, washing the dead, hating the war with a passion, thinking of my friend, wishing I had listened to him.

He was the only son of a divorced mother, and they were very close. His two sisters still lived at home when he died, but, as I recall, both were on the verge of marriage. His mother, who would never recover from such a loss, faced being left on her own. The house was eventually abandoned, and she never sold it as far as I know. After years of neglect, it collapsed into itself, and sat there like an unlived life, a reminder. When I saw it again, it had become an eyesore in a block-long row of modest, party wall Victorian houses with front porches separated by waist-high railings that my friend and I leapt every morning on our way to elementary school at full speed in our very hip engineer boots, one end of the block to the other, his neighbors screaming behind us.

During my visit, the neighborhood where the old library stood seemed to have fared better than our little section of North Side. It was spruced up and looked attractive, but blanched of its character. The rows of shops, the farmer's market, even the streetcar tracks were gone, and there were no milling crowds because everything had been funneled into a central, enclosed mall. But the surrounding parks, dating back to a period of wealth and prosperity, were well tended and in full bloom, my beloved railroad still ran nearby, and most of the landmarks had survived, including the library.

Near Allegheny River, arched by bridges to downtown Pittsburgh, in a neighborhood I knew as one where I could always get work on the loading docks, I came upon the recently opened Andy Warhol Museum, lodged in a refurbished factory building I vaguely remember working in. Andy Warhol, homeboy and outsider, is a pure product of the Pittsburgh working class, and his art has interested me uninterrupted since I discovered it after the war. We both broke away from the working class streets of Pittsburgh and made it through the Vulcan King's university (Carnegie Tech in Warhol's time, Carnegie-Mellon in mine), and that was a detail impossible to overlook when, in a puzzled state, I saw my first Warhol Campbell's soup can.

Until that day I wandered into my past, I had always been under the mistaken impression that Warhol was from South Side—he was definitely not from North Side, where he would have been pulverized at an early age for his geeky, nerdish looks—but after checking deeper, I discovered he was, in fact, from a tiny working class neighborhood above the north shore of Monongahela River near Oakland. Graphic master of the quotidian, he swept everything assumed unsuitable into the arena of subject matter and possible beauty, and as such approached Whitman in his perceptions. Regardless of his reputed and actual lifestyle proclivities, which have long fomented serious criticism and gossip ranging from outrageous to well-deserved to entertaining, he is an artist ignored at the peril of being completely oblivious to Whitman's sort of street level focus, as well as Buchomov's nose, and is Pittsburgh's greatest argument against provinciality, not to mention one of the most shining children of its history.

Across the street from the Warhol Museum, there's a bar & grill I recognized from the days when I banged through the neighborhood working on my father's ice truck. Sometimes he would take me there.

It's called the Rosa-Villa, which (unless actually a family name) strikes me as a bit of foreign lingo dyslexia—both Italian and Spanish would place the Villa first. I opened the door, almost forty years later, looked in through cigarette smoke and darkness, and swear the same workers who were sitting there the last time I came in with my father were still sitting there. They looked up at me, expecting, I suppose, some odd looking nervous art patron from the museum wandering in, someone to gawk at and rib, if only between themselves and under their breaths. But they seemed to sigh when they turned back to their drinks in disappointment, dismissing me through a form of recognition I could never explain, communicated in the way we nodded to one another. A fellow gawker.

I felt a wave of nostalgia, knowing that this new museum, like the Carnegie Library of my youth, would fall under their ax of criticism. Warhol was not from North Side, but a relatively distant, hated place across the rivers. His was the land of hunkies and pollacks, plus he was gay (it being a well-known fact that homosexuals have been nonexistent on North Side from the time of the dinosaurs), and this Warhola Monument (not Warhol) was just another inedible gift of the rich.

I suspected their favorite artist, like my father's (probably Warhol's at one point, and one of mine), might be the brilliant painter John Kane, so-called Primitivist (née Self-taught, etc.), a railroad worker who hobbled around one-legged after being run over by a train one tipsy night, and senior member of Pittsburgh's working class art pantheon. I'd heard about Kane from the time I noticed house paint could be of many colors, and he was probably the first artist I became aware of. The Rosa-Villa crowd would be wrong about his preeminence, but they would be worth arguing with on the subject, and I have no doubt they would be willing to argue, voices almost completely gone from the universe now, along with their difficult world, willing to be heard, wishing to be understood.

Nominated by Kevin Bowen

THE WEIGHT

fiction by RICHARD BAUSCH

from THE SOUTHERN REVIEW

THIS IS A STORY I would have told grandchildren—and great-grandchildren—if I'd had any. I had three wives, but no children. That's a mystery, I suppose. As it's a mystery that I've been around for more than a century and am still blessed with reasonably fair health. I also remember what I had for breakfast this morning and who I talked with. You might have to remind me who you are if you come back, but that was always true. They say the far past becomes clearer as you get older and the near past gets dim. Well, I remember some things clearer than others, and there doesn't seem to be a pattern I can figure. More than ninety years ago, when I was almost twelve years old, something happened that I knew nothing would ever erase from my memory.

When I tell you about it, you won't ever forget it either.

In the summer of 1903—that's right, just after the turn of the *last* century—we lived in a little three-bedroom house on the outskirts of Baltimore. My mother and father, my older sister Livvie, and me. In mid-June, Father came down with a bad fever. He was delirious for three days, and for a while everybody thought he was going to die. He was a young man, only thirty-four, but he got very dehydrated, and his fever kept getting higher. Then Mother came down with it as well, and Livvie and I were shuffled off to our neighbor's house.

That was where we got sick.

Nobody knew quite what to do with us. The neighbor, Mrs. Lessing, was afraid to move us, or be near us either. For all anyone knew, our parents were dying, we were all dying. Mrs. Lessing got so frightened that she went to the post office and sent a telegram to her

562

cousin, out in Frederick, and he came in with his wagon and mules and took her away. She left her maid, Anna Scott, to nurse us. Anna was a black woman of about thirty. I was nearly blind with fever and she seemed too large for the room—not heavy, but big-boned and tall, with thick features and long-fingered, smooth hands. At least the backs of them were smooth. The palms made a pleasant scratching when they moved across your face, or rested on your forehead. When the fever would let up, during the day, she told us about the heavy mists in London, and how she had seen the terrible Tower, where people were kept for years, some waiting to have their heads cut off. She knew all the names of the kings and queens of England—Plantagenets and Stuarts and Tudors—and in the brief respite from sickness there was something wonderful about imagining palace intrigue in a faraway place. Livvie wanted more about the executions. Anna would demur for a time, denying that she knew anything so gruesome; then she would go on and say there is nothing more gruesome than the truth, and she would tell us in that soft drawl about Henry VIII's unfortunate wives, or Mary Queen of Scots.

I liked her, liked listening to her soft contralto voice. She described for us the frightful conditions on the ship she came to America on as a little girl, the deaths at sea, and how they slipped the bodies over the side off a long wooden board. Her ancestors were free blacks who lived in Wales. She had stories about her father, who had trained in medicine down in Alabama, where she grew up, and had taught her some of what he knew. When she spoke of the mistress of the house, her eyes said more than her words. She had a low opinion of old Mrs. Lessing, who was as silly as she was cowardly.

"Y'all understand," she'd say quietly. "This world is, um, upside down."

Before it was over, she got sick, too. Her coal-colored skin gleamed with sweat, and when she sat down on the bed to put a cool rag on my head, it was as if she had collapsed there. "Lord," she said. "I feel low-down."

But she never stopped tending to us. She told us of growing up in Alabama, and coming north on the train, and meeting Thaddeus Marcus Adams, of Pratt Street in the city of Baltimore. She liked to use the phrase. "Listen to it, darlings," she said, running a cold rag over Livvie's cheeks. *"Thaddeus Marcus Adams, of Pratt Street in the city of Baltimore."* Sometimes she sang it, lifting my shirt from my back and washing me, her hands burning with fever. At night we

563

waited for her, and the sound of her in the house kept me awake. She moved through my dreams, and Thaddeus Marcus Adams got mixed up in them, too. I dreamed he spoke to me, and washed my forehead. I had a memory, which I am now fairly certain was not the product of delirium, of wandering out of the room and seeing a tall, powerful-looking brown man in the upper hall-way of the house. He wore a white shirt with the sleeves rolled above the elbow, and I saw the thick veins standing out on his arms.

I tried to ask Anna if this was Thaddeus. She was singing low, still feverish, spooning broth into my mouth. "Hush," she said. "Hush, child. You been dreaming."

"Is it Thaddeus?" I said. "Tell me."

"Thaddeus is away," she said. "You mustn't speak of him in this house. You must've dreamed it, child." But then she put her head down and rocked slow, as if she might slump over. "My head."

"Here," I said. And I took the rag from her hand and put it on her forehead. She raised her head slightly, and breathed. It was only a moment. She straightened and took my wrist. "I'm just tired, child."

Anna, I tried to say. I only wanted to say her name. But I couldn't get it out. I nodded, and felt there must be something between us, a secret. When Livvie and I had first come to the house, we didn't even know her. She was just the next-door-lady's person—kitchen help. I don't think we had even known her name until that week.

Mother was next door, dangerously close to dying. Father's fever had broken, but he was still very weak, and other neighbors were with them. For that strange week we were a sundered family, being cared for in separate houses. I seldom thought of my family. I spent dream hours, awake and asleep, with Anna Scott.

The worst night of my fever I thought I looked out the window of the bedroom where I lay and saw my father in his coffin in a flickering yellow light in the next house, hands crossed over his chest. No one standing near. I felt as though I had abandoned him to that fate. I lay crying and muttering that I was sorry. I'm sure now that I dreamed this, since I know the room I was in faced away from our house and the view out that window was of the fairgrounds, where the circus came every summer.

After the fever passed, Mrs. Lessing returned from the country, and a day or so later we went back to our house. At almost twelve and fourteen, we were not quite old enough yet to understand the particulars of the social setup in 1903. Obviously it was the air we lived in, but we had no conscious sense of that. We saw Mrs. Lessing ordering Anna Scott around, making her clean the surfaces of the bedroom with strong lye soap. And the old lady shooed Livvie and me away whenever we came near. We represented disease to her. That was what Father said when we went home. He was going to work again in the mornings. He had recently been made head teller at the Union Trust bank in town. Mother was still recovering, and the heat and humidity were no help. She lay on her bed in her long nightgown, gleaming not so much with fever, though a mild one did persist through the hot days, but with the windless summer heat. Women from other houses stopped by now and then to look in on her, and to bring her iced tea and books to read. People expected Livvie and me to keep out of the way, not to trouble Mother.

We sought chances to talk to Anna Scott. She would be out back, hanging wash.

"What do you children want with me?" she'd ask, half-smiling. "You're gonna get me into trouble, sure enough."

"In France," Livvie said, "they have a thing called a gillo-teen."

Anna corrected her. "You pronounce it gee-yo-teen. It's a terrible thing."

"It cuts off people's heads," Livvie said avidly. "And sometimes the eyes still look around after the head's rolling around on the ground."

"Who told you that?"

"I heard it," Livvie said. "I swear."

"The head falls into a basket," Anna said.

I felt lightheaded. I turned to Livvie. "Is that all you can talk about?"

"Tell us how it works," Livvie said to Anna Scott.

"I don't have any idea how it works, child."

"Why did they only use it in France, Anna?"

"I've never been to France."

"Would you like to go?" I asked, and felt as if I'd proposed that we go together.

She gave me a long look that seemed to reach down into my chest. I couldn't breathe. "Why, John, are you toying with my affections?"

I didn't know how to answer the question.

But then she was concentrating on her work. "Don't you children have anything better to do than pester me? You know Miz Lessing is gonna give me grief if she sees us."

"We don't have anywhere else to go," Livvie said.

This was true. The only other child our age who lived at that end of Market Street was Dewey Dumfreys, and she could not be depended on for entertainment. Dewey was an albino, but we didn't know this. I mean no one had said anything to us about it. We just knew she couldn't be out in the sun very much, that her skin was pale as paste, her hair a startling white, whiter than we could believe anyone's ever was, even when we were looking at it; and her eyes were a strange-looking pink the color of a rabbit's nose. She spent a lot of time writing in a journal. She seemed never to want to do anything else. She seldom left her front porch. But when she wanted company, she would call to us when we came out of the house. It depended on her mood, of course, and she was rather inclined to fits of unsociability.

The particular afternoon I'm remembering, we were fresh from fever, Livvie and I. That's how it seems to me anyway, recalling it—a hot, humid, cloudless day with a stillness about it, as if the earth had stopped spinning on its axis and was fixed in a searing pool of sun. Things seemed bright with an unnatural brightness, a feverish glare, perhaps because we had been ill and were now better. Mother had told us to go outside, and to stay in the yard. We were on the porch. Anna Scott was beating the dust out of a rug in Mrs. Lessing's side yard. The day was on fire, too hot for work. I held onto the porch post. Lines of heat rose in the air. Anna Scott turned and looked at us, her face gleaming, her eyes wide and white. In the window, Mrs. Lessing stood watching her like a hawk. When Anna glanced our way, Mrs. Lessing said something we couldn't hear, and Anna said something back that ended in "ma'am." She waved at us, went back in the house.

"I'm tired," Livvie said to me.

We knew that some people had died of this fever we had survived. Livvie stared at her hands. I think we were both experiencing the sense of how different it was to be on the other side of the sickness. Mother coughed upstairs, and I had a guilty moment of wanting to get away from the sound. The stillness carried every stirring, every breath. We went out to the end of the yard and looked up and down the street. In the distance, beyond the railroad yard, you could see the big, partially collapsed red-white-and-blue tent from the circus that had always come to town from mid-May to mid-July, and that a lot of people were unjustly blaming for this epidemic. That was why it was closing down early.

Dewey Dumfreys strolled over from her porch, wearing a floppy straw hat, a long-sleeved blouse, and a skirt that covered her feet. You couldn't see her feet. She appeared to glide like a ghost across the grass. "Know what happened?" she said, then didn't wait for an answer: "My Uncle Harry came in from work about an hour ago and told us there's been a terrible accident down at the rail yard. An elephant fell off the back of the train. They were coming to catch up with the circus, all the way from Scranton, and this one named Sport got playful and he backed against the door of the car and the door broke and he went flying off and landed on the track—off a moving train car. An elephant, think of it. Uncle Harry said he screamed a terrible scream. They were bringing them—two of them—to the circus."

"The circus is breaking up," I said. "Nobody went to it because of the fever."

"Well, they were getting two elephants and now one of them's dead and they're gonna have to kill the other one to put it out of its misery."

"What happened to the other one?" I said. "Did it fall, too?"

"No, the one that fell is still alive. But he can't move his legs, or stand up. The *other* one just up and died. Maybe from the shock. Maybe they love each other like people. Maybe the shock of her friend falling off the train killed her."

Livvie saw Anna Scott come from the Lessing house, wearing a white scarf like a bandana. We ran over to her, and Dewey repeated her story, adding the detail that the people at the rail yard had used a big freight derrick to hoist Sport back onto the train car. "They think his back might be broken. My Uncle Harry was there and saw the whole thing."

Anna looked up the road in the direction of the rail yard, then looked back at us. "My friend Thaddeus works there," she said in that voice I loved. "He'll know what happened."

"It's the God's truth," Dewey said.

"Oh, I ain't doubting you, honey."

We all stood there, looking down the street. You could see some of the apparatus of the rail yard, and across the road, beyond the houses, there were tracks that led there. There was a raised bed that was visible in the winter months, and when a train came through you could see it going by in flashes between hedges and houses and trees. We never paid much attention to the trains because they had been there all our lives. Their sound, roaring along in the wake of smoke and the blaring of a whistle, was as unremarkable to us as the clop-clop of horses' hooves in the street, the protesting of wagon wheels.

"I want to go see," Livvie said.

Anna shook her head. "Honey, you know your mother wouldn't want that."

"She'll let us if you take us," Livvie said.

"To the rail yard? Me? Young lady, you sure you still don't have fever?" She put her dark hand on Livvie's brow, which was almost as pale as Dewey's.

"Can we ask her?" I said. I was speaking with the confidence of one who was close enough to her to know about Thaddeus Marcus Adams.

Anna frowned. "I think you best let her sleep. Don't you, John?"

My name on those lips thrilled me. I felt the blood rush to my face. "Yes," I said, being responsible.

"Well, tell you what," Anna said. "I'll go on down there this afternoon and see what I can, and I'll come back and tell y'all about it, how'd that be?"

Livvie wasn't impressed. "It's not the same as seeing it."

"There's probably nothing to see, honey. It's over, whatever it was."

From inside, just then, came the voice of Mrs. Lessing. "You! Anna! What're you doing talking to those children? I asked you to go get some tonic for me."

"Yes'm," Anna called back.

"I don't have all day to wait for you."

"No'm, I know. I's going jes' as quick as I can, Miz Lessing." By this time Livvie and I were accustomed to the difference in Anna's speech when she spoke to Mrs. Lessing. I considered it part of our special relation to each other. Anna murmured to us: "I'll see if I can't find out something. Y'all stay here. And Dewey, you better not stay out in this here sun too long."

"Yes'm."

We watched her cross the street and go up the block, away from the rail yard and toward the old part of town, where the dry-goods store and the pharmacy were. She waved just before she went out of sight.

"My mother says Anna's a faithless heathen," Dewey said. "I think she's nice."

"I wish Mrs. Lessing would go back to Frederick," said Livvie.

We wandered to Dewey's front porch, where we sat in metal chairs. Nothing moved. There wasn't a breeze anywhere in the world. The leaves hung on the trees, wilting. The hottest day in the history of summer. Dewey's Uncle Harry was on the back porch, talking to her mother. We couldn't make out the words through the open windows, and we wanted to, so we said nothing, trying to hear. But they were two rooms and a corridor away. Finally we went around the house to where they sat with a pitcher of lemonade on the little table between their chairs.

"Hey, kids," Uncle Harry said. "Hot enough for you?" He took a sip of the lemonade and made a face.

"You kids stay close," Dewey's mother said. "There's trouble, serious trouble."

"We know all about it," Dewey said.

Uncle Harry sat forward. "What do you know, little girl?"

"About the elephant."

"Oh," he said. "That." He sat back. We waited for him to say more, but he sipped the lemonade and stared off. Dewey started talking about the circus. She had been twice, she said; her uncle had taken her. She went on about what she'd seen there.

I heard her mother say to Uncle Harry, "I think he's got himself a lady friend in the next house," and I stopped listening to Dewey.

"You're kidding me," Uncle Harry said.

"If I'm not mistaken. I've seen him at the back door over there, hanging around her. You know what kind of friend I mean."

"Of course."

"They're all so highly . . . they have no inhibitions where—well, I mean I think it's frightening."

Dewey's uncle said nothing for a moment. Then: "Does Mrs. Lessing know?"

"She'd fire her in an instant."

"Well, it's a small world."

"What do you think they'll do with him?" Mrs. Dumfreys asked, and I understood, with a shock, that they must be talking about Thaddeus Marcus Adams, of Pratt Street in the city of Baltimore.

I said, "What did he do?"

Uncle Harry looked at me.

"Uncle Harry," Dewey said. "Tell us about the elephant."

He shook his head. "I'm trying not to think about the elephant."

"Please?"

He turned to Mrs. Dumfreys. "I'm not kidding you, the worst noise I ever heard, that scream. I never thought an animal could make such a sound. I mean there was something *intelligent* about it." He sat there, with the glass of lemonade held to his lips.

Mrs. Dumfreys poured more and said, "Can't you children find something to do out front?"

"What did he do?" I repeated.

"Who?" Uncle Harry said. Then: "Don't be impertinent, young man."

I started to say the name Thaddeus, but thought better of it. I was afraid I might get Anna Scott in trouble.

"Dewey, take John and Livvie around to the front porch, please," Mrs. Dumfreys said.

"Can't we have some lemonade?"

Mrs. Dumfreys considered a moment. "All right, you can have some lemonade."

Dewey went in and brought out three glasses and filled them from the pitcher. We sat on the back-porch steps and drank the faintly stinging, sweet lemonade. The glasses beaded up immediately, and the drink looked even better than it tasted. After a while we saw Mrs. Lessing come out of her house and go along the alley to the street behind us.

Dewey was rattling on about the lemonade at the circus, and I kept my attention on Uncle Harry and Mrs. Dumfreys.

"You suppose Mrs. Lessing knows about it already?" he asked.

"She will soon enough."

"Would you keep a maid with a boyfriend who would threaten a white wom—" Uncle Harry stopped. Mrs. Dumfreys had caught me listening, and held her hand up. Very softly she said, "John, you and the girls go play."

We walked around to the front of the house. I felt restless and impatient to know more. Again we were listening, trying to hear what the adults were saying, and I thought I heard the word *impertinent* again.

"I'm sick of this," Livvie said. "Let's do something."

"I'm going to the freight yard," said Dewey. She stepped down off the porch.

We heard Mother cough from the bedroom window above the side yard. The sound made us pause. But she was in bed, half-dreaming. The white lace curtains of the window were still as stone. In that heat they looked as if they might burst into flame. Beyond the space of the window was the wall clock. It chimed once. We waited. It was as if we were waiting for the sound of the clock again. Or for Mother's cough. But there was only the murmur of the voices on the back porch.

"Come on," Dewey said. "If you're coming."

"You're not supposed to be out in the sun." Livvie said. "What about Uncle Harry and your mother?"

"I'm protected," said Dewey. "I'm tired of sitting around. They'll sit out there for at least another hour."

We followed her out to the sidewalk and on to the end of the street, then across. The rail yard was about a quarter-mile away, and we went slow, as if to hurry would reveal our true purpose. On one porch, someone darker than Anna Scott sat rocking a baby, the baby crying and protesting. We'd heard the cries a long way away. The woman watched us for a few paces, then gave over to worrying about what was in her lap.

The train yard smelled suffocatingly of coal and creosote and smoke. There were cars ranged along one wide group of about a dozen pairs of rails—the hold yard, as I later learned—and we went past this, on toward the office, where two men stood smoking. They were about the same age, both blond and with the grime of the yard on their faces, smudged where they'd wiped the sweat off. The tall one wore a vest and a short-sleeved white shirt. The other was shirtless, in overalls.

"We came to see the hurt elephant," Dewey said to them.

"Get on out of here," said the tall one. "The three of you, if you know what's good for you. Get."

We didn't move.

"Wait a minute, Jesse," the other one said. He leaned toward us, blowing smoke. He stared at Dewey. "What the hell, if you ain't the whitest child I ever saw. Look at this, Jesse. Man, this is the *opposite* of a nigger."

Jesse laughed. "Cal, you're a crazy sumbitch. You know it?"

"Watch your language," Cal said. Then he spoke into Dewey's face. "Ain't you the complete *opposite* of a nigger."

Dewey's lower lip shook, but she said nothing, staring back into the dirty, sweat-beaded face. Up close, I saw they were both older men.

"We want to see the elephant that fell off the train," I said.

The one named Jesse said, "Well, maybe you can and maybe you can't." He had brown teeth, and he spit through them, then wiped his mouth with the back of his hand. He had stepped closer to Dewey, who stiffened without giving any ground. I smelled tobacco and sweat. Jesse said, "You know, I bet these street urchins would taste good on a bed of lettuce, Cal."

"I bet they would," said Cal. He rubbed his stubbled face, then flicked the cigarette into the cinders of the yard. He brought a pouch and papers out of his shirt pocket and began to roll another.

"Heck," Jesse said. "Maybe they ought to see our little party. Might do 'em good."

"You're a damn philosopher, Jesse."

"Watch *your* language."

"Come on," Dewey said to us. "They don't know anything."

We walked away. After a few paces I turned, and they were standing there, staring.

"Hey," Cal yelled. And he pointed. There were more tracks ahead. A small group of men had gathered near an empty railroad car. They were moving with a quickness, as if struggling with something or trying to lift something. Cal whistled, and gestured for us to go over there.

"Well?" Dewey said to me.

"You go," Livvie said.

Dewey started, but then turned back.

"I'll go," I said. I kept to the edge of the rails. There were other cars beyond this one. I wondered which one held the elephant, and what these men I was approaching must have already done with the one that had died. The grass that bordered the yard was burned in the sun, stained with coal dust. The men had become still, their backs to me. I got to within about twenty yards of the car before one of them turned and saw me—a big man in a seersucker suit and a straw hat. He walked a few paces in my direction. "There's nothing for you here," he said.

The backs parted, and in the middle of the crowd I saw a brown man in what had been a white shirt. His face was battered and bleeding—you couldn't tell much about the features for the swelling of the eyes and the blood on his jaw and neck. The blood was all over the white shirt, which hung on his big chest in shreds. His hands were behind his back. He looked at me. They jostled him and closed in around him, moving to the other side of the car. I saw their feet there, a lot of confused motion and straining.

The man in the straw hat was coming toward me. "Shoo! Go home where you belong." It was clear that he meant to evict me physically if he had to. I backed away, then turned and ran. When I glanced over my shoulder, I saw that he was chasing me, big, lumbering steps, arms flailing at his sides. I yelled, and Livvie—who was always faster than I—left us behind, running far ahead. I caught up to Dewey, and we crossed the rails, then angled back toward Market Street through a field of dry knife-grass that stung our legs, and big blue stones—quarry stones, they looked like—that tripped us up. We climbed the roadbed and stumbled across the rails and down the other side, and went on between the houses, Livvie leading the way. Back on Market Street, we lay down on the grass of the first lawn, fighting for breath. My heart pounded in my neck and face, behind my eyes. For a long while we couldn't move or speak. Finally, Livvie said, "What was it? What were they doing?"

"We just wanted to see the dang thing," said Dewey.

"Tell us," Livvie said.

I said, "I didn't see anything." I remember thinking that it was my business, not hers or Dewey's.

We were quiet then. A wagon came up the street, two large drays pulling it, and a boy sitting on the bench with a piece of Johnson grass in his mouth. The boy looked at us as the wagon came by, and when he lifted a skinny hand to wave, I waved back.

"I bet the elephant's already shipped somewhere else," Dewey said.

We got to our feet and went along the street. When we reached Dewey's house, we walked through the airless hallway to the kitchen and onto the back porch. There wasn't anyone there. We drank water from the well and poured it over our faces. Then we sat on the porch steps as if waiting for the day to change. My head spun a little, probably from the running, but it frightened me. I felt sick. I watched the windows of Mrs. Lessing's house, and nothing stirred there.

Dewey said, "I wonder where they are."

"Probably looking for us," Livvie said.

"Why did that man chase us?"

"I don't know," I said. "How do I know?"

We were abruptly irritable with each other. They were looking at me. I wondered if what I had seen might be visible in my face. It was hard to believe they couldn't see it. I felt it in my cheeks like a bruise.

Presently, Anna Scott came into the alley from the side street where Mrs. Lessing had gone earlier. She came slow, hands knotted at her abdomen. I stepped down to the well with one of the lemonade glasses and filled it with water, then hurried across the lawn to meet her. She had seen me, and paused, her lips parted slightly. She was crying. I saw that she was standing there crying, and I wanted so to touch her. To say something, anything. She ran the backs of her hands over her eyes. I had the sense that I had known all along she would be like this when I saw her again.

"Hey," I managed to say. "Want some water?"

She spoke through her teeth. "Is that how you address a grownup? 'Hey?' "

"No," I said.

She sobbed.

"Anna."

Her lips curled back. "You get away from me." She sobbed again. Then she spit the words at me: "White boy." Her depthless eyes fixed me there, and held me out. I could almost see them shut down under the black irises. She said nothing more, but crossed to Mrs. Lessing's back door and went in.

"What was that?" Livvie said as I returned to Dewey's back porch.

I sat on the top step, silent, watching where Anna had gone. I guess Livvie knew enough not to ask me again. I think I understood most of what had already happened. And I wonder if it even needs retelling here. Thaddeus Marcus Adams of Pratt Street in the city of Baltimore had said something that a white lady considered flippant, and for this had been beaten to within an inch of his life and strung up on a street-lamp at the border of what everyone back then called Darktown. Some people from his neighborhood had cut him down, and he was not dead, but he was blind, he would never walk without a limp, and of course any kind of life he might have had was over forever. The lady who had been insulted had nearly run him down with her surrey as he came from lunch at a café on Market Street, walking toward the railroad yard to see about an elephant falling out of a livestock car.

The most unusual thing about that day took place in the evening at six.

They hanged the elephant. Livvie and I went with my father to see it. Dewey and her mother were there, too. A lot of people from the town came out. It was like a festival. They had got the elephant unconscious with ether, and they put a chain around his leathery neck and began lifting him on the same freight derrick they had earlier used to put him back up on the train car. He woke as the chain pulled him up to standing on his hind legs, so that it looked like a trick. He screamed, even through the tightness of the chain. It had disappeared where it was wrapped around the neck, but the line of it jutted from the loose flesh, on up to the top of the freight derrick, tight as a piano wire. The elephant's head was turned oddly to one side, and his screaming thinned out so that it was only a kind of hissing and gasping. The body stretched long, the rear feet still touching the ground; he was choking slow. They let the chain down again, with a rush, and the elephant was on his knees. I realized again that he couldn't stand or walk. A man I recognized as Jesse tried to administer more ether, but it was no use, so again they set the winch going, and the chain tightened and lifted, and they kept it going until the animal looked to be standing upright again, front legs hanging down, back legs supporting no weight but still touching the ground. An instant later the elephant emptied his bowels and bladder, and there was a gasp of alarm and fright in the crowd. I heard Livvie yell, a sound like a cry in a nightmare. I looked at Dewey and her mother. Dewey's eyes were wide, her mouth open. There was a blue vein forking up her white brow. The chain cranked loud, and startled me. It kept lifting, and the animal's hind legs trailed awfully through the pile of feces. When he cleared the ground he began to turn in the air, a slow rotation, the chain so tight into the flesh of the neck that I thought it might separate the head from the tremendous weight of the body. We watched the body rotating slowly, inanimate and limp. But the elephant was still breathing. A veterinarian, holding a handkerchief over his nose, put a stethoscope against the great side of the animal, then looked at the others and shrugged, and they all stood back and waited a while, trying not to breathe the effluvium of what had come from the body. Twice the process was repeated, at intervals of several minutes. Each time there was another shrug. Another wait. Finally the vet nodded, with his instrument, and the chain was slowly loosened, the hind legs and haunches settled into the mess, weirdly out of kilter—the front legs bending outward at a ridiculous and terrifying angle. They stopped the chain, and men began to disperse the

575

crowd. The release of the elephant's fluids had apparently not occurred to anyone as a hazard.

But it seemed so now. The crowd was ushered out, and soon Father and Livvie and I were walking along Market Street, toward home. Dewey and her mother were a few paces ahead of us. It looked like Dewey was helping her mother along. Livvie cried softly, and Father assured her that the elephant hadn't suffered. But we had seen the suffering, and we were not calmed by his words. I was carrying in my mind the image of Anna Scott's crying face, and the blood on Thaddeus Marcus Adams's torn white shirt. But there was the elephant, too—the stupendous, out-sized spectacle of its dying. I thought the world a terrible place, and I thought I had learned this in the space of that one day. I looked at the fading light in the sky and felt my equilibrium shift and go off. It was as if the fever had come back. As I had the thought, Livvie spoke it. "I feel feverish again," she said.

Father touched her forehead. "You don't feel warm."

We came to Mrs. Lessing's house, and there was a light in the window though it wasn't quite dusk yet. Mother was on our porch. She walked out to meet us. Mrs. Lessing came out, too. Dewey and her mother were already in their own house, shutting curtains.

"I've had to fire my maid," Mrs. Lessing said. "I'm afraid she was part of that business up the street."

"The elephant?" Mother asked.

"We'll talk later," said Father. "Good night, Mrs. Lessing."

"The animal is dead, then?"

Father nodded. "It didn't go off as smoothly as they'd thought. We never should've gone down there to see it."

"I wish we'd stayed home," Livvie said. She sniffled and wiped her nose. We crossed the lawn to our house. I looked back toward the rail yard. The first stars were twinkling above it.

"What was she talking about?" Mother asked Father as we went inside. "What business up the street?"

"Some black opened his mouth when he shouldn't have. And paid the price for it."

It was Father, many years later, who told me what they did to Thaddeus Adams. I had to jog his memory by explaining that it happened the day they hanged the elephant. He described it all, though he wasn't there to see it. In his estimation of things, it was unfortunate but necessary.

He worked hard to teach me honor, the love of one's family, the value of self-sacrifice, of kindness and concern, graciousness and thrift, industriousness and hard work, the love of country.

I never knew or found out what else might have happened, or how Thaddeus fared in his harmed life. And I never saw Anna Scott again, nor ever heard what became of her. Dewey moved away before I reached majority. One fall morning her house was empty, and new people moved in a week later. My parents lived to great age, into the early hundreds. We buried Livvie in the spring of 1958, after an automobile accident. She was sixty-seven. Mother and Father were still healthy, even strong. Livvie's family took good care of them that day. Livvie had raised three handsome and successful boys. They spoke with my father and me about all the trouble the coloreds, as they were then called, were causing. I went along with their talk, fearing the disapproval I might face if I said anything, and, I confess, agreeing with some of what was said. But then I remembered Anna Scott, talking to me in fever, in the year 1903. . . .

I've grown so old. . . . Everybody's gone now.

Sometimes, lately, I dream that I'm in that railroad yard and I can't see for the blinding hot light. The elephant is dangling from the chain, under the fretwork of the derrick, the iron supporting bars making a skinny black shadow on the red sky. I'm turning to look behind me; something awful is there, but I can't see it. Something weighs me down so heavily that my movements are terrifying slow. I move, but nothing seems to change. I'm a statue, utter stillness, trying to turn, trying to open my eyes in the blindness, and I never do see what waits in that dream that is so threatening—other men, a man, something not human, I never know in the dream. But I think I know. After I wake up, I think I know. And I try to gather the practical matters of my present life to myself like a protective cloak: the schedule here, the time, the coming morning. Betrayal can happen miles and years away. It can go on happening, down in the heart, in the dark. So these mornings are slow, and sometimes it seems the light won't come at all, and I lie here remembering that day so far past, when Anna Scott, crying, looked at me that way and called me "white boy," and later I stood in a crowd that had gathered to watch the death of the beast.

Nominated by C.E. Poverman

SPECIAL MENTION

(The editors also wish to mention the following important works published by small presses last year. Listings are in no particular order.)

POETRY

Snow Owls—L.S. Asekoff (Brooklyn Review)

Heart Beat—Frank Bidart (Raritan)

If The Blank Outcome In Dominioes Adds A Seventh Side To Dice—Brian Blanchfield (Seneca Review)

Still Life With Feral Horse—Lucie Brock-Broido (American Poetry Review)

Vermont—Dan Chiasson (Agni)

Two For A Journey—Carol Firth (The MacGuffin)

Xenophon's Soldiers—Nick Flynn (Bomb)

Two Children Are Threatened By A Nightingale—Julia Johnson (Poetry International)

A Dove! I Said—Li-Young Lee (*Book of My Nights*, BOA)

Valediction—James Richardson (St. Ann's Review)

We Were Horses Galloping Together—Marjorie Sandor (Prairie Schooner)

Pilar—Stephanie Strickland (Chelsea)

Moment—Rosanna Warren (*Bright Pages*, Yale University Press)

Parthenopi—Michael Waters (*Parthenopi*, BOA)

Road—Lisa Williams (Poetry)

Things To Do In The Belly Of The Whale—Dan Albergotti (Southern Humanities Review)

Degrees of Being There—Robyn Art (The Portland Review)

Difficult News—Valerie Berry (*Difficult News*, Sixteen Rivers)

To Twenty Canada Geese In The Palisades Industrial Park—Jenny
    Factor (Paris Review)
The End of Days—Gregory Fraser (Southern Review)
Eye—Beckian Fritz Goldberg (Journal)
Enamored—Jeff Hardin (Nimrod)
Deschutes River Confessional—Brent Johnson (Yale Anglers'
    Review)
A Small Song Called Ash From The Fire—Ron Price (Rattapallax 5)
La Vita Nuova—Christ of Scheele (Quarterly West)
Limited Time Offer—Beth Simon (Gettysburg Review)
The Landing—Katherine Soniat (*Alluvial*, Bucknell University
    Press)
My Mother's Name In English—Arthur Smith (*How Much Earth*,
    Roundhouse Press)
Letter from A Muck Farm—Leonora Smith (*Spatial Relations*,
    Michigan State University Press)
The Ghost—Karin Gottshall (Mid-American Review)

FICTION

Plane Crash Theory—Dani Shapiro (Ploughshares)
View of Kala Murie Stepping Out of Her Black Dress—Howard
    Norman (Conjunctions)
Porcupines—Liesel Litzenburger (*Now You Love Me*, Carnegie
    Mellon University Press)
Taughannock Falls—Bill Roorbach (Witness)
Meeting the Family—Mary Kenagy (Georgia Review)
Aral—Tom Bissell (Agni)
Blue Boy—Stuart Dybek (TriQuarterly)
Good Old Neon—David Foster Wallace (Conjunctions)
Egg Face—Mary Yukari Waters (Zoetrope)
Again—Stephen Dixon (Boulevard)
The Father Helmet—Matthew Derby (Fence)
Providence—Peter Orner (Epoch)
Eruption—Emily Hammond (Ploughshares)
Mystery Caller—Elizabeth Tallent (Threepenny Review)
My Stupid Harmony—Mark Wisniewski (The Sun)
Forty Steps—K. Anis Ahmed (The Minnesota Review)
Punch—Robert Coover (Conjunctions)

Zugzwang—Michael Griffity (New England Review)
Ordinary Pain—Michael Lowenthal (Witness)
I George—Duff Brenna (Frank)
Pony Car—Pinckney Benedict (Ontario Review)
The Canoeists—Rick Bass (Idaho Review)
Us In February—Christopher Tilghman (Meridian)
Arlo On the Fence—Mary Helen Stefaniak (Antioch Review)
Our Lady of the Height—Ha-yun Jung (Prairie Schooner)
The Last Thing I Remember—Ann Joslin Williams (Third Coast)
Joyce's Pupil—Drago Jancar (Kenyon Review)
Raincheck—Donald Lystra (Meridian)
Trees—Sylvia Watanabe (American Literary Review)
High Crimes—Christopher Torockio (Iowa Review)
Crazy—Laura Swenson (Kenyon Review)
Almonds and Cherries—Alicia Erian (Iowa Review)
Looby's Hill—Patrick O'Keefe (Doubletake)
Instinct—Natasha Ayala Garber (Threepenny Review)
The Gift—John Gilgun (Water-Stone)
A Tale of Love and Drowning—Diana Abu-Jaber (Tin House)
Lubing—Roger Hart (Natural Bridge)
100 Kisses—Chip Livingston (Art and Understanding)
Simple Machines—Michael Russell (New England Review)
Boom and Bust—Thomas McGuane (Harvard Review)
Snow, Ashes—Alyson Hagy (Virginia Quarterly Review)
Tell Me Something—David Jauss (Iron Horse Literary Review)
Ribs—Josip Novakovich (Tin House)
First Person—Judy Troy (Missouri Review)
Digging the Hole—Nancy Zafris (New England Review)
Sir Karl LaFond Or Current Resident—Christie Hodgen
     (Bellingham Review)
Beheadings—Kira Salak (Prairie Schooner)
(The) Only Lie—David Borofka (Mid-American Review)
His Blue Period—Valerie Martin (Conjunctions)
Seventeen 1960–61—Ursula Goodenough (Witness)
Yoyo—Eddie D. Chuculate (Iowa Review)
Biographers—Greg Ames (failbetter.com)
Then, Returning—Gina Ochsner (Chelsea)
Voodoo—Stephen Gibson (Boulevard)
The Good In Men—Jo Neace Krause (Witness)

Cleanup—Mary Guterson (ZYZZYVA)
Anna Passes On—Merrill Joan Gerber (Southwest Review)
Property Values—Aldo Alvarez (*Interesting Monsters*, Graywolf)
Wedding Night—Luisa A. Igloria (North American Review)
Watermelon Days—Tom McNeal (Zoetrope)
Seaworthy—Maud Casey (Gettysburg Review)
Blissful—Steven Huff (Hudson Review)
Carl, Under His Car—Christopher Chambers (Gettysburg Review)
The Raw Man—George Makana Clark (Transition)
Unknown Donor—Judith Claire Mitchell (Iowa Review)
Long Shot—Nolan W. K. Kim (Bamboo Ridge)
Eleanor Roosevelt and the Tornado—Kathy Karlson (Calyx)
Impossible Fruit—Valery Varble (Ascent)
Where The Bad Guys Are—Elizabeth Stuckey-French (Five Points)

NONFICTION

No After—Susan L. Feldman (Epoch)
A House In Florida—Lee Zacharias (Five Points)
Toward Total Recall—William H. Gass (PEN America)
Against Technique—Brett Lott (Creative Nonfiction)
Lost Things—Rachel Cohen (Threepenny Review)
Writer's Gift, Writer's Grudge—Norma Rosen (Raritan)
Notebook of An Artic Explorer—Dan Gerber (Fourth Genre)
from Japan Journals—Donald Richie (Manoa)
Refugium—Barbara Hurd (Georgia Review)
The Unauthorized Autobiography of Me—Sherman Alexie
    (Pleiades)
Defending the Land—Becky Bradway (*Pink Houses and Family
    Taverns*, Indiana University Press)
The Ass-End of Everything—Gary Fincke (Shenandoah)
A Boy, A Girl, Then and Now—Peter Stitt (Gettysburg Review)
Slow Flying Stones—Kate Kennessy (Doubletake)
Notes on Brodsky—Czeslaw Milosz (Tin House)

PRESSES FEATURED IN THE PUSHCART PRIZE EDITIONS SINCE 1976

Acts
Agni Review
Ahsahta Press
Ailanthus Press
Alaska Quarterly Review
Alcheringa/Ethnopoetics
Alice James Books
Ambergris
Amelia
American Letters and Commentary
American Literature
American PEN
American Poetry Review
American Scholar
American Short Fiction
The American Voice
Amicus Journal
Amnesty International
Anaesthesia Review
Another Chicago Magazine
Antaeus
Antietam Review
Antioch Review
Apalachee Quarterly
Aphra
Aralia Press

The Ark
Art and Understanding
Arts and Letters
Artword Quarterly
Ascensius Press
Ascent
Aspen Leaves
Aspen Poetry Anthology
Assembling
Atlanta Review
Autonomedia
Avocet Press
The Baffler
Bakunin
Bamboo Ridge
Barlenmir House
Barnwood Press
Barrow Street
The Bellingham Review
Bellowing Ark
Beloit Poetry Journal
Bennington Review
Bilingual Review
Black American Literature Forum
Black Rooster
Black Scholar

Black Sparrow
Black Warrior Review
Blackwells Press
Bloomsbury Review
Blue Cloud Quarterly
Blue Unicorn
Blue Wind Press
Bluefish
BOA Editions
Bomb
Bookslinger Editions
Boston Review
Boulevard
Boxspring
Bridge
Bridges
Brown Journal of Arts
Burning Deck Press
Caliban
California Quarterly
Callaloo
Calliope
Calliopea Press
Calyx
Canto
Capra Press
Caribbean Writer
Carolina Quarterly
Cedar Rock
Center
Chariton Review
Charnel House
Chattahoochee Review
Chelsea
Chicago Review
Chouteau Review
Chowder Review
Cimarron Review
Cincinnati Poetry Review
City Lights Books
Cleveland State University Poetry Center
Clown War
CoEvolution Quarterly

Cold Mountain Press
Colorado Review
Columbia: A Magazine of Poetry and
    Prose
Confluence Press
Confrontation
Conjunctions
Connecticut Review
Copper Canyon Press
Cosmic Information Agency
Countermeasures
Counterpoint
Crawl Out Your Window
Crazyhorse
Crescent Review
Cross Cultural Communications
Cross Currents
Crosstown Books
Cumberland Poetry Review
Curbstone Press
Cutbank
Dacotah Territory
Daedalus
Dalkey Archive Press
Decatur House
December
Denver Quarterly
Domestic Crude
Doubletake
Dragon Gate Inc.
Dreamworks
Dryad Press
Duck Down Press
Durak
East River Anthology
Eastern Washington University Press
Ellis Press
Empty Bowl
Epoch
Ergo!
Evansville Review
Exquisite Corpse
Faultline

584

Fence
Fiction
Fiction Collective
Fiction International
Field
Fine Madness
Firebrand Books
Firelands Art Review
First Intensity
Five Fingers Review
Five Points Press
Five Trees Press
The Formalist
Fourth Genre
Frontiers: A Journal of Women Studies
Fugue
Gallimaufry
Genre
The Georgia Review
Gettysburg Review
Ghost Dance
Gibbs-Smith
Glimmer Train
Goddard Journal
David Godine, Publisher
Graham House Press
Grand Street
Granta
Graywolf Press
Green Mountains Review
Greenfield Review
Greensboro Review
Guardian Press
Gulf Coast
Hanging Loose
Hard Pressed
Harvard Review
Hayden's Ferry Review
Hermitage Press
Heyday
Hills
Holmgangers Press
Holy Cow!

Home Planet News
Hudson Review
Hungry Mind Review
Icarus
Icon
Idaho Review
Iguana Press
Image
Indiana Review
Indiana Writes
Intermedia
Intro
Invisible City
Inwood Press
Iowa Review
Ironwood
Jam To-day
The Journal
Jubilat
The Kanchenjuga Press
Kansas Quarterly
Kayak
Kelsey Street Press
Kenyon Review
Kestrel
Latitudes Press
Laughing Waters Press
Laurel Review
L'Epervier Press
Liberation
Linquis
Literal Latté
The Literary Review
The Little Magazine
Living Hand Press
Living Poets Press
Logbridge-Rhodes
Louisville Review
Lowlands Review
Lucille
Lyric
Lynx House Press
The MacGuffin

Magic Circle Press
Malahat Review
Mānoa
Manroot
Many Mountains Moving
Marlboro Review
Massachusetts Review
McSweeney's
Meridian
Mho & Mho Works
Micah Publications
Michigan Quarterly
Mid-American Review
Milkweed Editions
Milkweed Quarterly
The Minnesota Review
Mississippi Review
Mississippi Valley Review
Missouri Review
Montana Gothic
Montana Review
Montemora
Moon Pony Press
Mount Voices
Mr. Cogito Press
MSS
Mudfish
Mulch Press
Nada Press
Nebraska Review
New America
New American Review
New American Writing
The New Criterion
New Delta Review
New Directions
New England Review
New England Review and Bread Loaf
    Quarterly
New Letters
New Orleans Review
New Virginia Review
New York Quarterly

New York University Press
News from The Republic of Letters
Nimrod
9 × 9 Industries
North American Review
North Atlantic Books
North Dakota Quarterly
Northeastern University Press
North Point Press
Northern Lights
Northwest Review
Notre Dame Review
O. ARS
O. Blēk
Obsidian
Obsidian II
Oconee Review
October
Ohio Review
Old Crow Review
Ontario Review
Open City
Open Places
Orca Press
Orchises Press
Orion
Other Voices
Oxford American
Oxford Press
Oyez Press
Oyster Boy Review
Painted Bride Quarterly
Painted Hills Review
Palo Alto Review
Paris Press
Paris Review
Parkett
Parnassus: Poetry in Review
Partisan Review
Passages North
Penca Books
Pentagram
Penumbra Press

Pequod
Persea: An International Review
Pipedream Press
Pitcairn Press
Pitt Magazine
Pleiades
Ploughshares
Poet and Critic
Poet Lore
Poetry
Poetry East
Poetry Ireland Review
Poetry Northwest
Poetry Now
Post Road
Prairie Schooner
Prescott Street Press
Press
Promise of Learnings
Provincetown Arts
Puerto Del Sol
Quaderni Di Yip
Quarry West
The Quarterly
Quarterly West
Raccoon
Rainbow Press
Raritan: A Quarterly Review
Red Cedar Review
Red Clay Books
Red Dust Press
Red Earth Press
Red Hen Press
Release Press
Review of Contemporary Fiction
Revista Chicano-Riquena
Rhetoric Review
River Styx
Rowan Tree Press
Russian *Samizdat*
Salmagundi
San Marcos Press
Sarabande Books

Sea Pen Press and Paper Mill
Seal Press
Seamark Press
Seattle Review
Second Coming Press
Semiotext(e)
Seneca Review
Seven Days
The Seventies Press
Sewanee Review
Shankpainter
Shantih
Shearsman
Sheep Meadow Press
Shenandoah
A Shout In the Street
Sibyl-Child Press
Side Show
Small Moon
The Smith
Solo
Solo 2
Some
The Sonora Review
Southern Poetry Review
Southern Review
Southwest Review
Spectrum
The Spirit That Moves Us
St. Andrews Press
Story
Story Quarterly
Streetfare Journal
Stuart Wright, Publisher
Sulfur
The Sun
Sun & Moon Press
Sun Press
Sunstone
Sycamore Review
Tamagwa
Tar River Poetry
Teal Press

Telephone Books
Telescope
Temblor
The Temple
Tendril
Texas Slough
Third Coast
13th Moon
THIS
Thorp Springs Press
Three Rivers Press
Threepenny Review
Thunder City Press
Thunder's Mouth Press
Tia Chucha Press
Tikkun
Tin House
Tombouctou Books
Toothpaste Press
Transatlantic Review
TriQuarterly
Truck Press
Undine
Unicorn Press
University of Georgia Press
University of Illinois Press
University of Iowa Press
University of Massachusetts Press
University of North Texas Press
University of Pittsburgh Press
University of Wisconsin Press

University Press of New England
Unmuzzled Ox
Unspeakable Visions of the Individual
Vagabond
Verse
Vignette
Virginia Quarterly
Volt
Wampeter Press
Washington Writers Workshop
Water-Stone
Water Table
Western Humanities Review
Westigan Review
White Pine Press
Wickwire Press
Willow Springs
Wilmore City
Witness
Word Beat Press
Word-Smith
Wormwood Review
Writers Forum
Xanadu
Yale Review
Yardbird Reader
Yarrow
Y'Bird
Zeitgeist Press
Zoetrope: All-Story
ZYZZYVA

CONTRIBUTING SMALL PRESSES FOR PUSHCART PRIZE XXVII

A

Adept Press, P.O. Box 391, Long Valley, NJ 07853
The Adirondack Review, 1200 Suoerior St, F-24, Watertown, NY 13601
Aethlon, English Dept., E, Tennessee State Univ., Johnson City, TN 37614
Agni, 236 Bay State Rd., Boston, MA 02215
Alaska Quarterly Review, Univ. of Alaska, 3211 Providence Rd., Anchorage, AK 99508
Algonquin Roundtable Review, Algonquin College, 1385 Woodroffe Ave., Nepean, Ont., K2G 1V8
    CANADA
Always in Season, P.O. Box 380403, Brooklyn, NY 11238
American Letters & Commentary, 850 Park Ave., New York, NY 10021
American Literary Review, P.O. Box 311307, Univ. of Northern Texas, Denton, TX 76203
Amherst Writers & Artists Press, P.O. Box 1076, Amherst, MA 01004
Ancient Paths, PMB #223, 2000 Benson Rd. S #115, Renton, WA 98055
Anthology Magazine, P.O. Box 4411, Mesa, AZ 85211
Antietam Review, 41 S. Potomac St., Hagerstown, MD 21740
The Antioch Review, P.O. Box 148, Yellow Springs, OH 45387
Apogee Press, P.O. Box 8177, Berkeley, CA 94707
Arctos Press, P.O. Box 401, Sausalito, CA 94966
Argonne House Press, P.O. Box 21069, Washington, DC 20009
The Armchair Aesthete, 31 Rolling Meadows Way, Penfield, NY 14526
Arsenic Lobster, P.O. Box 484, Pocatello, ID 83204
Artful Dodge, English Dept., College of Wooster, Wooster, OH 44691
Artifact Press, 1701 Stanley Rd, Cazenovia, NY 13035
Arts & Letters, Georgia College & State Univ., Milledgeville, GA 31061
Ascent, English Dept., Concordia College, Moorhead, MN 56562
Asterius Press, P.O. Box 5122, Seabrook, NJ 08302
The Aurorean, P.O. Box 219, Sagamore Beach, MA 02562
The Austin Chronicle, P.O. Box 49066, Austin, TX 78765
Axe Factory, P.O. Box 40691, Philadelphia, PA 19107

B

Ballast Quarterly Review, 2022 X Ave., Dysart, IA 52224
The Baltimore Review, P.O. Box 410, Riderwood, MD 21139

Bamboo Ridge Press, P.O. Box 61781, Honolulu, HI 96839
Barrow Street, P.O. Box 2017, Old Chelsea Station, New York, NY 10113
Bellingham Review, MS 9053, WWU, Bellingham, WA 98225
Bellowing Ark Press, P.O. Box 55564, Shoreline, WA 98155
Beloit Fiction Journal, Box 11, 700 College St., Beloit, WI 53511
Beloit Poetry Journal, 24 Berry Cove Rd., La Moine, ME 04605
Berkeley Fiction Review, 10 Eshleman Hall, UC, Berkeley, CA 94720
The Bible of Hell, P.O. Box 719, New York, NY 10101
Big City Lit., Box 1141, Cathedral Sta., New York, NY 10025
The Bitter Oleander Press, 4983 Tall Oaks Dr., Fayetteville, NY 13066
Black Dress Press, P.O. Box 1373, New York, NY 10276
Black Hat Press, 508 2nd Ave., Goodhue, MN 55027
Black Warrior Review, P.O. Box 892936, Tuscaloosa, AL 35486
Blink, P.O. Box 7387, Reynolds Sta., Winston-Salem, NC 27109
Blue Fifth Review, 267 Lark Meadow Cr., Bluff City, TN 37618
BOA Editions, Ltd., 260 East Ave., Rochester, NY 14604
BOMB Magazine, 594 Broadway, Ste. 905, New York, NY 10012
BoneWorld Publishing, 3700 County Rte. 24, Russell, NY 13684
Boston Review, E53-407 MIT, Cambridge, MA 02139
Boulevard, 7545 Cromwell Dr., Apt. 2N, St. Louis, MO 63105
Brain, Child, P.O. Box 1161, Harrisonburg, VA 22803
Briar Cliff Review, Briar Cliff Univ., P.O. Box 2100, Sioux City, IA 51104
Bridge, 1357 N. Ashland Ave., #3A, Chicago, IL 60622
Brilliant Corners, Lycoming College, Williamsport, PA 17701
Byline, P.O. Box 130596, Edmond, OK 73013

C

Cabinet Magazine, 181 Wyckoff St., Brooklyn, NY 11217
The Caribbean Writer, Univ. of Virgin Islands, RR2-10000 Kingshill, St. Croix, U.S. Virgin Islands 00850
Carve Magazine, see Mild Horse Press
The Chariton Review, Truman State Univ., Kirksville, MO 63501
The Chattahoochee Review, 2101 Womack Rd., Dunwoody, GA 30338
Chelsea, Box 773, Cooper Sta., New York, NY 10276
Cider Press, P.O. Box 881914, San Diego, CA 92168
Cimarron Review, Oklahoma State Univ., Stillwater, OK 74078
Clackamas Literary Review, 19600 Molalla Ave., Oregon City, OR 97045
Coal City Review Press, English Dept., Univ. of Kansas, Lawrence, KS 66045
The Comstock Review, 4956 St. John Dr., Syracuse, NY 13215
Conduit, 510 Eighth Ave., NE, Minneapolis, MN 55413
Confrontation, Eng. Dept., C.W. Post of L.I. Univ., Brookville, NY 11548
Conjunctions, Bard College, Annandale-on-Hudson, NY 12504
Connecticut Review, English Dept., So. Connecticut State Univ., New Haven, CT 06515
Copper Canyon Press, P.O. Box 271, Port Townsend, WA 98368
Crab Orchard Review, Eng. Dept., So. Illinois Univ., Carbondale, IL 62901
The Creative Connection, P.O. Box 97, Spruce Head, ME 04859
Critique Magazine, see Wind River Press
Crucible, Barton College, Wilson, SC 27893
Crux, P.O. Box 255, S. Londonderry, VT 05155

D

Dana Literary Society, P.O. Box 3362, Dana Point, CA 62629
Daniel & Daniel, P.O. Box 21922, Santa Barbara, CA 93121
Del Sol Review, 342 Parker St., Acton, MA 01720
Deviant Minds, 1903 Gardner St., Augusta, GA 30904
Diagram, 51 Cedar Crest, Tuscaloosa, AL 35401
Dial-a-Poem, 576 Horseshoe Tr., SE, Albuquerque, NM 87123
Diner, Box 60676, Greendale StA., Worcester, MA 01606
Disquieting Muses, P.O. Box 640746, San Jose, CA 95164
Dogwood, Eng. Dept., Fairfield Univ., 1073 N. Benson Rd., Fairfield, CT 06430
DoubleTake, 55 Davis Square, Somerville, MA 02144

E

Eastern Washington University Press, Cheney, WA 99004
Edge Publications, P.O. Box 799, Ocean Park, WA 98640
Eggplant Literary Productions, P.O. Box 2248, Schiller Park, IL 60176
Ekphrasis, P.O. Box 161236, Sacramento, CA 95816
Elixir Press, P.O. Box 18010, Minneapolis, MN 55418
Elysian Fields Quarterly, P.O. Box 14385, St. Paul, MN 55114
Emrys, P.O. Box 8813, Greenville, SC 20606
Epoch, Cornell Univ., 251 Goldwin Smith, Ithaca, NY 14853
Eureka Literary Magazine, Eureka College, 300 E. College Ave., Eureka, IL 61530
Evansville Review, Univ. of Evansville, 1800 Lincoln Ave., Evansville, IN 47722
Event, Douglas College, P.O. Box 2503, New Westminster, BC CANADA V3L 5B2
Exquisite Corpse, English Dept., LSU, Baton Rouge, LA 70803

F

Faultline, English Dept., Univ. of California, Irvine, CA 92697
Fauquier Poetry Journal, P.O. Box 68, Bealeton, VA 22712
Fells Point Poetry Books, 209 Academy Way, Columbia, SC 29206
Fence, 14 Fifth Ave., #1A, New York, NY 10011
Fiction International, Eng. Dept., San Diego Univ., San Diego, CA 92182
First Intensity, P.O. Box 665, Lawrence, KS 66044
5 AM, Box 205, Spring Church, PA 15686
Five Points, Eng. Dept., Georgia State Univ., Atlanta, GA 30303
5-Trope, 517 Lorimer, Brooklyn, NY 11211
The Florida Review, Eng. Dept., Univ. of Central Florida, Orlando, FL 32816
Foot Hills Publishing, P.O. Box 68, Kanona, NY 14856
The Formalist, 320 Hunter Dr., Evansville, IN 47711
Fourth Genre, Michigan State Univ., 286 Bessey Hall, East Lansing, MI 48824
Frith Press, P.O. Box 161236, Sacramento, CA 95816
Front Range Review, FRCC-Eng. Dept., 4616 S. Shields, Ft. Collins, CO 80527
Fuque, Dept. English, University of Idaho, Moscow, ID 83844
Futures Magazine, 3039 38th Ave. S, Minneapolis, MN 55406

G

The Georgia Review, Univ. of Georgia, Athens, GA 30602
Gettysburg Review, Gettysburg College, Gettysburg, PA 17325
Glimmer Train, 710 SW Madison, #504, Portland, OR 97205
Grain, Box 3092, Saskatoon, SK CANADA S7K 3S9
Gravity Presses, 27030 Havelock, Dearborn Heights, MI 48127
Graywolf Press, @402 University Ave., Ste. 203, St. Paul, MN 55114
Great Marsh Press, P.O. Box 2144, Lenox Hill Sta., New York, NY 10021
Green Bean Press, P.O. Box 237, New York, NY 10013
Green Hills Literary Lantern, P.O. Box 375, Trenton, MO 64683
Green Mountains Review, Johnson State College, Johnson, VT 05656
The Greensboro Review, P.O. Box 26170, Greensboro, NC 27402
Gripper Products, 787 N. 24th St., Philadelphia, PA 19130
Gulf Coast, English Dept., Univ. of Houston, Houston, TX 77204

H

Hampton Shorts, P.O. Box 1229, Water Mill, NY 11976
Hanging Loose Press, r31 Wckoff St., Brooklyn, NY 11217
Happy, 240 E. 35th St., 11A, New York, NY 10016
Harp-Strings Poetry Journal, 3444 S. Dover Terrace, Inverness, FL 34452
Harpur Palate, Eng. Dept., Binghamton Univ., Binghamton, NY 13902
Harvard Review, Lamont Library, Harvard Univ., Cambridge, MA 02138
Hats Off Books, 610 E. Delano St., Ste. 104, Tucson, AZ 85705
Hawaii Pacific Review, 1060 Bishop St., Honolulu, HI 96813
Hayden's Ferry Review, Arizona State Univ., Tempe, AZ 85287
Heart, P.O. Box 81038, Pittsburgh, PA 15217
Helicon Nine, P.O. Box 22412, Kansas City, MO 64113
Hermenaut Magazine, 179 Boylston St., Bldg. P, Jamaica Plain, MA 02130
The Higginsville Reader, P.O. Box 141, Three Bridges, NJ 08887
High Plains Literary Review, 180 Adams St., Ste. 250, Denver, CO 80206
Horse & Buggy Press, 303 Kinsey St., Raleigh, NC 27603
Hubbub, 5344 SE 38th Ave., Portland, OR 97202
The Hudson Review, 684 Park Ave., New York, NY 10021
Hutton Publications, P.O. Box 2907, Decatur, IL 62524
Hybolics, P.O. Box 3016, Aiea, HI 96701

I

The Iconoclast, 1675 Amazon Rd., Mohegan Lake, NY 10547
The Idaho Review, Eng. Dept., Boise State Univ., Boise, ID 83725
Illya's Honey, P.O. Box 700865, Dallas, TX 75370
In Posse Review, 239 Duncan St., San Francisco, CA 94131
Indiana Review, Indiana Univ., 1020 E. Kirkwood Ave., Bloomington, IN 47405
Inkwell Magazine, Manhattanville College, Purchase, NY 10577
The Iowa Review, 308 EPB, Univ. of Iowa, Iowa City, IA 52242
Iron Horse Literary Review, Eng. Dept., Texas Tech. Univ., Lubbock, TX 79409
Italian Americana, Univ. of Rhode Island, So. Washington St., Providence, RI 02903

J

The Journal, Eng. Dept., Ohio State Univ., Columbus, OH 43210
Journal of New Jersey Poets, CO. College of Morris, 214 Center Grove Rd., Randolph, NJ 07869
Jubilat, Eng. Dept., Univ. of Massachusetts, Amherst, MA 01003

K

Kelsey Review, Mercer Co. Community College, P.O. Box B, Trenton, NJ 08690
Kenyon Review, 102 College Dr., Kenyon College, Gambier, OH 43022
Kestrel, Fairmont State College, 1201 Locust Ave., Fairmont, WV 26554
King Wenclas, P.O. Box 42077, Philadelphia, PA 19101
Kings Estate Press, 870 Kings Estate Rd, St. Augustine, FL 32086

L

The Larcom Review, P.O. Box 161, Prides Crossing, MA 01965
The Ledge Magazine and Press, 78-44 80th St., Glendale, NY 11385
Licking River Review, Nunn Dr., Highland Heights, KY 41099
Literal Latté, 61 East 8th St., Ste. 240, New York, NY 10003
The Literary Review, 285 Madison Ave., Madison, NJ 07940
Livingston Press, Sta. 22, Univ. of Western Alabama, Livingston, AL 35470
Lyric, P.O. box 980814, Houston, TX 77098

M

The MacGuffin, Schoolcraft College, 18600 Haggerty Rd., Livonia, MI 48152
Magazine of Speculative Poetry, P.O. Box 564, Beloit, WI 53512
The Manhattan Review, 440 Riverside Dr., #38, New York, NY 10027
Manic D Press, 250 Banks St., San Francisco, CA 94110
Mānoa, English Dept., Univ. of Hawaii, 1733 Donaghho Dr., Honolulu, HI 90822
Many Beaches Press, 1527 N. 36th St., Sheboygan, WI 53081
Manzanita Books, 6357 Sharon Hills Rd., Charlotte, NC 28210
Manzanita Quarterly, P.O. Box 1234, Ashland, OR 97520
Margin, 9407 Capstan Dr., NE., Bainbridge Island, WA 98110
The Marlboro Review, P.O. Box 243, Marlboro, VT 05344
The Melic Review, 700 E. Ocean Blvd., #2504, Long Beach, CA 90802
Meridian, Univ. of Virginia, P.O. Box 400145, Charlottesville, VA 22904
Michigan Quarterly Review, Univ. of Michigan, Ann Arbor, MI 48109
Mid-American Review, Bowling Green State Univ., Bowling Green, OH 43403
Mid-List Press, 4324 12th Ave. S, Minneapolis, MN 55407
Midstream, 633 Third Ave., 21st fl., New York, NY 10017
Mild Horse Press, P.O. Box 72231, Davis, CA 95617
Mississippi Review, Univ. of Southern Mississippi, Hattiesburg, MS 39406
Missouri Review, Univ. of Missouri, Columbia, MO 65211
The Montserrat Review, P.O. Box 391764, Mountain View, CA 94039

N

Natural Bridge, Eng. Dept., Univ. of Missouri, St. Louis, MO 63121
The Nebraska Review, Univ. of Nebraska, Omaha, NE 68182
New England Review, Middlebury College, Middlebury, VT 05753
New England Writers/Vermont Poets Assoc., P.O. Box 483, Windsor, VT 05089
New Letters, Univ. of Missouri, 5100 Rockhill Rd., Kansas City, MO 64110
New Millenium Writings, Eng. Dept., Univ. of Tennessee, Knoxville, TN 37996
New Orleans Review, Box 195 Loyola Univ., New Orleans, LA 70118
The New Orphic Review, 706 Mill St., Nelson, B.C., CANADA V1L 4S5
New York Stories, LaGuardia Community College/CUNY, E-103, Long Island City, NY 11101
Night Rally, P.O. Box 1707, Philadelphia, PA 19105
Nightsun, English Dept., FSU, Frostburg, MD 21532
Nimrod, Univ. of Tulsa, Tulsa, OK 74104
96 Inc., P.O. Box 1559, Boston, MA 02215
North American Review, Univ. of Northern Iowa, Cedar Falls, IA 50614
Northeastern University Press, 360 Huntington Ave., Boston, MA 02115
Northwest Review, Univ. of Oregon, 369 PLC, Eugene, OR 97403
Notre Dame Review, Eng. Dept., Univ. of Notre Dame, Notre Dame, IN 46556

O

On Earth Magazine, 40 West 20th St., New York, NY 10011
Ontario Review, 9 Honey Brook Dr., Princeton NJ 08540
One Trick Pony, P.O. Box 11186, Philadelphia, PA 19136
Open City, 225 Lafayette St., Ste. 1114, New York, NY 10012
Orchises Press, George Mason Univ., Fairfax, VA 22030
Orion, 187 Main St., Great Barrington, MA 01230
Osiris, P.O. Box 297, Old Deerfield, MA 01342
Other Voices, Univ. of Illinois, 601 S. Morgan St., Chicago, IL 60607
Oxford American, P.O. Box 1156, Oxford, MS 38655
Oyster Boy Review, P.O. Box 77842, San Francisco, CA 94107

P

Pageant Press, 27 Chestnut St., Binghamton, NY 13905
Palo Alto Review, Palo Alto College, 1400 W. Villaret Blvd., San Antonio, TX 78224
Pangolin Papers, P.O. Box 241, Nordland, WA 98358
Parkett, 155 Ave. of the Americas, New York, NY 10013
Partisan Review, 236 Bay State Rd., Boston, MA 02215
Pathwise Press, P.O. Box 2392, Bloomington, IN 47402
The Paumanok Review, see Wind River Press
PEN America, 568 Broadway, Ste. 401, New York, NY 10012
Pen in Hand Press, 3665 SE Tolman, Portland, OR 97202
Penny Dreadful, P.O. Box 719, New York, NY 10101
Peppercorn Press, P.O. Box 122, State College, PA 16804
The Peralta Press, 333 East 8th St., Oakland, CA 94606
Perugia Press, P.O. Box 60364, Florence, MA 01062
Phantasmagoria, 1406 St. Clair Ave., St. Paul, MN 55105
Pleasure Boat Studio, 802 East Sixth, Port Angeles, WA 98362
Pleiades, Eng. Dept., Central Missouri State Univ., Warrensburg, MO 64093

Ploughshares, Emerson College, 120 Boylston St., Boston, MA 02116
Pluma Productions, P.O. Box 1138, Hollywood, CA 90078
Poems & Plays, Eng. Dept., P.O. Box 70, Middle Tennessee State Univ., Murfreesboro, TN 37132
Poet Lore, 4508 Walsh St., Bethesda, MD 20815
Poetry, 60 W. Walton St., Chicago, IL 60610
Poetry Center, Eng. Dept., Cleveland State Univ., Cleveland, OH 44114
Poetry Miscellany, 3413 Alta Vista Dr., Chattanooga, TN 37411
The Poetry Porch, 158 Hollett St., Scituate, ME 02066
The Poetry Project, Ltd., 131 East 10th St., New York, NY 10003
Porcupine, P.O. Box 259, Cedarburg, WI 53012
Portland Review, Portland State Univ., P.O. Box 347, Portland, OR 97207
Post Road, 19816 N. 49th Dr., Glendale, AZ 85308
Potomac Review, P.O. Box 154, Port Tobacco, MD 20677
Potpourri Publications, P.O. Box 8278, Prairie Village, KS 66208
Prairie Fire, 423-100 Arthur St., Winnipeg, Manitoba, CANADA R3B 1H3
Prairie Schooner, P.O. Box 880334, Univ. of Nebraska, Lincoln, NE 68588
Prairie Star, P.O. Box 923, Fort Collins, CO 80522
Prism International, Creative Writing Program, Univ. of British Columbia, Vancouver, B.C.,
    CANADA V6T 1Z1
Prose AX, P.O. Box 22643, Honolulu, HI 96823
Provincetown Arts Press, P.O. Box 35, 650 Commercial St., Provincetown, MA 02657
Publishing Online, 1200 S. 192nd St., Ste. 300, Seattle, WA 98148
Puerto del Sol, New Mexico State Univ., P.O. Box 30001, Las Cruces, NM 88003

Q

Quarterly West, Univ. of Utah, Salt Lake City, UT 84112
La Quasta Press, 211 La Questa, Woodside, CA 94062
Q.E.C.E., 406 Main St., #3C, Collegeville, PA 19426

R

Rain Crow Publishing, P.O. Box 11013, Chicago, IL 60611
Rain Taxi, P.O. Box 3840, Minneapolis, MN 55403
RALPH, Box 7272, San Diego, CA 92167
Raritan, 31 Mine St., New Brunswick, NJ 08903
Rattle, 13440 Ventura Blvd., #200, Sherman Oaks, CA 91423
Razorcake, P.O. Box 42129, Los Angeles, CA 90042
RE: AL, Stephen F. Austin State Univ., Box 13007, SFA Sta., Nacogdoches, TX 75962
The Reading Room, P.O. Box 2144, Lenox Hill Station, NY NY 10021
Red Brick Review, Eng. Dept., Penn State, 501 Station Rd., Erie, PA 16563
Red Moon Press, P.O. Box 2481, Winchester, VA 22604
Red River Review, 1729 Alpine Dr., Carroltown, TX 75007
Red Rock Review, Community College of So. Nevada, NO. Las Vegas, NV 89030
Red Wheelbarrow Literary Magazine, DeAnza College, Cupertino, CA 95014
Rendezvous, Eng. Dept., Idaho State Univ., Pocatello, ID 83209
River City, Eng. Dept., Univ. of Memphis, Memphis, TN 38152
River Oak Review, 734 Noyes St., #M3, Evanston, IL 60201
River Styx, 634 N. Grand Blvd., 12th fl., St. Louis, MO 63103
River Teeth, Ashland Univ., 401 College Ave., Ashland, OH 44805
Romantics Quarterly, P.O. Box 22543, Milwaukie, OR 97269

S

Salt Hill, English Dept., Syracuse Univ., Syracuse, NY 13244
Santa Monica Review, Santa Monica College, 1900 Pico Blvd., Santa Monica, CA 90406
Sarabande Books, Inc., 2234 Dundee Rd., Ste. 200, Louisville, KY 40205
ScribbleFest Literary Group, 542 Mitchell Dr., Los Osos, CA 93402
Seal Press, 3131 Western Ave., Ste. 410, Seattle, WA 98121
Seneca Review, Hobart & William Smith Colleges, Geneva, NY 14456
Sensations Magazine, 2 Radio Ave., A-5, Secaucus, NJ 07094
Shenandoah, Troubadour Theater, 2nd fl., Washington & Lee Univ., Lexington, VA 24450
Shearsman, 58 Velmell Rd. Exeter EX 440D England
Sheep Meadow Press, P.O. Box 1345, Riverdale-on-Hudson, NY 10471
Singles Network, P.O. Box 13, Springfield, VA 22150
6IX Magazine, P.O. Box 730, Kutztown, PA 19530
Skylark, 2200 169th St., Hammond, IN 46323
Slipstream, P.O. Box 2071, Niagara Falls, NY 14301
Slow Trains, P.O. Box 4741, Englewood, Colorado 80155
Small Beer Press, 360 Atlantic Ave., PMB 132, Brooklyn, NY 11217
Small Brushes, see Adept Press
Small Poetry Press, P.O. Box 5342, Concord, CA 94524
The Small Pond Magazine, P.O. Box 664, Stratford, CT 06615
Songs of Innocence, P.O. Box 719, New York, NY 10101
Southern Indiana Review, Univ. of Southern Indiana, Evansville, IN 47712
Southwest Review, Southern Methodist Univ., Dallas, TX 75275
The Sow's Ear Press, 19535 Pleasant View Dr., Abingdon, VA 24211
Spinning Jenny, see Black Dress Press
Story Quarterly, 431 Sheridan Rd., Kenilworth, IL 60043
Strange Horizons, 1012 E. 2nd Ave., Salt Lake City, UT 84103
Stringtown, 2309 W. 12th Ave., Spokane, WA 99224
The Sun, 107 N. Roberson St., Chapel Hill, NC 27516
Sundog, Eng. Dept., Florida State Univ., Tallahassee, FL 32306
Superior Books, P.O. Box 299, Indian Lake, NY 12842
Swan Scythe Press, Eng. Dept., Univ. of California, Davis, CA 95616
Sycamore Review, Eng. Dept., Purdue Univ., West Lafayette, IN 47907
Symbiotic Oatmeal, P.O. Box 14938, Philadelphia, PA 19149
Synaesthesia Press, P.O. Box 1763, Tempe, AZ 85280

T

Tale Bones, 5203 Quincy Ave. SE, Auburn, WA 98092
Talking River Review, Lewis-Clark State College, Lewiston, ID 83501
Tampa Review, 401 W. Kennedy Blvd., Tampa, FL 33606
Tar River Poetry, Eng. Dept., Eastern Carolina Univ., Greenville, NC 27858
Tatlin's Tower, 70 North St., Bristol, VT 05443
Tebot Bach, 20592 Minerva La., Huntington Beach, CA 92646
Ten Pell Books, 303 Park Ave., S, #500, New York, NY 10010
Thema, Box 8747, Metairie, LA 70011
Thorngate Road, English Dept., Pratt Institute, Brooklyn, NY 11205
Threepenny Review, P.O. Box 9131, Berkeley, CA 92709
Tin House, 120 East End Ave., #6B, New York, NY 10028
Tiny Lights Publications, P.O. Box 928, Petaluma, CA 94953
Towers & Rushing, Ltd., P.O. Box 691745, San Antonio, TX 78269
Transition, 69 Dunster St., Cambridge, MA 02138
TriQuarterly, Northwestern Univ., 2020 Ridge Ave., Evanston, IL 60208

Tsunami, Inc., P.O. Box 100, Walla Walla, WA 99362
Turtle Point Press, 103 Hog Hill Rd., Chappaqua, NY 10514
Two Rivers Review, P.O. Box 158, Clinton, NY 13323

U

University of Massachusetts Press, P.O. Box 429, Amherst, MA 01004
University Press of New England, 23 S. Main St., Hanover, NH 03755
Unwound Magazine, P.O. Box 835, Laramie, WY 82073
Urban Spaghetti, P.O. Box 5186, Mansfield, OH 44901

V

Valley Contemporary Books, P.O. Box 5342, Sherman Oaks, CA 91413
Van West & Co., Publishers, 5341 Ballard Ave., NW, Seattle, WA 98107
Verbatim, 7690 Hope St., Providence, RI 02906
Verse, English Dept., Univ. of Georgia, Athens, GA 30602
Verse Press, see Verse
Vestal Review, 2609 Dartmouth Dr., Vestal, NY 13850
Via Dolorosa Press, 701 E. Schaaf Rd., Cleveland, OH 44131
Vincent Brothers Review, 4566 Northern Circle, Riverside, OH 45424
Virginia Adversaria, P.O. Box 2349, Poquoson, VA 23662

W

Wake Up Heavy, P.O. Box 4668, Fresno, CA 93744
Washington Writers' Publishing House, P.O. Box 15271, Washington, DC 20003
Waterside Press, P.O. Box 1298, Stuyvesant Sta., New York, NY 10009
Water-Stone, Hamline Univ., 1536 Hewitt Ave., St. Paul, MN 55104
West Anglia Publications, P.O. Box 2683, LaJolla, CA 92038
West Branch, Bucknell Univ., Lewisburg, PA 17837
White Pelican Review, P.O. Box 7833, Lakeland, FL 33813
Wildside Press, 1120 N. 45th St., Waco, TX 76710
Willow Springs, EWU, 705 West 1st Ave., Spokane, WA 99201
Wind River Press, 254 Dogwood Dr., Hershey, PA 17033
Witness, 27055 Orchard Lake Rd., Farmington Hills, MI 48334
Word Wright's Magazine, P.O. Box 21069, Washington, DC 20009

Y

Yellow Man Press, P.O. Box 381316, Cambridge, MA 02238
Yuganta Press, 6 Rushmore Circle, Stamford, CT 06905

Z

Zoetrope, 1350 Ave. of the Americas, 24th fl., New York, NY 10019
ZYZZYVA, P.O. Box 590069, San Francisco, CA 94159

CONTRIBUTORS' NOTES

CAROLYN ALESSIO is the prose editor of *Crab Orchard Review*. She teaches at Cristo Rey High School in Chicago.

STEVE ALMOND's short story collection *My Life In Heavy Metal* was published recently by Grove/Atlantic. He lives near Boston.

JENNIFER ATKINSON is the author of two books of poems: *The Dogwood Tree* and *The Drowned City*. She teaches at George Mason University.

MARY JO BANG is past poetry editor of *Boston Review* and the author of three books of poetry. She teaches at Washington University in St. Louis.

RICHARD BAUSCH lives in Broad Run, Virginia. His stories have previously appeared in Pushcart Prize XXIII and XXIV.

JOSHUA BECKMAN is the author most recently of *Something I Expected to Be Different* (Verse, 2001). He lives in Staten Island, New York.

PHILIP D. BEIDLER is Professor of English at the University of Alabama. "Solatium" is part of a new book project joining personal memory and cultural reflection.

AIMEE BENDER is the author of the short story collection *The Girl in the Flammable Skirt* and the novel *An Invisible Sign of My Own*. She lives in Los Angeles.

ANDREA HOLLANDER BUDY is the author of two poetry collections from Story Line Press. This is her first published essay.

JANET BURROWAY's most recent novel is *Cutting Stone*. She lives in Tallahassee, Florida.

DAN CHAON's story collection *Among the Missing* was a finalist for the 2001 National Book Award. He lives in Cleveland Heights, Ohio.

TOM CRAWFORD's poetry collection *Lauds* won the Oregon Book Award in 1994. He lives in Portland, Oregon.

CARL DENNIS won The Pulitzer Prize in 2001. He is the author of twelve books of poetry and teaches at SUNY, Buffalo.

MONIQUE DE VARENNES is a graduate of Johns Hopkins writing seminars. She lives in Los Angeles.

CHITRA BANERJEE DIVAKARUNI's new novel *The Vine of Desire* was published in 2002. Her work has appeared in many journals including *The Atlantic Monthly* and *The New Yorker*.

JOSEPH EPSTEIN is the author of fourteen books, the most recent of which is *Snobbery: The American Version* (Houghton Mifflin). He writes for *Hudson Review*, *Commentary*, *The New Yorker* and *The New Criterion*.

GEORGE EVANS is the founder and editor of *Streetfare Journal*, a project which publishes and displays modern poetry and art on 14,000 buses in 16 U.S. cities. He is the author of five books of poetry from Coffee House, Curbstone Press and other publishers.

MIRANDA FIELD's first book *Swallow* is just out from Houghton Mifflin. She lives in New York City with her husband, the poet Tom Thompson, and their two children.

CHRIS FORHAN won the Bakeless Prize for his book *Forgive Us Our Happiness* (University Press of New England, 1999). His poems have appeared in *Poetry*, *Parnassus*, *Doubletake* and elsewhere.

CAROL FROST's poetry collection *One Fine Day* is due out from TriQuarterly Books. She is writer-in-residence at Hartwick College.

JAMES GALVIN's first novel is available from St. Martin's Press. His *Resurrection Update: Collected Poems 1975–1997* was published by Copper Canyon Press.

TED GENOWAYS is the author of *Bullroarer: A Sequence* (Northeastern, 2001) and three chapbooks. He has twice received the Guy Owen Poetry Prize from *Southern Poetry Review*.

DINARA GEORGEOLIANI is a linguist and assistant professor at Central Washington University.

MARGARET GIBSON is the author of seven books of poems, most recently *Icon and Evidence* (2001). *Autumn Grasses* is due soon from LSU Press.

GARY GILDNER's new memoir *My Grandfather's Book* (Michigan State University Press) includes "Where The Dog Is Buried." He was awarded a National Magazine Award and the Iowa Poetry Prize.

LOUISE GLÜCK received the Pulitzer Prize in 1992. Her most recent book is *The Seven Ages* (Ecco).

LINDA GREGERSON's latest book of poems is *Waterborne*. She has received grants and awards from the NEA, The Guggenheim Foundation and The American Academy of Arts and Letters.

SUSAN HAHN is a poet, playwright and editor of *TriQuarterly*. Her most recent poetry collection is *Mother In Summer*.

JOHN HALES teaches at California State University, Fresno. His work has appeared in *The Southern Review*, *Ascent*, *Hudson Review* and elsewhere.

MARK HALPERIN teaches English at Central Washington University. His fourth volume of poetry *Time As Distance* is just out from Western Michigan University Press.

JANE HIRSHFIELD's fifth collection of poems is *Given Sugar, Given Salt* (HarperCollins). She was a finalist for the National Book Critics Circle Award.

CHRISTOPHER HOWELL is the editor of *Willow Springs*. His poems may be found in recent issues of *Field*, *Poetry Northwest*, and *Third Coast*.

KARL IAGNEMMA is a research scientist at M.I.T. His first story collection is due from Dial Press soon.

JUNSE KIM teaches at the Academy of Art College in San Francisco. Work recently appeared in ZYZZYVA.

ALEKSANDR KUSHNER is a Russian poet and essayist. He received the Russian State Prize for literature. This essay first appeared in the journal *Novy Mir*.

MARK RAY LEWIS was a Wallace Stegner Fellow at Stanford. "Scordatura" is his first published story.

JEFFREY A. LOCKWOOD teaches in the Department of Renewable Resources at the College of Agriculture of the University of Wyoming. He lives in Laramie, Wyoming.

NANCY LORD teaches at the University of Alaska. She lives in Homer, Alaska and fishes commercially for salmon.

PAUL MALISZEWSKI's work has appeared recently in *The Baffler* and *McSweeney's*. He lives in Durham, North Carolina.

SARAH MANGUSO is the author of the poetry collection *The Captain Lands In Paradise* (Alice James Books). She lives in Brooklyn, New York.

BEN MARCUS is the author of *Notable American Women*, *The Father Costume* and *The Age of Wire and String*. He lives in New York City and Brooklin, Maine.

BRENDA MILLER's collection of essays *Seasons of the Body* is just out from Sarabande Books. She teaches at Western Washington University.

CAROL MOLDAW is the author most recently of *Through the Window* (2001). She lives in New Mexico.

NICHOLAS MONTEMARANO is the author of the novel *A Fine Place*. A story collection titled *Cancer* is forthcoming.

BRADFORD MORROW is founding editor of *Conjunctions* and author of *Trinity Fields* and *Ariel's Crossing*, among other novels.

CORNELIA NIXON is the author of two novels, *Now You See It* and *Angels Go Naked*. She teaches at Mills College near San Francisco.

JOYCE CAROL OATES is a Founding Editor of The Pushcart Prize series. She teaches at Princeton University.

JULIE ORRINGER lectures at Stanford. Her work has appeared in *The Paris Review*, *The Yale Review* and *Pushcart Prize XXV*.

MICHAEL PALMA has published a poetry collection *A Fortune In Gold*, and ten volumes of translations from Italian poets, including a fully-rhymed *Inferno* (Norton, 2002). He Lives in New Rochelle, New York.

MICHAEL PARKER is the author of two novels and a collection of short fiction. He teaches at the University of North Carolina, Greensboro.

ROBERT PINSKY was Poet Laureate of the United States. He lives in Cambridge, Massachusetts.

DONALD PLATT's second book *Cloud Atlas* is just out from Purdue University Press. His poems have appeared in *Shenandoah*, *New Republic*, *Kenyon Review* and elsewhere.

D.A. POWELL is the author of *Tea* and *Lunch*, both from Wesleyan. He teaches at Harvard.

LADETTE RANDOLPH is a senior editor at the University of Nebraska Press. Her short stories and essays have appeared in *Connecticut Review, Prairie Schooner, Passages North* and elsewhere.

GRACE SCHULMAN's new poetry collection is *Days of Wonder: New and Selected poems* (Houghton Mifflin, 2002). She lives in New York City.

REBECCA SEIFERLE is the author of two poetry collections from Sheep Meadow Press. She edits an on-line magazine *The Drunken Boat* and lives in New Mexico.

KATHERINE TAYLOR just graduated from Columbia University's graduate writing program. She lives in New York City.

ALEXANDER THEROUX appeared in the first *Pushcart Prize* in 1976 and twice since. He lives in West Barnstable, Massachusetts.

MELANIE RAE THON lives in Salt Lake City. Her most recent book is the novel *Sweet Hearts*.

WELLS TOWER's writing has appeared in *The Paris Review, Fence*, and elsewhere. He lives in New York City and North Carolina.

ELLEN BRYANT VOIGT was awarded a 2002 Fellowship from The Academy of American Poets. She has published six books of poetry, most recently *Shadow of Heaven*.

KAREN VOLKMAN's books of poetry are *Crash's Law* (Norton, 1996) and *Sugar* (University of Iowa Press, 2002). She is Springer Poet-In-Residence at the University of Chicago.

WILLIAM WENTHE's next book is due soon from LSU Press. He teaches at Texas Tech University in Lubbock.

DARA WIER is the author of *Hat On A Pond* (Verse, 2002) and eight other collections. She lives in Amherst, Massachusetts.

CHRISTIAN WIMAN teaches in the English Department of Lynchburg College. He lives in Lynchburg, Virginia.

ROBERT WRIGLEY directs the creative writing program at the University of Idaho. Penguin will publish his *Lives of Animals* soon.

DAVID YOUNG teaches at Oberlin College and helps out at *Field*. His most recent book of poems is *At the White Window*.

MATT YURDANA's poems have appeared in *North American Review, The Southern Review, Massachusetts Review* and elsewhere. He lives in Portland, Oregon.

INDEX

The following is a listing in alphabetical order by author's last name of works reprinted in the *Pushcart Prize* editions since 1976.

603

604

607

609

612

616

619

622

626

627

631